W9-CBM-177

The world is in turmoil. A new age is dawning. It is the late 1660s, a time of conquest and piracy. When fortunes can be made by importing teas and spices and silks from the exotic East—or lost through political intrigue and religious persecution. And England is about to become the greatest merchant empire the world has ever seen.

ROGER GRIFFIN—A man with two loves but only one overwhelming desire: to restore the family fortune.

NANCY WILMOTT—She had seen the worst of the London slums and knew that no adversity was too great to overcome.

RACHEL AHMET—The dark-eyed Eastern beauty who endured disgrace to carry Roger Griffin's love child.

BENJAMIN AHMET—Sensing a new wave of religious intolerance that would destroy the trading company he and Roger had worked so hard to create, he sought refuge in the New World.

SOPHIA GRIFFIN—A vision had promised her a Catholic king on the English throne, but the price she had to pay was her family's destruction.

THE OUTCAST

The Griffin Saga
Volume I

by

Beverly Byrne

FAWCETT GOLD MEDAL • NEW YORK

THE OUTCAST

Published by Fawcett Gold Medal Books, a unit of CBS Publications, the Consumer Publishing Division of CBS Inc.

ISBN: 0-449-14396-1

Printed in the United States of America

First Fawcett Gold Medal printing: April 1981

10 9 8 7 6 5 4 3 2 1

The Griffin is a creature with the body of a lion, the head and wings of an eagle....Like birds it builds a nest, and instead of an egg lays an agate therein. The Griffin finds gold in the mountains and builds its nests of it...for which reason it keeps vigilant guard....The Griffin's instincts lead it to know where buried treasures lay and to keep plunderers at a distance....

—*Bulfinch's Mythology*

THE GRIFFIN FAMILY TREE

In 1077 Emile LaGriffe, said to be the captain of the boat that carried William the Conqueror to England in 1066, comes with his wife Roselyn to "the wilde and desolate landes the natives call the moors of Yorke Shire" and founds the house which six centuries later is the residence of the family who now call themselves Griffin, and their home Harwood Hall.

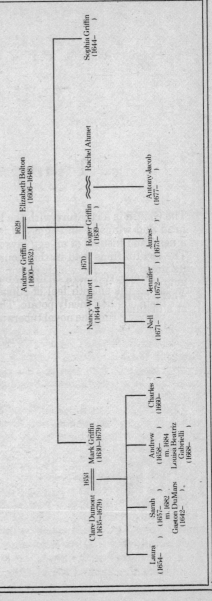

1660

Prologue

Forever afterward Laura Griffin would remember that historic day as the smooth feel of slippery pink satin and the exotic taste of a hot, mealy potato. The latter was purchased from a man roasting the novel tubers over a smoking charcoal brazier. The satin dress her mother had made a fortnight earlier, before they left Harwood Hall in Yorkshire on the long trek to London. In all Laura's six years such events had never occurred; little wonder that they were more clearly etched on her child's memory than was the return of a triumphant king.

"Will they be coming soon, Papa?" Laura's sister, Sarah, was only three; her impatience, even boredom, was undisguised. "I want to go home to the Hall. I want to wear my old dress again."

"Your old dress?" The child's mother sounded astonished. "Don't you like this pretty new one?"

"It's too ruffly. I want my other dress."

Clare Griffin had spent days sewing the new frock, but she had the grace to laugh. "She's a Roundhead child for all time, I guess," she commented wryly to her husband. "The Puritan influence won't be supplanted no matter how many kings are restored to the English throne."

Mark Griffin ignored her chatter and strained his neck

and shoulders to see the distant end of the path of gravel spread along the Strand. He could hear the measured tread of the horses and the muffled sound of drums, but as yet he could see nothing of the monarch, only the resurrected finery of those around him.

Sensing that her husband's impatience chafed as much as little Sarah's, for all it was better hid, Clare said gently, "Think how fortunate we are, my dear...to have seats when so many must stand...."

"Yes—we've Roger to thank for that. Were it not so I'd never have brought you in your condition." Smiling, he put an arm around her yet-slim waist. It would be some weeks before the coming child would announce its presence. At this moment Clare still looked a pretty young girl, despite the two daughters who flanked her and the toddling son asleep in her lap. "And if I had refused to bring you," Mark added pensively, "you'd have sulked for a month. Regardless of the fact that it was your best interests which moved me...."

Clare laughed gaily. "Oh, Mark, what a goose you are! You're getting angry about something that didn't happen and won't happen. How like you. We're here, aren't we? And none the worse for the journey. I'm only sorry Sophia couldn't come."

The mention of his moody younger sister and her endless vague complaints made Mark grimace. Before he could speak, Clare exclaimed, "Oh, see! They're coming." In the distance the flash of sunlight on a golden trumpet signaled the procession's approach.

Sensing the raised expectations of the crowd, Laura tugged at her father's velvet sleeve. "Will everybody see him soon, Papa? Will they see Uncle Roger?"

Mark Griffin chuckled. "It's not your Uncle Roger they've come to see, pet. They're here to welcome home our king and sovereign lord."

"I know." Laura repeated her lessons dutifully: "His most gracious majesty Charles II....But I still don't understand why he's coming home now, Papa. Where has he been before? And if he's Charles II, where's Charles I?"

Mark glanced round. The habit of eleven years was hard to break; to discuss such matters openly still made him nervous. The crowd, however, was concerned with the spectacle to come. None paid any attention to the child's questions. He spoke with quiet seriousness. "As for Charles I, God rest his holy soul, he's in a martyr's grave. Cruelly executed for no

8

crime but insisting on his God-given prerogatives as rightful King of England. Charles II has been in France all this time, waiting until it should be safe for him to come home."

"You mean the bad men who killed the other king wouldn't let him come home until now? Was it the Puritans, Papa? Did they kill the old king?"

"Not exactly, Laura—not all the Puritans. Only some who followed the lead of Lord Cromwell and his army. You mustn't think all Puritans bad."

The little girl sighed. She was often commended by her tutor for quick intelligence, but this was a very complicated story. "Oh well," she said simply, "it doesn't really matter now he's home—his gracious majesty, I mean. And since Uncle Roger's with him, I think it's all quite splendid. Just like a story...'and they all lived happily ever after.'"

Mark shook his head at childhood's trust. Then, before he could reply, the first part of the procession approached. As one body the crowd rose to its feet. Young Andrew still slept in his mother's arms, and Mark relieved his wife of the small, chubby burden. The little girls stood to see over the throng. Even blasé Sarah was infected with excitement. "Is that him?" she demanded, her voice lost in the rising tumult of cheers that greeted the advancing parade. "Is that the king?"

The man to whom she pointed was a trumpeter in golden helmet and full court dress. Only to the eyes of a three-year-old born into the somber gray-and-black landscape of Oliver Cromwell's Republic could he seem the long-awaited sovereign. No one bothered to answer her. They were conscious of nothing but the incredible river of pomp flooding the street before their eyes.

First came young pages strewing flowers and rushes. Their appearance was the signal for trumpeters and music makers of every sort to appear on the balconies of the surrounding houses. Then tapestries were let loose to flutter in the April breeze. Next came horsemen, a loud and lusty wave of humanity, filling the air with the sight and smell of glorious triumph, brandishing their swords and cheering as loudly as the watching crowd. Endless numbers of them; such an array as to make one wonder why Charles had not been able to wrest back his kingdom by force rather than waiting for Cromwell's sudden death, the brief rule of his incompetent son, and the invitation of Monck's "Free Parliament"...until one remembered that hundreds of those who now marched in jubilant parade had, until recently, sworn allegiance not to the king, but to the lord protector. Only when Royalist sentiment overwhelmed the land like a sudden winter thaw did thousands flock to this sunrise of the Stuarts.

It took hours for the horsemen to pass. Mark was later to learn there had been nearly twenty thousand of them. Finally the figure of the king came into view.

Charles rode a great white steed, as erect as if he'd mounted minutes, not hours, earlier. The wild cheering of the crowd seemed to refresh him at every step. Around him marched half a hundred footmen carrying maces of gold and silver and dressed in lace-trimmed reds and purples. The mane of the king's horse was braided with rubies and emeralds; they flashed an opalescent rainbow in the rays of the setting sun. Charles was hatless, his dark hair almost shoulder length. A cloak of woven gold spread across his broad back and rippled over the haunches of his horse. The garment cast a reflected glow over the king's swarthy features; they seemed bathed with almost celestial light. Not for a moment did he cease to wave and smile at the crowd. There was nothing of formality or duty in the gesture. For all his formidable reputation as a lover, for all the numerous bastard children he had fathered in his exile, this day Charles's passionate attention was wholly fixed on duty. He was lovingly attentive to his welcoming people.

"They say," an anonymous voice shouted in Mark's ear, "that over to King's Head tavern a goodwife was so excited she gave birth on the spot. And his majesty got down and greeted the babe as his newest subject." Of such stuff was a legend being created. Mark knew this was only the first of a thousand stories that would be told about this day.

"Look, Mark, look!" Clare shouted in her excitement, she who was always so serene and quiet. "That's the Duke of York, I think—just there behind the king. Roger must be nearby!" Then, as Clare spoke his name, Mark saw his brother.

Roger Griffin was twenty-one, and Mark had not seen him since he'd gone, at seventeen, to take up a commission in France with James, Duke of York, brother to Charles II. Somehow, through all the confusion and even lunacy that marked the efforts to restore the king by military means, Roger had distinguished himself and won James's favor. Today he rode just behind the Stuart brothers, a captain of the

Royal Navy, of which James, Duke of York, was now the lord high admiral.

He's aged well, Mark thought, seeing the broad shoulders and manly bearing of his young brother. Roger's dark good looks had achieved all the promise of his youth. Mark felt a moment of thanksgiving that the half-mad romantic gesture which had led Roger to join the Stuart exile had borne such happy fruit. Excitement spilled over, and he nudged his drowsy daughter. "Wake up, Laura, you'll miss everything. There's Uncle Roger just there beside the Duke of York!"

The little girl stared at the relative she had not seen since she was two. "Papa, is he really your brother? He looks so splendid. Is he really just a Griffin like us?"

"Just a Griffin! My girl, your ancestors have ridden beside English kings since the time of William the Conqueror. Griffins, you must never forget, are always loyal to the crown; and always rewarded for it."

Far from the elegant Strand with its contingent of nobles and landed gentry, in the warren of winding, narrow alleys clustered around Cripplegate and Moorgate, the king's procession had long since passed. The streets were strewn with refuse and litter; even these infamous slums had seldom looked so dirty. However, to a girl of ten who had never lived elsewhere, the remnants of the parade were a bonanza. "God almighty, Nance, here's another one!" The child stooped to pick up a crushed orange from the road and popped it into her pocket to join half a dozen others. "We'll not be hungry for a week."

"Pray God," the other girl retorted, "we'll not be hungry again. With this fine king restored there may be easier ways for such as you and me to live."

"Do you really think so, Nance?" The youngster placed her dirty little hand in that of her adored sixteen-year-old friend and protector. "Why should it be any different?"

"Because this king is said to like music and dancing and acting. All those things that haven't been allowed in this town since I was younger than you are now!"

Nancy Wilmott swung the little girl into an impromptu dance, jostling shoulders with the masses that still thronged the road, laughing loudest when a forward lad pinched her firm young buttocks. "Get along!" she shouted with good humor. "That's all you get for free, you rascal. If you want more it will cost you half a crown!"

The boy ran off chuckling, and Nancy turned back to her companion, who was sucking at an orange with self-absorbed concentration. "Listen, Nelly darling. I hear talk that the king's going to license a theater. Right in Drury Lane. Two gentlemen were saying so last night at the Crown tavern. And they said they were going to have girls on the stage. Like they do over there in France. I think we should become actresses. What do you say?"

Nell Gwyn soberly nodded her head in agreement.

BOOK I

1669–1674

PART ONE

The Taking

The king and court were never in the world so bad as they are now for gaming, whoring and drinking, and the most abominable vices that were ever in the world....

—Samuel Pepys
Diary Entry

1.

"Do you think," the queen said, twisting her rope of pearls around one slim finger, "that I don't know about his whores and bastards?"

Griffin hardly knew what to say. He had first met Catherine of Braganza when assigned by Charles to command the naval escort that brought his bride to England from Portugal in 1662. Somehow Catherine had conceived a deep affection for the young captain. Tongues often wagged at court, but Roger knew it was just friendship—a friendship for which he was grateful. Now his silence was straining the visit. Griffin searched for a polite reply, but only the truth presented itself. "I know you are aware of the ... women, ma'am. All London knows that."

"Yes, and thinks me a fool as well as a failure."

"No, milady, you mustn't say it, for it's not true."

"Oh but it is, dear Roger. I am perhaps both.... Yet, no woman has ever had a kinder, more thoughtful husband than the king is to me. That's the peculiar aspect of this strange cross I bear." She laughed bitterly. "Sadly, the cross is all I bear."

Roger stepped nearer her side and took her hand in a gesture of spontaneous warmth. At moments like this she was simply a young woman who had chosen him as confidant. Perhaps she'd done so precisely because he was sometimes able to forget that she was also his queen. "You're still very young," he said. "You mustn't despair of having a child...."

She sighed and managed a small smile. "I do not despair, I dare not. I will continue to beg Christ for an heir, and next week I go again to take the waters at Tunbridge Wells."

"You found them beneficial, then? When you went last year?"

"I think so, yes. And my lord found other amusements."

Again the wry smile that made her rather ordinary prettiness a grander thing. "Now, Roger, we will talk of other matters, and you will take a cup of tea with me. Last time you promised to taste the brew on your next visit." She rang a silver bell that was near to hand, and a lady-in-waiting appeared. They chatted in Portuguese, and Roger had a moment to observe them both.

The attendant, he knew, was old Ducetta, one of that retinue of Portuguese ladies and monks come to England with Catherine.

In '62, the new queen had looked as chaste and austere as a nun. Today her hair was dressed in the latest fashion, and her gown was as low-cut as that of any woman at court.

Finding herself wed to a man who shortly after their marriage publicly presented his current mistress to his new wife, Catherine had chosen to fight for the affection of her husband with the weapons any woman uses. She had gained that affection, although for a man like Charles it didn't imply fidelity.

At twenty-seven Roger Griffin was unmarried, too busy with his career to do anything but tumble the occasional wench who thrust herself at him. He knew little of deep emotions between a man and woman. Still, he understood something of the bond between the king and queen. Catherine forgave Charles his constant whoring, he forgave her for being sterile.

A tray arrived laden with silver and little red porcelain bowls from China. "See, Roger?" The queen smiled up at him with obvious pleasure. "The leaves are steeped in this jug, and then we pour the brew into these little bowls." He reached for one with an expression more of duty than expectation, and Catherine stayed his hand with laughter. "Not yet, Roger! First Ducetta will add the sugar and the milk. I know you've not yet tried tea, but surely you've come to appreciate sugar?"

It was hard not to laugh at that remark. Catherine of Braganza had brought to the marriage market the most fabulous dowry in all of Europe. At least so her mother claimed. But when Roger watched them load the ship in Lisbon it wasn't gold that filled the hold but sugar, tons of that exotic sweetener few Englishmen had even seen before the arrival of the Portuguese princess. Worth more than the promised five hundred thousand in cash, Catherine's mother claimed; worthless, the English insisted. The battle raged for years, though it didn't prevent the marriage. Now, hearing the queen refer so innocently to the virtues of sugar, Roger had difficulty containing his mirth. "I'm afraid I'm not concerned with such things, ma'am," he managed to say finally. "Whether food's sweetened with honey or sugar seems to me to matter little."

"Dear Roger! How very, very English you are.... It matters enormously. I'm sure you will come to see that."

While Griffin sipped tea with the queen, the king strolled in his privy garden and discussed Roger with James, Duke of York. "I saw just yesterday your young protégé's plan for improving the methods for requisitioning naval supplies. I'm not expert in this matter, but it seems to me quite clever."

"It is. He's a very promising young man."

"Yes, so you've said repeatedly. Has this Griffin chap a wife or sister you wish to bed that you press his case so diligently?"

The Duke of York chuckled. "Would you believe it, neither. He's unmarried, and I've never met his relatives. I think he does have a sister, but like all the family except Roger, she lives far off somewhere in the Yorkshire wilds. What charms the lady may possess are unknown to me."

"Then why..."

"Why do I urge you so heartily to give him authority and let him use it? Because he is a quite brilliant lad with both intelligence and imagination. I claim neither virtue, as you know, but the ability to recognize them is a talent I believe I have. Moreover, he is completely loyal to you. Your majesty has few enough men of brilliance and total fidelity."

"So." Charles slowed his pace along the grassy path they walked and idly twisted the gold-topped stick he carried, making a pattern of holes in the soft springy turf. "You have no special suit to press, and neither does he. I'm to believe you both act only in my best interests?"

"And England's. Do you doubt it?"

"When all is said and done, no, I don't. The queen sings this Griffin's praises as loudly as you do. And I know beyond question that she has no motive other than to serve me. But there are others..."

"Ah yes. Burton and Lord March, I expect."

"They are but two among perhaps a half-dozen who crave young Griffin's hide."

"I don't doubt it. His efforts have done much to reduce the profits they garner from supplying the ships."

"You say that with scorn, James, but you're wrong. Full money chests do as much to foster loyalty as do nobler sentiments."

The younger brother snorted in disgust. "My lord, I have much respect for your way of making the court and the people love you. But you cannot purchase love by allowing such disasters as overtook our fleet two years ago."

"Allow, me? I remind you, dear little brother, that it is you who are lord high admiral of the Royal Navy. Surely it's not my fault that the Dutch broke through our defenses, sailed up the Medway to the Thames, and captured and towed away our flagship, the *Royal Charles*."

James grimaced; the memory rankled him more than it did the king. Unlike his brother, for James forgiving and forgetting did not come naturally. "I admit my responsibility," he said stiffly. "But I told you then, and I tell you now, the entire fiasco was the fault of men like March and Burton and Randolf. We had ships carrying cannons without shot, muskets without lead. All because of profiteering whoremasters who use the Royal Navy to feather their own nests."

"All right, enough!" The king held up an elegant hand. "God knows you've told me this before. Very well. Young Griffin will have his chance. I pray both he and I don't live to regret it. I suggest you set him working with that young clerk you so admire. What's his name..."

"Pepys, sire. Samuel Pepys."

"Right. Put him and Griffin together and let's see what they can do."

Roger lowered himself between the woman's spread legs more from a sense of duty than from passion. An hour earlier the smell and feel of her had been an almost painful excitement. When first she'd thrust at him those full breasts, waving them like a flag of challenge in his face, and pressed her curved hips against his breeches, Roger had found the prospect of what she was offering delightful. Now he slid himself into the much-used cavern of her womanhood with a mix of boredom and distaste. At that moment he could not have said exactly why.

Every man who'd been with him at that little supper in

19

the king's private chamber was likewise engaged. It had been just ten o'clock when they'd all paired off, none so crude as to leave with his own wife, and gone to their separate but similar entertainments. Though some said he was tiring of her, Charles himself left with his mistress of many months, Barbara Villiers. In the seconds before nature overruled intellect, Roger wondered briefly if the royal assignation was more pleasurable than this one. Then his loins developed a life and will of their own. He thrust with increased vigor until he ended his exertions in shuddering gasps and a welcome sense of relief.

Beneath him the viscountess was moaning and gasping and writhing with enthusiasm. Honesty caused Roger to view her performance with a jaded eye. She so clearly intended him to believe that he had given her extraordinary pleasure and demonstration of virility that her act lost credibility by its excess.

Such thoughts caused him a moment's guilt, then the viscountess absolved him with her first words. She lay beside him, head cradled on his chest and fingers toying with his hair. "Sir, or perhaps now I may call you Roger..." She simpered rather than laughed. "I wonder if I may speak to you of something. I hope I've given you enough proof of affection to justify my boldness. Lord Randolf tells me you've taken from him the contract to supply meat from his estates in Cambridgeshire to the vessels of the fleet moored in Rye...."

So it was all clear. The viscountess was reputed to be Randolf's mistress. It must be at his lordship's behest that the woman had spread her legs for the young captain. Seeing her in that light, Griffin fought back a wave of nausea. Like everything in this stinking court she was overblown and opulent. She glittered, but beneath the facade was a disregard for any value other than money. Her great breasts seemed to him rotten, like too-ripe fruit, her pouting mouth not sensuous but servile.

Later, walking through the gardens of Whitehall Palace toward his apartment in the east wing, Roger knew a sudden pang of longing for the wild moors and hills of Yorkshire. It was so intense it cramped his gut, a real and hurtful thing. This was October. In the gardens of Harwood Hall the rowan trees were festooned with orange berries, and his favorite patch of wild bramble high in the hills was heavy with succulent black fruit. It was very special, that patch. Since boyhood he'd thought of it as his. No one else ever went there or gathered the berries. He had discovered the bramble thicket when he was out hawking. Often he'd returned to the spot to drink of its peace and beauty and isolation. In that place he had come to terms with himself and his life, made his most important decisions.

Roger Griffin had been nine when his mother died and thirteen when his father joined her. After that Mark, his brother and elder by nine years, became squire of Harwood Hall. Both boys had always known it would be so; Mark was the firstborn and legitimate heir. But never until the actual event did Roger understand what it meant to be the second son. He had little in his own right, only a monthly allowance from the estate. For anything more he must depend on Mark. The elder Griffin was generous; the boys had always been close. But Roger knew he would never be content to live in his brother's shadow. That much he recognized instinctively and without struggle—it was the consequences that flowed from it which were difficult to accept. For if he was not to be simply Mark's lieutenant and dependent, he must make a life for himself elsewhere—he must leave Harwood Hall.

The lonely bramble patch had been his host throughout the long weeks and months of wrestling with that truth. The Griffins were known for their steadfast loyalty. It was a characteristic that surfaced in each of them in every generation; vigilant guardsmen of what was theirs, like the mythical beast whose name they bore. In Roger the quality was somehow intensified, writ large. The Hall was part of his flesh, its aged stones his nourishment. To leave it was to cut off something of himself. But warring with that inbred attachment to the place his ancestors had occupied since the eleventh century was this new un-Griffinlike ambition to be his own man, to carve a mark upon his time.

When the answer finally came it was not a break with his heritage, but the affirmation of yet another part of it; that Griffin dogma which put fidelity to the crown above all other duties.

The broadside which announced Charles I's execution arrived in Yorkshire, and Mark insisted the rooms of the Hall be draped in black. The family assumed mourning dress with haughty disregard of the consequences such defiance of the new order might bring. Harwood was far removed from London; neither the Parliament nor the army, which had conspired together to murder a king and seize his power, were forces in the distant north. Instead the deposition of the monarch and Cromwell's assumption of rule confirmed the secret decision Roger had earlier made. He would offer himself in service to the new king, preferably with a military commission under the Duke of York. That the Stuarts were then in exile only made his choice seem a greater, more worthy thing. He was seventeen when he secured his brother's consent and took passage to France.

Walking this night ten years later in the grounds of Whitehall, disgusted with the endless intrigues and idiocies of court life, Griffin knew a moment's doubt about the wisdom of his choice. Then he remembered yet again the family motto, *Regum in Via Recta Dirige*—Guide Straight the King. Somewhere a cock crowed and dawn reddened the horizon. He shrugged, casually saluted the palace guard, and took himself to bed.

2.

"Mark..."

"Yes?" He looked up from a huge oak table spread with ledgers and accounts. "Oh, it's you, Sophia. Come in."

"I shan't disturb you, I promise. I just want to look at that old record again. May I?"

"Of course." He gestured to a shelf in the far corner of the study. "You know where it is." His sister made no reply. "Tell me, Sophia...what is it you're looking for? You've been through that book four times. Maybe I could help."

"Thank you, but I don't need any help." She removed a great leather-bound folio from its niche and spread it open on a small table nearby.

"Well," her brother said with a grin, "you're welcome to look. Though I'm damned if I can see what fascinates you in Samuel Griffin's accounts of the Hall. Endless detailed entries like 'Two shillings paid to Farmer Marsh's wife for eggs.'

Incredibly boring. Besides, shouldn't you be helping Clare with the children now?"

"She doesn't need me." Sophia ran a pointed finger along her great-grandfather's journal entries. He had kept fastidious records. That's why she was sure she would eventually find here some clue to her private mystery.

Mark seemed determined to distract her with conversation. "I wish you were as interested in the future of Harwood as you are in its past. You still haven't given me an answer about John Cannock."

"That's not so. I gave you my answer the first time you mentioned him."

"Sophia..." Her brother was growing impatient and a trifle angry. "That wasn't an answer. It was an ill-considered piece of childish nonsense. 'I don't intend to marry.' What kind of statement is that, for God's sake?"

"A true one. Anyway, I'd never wed John Cannock. He's four years younger than I, his teeth are rotten, and he's a Scot."

Mark rose and stood behind his desk, arms folded and color rising. Sophia had been only eight years old when he became squire. Now she was twenty-five, long past the marrying age, and still as obstinate as ever. "Dear girl, I hesitate to be indelicate, but you're not getting any younger, you know. And you're not..." He broke off. It wasn't in Mark Griffin's nature to say hurtful things.

"I'm not any beauty. Is that what you were going to say? Don't blush, Mark. I'm not offended. I can see myself in my glass as well as you can."

"Look, love, that's not important. You do exasperate me and I say foolish things, but you're a fine woman and you'll make someone a fine wife. Why in heaven's name must you be so stubborn? Cannock's a full-grown man in spite of being a bit younger than you. That he's a Scot isn't a fault. He's no kirk fanatic, after all. The family are Church of Scotland, as Anglican as we are in all but name. And Cannock's father owns land just north of us in Richmond. He proposes to build a house for you and his son there. It would unite our estates."

Throughout his long speech Sophia kept her eyes glued to the page of ancient trivia as if it were her only concern. But mention of the Richmond property caused her to raise her head. "That's really the crux of the matter, isn't it?" she said quietly. "More land for Harwood Hall."

"What in holy hell is wrong with that? You're the one so

suddenly enamored of our history." He pointed to Samuel's journal. "And if you read well you'll find mention of how the old man made arrangements for marrying all his children to mates of his choosing. Not theirs. I could insist, Sophia. You know I could."

"Oh, Mark..." This time she sounded genuinely distressed. "You wouldn't. You promised me you never would. And Clare said you wouldn't dream of it."

Griffin dropped back in his seat and ran his fingers through his graying hair. "Be calm, Sophia. For God's sake, no hysterics. I promised and I'll keep my word."

Brother and sister were silent for some minutes after that, each absorbed in the pages they studied.

Then Mark heard the girl gasp and looked up. If, however, she'd discovered something noteworthy she made no mention of it. Instead she calmly closed the book and replaced it on the shelf. "You've found something, then?" he asked at last.

"Perhaps." She started for the door, then turned back to him. "Besides," she added, "Cannock's teeth are rotten. You didn't deny it."

The door was closed behind her before he recovered himself sufficiently to speak. Then he muttered aloud in the empty room, "Lord protect me from this houseful of women...all of whom unfortunately know how to read!"

"You've come again, child?"

"Yes."

The old woman was exactly where she'd been the last time. Sitting at a rough table in the room that looked like a scullery, though it could not be, and shelling peas, though it was autumn and no peas could be found in all of Yorkshire. Sophia lowered herself to a three-legged stool in the corner and watched her.

"How is it with you today?" the nun asked after some minutes.

"Very well, thank you. That is..."

"Yes? You've some problem?"

"Dear God! You, you're my problem. What are you doing here?"

The old woman chuckled. "Just what I was doing when last you came. My work in this the kitchen of Kirkslee Priory."

24

"But it's not! It can't be. It's the west wing of Harwood Hall."

"So you've said before."

"And you and all your kind are gone from Yorkshire. From all England, in fact."

"Yes, you said that too."

"Then how can you insist so calmly..."

"Child." The nun held out her hand. "Touch me. My flesh is warm. If you prick me with this knife I promise you it's real blood you'll draw. I'm no ghost and neither are you, I'm sure of it."

"But I tell you it is October of the year 1669. Beyond that door is a corridor leading to the east wing of my home, Harwood Hall. In it are my family, my brother, his wife, their four children, the servants. None of them are ghosts either! Tell me if you can, when you go out that door, where will you be?"

"In the priory's south cloister, which leads to the refectory. Just as I was but a few minutes earlier. In the year 1510, as I explained on your last visit, and the one before that."

"What month is this?" Sophia demanded.

"July, the first of July, and we are keeping the feast of Our Savior's most Precious Blood."

Sophia buried her head in her hands. "How can you accept it all so easily?"

"Accept what, child? You? Your presence here? How can I accept that my Lord and God should have willingly hung on a cross for me? That He gives me Himself in Holy Communion? Is not that more marvelous? Yet I accept and believe it, base my life on it. But, I'll tell you the truth, the first time, the boy, well, that frightened me. Now it does no longer."

"What boy? When was it? You never told me anyone else had come."

"You never asked me. As to who he was, I do not know. We didn't speak. He simply opened the door, then ran away terrified."

"Was he a lad of ten or twelve?" Sophia asked, thinking of her nephews. "Tall with blond hair? They're both tall and blond."

"No. Not blond, dark. And a bit older than that, I think." The nun shrugged. "It doesn't matter."

"Yes, it does!" The girl rose and clenched her fists in anguish. "If someone else saw you I'll make them tell me. Then I'll know I'm not going mad."

"Mad? Of course you're not. Because one sees that which is inexplicable does not mean madness. Surely you know that."

Sophia ignored her words. "When was the boy here?"

"By my reckoning, a few weeks ago. By yours, I cannot say." She finished with the peas and placed the big bowl on the table, then stood and smoothed her shabby black habit. "Now I must go. It's almost time to chant the office."

"Come." Sophia held out her hand. "We'll go together. We'll walk out through that door together and see which of us is right about what's on the other side of it."

"No." The woman shook her head. "That we mustn't do. I know that much for sure. You must promise not to follow me, or try to step across the threshold at the same moment I do. You do promise?"

Sophia nodded her head. She did not know why she gave in on this point, only that she always did. She watched the nun move toward the door. It was open for a second. Beyond it Sophia had a fleeting impression of light and sunshine. Then it was closed and she was alone in the scullery. An ordinary place, filled with ordinary things, little different from the scullery of the Hall downstairs.

But there was no reasonable explanation for it, or for the woman's being here when all religious houses in England had been dissolved and banned since 1540. The only hint was that one entry she'd found in her grandfather's journal. A note dated 11 November, 1572, that stated, "Today were delivered six cartloads of stone from the ruined Priory of Kirkslee to be used for building the new west wing. Paid for them the sum of two sovereigns."

Sophia walked to the door and slowly pushed it open. The light and sunshine were there no longer. She had known they wouldn't be. There was only the passageway leading away from this west wing, which was supposed to be shut off and empty.

She didn't go back for nearly a week. Fear perhaps, or self-discipline. Better to leave such things alone, better to ignore what one cannot explain. But she couldn't stay away. This time the nun was sorting a basket of new-laid eggs. She smiled at Sophia and went on with her task.

26

"I asked both boys, Andrew and Charles, my brother's sons. Both swear they've not been near the west wing. I believe them."

"I'm glad they're truthful children."

Sophia picked up one of the eggs and held it gently in her cupped palm. It was still warm, decidedly no figment of her imagination. "How long is it for you? Since I was last here, I mean."

"It's afternoon. You were here this morning."

"No. It's six days. This is Sunday. I was here Monday last."

"Our reckoning is different, we know that. Sometimes too it seems to me a long time that we speak, but when you've gone my work is often just at the stage it was when you arrived, though my hands were not a moment idle. It's one of the strangenesses. Like the fact that no one ever interrupts us here, though my sisters otherwise come often to the scullery. Do not others of your household use this place you call the west wing?"

"No one, ever. I don't know why. It's been shut up since I was born. I'm told my mother ordered it. But she died when I was four, and I do not know her reasons."

"What brought you here the first time?"

"I don't know that either. An urge, more like a compulsion. I had to come."

"Yes. I understand. That doesn't surprise me."

"But why? Why is this whole mad business happening?"

"You mustn't call it madness. It's Our Lord's doing."

"How do you know that?"

"I know."

Sensing that she'd speak no more of that, Sophia changed the subject. "Tell me something else. You do not seem like any servant woman of my time. Why do you do this menial work?"

"It is the way of our order. All are servants of the Lord Jesus. All do menial work."

"It seems ridiculous to me. You should have kitchen maids for these things."

"Many agree with you. They go to other orders where that is the custom. We are but thirteen."

"I see...then that's why..." Sophia broke off and bit her lip.

"Go on. That's why what?"

"I didn't want to tell you. It's horrible. And I'm not sure it's true. I've been reading the old histories. They say that

27

when King Henry ordered all the houses of monks and nuns to close in 1540 there were only three women left in Kirkslee."

"But that's just thirty years hence by my reckoning. To think so few are left by then!" The nun shook her head in wonderment.

Anger at her calm acceptance of all Sophia found so deeply disturbing prompted the girl's next statement. When first she'd read the story she had vowed never to tell the woman about it. "Seven of them were hanged at York Castle, and three others ran away. That's why only three were left."

She had intended to shock, and she had. "Hanged! But why? In God's name, why?"

"Because they wouldn't take the oath when the king and the bishops said we were not subject to the Bishop of Rome. They wouldn't swear that Henry was the lawful head of the Church in England."

"Praise God!" the old woman exclaimed with feeling. "I feared witchcraft."

"Oh, you make me furious! Don't you even want to know if your name was among those that were hung?"

"I dare not ask. I might lose courage if I had to live expecting such a thing. But I'm already fifty. It's not likely I can live thirty more years, even to win a martyr's crown."

"I don't know anyway." The girl's tone softened. "No names were listed in the records."

"It's better that way." The nun transferred her basket of eggs to another table and sat facing her young visitor. "Listen to me, child. These meetings of ours, I know they disturb you greatly. Just as I know they're of God and not the devil. One cannot explain such knowing, but I'll try. I have prayed much over this matter, though I've discussed it with not another soul. When last I was shriven of my sins I thought to mention it to my confessor, but something stopped me. Now it occurs to me that time, all time, is like a great tapestry worked by the Lord God and laid over our world as a cloth is laid over a table. Somehow in this place there is a . . . how can I explain it . . . a fold, a wrinkle if you will, in the tapestry. We are part of a wrinkle in time."

"But why? To what end? I think that now I've told you the terrible things to come you must all leave this place. If you're not here none of it can happen."

The nun shook her head. "No, we must change nothing. If it were to alter the course of Divine Providence that this

28

had happened Our Lord would have chosen other instruments. Important people, kings and queens. Not an old nun and a helpless girl. Don't you see that?"

Sophia nodded. "I've thought about it since I read that awful story, and there seems to me nothing I can do."

"No, nor are you meant to. The answer lies elsewhere, child. In our hearts."

"I cannot find it there."

"You will. Trust God and pray. You will find it."

The next time she went to the west wing she found nothing but the drafty old rooms that were meant to be there. They were empty of all but a few sticks of unwanted furniture, cold and damp and tightly shuttered. Sophia felt relief, but also a sense of loss.

"Mark?" She didn't know what prompted the question. She had not intended to ask it. Not here at the dining table, of all places. "Why did Mother close the west wing? Do you know?"

He had been raising a beaker of wine to his lips when she spoke. Now he put it down and said with some impatience, "A superstitious nonsense. It's got nothing to do with you."

"But it must have," Sophia persisted. "Old Bess, the kitchen maid, told me it was closed just four days after I was born. It must have something to do with me."

"I told you, it's a ridiculous story. Not worth repeating."

"Oh Papa, do tell us! I've often wondered about the west wing myself. Why doesn't anyone ever go there?" At fifteen Laura Griffin was a sunny, sparkling girl, still like a child in her spontaneous enthusiasms. And still her father's favorite, though he was beginning to think he must look for a husband for her, not let her grow as set in maidenhood as had her aunt.

"It was nothing but an old fairy tale. Someone said they saw a ghost in the west wing. When your Aunt Sophia here was born with one eye brown and the other blue, my mother decided it must be true. She had the place sealed off."

"A ghost!" the two young boys shouted in unison. "A ghost at Harwood Hall?"

Sarah, thirteen and still the practical, plain-speaking

Griffin, said, "That's foolish. There are no ghosts. Leastwise not at the Hall."

Sophia paid no attention to the comments of her nieces and nephews. She only stared at her brother and asked quietly, "Who said they saw the ghost, Mark? Who was it?"

"Truth is, it was me, though I'm ashamed to admit it. I insisted I'd seen an old woman dressed all in black in the room just off the east passageway. I don't know why I said it."

Sophia dropped her wineglass with a loud clatter and watched unseeing as a purple river flowed out from the shards. The children went on gossiping. A footman appeared hastily at her elbow and mopped up the mess. When she looked up she saw Clare peering anxiously at her husband. He was staring at Sophia with the same expression of shock she knew masked her own features.

3.

"You sent for me, sire." He bowed low and stood waiting.

"I did. You need not be so formal, Captain Griffin. Sit down. Did you enjoy yourself the other night? You left with that dark wench, didn't you? The Viscountess something-or-other."

"Yes, your majesty. It was a most pleasant evening. Your majesty did me great honor to invite me to share such an intimate gathering."

Charles cocked his head and studied the younger man. "Why didn't I see more of you when we were in France in the '50s, Roger? Had my brother not told me you were with us then, I wouldn't have known it."

"I was very young, sir, just seventeen when I came in '57. And his grace the Duke of York kept me fully occupied."

For some reason the statement amused the king. He guffawed loudly and pounded his fist on the arm of his chair. "Indeed, as you were occupied the other evening perhaps?"

"Hardly with such attractive company, sire."

"No, I think not. You were asked to our supper"—his voice lost its undertone of laughter and grew serious—"to discuss your latest proposal. But the time didn't seem propitious, so we'd best discuss the business now." He withdrew a sheaf of papers from a drawer and spread them on the elaborately carved table. "I wish to hear this explained in your own words."

Roger drew a deep breath and marshaled his arguments in quick mental exercise. This unexpected meeting seemed likely to make or break his career at court. The king was sensitive to his young aide's concerns. "Don't spare the truth, Roger. Your frankness, according to both my brother and my queen, is your greatest virtue. It won't serve you ill now."

"By your leave, then, sire, your navy is in a piteous state. Not because of any lack of courage or loyalty among the officers or the men, nor because of any lack of ability on the part of his grace as lord high admiral. It's because those who purport to serve the needs of the fleet care only for their own purses."

Charles stroked his silky mustache with one ringed finger. "If that's truth, Roger, it's also treason. To subvert the king's navy is to undermine the king. Is such your accusation?"

"You are wiser than I in such matters, sire. You put a finer point on the issue than I would dare to do. I only know that at this moment most seamen are some fifty months behind in their wages. Men are dying regularly on all voyages. Not from any wounds inflicted by an enemy, but through simple starvation. In a battle, as your majesty well knows, they often find themselves out of ammunition before the second salvo is fired. If this be treason, then it is a crime only your majesty can deal with. I call it simply gross greed, inefficiency, and stupidity. That I propose to rectify."

"How?" Charles leaned forward and stared intently.

"It's all here, sire," Roger shuffled through the papers until he found the one he wanted. "Here, this bit on the victualing of the navy. That's the most pressing need."

The king pushed the paper aside. "Yes, I've read it. Now I want to hear you tell it."

"Look, right now we're letting out private contracts to all and sundry for supplying this or that. They deliver the goods to individual ships, and receipts are issued by individual

31

pursers. The opportunity for collusion, for every manner of graft, is obvious. I propose a central authority for all such purchasing, sire. And a series of central storehouses guarded by your own troops and manned by men accountable to his grace the Duke of York."

"And whence will come the money for all this purchasing?"

"From Parliament, sire. They must vote the funds to feed those whom they rely on for the defense of yourself and the realm."

"Must, Roger? I fear, lad, your memory is short where Parliament is concerned. They don't believe they 'must' do anything. My late father could attest to that."

"Sire, I'm beyond my own capabilities. I readily confess it. I was asked to create the structure in which it is possible to feed efficiently and economically your great fleet. This I dare to believe I've done here." He tapped the papers lying before him. "To make such a plan politically acceptable is not a task for which God's given me a whit of talent. Forgive me if I've thus failed you."

"No, Captain Griffin, you haven't failed me at all. I think your plan is brilliant. Others will have the job of getting Parliament to agree. That slippery business is not your province. Your colleague, Mr. Pepys, it's more his line of country."

He rose to signal the interview ended, but ruffled through the papers once more. "A final thing, this list of provisions per man—'daily, one pound of biscuit, one gallon of beer, two pounds of beef or pork, one pint of peas...' It hardly seems enough to keep a child alive, let alone a British tar. You're sure of these quantities?"

"I've questioned many, sire. Ordinary seamen and their betters. They all assure me it's enough."

Charles shook his head and laughed again. It was the warm, infectious laughter that had endeared him to so many. "A single gallon of beer for a whole day. And seamen are supposed to be a drunken lot. Not on eight pints of beer, I wager."

Summoned to the royal presence for the third time in as many days; sweet Christ, when was he expected to get any work done? Roger stood silently, listening to the king and hoping his distaste for the proposed errand didn't show on his face.

"You can't expect me to send Dewinters here," Charles

said. "Surely, Roger, even an innocent like yourself can see Sir John's no messenger to send to fetch a lady."

The aide in question made no response to this insult. His bloated red face, looking for all the world like a blood sausage squashed in the middle, didn't change. When the king turned to him and asked, "Don't you agree, Sir John?" Dewinters nodded meekly and didn't even bother to look at the young man who was witness to his humiliation.

Years in court had taught Roger that incidents such as this were never without a purpose. Charles wasn't a vengeful or a crude man. So what was this episode in aid of, and why was he involved? To go to the theater in Drury Lane and summon the actress Nell Gwyn to have supper with his majesty. That's what Charles said, at any rate. But why send Roger Griffin? Surely he wasn't reputed to have any special talent with ladies. Moreover, when the king sent for a wench like the celebrated Miss Gwyn no special envoy was needed. Charles could dispatch the humblest page in the palace and be sure the woman would come running. Everyone knew Nell had been warming the Duke of Buckingham's bed for the past year. And Buckingham's wife was James's present mistress. Lord, what a tangle these people got themselves into....

"Well, Roger...don't just stand there. Go get the girl." Charles poured himself a glass of wine before Dewinters could manage to do the service for him. "I'm lonely tonight. Miss Gwyn's company appeals to me."

"Your pardon, sire, for the delay. I'm on my way."

He bowed and started to leave, but the king's last words stopped him. "Oh, Roger, one bit of business. I sent your victualing plan to my brother today. With a note in my own hand commending its virtues."

And that, of course, was the object of the exercise. Dewinters was part of the clique that included March and Randolf and Burton. The very trio who had most to lose if the new plan was put into practice. This little drama in the king's sitting room was his majesty's way of letting all of them know he stood firmly behind Roger and the Duke of York in the matter. Christ! It must come with the blood royal, this gift for convoluted intrigue.

Griffin nodded, squared his shoulders, and stepped out into the evening. "You there, footman! A carriage, lad, and hurry! I'm on the king's business."

* * *

It was a still night. No breath of wind came to diffuse the ripe odor of the London streets. Behind the team of horses the driver's face was as dark as his livery. He hacked and wheezed until Roger feared he might lose control of the small vehicle, but he couldn't blame him. The stench invaded a man's nostrils, crawled down the back of his throat until he couldn't breathe. It wasn't just the human refuse or the horse dung that the road cleaners should have removed earlier that was so noxious. It was the pervasive, eye-stinging fumes of coal fires burning in tens of thousands of grates to warm the city of half a million souls. Tonight Roger fancied that he could smell as well the lingering stench of that larger conflagration, the Great Fire that had swept through the city three years earlier.

A jumble of wooden houses and shops cluttered the narrow road, made it impossible for any fresh air to disperse the stink. In '65 and '66 these very alleys and lanes had been ravaged by first the black death and then the fire, but they seemed unchanged for all that. The king and Parliament had passed numerous laws insisting that all rebuilding be done in brick or stone. Still, people needed homes and places of business. Most of them couldn't afford such fire-resistant materials, so they rebuilt in the familiar stucco and half-timber. They could only trust God to protect them from yet another disaster.

Roger pressed a linen handkerchief to his nose and rolled up the window of the little coach. This wasn't the king's grandest vehicle by any standard. But it had clear glass windows rather than leather flaps to keep out the elements. Roger was grateful for them. If the Gwyn woman returned with him, and God help them both if she didn't, he'd pull the curtains shut inside the glass. If Charles chose to make this new affair public, that was his concern; it wasn't for Roger to do it for him.

"Drury Lane, sir." The footman yanked the door open before Roger realized the carriage had stopped. "Shall we wait?"

"Yes. I don't know how long I'll be, however. Here..." He fished some coins from the purse at his waist. "Sixpence for each of you. Have a pint of beer while you're waiting, but see you're ready to leave when I am."

They left him standing before a single-story building lit by two flaming torches flanking a narrow door. Roger stepped inside and found himself in a kind of antechamber, stuffy and badly lit, leading to the theater itself. From behind heavy curtains he could hear a roar of voices and laughter. The audience was loud in its enjoyment and approval of the play.

A young page stood at the back of the small lobby. "You there, boy," Roger said. "I wish to see Miss Gwyn."

"So do all those folks inside." The boy gestured toward the velvet drapes that hid the audience. "That's what they paid their shilling for. Have you bought your ticket, mister?"

"Cheeky little devil, hold your tongue or you'll regret it. I'm on the king's business."

"Meant no disrespect sir, not to his majesty. But Nell's on stage now. Be through in about a quarter of an hour."

Suddenly Roger heard the clear, melodious voice of the famous actress. "Very well, I'll wait. But see she knows I'm here."

"I'll tell her friend Miss Nancy, sir. You wait right here."

Roger studied the small room. The walls were plastered with posters and broadsheets of previous productions; almost all had been Gwyn triumphs.

"They tell me, sir, that you come from the king." The woman's words were addressed to his back, for he hadn't heard her enter. "What is his majesty's wish?"

His first impression, and he was never to forget it, was of a shaft of sunlight having strayed into the dark little chamber. The girl wasn't beautiful; she had none of the curvaceous lushness that typified the women at court. She was tall, with slim hips and small breasts that made her figure appear almost boyish. Her hair glowed a rich, improbable auburn and hung straight down her back like a shimmering veil. Her smile was wide and generous, and her voice was edged with laughter. "Who," he asked, grinning broadly with sheer pleasure at the sight of her, "might you be?"

"Nancy Wilmott's my name. And who are you, milord?"

"Not 'milord' at all. Just Roger Griffin, captain of the Royal Navy."

"The Royal Navy indeed." The girl saw the way he looked at her and grew bold. "Have you a frigate tied up outside, captain? Or are you here to declare war on us poor players?"

"I'm here at the king's behest, Miss Wilmott." He made his face and voice serious, though the lass had a way of making him want to laugh aloud. "I've a message for Miss Gwyn."

"Oh, I see." She raised her eyebrows. "So his majesty's finally come round, has he?" She spoke more to herself than to him, then seemed to fear an indiscretion. "I mean..."

He liked watching her cheeks color in confusion. For some seconds he said nothing to put her at ease. Then, "Don't worry. I know what you meant. Has she been expecting this, then?"

The girl laughed. "Since they met at Tunbridge Wells last year. Nell was with a touring company, and his majesty accompanied the queen, who was taking the waters. But 'expecting' isn't the right word; 'hoping' is more correct, perhaps."

"Can I ask you something?" His sincerity was real. It could prove ill advised if his instantaneous judgment of Nancy Wilmott was inaccurate. "Why? Why hope to be his mistress? Is it just the presents and the money?"

"Plenty will say just that, but I know Nell better than they do. We've been together all our lives. To tell you the truth, she doesn't care much for wealth. Not if she has a pretty dress to wear, enough to eat, and a warm, dry bed. No, she took a liking to him. She'll be genuinely flattered that his majesty felt something the same. That's all there is to it."

"So," Roger spoke in amusement and wonder, "she fancies him, is that it? Like any milkmaid with a farm hand?"

The girl's chin came up in defiance. "You can mock if you like, Captain Griffin, but yes, that's it. She fancies him."

"Don't be angry. I'm delighted to hear it. Really I am. There are few enough that seek to please the king only because of affection. If Nell Gwyn's one of them I wish them joy of each other. When will she be ready to go?"

"I'm ready now." That famous, unmistakable voice. Close up, her dark good looks weren't as spectacular as they appeared on stage, but the vibrancy which illuminated her every word and gesture was even more overwhelming. So too the fun-loving sparkle in her eyes. "C'mon, ducks." She linked her arm through Roger's. "I've been ready for twelve bloody months."

4.

The following week Griffin went to the theater three nights running. They were doing *Antony and Cleopatra* in a version that had Nancy Wilmott acting the Egyptian queen. She didn't die in the end, however. She wed Mark Antony instead, and the pair lived happily ever after. Roger found Sir William D'Avenant's popularized version of the story ridiculous, but Sir Will was widely reputed to be Shakespeare's bastard son, so perhaps he had the right to such finagling. With Nancy Wilmott's performance Roger had no quarrel whatever. Except, perhaps, that the elaborate black wig she wore on stage hid her glorious hair.

"There you are." He stepped into her path as she left the playhouse after the last performance. "I like you better like this. Your own hair is magnificent. They should never have made you wear that wig."

"Oh." She didn't seem startled to see him. "You didn't care for my Cleopatra, then?"

"On the contrary, I cared very much indeed."

"Yes, I rather thought so. You came every night, I noticed."

Roger smiled. "I thought you saw me. I'd come every night for the next year if you were playing."

"Such pretty speeches! And from a navy man at that. They teach you well in Charles's court."

"I'm no protégé of court manners," he said and scowled. "Whatever you may think."

"A protégé of the Duke of York, I'm told. And good friend to both king and queen."

"You're well informed. You were sufficiently curious to inquire, I see." He smiled and ran a bold finger along her curved cheek. "Then I can be assured you'll have supper with me."

"You can be assured of nothing." She brushed his hand

away. "All London knows everything that happens at White-hall. I couldn't help but hear."

"Very well." He laughed and put the offending hand behind him. "I see you're not yet overwhelmed by my charms. Give me an hour to prove their worth, then. Sup with me, Nancy. I've made arrangements at the Golden Bull. It's not far. Please say you will."

"At last, the word I've been waiting for." She smiled, and it lit up her face in a way that made his heart beat like a young boy's. "You've said 'please,' so I'll say 'thank you.' 'Yes thank you,' in fact." She linked her arm through his. "Is it near enough to walk? I don't know the place, but I like to walk after the theater."

"Just over on the river, by the Temple. We can walk. I'll tell my driver." He spoke a few words to the waiting coachman and rejoined her quickly. "Now, tell me about yourself. Do you live nearby? You have the advantage of me, since, as you say, all London knows everything about the court."

"There's little worth telling. I have a room at the Cock and Pie over there. That small inn on the corner. The old widow who runs it isn't averse to renting chambers to theater people."

"You have no family, then?"

"None."

"Were you born in London? Your accent gives nothing away."

"Doesn't it?" She laughed. "Ach, milord, hae ye a penny fur a lass wot's fair starvin'?" More laughter, this time with a bitter undertone. "Would that tell you anything?"

"A child of the Moorgate alleys. But is that the real Nancy Wilmott, or just another role?"

"It's real enough. I spoke that way for sixteen years. Then Nell and I joined Killigrew and D'Avenant and learned to 'talk proper-like.' Actresses mustn't sound like street urchins."

"I'm glad you did. Learn to speak properly, I mean. A woman who looks like you shouldn't sound like a tart."

She stopped suddenly and turned to face him. A nearby torch cast a red glow over the dirty cobblestones and made her chestnut hair sparkle with hints of gold. "But I am a tart," she said. "Make no mistake about it, my high and mighty Captain Griffin. I was very lucky in 1660—I overheard some talk in the Crown tavern and wormed a place in the company for Nell and me. I managed that the same way

I've managed most things in my life. On my back with my legs spread. I'm not saying I'm proud of it, but if you plan to pursue me you'd best know the truth from the start. That way there won't be any misunderstanding."

Her words were calm and her voice expressionless. Only her heaving chest indicated that the frank speech cost her something. "Now, my fine Yorkshire gentleman, do we go on, or have you suddenly remembered business at White-hall?"

He wanted very much to kiss her. His arms almost reached for her of their own accord, but he knew the moment was all wrong. Instead he said quietly, "Come along, Nancy. Our supper will be getting cold."

It was four nights later, riding with her in the back of a hired hackney coach, that he finally gave in to the hunger she roused in him and took her in his arms. When he released her mouth she said, "At last," with that hint of laughter that always underlay her words. "I thought, in spite of this invitation to accompany you to the country, I'd caught an odd fish that wanted me for something other than the usual. Why has it taken you so long to kiss me, Roger?"

"Damn you!" He couldn't say why he was angry. "That's just why. Because I knew you'd think exactly what you're thinking."

"'Come away with me, Nance...I know a fine little country inn where we can be alone for a few days....'" She mimicked his broad Yorkshire accent with devastating fidelity. "What do you expect me to think?"

"Then why did you agree?"

"Because," she said and reached up to stroke his forehead, "I wanted to. I want you to kiss me, and more...."

"But you always mock me."

"It's my way, Roger. I mean you no personal insult. Try to understand....I guess if I'm honest I'd have to say it's my protection."

That confession was a peace offering, he knew, a gift of self. Then, when she took his hand and pressed it over her heart, he forgot everything except the fiery yearning this woman kindled in him. A hundred willing bedmates crossed his path daily at Whitehall, but he'd conceived a thirst for Nancy Wilmott that only she could slake. When he kissed her again it was with a fervor that left no doubt in either of their minds as to what it was he wanted.

Later, when she lay beside him, white and naked in the moonlight that came through the open window, she reminded him of some high-strung thoroughbred at Harwood Hall. She had small pointed breasts, long thin flanks. The animal simile fitted too the ferocity of the act they'd recently consummated. It had never before been like that for him. Not that total wrenching union that seemed to summon the essence of his maleness from some buried place deep in his gut.

She hadn't said a word since he'd uttered his last moaning groan and rolled away from her twenty minutes before. When finally she spoke, the mocking tone had gone from her voice. "You liked me?" she asked. It sounded like the question of an insecure child.

"God..." He turned and touched her shoulder, letting his hand play over her cool, silky skin. "Couldn't you tell?"

"That's no answer." She was laughing again. "Not for a woman. You're really not a Whitehall gallant, are you?"

"No, I told you I wasn't."

"Mmm...but I didn't believe it. Tell me some more about your home. I love to listen to you talk. Tell me about leaving to join the king in France." She caressed him while she spoke. Soft, gentle touches that spoke of experience but somehow avoided the stilted artifice of the ladies of the court. He found himself telling her stories of his youth he'd never told anyone. Things he'd never believed would interest anyone but him. She was an attentive listener, but that didn't slow her busy hands.

Time passed and still neither of them seemed sleepy. It wasn't long before she'd stirred him again. He was taut and heavy with desire, but when he turned to take her once more she whispered, "Wait," and guided his hand to the softness between her thighs. "Touch me here and here. Yes, like that. Oh yes!" She was the one moaning now. Soft, persistent sounds that soon changed to gasps of hunger. When he covered her body with his she arched to meet him and wrapped her legs around his waist in a grip so strong it was startling. Her motions matched his own; those thin, boyish hips replied to every thrust with a sure rhythm.

This time, perhaps because it followed so soon on the earlier effort, it took him longer to summon the shuddering tumult from his loins. He was less immersed in the sensations of his own flesh, more conscious of her. It was an awareness

40

that strangely heightened his pleasure. She too was building to a frantic climax of sensation. That gave him a sense of power and delight beyond any previous experience. Suddenly her teeth sank into his shoulder. The unexpected pain mingled with the explosive pleasure they shared, and produced something that could only be called ecstasy.

"But what in God's name does Charles see in her? A common little whore..."

"An actress," the viscountess corrected as she poured chocolate into fragile porcelain cups. "An *artiste,* my dear. You mustn't call Nell Gwyn a common little whore any more. Not these days. They say she's pregnant. You know that always makes men sentimental and protective."

"Well, small wonder if the Gwyn bitch is pregnant. The king drops his breeches by her bed at least twice a day."

"Yes, but he does as much for the queen, at least so they say. Such a virile man his majesty! Still, Catherine's not ever pregnant."

Her companion tittered. "One advantage of common blood, I think—they do breed easily. Like sows and mares."

"My, you're wicked today! I think you're jealous." The viscountess smiled sweetly and sipped her drink. "I have another tidbit for you. Our sovereign's not only virile but influential. His taste for common meat's become a contagion. Did you hear about that handsome Captain Griffin, the one who caused so much trouble about the naval supplies? They say he's followed the king's example and taken up with an actress too. The lengths some people will travel to curry royal favor!"

"I like your mouth." Roger traced the wide and generous outline with his finger. "It's a mouth made to laugh, Nance. And to say yes. Why do you continue to refuse me?"

She rolled toward him, leaning on her elbow so that one rose-tipped breast nuzzled his shoulder and her long hair hung over his chest like a perfumed curtain. "Because you're daft. Worse than that...totally mad."

"About you, yes."

"About the world. Love, for the twentieth time, men like you simply do not marry girls like me. Bed them yes, often and with vigor, but wed them? Never."

"Love!" Roger pushed her away and stood beside the bed. "So you call me...like any little costermonger selling fish from a barrow. 'Sell you 'alf a pint o' cockles, luv. Only tuppence.' Is that what the word means to you, Nancy? About two pennies?"

"My speech is common," she admitted, "for all my accent's been tutored. I don't claim to be better than I am, Roger. You know that. But I do love you. I think you know that too."

His anger left him as suddenly as it had come. "I know it." He knelt and gathered her into his arms. "And I love you. Worse, I'm besotted with you. That's why I can't bear these constant partings. What kind of life is this, Nancy? We snatch what time we can spare and come to some inn or other, then it's back to Drury Lane for you and Whitehall for me. Is that all you want for us?"

"It needn't be like that, darling." She smoothed his dark hair back from a forehead that lately seemed permanently furrowed with worry. "I told you, if you get us a small house somewhere I'll live with you openly. I don't care a farthing who knows how much I love you."

"No." He rose once more and reached for his breeches, still lying on the floor where he'd hurriedly dropped them an hour earlier. "London may think such arrangements quite ordinary, but I don't. I'm a Griffin, Nancy. A Griffin of Harwood Hall. To me that means something. I'm asking you to share that ancient and honorable name. Not be my whore."

"Please." She stretched out one long, slim arm and extended her hand in a gesture of pleading. "Don't let's quarrel. Not today. We have so little time. Tomorrow I play Desdemona. I must be at the theater by six. Come back to bed, Roger. Please..."

He gave in to her, as he always did. Nothing seemed capable of bringing this issue of marriage between them to any settlement acceptable to him. "Tell me," he said with a humorless grin, "in your version will Othello and Desdemona live on in wedded bliss?" She nodded. "I thought so. The world you live in is no part of reality, Nancy. It's you, not I, who's mad."

"Oh, that feels good!" the girl exclaimed happily. Lord Randolf laughed and thrust himself yet deeper into the wench bouncing so athletically beneath him. He didn't know her name. She was a serving maid who had arrived in his chambers carrying a flagon of ale and stayed to offer other pleasures. He moved yet faster, intending to finish the encounter in customary fashion. Suddenly the girl put both hands on his chest and with surprising strength stopped him from making the final lunge. "If you fill my belly with a bastard, milord," she said calmly, "will you pay the babe's upkeep?" He stared at her in astonishment, then nodded his head. "I have your word on it?" He nodded once more. "Then drive home, milord! Drive home!"

He wasn't, however, destined to spill his seed this night. Not in this willing cavern. There was a loud and demanding knock on the door. This further interruption, coupled with the girl's greedy question at a moment of such delicacy, ended both Randolf's desire and his ability to continue. "Bloody hell," he muttered, more in exasperation than in anger, and rolled off the wench. His tool, he noted sadly, was now flaccid and useless. "Get your drawers on. Here's a shilling for your trouble. And you won't have a full belly after this night's work, so don't go looking for more."

He hitched up his elegant satin breeches and walked to the door. "I'm coming, stop that damned noise! Oh, it's you, is it, Dewinters. You interrupt my fucking; I hope it's in a good cause. Look at the nice bit of arse you've made me miss."

The girl hurried by the two men, still lacing her bodice. Then, mindful of her rank and theirs, she turned to drop a quick curtsy. "Thank you kindly, your lordship." She held out a grubby palm and displayed the shiny coin. "For the gift and...for everything."

The permanently red-faced Dewinters didn't join the other man's laughter. "You're a whoremaster, Randolf. You're so concerned with pampering your cock you'll soon find there's not a farthing in your money chest to pamper your belly."

His lordship held up his hand. "Spare me, Dewinters. I don't share your Puritan worry of hellfire and brimstone. What brings you here?"

"I've news, a hint of something that may work to our mutual advantage."

"With you that can only mean money. There's no other advantage you care about."

"Not so, sir!" Dewinters adopted an expression of long-suffering patience. "My chief concern is to see this realm kept free of papist superstition and evildoing. If that sometimes brings me material gain it's only the Lord's justice being done."

"All right, all right. Come in, for God's sake, and tell me what you've come here to tell me. Here, you old fraud, have some wine. I won't tell your Roundhead cronies."

"I tell you again, milord! I'm no Puritan." Then, sensing that Randolf was only baiting him, Dewinters turned to the matter at hand. "I hear you've felt the sting of this upstart Griffin's tail. It's true?"

"It's true. His new plan for victualing the fleet makes no provision for buying from my Cambridgeshire estates. Though it's a contract I've had these past seven years."

"Well, mind you I'm not saying anything definite, but he's a Yorkshire man. You know that?"

"Of course I know it. I've spoken to him, haven't I?"

"His people are well known in their part of the world. Only country squires, of course, not noblemen. But supposed to be Norman stock, though God knows many who claim it have no right."

"Get to the point, man. I'm not interested in his ancestors or yours."

Dewinters had bought his baronetcy from the proceeds of a piggery. He hated to be reminded of that, but he managed to smile. "Popery," he said. "There's rumors of popery at Harwood Hall. No proof yet, of course, but I have friends in Yorkshire. One of them swears he saw a Catholic priest leaving the place. If it's true it might be what we need to pry young Griffin from his high and mighty perch."

5.

"My dear," Mark said, putting his arm around his wife's waist, "you are sure, aren't you? I wouldn't want to force..."

"Ssh." She covered his mouth with her hand. "You've forced nothing. Neither for me nor the children. Certainly not for Sophia."

"Sophia..." He moved away from Clare and stood alone,

looking at the open expanse of moor and dale spread before him. In the chill December afternoon it was a grayed purple landscape. Snow obliterated the signs of plowed and cultivated fields that in season tamed this great expanse; now it was only the wild and achingly beautiful thing it had been since primeval time. "Sophia..." he repeated. His sister's name seemed to fly over the hills.

"Look," he said, stretching out his hand to draw Clare closer to his side. "It's Griffin land as far as we can see in this direction."

"Yes." She knew everything her husband meant by the simple phrase. It carried with it that same sense of wonder and commitment she always felt when for the first time she held to her breast a newborn child. Destiny, permanence, wholeness. "Yes," she repeated softly, "Griffin land."

"And yet," Mark continued, "it's not enough to bind Sophia."

"I don't understand. Do you mean she wants to go away? Where?"

"No, no...you take me too literally. It's her spirit that soars to places I cannot know or understand."

"Nor I," Clare agreed. "But so do you sometimes. It must be a Griffin thing. We Dumonts are a practical, earthbound lot."

He laughed and kissed her cheek. She smelled of lavender and fresh, cold air. "Thank God for that. One woman visionary in the house is enough for any man."

"Yes, but look where her vision has taken all of us."

"Look indeed. But that's just it. That's what I brought you up here to talk about. It mustn't be Sophia's vision, my dearest, that leads you on this course. Nor even mine. It must be your own."

"It is. It's not like hers or even yours. I don't share that gift. But when both my head and my heart tell me something is right and true, then that's enough for me."

"It may cost, Clare. It may cost dearly. At this moment I can't say how, but I've a feeling...that is, Sophia has a feeling. She told me this morning that she senses something. Something awful."

Clare's mood changed abruptly. She was once more the practical mistress of the manor. "That's quite enough of that, Mark. Even Sophia mustn't claim more for her gifts than their due. I'll have no part of seers and prophetesses and predictions of doom and gloom. 'Sufficient unto the day is the evil thereof,'" she said with finality.

Later, back in his study, Mark considered her choice of quotation. The Lord had also said, "If any man will be my disciple let him take up his cross and follow me." It seemed to him equally appropriate. Sighing, he reached for his pen.

"There is a matter of some importance," the note began, "which I wish to discuss with you. It is family business and your counsel is needed, but it is rather too delicate for a letter. Can you come to spend a few days at the Hall as soon as convenient?"

Roger read the letter over a second time, then set it aside. The business to which it referred sounded very mysterious. Matters to do with the management of the estates were all strictly Mark's concern; they never involved him. What, then? Something about Sophia, perhaps. Maybe Mark had finally persuaded her to a match. Strictly speaking, that wouldn't involve him either. Sophia, like everything else at Harwood Hall, belonged to the squire. But if his sister needed convincing, it might be Mark's idea to marshal the full force of the family to the argument. Yes, that must be it. Sophia's consent wasn't necessary in the matter of her marriage, but it would be important to Mark.

"I wish to God," he said aloud in the empty room, "these modern women weren't so damned independent." But even if Nancy were not convinced that she could choose her own destiny, what good would it do? She had no father or brother with whom he could conclude arrangements for a wedding despite the bride's reluctance. No, if Roger was going to marry Nancy Wilmott, she must be made to agree of her own volition. That was the thought that fathered the plan. He would go to Harwood within the week. And he'd take Nancy with him.

It was an idea of genius, he told himself immodestly. First, once she had made such a journey with him—at least six days traveling together publicly on the open road—her position as his acknowledged mistress would make a nonsense of all her concerns with "the done thing." Of course, she'd already agreed to live openly with him, but surely she must see that if he cared about public opinion he wouldn't take her to his family home. And once she'd met the other Griffins, seen how happily married Mark and Clare were, seen the

46

Hall and met the children.... Truly an idea of genius. He set about the arrangements.

Roger had everything well in hand when he met Nancy that evening. "I've a surprise for you." He spoke the words before they'd broken from the first, hungry embrace in the sheltering darkness of the street.

"Mmm, that's lovely. I like surprises. Will you tell me now?"

"Not yet. I want the proper setting."

"Where are we going?" she asked as he hurried her along Drury Lane to a waiting carriage.

"The Golden Bull. I've hired a private room for supper and told the landlord we're not to be disturbed." Then he turned to her with all the pent-up longing of the two days since last they had been together, and for the rest of the brief ride they spoke no more.

The tavern was noisy and crowded. Full of massed and milling humanity, awash in ale, quivering with high spirits. "This way," he said, leading her up a back flight of stairs and grateful that no one paid them any attention. This night he didn't want to share Nancy with admiring throngs. "Here we are." It was a small chamber on the second floor. Three candles lit the interior. The one small window was securely curtained, and the door could be bolted from the inside. "Now, we're quite alone and private. As I meant us to be."

"Fine." Nancy took off her cloak and stepped nearer the blazing fire. "But before you satisfy your appetites, I intend to satisfy mine. I'm ravenous." The table was laid with cold venison pie, crusty brown bread, a mound of pale-yellow butter, and a generous wedge of blue-veined Stilton cheese. The rich and delicious scent of the repast was enough to make a statue salivate, but Roger was oblivious to the food.

"Can't it wait?" He reached for her and fumbled with the bodice laces of her blue velvet gown.

"No," she said, laughing as she twirled away from his grasp. "It can't. I haven't eaten since breakfast. But"—she lifted a thick wedge of the savory pie to her lips with one hand and finished loosing the ties with which he'd been fumbling with the other—"I don't mind getting ready for the course that's to follow." In minutes she had managed to devour half the food in sight and at the same time take off all but her thin silk chemise. Most fashionable women wore tightly laced corsets under their dresses, but Nancy never

47

did. Beneath the gauzy undergarment her small firm breasts announced proudly that they required no such support.

"You devil!" Roger exclaimed, laughing and taking the flagon of ale from her hand. "I'll teach you to tease me." In seconds he'd turned her over his knee and delivered three sound smacks to her bare rosy buttocks. She yelped and pummeled his legs with her fists, but she stopped even the pretense of resistance when he laid her full-length on the carpet and stretched his hard-muscled young body over hers.

"I love you, Roger, oh how I love you. Take me. Hurry, for God's sake, hurry...."

Later she agreed with surprising alacrity to go with him to Yorkshire. He'd expected protest, but there was none. "It's a good time, as it happens. Nell's pregnant. She's going to do two weeks' consecutive performances at the theater, starting this Monday. Then she'll be too stuffed with Charles's fruit to go onstage. The public like their heroines to have slim waists and flat bellies."

"You speak of it so casually. Does it bother her?"

"Nell? Bother her to have Charles's bastard? I should say not. Why should it? She loves him. He's fond of her, good to her. He'll acknowledge the child and support them both. Why should it bother her?"

"The queen's left Whitehall. She's gone to her residence at Somerset House again. I'm afraid it bothers her."

"Yes, I understand that. And I feel sorry for Catherine. Nell says she's rather nice."

"Very nice. As fine and noble a lady as I've ever met."

"All right, but it's not Nell's fault the queen's barren. If he wasn't lying with her Charles'd be in some other bed. Everyone knows it."

"I suppose so. But you women are a puzzle to me. Your sense of what passes for honor is quite different from anything I know by the name."

"Honor!" Nancy made a disparaging sound and reached for the last bit of pie on the plate. "Honor doesn't fill your belly when you're hungry, or warm your flesh when you're cold."

"What do you think does, then?" He ran one finger lightly over her breast and watched intently as the dusky nipple stiffened beneath his touch.

"A decent meal for the one, whether you have to beg, borrow, or steal it. And love for the other, if you're blessed or lucky enough to find it." She turned and twined her arms

48

around his neck, pressing full-length against him as if she wanted to mark forever his being upon her own.

The rider came toward them down the brow of a hill purple with late-afternoon light. Even at this distance it was possible to see that the flanks of the black horse were sheened with sweat. They glittered and flashed as if bejeweled. Above those pounding hooves a great cape billowed from the horseman's shoulders, spread by the wind into a pair of wings either side of the steed.

"Who's that?" Nancy pressed her face to the window of the coach and watched the horseman approach. "He seems to be making straight for us."

"That"—Roger only looked for a second, then settled back in his seat—"is most likely my sister Sophia."

"Your sister! It can't be. That rider's seated full astride the horse. It must be a man."

"No." The horse was nearer now. "It's Sophia." He signaled to the driver to halt the coach and wait. In a few moments the meeting was accomplished. Sophia, for it was she, didn't get down, she only pulled off her wide-brimmed hat and leaned forward to look into the carriage.

"Hello, Roger."

"Hello yourself. May I present Miss Nancy Wilmott. Nancy, my sister Sophia. Who, as you can see, has her own, somewhat unorthodox, ideas of propriety."

Child of the London slums she might be, even a woman grown accustomed to the excesses and indulgences of pleasure-mad London, but Nancy stared at the man's black breeches worn by Roger's sister, and her shock was plain on her face. "How do you do," she managed after some seconds. "I . . . we . . . hadn't thought to meet you here."

The girl ignored Nancy's obvious surprise and disapproval. "I've been up there for hours," she explained. "I saw your coach when it was miles down the road and waited for you."

"That's a pretty welcome, Sophia." Roger smiled at her. "In spite of the effect your dress, or rather lack of dress, is having on Nancy. Come inside. Your horse looks done in. One of the grooms can bring him along."

"No thank you. I'll ride home. I just wanted to ask you something. Now, before you get to the Hall and talk to Mark.

When you were a boy, before you went to France, did you ever go into the west wing?"

"The west wing of the Hall? No. Of course not. It was closed. Unused. Isn't it still?"

She didn't answer his question, only posed another of her own. "Do you know what this place is?"

"What place?" Roger gazed around him at the empty hills. "It's not our land. I know that."

"No. We're shallow this south side of the boundary. Mark tried..." She broke off. It wasn't to discuss land she'd come. "I've been up there looking for a sign of the ruins, but there are none that I can see."

"Ruins of what, Sophia?" Roger's patience was wearing thin. It always did with his sister. "If you want to talk, why can't you ride with us? We've been many hours on the road today. I want to get Miss Wilmott to the Hall."

"Yes, of course...I'm sorry. I just thought you might know. I remember that you used to wander for miles around when you went hawking. According to the old records there was a nunnery up there. Just on that hill, as near as I can read the maps. Kirkslee Priory, it was called. There doesn't seem to be a stone left."

"That's just as well." He spoke with feeling. "If you knew the intrigues the papists cause at court, the trouble they stir up, you'd not be looking for them here in Yorkshire."

Sophia didn't answer. She only stared for some seconds, then gave her mount a sharp spur and galloped away. Roger watched her a moment longer, then turned to Nancy. "She shocked you, didn't she?" He chuckled softly. "My wise woman of the world left gaping by a country girl....Can't say I blame you though. Sophia's unique. Now you've met her you'll find everything else at Harwood small beer. The rest of the Griffins are decidedly ordinary when compared with Sophia."

"Well, what do you think of it?" He dropped to the ground next to her and reached for her hand. Across the narrow valley at their feet, higher in fact than the hill which they'd climbed to get this view, was Roger's family home. Like a magnificent ship riding the topmost crest of a wave, powerful, defiant. Its gray-black stones, hewed from Yorkshire granite, seemed fixed in their places with the finality of revelation. The Hall looked like nothing so much as eternity.

"I always think you can see it best from here," Roger said after some minutes of silence. There was worship in his voice.

"Yes, you can. Why did they build it up there and not in the shelter of the valley below?"

"Because the valley's too hard to defend. From that hill they could repel an attack with ease."

"Have there been attacks?"

"None are spoken of in the family records. But when they started building Harwood six hundred years ago, this was rugged, half-savage country. The natives weren't expected to roll over and play dead for the Norman conquerors. Look, you can see the E shape plainly now."

"Yes, I do see it. Like the letter E lying on its side. The long part at the back and the three wings coming forward. Was that part of the defense plan?"

"No, not at all. That came much later. After they'd ceased to think of the place as being in hostile territory. The oldest part is really the east wing there on your left. That was put up around 1100. Then came the long bit that looks like the spine of the E, about a hundred years later. Soon after that they built what we call the middle wing. The west wing's what makes it look like the letter, though. And that's the newest part. My great-grandfather Samuel Griffin added it in 1572 in honor of Queen Elizabeth. Apparently it was a popular thing to do. I'm told England's full of houses built in the shape of the letter E. According to Sophia, he used the stones of an old nunnery from which Henry VIII had evicted the occupants. That's what she was on about when we met her that first day."

"I can't imagine," Nancy said, twisting the tassels of her cloak between her gloved fingers, "what it must be like to know where your family's been for six hundred years. What they were thinking, dreaming.... Look at it! God, it's so beautiful it takes my breath away."

"Sweet Christ, Nance! Don't start that again. You've been saying things like that the whole time we've been here. That's not why I hauled you all the way to Yorkshire. I love it, yes. And I'm proud to be part of it, to be a Griffin. But I love you too. And I don't give a damn who your parents were or what they were. When you marry me you'll be a Griffin. And our children will be Griffins. Why do you make it seem so important about the past?" He was close beside her now, both hands on her shoulders, near enough to see her eyes glow with tears. Nancy Wilmott, who never cried.

"Because it is important, my dearest. I know it even if you don't. Gentry marry gentry. When they don't it means trouble. You'd soon resent me, Roger. All the things I don't know, can't do. You'd be discontent, take a mistress, and I'd hate her and eventually you...."

"It doesn't have to be like that. You've met Mark and Clare. Have you ever seen two happier people? Mark doesn't have a mistress. You're so jaded by those degenerate Londoners you don't know what the rest of the world's really like."

"I think your brother and his wife are wonderful. But they prove my point, not yours. Clare knows everything about managing a place like that." She gestured over to the Hall. "I know nothing."

"You'd learn. Clare would help you. I can tell she likes you. Listen, darling, there's a bit of land just south of here— you saw it. The place where we met Sophia the first day. It doesn't belong to the Hall yet, but Mark told me he's buying it. And he'll make it over to me if I want. We can build a house there."

"You'd leave court? Leave Whitehall and the navy?"

"With pleasure. I'm not cut out for all that, Nancy. I have an obligation to serve his majesty, but when this business with the supplying of the fleet is finished I'll have done all I can. He'll release me. I've already hinted as much to the Duke of York."

"Oh, Roger...you have it all figured out, haven't you?"

"Indeed I have. And you're the biggest part of it. Now, when will you marry me?" She started to shake her head, but he smothered her against his chest. "All right, all right...just don't say anything. We'll talk more about it later. Now I'm so hungry for you I can't be satisfied with words." He covered her mouth with his own and pressed her full-length on the hard, cold ground. The sun was warm on his back, and for a few moments it didn't seem like winter.

6.

Nancy felt particularly tall standing next to Clare Griffin. The other woman was small and gentle; she roused protective instincts in Nancy despite being the older of the two and having a far superior station. But Clare spoke to her guest as if they were peers, young girls together sharing confidences. She seemed to accept Nancy's status as Roger's mistress with quiet tolerance. "Have the children explained that to you?" She pointed to the huge tapestry that hung on the wall of the great hall in which they stood.

"No. There hasn't been time. It's your family coat of arms, isn't it?"

"The Griffin coat of arms. My family was Dumont. Since I've no brother, I have a right to their arms too. But I'll show you that some other time. The Griffin arms are much older and more important. Mark's great-grandmother worked this tapestry in 1560. According to the family records she copied it stitch for stitch from a much older one that was damaged in a fire here at the Hall."

"It seems—I mean no offense—it seems a very simple design. Compared to what one sees in London, I mean." Nancy blushed. The statement hadn't come out at all the way she'd intended it. It sounded as if she were deprecating the Griffins, comparing them to grander London folk. Clare only laughed lightly.

"It is simple. That's because it's so very, very old. Everyone in England wants to say they're of Norman stock, and that's why they invent all kinds of elaborate proofs of ancestry. The Griffins really are Norman descendants. Their arms were awarded centuries ago when it was the custom to use very simple markings. In heraldic language they say, 'Azure, a bend or. With two griffins rampant.' The blue field of the shield is the 'azure.' The 'bend or' means that gold line, and the 'griffins rampant' are the beasts that look like lions with eagles' heads and are reared back on their hind legs. The Latin motto below the shield is of later origin. Around 1400, we think. It means 'Guide Straight the King' and refers to the fact that the first Griffin who came to England was master of the ship that brought William the Conqueror."

Such a long speech for Clare, such pride in her voice. Then her tone lightened. "Come." She linked her arm through the younger girl's. "Let's walk in the portrait gallery. I'll show you funny-looking old pictures and you can tell me about London. I've only been there three times, but I thought it was splendid."

Mark saw the two women pass his study door. "They're getting on quite well," he commented to his brother. "Clare's telling her about the house. That's a certain sign of affection."

"Clare's been marvelous. Nancy had all kinds of fears about coming here, and Clare's made her forget them all."

Mark refilled their glasses with blood-red claret and smiled slightly. "You must admit you've put the girl in an awkward spot, Roger. Traveling openly with her the length of England, staying here together like this. Any woman would find it embarrassing. Do you mind my asking what are your intentions?"

"I don't mind in the least. I want to marry Nancy. Truth is, it's not I who keeps our relationship without benefit of clergy. It's she. She thinks she's not good enough for me. That I'd tire of her and take a mistress, a woman 'more of my station'—at least that's what she says. Sometimes I wonder if what she's seen in London has just soured her on marriage in general. There's hardly a man from Tower Hill to Westminster goes to bed beside his lawful wife two nights running."

"Yes, so everyone says. Now that the Puritans have fallen from grace, England's mad to make up for eleven years of virtuous boredom. London, I expect, is the worst. It always is."

Roger nodded. "What do you think?" he asked quietly. "About my marrying Nancy, I mean. She's penniless, you know. She's an actress at the Drury Lane Theater. Not much of a wife for a Griffin, most would say."

"But not me." Mark swirled the wine in his bulbous glass and leaned back in his chair. "If a man has great need of a

54

dowry...well, I suppose that's another matter. You do not. Harwood Hall doesn't. Our affairs are in good order, Roger. I never thought we'd recover so fast from the losses people like us suffered under Cromwell, but we've been fortunate. That's not pride speaking, it's the truth. I'll show you the accounts if you like. As for Nancy, she worships you. It's plain to any observer. And there's a kind of direct honesty in her I admire. She'd make a fine wife for you. Better than I could have hoped you'd find down there at court. You have my blessing."

"Thank you, that pleases me greatly. But it's premature. Nancy Wilmott's a woman of our new age, an independent female. Insists on deciding her own future, if you can credit it. And so far she won't agree to wed me."

"You'll bring her around. I've no doubt of it." Mark chuckled. "What she needs, if you'll forgive my crude speech, is a swollen belly to convince her what a woman's place should be. I trust you know how to manage that?"

"Oh, I've learned a thing or two about it," Roger admitted, laughing. "And I admit the thought's crossed my mind....Speaking of women who want taming, what are you doing about Sophia? She seems to grow wilder by the day. She's still riding around the countryside in man's breeches, I see. And what's all this about nunneries and the west wing?"

Mark's face darkened. "Sophia is wild, I admit it...and I've never had the heart to break her spirit, though I suppose I should have. She's like some strange bird, born out of time. I don't understand it, but, truth is, it touches me."

"Yes, I know what you mean."

"Do you? Then it will make what I have to say, my reasons for summoning you here, easier to explain."

"I wondered when you'd get to that. Four days and you've not said a word."

"I've been a coward. I admit it."

"A coward, you? Don't talk rubbish, Mark. You needn't be afraid to tell me anything. You know my opinion of you, and nothing can change that."

"Thank you." The older brother smiled warmly. "We've been lucky in our feelings for each other, we Griffins. That's why..."

"Yes?"

"Why I hope you'll understand when I say that I...all of us..." He drew a deep breath, "We're becoming Catholics,

Roger. Me, Clare, Sophia, and the children. We'll be received into the faith sometime next month."

There was silence for some seconds. Finally Roger found his voice. "Do you mean Roman Catholics? Papists?"

"I'm afraid I do."

"In God's name, man, why?"

"Precisely that. In God's name."

"God's... Mark, listen to me. You're very isolated up here. I know you're the eldest and the squire, but I've been four years in France and nine years in London. I've seen papists at first hand in a way you never have. God's truth, Mark, they're a loose-living, greedy, profligate bunch of whores and whoremasters. Charles tolerates any number of them at court, because it's his way and there's his mother and his wife to consider. You can't imagine what they're like or you'd not be telling me something this daft. Far from being better than other men because of their 'holy faith,' they're worse, much worse."

"I don't doubt it. In spite of the innocence of which you accuse me, I've learned a bit about human nature up here in the wilds of Yorkshire."

"Then why..."

"Roger, let me ask you something. Do you think in all the realm it is possible to find a man more able to rule than Charles? A man more noble, honest, wise, courageous? Does such a man exist, do you think? If we could search the entire kingdom?"

"I don't doubt it. But what..."

"Wait, let me finish. Supposing someone found this paragon and proposed him to wear the crown. Would you, if convinced of all his virtues, would you rush to his side, bear his standard, wage war to give him the throne?"

"I bloody well would not!"

"No, neither would I. And why not, Roger? Why wouldn't you support such a saint?"

"Because, as you know full well, Charles Stuart, for all his faults, is the true King of England. No one can take that from him."

"Exactly. And we believe we've found the true Church. The parallel must be obvious."

Roger leaned back in his chair and ran his hands through his hair. "This is something to do with Sophia and her crazy prattle about the west wing, isn't it?"

"Not in the way you mean. I'm not such a fool as that, Roger. Nor is Clare. Don't sell us so short."

"I don't mean to. But to take such a risk because Sophia says she's seen a ghost...it's madness."

"First, it's not because of anything Sophia says. Which is not to say I don't believe her story. I do. I think I saw the same ghost once myself. Years ago. Though it didn't send me rushing to the Catholics then, and of itself it wouldn't do so now. Sophia's visions were but the means of starting us down the road. She asked permission to bring a priest here to exorcise the west wing, and I agreed. You know old Solomon Swale over at Grinton a few miles east. He's a known Catholic and keeps a chaplain at his house. I sent for him."

"And did this priest say his Latin mumbo-jumbo over the old storeroom in the west wing?"

"No. It didn't seem important once he got here. We talked. We've talked often since. All of us. The decision's made, Roger. I hope you can accept and understand it. I even hoped you'd think about joining us."

"Not on your life! Have you thought about what this may mean for the future, Mark? The Catholics are tolerated, as I said. Swale even has a seat in the Commons if it comes to that. But the laws against those who don't conform, against recusants, are hard laws, Mark. If someone chooses to enforce them..."

"We'll try not to make any fuss. We are isolated here, as you pointed out. Few need know."

"And will you go to the Anglican service? Take Anglican communion?"

"No. That we can't do."

"I thought not." He stared at his brother. Sound, sane Mark. Always, until now, the repository of good sense and wisdom, while he himself was the mad adventurer. Roger shook his head in disbelief, but there was nothing more to say.

The following day they began the long trek back to London. It was scarce sunup when they loaded their baggage atop the small coach. The team of six matched bays which Roger had purchased in Kent, and which had excited Mark's admiration, pawed the cobbles of the forecourt, anxious to make a start. "Move them out," he said softly to the driver, and turned to take a last look at the household, who, in spite

57

of the early hour, stood massed by the front entrance to bid them Godspeed. Sophia, he noted with a grimace of distaste, stood apart from the waving throng, her hands fiercely clenched beneath her breasts and her head tipped back, revealing closed eyes and moving lips. Hysteria, he'd call it. In his present mood Mark would doubtless insist it was a vision.

Roger felt the cold sweat of fear on his forehead. It was a new experience. In all the years of exile, the skirmishes, even the battles waged under the flag of Spain or France in the Royalist cause, he'd never really been afraid. Always in some secret place deep inside himself there lodged the memory of England and Yorkshire and Harwood Hall, safe and waiting. Only now did the rot of men's prejudices and stupidities seem to threaten this essential core of his reality. He trembled with fear, and dripped sweat like a coward mounting the gallows.

It had seemed at first a surplus of horseflesh. The carriage was light and small, a marvelous new French design, and the bays dwarfed it in ridiculous disproportion. But the trip up had proved the wisdom of the stablemaster on whose advice he'd selected a team of six. For most of the journey the road was only a track of beaten earth. Where rain or heavy traffic had been the order of the day it became a sea of mud and the power of the mighty bays a blessing. Now, heading back to London, they were lucky. At least the first day. There had been a frost, and the earth was firm beneath the wheels and hooves. They made the great city of York by midmorning. Griffin asked Nancy if she wanted to stop, but she shook her head and settled quietly in her corner, sensing as she had for some hours past his black mood. They pushed on and were at Houdon by scarce one o'clock.

"We'll lunch here," he said, interrupting the long silence of the morning. "There's a decent inn just over the hill."

It was, Nancy thought, more than decent, though its droll name, the Cock Rampant, seemed to her quite the opposite. It was a charming place nonetheless. A great thatched roof overhung half-timbered walls, and the scent of burning wood mingled with that of roasting duck. The landlord welcomed them warmly and brought a bottle of claret without being asked. She almost suggested they spend the rest of the day and the night in this place. Not go on until tomorrow and see if the Cock Rampant lived up to its promise. But Roger's dark scowl didn't encourage such a frivolous idea, and she said nothing. Whether his black humor was caused by something she had said or done, or the long hours he'd spent with his brother the day before, she didn't know. It seemed better not to ask.

By nightfall, however, they were only in Doncaster. They'd been delayed by a mounted sheriff and his retinue, all in full state regalia and going, so they said, to the county border to meet his majesty's judges come to sit the quarter sessions. The officials had looked suspiciously at Roger and Nancy in spite of their elegant equipage and dress. Strangers always caused a prickle of hostility in these parts. Then, when Roger spoke to them in accents as Yorkshire-broad as their own, things changed.

"Are ye from hereabouts, then?" the sheriff asked with some doubt. "I don't know yer face."

"I know the gentleman." Another rider urged his horse forward. "At least I know the family. Yer a Griffin, ain't ye? Brother to Squire Mark Griffin up to Harwood Hall. The young lad wot's been away with the king."

"Captain Roger Griffin." He bowed as graciously as the small carriage allowed. "Your humble servant, sir."

"Beggin' yer pardon, Captain Griffin," the sheriff hastened to regain the initiative. "Me and me men's a bit edgy today. There's talk of highwaymen round here lately. Yer armed, I hope."

"I am." Roger patted the pistol beside him on the seat. "And ready. Thank you for your concern."

The horsemen rode on, but the sun was a dull-red glow on the horizon and he instructed the driver to stop at the next inn. "I seem to know this place," Nancy said half to herself. "I don't know why. We didn't stop here on the way up, did we?"

"No. I can't think why it should be familiar. You've really never left London before?"

"Never."

He smiled, the first warm look he'd given her since morning. Her strange little pockets of inexperience, hidden beneath the sophisticated facade she affected, delighted him. Made him feel superior and protective in spite of her stubborn independence. "Perhaps..." It seemed a farfetched literary notion, and he didn't finish the thought. But she did.

"Oh, Roger, I know! It's the Richards... *Richard II* and

Richard III. The company's done them both any number of times. They're both set just here. In this very part of the country. How strange that I recognized it."

"I think," he said, laughing, "that's what's meant by art. The genuine sort, not what sometimes passes for the same. If you ask me, D'Avenant makes rubbish of his reputed father's genius with all his changes, but the plays themselves will be around for generations, I'll wager."

Then, because the coincidence seemed to have lifted the scowl from his face, she asked, "What's troubling you? Is it something I've done?"

"No, I'm sorry if I gave that impression. It's nothing to do with you, Nance. I can't discuss it, however. Be patient, will you? Please?"

"Of course." She smiled, and he kissed her cheek. Somehow now she was inside his anguish, part of it without needing to know the details. That unacknowledged fact comforted them both. They slept twined close together with no need of passion.

In the morning he seemed better. More civil, certainly. "We made close on fifty miles yesterday. That's not too bad. At that rate we'll be in London by the end of the week."

It proved an accurate estimate. They traveled ten to twelve hours a day, stopping only for lunch and, when necessary, to relieve cramped limbs and meet nature's demands. They passed through small villages of stone the color of spent ashes, and yet others built of daub and wattle and thatch. Between the far-flung settlements lay the open country of forest and fen, hill and valley. Tilled fields seemed scarce, but it wasn't really possible to tell in winter. The towns and villages, on the other hand, had in common a prosperous look—shops and houses in good repair, people that looked healthier and better-fed than the London masses. "Charles has been good for England," Roger said suddenly one afternoon. "Don't you think so?"

"I do. Good for the likes of me, God knows. Can you see me a proper Puritan? All dressed in black and looking doleful."

"No, I certainly can't!" Then, because the thought had implications that touched a nerve now sensitive, "What do you think happens to people who don't fit in with the mainstream? How do they survive?"

She shrugged. "Some by their wits, I guess. Others not at all."

"Do you suppose," he asked without really intending to do so, "that many of the folk we pass on these roads are recusants? Dissenters from the Church of one type or another?"

Religion wasn't a subject she thought much about. God, she had decided years before, was for the rich and mighty. He wasn't interested in the Nancy Wilmotts of the world. "I don't know. Maybe. But why? It's dangerous, isn't it?"

"It can be. Charles has a lot of advanced notions about tolerance and freedom of conscience, but the good bishops won't have any part of it. The House of Lords votes down every toleration act he proposes."

"They must be very sure they're right," she said with simple wisdom, "But how can they be? How can any human being be?"

"I rather doubt that real belief's got much to do with it. It's all politics, mostly. One can't trust the Catholics because they're loyal to the pope and probably supporters of the French. The Puritans and the Quakers and the Anabaptists seem opposed to the monarchy and the established order—"

"Stop!" She shook her head in consternation. "You're confusing me. Why are we talking about such gloomy things? Let the preachers settle all that." He smiled and took her hand and they traveled on in silence.

"I thought you'd never get home!" Nell hugged her with enthusiasm. "Old D'Avenant's livid because he wanted you to play some new role this week. He's got the latest comedy from Dryden."

"Oh God! Is he really very angry? I was longer than I told him I'd be. Will he sack me, do you think?"

"Sack you! Not a chance." Nell moved toward the glass and tugged at one recalcitrant dark curl. "He wouldn't dare. Not now. The old buzzard knows very well what I'd say to the king about that. And don't you go thinking you have to warm his bed, or anyone else's you don't fancy, Nancy love. Not any more." She whirled about to face her friend, and her eyes shone with happiness and something Nancy had never seen in them before, something remarkably like the security and pride of place she'd observed in the face of Clare Griffin. "We're safe now, Nance. For all time. Charles cares for me, he really does. I'm to have my own house soon. In Pall Mall. With all the gentry. What do you say to that?"

"I say marvelous. Oh Nell, I'm so happy for you."

"Not just for me. For yourself. You know that anything I have is yours. Just as it's always been with us. Come live with me, Nance. We'll be fine ladies on Pall Mall and thumb our noses at the common folk. Look"—she patted her slightly swollen stomach—"I've got royal blood in me now!"

"So you have." Nancy laughed with her. "So you have. But I won't come to live with you, darling. I need my own little corner. My room across the road suits me fine. You understand?"

"Yes. I hoped it would be different, but I knew you'd say that. Very well, but don't you ever dare not to ask me if you need anything. Anything at all. Promise me that, Nancy. Swear it."

"I, Nancy Wilmott," she said with mock seriousness, "do swear to Nell Gwyn by the Holy Bible, or whatever, that I'll come running to the same Nell Gwyn the minute anyone says no to me ever...about anything. There, will that do?"

"It will if you mean it. You're joking now, but I'm serious. Just you remember that."

"I've had word from Yorkshire. It's true. The Griffins are secret papists." Dewinters puffed out his veined cheeks and looked smug. "My informant saw a Jesuit priest, one Father Joachim MacTavish as he styles himself, leave there after a three-day visit just last week."

"What does it really prove?" Randolf wiped his fingers on a linen napkin, then reached for another of the sticky French sweetmeats. "You should try one of these...no? Very well. About this Jesuit, it can't be a crime to receive one. The queen's got a whole flock of 'em living with her over in Somerset House. And a convent of Mary Ward's Jesuitesses too, if it comes to that."

"The queen's another matter." Dewinters dismissed her with a wave of his hand. "There's a justice of the peace up in Yorkshire whom I know, a friend. Owns a piece of land on the border of the Griffin place. He'd not be averse to acquiring a bit more. Say the half of what's now Harwood Hall."

"And the other half?"

"Well, I've been wanting some holdings up north. It's good country. Fine pasture for sheep, they tell me."

"I see." His lordship burped noisily and leaned forward. "I still don't understand two things, however. One, how are you going to get this land from Griffin? And two, what good is it to me if you make the elder brother sweat when it's the younger, right here in court, who's the thorn in my side?"

"There are ways, milord. To accomplish both ends, there are ways."

7.

By the middle of January the knot of fear in his stomach began to loosen. There'd been no word from Mark, and he'd have heard if there was trouble. His own work was going well; the plan for supplying food to the navy was almost ready for implementation. Moreover, he and Nancy ushered in the year of 1670 at a private party given by Nell Gwyn in her new house on Pall Mall and attended by both the king and the Duke of York. On that occasion the royal brothers had been markedly friendly to Roger. He didn't think such would be the case if news of the Yorkshire affair had reached London. Whatever decision Mark had finally taken, he had apparently been discreet.

"You've a fine wench there," Charles had said heartily, watching Nancy, who looked particularly lovely in an amber gown. The frock had been Roger's Christmas gift, a filmy, ethereal thing beautifully set off by his other gift, a string of pearls. "First time I've ever met her, isn't it? Been keeping your pretty bit of fluff away from the court, have you?"

"Meaning no disrespect, sire, it seems wise. And she prefers it that way. She's an actress at Drury Lane. One of that new breed of independent women, I fear. She won't leave off performing with D'Avenant's troupe of players."

"Hah! I know just the sort you mean." Charles laughed loudly and gestured toward Nell, sitting in a corner conversing with a noble gentleman who seemed to be mightily enjoying the sight of her full breasts displayed above a low-cut gown. "And I agree it's wise to keep some things to oneself. But your tall young filly looks to need breaking." The king moved closer, and his swarthy good looks were lit with spirited humor. "Take some advice, lad, give the girl a foal to nurse. Does wonders for 'em." Then, still laughing, he moved away to reclaim his Nell.

Later that same night he'd asked outright, "Have you ever had a child?"

The question angered her. She bounded from the bed and stood facing him in nothing but her skin and dignity. "Don't you ask me questions about the past, Roger Griffin! Don't you ever ask me. I told you long ago what I've been, what I am. But no man's touched me since the first night I lay with you, and that's all you need to know."

"Come back to bed, Nancy." He stretched out his hand, too full of wine and lovemaking to argue. "I'm not trying to probe your past. I don't care a farthing for it, you know that." Then, when her head was nestled on his shoulder once more, "I only wondered because...well, because it seems surprising there's no child of mine growing there."

She put her hand over his where it lay on her flat, hard-muscled stomach. "I know. I've thought as much often these past weeks. I wish there were. I'd love to have your child, Roger." She moved his hand over her flesh in slow, widening circles. "Sometimes I think perhaps I'm barren. You see, the answer to your earlier question is no. I've never had a child. Fill me with yourself, my darling. Keep filling me until the seed bears fruit."

Later still he whispered, "When you do, Nancy—when you bear my child—it'll be a Griffin, not a bastard. Remember that."

The morning of January 27, 1670 was misty, dull-gray. Leaden sky and frozen earth. No broken cloud interrupted the dense fog that hung close around Harwood Hall, no ray of sunlight pierced its dripping shroud. The sound of pounding hooves was muffled by sodden air when horses thundered into the forecourt and drew even with the door. "I've come to see the squire," a rider shouted to a startled footman. "See, he knows I'm here."

"Who shall I say, sir?"

"John Lane. Justice for his majesty's peace."

"Come in, John." A few minutes later Mark Griffin ushered his uninvited guest into the great hall. There was a hint of amusement in his eyes. "You've never before called in full regalia. Do you think that sash and chain of office are likely to make me more willing to sell you some of my land?"

"Don't make light of me, Mark. Not this day. I've come on the king's business."

"Indeed. Well, none knows better than you that I'm the king's good servant." Years before Lane had capitulated to Cromwell while Griffin stood quietly firm in his Stuart loyalties. Both men knew it. "I've never shared your gift for bending with the wind," Mark said now. "What does his most gracious majesty wish of me?"

"To take this oath," Lane replied softly. "That's all, Mark. You and all your family and household are to take this here oath of allegiance. 'Tis a simple thing, isn't it?"

Griffin stared at the paper the justice of the peace proffered and went very pale.

"I just don't understand!" Nancy thudded the arm of the chair with her closed fist. "What does this bloody oath say, then? Why couldn't they take it?"

"I'm not sure...at least not really." Nell, her body now thick with pregnancy, seated herself rather awkwardly on a corner of the narrow bed that, with one chair, a chest, and a washstand, composed all the furnishing of Nancy's room. "It's something to do with the pope."

"The pope! The Bishop of Rome? In God's name, Nell, what has that to do with them?"

"Don't shout at me, Nance, please. I'm trying my best to explain. As near as I can make out it's an oath to prove you're not a papist. That you're loyal to the crown, not a foreign prince. Someone accused Mark and Clare Griffin and all the family of having a Jesuit in their house...in that Harwood Hall place. So a justice of the peace went and asked them to swear the oath, and they wouldn't."

"But they're not papists. I was there, I met them, I'd have known, Nell, surely I'd have known."

"Don't cry, Nance, you mustn't. I've got to make you understand. It's important."

Nancy made an effort to control her threatening tears. Had she been asked, she would not have predicted the violence of her own reaction to this news. But somehow, in the few days she had spent in their company, the Yorkshire Griffins had wormed their way into her affections. It wasn't just because they were Roger's kin, it went deeper than that.

"They were so happy, Nell. Such good people. And you should see the Hall. It's the most beautiful place in the world. It must be."

"Yes." Nell's full lips were pressed into a thin line of anger. "That's a big part of it, make no mistake."

"I don't understand," Nancy repeated for something like the fourth or fifth time.

"Oh, you can be such an innocent sometimes! Look, love, they're filthy rich, aren't they? Piles of money and land and what all?"

"Yes, I guess they are. They're gentry. The real kind that go way back to hundreds of years ago."

"Don't you see? That's why there are always people so jealous and greedy they're willing to do anything to hurt them."

"It's very bad, then? The consequences of refusing this oath?"

Nell drew a deep breath. Her friend had taken the first of the news so badly she dreaded telling her the rest. "It's bad. Brace yourself, Nance. They're taking Harwood Hall, all the land, everything."

"Taking..." For the first time Nancy Wilmott's common sense asserted itself, mastered her shock and her anger. "Who's 'they,' Nell? I don't believe this is the king's doing."

"It isn't. I swear that. Mostly that's why I came to you the minute I heard. You mustn't think it's Charles that's done this. It wasn't clear right away who had. When I first heard the story it seemed to be just some pig of a justice of the peace in Yorkshire. But I've been nosing around all morning and I think it's something to do with Sir John Dewinters."

"And who might he be?"

The other girl made a face of distaste. "A loathsome, ugly brute. Just the sight of him makes my skin crawl. He's like a leech, full of other people's blood. The king can't abide him, but..."

"But what? If this Dewinters is so awful and Charles doesn't like him, then how can he get away with this? Can't you ask the king to make him leave the Griffins alone?"

Nell shook her head. "I wish to God it were that simple. Or that this were the end of it. Nance, listen, I'm not very clever about court business. But I know they're all pulling Charles in a dozen different directions. Sometimes I'm so afraid for him I can't sleep. Still, he's smarter than they are. He keeps Dewinters right by his side, says that way he always knows what he's plotting. The thing is, Dewinters has a tremendous amount of influence with Parliament. Charles needs him. And you see, the Griffins have admitted it all. Plainly and openly. They are papists."

The other girl shook her head stubbornly. "Well, even if it's true, what of it?"

"Stop asking me that. I don't know. I don't know why it's so important sometimes and doesn't matter a damn others. There's something else you have to know. I talked with one of the kitchen maids this morning. She used to be at the palace, then Charles sent her to me a while back. She told me she once heard Dewinters talking to Lord Randolf. She says it's Roger Griffin they're really after. He's taken money out of Randolf's pocket with all his new plans for the navy, and it's Randolf who wants revenge."

"Oh my God. Does Roger know?"

"I can't say for sure. I heard it late yesterday afternoon, and I guess it's all over Whitehall by now. Did you see him last night?"

"No. I waited for half an hour after the show, but he didn't come. I thought it must be court business. That's happened once or twice before."

"Well, it could be, I suppose. But it could be all this. I knew you'd want to know, Nancy. That's why I came."

"Yes. Bless you, Nell. I'm grateful."

"No need of that." She rose and gathered up her fur-lined cloak. In her present condition the garment made her look like a round little doll that would tumble over at the first touch. "I have to go now, darling. But if there's anything I can do, or if I hear any more..."

She found him walking in the small private garden behind his chambers. A footman took her as far as the gate, gestured toward Roger a few yards away, and left her there, pocketing the generous bribe she'd paid to get this far unannounced and unbidden. Nancy simply walked forward and fell into step beside him. "What are you doing here?" was his only greeting.

"I wanted to be with you. Nell told me earlier. I waited a bit, but there was no word from you, so I came. It's true, then?"

"It's true." Silence for some minutes. A kestrel circled overhead, seemed to decide the frozen garden offered no bounty, and disappeared. Finally, "Are you too cold out here? Shall we go inside?"

"I'm all right. We can do whatever you want."

He took her hand, and it was like ice. "You are cold. Come." The door to his rooms was just a few feet away. Inside a fire glowed on the hearth, and he led her to it, then poured a glass of claret. "Drink this. It'll warm you." He looked ruefully at the wine. Only a few inches of the dark-red liquid remained at the bottom of the jug. "I've made a dint in this today."

"Roger, what does it all mean? If you don't want to talk about it, I'll understand, but..."

"It's all right. I don't know why I'm so calm, but I am. It hasn't hit me yet, I think. And I've been somewhat prepared. Mark told me they were all going over to Rome when we were there last month. That was why I came home in such a foul mood."

"They are papists, then?"

"Yes. They intended to be discreet. Not attract any attention. But there are spies all over the country. Someone found out, obviously."

"And this oath? I can't see why it matters. Nell said they refused to swear. But what about the queen? She's a Catholic. And there are others. I know there are. One hears about it sometimes."

"Sit down, Nancy. You're somewhat involved in all this, so you'd best know a few things. The queen, and the queen mother for that matter, are a different case. Their marriage agreements stated that they'd be free to practice their Catholic religion as long as they didn't incite anyone else to do so, and as long as their children were raised as Protestants. Others, as you say, are known to be papists and yet left alone. It's politics, Nancy. Some people are adept at walking such a tightrope. They wiggle and squirm and play one side off against the other, and always come out on top. Mark's not made of that kind of stuff. He's been such a damned fool...."

Roger ran his fingers through his hair, and for a moment it appeared he might lose his thin veneer of control. But only for a moment. He was calm again instantly. "What I can't believe is that when they threatened to take the Hall he still persisted in this bloody-minded madness. Apparently Sophia even made an impassioned speech telling the justice and all his men they were going straight to hell for their heresy, and that she'd support the claims of the Bishop of Rome until she died. And my gullible fool of a brother let her go on."

"Can they do it? Take the Hall, I mean."

His laugh was bitter. It rang in her ears like the sound of breaking glass. "Oh yes. Why not, when the squire himself practically gives it to 'em with an open hand? Do you know what the laws concerning recusants say? Do you?" She shook her head. "Well, I do. I looked them up when we first came back to London. They made me sick at my stomach for a week. To refuse to take the oath of allegiance is a felony punishable with life imprisonment and confiscation of all property. Catholics caught at their damned Roman Mass or using their ridiculous rites and beads and waters can be fined a hundred pounds for each offense. They're not supposed to travel more than five miles from home without a special permit.... I could go on; what's the point?"

"Life imprisonment..." She had heard nothing beyond that. "Will they..."

He shook his head. "Not so far. Not ever, so the Duke of York tells me. He has enough influence for that. And he's arranged a brief time of grace for them, before they must leave the Hall. All in all, York's been damned decent. But faced with Mark's idiocy, there's little anyone can do. The laws exist. They're true laws of the realm. If someone makes a point of enforcing them, and if the accused give them the ammunition my brother's given..." He shrugged.

"Will you be going to Yorkshire?" she asked. "I'll come with you if you like."

"To Yorkshire! To what, Nancy? I've nothing left there. My home's gone, everything the Griffins have spent six hundred years building is gone. Because of one man's lunacy and the influence of one hysterical girl. No, I'll not be going to Yorkshire. I don't want to see my brother or any of them. Not now...not ever again." He was weeping at last, great wrenching sobs like a woman or a child. She cradled his head in her arms and let him cry.

Of course that wasn't the end. Friends avoided him, servants seemed always to be whispering and snickering. Roger adopted a rigid self-control, so tight and inflexible it frightened Nancy more than had his single concession to tears. It seemed to border on madness. And when he took her, night after night in a kind of punishing, mindless rage, there was nothing of love or tenderness in him. It will pass, she told herself repeatedly. It must pass. The old Roger's not dead, just mortally wounded.

Yet, despite this new side of his character, and despite the cold, almost cruel way he treated her of late, her love seemed to grow. She'd not have thought that possible, not have imagined she could love him more. Eventually she realized that what she felt before was tainted with a sense of impermanence. She had believed their affair an inevitably transitory thing. For all his talk of wedding her, it had never occurred to Nancy Wilmott that she might really spend the rest of her life with Roger Griffin. Now she saw for the first time that he didn't just love her, want her...he needed her, and that was quite a different thing.

She waited for him to renew the proposal of marriage he'd made so frequently, but he didn't mention it. One evening ten days after the blow had fallen, she said, "I want to marry you. Now. Right away." He'd looked at her in silence for some seconds, then laughed mirthlessly.

"Now, Nance? When I've so little to offer you? Your generosity astonishes me. Do you have any idea what a navy captain's pay is? Or how seldom he gets it?"

"I don't care. I love you."

"Yes." There was a moment of sweetness, an echo of former days. He touched her cheek with gentleness, and his voice was soft. "Yes, I know you do." The moment passed. "But you're a fool. I can't marry you or anyone. I've no means to support a wife. I no longer have an income from Harwood Hall. My apartment at Whitehall is the only bonus of my job, and it's strictly bachelor quarters. I'm thinking of putting out to sea."

"No." She held him then as if the demons of hell pursued them both. "Don't leave me, Roger! Don't ever leave me!" He made no reply, only turned to her with that fierce, inhuman hunger that was all he had to offer these days.

It was perhaps merciful that this period lasted only a fortnight. Since the worst was yet to come, it was better that it come quickly. It was the Duke of York, not the king, who summoned him. "Sit down, Griffin." The older man peered at him intently. "You don't look well."

"It's not been the best of times, your highness."

"No, I guess not. Here." He poured a flagon of ale. "There's too damned much wine drunk in this place. Try this to put some strength in you."

70

Roger reached for the glass and said wryly, "I've not neglected its virtues, sir, I assure you." In fact his eyes were red-rimmed with drink, and the duke seemed to notice it.

"It's odd counsel for these times, but...be careful, Roger. Alcohol can be dangerous to a man facing trouble. It clouds his wits."

"And dulls his senses. That's the good part."

York shrugged. "No doubt. Lad, I've an unpleasant job to do, and I propose to do it quickly and cleanly. His majesty wants you to resign your commission and leave the court."

Roger stared at the man to whom he'd first offered his services when the latter was an exile with a price on his head and no apparent prospects of regaining his heritage. He said nothing. There was nothing he could find the words to say.

"I know what you're thinking. What any man would think," James continued softly. "It's a foul reward for thirteen years of loyalty and devotion. Frankly, it makes me want to vomit. And in fairness to the king, he feels the same. But our hands are tied in this matter. Your brother's obstinacy was monumental. It took all my influence just to keep him and his family out of a dungeon in York Castle. The dust raised by his spectacular gesture, by your sister's speeches, hasn't yet settled. And it won't for a time. Moreover, you yourself have made powerful enemies here at court. You should have cultivated Randolf and March and their ilk, not let them know what rogues and fools you believed them to be. I told you as much many times."

"And told me too," Griffin said at last, "to clean up the stinking mess they'd made of the business of supplying the fleet. Which did you want, your highness? Another arse-kissing lackey, or a job of work done?"

"Enough. I don't hold your words or your anger against you, Griffin. I've too much respect and affection for you for that. But mind you, say nothing of that sort outside this room. I'd be forced to move if you did. You understand that?"

"As God is my judge, I don't understand anything any more."

The duke rose and stepped toward him, laying a broad hand on his shoulder and forcing a small leather pouch into the sleeve of his jacket. "Take this, Roger. It'll see you through a bit. Go to ground, man. Maybe to France. Wait till all this blows over. Then we'll see. My friendship's not a sometime thing, you know. You can count on it. Always."

8.

The Duke of York gave excellent advice. But to profit by it, Roger needed a cool head, and a calculating frame of mind. He had neither. Instead Griffin did what men have done since time immemorial when the world collapses in disaster. He went to the most derelict public house he knew, an evil-smelling hole in the shadow of hulking Newgate prison, a place called, with fine irony, the Free Man. He took a seat in a remote corner and ordered a jug of rum. It was the strongest drink available; Roger proceeded to get quietly, stupefyingly drunk.

Nell's footman was waiting when Nancy came offstage. "Someone to see ye, Miss Nancy, in t' Green Room. Been waitin' fifteen minutes. All done up in fancy livery 'e is. Says 'e comes from Miss Nell. Think on it! Miss Nell wit' a footman!" The old man had been jack-of-all-work with the company since its formation. Now he chuckled malevolently. "Fancy wot a lass can get wit' 'er legs spread."

"Be quiet, you villain." Nancy wasn't really angry, she was used to the man's evil humor. "You daren't speak about Miss Gwyn like that now. Is there any word from Captain Griffin?"

"Captain Griffin, eh ..." He chuckled again with more feeling. "Captain Griffin ..." But he walked away without giving her an answer.

Nancy clinched her fists in exasperation, then headed for the belowstairs dressing chamber they called the Green Room. The waiting footman's message was simple: Nell wanted to see her. Right away. There was a carriage outside.

"I just heard, darling. I sent for you immediately." Nell

poured a glass of wine for her visitor, made her drink it and take a seat before she'd continue. "Brace yourself, Nance. It's bad news again."

"I begin to think there isn't any other kind. Don't spare me, Nell, I'd rather know. Is Roger hurt? Has something happened to him?"

"Not the way you mean. He's been asked to resign his commission and leave court. The Duke of York spoke with him this morning. James sent word to me because he knew I'd tell you. He's trying to be kind, Nancy. You must believe that."

"Kind? So he sends Roger away in disgrace, when he's done nothing? My God, Nell! Do you know that he joined the Stuarts when they were still in France? He risked everything for the king. Now Charles rewards him like this. It makes me sick."

"Don't do that, Nancy. Don't ever do that." Nell rose and spoke in an even, quiet voice. In spite of her misshapen roundness in this the sixth month of her pregnancy she looked eminently dignified and imposing. "Not even you can speak ill of Charles in my hearing. You have no idea what he goes through, what he must do to preserve his God-given rights from those Parliament buffoons and plotting court advisers. He's dismissed Roger because they left him no choice. Had he refused it would have been worse all around. For everybody. Do you want to see the Roundheads back in power? Another civil war, perhaps? Do you?"

"Of course I don't. I just want Roger safe and happy again."

"I know." Nell's anger faded quickly. "I know, pet... and you shall. I'm sure of it. Charles told me a few days ago he might have to do this. He says it's just for a time. Just until things blow over, calm down as it were. James gave Roger some money. They think it's best if he goes away for a while. To France, perhaps. But no one's seen him since he left York's chambers. He just walked out of Whitehall and disappeared. I thought you might have heard from him."

"Not a word." The color left Nancy's cheeks, and her tall slim figure crumpled in the chair like a rag doll discarded by a careless child. "He's been in such a terrible mood since all this started. I'm frightened, Nell. I don't know what he might have done."

"Then it's up to you to find him and see he doesn't make any awful mistakes. Have you any idea where he may have gone? To Yorkshire, perhaps? Or to France? They say he took

73

nothing from his rooms. Just left in the clothes he was standing up in."

"He'd not have gone to Yorkshire. I'm sure of that. He says he never wants to see his family again. I think he'll get over that, but right now he means it."

Nancy rose and paced the exquisite drawing room of Nell's fine Pall Mall house. Beneath her feet a sumptuous Turkey carpet glowed with jewel-rich colors. The windows were curtained in silk brocade and the graceful chairs and sofas upholstered in damask. It was a beautiful room, the epitome of Stuart elegance and lavish taste. But it had about it a sense, a smell almost, of unreality. A startling firework that would light up the sky for a few seconds, then disappear. Unbidden there came to her mind the contrasting picture of the dark oak grandeur of the great hall at Harwood. That was permanence. That was the essence of a code of behavior bred for six hundred years. It would outlast the flamboyant brilliance of any royal house of whatever name. "He'd not have gone to France without seeing me first," she said slowly. The conviction, the knowledge, that she had found a wholly reliable insight into Roger's sense of honor was born as she spoke. "He's a Griffin to the tips of his fingers. Landed gentry. They can take away his land, his position, his money...they can't change him inside. If he were leaving England he'd come to me and tell me himself."

"Very well. I think I see what you mean. But where is he, then?"

"I don't know. But I mean to find out." She was charged with new vitality and determination. "Nell, have you any money? I don't need a lot. Just a few shillings to get on with. Looking for him may cost a bit, and I haven't a ha'penny, as usual." Nancy lived for the moment, as she always had. Putting money by against a possible emergency was no part of her world. Now she accepted with a grateful smile the three pounds Nell thrust into her hand, refused the offer of a carriage, and hurried away.

The streets were broad and pleasant in this the most elegant part of London. She was anxious to return to the small, narrow paths around Drury Lane. She forced herself to slow her steps. The irrational urge to hasten conflicted with the need to think and plan.

The secret knowledge that she didn't walk alone kept Nancy from panic. Within her there lodged a living part of Roger. She was pregnant. A wondrous truth, a blessing for

74

both of them. He wanted children. He'd admitted as much a number of times. And he wanted her to bear his children. When she told him it would give him hope, courage. All that remained was to find him and offer her gift.

But where in this great city was he likely to have gone? To what den had he retired, a battered animal needing to lick his wounds? That must be his state of mind. If he'd been angry, furious with the duplicity and weakness of the king and his brother, he'd have come to her, used her as a kind of sounding board for his fury. He'd have poured his rage into her body just as he had these past weeks, then risen from her bed able to control himself and fight on. Instead he'd gone to ground. That meant he felt not anger but despair. That could be a dangerous thing. For Roger Griffin it was also a shaming thing, and that was why he wasn't with her now. Very well. It was time she took the initiative.

No lady would have been welcome in the kinds of places Nancy visited in the next forty-eight hours. It had been surprisingly easy for her to shed the surface gentility of the past nine years and become once more the guttersnipe she'd been born. Her dress was borrowed from the theater, a tattered brown muslin garment she'd once worn in the role of a street urchin. Her legs were bare, and though it was February she had only wooden clogs tied with ropes on her feet. Her cloak was of rough stuff and an indeterminate color, but it kept the worst of the winter wind away. Nancy had hidden her thick auburn hair beneath a woolen cap and left behind her broad-brimmed hat with its dashing feather. She was, in fact, as drab and colorless as any costermonger pushing her barrow in the poorest part of London, and that was exactly what she intended. Dressed thus she could wend her way through the fetid alleys of the city slums around Moorgate and Cripplegate and Newgate unremarked and unmolested.

She was almost certain he was somewhere here. It was in these parts that Roger could be sure of anonymity, and she knew beyond question that was what he sought. Yet the first day's search was without reward, though she pursued it beyond midnight. In the morning she started on her rounds once more, going slowly, looking in every corner and doorway for a familiar figure huddled against the cold. She didn't really think to find him like that. More likely in some tavern, drinking up the bribe the Duke of York had paid him in exchange for his honor. But no opportunity must be overlooked. So she used precious time investigating every filthy hiding place she passed.

It was night, close on ten o'clock, when she came to the Free Man and stepped inside its dank and uninviting hall. "Looking for some'un, luv?" the barmaid said and inspected Nancy with a disapproving eye. Even in places like this women didn't come to drink alone. "You'd best state yer business and be gone. They're a surly lot in 'ere this night. Must be the weather. Snow's comin'. No mistake about it."

"Is there a man 'ere? A stranger? Upwards of two yards tall 'e is...and dark. Dressed like a gent. There's tuppence in it for ye if 'es the right 'un." She tapped the coins on the counter and waited for the other woman to speak.

"Oo wants 'em?"

"Wot's it t' you?"

The barmaid shrugged. "Folks as come 'ere knows they won't be bothered. 'Tis the landlord's rule."

"I'll not be a bother t'im. Not if I find 'im, that is." Nancy giggled wickedly and leaned forward to whisper. "'E's my man. S'truth. 'E is."

"Yer man? And a gent? Get on wit' ye, lass."

"S'truth, I tell ye. Me belly's full of 'im and all."

"Is it now?" The woman guffawed loudly. "Well, that's different. Even gents gotta pay fer their fuckin'. Would that be 'im? Over there in yonder corner. Been sittin' by hisself drinkin' fer two days. Didn't take no room or nothin', just sits. And pays fer 'is drink wit' a fat purse. That is, 'e did. Ole Willy Granger relieved 'is lordship o' t' purse an hour ago. Ain't even missed it yet. But 'e will." She chuckled loudly. "Wait till 'e tries to pay fer the next bottle...."

Nancy hardly listened to most of this speech. She'd recognized Roger as soon as the barmaid directed her attention to a shadowy corner in the rear. Leaving the copper coins on the counter in payment, she moved through the throng of drinkers, ignoring their lewd comments and exploratory hands.

"Hello, darling," she said softly when she reached his table and took the empty seat beside him.

Roger had gone beyond drunkenness. He'd passed out and come to a number of times, and each return of consciousness had caused both stupor and reality to retreat yet further. Now he was simply numb. The world, even the small odorous world of the Free Man, was a distant dream. He could see and hear, but reason had deserted him. He no longer knew why he was there, what was the cause of the great aching void inside himself. He only knew that he was terribly sad. At odd moments his eyes would overflow with tears he could not explain. It was the first such experience of his twenty-seven years, and he could put no name to it.

Into this sham reality there suddenly came a creature wonderfully familiar. Despite the odd way she was dressed, despite the incongruity of her appearance in this place at this time, the absolute rightness of her presence filled him with sudden happiness. "Nancy," he said in tones of wonder. "Nancy..."

He went with her as docile and uncomplaining as a child, following her into the chill night with his hand locked in hers, feeling as if a fairy godmother had materialized to drive away the terrible demons that beset him.

He slept for endless hours, stirring only when she sponged his sore muscles with a cool, scented cloth, or held a cup of broth to his lips. When he woke the first time, his head so pained him he wanted simply to die. The second time she wasn't there, and alone he rolled to the edge of the narrow bed and vomited endless streams of putrid green fluid onto the floor. Then, too ill and tired to feel either shame or fastidious revulsion, he turned back to the wall and slept. Sometime she must have returned and cleaned up the mess. The next thing he knew he was sipping a hot, nourishing drink and there was neither sign nor smell of his earlier sickness.

Real consciousness didn't come until the morning of what he later learned was the third day of his recovery. He opened his eyes to find that the sunlight pouring through the window didn't sere his eyeballs and the terrible pain in his head and gut had gone.

He'd never been here before, but he realized instantly that he must be in Nancy's room. He recognized her gowns hung carelessly on hooks hammered into a cracked and dirty wall. The washbasin was still full of the water she'd bathed in earlier, and a clutter of her familiar toilet articles lay nearby. Always before this the many hours they'd spent together had been on neutral ground, neither her quarters nor his. Except for that one time she came looking for him when the news broke about Harwood Hall, they had shared rooms only in inns and coaching houses. Griffin's first thought was that the

77

small chamber Nancy was satisfied to call home was incredibly shabby and squalid.

His next was that the nightmares which had flitted through his long sleep weren't figments of his imagination, they were real. Mark and all the family in their stupid, stubborn apostasy. The Hall stolen by thieves engaged in legal plundering. The Duke of York telling him that notwithstanding thirteen years of loyalty he was now *persona non grata* in the Stuart court.... And he, faced with all this rottenness, had wallowed in self-pity and taken refuge in drunkenness. A mere woman had to find him, nurse him back to health like a helpless calf. The thought was revolting. His disgust with himself was somehow personalized and given shape by the appearance of this ugly little room. Its evidence of slovenly disregard for the kind of gracious, careful housewifery to which he was accustomed was a somber omen.

Forcing back a wave of distaste, Roger rose and dressed. He found some shaving gear that Nancy had obviously left for him, and clean breeches and a shirt. He'd not seen any of the items before. Finally, looking and feeling a little more like his old self, he settled in the one chair to await her return.

9.

"Sweet Christ, Nancy! Are you sure?"

"I'm sure. Can't you try to look happy about it?"

"Happy? Sorry, it's not a word I've much knowledge of these days." Roger grimaced and took a long pull on the tankard of ale she'd brought him when she'd returned a few minutes earlier.

"I understand. But the baby's a fact nonetheless."

Something in her tone made him aware of his tactless behavior. "Nancy...I'll own the child. Surely you realize that." She made no reply, and the conversation seemed suddenly like an awkward confrontation. He groped for a change of subject. "Where did these clothes come from? They're not mine."

"No, I borrowed them from a fellow at the theater. Your own things will be here sometime this afternoon. Nell's managing to get them out of Whitehall."

"Managing? I'm a criminal, then? In hiding?"

"Of course not. It's just that your friends think it best you aren't seen about for a while. York wants you to give things time to settle."

"He does, does he?" Anger was a pain in his gut. "Time to settle! God, the bloody bastards! I'd never have believed it, Nance. I fought at York's side at Ardres and Dunkirk and Nieuport. He was magnificent, afraid of nothing. Saved my life more than once, and I his, if it comes to that." He was pacing now, talking more to himself than to her. "Then just four years ago, in '66... the Great Fire... Do you know that after it became obvious that the jackass calling himself Lord Mayor of London would do nothing, Charles put James in charge of saving the city? My God, he was brilliant! The king too. Neither of them were out of the saddle for something like two days and nights. Checking everything, seeing to every detail, no thought for personal risk. I thought then that to serve two such men was as much as anyone should look for in this life. And now this..."

"But you wanted to leave court anyway. You told me as much three months back."

"Leave court! Do you think it was this kind of leaving I had in mind? To lose not only every farthing but my good name?"

"You know," she mused softly, "I've never before realized that to be born into a family and station like yours, to be so very secure from the first breath you draw, it can be a disadvantage. You expect life to be fair, and you're shocked when it isn't."

"Fair? Because I believe in things like justice and duty and honor? Is that unreasonable?"

"What would you have the king and York do? You speak of their great courage in war. Would you have Charles secure the throne by fighting pitched battles in the streets of London? Hasn't there been enough fighting and killing? I admit I don't understand it all, but surely it's politics and diplomacy that are needed now."

"Diplomacy! To kowtow to scum like Dewinters and Randolf..."

"Stop it, Roger!" She faced him with a sudden flare of impassioned anger that made her eyes glitter and her breasts heave. "Stop bemoaning your fate! It's done and that's that. You have to pick up the pieces and go on. As for justice and duty and honor...do you remember what you told me weeks ago?" He stared at her in blank silence. "About the baby, our baby. 'It won't be a bastard, Nancy,' you said. 'It'll be a Griffin.' Where's your justice and honor now?"

"I told you I'd acknowledge the child," he said stiffly. "Give it my name."

"You miserable whoring son of a bitch!" She spoke with teeth clenched, no trace of color in her face. "How dare you! Where does that leave me, my fine gallant gentleman? The mother of your bastard, that's where. Good enough for Nancy Wilmott, is that what you think? Is that what all your pretty speeches meant?"

"Nancy, you don't think that, you can't." Most times when she got into a rage he became equally angry. This was different. He saw too well how his words could be interpreted thus. Remembered too well how often he'd asked her to wed him, insisted her background didn't matter, said he hoped she'd have his child. "I love you," he said softly. "You know that. Since the first moment I saw you I've wanted you to be my wife. It's just that now..."

"Now? Because you've come on a rough patch in your life you want the rules suspended? The words taken back? It's not on, Roger. It can't be." She pressed her hands over her belly. "The child in my womb won't wait for its father to straighten out his affairs before being born. Either you take us now, Roger Griffin, me and the child, openly and honestly before God and man, or not at all. I swear to you, if you don't wed me now you'll never see me or the son or daughter I bear you ever again."

It was, of course, a quiet wedding. Nell stood beside Nancy, Roger stood alone. The vicar mumbled and guffawed, seeming bored by the proceeding. Only because his church, St. Catherine Cree on Leadenhall Street, was far from the precincts of Whitehall did Nell suggest it. For this same reason mistress Gwyn was a source of interest to the vicar. It was the first day of March in the year 1670; she was two months away from "dropping her foal," as Charles had put it recently. It might well be two foals, judging from the size of Nell. The minister of the Gospel gazed with wondering eyes on this lavish proof of his sovereign's prowess in bed, and droned on the words of the ceremony. "I now pronounce you man and wife," he said at last. It was the first time he'd looked directly at the bride and groom.

Roger led Nancy down the nave of the church with a sense of profound relief. It was all over; he had the satisfaction of having done his duty as a gentleman. When he went to signal the waiting coachman, Nell and Nancy had a few seconds alone.

"I must say," the younger girl remarked with customary directness, "your husband doesn't look all that thrilled with his new estate."

"I know. He thinks I'm mad to hold him to his promise of marriage now that he's a pauper." Nancy adjusted the sleeve of her amber gown and didn't seem much concerned. "But he'll get over it. He loves me, Nell. What's more, he needs me. Now, at least. I warrant it's the first time he's needed anyone."

"And that's why you married him? Because he needs you?"

"No. Because I love him. But that wouldn't have been enough. Do you understand?" Nell had no chance to answer. Roger returned and ushered both women to the waiting carriage.

They stayed on at the Cock and Pie mainly because there didn't seem anyplace else to go. Their only income was the few shillings that Nancy earned at the theater. Cheaper lodgings than her small room didn't exist. She seemed unworried about the future, about what they would do when she was too obviously pregnant to continue performing, when there was no income at all. Roger was deeply concerned. His plan was to obtain a commission with either the French or Spanish forces, or an officer's berth on a British naval vessel. The negotiations, however, for one so out of royal favor, were long and delicate, and he had no intention of telling her his plans until they were an accomplished fact.

Later he was glad he had no need to reproach himself for upsetting her. He wasn't to blame for the tragedy. But he was with her in the squalid little room three weeks to the day after their wedding, when she suddenly doubled over with pain and let loose an agonized scream. "What is it, Nance? What's the matter?"

"I...don't know," she managed to gasp when the sudden and terrible pain subsided. "It must be something to do with the baby.... Get Moll..." Then she was writhing once more, her knees drawn up almost to her chest, her face red with the enormous effort of breathing.

Moll Blake, Old Moll everyone called her, was a great fat battle frigate of a woman. Her flesh hung in gray and quivering folds from a frame that would have been oversize regardless of how much she weighed. She hadn't a tooth in her head, and her tongue was as evil as the sight of her. A creature to frighten small children and put the devil himself to flight—but no one in London had a better, surer touch with a woman in labor.

Old Moll could take a babe from a woman with her two hands if nature didn't seem able to do it alone, and neither mother nor child any the worse for the intervention. She kept great crocks of foul-smelling brews and powders in her cottage, and grew the herbs from which she concocted them in the patch of earth behind. Regardless of how noxious her potions seemed, women took them gratefully. Dozens swore that it was Old Moll's "physicks" made them conceive when they thought they couldn't, gave them sons when only daughters had arrived before, eased the pain of birth until it was little more than a pinprick, and at least half a hundred other marvelous claims. It was rumored that Queen Catherine herself had sought a cure for her barrenness from Moll Blake, though obviously to no avail.

Roger knew the harridan's reputation the way one always knows such things, by simply living in a place where the legend was in the air. He didn't need to question Nancy's request or ask the whereabouts of the woman she wanted. He pounded down the two flights of narrow winding stairs that separated him from the street without stopping for cloak or jacket. And he thanked God that the miserable hovel he and Nancy called home had the single advantage of being just yards away from Moll Blake's house in Crown Court.

"My wife...please..." He'd run all the way, and his breath came hard.

"Calm yerself, laddie." The woman slowly heaved her bulk out of a chair and reached for a shawl hanging nearby. "Tell me wot's doin' so's I'll know t' bring right med'cin."

"She's expecting a child..."

"I guessed that much. Is her time come?"

"No...it's just two months or so...I'm not sure."

Moll's face clouded. "'Tis bad, that. Bearin' out o' time can cost a gel all t' babes she mighta borne...."

"For God's sake, don't stand there chattering! Just come."

The woman ignored this reproach, started accumulating little jugs and packets from a shelf in the corner. These she put in a great black satchel, as stained and tattered as the shapeless gown that covered her massive frame. "All right," she said at last. "I'm ready. Have ye a carriage waitin'?"

"No. It isn't necessary. We live just down the road at the Cock and Pie." Moll raised her eyebrows at this announcement—he didn't look the sort to live in such a place—but she followed him. In fact, once they were set out on the brief trip Roger was astounded at the speed with which the woman moved. Like a ship under full sail she traversed the short road almost as quickly as he'd come running to fetch her.

"It's Old Moll come to ye, gel," she said when she stood beside the bed on which Nancy lay twisted in pain. "Stop yer frettin' and try to breathe easy-like." Moll paid no further attention to Roger. He stood in frozen panic by the door, not knowing whether to go or stay. The woman stripped the girl bare, probed with practiced touch her barely rounded stomach. "Ah..." she breathed finally. "I kin feel it now. Like a great knot in yer belly. Shouldn't be so for six or seven months yet, but there it is. Yer babe's a-bornin', gel. We's just gotta wait a bit and see if it comes of itself like it should."

Roger listened with incredulity to this announcement. "How can it?" he ventured. "I mean, it's not time. How can the child..."

Moll didn't look at him when she answered. She might have been discussing the time of day for all the emotion in her voice. "It cain't. Too small yet, not even a real babe. But whatever it is, it don't mean to stay put inside this gel any longer. That's plain."

He realized then that she'd spoken the child's obituary. The knowledge hit him like a blow to the midsection. Until this moment he'd not realized that he genuinely cared about the baby. It had announced its presence in such a time of crisis that he'd never consciously thought of it as anything but a damned inconvenience. Then Nancy's stubborn insistence on holding him to his word in spite of the totally changed circumstances had made him resentful, without affection for the idea of fatherhood. But beneath this surface anger and disregard had grown another stronger, albeit less rational, feeling—a secret hope that somehow siring an heir would give him back the will to fight for its birthright and his, the birthright of a Griffin. The notion had not been conscious until he'd heard this obese ghoul tell him he was to forfeit his child along with everything else.

"We'll save t' mother, though," Moll added, as if realizing that her words had shocked and grieved him. "She's young 'n' strong. We'll save her." And having said that she began pottering among the evil-smelling powders in her bag. Some she made Nancy swallow, others were smeared on her stomach and over her thighs. "Won't be long now, gel...." she whispered. "Push hard wit' t' next pain...."

Her whole body trembled and seemed to contract in agony before his eyes. One long scream—then silence and a bloody, seething mass between her legs.

In that gory mess there was one small but distinguishable lump of something that couldn't be called flesh, though Roger knew no other word for it. He watched in fascinated horror while Moll Blake scraped this thing into a piece of filthy cloth and dropped it unceremoniously into her satchel. Then she quickly and efficiently wiped Nancy clean and covered her with a blanket. "Let 'er sleep now. Best thing. Give 'er a sip o' this when she wakes. You owe me fourpence, laddie."

He fished some coppers from his pocket and silently handed them to the woman. He was equally silent while he watched her leave the room and descend the stairs, carrying in her bag what should have been his child.

PART TWO

Children of Agate

As when a Griffin through the wilderness
With winged course, o'er hill and moory dale,
Pursues he who by stealth
Hath from his wakeful custody purloined
His guarded gold...

—John Milton,
Paradise Lost

1.

A long, long journey. And at the end, what? Mark didn't know. Sanctuary, perhaps. A roof over Clare's head. Some place for the children. Not such small children any longer; Laura was sixteen, Sarah thirteen, Andrew and Charles twelve and ten. They plodded beside their parents along this cart track the spring rains had made a sea of mud, and their faces looked to him neither young nor discouraged. They were grimy and exhausted, of course; they had been walking for seven days. Sleeping rough under the night sky with only the underside of their wagon loaded with goods for shelter, eating cold meals from Clare's carefully apportioned store of foodstuffs, taking turns guiding the old horse that pulled the wagon. Yet despite these things, a state of life that a few months earlier they would all have been unable to imagine, the children looked wise beyond their years, reconciled to their condition. Whatever it was that had made them all so willing to set out on this course, take the risk, become Catholics, now animated them, gave them an inward courage and strength. Mark was proud of them.

"We'll stop just under those trees," he said, seeing the fatigue they couldn't hide. "There's plenty of daylight left. We can afford a few minutes' rest."

"Are we out of Yorkshire yet?" Sophia asked. They were her first words since morning.

"I think so," Mark answered. "It's some four hours since we left Sheffield. I hope we see Chesterfield Castle before dark."

"And we'll be in Nottinghamshire then?" Clare's knowledge of geography was limited to the boundaries of Harwood land.

"Yes." Her husband smiled gently. "Just your fourth time

away from home ground, my dear. I'm sorry this isn't a happier journey."

"Happy enough." She smiled more warmly than he. "We're all together, Mark. All well and alive. Sooner or later we'll be in London and Roger will find some way to help us start anew. We'll manage till then."

"No he won't." Sophia's voice was flat, without expression.

"That's nonsense, Sophia! You must stop saying such things. Roger's your brother, uncle to these children. Do you think he'll see us starve?" Clare was busy even while she scolded. "Here, pass this drink around. It's a rose-hip cordial I made last summer and will do us all good."

Mark shook his head in wonder at the variety and practicality of the things she'd managed to load on this single wagon the authorities had allowed them to take. But his pleasure in Clare's eternal housewifery didn't dispel the knot of fear Sophia's words caused to form in his gut. "Why do you say such things?" he asked his sister. "Has Roger ever given you cause to believe him hard-hearted or callused?"

The girl shook her head. "I don't know why...only that Roger can't help us. It's folly expecting him to."

"That's enough, Sophia! I'm still master of this family, and I make the decisions."

"So you do, Mark." She sighed and shrugged. "But that won't change the facts."

"How do you know they're facts, Aunt Sophia?" Sarah was as outspoken and serious as ever. "You sound so sure."

"I am sure. But not of anything else. It isn't given me to know everything, just...."

"Just what your 'voices' tell you," young Charles interrupted with a child's acceptance of the most improbable claims. "Like Joan of Arc. Right?"

Sophia didn't reply, but Andrew did. "Not like her, I hope!" he said with feeling. "She was burned at the stake for a witch, thanks to her ruddy voices!"

"Andrew! Mind your language. And don't go making drama where none exists. There'll be no voices in this family. I won't have it." Clare looked for support to her husband, but he ignored her and continued to stare at Sophia. Then he rose and signaled them to move on.

Given the facts of their situation, it wasn't surprising that Mark was uneasy. But he knew it was not because they were homeless fugitives that he felt so unquiet inside himself. They were in this condition because they had heeded the words of the Holy Gospel: "Whoever confesses Me before men, I shall confess him before my Father who is in heaven...." If acknowledging the Lord Jesus and His true Church meant losing all material things, so be it. God would provide. No, his anxiety was based on something else.

For one thing, there'd been no word from his brother since the day John Lane arrived and demanded they take the oath. What effect on Roger the family's recusancy had produced, Mark didn't know, neither how he'd fared at court nor what he thought of it all. He did know that it was Roger's patron, the Duke of York, who had seen to it that the Griffins weren't sentenced to life imprisonment. Lane had told him so with a malicious sneer. "Takes one to know one," the justice of the peace had said disdainfully. "They tell me York's wife won't take Anglican communion these days. It wouldn't surprise me if he's a papist too. But if so, you can forget your Stuart kings. No Catholic will ever rule this realm, depend on it." Mark wasn't concerned, however, with rumors about the goings-on at court. What nagged at his peace this April afternoon was the fact that none of his letters to Roger had received a reply.

Another worry was the meeting he'd had with Father Joachim MacTavish the week before they'd left the Hall. The Jesuit had come secretly, insisted they descend to the wine cellar to speak. Then he whispered cautious, vague advice Mark still wasn't sure was sound. "Go to London when you leave here," the priest said. "But don't enter by the Oxford road, though that's the most direct route. Go across the moors till you reach the Islington road and enter thus. When you've come to a place called Cripplegate, look out for a friend. I can't tell if 'twill be man, woman, or child. Whoever, they'll say, 'The air's not so fine as in Scotland,' and you'll know they've come from me."

It all sounded so farfetched and theatrical. Mark had doubted the advice then; he doubted it still. To involve others in their plight was to burden his conscience with more innocent victims, when he already feared Roger might be the first. In fact he was so unsure of MacTavish's suggestion that he'd told no one, not even Clare, about the priest's instructions. Now his uncertainty was intensified by Sophia's warnings. He tried to ignore them, but he kept casting sideways glances at her.

Something had happened, was happening, to his sister. Clare might dismiss it as nonsense and odd fancies; he knew otherwise. Sophia had been a wild and willful girl, spoiled, stubborn, given to airs and disobedience...all true. But this was different. In the months since she'd set them on this course, Sophia had changed. She was painfully thin; he suspected her of keeping secret fasts and God knew what other hidden penances. Yet there was a peace about her that he'd never seen before. Not that it could be called quiet. The girl burned with some white-hot inner flame, some hidden conflagration. She spoke seldom, and when she did it was only to tell them what she thought she must, with no real effort to argue or persuade. She was...Mark searched for the word and finally found it: she was "abandoned" to a kind of obedience he could never have claimed and didn't understand.

"Sophia..." The girl turned restlessly in her sleep. "Sophia. Wake up. I must speak with you."

"Who's there?"

"Don't be frightened. It's me."

She recognized the voice. "Sister? Where are you? Why can't I see you?"

"That's not possible. Not now."

Sophia sat upright and peered into the darkness. Nothing. Just the voice, and the sense of familiar presence. "How can you be here?" She was in the same small copse of beech trees Mark had selected earlier as their campsite for the night. She must be dreaming. Then she heard the tinkling laugh she'd heard before in that place that was, and was not, the west wing of the Hall. "It is you. But so much has happened...I've much to tell you..."

"There's no need. I know everything. I told you, it's different now."

She shook her head. "I don't understand."

"No, you won't. Not for many years yet. But trust me. It's very rare, Sophia. This privilege we have. This ability to talk together. You've been given much grace. It joys my heart. You must not mourn the loss of your home, the present difficulty."

"I don't. We're going to London. I think it's lunacy. Roger can't help us."

"No. Not yet. But it is right that you go to London. What will you do there?"

"I don't know. Mark won't say anything except that we are going to Roger."

"For your brother and his family that may be wise. I don't know anything about them. Only you. There's something you must do."

"What? Why?"

"You must sacrifice your life. For the sake of your own soul, and many others. For England." Calmly, without drama, as if she were suggesting a hot drink.

Sophia's voice shook. "I'm to die, then? To be a martyr like the Kirkslee nuns in 1540?"

That same tinkling laugh. "Nothing so dramatic. But yes, you must be one of us. The reward will be great. Later perhaps I can tell you."

"Later!" The girl was suddenly impatient. "This is a mad conversation. Is it the best you can do now that you're a ghost?"

"Is that what you think? Silly child. I'm a person. Alive as you are. I told you all that long ago."

"Then why can't I see you?"

"We're..." The voice hesitated, seemed unsure. "We're separated. By time. A sort of time, at least."

"I don't understand," she repeated.

"It doesn't matter. Only remember what I told you. Good-bye."

"Sister, wait! Will you come again? Can I see you?"

There was no reply. The sense of presence was gone, the nun was gone. Around Sophia the shadowy, humped figures of her family huddled in sleep were miniature hills in a black and starless landscape.

They went on. Nights and days ran together, a river of time. They walked, they slept, they ate. Clare was composed and efficient. Laura was merry; nothing could dampen those high spirits. Sarah was prim and fastidious; eating cold bread and cheese by the roadside with the same attention to propriety and detail as if she sat in the dining hall at Harwood. The boys chased rabbits, engaged in mock duels, chatted incessantly, in short, they treated the whole affair as a kind of adventure. Sophia said little, and neither did Mark. Miraculously, or so it seemed to him, they met no one, were stopped or questioned by none. At last they reached the brow of a hill and saw the clutter of London on the horizon. Below them a broad road of hard-packed dirt snaked in from the west and stretched in a direct line toward the city. The Oxford road. "That way, Mark." Sophia pointed away from the inviting route and across the fields.

"I don't know...." He looked at her with a dozen questions in his eyes. No one but he knew of MacTavish's advice.

"I do," she said. "We have to go that way."

"But why, Aunt Sophia? This is ever so much better a road than we've been on. It'll be easier and faster." Laura gave voice to the thoughts of all of them.

"We have to go that way," Sophia repeated quietly.

"Sophia's right." Mark didn't know until he spoke that he'd made the decision. "Come along, everybody. Across these fields."

Hot sun. Hotter than he ever remembered for this time of year. A track that was little more than a footpath, the wagon wheels gouging great ruts either side of it, the horse straining with the effort. Clare's lips pursed in stern disapproval of his impractical choice and the credence he gave Sophia. The children were mildly annoyed at first, then began to enjoy the wild flowers and the varied insect life of the open moor. They managed. Soon after lunch they came on a better road, not as wide or well traveled as the one leading to and from Oxford, but better than they'd been on before. He saw a sign reading "To Islington" and pointing back in the direction they'd come. "Here, the Islington road. This is what we want." He half expected some comment from Sophia, but there was none.

London seemed to creep up on them. A few isolated farmhouses, an open space with a market cross and signs of occasional busy activity, then a shanty town of tents and hovels like a gaping mouth ready to swallow them. "Is this the city?" young Charles asked in tones of disbelief. "Is this London?"

His sister laughed. "Don't be a goose." Laura tossed her head and tried to shake the dirt from her skirt. "This is just the beginning. Wait till you see it!" Her image of the town was that fairyland of pomp and panoply she'd witnessed ten years earlier on Restoration Day. With that picture before her eyes she could forgive the misery of the slum they were in now. "Where exactly are we going, Papa?"

Clare was watching him too. She'd not had the boldness to ask the question her daughter posed so innocently. Mark shook his head and said, "Don't fret. It's all arranged," with more conviction than he felt. He was grateful that the rising crescendo of tumult made further questions impossible.

The farther toward the city they progressed the more

crowded, noisy, and filthy were the streets. People were everywhere, none with the time or inclination to be curious about one more band of ragged travelers with a wagon. It was then, for the first time, he saw fear in his wife's face, and felt guilty about his cowardice in welcoming the diversion. "It's all right, my dear." He stepped closer to her side and took her hand. "I promise you it'll be all right."

"I know. I trust you, Mark. It's just so disorderly."

Not surprising she felt thus. Clare, torn from her world of linen sweet with lavender, oak rubbed with beeswax, house and garden arranged to perfection. All snatched away in a moment and replaced with this sodden, noxious lump of humanity, swallowing them up like a mass of sour, overrisen dough.

They came to a stone church bearing the inscription "St. Giles." Next to it was an ancient aperture that had obviously been a gate in the medieval London wall. The wall had disappeared amid cluttered rows of houses and shops, but its old entry points still lived in the speech of London folk. "That's Cripplegate, I think," Mark said.

"It's that indeed, mister." A small child darted out of the crowd to stand next to Mark and tug at his sleeve. "Ain't ye never seen it afore?"

Mark smiled at the boy, younger than his own sons, and less nobly born, but bright-eyed and alert. "No, I've not."

"Yer from the north I'd guess by yer talk, mister. From Yorkshire, p'raps?" The question unnerved Griffin; anonymity was the one protection he sought for his family. He didn't answer. "The air's not so fine here as in Scotland, I'll wager," the lad said and waited.

He recognized the phrase instantly. Too late to question the wisdom of the Jesuit's advice now. "No, it's not. I'm Mark Griffin, and this is my family. What's your name?"

"Tom, sir, Tom Cuttlebone. I've been waiting all this past week. Me father said a man, two boys, and four women with a wagon, so's I knew it must be you lot. Follow me. T'ain't far to Marden Lane."

"Sit down, squire, milady. A hot drink first, then a wash, I reckon." The woman smiled and bustled and treated them like the gentry she knew them to be. But there was nothing of the fawning servant in her manner. "'Tis a poor place compared to what yer used to, I know, but yer safe here. And warm and dry. There'll be good hot soup and a bit of bread and cheese fer yer supper soon."

Clare rose and swiftly put her arms around the chubby woman. "God bless you, Mrs. Cuttlebone. We're very grateful indeed, and you mustn't fuss." Then, recognizing a kindred soul in spite of the differences in their station, Clare's eyes regained their normal sparkle. "I've some things in the wagon will help to replenish your larder for all our extra mouths. Can I show you?" Arm in arm the pair walked to the street, where young Tom stood guard over the Griffins' remaining possessions.

In the following days the children accepted it all as quite natural. Sophia remained lost in her private world. Clare fell into camaraderie with Mrs. Cuttlebone, sharing domestic business and women's chatter. Mark felt that he alone was conscious of the strange unreality of this new world. At night, lying beside his wife in the room they shared with the children and Sophia, he longed to talk about it. But he didn't dare for fear of alarming the others.

It wasn't exactly the family Cuttlebone themselves who made him feel thus. They were as normal and sane as ever he'd met, as solid as any of his tenant families back in Yorkshire. He understood them at once and instinctively—hardworking folk who knew their place and were content with it, but not servile in spite of that; decent in the true sense of the word, with the dignity that only such wholesome decency conveyed. It was the contrast with that familiar identity that Mark found alarming, unnerving. For behind that thoroughly English exterior another, secret identity lurked. They were recusants, Catholics. Not the type known as Church papists who survived here in London by dint of their wits and their ability to pay enough lip service to Anglicanism to keep the sheriff at bay. These were fervent believers, devout supporters of the pope. They'd come under Jesuit influence years before and since then led a double life of breathtaking danger.

Josiah Cuttlebone was general dogsbody in a bookbindery in Cornhill. It seemed an innocent enough occupation until Mark learned that most of the books they made were forbidden Catholic treatises which Josiah delivered about the city at daily peril.

Every night the family gathered in a hidden corner of the storeroom behind the house and spent an hour or more in pious prayer which included such petitions as hopes that the

Almighty would soon depose this terrible Stuart king and cast him into the hellfire he deserved. "But Charles is rightful King of England," Mark protested one night after the children had gone to bed and he and Clare and Sophia sat with Mr. and Mrs. Cuttlebone before the kitchen fire. "You must see that. He's your sovereign and mine. You should be praying for his health and well-being."

"Beggin' yer pardon, squire, but he ain't. Rightful king, that is. Not any more. Not since the pope said Elizabeth weren't rightful queen. All is been kings since then is frauds. Pretenders. Them and their heretic Church..." The old man spat into the coals.

"The Bull of Deposition, yes, I know. But it's a hundred years since that was issued. The time, the situation, is changed. To hear you talk one can't be a loyal English subject and a good Catholic at the same time. I don't believe that."

The Cuttlebones listened and looked attentive, but Mark's arguments made no difference in their attitudes. The nightly prayers still called down a pox on Charles and his house, still made veiled reference to secret plots to overthrow him, the success of which was made the object of much earnest petition.

"We've got to get away from here," he said to Clare on the fourth day after their arrival. "These people are good and well-meaning, but misguided. What they're doing is terribly dangerous, and I can't put you and the children at such risk."

"But where will we go? Besides, it seems so mean and petty. Look at the sacrifices they've made by letting us stay here."

"I know. I've thought of all that. It doesn't change anything. Tomorrow I'm going to try to find Roger."

"Tomorrow? But it's Sunday. Mrs. Cuttlebone says there's to be Mass not far away. She's going to bring us."

"Fine. I'll wait till after Mass, then."

2.

Throughout the service Mark wondered why the priest looked so familiar. Later, talking with him privately, he knew. They were in the home of people slightly higher-placed than the Cuttlebones, the owners of the book bindery, in fact. There was a small study where men could meet, and Mark was taking advantage of that situation. He marshaled his thoughts and watched the priest over the rim of a glass of Rhenish wine. The man had that same burning-eyed luminosity as did Sophia; he gave the same impression of being lit by some curious inner fire. "We heard all about it here," he told Mark with what could only be described as relish. "All about your giving up your home and land and everything for the faith. It's marvelous, my son, quite marvelous."

"Do you think so?" Mark grimaced. "I don't. Frankly, father, I think it's bloody awful."

"But..."

"But nothing. Don't you see? I wouldn't do anything differently if given the event to live over. Neither would my wife, or children, or my sister. We did what we had to do because of what we believe. That doesn't mean we like it. At this moment, sir, we have the clothes on our backs, the household goods my wife could load onto one small wagon, and about one hundred and fifty pounds I managed to get out of my money chest before it was commandeered. That's damned little for a man with a family to be getting on with, father. You'll forgive me if I don't think it's marvelous."

"I didn't mean... only that..."

"Listen." His anger interfered with his sense of the reverence due the old Jesuit. "We were saved from life imprisonment by the intercession of the Duke of York, who is a friend to my brother. I have no shame in telling you that I wept tears of joy when word of the reprieve came. I will do as my God commands, and so will my family. But neither I nor they have any desire to be martyrs. I fear, father, that you and our kind hosts here differ from me on this matter. Frankly, you all seem to me quite mad. And the end of your little drama is likely to be a rope at Tyburn Tree."

The priest wasn't angered by Mark's outburst. He was too old and too familiar with the gap between words and deeds. "I take your meaning, sir. I think no less of you for it."

"Thank you, father. I have no wish to offend, nor am I ungrateful for the enormous kindness done us by these people. But I think it far better if we leave Marden Lane as soon as possible."

"But where can you go?"

"I must find work, obviously. Not an easy thing for a man whose only training is as a country squire." He had enough sense of proportion left to laugh. "Still, I have hope. God won't desert us, surely. And if you will, you can help."

"Anything."

"I want to reach my brother. Captain Roger Griffin, special assistant to the Duke of York. Last I heard he had an apartment at Whitehall. I've had no word of him in many weeks. In the circumstances it seems unwise for me to simply walk in the palace gate, announce myself, and ask to see him. Can you suggest someone who might be able to carry a message for me?"

The Jesuit thought for a moment. "I can do better than that. There is a man, a priest in fact, privy to all court business and yet trustworthy. With your permission I'll arrange for you to meet with him. He can probably give you news. In any event he can carry your message."

Huddleston arrived the evening of the same day. It was young Tom Cuttlebone who came to tell Mark that the priest was waiting downstairs. He spouted a bit of the man's extraordinary history as well. "Him it was, squire, wot helped King Charles in '51 when the king was runnin' away from them Roundheads after the Battle of Worcester. You knows the story, sir, how the king 'scaped dressed as a servant and took sanctuary in that there house in Shropshire, the one they call Boscobel House. And how he hid under floorboards, and later in a tree, while soldiers looked everywhere."

"I do indeed know the tale, my young friend. And don't you think that shows his majesty's bravery and proves he's our true king and merits our loyalty?" Mark couldn't resist an opportunity to temper the virulent anti-Stuart feeling with which the boy was raised.

"I sees wot yer meanin' be, squire, but that's why it's so good 'bout Father Huddleston. He helped the king then and his majesty ain't never forgot it. He lives right there in court with 'em. If he makes the king a Catholic then everything'll be fine, won't it?"

"Yes, Tom, just fine." It was pointless to try to tell this simple lad more of the realities of life. "Now, take me to see this famous priest."

He found a man in his late sixties with white hair, a florid complexion, and sparkling blue eyes intensified by his somber black robe. Somehow he looked an utter incongruity seated by the wide hearth in this simple kitchen. "Thank you for coming, father. I hope I cause you neither embarrassment nor inconvenience."

"You do not, squire. But I wish I brought you better news. In my experience, son, it's better to tell evil tidings quickly. Brace yourself."

"Oh lord! Something's happened to Roger, then? Is he dead?"

"No, not dead. But dismissed from court in disgrace."

Mark buried his head in his hands. "That's my fault. If we weren't recusants this wouldn't have happened. So Roger suffers for beliefs he hasn't the privilege to share....Sweet Jesus! What justice is there in this damned world?"

"Precious little, son. I expect you know that. Justice comes later, but it does come. Console yourself with that. In fairness, it's not really the fact that you've become Catholics that cost Captain Griffin his place. He was asked by the king and the Duke of York to do a dirty, thankless job—to rectify the appalling business of supplying the navy. He did it too well and made many enemies. Your actions merely gave them a lever to use in getting rid of him."

"Where is he? Can I see him?"

"I don't know for certain where he is, though I'm told he's still in London. There is one person who will know, however. Are you familiar with the name of Nell Gwyn?"

"No. I know little of this city and its people."

"She's an actress. Quite a famous one. That is, she was. At the moment she's heavy with the king's child and living in retirement. To get to the point, your brother is married to a woman also an actress."

"Nancy? Nancy Wilmott? He did marry her, then?"

"You know the woman?"

"She was with my brother when he came to the Hall December last. He said then he wanted to wed her."

"I see. Well, the word I have is that he did. And this girl, your brother's new wife, is a close friend to our Nell. So, if you wish, I can probably send him word through her."

"Thank you. I do indeed wish it. But..." He was embarrassed by the question, yet couldn't resist asking. "You seem most tolerant of this woman, this Nell Gwyn. It doesn't disturb you? That she...that the king..."

"That she's Charles's mistress, you mean?" Huddleston laughed. "Of course it disturbs me. But so do my own sins disturb me. When I've eradicated all those, sir, I'll start feeling able to judge the conscience of others."

"A good answer, father. One I expect I can profit by if I've the sense to."

"That's as may be, squire. For now we must do what we can to see you and your brother reunited. You'll hear from me as soon as there's word. I'll find you here?"

Mark shrugged. "I don't see where else is possible. Though frankly it troubles me greatly to impose on these good people, and..." He took a deep breath. "To be honest, I fear for my family in this place. You're not a Jesuit, so I dare to speak. These are good, holy folk, and so are the priests who guide them. But they're treading a dangerous path. I've no wish to follow them down that road."

Huddleston put his hand on Mark's shoulder. "I know more than you think. Be patient. I shall do what I can as quickly as I can." He turned to go then paused at the door. "There is one more thing. While I was waiting for you your sister came in. Miss Sophia, I believe the lady's called. She asked to speak with me in private when we're able. Have I your permission to permit such an interview?"

Mark smiled. "If Sophia's made up her mind to talk with you, there'd be little point in my forbidding it. You may see her whenever you wish."

The meeting took place in broad daylight in that green and pleasant oasis known as St. James's Park, which the king had lately opened to the use of his subjects. Sophia was too wrapped in her own concerns to register the remarkable fact that she, a known recusant, was meeting a known Catholic priest in this public place a stone's throw from the palace. Had she been more knowledgeable of politics she would have recognized in this incident the essence of the religious ambiguity that marked the times. As it was she merely thought of her reasons for meeting Father Huddleston.

"Tell your brother," the man began before allowing her to speak, "that Miss Gwyn was delivered of a son yesterday morning. It will therefore be some days before I can use her good offices for the matter he and I discussed. You will remember that? It's important."

"I'll remember. But father, it's not on family business I've come. Not really."

"No. I thought not. Speak your mind, Miss Sophia. I'm listening."

"I wish to become a nun." There. At last the bald words she'd not had the courage to speak aloud before now.

"Indeed. A most admirable wish. Is there some obstacle—other than the laws of our land, I mean—some family opposition? You're not married, are you?"

"No, nor ever have been. Or even betrothed. I always knew I should never marry. But not why. That is, not until recently. Now I do."

"Yes, I see. But have you told your brother? He is your legal guardian, is he not?"

"He is. I haven't told him, though. Not yet. I wanted to speak with you first. To see if it's even possible."

"Possible, yes. But very difficult. Surely you understand that?"

She nodded her head. The early May sunlight played on the full skirt of her pale-lavender gown. It was a fine gown, one that looked quite at home here in St. James's Park; patterned silk cut up the front to reveal a lace underskirt. Sophia fingered its folds and thought briefly of how odd it was that though she was now a pauper she still had clothes that bespoke her former station. Then her glance roved to a nearby flower bed in which stately ranks of golden tulips blossomed within a pristine border of boxwood. "They're the more beautiful," she half-whispered.

"I beg your pardon?"

"Nothing. Forgive me, father, I was distracted. You ask if I know the difficulties of pursuing this choice. I do, of course. But you do think it's not impossible?"

Huddleston shook his head. "No, it's not. At the queen's residence in Somerset House there's a group of women called the English Ladies—some refer to them as Jesuitesses, but that's not correct. At any rate, these women have a convent and are under the queen's protection. They're allowed to go out and nurse the sick; that permission was granted when they were so desperately needed during the time of the plague five years past. Soon they hope to be able to take children into a school. I could speak with the mother superior about you if your brother gives his permission. Given our present straits, they will often take women without the usual dowry."

Now she was coming to the most difficult part. "Thank you, but that won't do. Not the English Ladies, I mean."

"Indeed? Why not?"

"Because it's a very particular convent I must enter. A priory."

"A priory? Like the Dominican nuns or the Poor Clares, you mean? My dear child, there haven't been any such in England these past hundred years."

"I know. And I don't know if it's Dominicans or Poor Clares or whatever you call them. I know nothing of such things. But father, do you know the history of a place called Kirkslee Priory? In Yorkshire. Not too far from my home...that is, my former home."

"No, no, I'm afraid I don't. Do I understand that you want to enter this Kirkslee Priory?"

"Not exactly. There's nothing there now but a field. Not even the ruins are left. But I thought, that is I hoped...well, isn't it possible there are nuns of this order somewhere still? On the Continent, I mean?"

The priest eyed her speculatively. He hardly knew what to make of this rather homely young woman with her broad Yorkshire accent and her strange ideas. Better to send her home to her brother, with instructions to forget all this and settle down to her needlework or whatever spinster ladies did to pass the time. Something held back his words. A look in her eyes, perhaps. A feeling, born of his own long years trying to understand the mysterious ways of God with souls, that there was something here. Something precious he must not destroy. "Miss Sophia, I must speak to you honestly. First, all that you say may be true. If we knew what order of nuns lived at this Kirkslee Priory of yours we might find that some of their number still exist in France or Italy. But surely you see the difficulty? How would you get to them? A young woman on her own...what dowry could you bring? Considering your brother's present circumstances, I mean."

"I can't answer those questions, father. I can only tell you what is in my heart, what the Lord tells me in prayer. I swear to you I'm telling the truth."

Her tone was sufficient proof. "Yes. I don't doubt you are. In any event, my dear, if it is truly the voice of God that directs you on this path we need have no care for the practical problems. He will arrange things in His own way. For my part I can only promise to investigate a bit for you. I shall consult the old records and see if I can learn the name of the order you seek. Will that do for now?"

"Yes. Thank you very much." Then, regardless of the time, the place, and the circumstance, Sophia sank to her knees before the priest. "Pray, father, give me your blessing."

Despite the debt Charles owed him, Huddleston had not survived this long without learning a healthy sense of caution. He was no fanatic, no radical Jesuit pursuing a single-minded quest for martyrdom. That was one reason he enjoyed his singular freedom and privileges. But at this moment he didn't care. Something in the girl reached out to him, making him conscious of realities beyond the seen. He lifted his hand. "*Benedicat te omnipotens Deus,*" he intoned softly, while his hand firmly traced the sign of the cross in the air above her head.

3.

Usually Roger would meet her after the theater. They'd go with other members of the company to the Lion's Rest or the Boar's Head for a late supper, or sometimes, if they particularly wanted to dine alone, their old haunt the Golden Bull. This night there was no sign of him, and after waiting a bit Nancy refused the many invitations to join the others and walked across the street to their room at the Cock and Pie. "What happened?" she asked, finding him sprawled on the bed and staring into the dark. "Are you ill?"

"No. I just didn't feel like going out this evening. Sorry if I worried you."

"It doesn't matter." She lit a candle. "Aren't you hungry?"

"No." Then, realizing that some kind of explanation was called for, "I had a note a few hours back. It left me rather sick to my stomach. That's all."

"Literally or figuratively?" she asked softly, seating herself next to him and stroking the dark hair back from his forehead. "Do you want to tell me about it?" She expected to hear that it was some new and degrading message from court. She wasn't in the least prepared for the truth.

"It was from Mark. He and the rest of them are in London."

"Your brother? And his family? They're here? But Roger, that's marvelous!"

He was incredulous. "You must be joking. What in hell's marvelous about it?"

"Well, you can see them. We can tell them about us, make sure they're all right..."

"Nancy..." He rose and strode across the tiny room to stand facing her with his back to the candle so he cast an elongated and grotesque shadow on the wall. "You'd better get something clear. Something I thought you understood. I have no intention of seeing or speaking to my brother or any of them ever again. I told you that."

"No, I don't understand, not a bit. You said those things when the news first came, when you were shocked and upset. I never thought you'd take such a hard view once you'd had time to adjust. In God's name, Roger, he's your brother! Your own flesh and blood. Where are they staying?"

He chose to ignore her harangue and respond only to her question. "I don't know where they're staying. The note was delivered by a messenger who said he could arrange a meeting. It was a young man. I think I've seen him before, as a matter of fact. One of the queen's household."

"The queen! But how..."

Roger shrugged. "You don't know these papists my brother's thrown in with. A regular little army of spies and intriguers they are. Many attach themselves to her majesty, for obvious reasons."

"I'm very confused." She shook her head, and her auburn hair glittered like some exotic jewel. "How did this messenger know where to find you?"

"That part's easy. Nell knows where we are. She must

have passed the information on. She's our only tie to the court at present."

"So now I suppose you're angry with her too."

"No, why should I be? It's not her affair whether I want to see my brother."

"But it is mine. What did you tell him, Roger? What did you tell the messenger?"

"I told him nothing. I'm not given to discussing my private life with every stranger. I gave him a note to take to Mark."

"And...?"

"And I told my dear brother just what I've told you. I want nothing to do with any of them. No, Nancy." He held up his hand to forestall her next words. "You've said enough. On this matter I'll brook no further interference. It's done and over. Pray God I'll not have to hear any more about it."

Roger seldom commanded her in that peremptory manner. That he did so now was enough to make her bite back her angry words. "Very well. Why don't we go downstairs for a drink and something to eat, then? There's no point in brooding about it."

He nodded in agreement and said no more till they were halfway down the stairs. Then, without preamble, "I had another message today too. The queen commands my presence at Somerset House."

"State your business." The voice was matter-of-fact, the livery too elaborate to be battle dress, but the drawn sword showed a sharp and threatening edge and it was a hairbreadth from the buttons of his coat.

"To see the queen, in answer to her summons." Roger had never before visited Catherine at Somerset House. All their meetings had taken place at Whitehall. He wasn't surprised that this guard didn't know him by sight. "My name's Roger Griffin," he added.

The uniformed man checked a list posted on the wall next to his station, then snapped to attention and waved him up an angular staircase that rose steeply from the waterside level to a small landing. At the top there was only one direction possible, straight ahead. He walked slowly, examining his surroundings as he went. This palace still retained its Tudor intimacy; the grander Stuart stamp hadn't yet touched the residence that belonged officially to England's queen. There was a disregard for the demands of classical symmetry. Instead there were low-pitched ceilings that made one feel somehow protected, enclosed. There was worn red brick and oak black with centuries. In all it suited the little Portuguese woman more than did that labyrinthine sprawl upriver.

The chamber they called the Presence Room was long and narrow, lit by diamond-shaped panes of odd purple glass that made glimpses of the bordering Thames seem like images of a stygian underworld. Catherine sat at the far end on a brocaded dais beneath a heavily embroidered canopy. Her gown was of black silk, one of those somber frocks she never wore in Whitehall, and by contrast her skin seemed paler than usual, her eyes darker, sadder. "I am pleased to see you, Captain Griffin," she said with that lisping Portuguese accent she'd never lose.

"Your majesty's summons gave me joy," he replied. "Is there some way I can serve you?" It was a question that he'd been puzzling since the message came the day before. Surely even Catherine of Braganza, remote and removed from politics though she tried to remain, knew of his fall from grace. What could she want with him now?

"Perhaps," was all she said. "Come, we will talk in less formal surroundings." She stepped down from her royal perch and led him out of the room, ignoring the bowing and scraping of the minions that surrounded her.

Following in her wake, Roger glimpsed a man in a rough brown gown tied with a knotted rope. Doubtless one of those Spanish Capuchin friars that Catherine kept here. Another foreigner caught his eye, a corpulent, red-faced chap wearing the sumptuous robes of a Romish bishop; purple velvet, sable, a jeweled pectoral cross that swung out over his well-fed belly when he bowed to acknowledge the queen's passage. This prelate looked neither Spanish nor Portuguese, however. Roger wondered who he might be, but his curiosity evaporated as soon as they were out of the Presence Room. He was too overwhelmed by the warmth with which Catherine turned to him and clasped his hand.

"My dear Roger. I've wanted to send for you for months. First it didn't seem in your best interests to be seen here, then I felt sad that I'd so little influence, so little help to offer.... You never doubted my friendship? You knew how much you were in my prayers?"

"I dared to hope, milady."

"But of course, Roger. Now, come this way." She took his

hand and almost pulled him along the corridor like a child urging another to join in play, her enthusiasm barely concealed. "I have something to tell you, a marvelous idea.... But wait, we can talk out here." She led him to a balcony overlooking the privy gardens that filled the strip of land between her private apartments and the river. It was said that these gardens had been laid out by Queen Elizabeth and never changed—intricate knots and parterres, angular terraces and neat little sets of steps, the whole limned with the pale lime green and delicate yellow of May. "Look, Roger," she said quietly. "It's rather a charming place in which to be exiled, don't you think?"

"Exile, your majesty? But, surely..."

"Oh, not official exile. I've not been banished from court as you have, my poor friend." Her laugh was brittle. "My punishment is self-imposed. I flee here to hide whenever the pain becomes too great." He didn't know what to say, and it showed on his face. "It's all right, Roger. You needn't comment. In the circumstances you can't be expected to say anything about Mistress Gwyn and her bastard son."

"It doesn't really touch you. You know that." How often he'd said this same thing to her in the past. Now, knowing for himself that external events can't be so easily ignored, he felt a fool. "I mean..."

"It's all right. We'll speak of something else. I didn't bring you here to offer sympathy or to ask for it. Tell me..." Her mood changed, became suddenly less open. "What are you doing now? I hear you've married."

"Yes, milady. Two months past." The best thing seemed frankness. "My wife is a member of the King's Company of Players. You may as well hear from me that she's a close friend to Mistress Gwyn. They were children together."

"Yes." The queen smiled as if for once she was amused by his naiveté. "Do you doubt that there were many at court who hastened to inform me of that fact?"

He grimaced. "I should have expected as much. You know that it doesn't affect my admiration for you, ma'am. Nancy— my wife, that is—she's not a political sort. It's perhaps hard to understand, but she thinks of herself as your loyal subject as well as Nell's best friend."

Catherine giggled. "Funny, that's rather like my husband's point of view. He doesn't see why fathering a bastard or two has anything to do with me either." She seated herself on a stone bench near the balustrade and patted the place next to her. "Sit down, Roger. You didn't answer my question about your present career. What plans have you now that your family have tumbled themselves into the pope's bed and you out of yours?"

"I'm not quite sure yet. At the moment nothing. I've been thinking of requesting a commission in some other navy. Frankly, I'd have thought of Portugal if I'd dared to ask for your help."

"The Portuguese navy! You're mad, Roger. It wouldn't suit you a bit. No foreign land would suit you. You're as thoroughly English as any man I've ever met."

"I love my country, milady. I make no apologies for that. But what other choice have I?"

"One other, perhaps. A better one. There's someone I want you to meet. His name is Alphonso da Gama, and he's my kinsman. My cousin's husband, in fact." She clapped her hands, and a man joined them as rapidly as if he'd been waiting in the wings for his cue.

Da Gama was a small, slender man, little bigger than the queen herself. He sported a carefully groomed mustache and pointed beard, and his hair was hidden under an elaborate wig of shoulder-length curls. Apart from his size, everything about the man seemed overstated, theatrical. His bucket boots of gold suede had fanned-out tops that touched the hem of a knee-length blue velvet coat with a waist too tightly nipped and flared satin cuffs reaching almost to the elbow. At his neck was an elaborately bowed silk fichu, and the hat he doffed as he bowed deeply was almost hidden beneath waving ostrich plumes. A puffed-up popinjay of a man; Roger didn't like him on sight.

"Captain Griffin"—da Gama's English had only a trace of accent—"her majesty has told me much about you. It is her belief we may be of some service to each other at this moment."

"Oh," Roger looked inquiringly at Catherine, but she only smiled coyly into her lace fan. "And how is that, sir?"

"If your majesty will permit..." da Gama touched his mouth with a lace-edged handkerchief and waited for a royal nod before continuing. "Forgive my indiscretion, captain. I'm told you are, how shall I put it, between employments just now. Some religious matter I do not pretend to understand."

"That's no secret, man. Get on with it." Then he felt a cad.

This meeting had been arranged by the queen. It was rude, as well as folly, to seem impatient and disinterested. "You speak of some mutual service...are you too 'between employments,' to use your delicate phrase?"

Da Gama laughed. "Not quite in the same way as you, captain. I am a man who suddenly finds himself with, what is your English phrase, an embarrassment of riches."

"Then I envy you, sir. My own condition bears no resemblance to that."

"But you misunderstand me. In my case the embarrassment is greater than the riches."

Catherine seated herself on a bench and watched the two men square off and take each other's measure. Griffin stood his ground, both feet planted firmly in one spot, arms folded. Da Gama pranced and circled, a feline stalking prey. "You see," the Portuguese said, "at this moment I am sole owner of the largest single shipment of coffee ever to come out of Ceylon."

"I congratulate you on your good fortune."

"Ah, thank you. But your felicitations are premature. This treasure presently costs me so much each day that I am on the edge of bankruptcy. To deny it would be stupid."

"And why is that, Senhor da Gama?" In spite of himself Roger was fascinated. The man danced about on the balls of his feet and gestured broadly with beringed hands. He was a ludicrous figure, an undersized peacock, but something in his eyes commanded attention, a metallic gleam that spoke of determination and wit behind his ridiculous facade.

"Because"—broad gestures with the handkerchief once more—"I came by the goods in a manner that could prove, I speak frankly, dangerous."

They were getting to the crux of the story at last. And, as if to confirm this fact, da Gama stopped moving, leaned back against the balustrade, and stared at Roger like a man about to issue a challenge. "I do not think, captain, that it is necessary for me to give you lessons in either politics or geography. But just to have everything clear between us, Ceylon is a Dutch colony. The coffee left the island in a Dutch ship. Certain persons relieved the ship's captain of his cargo without, shall we say, his cooperation."

"Piracy." Griffin's voice betrayed his distaste. He was still too much of a navy man for it to be otherwise. "And were these pirates in your employ?"

The Portuguese chuckled. "Pirates are in no one's employ.

And if they were I should scarcely admit as much here and now. No, captain, let us just say that the man who found himself in possession of the coffee suspected that I would be a likely buyer. He was correct."

"Doubtless a judgment based on past experience." Da Gama shrugged, and Griffin went on, "I'm afraid I still don't see why this is a problem to you, or what it has to do with me. I'm not interested in captaining any pirate ship, if that's what you have in mind."

"I didn't for a moment think you were. No, captain, as you say, you don't understand. The man's instructions were to off-load his booty in a neutral port. Either he was drunk or stupid, and he brought it instead to Lisbon. There it sits now. In a warehouse I must pay a fortune to have guarded day and night. My king, milady's noble brother"—another bow to Catherine—"has treaties with the Dutch, trade agreements. This is, as I've told you, a spectacularly large shipment. Inquiries have already been made, denials issued. Moreover, my wife is related to our king, as perhaps the queen here has explained. It could be most embarrassing. More than that, disastrous. For me, at least." Roger waited, and da Gama went on. "I came here to seek an outlet for my coffee, senhor. I dared"—he bowed deeply in Catherine's direction yet again—"to presume on our relationship and make inquiries of this most gracious lady. She tells me you may be the man I seek."

Griffin's mind was assembling facts, innuendos, and suppositions. Here was a tactical problem such as he'd spent the last decade dealing with. Supply at point A, demand at point D. How to negotiate the ground between? There was hardly a pause between da Gama's last words and Griffin's first. "Do you propose to sell me the cargo outright?"

"Oh no, my young friend." A laugh as shrewd as his eyes. "The price of this coffee is as volatile as its aroma. It rises daily. Right now they're paying three shillings a pound for it at the exchange, and getting six and seven shillings a pound from the merchants. No, I'll not sell it outright. I suggest that you and I market the coffee in England and split the profit. Shall we say sixty-forty?"

"The sixty to you, I take it." And, not waiting for the other to nod, "Precisely what am I to do to earn my forty percent? That part's still not clear, Senhor da Gama."

"But it's obvious, Captain Griffin. You must send a ship to Lisbon, load the cargo, and bring it to London. Once it is here you must negotiate its sale. I can't afford to have even a whisper of my name in the matter. That must be understood."

"Ah, I see. I am to take all the risks and you are to take the lion's share of the profit. So piracy is your game after all."

"Not at all, dear fellow. I will see to the security at my end. If your ship lands in Lisbon I will guarantee that she will sail away loaded with coffee and unmolested. Moreover ... I hesitate to be so blunt, but as we stand here, captain, it's I who have the coffee."

It was at this moment that Catherine rose. "You have said quite enough, Alphonso. Now leave us. I wish to speak with Captain Griffin alone."

"Your humble servant, milady." Da Gama bowed his way out of the room, leaving behind a faint scent of rosewater and corruption.

The queen made a face of distaste. "He's a horrible little man, Roger. I can't see how my poor cousin Dorothea stands him. But that isn't important now. You do see what an opportunity this is for you?"

"Frankly, your majesty, no, I don't. Forgive me, but the man inspires me with no confidence. I wouldn't trust him as far as that wherry over there." He gestured toward a small boat pulling up the Thames against the tide. "Certainly not Lisbon. And what's more, I have no ship to send on this venture."

"Both points are unimportant, Roger. I will assure you that in this instance at least, Alphonso will do as he says. He will know quite well what it will mean if he doesn't. One word from me to my brother and little Senhor da Gama will be preening himself before the *auto da fé*. And I propose to lend you the money to buy a ship."

Her words were as offhand as if she were commenting on the weather. Roger could only stare at her for some seconds before he found his voice. "Milady ... I hardly know what to say. I wonder, do you have any idea of how much money is involved? And if this venture should fail I would have no way to repay you. You know that." She made as if to answer him, but he went on, "Wait, there is something else. I presume on your friendship, but I must speak my mind. It isn't safe for you, milady. Not now. I'm tainted, *persona non grata* with everyone who matters in London. Your own enemies could use this against you if it came out."

"Oh yes." She smiled, but not with her eyes. "My enemies. Those who want Charles to divorce me and find himself a Protestant queen who will produce a Protestant heir and neatly remove the Duke of York from the prospect of being king after my husband. Never fear, Roger, I'm no longer the innocent maiden you brought here from Portugal. I know all about their schemes. But neither you nor they can know my real strength in this issue. Charles will never divorce me. No matter how many women he beds or how many bastards he sires. I am his wife in the sight of God, and he is Henrietta Maria's son. The king, my dear Roger, shares Catholic belief in the indissolubility of marriage. He'll not put his immortal soul in peril to satisfy political expediency. He fears too much for it already."

She wouldn't listen to any more protests. Griffin left Somerset House possessed of an understanding with da Gama and an exchange order for three thousand pounds drawn on a discreet goldsmith in Pope's Head Alley across from the Royal Exchange.

4.

Walking up the Strand to where he'd arranged to meet Nancy, Roger was like a man awakened from a dream. This was the first time in months he'd actually seen London. Here, in a part of town that had mercifully been just beyond the fire, was a city old but ever new. Alive, vital, constantly changing. Why hadn't he realized this before? What if the bastards had stolen Yorkshire from him? Here was a way to beat them at their own game, to possess their city, make it his own. The idea was exhilarating. He felt drunk, but not befogged. Things appeared to have a new clarity. Money and power, that's what life was about. In his pocket was a slip of paper that would buy him everything else if he used his wits.

He would have liked to go at once and trade the exchange order for solid currency, but for one thing Nancy expected him, and for another it occurred to him that he had no money chest. Morever, the little room in the Cock and Pie was not sufficiently secure for such a treasure. It was a problem requiring thought. Tomorrow would be time enough to begin. He turned left on Arundel Street, then made his way through Spite Alley to a small tavern called the Lion's Rest. This was a favorite haunt for the players of the King's Company, and this afternoon Sir Will D'Avenant had invited them all to celebrate the tenth anniversary of the theater's founding.

Roger had earlier learned that when this group were together offstage they spent their time entertaining one another. Therefore he wasn't surprised to hear Nancy's voice singing a ballad when he entered the taproom. The light was poor. This was a very old inn; some said it went back to the time of the Plantagenets and took its name from Richard the Lionhearted. The ceilings were so low he had to stoop, the beams enormous, blackened by generations of soot and smoke. What windows the place boasted were high and narrow, with panes embedded in lead thick enough to eliminate all but the most persistent sunshine. It was crowded nonetheless. Not just the Drury Lane party, but dozens of local folk were engaged in more or less serious attempts to drain the landlord's barrels of ale.

For a moment he remained unobserved by the door and watched his wife. She was finally rid of the sick pallor that had lingered after she lost the child. Today her cheeks were flushed and her brown eyes sparkled. There was nothing Nancy liked better than performing for her friends. Her voice wasn't great, it never had been, but it had a combination of sweetness, vibrancy, and warmth that made her a popular singer. "C'mon, Nance," someone called. "Give us another one." Then, spotting him, "Here's your handsome husband come to join us. Sing him a love song, girl, you never know where it might get you." There was loud laughter while he made his way forward to sit next to Sir Will, and she launched into another tune. This time young Kevin Mitchell joined her on the lute as he often did onstage.

The song was an old one, known to them all. "Oh do you remember sweet Nellie from Feif..." Suddenly a stranger pushed forward, obviously drunk, buff leather breeches and jerkin bespeaking his laboring origins.

"Hold on," he shouted in a voice thick with the cheapest

ale. "I'll sing ye a new set of words fer that old tune." His mates egged the man on with comments.

"You tell 'em, Curtie. You tell 'em 'ow it really goes."

"Aye, that I will. Play on yer lute fer me lad.... See, it goes like this:

"Hard by Pall Mall lives a wench call'd Nell ..."

"Stop! Stop this instant!" Nancy got to her feet, her fists clenched. Instantly Roger moved forward and pulled her to a seat.

"Be quiet. He's a drunken lout. Are you going to brawl with him?"

"I'll not listen to any insults paid Nell. I'll not!"

"Roger's right, my dear." Sir Will covered her hand with his in a soothing gesture. "Let the fellow have his fun. Nell'd be the first to join in. It doesn't pay to make a scene."

The singer, of course, was continuing regardless of their comments. He seemed oblivious to the fact that his ditty was inappropriate to entertain this particular group.

"King Charles the Second he kept her,"

he roared in a voice both tuneless and loud.

> *"She has got a trick to handle his prick*
> *But never lays hands on his scepter*
> *All matters of state from her soul she does hate*
> *And leave to the politic bitches.*
> *The whore's in the right, for 'tis her delight*
> *To be scratching just where it itches!"*

Finished at last, he staggered back to the bar to laughter and even applause. Nancy looked around at those who were supposed to be Nell's friends but didn't mind this joke at her expense. "Let's go," she said imperiously to her husband. "It stinks in here."

Roger's lips were set in a thin angry line, but he rose to follow her. "My thanks, Sir Will." He bowed slightly in the old man's direction. "My wife seems in need of some air." He caught up to her as she left the tavern, and they walked silently for a few feet. Then his mood softened. He didn't like Nancy's making a scene in a public house, but he couldn't blame her for being loyal. "It's not really an insulting ballad, you know," he said quietly. "The ordinary folk prefer Nell to Barbara Villiers because she doesn't meddle in politics. Sir Will was right. She'd be the first to join in."

"I don't care. I hate to hear them toss her name about like some kind of bawdy joke. What business is it of theirs?"

Roger shrugged. "Whatever the king does is his subjects' business. In the end they pay the piper regardless of who calls the tune."

"Money, that's all they care about. Pounds, shillings, and pence where their hearts should be."

"It's a fault none can accuse you of, anyway." His irony was lost on her. "It really doesn't bother you, does it?"

"Does what?"

"This." He waved his hand to indicate the shabby facade of the Cock and Pie. "Our less than palatial room at this less than illustrious inn. The not quite princely sum of five shillings a week on which we live and which is earned not by your fine, strong husband but by you."

"Stop it!" she whirled to face him, ignoring the fact that the mud of the street splashed her yellow silk gown. "I don't want to listen to that dismal story again. I've heard it too often. We can't spend our lives crying over spilt milk, Roger. We've got to accept things as they are and go on. It's not a bad life, whatever you say. And until that lout with his foul mouth ruined things, I was having a good time. What else matters?"

"Good God, Nancy! Did you think I'd be content to go on like this forever? Living off my wife. Letting her earn our daily bread by flaunting her tits in front of every buffoon with the price of a theater ticket."

"Flaunting...is that what you think of my acting? And is having a star's role in the King's Company of Players nothing but entertaining buffoons?"

"The noble Charles, my dear, may patronize your company and even reach into its ranks for his bedmate on occasion. But he doesn't marry thus. Nor live in a room above a tavern."

An answer was on the tip of her tongue, no doubt words as well designed to wound as his. But he didn't let her speak. His mood changed abruptly. "Don't let's quarrel, Nance. Please. I'm sorry if I hurt you. It's been an extraordinary day. Don't you want to know about my afternoon?" He took her arm and guided her quickly up the stairs. Only when they were in their room, the door safely bolted, did he continue speaking. "I spent three hours with the queen. She had a marvelous plan to propose. It will change everything."

"The queen? Catherine?"

He laughed. "She is still the queen, you know. Despite Nell's favored place. No, don't start that again." He saw her expression and raised his hand to forestall another outburst. "I'm trying to tell you something important. To understand it you have to know a bit of the background. I was in the party that fetched her majesty from Portugal in '62. She's been fond of me ever since."

"Fond? How fond?" Her eyes narrowed and he could see the jealousy.

"Don't, Nance," he said quietly. "Green doesn't become you. And I won't have anything ill said about the queen. Catherine's a remarkable woman, a fine and noble lady."

She couldn't seem to help herself. "Maybe that's her problem. Too noble to spread her legs. That's why Nell had Charles's son instead of her."

"That"—he was finally as angry as she—"is the remark of a gutter bitch. Sometimes I think that's all I can expect from you. Besides, who are you to throw stones at the queen? I seem to recall you didn't manage to produce a live child either."

"You bloody bastard!" Her cheeks were flaming and her breasts heaved in anger, threatening to escape the tenuous control of her bodice.

Suddenly he realized that her anger excited him, made his breeches draw tight with desire. He took a step forward. She stood her ground, looking as if she expected him to strike her. Roger fought back the urge to tear at her dress, as some sane corner of his mind warned that such an act might never be undone. "I want you," he said instead. "Now. Take your dress off."

"Are you commanding or asking?" she spoke softly but with an element in her tone he'd never heard before.

"Commanding."

She reached up and pulled the garment over her head with slow deliberation. When she'd dropped it to the floor behind her and removed her shift she said coolly, "See, Roger, I'm quite experienced at this sort of thing. Men have been commanding me to bed for years."

He did strike her then, one swift open-handed blow that left an ugly red stain on her cheek. "If you want to talk like a whore then I'll treat you like one." There was no further speech. Just the sounds of flesh rubbing against flesh after he stripped off his own clothes and threw her across the bed. For the first few seconds she was passive, removed. But that didn't last. Soon he could feel her twisting beneath him, straining to bring his heavy maleness into contact with the sensitive, moist folds of her womanhood.

"Oh God," she muttered through teeth now clenched not in anger but in passion. "Why is it always like this with you . . . no matter what . . . deeper . . . please . . . harder . . . harder, damn you!" And when it was over only silence. He rose, pulled on his clothes, and left the room.

It was morning when Roger returned, a gray misty morning that shed a dirty light into their small room, and made it look even meaner and more squalid than usual. "I'm sorry," he said without preamble. "You know I never intended that to happen. Did I hurt you?" It was the first time he'd touched her since the miscarriage, and during the long night just past that fact had bothered him most of all.

"No. I'm all right. For what it's worth, I'm sorry too." She pulled herself up in the bed and drew the thin cover over her breasts. "Sit down," she said, patting a place beside her. "You look exhausted. No sleep, I'll warrant."

"No. I've been walking, thinking."

"Do you want to talk?"

"Yes, I do. Nancy, why did it happen? Why do we fight so these past weeks?"

She shrugged. "I can think of a hundred reasons, but I don't know if any of them is the real one."

"What reasons? Tell me."

"First that you resent my forcing you to marry me when you had decided against it. Second that we lost our child. Third that you're bitter about everything that's happened to your career. . . . Shall I go on?"

"No. That's not what I think is the real cause. None of it. True, I'd not have married just when you decided we must. But I wanted you for my wife the first moment I laid eyes on you—the timing's not all that important. And losing the baby was sad, but we can hope for more children. Neither is bitterness involved. What it's been is more . . . more a sense of impotence. Losing because of circumstances that were no doing of mine, that I couldn't control. Yesterday, when I met

115

you, I was full of wonderful news I wanted to share. Instead..."

She pressed her finger over his lips. "Never mind that. Yesterday's past. Tell me now."

"I told you before, you have to understand a bit of the background. You must have known I'd been making some plans, figuring out a way to build a future for us."

"I like our life now, Roger. I like my work at the theater. That's the part you never reckon with."

"All right. Leave that aside or we'll just start quarreling again. What matters is that I've been casting about to find a way to support us and the family we hope to have. I'm not like you, Nance. I can't just live from day to day."

"No, I do understand that. One must be born to that kind of existence, and you certainly weren't."

"Well, I decided to seek a commission in some foreign navy."

"What!" She sat bolt upright, paying no attention to her nakedness. "Are you mad? What kind of life would that be, for God's sake? You off for months and years at a time. Me here on my own and worried half to death..."

"Ssh. Stop shouting. It isn't going to be that. I only considered it because there seemed no alternative. Now there is. A marvelous new scheme. I'm going into business, Nancy. I was offered the chance yesterday afternoon. The queen introduced me to a Portuguese chap. He...never mind all that, it's complicated. The thing is I'm going to organize a trade in coffee. You are looking, my dear, at a merchant. The sole owner and head of Griffin's Importations."

5.

"Are you daft, son?" The old man sat back on his stool and eyed the client standing before him. "Ain't you never heard of the East India Company? No one but them's going to hawk coffee on the floor of the Exchange. Not if they have any say."

"I know that. But it's my worry, not yours. All I need to know from you is can you build the ship I want."

"Have you got the money to pay for 'er?"

"I have."

"Then I can do better'n that. Come down to the yard with me."

His name was Cecil Towne, and he was quite possibly the best shipwright in England, certainly the best in London. Roger had known him for years, coming to his place here in Deptford dozens of times on navy business. When he arrived this morning Towne didn't seem unfriendly, but neither had he failed to let Griffin know that he was aware of his changed fortunes, and would not work on credit. With that established, he listened quietly to Roger's description of the craft he wanted. Fast enough to do a journey in record time, yet broad-beamed enough to carry a substantial cargo.

Now Towne led him through a maze of masts and struts, a forest of timber and nail kegs, with the surefooted gait of total familiarity. They moved toward the open water that lapped at the foot of the yard, and when they got to the very edge the fellow stretched out his hand and pointed. "Feast yer eyes, lad. Ain't nothin' finer afloat for your purposes, and ain't never gonna be."

Riding at anchor in the scummy churlish river was a craft Roger recognized instantly. He ought to, for he'd been in the official welcoming party when the ship first reached England.

"Dutch," Towne said unnecessarily. "One o' them wot's called a pinnace."

"How did you come by her?" Griffin's voice gave nothing away.

Towne scuffed the toe of his boot in the mud and clasped his hands behind his back. "Bought 'er. Fair and honest."

"You're a lying bastard." There was neither anger nor excitement in the words. "She's the *Von Ruyter*. Captured by Rear Admiral Holmes in the Channel off the coast of Vlie, on the eighth of August '66."

"Ye know a bit about it then." Towne sounded not the least repentant.

"I should. I took command of her from Admiral Holmes on behalf of the Duke of York a month later. In Rye. She's the property of his majesty's navy. But you know that as well as I do."

"I know nothin'." The old man spat into the water. "I bought her from a gentleman wot had all the papers provin' she was his. Paid good English money for 'er, too. That's all I care to know."

Griffin turned away and walked a few yards downstream. Here, writ large, was everything he'd spent the last ten years trying to rectify. Anchored in front of his eyes was proof of the monumental combination of incompetence, greed, and thievery that was plaguing the English navy. If confirmation was needed he had it in the audacity of Cecil Towne, who, knowing full well the ship's history, didn't hesitate to offer her for sale to one so lately the confidant of the navy's lord high admiral.

Christ! Where would it end? He'd seen Pepys just a few days ago, run into him in the Fleece Tavern by the Exchange. The man had dolefully told him the latest news. The master plan for supplying the fleet was scrapped. Randolf, March, Burton, and a dozen others just like them had their contracts back with only token reforms. All their work was gone up in smoke. And why? Because when the crunch came the brothers Stuart valued their royal prerogatives over the needs of the kingdom. He'd never before believed that to be true; now he did.

Overhead a gull's raucous call pierced the sounds of the busy yard and drew his eye. The scavenger bird dropped low while he watched. Swiftly it grasped a bit of biscuit from a workman's lunch and flew away. The incident happened in the wink of an eye, was remarked by no one but himself and the victimized chap who was shaking his fist in the gull's direction. Griffin made up his mind and turned back to Towne. "We'll need some modifications," he said. "I'll tell you what I want, and you give me a price for the vessel and the necessary work."

The *Von Ruyter* was seventy feet long and could carry perhaps seventy tons. She had a flat stern, a single deck, a short quarterdeck, a high forecastle, and three masts which could support enough square sail to make her incredibly fast when fully rigged. These pinnaces had long been used by the Dutch not as fighters, but as merchantmen. Still, like others of her class, the *Von Ruyter* had a series of high bulwarks around her open deck, and in two places on either side they were pierced for guns. Pinnaces were designed to defend themselves, not go looking for trouble. Roger wanted more insurance than that. "Six more gun mountings," he said.

"There's to be four either side. And I want fore and aft sails on the mainmast. Plus a spritsail."

"That's a lot o' sheet, laddie. And a lot o' guns. Where ye plannin' to take this lady? All the way to Brazil fer yer coffee?"

Griffin ignored the question. "Can you do it?" he asked. "And adapt the crew's quarters so she can carry a complement of twenty with some comfort?"

"I kin do it."

"How long will it take?"

"'Bout a month or two. Could be three if the weather gives trouble."

"No more?"

"No more."

"You'll sign a contract to that effect? With a forfeit to be paid for every day over ninety before she's ready for launch?"

"I will."

"How much?"

Towne licked his lips and squinted in the high noon sun. "Eight hundred," he said at last. "Half now. Rest when she's finished."

"Done." They shook hands. "Oh, and Towne, one more thing. She's to be called the *Queen Catherine* from this day forward. Put someone on carving an appropriate figurehead."

Somehow it seemed fitting that Nancy realized she was pregnant again at the same time Roger was so full of plans for the venture he now called Griffin's Importations.

"It is rather a grand name," he admitted sheepishly when he first told her about it. "More than is warranted by a single cargo of coffee. But it's a promise, Nance, a promise of bigger and better things to come. What do you think of it?"

"I think it's splendid," she said, smiling at his enthusiasm. "I rather fancy you as a merchant, to tell the truth."

"You do?" He seemed surprised at this. "You don't think it's dull and boring?"

"Not in the least. I remember as a child how I used to press my nose against the shopfronts and watch the men inside. Just imagine, I'd tell myself, they own all those things and they can eat and drink whatever they want whenever

119

they want...marvelous." She sighed and lay back against the pillow.

Her husband laughed and turned toward her in the darkened room. Often at night like this they were closer, happier, than they'd been since they married. The darkness hid the flaws in their relationship as it hid the cracks in the wall and the shabby furnishings. "That's not quite what I have in mind. I don't fancy myself coatless behind some counter bowing and scraping to all the housewives and maidservants of London. Not a bit of it."

"What then?" Her only idea of tradesmen was confined to just such an operation as he was belittling. "Roger, what are you going to do with all that coffee once you get it to London?"

"Look, love, there are two choices. The first is to do the usual thing and go to the floor of the Exchange and battle with the wholesalers for the best price I can get. That's what everyone, even my must-be-nameless Portuguese, thinks I plan to do. But if I do I run head on into the East India men, and they'll not take kindly to my presence, I assure you."

"What can they do? If the coffee is yours legally and you want to sell it, how can they prevent you?"

"They can't, really. But they can exert so much pressure on the buyers, all of whom are dependent on the East India Company's imports for the bulk of their goods, that I'll be forced to sell at a low price. I don't intend to give them that opportunity. Nance"—he raised himself on his elbow and toyed with a lock of her hair while he spoke—"It's little different from planning for the navy. You have to be willing to examine new ideas, look for new methods. My new idea in this case is to skip the wholesalers altogether. That means I'll skip the Exchange. I'm going to find warehouse space of my own. Then I'm going to go around this city up and down and crosswise and deal with the retailers direct. I'm going to give them a price they can't possibly get from the wholesale men because I'm eliminating a step in the chain. Do you see?"

"Yes..." She was hesitant. "I think I do. But isn't it an enormous task? For one man, I mean?"

"Good God, girl, it certainly would be. I don't mean to do it alone. I mean to hire people to help me. That's why I've given the business a name, in my mind at least. It's going to be a permanent fixture in London before I'm through."

"I see." Her voice was low, perhaps more serious than the discussion warranted. "And then?"

"Then..." He hesitated, was almost reluctant to give voice

to this part of his dream. "Then...the truth is, I hadn't planned to say anything just yet, but you might as well know. I intend to buy back Harwood Hall, Nancy. I shall do it if it takes me a lifetime."

"Buy back..." She was stunned. "But how can you?"

"With money. What the hell else? John Lane is a greedy, cowardly whoremaster. All Harwood means to him is land and profit. I'll find myself some smart London solicitor and have him make an offer for the place. That bastard Lane won't be able to resist."

"And we're to live there? In Yorkshire?"

"Eventually, yes, of course. Don't you like the idea?"

"I thought Harwood the most beautiful place I ever saw, but...Yorkshire..."

"Great God, girl, it's not the back of beyond. You make it sound as if I'm suggesting you live in Cathay. It is England, you know."

"But it's so far, so different from London."

"Yes, it is, thank God. You'll love it, Nance. Once you actually live there you'll feel very differently. You'll see."

"But..." She hesitated, unsure if this was the time to press an argument that might go on for years. "If your business, this Griffin's Importations, is to be in London, how can we live in Yorkshire?"

"Oh, don't worry about that." He dismissed the query with a wave of his hand. "I'll think of something. It may mean that I'll have to travel a lot, but that's not so bad. We'll manage some arrangement. A town house here, probably."

She couldn't resist saying, "It all sounds very grand for two people who haven't more than a farthing between them at the moment."

Roger was silent. The innocent remark wasn't meant as a reproach, but it stung anyway. He hadn't told Nancy how much money Catherine had lent him, how much he still had after paying Cecil Towne a deposit on the Dutch ship. Even when he'd paid the balance and taken delivery his money chest wouldn't be empty. But the chest itself was lodged with Levi the goldsmith, and Nancy didn't know what was in it or even that it existed. It had been on the tip of his tongue to tell her—enthusiasm alone prompted it if nothing else—but he'd kept silent.

His wife, he'd realized over these past few months, knew nothing of the value of money. She spent her wages within twenty-four hours of receiving them, and didn't worry a minute about how to survive until the next lot was earned. Money was of interest to Nancy only as something to buy a new frock or pay for a venison pasty from the baker. Thrift was as much a mystery to her as housekeeping. Roger told himself this was only to be expected considering her background, but it rankled nonetheless. And so did his own silence about the present state of their finances. It seemed dishonest not to share their changed fortunes with her.

Nancy mistook the silence that this guilt produced as a reproof. "Listen, darling," she said earnestly, "you mustn't think I don't have faith in you. I do. I don't doubt for a moment you'll do everything you say you'll do. It just took me back, the idea of living in Yorkshire, having a place as grand as Harwood."

"Harwood's where we belong," he repeated with iron in his voice. "We're Griffins. It's the Griffin home."

"That's as good a cue as you're going to give me, love, so now you be quiet and listen to me for a minute. I have something to tell you."

"Mmm..." He wasn't really paying attention, too full of his plans and dreams and getting sleepy to boot. "What?"

"There's going to be another Griffin soon. I'm pregnant."

And later, after all the tender things had been said, the caresses exchanged, "There's one thing, Roger...I went to see Old Moll yesterday. Told her I was having another child and asked her advice. I was worried, after the last time and everything."

"Of course, I understand that. What did she say? Did she dose you with some of her evil-smelling powders?"

"No, nothing like that. She said that I should have lots of rest, fresh air, and sunshine."

"That's all?"

"Yes."

"Well, that's easy enough. You'll have to stop working now, Nance. That settles it."

"But how will we live? Until your coffee cargo arrives, I mean?"

He felt like a cad for his past silence. "That's not a problem any longer. I've a bit left of the money the queen lent me. Enough to see us through."

6.

Huddleston peered earnestly at Mark Griffin and waited for an answer. The Yorkshireman looked gray with fatigue. For a fellow like Griffin to have lost everything, to be thrown into the mare's nest of folly and intrigue that buzzed around the Cuttlebones and their friends, all that after being, like St. Paul, knocked from his horse by a revelation of truth he probably never sought nor wanted... it was asking a lot. Now the priest brought the squire a new problem to deal with.

"You're sure," Griffin said at last. "This French bishop can definitely get her into this nunnery she wants to join?"

"I have no reason to doubt it. It's in his diocese, under his jurisdiction. The nuns couldn't refuse, and they're not likely to want to anyway. Why should they?"

"I don't know. It just sounds so bizarre. Locked up somewhere in a foreign country. Good God, Sophia doesn't even speak particularly good French. A nunnery... and she never said a word. Not to me or to my wife. You don't think it's just some passing fancy?"

Huddleston shrugged. "You know the young woman better than I do. But for myself, no, I don't think it's a passing fancy. She didn't even know the name of the order. Just that she must enter one of their houses wherever it might be."

"And the one she wanted, the one that used to be at Kirkslee is this, what did you call it, Order of St. Savior?"

"Yes. Properly speaking, the Hermit Nuns of the Order of the Holy Savior and His Most Blessed Mother. According to his lordship, Bishop Fermeau, they're commonly called just the St. Savior nuns. A small group. Very austere, very special. Founded in the Holy Land some seven hundred years ago. The first nuns of their order to come to Europe returned with the crusaders in the twelfth century. Now they have this abbey in France, the one just outside Paris in Fermeau's

123

diocese, and two or three small priories scattered over the continent. Kirkslee was their only English foundation, and it was never very big. At the time of its dissolution in 1540 there was only a handful of women there. Your sister claims she's called to this order. And I must admit, finding Fermeau a guest at Somerset House at precisely this moment did seem to me a strange coincidence. It's hard not to call it Divine Providence, don't you think?"

"Yes, I do. And there's more to it than just that. Did Sophia tell you how she knew of this old priory in Kirkslee?"

"No. Just that it had been near your former home. I didn't think it important. Was I mistaken?"

"No, father, not mistaken. It's not important." Mark couldn't say more to this practical, kind man. "Tell milord bishop my sister and I will call on him at his convenience." He sighed and leaned his head back against the wall of the fireplace. The stones felt warm, comforting, and real. Unlike the stones of the west wing, they didn't seem capable of causing anyone to see ghosts and visions, to set an entire family on a path of ruin.

"Forgive me," Huddleston said and reached out a hand and touched Mark's shoulder, "it's none of my affair, but you seem very tired and worried. No news from your brother yet?"

"Oh yes. I expect it's fair to call it news." Griffin's tone made the nature of the reply painfully obvious. "He wants nothing to do with any of us and he'll thank me not to try to communicate with him ever again. I'd say that's news, wouldn't you, father?" Huddleston obviously didn't know what to answer. Mark looked at the older man's expression of shock and added, "Not that I really blame him. Don't you see what it must look like from his point of view? Frankly, if the situation were reversed, I'd probably have done the same. Still..." A sadness crept into his voice. "I can't deny it hurts. We were always very close."

"Tell me." The question was unthinkable coming from a Catholic priest, but he asked anyway. "Do you ever regret it? This terrible price you're paying for what some would see as so little reward?"

It was a query born of his own doubts, his own fears and failures. Mark understood that with a visceral, wordless intuition. "Regret it? You might as well ask me if I regret the fact that the sun comes up or that it rains. What no one understands is that we had no choice. Our decision wasn't some carefully weighed thing in which all the pros and cons were totted up and measured. We did what we had to do. The rest was beyond our control."

Huddleston felt small and more than a little awed. In thirty years of priesthood he'd heard about this sort of thing, but never seen it quite so naked and exposed. He could think of nothing to reply. They parted in silence.

They met the French bishop in the garden of Somerset House. It was a quiet, uneventful discussion without witnesses. Fermeau, a heavy-set jolly little man, looked as if he thoroughly enjoyed all the privileges of his office. He didn't strike Mark as a spiritual type, but he was pleasant, even gracious. "You are sure, my child?" he asked Sophia.

"I'm sure," she answered. None of his warnings about the austerity and difficulty of life in this particular order had made any difference to her. She hardly seemed to hear them.

"Then," the bishop said, "You will leave with me. Be here at six in the morning of the day after tomorrow. We will take a coach to Dover and sail for France from there."

"One further thing, milord." Mark had said little throughout the interview. Now he spoke with quiet insistence. "Please tell the lady abbess of these nuns that my sister's dowry will be paid whenever it becomes possible. Pray God our condition will not always be as it now is. At that time we will make good all debts."

"I will tell her, sir. But you need not trouble yourself overmuch about this. The St. Savior nuns are poor and choose to be so. It won't matter a great deal." The bishop made a vague gesture of blessing over their heads and waddled back in the direction of the palace.

It seemed to Sophia but a continuation of that long journey begun two months earlier when they left Harwood. She arrived at Somerset House shortly after dawn on Wednesday morning. Standing before the palace gate with the woven straw trunk that carried all her possessions at her feet, she had no idea of how to proceed. There wasn't a soul in sight; her only companions were a flight of skylarks twittering gaily in the trees over her head. Perhaps she should have let Mark accompany her. But it had seemed so unnecessary. And after the scene Clare made when she learned of Sophia's plans, unwise.

Her sister-in-law had displayed a rare case of hysterics. In all her lifetime Sophia had never seen Clare thus. "It's mad," she kept shouting. "Utterly mad! Who are these women? Why should you shut yourself up with them in a foreign country? What will be said of us if word gets around that you've done this thing?" Her objections had been endless and uncharacteristically loud. And they'd been voiced against a counterpoint harmony equally as bizarre.

Mr. and Mrs. Cuttlebone, on hearing of Sophia's impending departure to enter a nunnery, had proceeded to kneel down in the middle of the kitchen floor and tell their beads. The *Aves* were interspersed with spontaneous prayers of joy and thanksgiving that England would soon have another martyr to her credit. Even Sophia in her present mood, withdrawn, self-absorbed, and introspective, had found the experience unnerving. Small wonder that the children ended the evening in tears and hysterics like their mother's. Of course it all calmed down eventually. Clare had no choice but to accept a decision taken jointly by her husband and his sister and sealed with the approval of no less a personage than a bishop.

After all that upset, Sophia wanted only to slip away quietly and alone this morning. Mark hadn't liked that, but he was afraid he'd be needed at the Cuttlebones'. The household had indulged in such noisy goings-on the night before that there was no telling what morning might bring. Sophia had her way and left unescorted. Only Mark rose when she did, shared her breakfast of mulled cider and a bit of cold rabbit left from the previous day, and kissed her farewell at the door. Of the rest of the family there'd been no sign, except that Laura ran down the stairs at the last moment and enveloped her aunt in one fierce, long hug before Sophia went out to the deserted street.

Now, standing before the locked gates of Queen Catherine's residence, Sophia wondered what to do next. She hadn't long to worry. A guard appeared, rubbing sleep from his eyes and asking her business in words muffled by a huge, disinterested yawn. "To meet his lordship Bishop Fermeau. He told me to come here," Sophia said.

"Aye, that's the French chap, ain't it. The fat one with the fancy robes. Wait here, lass, I'll see if he's up and about." The guard's words had a decided Scots twang, and for some reason that amused her. She was smiling broadly when he returned and unlocked the gate. "Up with the birds is the bishop, just like you are, lassie. C'mon, then, his lordship's waitin' for ye." And that was the first problem solved. As far as she was concerned there seemed to be no others.

They were on the road by seven, traveling in an elaborate gilt coach bearing the queen's arms on its door. Four mighty chestnut mares pulled the vehicle as if it were a toy. They were riding on the finest road in England, the much-traveled thoroughfare from London to Dover. They lunched in Maidstone and made Canterbury by nightfall. There they were expected by the innkeeper of a small establishment nestled in the shadow of the towering cathedral. He had their supper ready and waiting, as well as a welcome bottle of Burgundy wine.

Besides Sophia there were half a dozen clerics traveling with Fermeau. At the supper table they talked of subjects of which she knew little, in a language that she had difficulty understanding. It made a welcome excuse for staying out of the conversation. She ate her meal and went to her room within half an hour.

Sophia was wakened shortly before dawn by a light tap on her door. "It's only me, mademoiselle. Father Lille, his lordship's secretary. I thought you'd want to know there will be Mass in the bishop's chamber in ten minutes."

Sophia found the service extraordinary. She was accustomed to seeing the holy sacrifice offered hastily and in secret, by priests who half expected to be arrested at any moment. Admittedly this makeshift altar was only a table customarily used to hold a washbasin, but in every other particular the ritual was more elaborate than anything she'd previously witnessed. Fermeau's vestments were of heavy embroidered satin, his chalice and paten thick with precious stones. The priests of his traveling household performed their appointed roles in the ancient rite with the finesse and elegance of a trained *corps de ballet*. No fear of spies or informers need distract them. As Frenchmen traveling under an authority signed by Queen Catherine, Fermeau and his company had nothing to fear from laws that forbade the celebration of Mass.

Moreover, they seemed to feel not in the least unnerved by the presence among them of an Englishwoman officially branded an outlaw. On the contrary, they were extremely kind and thoughtful. "You will wish to take communion, mademoiselle," the one called Lille whispered before the service began. He crossed himself piously and added, "The Channel can be treacherous; this may be our last opportunity...." Sophia heeded his warning, and before the Mass started she quietly confessed her sins to him in a private corner of the room.

Thirty-six hours later they clambered into a small boat manned by four oarsmen and headed for a French brigantine lying a mile out. The ship was present expressly for the purpose of carrying the bishop and his party the twenty-two miles to Calais. No prelate of Fermeau's standing need wait for the regular packet that plied this much-used route.

"The good God is with us, *chère mademoiselle*," the bishop said as they boarded. They were the first words he had spoken directly to her since the journey began. "See, the tide is just now at its ebb, and the wind freshens. If the good God is willing we will be on French soil by nightfall."

7.

Perhaps she'd thought it would look something like Canterbury Cathedral or York Minster. But the Abbey of St. Savior was nothing like either of them. Riding toward it through the misty light of the French countryside, Sophia was reminded of a pile of stones left by workmen and artlessly formed into a pretend fortress by children. The building was neither gracious nor imposing. It was simply there. The carriage pulled into the forecourt, and a bored footman handed her out. "This is the place, mademoiselle," the servant said. "Have you any further need of me?"

"No, nothing more. Thank you." She was alone, deposited by the silent entrance like a cartload of turnips. Sophia looked long at this ugly stone eruption in the gentle blue-green hills of this countryside known as the Île de France. She shivered, and her palms grew damp with sweat.

When she had gone to meet the bishop at Somerset House she had insisted on going alone; this morning she would have been grateful for an escort. Some official Church personage perhaps, who could guide her through the unfamiliar territory that awaited. But, having brought her to Paris and installed her as a guest in a convent of nuns who took charge of the housekeeping at his palace, Fermeau had seemed to forget about her existence. Except that he couldn't really have done so. Less than a week after she arrived in France a note had come for her from the lady abbess of St. Savior's. "We are informed," the message read, "that you are an Englishwoman who, given the sad circumstances in your own dear country, wishes to join us in our life of penance here. Please come to the abbey on the morning of Tuesday the tenth of June at nine o'clock." The signature read simply, "Germaine, Abbess."

So Fermeau had remembered her presence. But having put Sophia and the nuns of St. Savior's in contact with one another, he obviously believed his duty done. She heard nothing further from him or anyone else until, on Monday afternoon, a young nun approached her and told her a carriage would be waiting for her the next day after Mass. "Sister, wait a moment, please." Sophia had barely said half a dozen words to these silent black-robed women who crept about their duties with downcast eyes and folded hands. "I don't mean to trouble you, but I need some advice. Should I bring anything with me? I don't know what is proper in such circumstances."

"I believe everything is arranged, mademoiselle. You needn't worry." Then, for the first time, a bright smile caused the nun's face to seem young and familiar. "I wish you much joy of your vocation, mademoiselle. It is very courageous of you."

"Courageous?" The choice of words surprised her.

"You know, of course, that you have chosen the most austere order in the Church. To sleep in one's coffin every night and eat one's meals from the floor..." The nun shuddered. "I confess I don't think I could do it. May God and Our Blessed Lady sustain you." Then she was gone, leaving Sophia with a sense of elation that bordered on euphoria. The bishop had told her that the order was penitential and strict, but this was beyond her hopes. It was exactly what she'd prayed for. She spent the rest of the day on her knees in thanksgiving.

Only now when she stood before the door to this new life

of sacrifice did she know a moment's fear. What if she failed? What if she wasn't strong enough? Sophia took a deep breath, marched purposefully to the bell chain, and gave it a strong, hard pull.

The woman who opened the door quite took her breath away. She was an exact replica of that old nun she had seen in the west wing of Harwood Hall. Sophia actually whispered, "But it can't be you..." before she realized that the resemblance occurred only because the nun was around the same age and wore the same habit as the other one.

"I don't know why it can't be me, *ma petite,*" the doorkeeper said, laughing. "I'm Sister Imelda. You must be Sophia Griffin."

"I am. And I'm sorry—about what I said. It's just that you reminded me of someone."

"Oh, think nothing of it. People say all kinds of weird things at this door. Particularly girls coming to enter. It's a bit unnerving, isn't it? But don't worry, child, it's painless." And still laughing with a kind of bonhomie that seemed wholly out of keeping, the nun bustled Sophia inside to a small parlor filled with sticks of old furniture and hung with faded draperies. The only comeliness in the place was that it was immaculately clean; the only bits of nonfunctional decoration were a massive wooden crucifix and a tiny painting of the Madonna.

"Now, I'm sure you've had a long journey, and you must be cold and tired. Here, Miss Griffin, drink this." It was mulled red wine with spices, and Sophia sipped it gratefully while the other woman explained that unlike the rest of the community, she was dispensed from the vow of enclosure, free to take care of the abbey's business with the outside world. "Someone has to do it," she said with a sigh. "Though I admit I'd rather be inside."

"You would?" Sophia didn't intend the remark. It just slipped out. She couldn't quite believe that anyone else shared her longing for a life of unremitting penance and hardship.

"Of course," Sister Imelda said. "Out here you always have to deal with the doom and gloom of the world. Inside it's so much more joyful." She didn't seem to notice the astonishment this produced in her listener. Instead she hurried over to a table and brought a slip of paper to where Sophia stood waiting. "You can read, can't you? Good, then read this. It's the words of the entrance ceremony. You can keep hold of it and read your bits. Now, child, are you quite ready? If so, I'll ring."

Sophia nodded and ran her eyes over the flowing script of the paper she'd been given. Her Latin was passable, and the words weren't difficult. Yes, she'd manage. She looked up just in time to see Sister Imelda go to a rope hanging in the corner and pull it in slow measured tugs.

All at once the building seemed to come alive with sound. A deep resonant pealing filled the abbey, and the stone walls seemed to reverberate with its echo. "This is the St. Martin's bell," Imelda explained breathlessly as she worked the rope. "It's rung twenty-seven times exactly. And only for the entry of a new postulant. That way the nuns inside know what's happening and can come and assemble by that door over there." She lifted her chin in the direction of a heavy oaken portal Sophia hadn't yet noticed. There was no sign of a handle or any other means of opening the door.

Imelda seemed to read the question in the girl's face. Or perhaps she simply expected it. "It's only opened from the other side. Like the St. Martin's bell, it's only for a postulant to enter. Or a novice on her clothing day. After she comes out here to change into her bridal dress, that is. But then you don't know about any of that yet, do you? There." She heaved a last sigh and straightened the stiff linen wimple the bell ringing had knocked askew. "That's twenty-seven, I think. Now, child, you come kneel over here and wait."

Sophia did as she was bidden. The bare tiled floor was cool; she could feel it even through her skirt and petticoats. It was some moments before a piercingly beautiful voice intoned, *"Benedicamus Domine,"* from the other side. The extraordinary voice startled her, and she had to be prodded by Sister Imelda before she glanced hurriedly at her paper and croaked the reply, *"Deo gratias."*

After that she paid attention. It was hard not to do so. The ceremony she was going through was obviously designed to impress her with the solemn nature of her undertaking. it could hardly fail to do so.

"What do you seek in this place?" the hauntingly beautiful voice asked.

"Jesus Christ," Sophia read.

"He is here, crucified. Wilt thou share His Passion?"

"With God's help I will."

At that point the door swung open on noiseless hinges and Sophia looked up to see a double file of black-robed nuns headed by a tall, regal-looking woman. It was she who had the voice that made speech seem like song. "Art thou willing to live according to the Holy Gospel and according to the rule of this the Order of the Hermit Nuns of the Holy Savior and His Most Blessed Mother?" she asked.

"With God's help I am."

"And will you forsake all others and be obedient only unto Him who was obedient for you even unto death?"

"With God's help I will."

"Then enter, child. Enter into the foretaste of that joy He has prepared for you."

They lifted her up then, Sister Imelda and the tall one whom she guessed to be the abbess, and led her to the front of the line of nuns. Someone took her hand and guided her on a slow, measured walk down a long corridor of yellow stone that seemed to glow in the morning sun. Behind her Sophia could hear the cadence of plainsong as the nuns chanted a hymn she couldn't identify.

They reached a set of double doors that her guide threw open, and she was being marched down the nave of a white-washed chapel, bare of everything except rows of wooden choir stalls and a great iron grill that hid the altar from view. As one the nuns genuflected, and Sophia found herself incorporated into their collective rhythm and movement.

"Accept this child, Lord," the abbess's voice intoned behind her. "Accept her sacrifice and ours that together we may make up in our bodies what is wanting in the sufferings of Christ."

The ceremony was over. Sophia stared at the tabernacle, whose outlines she could dimly perceive through the grill. "I'm here," she whispered. "I promised you, and now I'm here...." She had no doubt that the Kirkslee nun was there too.

Sophia had her first actual meeting with the abbess some days later. By that time she no longer wore the lavender frock in which she'd arrived. The mistress of novices, a rather forbidding, silent nun called somewhat inappropriately Sister Angelica, had given her a shapeless black dress and a white bonnet, the customary garb of postulants. And, Sister Angelica informed her, that's what she now was.

The summons to the august presence of the abbess was carried by a young sister whose name Sophia hadn't yet learned. "Mother bids you come to her office, Miss Sophia. It's just there at the top of those stairs. She's expecting you."

"I'll just finish this bit of floor," Sophia said, wielding the mop with more speed.

"No." The nun took the tool from her hands. "When mother calls you it's the voice of God. You must go at once. The floor will still be here when you return." She smiled, so there was no sting in the reprimand, and Sophia hurried up the stairs as she was bidden. It was an entirely new experience, this being ordered about like a servant, being at the beck and call of all the others. She wasn't sure she liked it much. Nor had she yet been introduced to those heroic penances she'd come here to undertake. The girl had a worried look on her face when she entered the abbess's chamber and stood waiting.

"Come in, child, sit down. I've been meaning to send for you for some days, but we're very busy in the garden just now. So much to do this time of year...." As if to verify her statement, the woman was hastily removing an outer apron soiled with grass stains. Beneath it her habit was shiny with age, the cuffs much mended with neat, careful stitching. "So, how are you finding us, Miss Sophia? You're warm enough? There are sufficient blankets on your bed? The food is acceptable to you? It must be difficult to enter not only a new life but a new country at the same time. Never doubt that your novice mistress and I are aware of that. We want to help any way we can."

What an extraordinary speech! Sophia's eyes widened. This was exactly opposite to what she expected. "I'm quite comfortable, lady abbess, thank you. But..."

"Wait." The hand the woman held up was slim and elegant, an aristocrat's hand in spite of its familiarity with a spade. "First I must explain that here at St. Savior's we do not use such grand titles. It is the custom in our order for the nuns to call the abbess only 'mother.' I hope you will feel comfortable with that soon, Sophia. I genuinely wish to be a mother to you. Your own died when you were very young, I'm told."

"Yes, lady...yes, mother. And you're most kind, but I do have some questions. If I might be permitted?"

"Of course." Mother Germaine smiled encouragingly.

"It's just all of you, this place...it's not what I expected. What I was led to expect."

"Oh? It isn't?" The nun's expression made her surprised tone seem a bit put on. "Let me see." She consulted a slip of paper on her writing table. "It's just five months since you renounced your apostasy and were received into Holy Church, isn't it? Hmm...I had some doubts about that. Frankly I would have suggested you spend a year or more living your faith in the world before trying your religious vocation, but his grace Bishop Fermeau seemed quite sure. And given the circumstances of your life in England he thought it best you come to us immediately. But now you have some doubts, is that it?"

"Not about being a nun, mother. I'm quite sure about that. It's just that things here are not what I thought they would be."

"No." Mother Germaine was giggling now. There was no other word for it. "Of course they're not. You thought we would give you a coffin to sleep in and a hair shirt to wear, and serve you your dinner from a trough, like a pig. Or did you hear the story about eating on the floor like a dog? Both tales are in circulation, I'm told."

Sophia's cheeks were red with embarrassment. "I meant no offense, mother."

"I know that, child. I take none. All these silly stories amuse me, though I don't know how they get started, and sometimes I fear they may do real damage. But not to those whom the Lord calls to this place. His voice is not to be shut out with the nonsense of the ignorant." Mother Germaine rose and drew Sophia to the high window that looked out over the gentle French countryside.

"Out there, Sophia, are men and women loving, fighting, living, dying. There is incredible suffering, incredible heroism, incredible sin—all existing side by side, all part of the tapestry of God's plan for man's salvation. Here at St. Savior's our part in that tapestry is to pray without ceasing. We are to offer our lives, our sacrifices, on behalf of all humanity. Do you understand, Sophia?"

"I thought I did, mother. It's only that when you ask me if I've blankets aplenty and enough to eat...well, it seems contrary to the very things you mention."

"That's the error everyone makes, child. If you came here seeking heroics and martyrdom, you came to the wrong place. It is extremely unlikely that you'll find either. What you'll find is the constant penance of living with forty other women with whom you may not be compatible, the daily effort to sacrifice your own will to the will of the community. You'll find the tedium of a diet of stern simplicity which is wholesome but admittedly boring. You'll find the endless chafing of doing not what you want, but what someone tells you to do, the tyranny of the bells, the endless demands of the liturgy. Those are our penances, Sophia. They are also our great joys. Here you will be forced every day to come face to face with yourself and your own failings. Here you will have the example of women who have turned their backs on all the pleasures of the world to be hidden with Christ in God. It is an example that you may come to see as worthy of emulation. For those who are called, Sophia, this house is a bit of heaven on earth. Those not called are unlikely to stay. Do you begin to understand?"

"I think so. I will try to understand, mother."

"Good. For the moment that's all that is asked of you. Now, go back to your work." Then, just before Sophia pulled the door shut behind her, "One last question, if I may. Why did you come here, Sophia? Why to this particular place?"

She didn't hesitate. Only the truth would suffice. "I was told to come. I met a nun of the order, and she told me."

"A nun of our order? In England?" Germaine lifted her eyebrows. "I see. And did this nun tell you why you must come here?"

"Yes, mother. To pray for the conversion of my country. God is going to put a Catholic king on the throne of England. He told me so."

135

8.

The end of June, the weather fickle as only English weather can be. What had been an unseasonably warm spring had become a horrible cold and rainy summer. Nancy looked at the gray sheet of mist outside the narrow window of her room and clenched her fist in frustration. Yesterday she'd gone to Old Moll to seek some relief from the weakness and nausea that plagued her in this the second month of her pregnancy, but with no success. "There be nowt I can give ye, gel," the old woman said while she continued to rock rhythmically in her chair. "Ye ain't ill. Leastwise not as I can cure. Ye need sun, air, rest. Like I told ye afore. I've seen cases like yours many times. Some gels ain't able to birth a live child in the city. They's only gonna do it in a country place."

"But that's ridiculous," Nancy protested.

Old Moll shrugged. "Ye kin have wot opinion ye wants. Ain't nothin' to me if'n ye takes my advice or no." The rolls of fat that hung from her body quivered with mirth as she chuckled. "Mebbe ye ain't so keen to carry yer babe nine months anyhow. Mebbe ye'd rather keep yer figger and have the fun o' startin' a new one."

"Don't you talk like that to me, you old witch! Of course I want my child."

"Well, 'n' its plain wot yer gotta do, ain't it? That is if ye thinks I'm tellin ye truth." She held out her hand for the tuppence Nancy owed her and continued to chuckle while she watched the girl walk away.

Thinking back on that conversation, Nancy knew she did believe Moll Blake, whether she wanted to or not. No one could have established a reputation such as that old woman had without having been right more often than wrong. Besides, hadn't she already lost one child? And wasn't the way she felt now proof of the accuracy of the diagnosis? But neither of those arguments convinced Roger. "You'll have to hang on a bit longer," he'd said. "I'm sorry, there just isn't enough money to move us out of London yet. Not until after the coffee arrives, Nancy. You know that."

When she pressed him for a date, he gave vague replies. The ship he'd dubbed the *Queen Catherine*, a name that annoyed Nancy in spite of herself, was still in Deptford being fitted to Roger's specifications. God alone knew when she'd sail for Lisbon. Probably even He didn't know when she'd return with her cargo. Meanwhile the child in Nancy's womb was being poisoned by the evil London air, starved for the kind of environment it needed to survive.

She pressed both hands over her belly. It was still flat. Should it be? Was this another sign of sickliness? Was the baby growing too slowly? How could she know? She'd never been exposed to such things before. But it did seem to her that at this same stage of pregnancy Nell had been plumper. God knew she'd been the picture of rosy good health from start to finish of the business.

Nancy hesitated a moment more. Then, her mind made up, she reached for her shawl. There was one woman she would dearly have loved to talk with just now—Clare Griffin. The only time she'd met her sister-in-law she'd realized that Clare was everything she herself was not, an efficient and capable wife and mother, expert at all things connected with housewifery, warm and sympathetic too. Clare was only nine years older than she, but in some ways seemed the mother Nancy had never had. Still, none of that mattered. Roger would be enraged if she went to Mark's wife, even supposing the Yorkshire Griffins were still in London and she could find them. She dared not risk it. Not these days, when he was so preoccupied and so short-tempered with her. There was only one other person to whom she could go. Nancy pulled her shawl over her head in a feeble attempt to stay dry and walked out into the street.

From Drury Lane to Nell's house in Pall Mall was a distance of some two miles. Normally she would have walked. But today she felt unusually tired, and the streets were a muddy mess as a result of all the rain. No, she'd go by water. She fished her hand into the pocket of her frock and felt a few coins. Roger had given her four shillings just two days past. He'd be furious if he knew how little she had left. What he doesn't understand, Nancy thought grimly, is how dear everything is. The mutton pies she'd brought in for their supper last night cost tenpence. And he'd complained that they weren't properly done, implied that she should cook their meals herself rather than buy them from the baker. But that was silly. She'd never cooked in her life. And how was she to do it on the little charcoal brazier in their room?

These thoughts occupied her as she made her way past St. Clement's toward Milford Stairs. By the time she got to the river she was soaked through despite her shawl. "Boat, miss?" the man asked, eyeing her up and down with frank interest. He was an evil-looking character, unshaven and dirty as these types often were, big gaps in his mouth where his teeth had rotted away. Nancy looked at him with distaste, but she climbed into his small wherry anyway. "Hungerford Stairs," she said. "And for heaven's sake don't dally." The man whistled for his partner, and swiftly the pair took up their positions at the oars. The tide ran with them, and they were away in a matter of seconds.

There would come a time, many years later, when she would marvel at the events she set in motion that wet June day of 1670. Was it all really only coincidence? Or was it something more, rather like fate or Divine Providence? She was never to make up her mind about that. But in any case, on the day itself her thoughts were of nothing beyond the immediate need to protect her unborn child. Only that instinct, so newly surfaced yet so strong, guided her actions.

"Tell your mistress it's Nancy Griffin," she instructed the footman who answered her tug at the bellrope. Perhaps it was her wet and bedraggled appearance that made the servant leave her standing on the doorstep while he went to convey the message. When he returned his expression was rather different and his step had a good deal more spring. "This way, ma'am, if you please. Madam's upstairs and bids you join her."

Nell's boudoir was like the rest of the Pall Mall house, luxurious to the point of opulence. A great four-poster bed was hung with damask, the floor was swathed in Turkey carpets, delicate French furniture and bibelots of shimmery crystal caught the fire burning in the grate and reflected a rainbow into the storm-darkened room. "Nancy, darling!" Nell stretched out her arms. "It's marvelous to see you. I've waited and waited for you to come."

The two hugged with all the old warmth and familiarity.

"I wanted to visit weeks ago, but I dared not. I've not been well, and you with a new baby and all. It didn't seem wise."

"Not well? I shouldn't wonder. Look at you, Nancy. You're soaked to the skin. Get those clothes off right away. Here, you!" She gestured to a footman. "Get out. And send the maid." She issued orders in a manner as imperious as any lady born to her station. There was no hesitation in her playing of this new role.

Nell couldn't keep a grin from her face while she watched Nancy peel off her clothes. She eyed her old friend's figure with the frank intimacy of past days. "Nancy Wilmott, or I should say Griffin, you're getting fat. Is that what married life's doing to you?"

Nancy giggled. "You might say that. Do you really think I'm getting fat? That's wonderful."

"It most certainly is not. You should see Moll Flanders these days. Or Frances Stewart, for that matter." She mentioned two of Charles's former mistresses without rancor. "They're as pudgy as a brace of pouter pigeons. It's disgusting. Look at me." Nell tossed back the covers and ran her hands along her tiny waist and curved hips. "And my son's just two months old."

The maid came in just then and offered Nancy a velvet dressing gown. After she left the older girl turned back to Nell. "But you didn't look like that a few months ago. When you were pregnant, I mean."

"No, of course....Oh, Nance! Is that it? Are you having a baby?" Nancy nodded and clambered up to sit beside Nell on the curtained bed. "That's marvelous," Nell continued. "At least I think so. Do you?"

"Yes, I do. But I need advice. That's why I came here." She began telling Nell how sick she'd been, what Old Moll had said. The story didn't take long to relate. And, as if to prove her tale, even while she spoke the terrible nausea was returning.

"Stop talking, darling, and lie down for a bit. You look awful."

"Oh, dear, I'm sorry, Nell. I do feel quite queer...." She didn't say any more. She couldn't. At that moment Nancy rolled from the bed to the floor in a faint.

"Lucy!" Nell shouted for the maid again. "Send for the doctor immediately. Tell him to hurry...."

* * *

It was ten days before she rose from Nell's bed. During that time Nell herself slept in another room, but she spent hours sitting beside her friend. And yet more time talking with the doctor, and with Roger Griffin, whom she summoned to her presence that first day and half a dozen times thereafter, and ultimately with the king himself. By the time Nancy was well enough to sit by the window and admire the stray sunbeam that was probing the eternally gray sky of the season, Nell had everything arranged.

"You're leaving here the end of the week," she announced with finality.

"Of course, Nell. I'm sorry to have been such a burden. Couldn't I leave today?"

"Don't be a fool. That's not what I mean. I'd keep you here until the baby's born if that would do any good. But the doctor says it wouldn't. He's Charles's own doctor, you know. So he should know something. And he confirms what Old Moll told you. You've got to get out to the country if this baby is to see the light of day. So I talked with the king and it's all arranged."

"You talked with the king?" Nancy's eyes widened. "About me?"

"Well, not about Old Moll, you goose. And don't look so awestruck. Charles is the same as any man when he's got his breeches off. Easy to persuade." Nell giggled, but her affection for her royal lover was obvious. "Besides, he's really a dear, you know. Very sympathetic and understanding. He realized at once what had to be done." She patted her full bosom, and for the first time Nancy noticed the thick creamy envelope that lodged there. "I've got the quitclaim deed right here."

"Deed? What deed?"

"Why, to your new home, of course. It's a cottage in Surrey. Just a few miles from Hampton Court Palace, so I can visit you when Charles and I are there." She peered into the mirror and tugged at one dark curl in a gesture Nancy knew well. It always meant she had something on her mind other than what she was talking about. As if to confirm that opinion, Nell suddenly changed the subject. "I hope he takes me there this month. Catherine's still at Somerset House, so that's all right. But there's talk of his having spent a lot of time with that French bitch Louise de Kéroualle while I was flat on my arse birthing his bastard son." She slammed a comb down on the inlaid mahogany dressing table and turned to face her

140

friend. "He does care for me, Nancy. I know he does. But that court! You can't imagine what it's like. Always plots and intrigues..."

"Nell, look, darling, I'm not following this at all. Is there trouble between you and Charles? Have I caused it in some way? What is this cottage you're talking about?"

"Sorry, love, I'm wandering. And this isn't the time to involve you in all this anyway. Don't fret about Charles and me. He still says I'm the best thing he's ever had in bed, so I'm not afraid of that French tart whatever she does. Anyway, the cottage is a royal gift to you. It belonged to the crown until yesterday. It was Wolsey's originally. Then Henry VIII took it when he took Hampton Court. Charles says it's been crown property ever since. But as far as he knows no one's lived there in donkey's years. I only hope it's still sound. The last inventory described it as 'livable.' Whatever that meant to the surveyors."

This flow of information was just beginning to get through to her listener. "Do you mean Charles has given you a cottage? In Surrey?"

"No." Nell shook her head impatiently. "You haven't been listening. He's given it to you. To,"—she withdrew the paper and read from it with some difficulty—"Goodwife Nancy Griffin, nee Wilmott. That's you, isn't it?"

"But I can't! What will Roger say?"

"Oh, that's all arranged. I talked with him too. He understands that the king had to give it to you in your own name or raise all the eyebrows at court. Roger's enemies haven't forgotten him, I'm afraid. But I told him too what Charles told me. That he was specially glad to do it because he felt badly about what happened to Roger. So you see, everything's settled and you leave at the end of the week.

"The house is called Tassels, by the way. Funny name, I know, but it has a story." She moved from the dressing table to sit on a stool next to Nancy. The wide skirt of her red gown made a pool of color on the carpet. "Seems when the pope made that rascal Wolsey a cardinal and sent him his red hat, Wolsey insisted the papal delegation wait in this little cottage while he assembled a huge procession and fête. Wanted everyone to see him get his Roman prize." Then, when Nancy still looked blank, "Don't you see? Tassels. Those funny braided ropes that used to hang down the back of the cardinal's hats. The house is named for them. And that must be all that's left in England of Wolsey or the Bishop of Rome."

9.

They both said they would accompany her, but in the end she went alone. Roger, who had been with her the previous afternoon, sitting in Nell's elegant drawing room and looking somehow more himself there than ever he did at the Cock and Pie, was supposed to arrive by eight in the morning. Instead a messenger brought a hurried scrawl saying he was urgently required in Deptford and would join her in Surrey as soon as possible.

"It's that damned *Queen Catherine*," Nancy said, crumpling the note in anger.

"The queen?" Nell looked astonished. "What's she to do with it?"

"I don't mean her. That ship he's bought. He named it the *Queen Catherine*. If Roger's urgently needed in Deptford, that's what it's about."

"Oh yes, you did mention something. What's he doing with a ship, anyway?" Nell was folding a linen shift while she spoke. The hamper she was packing was the last of the mountain of luggage she was sending with Nancy to the country. Nancy herself had no idea what was in the array of trunks, and at the moment she had little interest in them.

"I can't say. I only know a bit about it myself. And that bit I'm supposed to keep totally secret. It seems ridiculous, but I did promise. You're not offended?"

Nell laughed. "Of course not. What do I care? Men love secret deals and intrigues. Like little boys."

Nancy wasn't feeling so indulgent, and she didn't reply. But there wasn't time to continue the conversation anyway. A maid knocked at the door and whispered a message to Nell. When she turned back to Nancy, it was with a worried frown. "Darling, I feel awful. Word's just come from Whitehall. The king commands my presence at once."

"Don't apologize, Nell. Of course you have to go."

"I do, Nancy. Just now I can't play high-handed with Charles. Not with that French bitch sniffing at his heels." She was patting her curls into place and adjusting her frock even as she spoke. "You'll just have to go alone. I don't think it's wise for you to delay. Your health and the baby's are all that matters now. Will Smith's going with you to handle the luggage and the details. You'll be all right." She hugged Nancy swiftly. "Courage, pet; I'll come to visit as soon as I can. Godspeed."

"Nell, be careful."

"What do you mean?"

"That court, the king...it can be very dangerous. Don't let them hurt you, Nell."

"Don't worry about me. I'm a pussy cat, Nancy. I always fall on my feet. You should know that better than anyone."

She always thought of Nell's general dogsbody, Will Smith, as an old man in a young man's body. What his true age might be Nancy had no idea, but he was as wily and tough as a boy despite his gray hair and rheumy eyes. Unlike the rest of the elaborately liveried, fawning staff, Smith wore no uniform and offered no deference. Nonetheless he was Nell's most trusted retainer. He was waiting in the hall when Nancy came down the stairs, leaning against the pile of trunks and picking his teeth with a splinter of wood. "Be ye ready then, gel? Just as well it is. Tide don't wait for no lass fair or ugly. Here you!" He grabbed the collar of a passing page. "Help me get these bags into the coach. Hurry up, lad, or I'll box yer ears."

The job was done with dispatch. In less than twenty minutes they were at Hungerford Stairs, where a boatman was waiting. Five boatmen, in fact—four rowers and a steersman. Nell had arranged a tideboat for this journey, twenty feet in length with two sets of oars as well as two square sails. "Good tide, good breeze, miss," the steersman commented. "'Twill be a fast journey if it holds."

It was. They made the thirty miles to Hampton Court in just under four hours. "Will ye look at that," Will Smith muttered, spitting over the side for emphasis. "Bloody lot o' money and blood's gone into that pile o' brick, I'll wager."

The palace squatted at a deep bend in the river amid flat

countryside that made the Tudor squareness of the place seem massive and heavy. From the vantage point of this waterside view, Hampton was sited at an angle, its series of low turrets and towers reaching back into the landscape like a red brick sea monster slithering up the bank and headed toward the distant hills. But it was not ugly for all of that. If nothing else, the lush greenery which billowed like a skirt around the edifice ensured its beauty. While they rowed steadily by, Nancy had the impression of a riot of colors dappling the gardens of the palace, softening its bulk. She could see too the web of scaffolding that crawled up the side of one exterior wall.

"King Charles don't like it how it is," Smith said. "Got a fancy architect feller workin' on it. I fergit 'is name... Somebody Bird, I think."

"Wren," Nancy corrected, chuckling. "Christopher Wren."

"Aye, that's 'im. Gonna get the place all modern and fancied up fer 'is majesty, this Wren is. After all, king may want to visit the place once or twice a twelvemonth." Smith spat again.

"You don't approve?" Nancy trailed her fingers in the water. It was warmer than she expected. "Don't you think the king's got a right to do as he wishes?"

The old man shrugged. "Ain't nothin' to me wot the king does. I gets me wages regular. That's all I care 'bout. King pays Mistress Nell and she pays me. Long as there's coppers enough fer that, 'e can spend wot 'e likes on palaces."

It was hard not to laugh at the surly old codger, but he looked as if he might take offense at her amusement. She was just as glad when the steersman created a diversion. "This here's the place we turn, ain't it?" he inquired of his passengers while pointing to a bend below them.

"S'pose it is." Smith answered. "Yer the one's s'posed to know. Ain't ye been given directions?"

"The lady said a place below Hampton Court with a stand o' pine on the right. That's it near as I kin see." The place he indicated was a juncture between the Thames and a narrow ribbon of water. They joined in a rippling eddy of white-frothed spray.

"Ye'll have to get out here," the steersman explained while the rowers guided the tideboat close to the bank. "Walk through them trees and meet us t'other side."

Even while Nancy and the old man clambered up the muddy slope to the land, the boatmen were busy with lines and hooks. In a matter of minutes only one man remained aboard. The others were on the shore hauling and straining at massive ropes secured to the craft's side. "Gotta pull 'er round the bend, miss," one of them called in explanation. "Can't row round that wash. Walk ahead. We'll meet ye."

It took half an hour. It would have been longer were the men less experienced or less brawny. But as it was the sun still rode high overhead when they were back in the boat and heading down the new stream. The land changed now. It was hillier, more lush, a sylvan green forest of beech and birch and occasional stands of pine. Bright-hued birds darted among the trees. Nancy had never seen most of them before. She could put no names to either the winged populace of this place or its flowers. A strange new world. How would she fit here? For the first time she felt a pang of fear. How could she of all people live by herself in a country cottage, she who'd never been out of London except for that one visit to Yorkshire? Where was Roger, anyway? What good was it having a husband if he wasn't present when needed?

"This be the place." The steersman intruded on her sudden melancholy. "Lady said a set of stairs 'bout a mile down the stream with a lion's head on the rail." Sure enough there was yet a carved lion gracing the ruined jumble of stone that jutted into the water's edge.

"Are those stairs safe?" Nancy asked doubtfully.

One of the rowers poked his oar at the granite pile. "Seem safe enough," he said. "You wait, miss, I'll try 'em."

In a few seconds they were pronounced secure. The boat was tied not to the pillar, however, but to a nearby tree. It seemed the wiser course. Then two of the men handed her up to the embankment, and she stood and watched while they off-loaded the heap of trunks and cases.

They hoisted the luggage to back and shoulder and set out along the narrow path that wound up the hillside. It was heavily overgrown, but like the stairs it remained, however vestigially, a walkway, separate from the natural wilderness surrounding it. Nancy was the last in the line of figures that stumbled along that track, the last to come to a broken-down gate half off its hinges. A gate of oak, black and iron-hard with age, and on its front panel, just at eye level, a crude carving. It was of a broad-brimmed, flat-crowned hat trimmed with long ties, each of which ended in an elaborate tassel.

* * *

It was hard to imagine that anything had changed in this house since that time almost a century and a half earlier when Wolsey insisted a papal envoy wait there on an Englishman's pleasure. Perhaps that's why Nancy found herself alone within thirty minutes of coming through the door. Smith and the boatmen had sniffed the musty, decaying odor of the cottage, deposited the luggage, and, to use Roger's favorite naval expression, beat a hasty course windward. God, she longed for Roger. What would he make of this place when finally he saw it?

Viewed from outside the house was a rambling structure with a queer double set of entrance steps at either side of a tall towerlike chimney. There were angles everywhere, at least half a dozen different pitches to the roof, and wings that jutted in every direction. Yet for all this it seemed a small house. She didn't explore or count the rooms. She had no taste for clambering around the dirt that years of vacancy had deposited in every corner. But in the big front room where the men had left her luggage Nancy began to feel a kind of intimacy with the place, as if it were settling around her. She half expected to look up and find the rampant vines and shrubs of the neglected front garden encroaching on her, walling her in. It was a most peculiar sensation, but for all that, not unpleasant. It was high summer. The country air was sweet and had turned warm. The sun managed to fight its way through the plethora of greenery that curtained the windows and salve the ancient room with gold. Moreover, she was so tired. Nancy prodded a pile of rugs that lay in one corner. Dust rose in thick choking clouds, but no scurrying vermin emerged to frighten her. Sighing, she sank down on the makeshift couch and fell asleep.

Nancy Wilmott had never been given to introspective self-analysis. Becoming Mrs. Roger Griffin hadn't changed that. Born to the city streets, on her own as far back as she could remember, she'd learned early to live by her wits and take her pleasures where they came. Years ago, when Nell had first started hanging on her skirts, Nancy had all but ignored the little girl. Then she'd conceived a protective affection for her and become Nell's self-appointed guardian. Now, alone in this deserted old house hidden in the woods, she consciously examined that facet of her character for the first time.

At twenty-six the one thing Nancy felt sure of was an instinct for making do, shaping events to whatever was necessary for her survival. And she knew that when she set her mind to it, she could see reality with a clarity that often evaded people better cushioned against the shocks of living. She knew, for instance, that it was when Roger was suddenly revealed as being not omnipotent but in need that her love for him became permanent. She understood that this same instinct had caused her to befriend Nell. And when, watching the moonlight trickle through the canopy of leaves and branches that overhung Tassels or seeing the rising sun turn the green landscape to flame, she admitted these things to herself, she understood her fierce determination to bring this child alive and well into the world. The baby needed her beyond any need she had previously experienced. She didn't intend to fail.

In the first twenty-four hours she spent in the place she came to believe that Tassels was inextricably bound up with that promise. The house wrapped itself around her, enveloped her, supported her. Until she sensed that support she hadn't realized she was longing for it. Now she understood all that and more. She remembered once finding a stray cat and taking it to whatever hovel she was calling home at the time. Funny, she couldn't remember where it was...it didn't matter. In her lifetime she had lived in a hundred such featureless rooms, moving on when she couldn't pay the rent. That wasn't important. But the cat was. She remembered it very clearly. An ugly, mangy beast with scars and a vicious disposition. She'd found it half drowned and taken it home. Soon after that she realized the thing was pregnant. She watched while it created a nest in a hidden corner. A thing of rags and refuse, but isolated, warm, and dry. Here the puss retired to wait the birth of her kittens, and God help anyone who violated that territory. Well, she felt just like that now. Tassels was her nest. Here she would wait the borning of her child. Here they would both be safe.

Beyond a few halfhearted attempts to clear the one room in which she spent all her time, Nancy did nothing further about exploring Tassels or making it a home. When Roger arrived four days later she was still sleeping on the pile of rugs in the corner and eating cold meals from a hamper Nell

147

had packed back in London, a diet she supplemented with the berries that grew wild just outside the door.

"Sweet Christ," were Roger's first words. "Is this it?" He stood in the doorway staring at her in disbelief.

"Yes, this is it." Then by way of pointing up his lack of greeting, "Hello, Roger. I'm glad you finally managed to come."

"So am I. And don't take that tone, Nance. I'm sorry I couldn't leave with you, but all our future depends on the work at Deptford. You know that."

"And all the queen's money and favor."

His lips set in a thin angry line. "Don't start that again. We've more important things to discuss now. Getting you back to London, for one thing. How could that old villain Smith leave you here alone? I'll have a few things to say to him, I assure you. Not to mention his lunatic mistress."

"I don't know what you're talking about. Smith left because I ordered him to. That's what was agreed. And how can you call Nell a lunatic when she's done so much for me?"

"Done so...for God's sake, Nancy, open your eyes? Have you gone mad? This place is a derelict old cesspool in the middle of nowhere. It sure as hell is no place for a sick woman alone."

"I'm not sick. Not any more. I've never felt better since I was pregnant." She nibbled at a juicy black cherry from a pile on a bench that was propped precariously on its three remaining legs. "Have one. They're delicious. I just picked them this morning."

Her husband stared at her. "I've eaten, thank you." After some seconds he shook his head and decided to try another tack. For the first time he came close and took her in his arms. "Look, darling, I'm more sorry than I can say that you've had such a bad time. I'll make it all up to you, I promise. We'll go home this afternoon. I've just the one horse I rode down, but I must be able to hire a boat in the next village." He was nuzzling her hair as he spoke, feeling again the familiar warmth she always inspired in him. "We can break the journey somewhere at nightfall. Stay in an inn. Then tomorrow I'll see about getting you a place to stay in town. Something a little more comfortable than the Cock and Pie."

"But we don't have to do any of that." Nancy put her hands on his broad shoulders and leaned back to look at him. "I'm fine here, Roger. Really I am. Besides, I like the place. I never thought I'd enjoy being alone like this, but I do. I miss you, of course, but that's all. And it's good for the baby. It must be. I feel marvelous."

He was speechless, angry, yet feeling he had no right to be; loving her, wanting her, and feeling he had no right to that either. At last he moved away and leaned against a wall that looked the only thing in the room sturdy enough to support him. "Nancy, listen to me. You've had a lovely little adventure, and I'm glad it was pleasant. The weather's been fine, and Nell sent enough food to last you." He gestured at the hamper that lay open nearby. "But you must realize that you can't stay here alone like this. It can grow cold at any moment. Your provisions won't last much longer, from the look of them. What will you live on? Nuts and berries like some half-wild animal? It's absurd. You must see that."

She shook her head stubbornly. "I'm not going back to London. What you don't see is that I'll lose my baby if I do. Don't you care about that?"

"Of course I care. But how can you be so sure? Because a crazy old crone told you so?"

"Not just Moll Blake. The king's own doctor said the same thing. You know he did. Besides, there's a village nearby. I can walk there and buy more food when this is gone. I've got money." She rummaged in her pocket and withdrew a handful of coins. "See? It's plenty for a while."

He stared at her in amazement. Nancy wasn't a practical or efficient woman, he'd known that for months, but she'd never before been so totally unrealistic. It must be her pregnancy, distorting her reason. He'd have to be gentle. "No, love," he said with finality. "It just won't do. I must have you in London with me so I can look after you. This was a good idea, but the place just isn't livable. You've had a fine holiday. Now we have to go home."

He was totally unprepared for the way she looked at him and pressed herself against the wall of the cottage as if terrified. "I mustn't leave here, Roger," she whispered in a voice hoarse with emotion. "I mustn't. My baby will die. Please, I'm begging you...see, on my knees. I've never gone on my knees to any human being before. You mustn't make me go back to London. Don't do this to me...please..."

He pulled her to her feet and wrapped her in a close embrace. She was weeping now, with her face buried in his shirtfront. "Don't, love. Don't cry. You mustn't get yourself in a state like this. It's not good for you or the baby." But he couldn't calm her until he carried her out of the house to the overgrown garden and found a spot beneath an old chestnut tree where he could sit rocking her and murmuring endearments into her hair. When she was finally quiet, he said, "All right, darling. If you're so determined, we'll find a way. What direction is this village you mentioned? Any idea?" She shook her head, unwilling to tell him she'd gone no farther than the front gate in all the time she'd been here. "Very well, it doesn't matter. I'll find it. I'm going there now. I won't be gone long. Will you be all right?" When she assured him that she would be, he rode off, leaving her sitting beneath the chestnut tree with the sun shining on her auburn hair.

It was dusk when he returned. Nancy was inside the house, making an obvious and hurried effort to effect some order out of the chaos, as if to convince him that she could manage alone at Tassels. The floor was swept after a fashion, and one of the trunks had been opened to reveal a store of blankets and bed linen. "There must be dishes in here, I think," she said brightly when he entered the room. "It's too heavy to be anything else. Help me get it open."

He did as he was bidden, smiling at her enthusiasm when the chest proved to be full of crockery as she'd predicted. "See?" she was like a child in her eagerness. "I've everything I need. Nell said she'd sent all that was necessary, and she did."

"Yes, I see. But stop all this now and listen to me." He held up the bulging saddlebag he'd brought in with him. "There's plenty of food in here. At least for a few days. More important, I've found a cottage just half a mile down the road to the west. A couple named Wadden, Ellen and Michael Wadden, farm a small piece they rent from some local squire named Lord Sheldon. Apparently your little country retreat here abuts his lordship's estate. Anyway, this Wadden pair seem all right. I've engaged them to come here daily. The woman will cook and tidy the place up, and the man's been told first to get that fireplace cleaned out and in working order and next to chop some wood and tackle that jungle out there. It's not much, but it's a beginning. More important, it means people arriving every day to check on you and see you're all right and have everything you need."

Her smile lit the room and kindled a blaze in his heart. "Thank you," was all she said. The simple words conveyed more meaning than a speech. He stroked her cheek with one finger, and she took hold of his hand, pressing it to her lips.

150

"I've spread clean linen over the rugs." She indicated the couch. "You will stay with me a bit?"

"Until tomorrow morning. I'll wait till the Waddens arrive and make sure the arrangement's going to work. Then I'm back to London. We hope to have the *Queen Catherine* ready to sail in two weeks' time. It's..."

"Ssh." She placed her finger over his lips. "No business now. You can tell me all that later. Now just hold me. Lie with me. It's been so long."

She was unbuttoning his shirt and unlacing her own bodice while she spoke, silencing him with kisses. Still he managed to ask, "You're sure it's all right? I won't hurt you?"

"Not a bit." She giggled and said, "I asked Nell. She's experienced in such matters now. Mmm...you taste good." She was biting his lips, teasing him, laughing all the while. "You won't believe the things she told me. You know how big she was at the end? Everyone thought it was twins." They were both naked at last, but even while she led him to the couch, acting the aggressor for the first time in months, she kept telling him with much detail how Charles had managed to have Nell even while her swollen belly seemed to make it impossible. The story was both amusing and titillating, but it made him a little angry too.

"You women! Do you always tell such intimate details? It's shameless."

"Do you think so?" She laughed. His reproach didn't embarrass her in the least. "But you already know I'm shameless. See, I like to touch your cock when it's like this. You know I do. Isn't that shameless? But you like it."

"Yes, yes I do." He ran his hands along her midriff, cupped her high pointed breasts in his hands. "I like everything about you. God, I've missed you, Nance."

"Don't think about that. Just that we're here together now. Nothing else matters. No...no, let me..." She resisted his attempt to roll her beneath him. "I want to be the one to ride this time." She was kneeling over him now, her long hair a web of spun silk that tickled his shoulders and smelled of the herbs and flowers with which she rubbed it daily. He felt drunk with the scent and feel of her. When she clasped her knees around his hips and lowered herself on his turgid member she and this strange place seemed the only reality in the world.

10.

No one could accuse the Wadden couple of being overzealous in their duties, but they kept Nancy's life at Tassels sufficiently civilized to make Roger worry less about her determination to remain there. When he came back a week after his first visit the single room in which his wife still slept and ate was aired and clean. A bedstead had been procured from some other place in the house and properly made up. There was now a sturdy table in one corner, and two chairs that looked capable of actually holding a man stood nearby. Most important, the hearth had been swept, the chimney cleaned, and a good-sized pile of logs was ready and waiting for the first day cool enough to warrant a fire.

"Have you someplace to cook?" Roger asked. "You can't live on cold food. It's not healthy."

"Oh yes. Look, this was in the trunk with all the dishes." Nancy pointed to a small brazier of heavy metal with a firebox full of charcoal and a hob big enough to hold a small kettle. "See, there's soup heating now. Will you have some?"

She ladled out a thick porridge of vegetables and oats without waiting for his reply, and he felt duty-bound to taste the unappetizing mess. It was surprisingly delicious. "Did you make this?"

"Me! Don't be daft. I haven't learned to cook just because I've moved to the country. Ellen made it. She prepares something like this every morning, and I need only heat it to have a hot supper. We're managing beautifully, Roger. Really we are."

"Very well. Here." He handed her a small bag of coins. "There's ten shillings in there. You're paying the couple two shillings a week as I promised them?" She nodded. "Good. Then this will do for you until I return next week with more."

"Roger..." Her voice was hesitant, almost as if she was

afraid to ask the question. "Couldn't you stay longer? Or come more frequently? Can't we live together here? I do miss you."

"And I miss you, my pet. But if you're still determined to be a country recluse we'll have to content ourselves with visits for a while longer. I've got to be in London if Griffin's Importations is to succeed. Which brings me to my biggest news—the *Queen Catherine* sails Wednesday next."

"Oh! That's marvelous. How long will the voyage take?"

"Less than two months to Lisbon and back if we're lucky. That's allowing plenty of time to load, too."

"Two months! And shall I not see you in all that time?"

"Not see me?...Wait a minute. Nancy, do you think I'm captaining the vessel myself? Is that what you've expected all along?"

"Well, yes, I just presumed..." She felt suddenly very stupid. But when he threw back his head and laughed so hard his whole long lean frame shook with mirth she couldn't keep from smiling too. Eventually she said, "I don't see why that's so funny. You are a naval captain, after all."

"Not any more, my sweet. Now I'm a merchant. I can't go sailing off to Portugal or anywhere else. Not if I want to succeed. My place is in town, where the decisions are made and the money won or lost. Nance..." He leaned forward and spoke with compelling enthusiasm. "You'd not believe how it is these days. Parliament's so busy making new laws to facilitate trade the *Gazette* hardly has time to announce them. Just to give you an example, two days ago the *Golden Felicity* landed from Bombay with a hold full of silk and cotton, more than has ever arrived in one shipment. The floor of the Exchange was like a carnival. The whole cargo was sold in three hours' time. Nance, more gold changed hands on that one deal than's been circulated in a month up till now. And the East India Company saw more profit than they'd had on their last six shipments combined. Everyone's wild to get into the play. There's a new day dawning for England, love, and its name is commerce."

"Tell me more." There was a slightly wistful tone to her voice, despite her determination to remain where she was. "More about the city. What plays are they doing at the theater this week? And what's the news from court? Are they still at Whitehall?"

"Court." He made a face of distaste. "Those fools are so blind they can't see their own faces in a glass. They're all off to Windsor this week. And last week Charles spent four days at Newmarket betting on the ponies. The Cabal rules all, and neither the king nor York seems inclined to keep them in check."

Nancy knew he referred to Charles's group of five advisers. Their names were Clifford, Arlington, Buckingham, Ashley, and Lauderdale, hence the Cabal, but she wasn't interested in politics.

"Did Nell go to Newmarket? I've been expecting word from her, but nothing's come."

"No, I don't think so. I heard he took some French wench instead. Louise de Something-or-other. She's a gift from Louis of France, if you can believe it. Like an oriental pasha offering a new piece of flesh for the harem."

"Oh dear." Nancy shook her head. "Nell was afraid he was getting interested in her. I hope she's going to be all right."

Roger shrugged. "Nell's playing a game many have played and lost before, Nancy. She must know that. In the end Charles finds new pastures and moves on. He always has."

"Well..." Nancy was determined to be cheerful. "It probably won't matter. The house and all the jewels are hers forever. The king told her so. They're outright gifts. And she can always go back to the theater. Sir Will would be only too pleased. All London would be wild to see her."

"No doubt. London feeds on court gossip rather than bread. If it's not whores and mistresses it's the intrigues of the Cabal, and failing that, the papists can always be relied upon to provide some new scandal. There's talk of something afoot with James's wife now. Jesuit intrigues, as usual."

No matter how hard he tried, it was impossible for Roger to convey to Nancy the intensity of the mercantile frenzy that gripped the city in this summer of 1670. After the lean years of Cromwell's Puritan Republic, after the restoration of the monarchy and the torrent of pleasure-seeking it loosed on the London scene, the English had begun to flex their commercial muscles. A few years ago they were without sufficient cash or ships or goods to compete with the Portuguese, the Spanish, or the Dutch. Those nations had commanded the seas and thus trade. But lately English circumstances had improved, in part helped by their victories in wars with the Dutch, even more so by the fabulous dowry of Catherine of Braganza.

When Roger was assigned to the party that went to fetch

Catherine in 1662, he had heard much talk of the cargo they were to bring back, substantially more than one infanta. Some claimed the most important item to be collected in Portugal was five hundred thousand pounds in cash. No one was particularly impressed with the gifts of the cities of Bombay in India or Tangiers in Africa. Less did they value the promised free trading rights for English shipping in the Portuguese ports of Brazil and the East Indies. In the event, the money never actually materialized, and Catherine's mother filled the hold of the ship sent to fetch her daughter with sugar in its stead. It was Bombay, Tangiers, and trading rights that changed the entire fabric of English life.

Since Roman times sheep had grazed the English hills, and their wool was spun into cloth in the thousands of tiny cottages that lined the nation's highways and byways. Then the British East India Company, first founded in 1600, got a new lease on life with the acquisition of Bombay. The city was ceded to them by royal charter, and they were charged to do whatever was necessary to squeeze from it and its people every drop of profit possible. After that wool became a nonstarter in the fashion world. Who would dress in drab serge or worsted when the brightly colored chintzes and calicoes of India were available? Certainly not even the meanest subject of a monarch as flamboyant as Charles II. Nor did the vivid new cottons find favor exclusively for dress. Hardly a bed in the land lacked its chintz coverings and hangings. East India Company ships plied the oceans in numbers that began to rival the foot traffic on London Bridge. What if pirates and Dutch men-of-war sank and burned the majority? Those few which got through brought their owners enough return to replace the lost vessels and garner a handsome profit besides.

The plague in '65 and the fire in '66 slowed this tide of wealth, but not for long. If London herself was regenerated not according to Charles's elaborate plans, but willy-nilly as individual taste or expediency dictated, the magnificent new Exchange building on Cornhill typified the ascendancy of the East India Company in particular and trade in general, as did the endless building of new docking facilities.

Roger often spent hours standing on those docks watching the incoming traffic. These days it wasn't just cottons from India the burly stevedores hauled out of the enormous holds. From the fabled land of China came lacquered cabinets of dazzling workmanship and, as ballast for that precious cargo, exotic pottery from the kilns of Shanghai. Moreover, those trading rights in the Portuguese East Indies were the source of two commodities now in great demand, mahogany wood and bundles of cane. With these new materials the joiners were creating a revolution in English furniture.

Observing all this, Griffin was astounded to find in himself a characteristic he'd never known he possessed. For the first time he burned with greed. It wasn't the things themselves he coveted, nor even the money exactly. It was a role in this new world he sensed a-borning. England, he told himself repeatedly, was never going to be the same. Never again would it be the essentially pastoral place it had been when he was a boy in Yorkshire. The part of him that belonged exclusively to Harwood Hall and the Griffin legacy was unbreached. It was a separate thing, a commitment so elementary it could not be altered. But beyond that was a new dream, one he had just as much determination to make reality. He intended to be part of this world of trade and commerce that was so obviously the shape of things to come.

Griffin didn't expect Nancy to understand such things. She was a woman, after all. How could she be expected to see what he saw? She thought him indifferent to her and their child. He knew that even though she never voiced the accusation. What she didn't realize was that she and the child in her womb were part and parcel of his dream. They were the future. Mark might have been willing to forfeit everything the family stood for in pursuit of some promised reward in the hereafter, but Roger was not. He intended to carve a new destiny for generations of Griffins yet unborn. And he would do it right here in London by besting the traders at their own game.

He approached the issue like an admiral planning the tactics of a great battle. There was little point, he decided, in seeking a foothold in the goods already monopolized by those who had preceded him into the fray. He intended to tap a source and a market that was as yet little known. While the others scurried to clothe their countrymen and furnish their homes, Roger planned to pay attention to their bellies. He was convinced that the same taste for the new and different that made people lust after chintz and mahogany could extend to exotic edibles not before seen in any quantity on these shores. Coffee was only a beginning. It would provide his stake, and as such it was vitally important, but from the deal done with Alphonso da Gama Roger intended to extract a far more lasting payment than mere money.

In Nancy's Surrey wilderness the sudden hot spell of August was paradise. For Roger and those like him in London it was something to be overcome. It made workmen slow and torpid and spread languor over the Exchange. A mile or so away, in Marden Lane, the heat meant something entirely different. "'Tis the judgment of God," Mrs. Cuttlebone murmured as she mopped the sweat from her face. "A sign from heaven."

"How do you figure that?" Clare looked with distaste at a lump of butter that was fast melting on the table. "It's just a nuisance as far as I can tell."

"No, ma'am, not that." Mrs. Cuttlebone hadn't lost her awareness of the superior station of her houseguests in the three months they'd lived with her, but she was easy enough with Mistress Clare to openly disagree. "God makes the sun to shine because of her grace. It's His way o' tellin' folk the Duchess of York's done His will." The whole idea seemed to Clare too absurd to require further comment. She went on with the preparation for lunch in silence.

Outside her husband was discussing the matter more directly with his visitor, Father Huddleston. "I can't delay any longer," Mark said with finality. "This is going to make it yet more dangerous for the Cuttlebones and their crowd. Even those mad Jesuits must see that."

"They see what they wish," the priest said. "Ann is James's wife and as such next in line to be Queen of England. Naturally her conversion to Catholicism is a coup in their eyes."

"And in yours?" The two men were friends now. Mark didn't hesitate to ask the question.

"I think," Huddleston said slowly but with conviction, "in the long of it, 'twill make little difference. Except to her grace, of course." He allowed himself a small chuckle. "To her it will make all the difference of eternity. But for England? Well, the last two queens have been Catholics. What will it matter if the next is also?"

"But the short of it?" Mark persisted. "You think it will make some difference there?"

"Yes." The old man looked grave. "I do. That's what brought me here today, Mark. I think you and everyone in this house is in great danger. The Cuttlebones won't care;

157

they've decided to quest after martyrdom. I suppose one must respect, even admire, their courage. It is not, I think, the only way to serve God and Holy Church. You see, I agree with you. If there's any way, you must leave here at once."

Mark ran his fingers through his hair, in a gesture of frustration common of late. "That's just the bloody hell of it. Excuse me, father—the times make me forget nice speech. If I had any place to take them, I'd have removed my family from here weeks ago. God help me, I just don't know where to go."

Huddleston hesitated. "You never had word from your brother, did you? After that first note?"

"Hardly." Mark snorted in derision. "After that there was little left to say. Not that I blame him. I can understand full well how it all looks to him. You'd have to know more of our family to appreciate the position. We were suckled on the notion that nothing in this world mattered more than being a Griffin, preserving the legacy of the Hall and our lands. To Roger I must look like the basest traitor that ever swung at Tyburn."

"You continue to amaze me, squire. I shall never cease to marvel that you could see past all that to take the step you took. And to have so little bitterness..."

"I said 'nothing in this world,' father." Mark grinned in spite of his black mood. "No one ever tried to convince me that name and property were more important than heaven. Once that issue is joined, the rest is self-evident."

"Yes, for Ann too, it seems."

"How is it with her? How does York seem to have taken it?"

"With less fury than the rest, apparently. He's a funny one, our James. I must admit, I find nothing to like in the man. He hasn't his brother's charm or warmth. But beneath all the temper and pettiness there is something else. A kind of loyalty...I don't know. It may all be my imagination. At any rate, he's said flat out that she's his wife and will remain so. Any that don't like it can answer to him. Sometimes I think..."

"What?"

"I shouldn't say. Again it's probably just my imagination. But in spite of all his personal excesses..." He saw Mark's smile. James was known to have a string of mistresses. "Well, sometimes I wonder if some deep religious hunger exists in the man. An attraction even, to the faith. But don't pay any attention to me, squire. I'm an old man, probably getting senile."

"I doubt that. But we digress, father. We were discussing my family and their future. Do you have any suggestions?"

"Yes, as a matter of fact I do. First let me tell you why I'm so sure you must take steps, however drastic they may be. You may not realize it, sir, but your sister's journey to France and the reason for it didn't go unremarked at court. The French bishop said something at Somerset House, apparently. After that, well, you know how gossip spreads. Everyone knows that Sophia Griffin left England to become a nun. There are those whose enmity to our faith is such that even so personal a choice angers them. With the duchess fanning the flames once more, the witch hunters will be seeking new victims. Miss Sophia herself is beyond their reach. You, your wife, and your children are not."

"Good God!" Mark was stunned. Never had he imagined the position to be so grave. "I needn't ask you if you're sure of all this, father. And there's something else." He drew a deep breath. "The situation is reversed. In this turn of events we become more of a danger to the Cuttlebones than they to us. Dozens of people know where we are. If any come looking for us here…"

"Exactly." The old man nodded. "That's why I am going to propose a plan that even to me seems half mad. Just as news of your sister became common knowledge at court, your brother and his affairs are spoken of. Charles and James both have a certain fondness for him, as does the queen. Moreover, as I told you before, his wife is close friend to Nell Gwyn. Recently a royal gift was bestowed upon Mrs. Griffin. She's acquired a cottage down in Surrey. That's far enough from London to offer some safety, it seems to me."

"But I've told you, Roger wants nothing to do with us."

"Your brother doesn't live in the place. He's in London, occupied with some new business venture. I'm given to understand that he only visits his wife on occasion. They're not estranged, as I heard it. It's just that Mistress Griffin's with child and her health demands country air. You said once that you'd met her. Tell me, Mark, do you think you could ask her to hide your family? Just until this business calms down?"

PART THREE

Pursuit of Treasure

The thing which is nearest to the heart of this
nation is trade and all that belongs to it. . . .

—Charles II,
Letter to his sister

1.

Clare's repeated thanks made Nancy more nervous than her sister-in-law's presence or that of the four young Griffins. "It's nothing...really," Nancy insisted. "There's plenty of room. You can see that."

"Oh yes." Clare glanced around her at the spacious chamber Nancy had said was to be exclusively for her and the children. "How many rooms have you here, Nancy?"

"I don't know," she said, smiling. "It seems odd, I realize, but I've not yet bothered to explore the place."

"Well, in your condition that's understandable. And we've kept you standing far too long." She led Nancy back to her own room and waited till she had settled on the couch. "How have you been feeling?"

Perhaps because she was tall, Nancy, even in this her fourth month, barely showed her pregnancy. "I'm quite well, thank you. But how did you know? The squire didn't seem to guess when he was here."

"Oh, Mark!" Clare giggled; it made her look like a young girl. "He's a fool about such things. Most men are. And by the way, you mustn't call either of us by any stuffy old titles. We're kin now, Nancy. I'm Clare and Mark's Mark. Agreed?"

"Agreed." She smiled warmly. "I'm glad you're here, Clare. Really I am. It has been rather lonely, though I'd never admit it to Roger."

At the mention of her brother-in-law, Clare frowned. "How is he?" Her voice betrayed the depth of her concern. "You must know how terrible both my husband and I feel about what our actions have cost Roger. That's why I'm so overwhelmed at your generosity in having us here."

"Now, you promised, no more of that. Roger's fine. As to his getting bounced out of court, it's not such a bad thing. He was never really happy there. Oh, he made a fuss, of course. And

162

even felt quite sorry for himself for a time. But he's over that. Frankly, Clare, I think this whole thing may be the making of Roger. You know he's involved in a business venture of his own, don't you? Griffin's Importations, he calls it."

"Yes, Mark told me. I pray that all will go well with him. And with you. Perhaps I can repay your kindness after all, my dear. A woman expecting a baby shouldn't be alone." With that she carefully adjusted the bolster behind the girl's head and in her capable way began to put the room to rights.

When Mark Griffin arrived unannounced on Nancy's doorstep the previous week, she'd hardly been able to contain her surprise. But she was glad too. Nothing had ever made her comfortable with the decision Roger had made when his brother's letter came months before. Blood ties, she firmly believed, must not be treated lightly. Perhaps she felt stronger about this for having none of her own. At any rate, she had brooded about the matter for a long time.

That's why it hadn't required more than ten minutes for her to make up her mind to agree to Mark's request. Clare and the children would stay with her in Surrey. She'd have welcomed Mark too, but he insisted he must remain in London and seek some kind of work that would eventually make the family independent. Mark had gone to great pains to explain that he would pay for his wife and children's upkeep. He could manage that, he insisted, from his savings. Just as he had at the Cuttlebones'. Four shillings a week to pay their room and board.

Nancy would have none of it. "I don't have any need," she said firmly, shaking her head and looking as if nothing would move her. "It's not right to take money from you. I just won't do it, so you can simply drop the subject." In the end he agreed, gratefully. She'd guessed how limited his resources probably were, and she wasn't wrong. Soon they'd moved from that bit of disagreement to considering the practical terms of the Griffins' tenancy.

When Nancy explained that the servant couple Roger employed for her came for only a few hours daily, Mark seemed relieved. Nancy would simply tell them that some of her family were paying a visit. As long as the Waddens weren't in the house day and night they were unlikely to overhear anything that might make them suspicious.

Just before he was ready to leave, Mark broached the real problem. "What will Roger say, Nancy? I can't let you do this if he wouldn't approve."

She didn't try to temper the truth. "Roger is very angry,
163

squire, and very hurt. You must forgive him. I don't think he'll always feel so."

"Yes, I do understand, believe me. I bear my brother no ill will. But that doesn't reassure me about his reaction to Clare and the children's being here."

"No, it wasn't meant to. He'd not like it. I'd be a fool to tell you otherwise. That's why I shan't tell him for the present."

"But even if I agree to your deceiving your husband, a matter that seems wrong to me, how could you do it?"

"First, I'm not deceiving him, just keeping certain facts out of his range for a bit. Believe me, squire, I've lived by my wits all my life. Had to. There's no sin in doing what's needed for survival."

"That's true." He spoke softly, peering at the handsome and rather remarkable woman his brother had married. "And I admit that all this bobbing and weaving is new to me. How will you do it?"

"Easy. Once a week a messenger comes to Tassels from London, a young lad my husband has hired in connection with his business affairs. His name's Sam Ludlow, and he's a bright, quick boy whom Roger believes wholly trustworthy. He comes just before noon each Monday and brings me money and a letter. The letter always tells me what day of the week Roger will visit. On that day your family will have to arrange to absent themselves. Surely we can manage that in this remote place. And the Wadden couple won't come that day. That way there'll be no chance of Roger's hearing anything from them."

"You astound me, Mistress Nancy." Mark smiled, and she could see the strong resemblance between the brothers. "I think your scheme will work."

"Yes, it will. For a while. We must trust that it will be long enough."

So he'd gone, and today Clare came with her four lively offspring and her Yorkshire woman's common sense and capable hands. Watching her buff a wooden trencher to glowing life almost without thinking about it, Nancy smiled. It would be good to have them here. Already she felt safer. Smiling, she closed her eyes and slept.

Perhaps it was the simplicity of Nancy's plan that made it successful. In any event, they settled to a routine. The children were gone most of the day, exploring the surrounding woods and fields and coming home in the evening to tell of their adventures chasing a deer or watching an otter at play beside some stream. Once they reported seeing a tall handsome man galloping a white horse across the country-side, but apart from that they saw no other human being. They carefully avoided the village and the isolated farm-houses scattered throughout the countryside.

"Did the man see you?" Clare asked, not looking up from the mending in her lap.

"Not a glimpse, Mama, never fear." Laura hugged her mother reassuringly. That spontaneous affection was the only indication ever given of the danger the Griffins knew themselves to be in.

"Good. Now, it's time for supper. Set the table, Sarah. And you, Charles, see to the fire." Clare had taken responsibility for the domestic tasks that were required in the household. Nancy was content to have it thus. By day she sat with the older woman and watched her sew or simply sit, hands folded in calm repose. They didn't speak a great deal. Clare wasn't the chattering sort, and Nancy was still in that self-preoc-cupied fog wherein only she and her unborn child had real meaning. On the days that Roger came to Tassels, Clare went into the woods with her children, carrying a picnic lunch and carefully checking before she left that all signs of their oc-cupancy were hidden away.

Nancy assured her she needn't fret about that. She and Roger always remained only in the one room that was her living quarters. He was preoccupied with his London affairs, and not interested in the house. Later, when he'd gone and she and Clare were alone again, she'd tell her sister-in-law the news Roger had brought from the city. They never spoke of the estrangement between the brothers, or of plans for the future.

The days began to grow shorter, and autumn bronzed the countryside. Nancy was at last showing her pregnancy, but she was not as clumsy or heavy as a shorter, less graceful woman might have been. "Childbearing suits you," Clare said one day. "Would you like many children?"

"I don't know. I've never thought much about it. Only about this one." She patted her swollen belly. "I'll tell you something." Her smile was shy. "It's a girl."

"Oh? How do you know?"

"I know."

Clare nodded. "It is like that sometimes. If so you must

thank God for her and pray for another right away. I think Roger would like a son."

"Yes, he would. To carry on the Griffin tradition and..." Nancy bit her lip. She'd almost said to be squire at Harwood after him, but she'd never confided to Clare Roger's ambition to regain the Hall, and she didn't want to do so now. It might seem too much like a reproach.

If Nancy was at pains to spare her guest any talk that would prove painful, Clare nonetheless was aware of more than Nancy ever said. Living with this newest Griffin bride, she came to appreciate the girl's charm and intelligence and generosity. But she saw too that many things about her would be irritating to a man like Roger after the first blush of romance had passed. "Why doesn't she do something about this place, Mama?" Sarah often inquired in critical exasperation. "It's a scandal. This whole big house going uncared for. Nothing done in the garden. Do you know there wasn't anything grown there this whole summer that can be put down for the winter? Not one blessed thing."

"Hush, Sarah. We owe your aunt much. It won't do to be critical." Still, she knew Sarah was right. Of course it was the young girl's passion for gardening that caused her to fasten on that aspect of the mismanagement of Tassels. Sarah had been born with "green fingers," the head gardener at Harwood had said repeatedly. From earliest childhood she'd been fascinated with seeds and plants and flowers of every description. But Clare knew that the child's criticism was valid despite her preoccupation with her own chief interest.

Nothing at the cottage was arranged as it should be. Most of the trunks of household goods that had arrived with Nancy from London were still packed, standing in an ignored corner. In all but the two rooms they occupied the dust lay thick everywhere. Rot and woodworm, and heaven knew what else, were unchecked. The two servants were managed so casually they had soon realized little was expected of them, so little was given. It was a sloppy, slovenly existence, and none knew better than Clare that sooner or later a man of Roger Griffin's sort would rebel. He'd either demand that his wife do her duty or leave her for someone who would. Still, she couldn't see that she had any right to say these things to Nancy. Particularly not now. She kept her counsel and insisted her children do likewise.

* * *

The first hint of trouble came one day in late October. The previous week Mark had come to Tassels to visit his family. Since he'd managed to do so three times since their arrival in Surrey, this last occasion was like a holiday. They all sat together in Nancy's room, where Mark told them funny stories about his job as porter at the Spanish embassy. Huddleston had found him the post, and neither the squire nor his wife was disturbed by the menial employment. They were too grateful for the relative security he enjoyed in a place that was treated as Spanish property not subject to English law. "Mass in St. Margarita's Church every day," Mark said in wonder. "As open and free as you please. And outside so-called recusants are being fined and imprisoned for the same thing. It's crazy."

"Mass every day..." There was a dreamy quality to Laura's voice. He looked questioningly at his eldest daughter, but Clare's warning look prevented him from saying more. It wouldn't do to discuss such things in front of Roger's wife. She didn't share their beliefs.

"I hear good things about your husband, madam," Mark said to cover the awkward silence. "Roger seems to have set a lot of tongues wagging in the city."

"That surprises me," Nancy said. "The ship sailed only last week. There were many delays, and he was worried."

"That's as may be, but apparently he's not been idle while waiting. Everyone's heard the name Griffin's Importations now. Seems he's hired a bunch of down-and-out watermen. Though no one knows what for."

"Yes." Nancy reached for her mug of spiced ale and gestured with it while she spoke. It had been many months since she'd appeared onstage, still her vibrant voice and elegant mannerisms were compelling. "There's been much trouble for the watermen, you know. First, many are out of work because of the hackney carriages for hire all over London. Secondly, the press has been very bad this year."

Clare shook her head. "I think the press is evil. It's a terrible thing to pounce on peaceful English subjects and carry them off to serve on men-of-war. Parliament should make a law against it."

"But Mama!" Young Charles was indignant. "His majesty's ships must be manned. Would you have the Dutch beat us again?"

"There should be some other way." Clare was adamant.

"Roger agrees with you," Nancy said. "He told the Duke

of York ages ago that the way to staff the navy was by paying wages when they were due and encouraging men to join the service. But he got nowhere."

"So what is his plan for the watermen, Nancy?" Mark brought them back to the starting point of the discussion.

"I don't know exactly. But he's going to use them in his business in some way. Meanwhile he has James's personal word that no man wearing the livery of Griffin's Importations will be bothered by the press. That's one reason they're anxious to work for him."

"It'll go a ways toward inspiring loyalty, certainly. Speaking of that, James is still his friend, I gather?"

"Yes. Frankly"—she dropped her eyes but spoke her mind anyway—"Roger says that James is even more friendly toward him now that the Duchess of York is known to be a Catholic. He even received Roger openly at the naval office."

There seemed no adequate answer to that. Clare hastened to change the subject. "You must come for a walk with us, darling," she said to her husband. "The children can show you all the delightful haunts we've found in the woods here."

"Right." Andrew was never one for cautious speech. "We go out there and hide when Uncle Roger's expected. It's great fun."

"Andrew!" His mother used that sharp tone she reserved for this sometimes difficult twelve-year-old. "You mustn't say such things. It's just that Uncle Roger..."

"Now Clare, I'm sure Mistress Nancy is accustomed to his plain speaking by now." Mark had a special fondness for this hot-headed youngster. He didn't want his wife to break that independent spirit. "Besides, he reminds me of a problem I've been worrying for some time. What are you to do after the weather turns cold?"

There was a long silence. Finally Clare answered, "I don't know. I guess we just hadn't thought about it."

"I did." Charles, usually overshadowed by his elder brother, suddenly commanded all their attention. "I thought about it and I've made arrangements. I've found a house for us to use."

It turned out to be a deserted structure more like a hut than a house. Mark went with his son to inspect the place and came back announcing that it seemed a good lair to be used when required. "It's pretty crude. Doesn't look like anyone's been near the place in years. An old woodsman's hut, or a gamekeeper's, most likely. But it'll do for a few hours' shelter when you need it. No chimney, but there's a hole in the roof to let smoke out and a kind of firepit that can still be used. I've told the boys to fell some logs and get them under cover. You'll be all right there. My mind's easy."

Had those instructions been followed, they might indeed have been all right there. But Mark reckoned without his wife's overdeveloped nesting instinct. She trekked up to the cabin the following day and every day thereafter for a week. When she was finished the erstwhile hovel was scrubbed and shining and boasted a kettle for making hot drinks, a few blankets against whatever necessity might arise, and a tin-lined chest of emergency foodstuffs.

They first took shelter in the place they'd dubbed White-hall—"You see, Aunt Nancy, Charles discovered it, so it's his palace"—on a Thursday in early November. Roger was visiting his wife, and the other Griffins were in the woods as usual. A storm suddenly blew in over the low hills that sheltered Tassels. Clare surveyed the threatening sky and drew her woolen shawl close around her shoulders. "Come, children," she said firmly. "It's too soon to go home, and if we stay out here we're going to be soaked. We'll go to the cabin." She hurried her brood along the path, and they reached their Whitehall none too soon. The rain was coming down in blinding sheets by the time they got through the door. "Quick, Andrew, get a fire going. Sarah, get the blankets..."

She'd not finished speaking before a man stepped out of the shadows. "One moment, madam. Your concern for these children is admirable, but I have some concerns too."

He was the tallest man she'd ever seen. Taller even than her husband or his brother. And thinner. It was a strange word to describe a man, but she thought of him instantly as "willowy." Nonetheless, he terrified her as she hadn't been terrified since that morning John Lane had stood in the Great Hall and demanded she swear an oath she could not swear.

"Who are you?" she found strength to ask at last. "What do you want?" Even while she spoke she was praying, Sweet Jesus give me strength and courage. Protect my children, holy Mother of God...

"I am Antony Blair Sheldon. Lord Sheldon, to you. And this is my property, so I'll ask the questions. Who, pray, are you?"

"You have a white horse..." Laura interrupted.

169

Sheldon turned and bowed in her direction. "That I do. And a black one and some that are chestnut-colored. Do my horses interest you?" For all the civility, nay inanity, of the remark, it didn't reassure Clare. His eyes were black and sunk into his thin face. They were burning, fanatical eyes.

"I beg your pardon, milord." She stepped in front of Laura as if to protect the girl from the man's glance. "We had no idea we were trespassing. The hut seemed deserted, and we required shelter from the storm. That's all."

"No, madam. That isn't all. If it were, you would be of no interest to me. The young lady...she's your daughter, I presume?" Clare nodded. "Well, she seems to have observed me for some time. I have likewise observed all of you. Forgive me if I seem inhospitable, but there is a decidedly suspect cast to all your activities. I repeat, who are you?"

Andrew was staring at the stranger, particularly at the long-barreled pistol he wore strapped to his side. Andrew had handled a pistol many times. His father had taught him to shoot when he was barely strong enough to cock the weapon. Now he moved cautiously to Sheldon's side. If he could just get his hands on that gun...He was the eldest son. It was his duty to protect the others when his father was absent. "We're Griffins," he said firmly, in hopes of distracting the man. "My name's Andrew."

"Very well, Master Andrew, since you seem to be the only member of this group willing to talk, I'll address my questions to you. What are the names of the others?" Lord Sheldon looked at the boy with something like amusement. "And you can stop staring at my pistol. I should have to shoot you if you attempted to take it, and that would distress us both."

Andrew retreated into silence. Red-faced and miserable at being so easily found out, he was now totally unwilling to speak. Sheldon seemed to guess that they had reached an impasse and some action was necessary. Slowly, almost casually, he withdrew the weapon from its place at his side. "Madam, if I shot your son, or any of you, the law would be completely on my side. You are trespassing, as I told you. Now will you satisfy my curiosity or not?"

"You can put away that weapon, milord." His overt threat gave Clare more courage than his previous hints. Besides, she'd had a few moments to assess the situation. This was no sheriff's man, whatever else he might be. Nor did he look like an outlaw for all his flamboyant garb of hose and doublet like her grandfather used to wear. "We're no threat to you or your property. My name is Clare Griffin. These are my children, Laura, Sarah, Andrew, and Charles. As I told you, we merely took shelter here. We'll leave immediately."

"But," Sheldon said, ignoring her comment about leaving, "if you 'merely took shelter,' as you put it, why is the place so well prepared? And why have you been skulking about these woods for three months past? That you live at Tassels with its beautiful new mistress I know, for the Waddens are my tenants as well as her sometime servants, but it seems to me your story is a bit more complex than that."

"Why is it any of your business?" Sarah's direct question was typical of her.

"Because I choose to make it so. I'm a law unto myself here, miss. For all that"—he twirled the pistol idly on one finger—"I do get bored. At the moment you interest me. I intend to know your story, you see, so it's pointless to delay. I could have the flesh whipped off that small boy's back, for example. And have all of you made to watch. Will that be necessary?"

"You wouldn't!" Laura pulled Charles close to her even while he struggled to get away and stand manfully on his own. "I think you're just talk. I've watched you, just as you said. Plenty of times. You're not the sort of man to do anything like that at all. So stop trying to frighten us."

Sheldon started at her in smoldering silence. For almost half a minute none of them spoke, The only sound was the howling wind and the pelting rain still beating down outside. Then his lordship threw back his head, and his laughter rang round the tiny hut. It was a brittle, strange laugh, but it broke the tension. "No, Miss Laura, you're quite right. I detest the sight of blood. It sickens me. And this thing"—he dropped the pistol contemptuously on the table—"isn't even loaded. Come, madam, you have supplies enough in there to brew a posset. I know, because I examined it all yesterday. Pray do so and we'll drink together. It's quite beastly outside, and no day for wandering in the woods."

Clare did as she was bidden; the children made a fire and arranged themselves near its warmth. But she wasn't easy for all that. This Lord Sheldon struck her as a dangerous sort of man. Their safety at Tassels was based on anonymity and seclusion. If that was breached, then everything might change. "Your good health, milord," she said at last, handing Sheldon his drink of hot milk and wine.

"And yours, madam." He lifted the tankard in her direction before draining it dry. "Now will you answer me one question, at least? Have you always been Catholics?"

2.

"But how could he know?"

"I can't say, Nancy, really I can't." Clare settled herself next to her sister-in-law. "He said he just guessed. I suppose we've no choice but to believe him."

"He's telling the truth, Mama, I'm sure of it."

Laura had shown an unusual degree of interest where this stranger was concerned. Now her mother looked at her questioningly. "Why do you say that?"

"Because it's logical. Look, he said he had observed us for weeks, and we've no reason to doubt that."

"No," Clare said, "nor his claim that people fascinate him. I suspect Lord Sheldon to be a man of whims and fancies. Certainly his eccentric clothes indicate as much. Sneaking around the woods and spying on us would fit right in."

"You're too hard on him, Mama. I think he's . . . well, rather lonely. And as he said, he watched us enough to decide we were deliberately, how did he put it, 'avoiding observation.' In other words, he knew we were hiding. And he could tell by watching us we weren't criminal types. So what could we be but recusants? His logic is quite sound."

"But recusants," Nancy said, "can be many things besides Catholics. How was he to know you weren't Puritans or Quakers or God knows what else?"

"Logic again. We just don't look like any of those."

"That's the part I don't care for," Clare added. "I admit he could have guessed the rest, but to know we were Catholics it seems to me he'd have to have some additional information. Something he's not admitting."

Laura shrugged. "What does it matter? Really, Mama, you

must believe him when he says he means us no harm. Why should he? And he did say we could use the cabin whenever we liked." Suddenly her defense of the man was interrupted by a loud groan from Nancy. "What is it?" the girl demanded, reaching her aunt's side before her mother did. "What's the matter, Aunt Nancy?"

"Nothing's the matter," Clare said quietly. "Nancy is going to have a baby, that's all. I've thought for some days the time was getting close. Go, child, fill the kettle. And get clean blankets. Hurry." Then to the young woman who was still struggling to regain her breath, "Lie back, dear, and don't worry. I'm here and it's all going to be fine."

"But it's too soon, Clare!" Nancy's voice was a throb of fear and anguish. "It's just seven months. Am I to lose this baby too? Oh God! I can't bear it..."

"Shh. If you get yourself in such a state you will lose the baby. But it's not necessary. Have you not noticed how the child dropped this past week? I could tell just from looking at you. Many babes are born before nine months are passed and are fine healthy tykes for all that. Courage, Nancy, and prayer. That's what's wanted. Now, girl, we'll see if you're a Griffin wife." Clare smiled warmly. "I rather think you are, Nancy, I've thought so for some time. Let's get to it."

In London, Roger Griffin had no idea that just hours after he left Tassels his wife was in labor. Had he known it's unlikely he'd have rushed back to Surrey to wait by her bedside. First, he tended to think of that as woman's work in which he had no part. Being witness to the time Nancy lost their first child had left him sick for days. And he believed that Ellen Wadden would be there when Nancy's time came. Best leave it to them. Secondly, on this particular evening he returned to the city to find news of far more import than the borning of any child, even his own.

A letter awaited him in the shabby room at the Cock and Pie which he still occupied. "The *Queen Catherine* left Lisbon this twenty-first day of October," he read. "I send this message with a friend posted to our Portuguese legation in London and hopes it reaches you before the *Q.C.* docks. Cargo loaded as arranged and all well disposed here. May God sail with her. Your humble servant, Nightingale." Nightingale was the code agreed for Alphonso da Gama. Griffin was Thrush. He'd thought the ruse silly when the Portuguese proposed it and he thought it silly now. But that didn't matter. The coffee was on its way. Now they needed only God or luck or whatever it was that determined men's fortunes. If they had it, he was one step closer to climbing back up that ladder from which Mark's idiocy had toppled him.

From the time he'd received Catherine's loan and found himself with the sudden advantage of capital, Roger's horizons had broadened daily. At first he'd thought only to do the deal with da Gama and take the profits to try to regain Harwood. But in a short time he'd seen the folly in that approach. No matter how profitable the coffee sale might prove to be, the money couldn't possibly amount to enough to make John Lane part with the Hall. It would take a truly fabulous sum to oust that usurper from the place he'd so long coveted. In addition, Roger had realized quite early that the opportunity he was facing could, if properly exploited, change the future for generations of Griffins yet unborn. The Hall could come later. It had stood in its Yorkshire isolation for six hundred years; surely it could wait a little longer for the return of its rightful owners. He must use this money to build a business that would outlast him, to make a place for himself in the new mercantile England evolving before his eyes.

Thus, in Roger's mind at least, was Griffin's Importations born. Soon he'd managed to make the name known all over London, despite the fact that not one item of merchandise had yet been traded by the infant company. A primary element in that growing reputation was the small house across from the Exchange he'd leased weeks before. This was the headquarters of the venture.

It was a poor place when he got it, one of those shabby structures built after the fire on the ruins of its predecessor. The owners had flouted the instruction to use brick or stone, as had almost everyone else. 7 George Alley was a two-story house of stucco and half-timber with two small rooms below and two above. When Roger took over, the furnishings had been so primitive and broken as to be useless. He'd had them all carted away and hired a joiner to make him adequate if modest appurtenances—a desk, bookcases, a few chairs. Only the downstairs was furnished, but none who called on him there knew that. 7 George Alley now presented a highly respectable and even prosperous face to the world.

The cash for all these things had been a worry to him for a while. If he used the remains of his hoard in the money chest in Pope's Head Alley he'd have precious little left. But that hadn't proved necessary. The goldsmith to whom Queen Catherine originally sent him, and who was yet guardian of his coins, was a man named Solomon Levi, a Jew, as were so many in his trade. Levi's connections with Catherine's family went back generations. His ancestors had been in Portugal for centuries. Throughout the long and bloody history of the relations between his race and their host nation, the Levis had managed to survive. Most avoided either forced conversion or burning, the lot of so many of their fellow Jews, and instead became first jewelers, then moneylenders to the ruling family. Solomon Levi himself had come to England shortly after Catherine. It had simply been good business for the Levis to have a representative in the country where a Portuguese princess had become queen.

At their second meeting the goldsmith had managed to hint to Roger of his resources, and his willingness to put them at the disposal of a young man who looked likely to produce a profit. "We Jews have a function, you know," he explained in heavily accented English. "Our very misfortune in being scattered over the world without a homeland can be useful. I myself have relatives in half a dozen different nations from Holland to Turkey. Between us we've managed to amass some facility to finance men of affairs when their own capital is tied up elsewhere. Her majesty speaks very highly of you, Captain Griffin. That is sufficient recommendation for Solomon Levi. Please call on me whenever you have need." The little man was as round as he was tall and had the prominent nose and swarthy skin associated with his people. When he bowed deeply to Roger, he looked comical, even a ludicrous figure. But there was nothing ludicrous in his offer. Roger was wise enough to see it as invaluable, and so it had proved.

Levi had advanced him a thousand pounds on the strength of only his signature and the promise of repayment in six months with an interest of sixteen percent. The loan went toward furbishing 7 George Alley and left him with ample reserve, which he lodged in another small chest not at the goldsmith's but under the floorboards of his new office.

He'd hired a burly old ex-sailor named Hart as night watchman for the place, and a lad to act as general dogsbody. The boy, Sam Ludlow, ran errands, kept the premises tidy, and took Nancy her weekly letter and supply of household funds. Fortunately he'd proved trustworthy and now slept in one of the two upstairs rooms on a bed that, for all it looked to Roger like the most uncomfortable couch possible, he claimed was more splendid than anything in his past.

Lately Roger had been thinking of fitting up the second upstairs room as a living chamber for himself. He'd resisted this idea at first; it didn't seem suitable for the impression he was trying to create. But he would be far more comfortable at George Alley than at the Cock and Pie, and no one ever went upstairs. On the ride back from Tassels the evening that, unbeknownst to him, Nancy went into labor, he made up his mind to the move. Da Gama's letter merely confirmed his decision. He'd need to be at the heart of things now. The months of planning and working were about to yield their first fruits. If Roger had known about his wife he'd have considered the timing remarkably prophetic; as it was, he would learn of the birth the same day he received very different information.

"Here she is, love." Clare placed the swaddled infant in Nancy's arms. "Tiny little mite, but fine and healthy for all that. Isn't she beautiful?"

"Yes, yes, she is beautiful...." Nancy looked long at the sleeping baby, then sighed with deep contentment. "You're sure she'll be all right?"

"I think so, yes," Clare said, nodding gravely. "Laura's made her a little bed just next to you. And I've sent Charles to gather as much rosemary as he can find."

"Why rosemary?" Nancy asked sleepily.

"To burn in the fire and strew around the baby's bed. It's an old practice I learned from the Scots woman that nursed all my babes when they were small. She said the herb was most salutary for cleansing the air of evil humors. And as I told you, Andrew was born early too, just like your little one. I know it helped him. Now you must rest, but tell me first, have you decided on a name for her?"

"Oh yes, I've known that for some time. She's to be Nell. Nell Griffin. It sounds fine, don't you think?" Nancy was asleep before Clare could reply.

It had been Clare's intention to summon Michael Wadden and send him to London with the news. Nancy rejected the idea. "Roger's business affairs are at a critical state," she said with what seemed like only half interest in the words.

"We can wait till the Ludlow boy comes on Monday." Clare didn't approve, but it wasn't her decision to make. "Besides," Nancy added, "I like having her to myself for a bit. Roger can meet his daughter next week." Therein lay the truth of her reluctance to inform her husband of his daughter's birth. Clare pursed her lips but held her tongue.

When Sam Ludlow came three days later he brought news he seemed to feel was as important as that he was to convey back to London. "Cap'n Griffin said to tell ye he was right sorry, ma'am. He'd no time to write no letter and he can't come this week. There's trouble o' some sort. 'Tis the *Queen Catherine*, I think. Cap'n didn't say, but I heard him talkin' with old Hart."

"What trouble?" Nancy inquired anxiously. "Is Captain Griffin well?"

"Oh, well enough, ma'am. 'Tain't nothin' like that. It's the ship, like I told ye. She was due in tomorrow or next day, but Cap'n heard she ain't comin'. Sunk she was...sunk by pirates off the Isle of Wight."

"I don't think it was pirates, Nancy," Roger said, pacing the small room. "There aren't any operating from the island. It's the Wighters themselves that do it. They set up false lights on a stormy night and bring ships to grief on the rocks off St. Catherine's Point. That way they get the salvage. It's an old trick and every seaman knows about it, but if the weather is dirty enough it's all too easy for even the most experienced to fall into the trap. I can't blame the captain, poor bastard."

"Were none of them saved?"

"One or two, I'm told. I've not seen any of them yet, so I can't be sure."

"Roger, what are you going to do?"

He looked at her for some moments before answering. This was Nancy's first visit to George Alley; that she was here was proof of what a remarkable woman he'd married. Just two days past Ludlow had returned from Tassels with the news that she had borne him a daughter. This afternoon Nancy herself walked through the door. "I had to come," she had said simply. "I've been worried sick about you since Sam told me the news. I went to the Cock and Pie and they told me I could find you here."

He'd protested, of course. Exclaimed about the fact that

177

she'd given birth just a week previously and had no business taking river trips in the December cold. She brushed away his objections and insisted on hearing the story of the ill-fated ship. Now he smiled and cupped her chin in his hand. "It's going to be all right, Nancy. You mustn't worry. It's a setback, of course. A huge one. But I don't intend to give up. Now, enough of that. Tell me about our little girl."

"She's perfect and beautiful. I've named her Nell. Do you like it?"

"It will do if it pleases you. And now, my sweet, I'm going to take you to a decent inn and see you have a meal and some rest. Tomorrow I'll take you back to Tassels and meet this little Miss Nell."

Later, while they sat over a meal of oyster stew and spiced ale, she broached the subject she'd really come to London to discuss. The idea was born when she heard about the loss of the cargo. Why she'd never thought of it before she couldn't imagine—probably because she'd been so preoccupied with her pregnancy, and because Roger seemed to be managing well enough without advice from her. Only when this happened, when she found that Roger needed her again, had she thought of Benjamin Ahmet and cursed herself for a fool for not remembering sooner. "Darling," she said quietly, "may I make a suggestion to you? I don't want to intrude in your business affairs, but I do have an idea."

"Intrude away," Roger said quickly. "God knows, ideas are welcome at this juncture. Yours as well as anyone's."

"Have you ever heard the name Benjamin Ahmet?"

He thought for a moment. "No, can't say I have. Sounds like a Jew."

"He is. From Turkey originally, though he's been in England for many years. I've known him since he first came. Around '62, I think." She refilled both their mugs from the jug on the table and watched Roger closely while she spoke. There were things she'd rather not say, but she would if she had to. The important thing was to convince him that Ahmet could be trusted. "He's a merchant, that is, a trader. At least that's what I think. I've never been much interested in such things, as you know. But Benjamin..."

"Oh." A new tone crept into his voice. "You're on first-name terms with the man? You know him well, I take it."

Nancy drew a deep breath. This was just the line she had wanted to avoid. "Yes," she said frankly. "At one time I knew him very well. But that was years ago, Roger. It's not important now. What is important is that Benjamin can be useful to you. I'm sure he can. I thought of it the other day, and that's why I had to come."

"I see." He hated himself before the words were out of his mouth but he couldn't stop. "You thought this Ahmet chap important enough to leave a newborn infant with a simple peasant woman like Ellen Wadden, did you?"

"She's not..." She bit back her words. This wasn't the moment to tell him it was Clare who had charge of the baby, not Ellen. "Nell is fine," she said instead. "We found a wet nurse in the village. Please don't change the subject, Roger. And don't get angry over something that existed years ago, before I even knew you. You must go see Benjamin now. I'm sure it would help your business."

"No, thank you," he replied stiffly. "I have my own sources, and I don't need your old lovers as associates." He left soon after that remark, though she had hoped he would spend the night, and didn't return until the morning.

"I've arranged a wherry for the trip back to Tassels," he said by way of greeting. "It's waiting at Trigg Stairs. Are these all your things?" He hoisted her small bag and waited by the door.

"Yes, that's everything. I thought perhaps to shop a bit in London..."

"Not today, Nancy. I have to see you safe home and get back to the city by nightfall. There's much work for me here now."

"You needn't come all the way to Surrey, then. Just put me on the boat and I'll be fine."

"No. I don't want you traveling alone so soon after the child's birth. Besides, I would like to see my daughter, you know. Even though you don't seem to think that's important."

It was pointless to reply when he was in such a foul temper. Nancy flung on her cloak and followed him into the street. Only later, when they were almost at the place where the boat waited, did she realize she would have to tell him more unpalatable truths. Coming with her to Tassels like this, unexpected and unannounced, he would be face to face with the facts. Better to hear it from her first. "There's something you must know, Roger. Something I haven't told you until now. Clare is at Tassels with me. She and the four children. They've been there since London became unsafe for them last August."

179

He greeted her news with an incredulous silence that reverberated throughout the five-hour journey home. Once or twice she tried to break through his icy reserve and make him see how helpful it was for her to have the others with her at Tassels, even if he didn't feel any responsibility for them. It was useless; he wouldn't talk, and when she tried for the third time to speak he cut her off with a command so harsh she dared not disobey. At last they reached the pile of rubble that passed for a landing at Tassels and started up the path to the house. "I want you to know one thing," he said, turning to face her in the wan midafternoon sunlight. "They will have to leave immediately. I'll tell that to Clare myself. As for your deceit and disobedience, I don't feel able to discuss that now."

Nancy's chin came up. The anguish she had been feeling was replaced with indignant determination. "You will do no such thing, Roger Griffin. I'm your wife and subject to your will, I know, but you forget one thing. Tassels is mine. The deed was given me in my own name by the King of England. What do you mean by telling me who I can and cannot have under my roof?"

"I..." Speechless, he couldn't do more than stutter in his fury. The claim she made to legal ownership of the house was nonsense. As his wife, all her property was his. But he didn't want to argue such matters of law with Nancy. What made his heart race with rage was the fact that she would persist in defiance of his express commands. "You'll do as you're told, madam," he finally managed to say.

"No, Roger, no I won't." She was calmer now, her voice low and sure. "Oh, you can probably make me do so up to a point, I know that. But unless you propose to imprison me and little Nell somewhere, you'd best hear what I have to say. I love you in spite of the beastly attitude you've taken on this matter of your brother's family, but I also love Clare and her children. They've been good to me, they do no harm here, and if I let you turn them out now it would be tantamount to signing their death warrants. I can never agree to that, nor allow you to do something I think you'll come to regret bitterly. You have your life in London, your business to tend to. I must make a safe place here for the baby and myself. Leave us be, Roger. There's nothing to be gained by great dramatic gestures proving your disapproval of all

Mark's done. This arrangement is only temporary anyway. They say that once the furor over the Duchess of York's conversion has died down London will be safer for Catholics. Mark is trying to find a home for his family. You mustn't turn them out now. What will be gained by doing such a terrible thing? A thing for which I don't think I could ever forgive you?"

For some moments he stared at her, then he turned and walked off the path to stand rigid and unapproachable among the trees. Nancy neither did nor said anything. He must make his own decision. Finally he turned back to where she waited. "I want to see the baby," was all he said.

Clare was alone with the infant; her children were off in the woods as usual. She looked up when they entered, but her face betrayed shock for only a brief moment. "Hello, Roger," she said quietly. "I am glad to see you, though I doubt you feel the same." She rose and went to her room, leaving Nancy to lift the infant from her beruffled basket and place her in her father's arms.

3.

On Birching Lane, between George Alley and the Exchange, were two tobacco shops. Roger passed them daily as he prowled around the city. One had a large sign proclaiming, "The best tobacco by Farr." The next bore the legend, "The very best tobacco. Better by far than the best tobacco by Farr." He'd not adopted the craze for pipe smoking, and he'd never entered either establishment, but their rivalry always made him chuckle. It was perhaps the epitome of that lust for trade which gripped London.

It was a consuming lust, Roger understood that now. He'd run into a fellow Yorkshireman a month or two back who expressed amazement at his change of loyalties. "What in God's name do ye mean, Roger Griffin?" the fellow said in shocked tones when they shared a pint at the Blue Boar. "Are ye daft, man? Land's the only thing that counts. Never mind that foolishness of yer brother's. It's nowt to do with ye. Come home to Yorkshire and buy land. These maniacs down here will ruin themselves with their buyin' and sellin' and bringin' into England what God never put here." They'd parted after half an hour with neither able to convince the other of his point.

When the news of the *Queen Catherine*'s disaster first reached him, Roger had thought instantly of that man. Maybe he was right. Land was permanent, solid. It couldn't be dashed on the rocks off any island, nor spill its cargo and his dreams into the muddy tide. That notion, however, stayed with him for only a matter of minutes. He knew too well what drought or frost or blight or disease could do to livestock or crops. The land was no stranger to calamity; even rents were uncollectible if the tenant farmers had nothing to bring to market. His vision of a new age, that vision born in him after his first meeting with Alphonso da Gama, was deep and sure. It wasn't a passing fancy that could be blown away by the first ill wind. Twelve hours after the news of the sinking reached him, Roger was at his desk making fresh plans, drawing endless columns of figures and balance sheets and schedules. When Nancy arrived so unexpectedly he found it unnecessary to show confidence for her sake. He was confident. His basic idea was sound. It needed only a quick new cargo to replace the coffee and he'd be able to absorb the loss of the ship and go on.

Walking to his premises after the trip back from Tassels, he stopped to look at the tobacconists' signs and reminded himself of that resolve. By the time he crawled into bed he'd promised himself two things. The one was that he would spare no time or emotion on the situation in Surrey. His wife and child were housed and fed; he need not worry about them. Nancy's defiance was a problem of a different order. It reflected on the nature of their relationship and the future of their marriage, but it required no immediate action. His task was to concentrate on Griffin's Importations. From that flowed the second resolution. He would go to see Levi tomorrow morning. The loss of the *Queen Catherine* and her cargo had put him in serious trouble so far as short-term capital was concerned. The goldsmith was the man to put that right.

"I understand of course, Captain Griffin." The Jew had a long and unfashionable beard that he stroked lovingly all the while he spoke. "Naturally a man in my position has seen such tragedies all too often. It's the luck of the draw, as you English say."

"Luck's only part of it, Mr. Levi, I assure you. A man must make his own most of the time. I intend to do so."

"But how?" A gesture of open hands spoke both sympathy and doubt. "Forgive me, captain, but I do not see what you can do."

"Buy another cargo, of course. Don't you understand, Levi? It doesn't matter what goods I sell. My whole plan is based on a unique distribution system. That's unaffected by the shipwreck."

"I see. And what, may I ask, is that distribution system?"

"Sorry. I'm afraid I can't be any more specific about that now. You'll have to trust me."

"No. Captain Griffin, it's I who am sorry. More so because I do like you. You've all the best of the English qualities. Swagger and nerve and a pirate's conscience behind a gentleman's facade. No, no...don't take offense. That's a compliment, truly. But to lend more money on the basis only of such feelings on my part and some vague hints on yours—that I can't do."

Roger had anticipated this response. Trying again for a loan on the basis of only his signature had been a shot worth taking, but one he hadn't truly expected to hit home. "Very well, Levi. I understand, of course. Tell me one further thing: Will you extend the time of my original debt repayment? Say six months more, at three percent additional interest for the extra time?"

Levi looked at him and stroked his beard. "Seven percent more," he said at last. "And on the whole term of the loan."

"That's twenty-three percent in all. Rather steep, wouldn't you say?"

"Yes, no doubt it is. My terms nonetheless."

Roger stuck out his hand. "Done."

"Done."

It was merely the beginning of a solution. He'd bought time, nothing more. His mind was racing when he left the goldsmith. It was cold out, the first brisk day of the winter. He turned into a nearby coffee house and ordered a bowl of the brew with no thought for what might have seemed irony. His attention was occupied with the problem of buying a cargo before it came to the floor of the Exchange. That meant buying at point of origin, not an easy task. Particularly now that his cash was in short supply.

"Captain Griffin, isn't it?" a voice said at his elbow. "Permit me to introduce myself. I'm Benjamin Ahmet. We've not met before, but your wife is an old friend."

He looked up to see a slim, wiry chap about ten years older than himself, elegantly dressed, sporting one of those long curly wigs the king had made so popular. "Yes," Roger said more shortly than he intended. "So I heard."

Ahmet ignored the unspoken meaning of the words. "May I join you?" He seated himself without waiting for a reply. "I've wanted to meet you for some time. You're making quite a name for yourself in the city these days. Frankly, I like what I hear."

"Kind of you to say so. What are you drinking?"

"Coffee, thanks. I see the latest events haven't turned your taste from the stuff."

Roger grinned and motioned to the man behind the counter to bring two more bowls of coffee. "Not much point in that, is there? What do you do, Mr. Ahmet? My wife tells me only that you're a trader."

"That's a vague but easy title, isn't it? Still, I guess it's as accurate a description as any. In a word, I buy cheap and sell dear. When I can, that is."

"That's what we all try to do, isn't it?"

"Quite so. Some more successfully than others." Nancy had said the man came from Turkey, but his English had only the slightest hint of an accent. "What success have you had lately?" The question was beyond frankness. It was patently rude. Roger didn't reply. "I've offended you," Ahmet said with easy good humor. "I won't apologize. I intended to."

"Why?"

"Because"—the man sipped his hot drink, then set the bowl down carefully—"I want to cut through the formalities. I wish to discuss important business with you, Captain Griffin. This place is pleasant enough, but not sufficiently private. Will you accompany me to my office? It's not far."

"Why the devil should I? At the moment, sir, I have no reason to think you anything but an impertinent stranger. My time is valuable, to me if to no one else."

"Yes, I see that. And you left out another reason for being rid of me. I'm a Jew. Everyone knows we can't be trusted. Didn't old Levi just rob you of seven percent extra interest?"

Roger jumped up and leaned menacingly across the table. "How in hell do you know that?"

"Please, Griffin, no violence. I merely wish to provoke your curiosity. It is in both our best interests that we talk. Shall we go?"

"As for knowing of your deal with Levi, that's simple." Ahmet poured something that resembled molten gold into two exquisitely cut glasses. "Here, try this. It's called brandy. I've a taste for the stuff, though it doesn't find much market in England. Careful, it's potent. Like it? Good, a man of taste. To return to the matter at hand, Levi's young dogsbody is my nephew. We Jews are clannish, as you've no doubt heard. We hire our own kind whenever possible. The old man knows full well that little Abraham comes running to me with news of his dealings." Ahmet shrugged, "It doesn't bother him. Why should it?"

"There is such a thing as confidentiality," Roger said stiffly.

"Oh yes. A very English notion, that. Not highly prized among us, I'm afraid. But in this case, if you'll hear me out, I think you'll agree it worked to your benefit."

"So you keep saying. So far I've not heard a word that makes me think I'm doing anything but wasting my time."

"Very well." Ahmet seated himself on a chair upholstered in fine cut velvet. His small office was like an elegant Whitehall drawing room. Roger couldn't help but be impressed, even though he realized he was meant to be. It had, after all, taken a large amount of money to create this place. The Jew seemed to read his thoughts. "As you can see, captain, this room is designed to create an impression of prosperity. You recognize it as such, for you've worked the same trick yourself."

"You give me more credit than I deserve. George Alley isn't half as grand as this."

"No. But that it exists at all is tribute to your, shall I say, imagination. You've not a farthing of your own. It's all front, a facade erected with borrowed capital. This Griffin's Importations everyone's talking about hasn't bought or sold a thing. Not a loaf of sugar or a yard of cloth. But it's earned you a reputation as a man of affairs. And now, with the cargo of pirated coffee you were promised by da Gama spirited away by the Isle of Wight smugglers, you've nothing at all. But look at you, dressed in your finest and parading about the city. A man like me appreciates that kind of bravado, captain. It's rare even among the English."

"This is the second time this morning I've been called a charlatan and told it was a compliment," Roger said, grinning. "You're a remarkable man, Mr. Ahmet. I suspect you've more secrets locked away in your head than the busiest *agent provocateur* in Whitehall. But what is it all in aid of? As you seem to know so much of my financial position you must surely know I'm not worth holding to ransom. What do you want of me?"

"A business deal, sir. One I've been sitting on for over a month. It will take much courage and ingenuity to make this particular arrangement profitable. I've been looking for the right man. I think I've found him."

"Wait. Before you go any further, Ahmet, tell me something. Did my wife put you up to this?"

"Your wife? Hardly, sir. I haven't seen her in five years. At least not to speak to. I've seen the lady on stage frequently, of course."

"Somehow I don't believe you." Roger stared at him intently. "It's too much of a coincidence that she mentioned you to me for the very first time just three days ago."

"Did she? I see." Ahmet rose and refilled their glasses. "I suspect I've blundered into the middle of a family quarrel. That's too bad, because it could color our relations, for one thing. And for another, your suspicions are mistaken. All of them." He waited for a reply, but none was forthcoming. "Very well, let me speak plainly. When I tell you I've not communicated with Mrs. Griffin for five years it's the truth. Whatever coincidence is involved is just that. Your jealousy is foolish and without basis in fact. I met Nancy years ago, when I first came to England. She was just starting with D'Avenant and anxious to learn to be a 'proper lady,' as she put it. I was a foreigner. I knew no one, and my presence here wasn't really legal. Cromwell simply allowed some Jews into England because he was impressed by their biblical prerogatives as the 'chosen people.' The lord protector's Protestant conscience was sometimes his worst political enemy. We were unpopular here; life wasn't easy for Jews in England regardless of sermons and tracts about biblical verities. Then Charles returned and he let it be known almost immediately that as long as our mercantile efforts were beneficial for the realm Jews could remain. So, in that mad climate of the first days of the restoration, I and my people found ourselves enjoined to produce a profit, or swing at Tyburn. That was the situation when Nancy befriended me. We helped each other. We were not in love, and, in the true sense of the word, we weren't lovers. Now, captain, does that explanation satisfy you? If it doesn't you'd best leave. No business alliance such as I'm proposing can flourish without trust."

For some moments Roger sat in silence. Finally he threw back his head and drained the last of his brandy. "State your offer, Ahmet," he said at last, setting the empty glass firmly on the table. "I'm listening."

The cargo was dried figs, dates, and raisins from Turkey. It was aboard a Dutch *fluyt*. The ship, a fast vessel used exclusively for cargo, was owned by relatives of Ahmet in Holland. At the moment she was seven miles off the coast of Bristol waiting only word from Ahmet to dock. The problem, he'd explained, was an old one for him. His far-flung family connections made it possible for him to purchase and transport many such cargoes, but his quasi-legal status in England was a weapon that anyone could use against him. Once he got his goods to the floor of the Exchange the East India men could freeze him out, force him to sell at a minuscule profit. It was either that or see the lot rot with mold while he held out for a better price. "Why do you stay in England, then?" Roger demanded. "Why not go someplace where the conditions are more favorable for Jews?"

"And where might that be?" Ahmet asked softly. Then, after a few seconds, "You can't make any suggestions, can you, Captain Griffin? There is no place where my people aren't merely interlopers. We've had no homeland of our own for fifteen centuries. Besides, I have my sister here with me. She is attached to England, and it wouldn't please her to leave. I'm very fond of her and am her sole guardian, since our parents are both dead. No, there's no point in my leaving England. I must find a way to defeat the East India Company right here in London."

And that, of course, was where Roger came into the picture. Ahmet's incredible intelligence network had told him about the watermen and the special arrangements that protected them from the press. It hadn't taken him long to guess most of what Griffin was planning.

Through all the long weeks during which he had put the

scheme together, Roger had discussed its totality with no one. Certain persons knew one part or another because they had to in order to make it work, but only he knew the whole story. Now he was faced with a choice. Benjamin Ahmet had managed to discover a good deal of the plan, enough to make him come up with an offer. If, however, they were going to enter into this proposed partnership, Ahmet would have to know everything. Should he trust the man? There was one possible means of avoiding that question. He tried it. "Why don't you simply sell me your cargo? You can name your price, say double what you know you can get on the Exchange."

"Oh no, my good captain," Ahmet said softly. "None of that. I'm not some Arab street trader to be fobbed off with quick cash. Don't you think it's best if we both admit to ourselves that the other isn't a fool? I know you have a plan designed to reap bigger returns than are presently dreamed of in this city. I want a part of that pie, Griffin, not the crumbs. What's more, I can be enormously useful to you. I can buy goods in a dozen different ports at better terms than you could hope to secure. That advantage has to be worth something more than a few pounds extra profit on a single cargo."

After that speech it took Roger less than thirty seconds to make up his mind. He'd needed a new opportunity; here it was.

"You have a list?" Ahmet asked after the scheme was explained. "You know where to go with your offer?"

"Every last grocer and food merchant in the city. I've divided them into territories and have maps and plans for the lot."

"And the watermen will be used to deliver the merchandise?"

"Yes. Once the orders are secured and the money has changed hands the goods will be landed right at the merchant's front door. It's the best deal he can hope to get anywhere. Much better than having to hire a drayman to cart stuff home from a warehouse."

"Yes, that's another problem. What about warehouse space? If one is to bypass the Exchange one can't expect to use its facilities at the docks."

"Naturally not. I've leased storage space in Wapping. It's big enough for any needs I can foresee, and it's mine until January of 1680. With an option to purchase then if I wish."

Soon after that Roger closed a deal with a handshake for the second time in two hours. It had proved a most remarkable morning indeed.

Perhaps it was because Ahmet's cargoes were almost always foodstuffs that he had seen the simple brilliance of the plan as well as Griffin did himself. The trading method of the East India Company was cumbersome, but not fatal for the supplies of soft and hard goods they imported. For perishables it could be disastrous. By eliminating a whole step of the process Griffin's Importations would move from dock to retailer twice as fast as the competition. But Ahmet didn't see quite the scope that Roger conceived. He thought the linchpin of the idea to be the watermen. He understood that guaranteeing them a regular weekly wage and freedom from impressment assured the loyalty of even that notorious crowd of thieves. What he didn't understand was how the second group of men on Griffin's payroll were as important, or as readily trusted.

The reason the East India Company could use the floor of the Exchange to hold so many different classes of people to ransom was simply that hundreds of small shopkeepers all over the city had no other way to obtain the stock that kept them in business. Griffin's Importations was proposing a change in that system. It wouldn't please the masters of the Exchange, but it would delight the independent retailers from one end of London to the other. A Griffin representative would call on them, discuss the latest goods available, and take their orders without their having to venture beyond their own front doors. And the goods would be delivered the same way. For the merchants it would be an answer to prayer. For Roger Griffin it would be a huge profit opportunity. To ensure that, he hand-picked a crew of seven men and dubbed them "company representatives."

Chief among them was a chap named Montague Kendal. Close on fifty, with graying hair he hid beneath an elaborate wig, he had twinkling blue eyes and a deep resonant voice that betrayed his true profession. Kendal was an actor, one of a large coterie of members of that trade who had the frequent misfortune of being out of work. In Monty's case the reason was that he'd grown too old to portray virile young heroes on the stage. Griffin recruited him by the simple expedient of promising him a shilling and sixpence each week to be supplemented with a commission of one percent of the value of every order he wrote.

He soon spread the word of this untapped bonanza among others of his circle of idle performers. In a fortnight Roger had selected six more to work under Kendal. Each had a territory of his own, with names and addresses provided from the George Alley headquarters. They were personable men of glib speech and ready charm, just the types to inspire confidence and expansive good humor. Roger believed those things, coupled with unbeatable prices, were exactly what was needed to produce sales.

Roger was shouting for the young errandboy before he closed the door on George Alley. "Ludlow!" he bellowed up the narrow staircase. "Come down here. And hurry, or I'll ship you back to the dung hill you came from."

"Here I am, captain." The lad snapped a naval salute in the manner he'd observed Hart using. "At your service, sir."

"Good lad. Here, take this off to Monty Kendal. You know where to find him?"

"Sure do, captain. Lives in a room on York Street, he does. But this time o' day he's sure to be at the Lion's Rest with all them theater folk."

"Right. Well, get him and bring him here. And see you don't dawdle. There's work for Mr. Kendal. Work for all of us, and about time."

In less than an hour the boy and Kendal returned to the office. They found Griffin ruffling through sheafs of paper and committing each to separate piles on his big oak desk. "Good to see you, Monty. That will be all for now, Sam." He dismissed the boy with a wave of his hand. "Now, my fine fellow, are you and your troop of company representatives ready to go out and earn yourselves a bit of money?"

"That we are, Captain Griffin. You've something for us to sell, then?"

"I have, Monty, I have. A sweet taste of the mysterious East. Succulent dates and figs and raisins, dripping with the honeyed sunshine of exotic Turkey. And we can deliver them to the shops just in time for all the goodwives planning their Christmas feast."

It wasn't until late that night, after all the storm of activity loosed at George Alley had died away, that he thought again of the infant daughter he'd met yesterday. Suddenly

190

it seemed to him a very good omen indeed, this deal with Benjamin Ahmet coming hours after he'd first made his daughter's acquaintance. Never mind her mother's stubbornness or the family of Yorkshire lunatics the poor little thing had inherited. Young Nell had one thing very much in her favor—a father who was determined to see she had a secure future to grow up into. And sooner or later he'd manage to move her back to the home that was hers by right. Back to Harwood, where, like all Griffins, she belonged.

That night, and in the busy days that followed, Nancy's disobedience receded into a place of less importance in his consciousness. When he allowed himself to think of it at all, he remembered not his wife's defiance of his wishes, but the way Clare had looked in the moment he'd seen her. Sweet and gentle as always. Gradually there grew a separation in his mind. On one side was Mark and the behavior he could never forgive; a man's choice carrying man's consequences. On the other were Clare and Nancy and his daughter and nephews and nieces. They were women and children and needed protection. If Mark had forfeited the role, that made the responsibility his. Without realizing it and without experiencing any dramatic moment of decision, Roger came to terms with the ménage at Tassels. Slowly they emerged as the background against which he was acting his drama.

4.

"Will he come for Christmas, do you think?" Clare adjusted the mending in her lap and moved closer to the fire.

"I don't know. I wish he would, but..."

"Yes, I understand. Nancy, are you sure it's wise? This insisting that we remain, even though it angers Roger so?"

"I told you what I think of that." She reached over and adjusted the blanket covering little Nell. Outside, snow was blowing in great wet chunks against the window, and the voices of Clare's children could be heard above the storm. They reveled in this first breath of winter. "If I gave in to Roger on this it would be the end of everything for us." She broke off. It was impossible to say everything she felt so sure about.

"Very well." Clare nodded. "And I'm more grateful than I can say. No, no," she said to stop Nancy from interrupting. "I know it's not just for us that you take this stand. I do understand, my dear, more than you realize. But there is something else you could do, something we could do together."

"What do you mean? Do about what?"

"About the way things are between you and Roger. Look, I'm not prying, and you needn't tell me anything. But I've been married for eighteen years, and I know a thing or two about men, Griffin men at least. Let me help you, Nancy." She left her chair to kneel beside the younger girl and take both her hands. "Let me help you make Tassels the kind of home it should be. Then at least Roger will see that you mean to be a wife to him. . . . I'm sorry, I've said more than I should."

"No, you haven't. Not at all. It's no secret that I know nothing of making a real home for Roger. I told him that long before we were married."

"But it doesn't have to be that way, Nancy. The children and I would love to do so many things at Tassels. We haven't because it seemed none of our affair, but if you let us we could accomplish a great deal. And I could show you so many things. There's nothing missing in your head, dear girl. You've just never had an opportunity to learn. It's as if I were taken to a theater and told to act a role. I'd not have the faintest idea how to do it. But you could teach me if you had to, couldn't you?"

"Yes, of course I could. The essentials, at least."

"There, that's just what I mean. Everything's only a matter of having someone show you the whys and wherefores. So let's do it. It'll take time and hard work, but isn't that better than sitting here brooding about your problems?"

Nancy stood up and walked to the window. It was impossible to see more than a foot or two in the storm. She stared into the swirling white morass for a few moments as if she could read the future in the snowflakes. When she turned back to Clare, her cheeks were flushed and her eyes sparkled. "Very well, love. You've got yourself a pupil in the art of housewifery. Where do we start?"

* * *

They began with the long-overdue tour of the house. It was, as it had first been described to her, essentially just a simple country cottage. On the ground floor were the two big rooms they were presently living in, two more slightly smaller, a huge dark cavern of a place Clare said must be the kitchen, and half a dozen small workrooms designed for functions Nancy couldn't even imagine. The larders, the still-room, and the dairy, Clare explained. And she was equally decisive about the second floor.

"This is the master bedroom, obviously," she said when they entered a spacious chamber at the top of the stairs. "Lord! I wonder when was the last time there was a fire in that grate. And look at that pile of rubble in the corner. It must have been furniture once, just a home for vermin now. We'll have to pitch it all out. That's a good job for Andrew and Charles." She hurried on to the next doorway. "This must be another bedroom...yes, it is. And there are three more. If we go up that narrow flight of stairs there, I'm sure we'll find the servants' quarters." They did, but she hurried Nancy out of that part of the house. "Too much to take on just now," she said firmly. "We'll leave that for last and concentrate on the first and second floors."

"You've been around this place before, haven't you?" Nancy asked suddenly. "I can tell you have."

"Yes," Clare admitted somewhat sheepishly. "I couldn't resist having a look when you went to London. It just tormented me not knowing what the rest of the place was like. Do you mind?"

"Not a bit." Nancy hugged her and laughed. "You must think me a real dullard without a spark of curiosity."

"No. I know that some people think such things boring. But it needn't be, Nancy. It can be a great challenge. I aim to prove that to you."

In the following days a storm of sweeping, dusting, and scrubbing descended on the cottage, a tornado of activity with Clare at its center and Nancy close beside. The Wadden couple had become accustomed to doing little for their two shillings a week, but soon they realized that the old order had passed. Clare used a combination of bullying and cajolery to effect the transformation, and in a few days' time Ellen and

Michael were working beside the Griffins with energy and determination.

They began on the second floor, heaving out through the windows sticks and rags and broken bits and pieces of bedsteads, chests, and what-all. "It looks like a battlefield," young Charles commented, surveying the turmoil in the gardens below. He wasn't far wrong. Legs and cushions and drawers were scattered around the foundations of the house, trapped in overgrown shrubbery, sticking out of flower beds and borders at exotic angles.

"In that case," his mother answered, "you and Andrew are the generals. Now get that mess cleared away. Cart it down to the field below the sycamore trees and burn the lot. And hurry—there's more to come."

"Tell them they must be careful," Sarah said quickly. "I've been checking and there are some good plants left in that garden. I don't want them clomping around with their clumsy big boots ruining whatever's left."

"That can't be helped now," Clare said briskly. "You can have your way with the gardens later. We have to make the inside livable."

"You're the general, Mama," Andrew called out, laughing. "This is your war; we're just foot soldiers."

They called it "Mama's War" from then on, and the analogy was apt. Clare gave orders and commands so fast the rest couldn't keep up. Nancy felt sure the dust would never settle and peace never return to Tassels. However, she had little time to mourn the loss of her tranquil retreat. Early in the morning of the second day of the attack Clare buried her head in a deep trunk she had brought with her from London and emerged holding a tin canister aloft like a trophy. "Here it is, I knew I had it!" She prized off the lid and held the article under Nancy's nose. "There, isn't it lovely?"

"It smells delicious," Nancy said in surprise. "Whatever is it?"

"Polish. My own special blend of beeswax, lavender, and a few other things. I'll teach you to make it in the spring. First," she added, laughing, "you have to learn to use it. You and Laura can work together. She's done it before, I assure you. I never believed in letting my girls grow up idle."

So every exposed bit of wood in the house was rubbed and buffed to a sweet-smelling shine. Exposed timbers, stair rails, floors, and the few bits and pieces of furniture that were in good repair came under the waxen assault. "It's like a fairy

194

princess's castle in here," Nancy commented in wonder after they were through. "I've never smelled anything so homey in my life."

"Wait till summer when we can make potpourri, then you'll see how sweet a house can smell." Sarah never missed an opportunity to remind them of the garden's promise.

At the end of a week Clare pronounced the cottage clean to her satisfaction. She wasted no time in setting the boys and Mr. Wadden to repairing the steps of the river landing and widening the path to the house, then she turned to the women assembled inside and announced, "Right. We're ready for the next step."

"Wait a bit, Clare," Nancy said. "Tell me one thing, please. What are we going to do for furniture in this place?" They were still living in just the two rooms they had always occupied. The rest of Tassels was now scrupulously clean, but empty.

"Some simple things the boys and Mr. Wadden can make. For the rest you'll have to wait until you can ask Roger to send a joiner."

"I see." Nancy turned away and busied herself adjusting little Nell's coverings. She'd not heard from Roger in ten days. When he left on the disastrous day that he'd seen the baby for the first time he had given her three pounds. She had money enough not to miss Sam Ludlow's weekly visit, but she sorely missed having word from her husband. "Well," she said as she turned back to Clare, determined not to give in to melancholy, "what do we do next, then?"

"The kitchen and the workrooms. No household can function properly without them."

They had already completed the basic cleaning in that wing of the house; what remained was to put the domestic offices in working order. They were fortunate in that most of the equipment was of metal and stone. Such things had stood the passage of time better than the furnishings upstairs. The heart of the kitchen was a fireplace big enough for a tall man to stand upright inside, with three baking ovens built into the rear. It had been swept and scrubbed from the hearth to the top of the chimney. Now Clare set about sanding and greasing the cranes and trivets and hooks and chains that cluttered the interior and looked such a mystery to Nancy.

"It all has a purpose," the Yorkshire woman explained. "I'll show you everything as we go along. See, this kettle fits on this hook." She dragged an enormous caldron forward. "Help me get it in place. And this," she added between gasps of breath as they struggled with the heavy utensils, "is the spit to take a joint of beef or a bird. You turn it with this crank."

Nancy thought she could actually savor the aroma of roasting meat and bubbling broth. "Lord, Clare! It's like a stage set. It wants only the actors to come alive."

"Actors indeed!" The other woman was offended. "This isn't make-believe, Nancy Griffin. This is real life!"

Certainly the work was real enough. By nightfall Nancy was soaked in perspiration and every muscle in her body ached. But she had a surprising glow of satisfaction, too. None of their previous efforts gave her as much pleasure as seeing the shelves of the larders filled with their supply of foodstuffs and the dairy ready to function. The latter room was admittedly tiny, but big enough to hold an old churn that still functioned perfectly, a stone-topped table for working butter, and deep kegs for storage.

"As soon as the boys and Mr. Wadden are done with the boat landing they can put that first barn to rights," Clare had said. "Then you can buy a cow or two and the house will be well supplied with milk and butter and cheese. It just doesn't do to buy such things ready-made, Nancy. It's far too dear, and no housewife worth her salt does it."

"But who'll milk the cow?" she demanded in horror. "I can't, Clare...I just can't! I've never done such a thing in my life."

"No, of course you can't. Shouldn't, either. Look, my dear, you must be mistress of this house, not maid of all work. As long as we're here, the boys can do it. It's good for them. When we're gone, you'll hire a lad to take care of such things. Don't fret, Nancy. I shan't leave until I've explained everything, including what servants you need and how to train them."

Now, lying in bed and remembering the pleasure the day's events had brought her, Nancy thought of that statement. Of course she knew that sooner or later Clare and the children must go to rejoin Mark, but the idea of being alone again saddened her. Determinedly, she pushed the notion away and rolled over to where she could see Nell's tiny form in the basket beside her bed. It was far nicer to think instead of the visions all this activity had conjured up in her head, visions of herself and Roger and a flock of happy healthy children living at Tassels in peace and security. It was a lovely dream.

"Will Uncle Roger be here for Christmas?" Sarah asked as she chopped apples for mince tarts.

"Hush, Sarah," Laura said quickly. "It's none of your affair."

"I just want to know if we're to have Christmas here or in the cabin in the woods," the younger girl persisted.

"Sarah!"

"It's all right, Laura. We all know Sarah will never be a diplomat." Nancy gave the pastry a final roll and stepped back to admire her efforts. Not bad for a first time, she thought as she said, "Besides, I thought you knew. Your uncle knows now that you're all here."

"You mean he will come, then?" Laura, taking a leaf from her sister's book, asked the direct question. "It would be lovely if he and Papa were both here and we could have a real family Christmas just like the old days."

When the holiday came, however, Nancy and Clare and the children were quite alone and thought they would remain so. Until midafternoon of Christmas Day, when Roger suddenly arrived. Nancy had given up hope by then. When she looked up to see him standing in the doorway with a dusting of new-fallen snow frosting the shoulders of his heavy cloak and whitening his hair, she had to catch her breath hard to keep from gasping. The physical sensation of joy his presence gave her was as unexpected as it was intense. "Roger, oh darling! I'm so glad..." She rushed to his arms as though they were totally alone. For the moment he was the only thing in her world.

"I had to come," he said simply. "It's Nell's first Christmas."

The others watched their kiss of greeting for a few seconds, then turned to their own conversations with slightly too much enthusiasm. Their embarrassment was apparent to Roger. He released his wife from that hungry embrace of reconciliation and said, "Hello, Clare. You look well. And look at the rest of you! Just a year since I've seen you, and Laura's a full-blown beauty and the boys almost men. As for you, miss..." He turned to Sarah with false severity. "You can

197

stop gaping at me with that look of disapproval. I rode all the way here from London without a rest, and I'm starved. Can you find some remains of Christmas dinner for me? Andrew, is there someplace in this tumbledown old ruin you can tether my horse out of the weather? The poor animal's as tired as I am. And see he has something to eat."

Later, when he was full of goose and sage and onion stuffing and sipping contentedly on a mug of mulled cider, he looked around him and saw for the first time the transformation the past month had wrought. It wasn't just the Christmas greenery with which they'd decked the big front room that made it look so different. There wasn't a bed in here now; it almost looked a proper drawing room, despite its poverty of furniture. "What have you done to this place?" he asked. "It looks quite different."

"It's about time you noticed," Nancy said. "Come and see. You simply won't believe it all."

It took half an hour to show him each nook and cranny. He did the tour carrying his infant daughter and crooning to her between comments about architecture and building materials. Only when it was finished did Nancy ask, "Well, what do you think?"

"I think," he said, looking at her with something quite new in his eyes, something rather like the respect he usually reserved for other men, "it's bloody marvelous."

"But how did you manage it all?" he asked when they were alone in the master bedroom late that night.

"Clare did most of the managing. I just tagged behind and did as I was told. But I am learning, Roger. She's simply wonderful, so patient and good. And she knows endless things I never knew existed. Like what herbs to put in the cupboards so moths won't come and how to store butter and..."

"Yes, yes..." He was laughing and stopped her words with a brief kiss. "I know Clare's armory of lore. Don't forget I wasn't quite fourteen when she married Mark and came to the Hall. She's a formidable mistress of the manor. You couldn't have a better tutor."

"You approve, then? Of my efforts, and Clare and the children's being here?"

His face darkened and he turned away from her to stand staring out the window. "Snow's stopped," he commented before replying to her question. "It'll be clear tomorrow, I expect. And damned cold." Then, because she was obviously still waiting for an answer, "I've thought quite a bit about it. Even though I've a lot of other things to think of right now, which I'll tell you about later. You were right in saying that if I forced Clare and the children back to London and something happened to them there I'd never forgive myself. In the end my quarrel is with my brother, not his wife or sons or daughters. Besides, it's also true that you and Nell are much better off not being alone here. So..." He shrugged and turned to face her. "You shall have your way, Nancy Wilmott. Just as you always do."

"I love you," she said. And watched while a smile lit his face. "I love you so much it hurts. And I'm not Nancy Wilmott, not any more. I'm Mrs. Roger Griffin. So come here and claim your marital rights, why don't you."

"Right," he said, stripping off his clothes and dropping them on the floor, since there was no place else available. "I note that empty as this room is of furniture, it has the one thing necessary in a sleeping chamber, a bed."

She giggled as he crawled in beside her. "Mmm, it's nice to have you home. You make the bed so much warmer..."

"Is that what you want me for, then! Well, we'll see about that..." There was no further talk for a while, only their wordless murmurings and the whispered sighing of flesh against flesh. Despite the fact that they had been so long apart, despite the tensions that had made the past month so difficult, this coupling was neither hurried nor dramatic. It was as if the cozy domestic scenes of the day had settled over them, blanketed them with a special husband-and-wife kind of familiarity. Each kissed, tasted, probed the other with slow deliberation, seeking new ways not to possess but to please. Somehow he appeared prepared to grant her more equality than at any time in the past. It seemed to her strange that she felt for the first time more wife than lover, and that change in role made her more venturesome.

"My God," he murmured when she explored his maleness with her mouth and tongue. It wasn't an expletive but somehow a prayer, a benediction of this new thing between them. For a long while he allowed himself to drift in an ecstasy of feeling, allowed her to play the part of aggressor. Until, "Stop, come back here to my arms. If you go on I won't be able to wait."

"Don't wait, Roger. Don't wait any longer. Take me." He buried himself deep inside her and claimed what was his in an explosion of feeling that shook them both.

5.

Roger woke to find sun streaming through the windows and Nancy sitting beside him fully dressed. "Here," she said, offering him a steaming mug. "It's only hot milk and honey. We live simply at Tassels, with none of your London fancies like coffee, tea, or chocolate. Speaking of coffee, do you want to tell me what's going on with Griffin's Importations?"

"Yes, I do. But not now, later. When I'm decently dressed and can muster some businesslike dignity. Sweet Christ, Nancy, this room is cold! Why haven't you a fire in here?"

"That," she said, pointing to the small fireplace, "smokes like a pitch blaze every time we try to light it. The boys have had a look and so has Mr. Wadden, but so far no one can fix it."

"I'll see about getting a proper chimney sweep before I leave. There must be someone in the village. And you need hangings, too. Curtains for the bed and the windows, not to mention some furniture. It would all help to warm the place up."

"Yes it would, but I haven't done anything because I didn't know if you'd approve and if we could afford it. Can we?"

"Not a lot. Not yet. But you can spend a bit on the place now, and there'll be more later. I've..." Then, remembering his plan to tell her the whole story later, he changed the subject. "Nancy, tell me something. Where is Mark? How come he wasn't with the family for Christmas? You couldn't have known I'd be coming."

"I didn't, but I hoped. Anyway, that isn't the reason Mark's not here. He had to remain at his job at the Spanish legation."

"What does he do there?"

"He's a porter."

Roger's face went grim. "A porter. Squire Mark Griffin fetching and carrying for a lot of bloody foreigners! Jesus."

200

Nancy shrugged. "He was glad to get the work. And it's the safest possible place for him. The legation is considered Spanish soil. He's safe from the wolf pack while he's there."

"Wolf pack indeed. But it's getting better. They've got new things to talk about in London now. Charles has just signed a treaty with the French. They're to be our allies in the war against the Dutch."

"How can that help Catholics?"

"They say the treaty includes promises of toleration for Catholics in England. There's even talk that the king has secretly promised to embrace the 'old faith' sooner or later."

"Do you think he will?"

"Frankly, no, I don't. More important, I don't think it really matters. What's important is free trade and peaceful waters so we can move goods without needing a flotilla of warships to accompany each merchantman. If we get that, London will be too absorbed with money to hound religious fanatics."

"Is that what you think they are? Fanatics? Clare and Mark and the others like them?"

"What else? It's not a matter I wish to discuss, Nancy. But tell me, does Mark ever get down here to see the family? Or write to them?"

"He's come a few times. He daren't write. He has no one he can trust with the letters. That is, no one he wants to know their whereabouts."

"Yes, I see that. Very well, you get word to Mark. Tell him I'll send young Sam Ludlow to his Spanish fortress once a week. Ludlow can collect a letter from Mark and bring it down here when he brings mine."

"Oh, Roger, that's wonderful! Clare will be so grateful."

"Never mind that. There's one more thing. I don't want to have to see him. Not anywhere, but especially not here. If you see to it that never happens, then this arrangement may work."

By morning light the house looked even more changed than he'd realized yesterday. Roger paced its rooms in silent admiration of all they had accomplished. Tassels remained a simple country cottage but a cozy home as well. "Come see the boat landing, Uncle Roger," Charles said. "We've almost finished with it, and it's super."

"Is it now? Then indeed I must see it. Nancy?" There was no reply, and he called louder, "Nancy! Come here a minute."

She hurried in from the kitchen, her nose smudged with flour and her frock covered by a voluminous apron. "What is it? Do be quiet, you'll wake the baby."

The sight of her made him grin. "You look a proper domesticated wench now," he said, laughing. "Tell me what you've done with my cloak. I mean to accompany this young man down to the river and see the marvels he's worked with that decrepit old landing. Everyone in this place seems able to make a silk purse from a sow's ear. I should take the lot of you back to the city and turn you loose on the floor of the Exchange. God knows what'd happen."

"Well, God will have to be the only one to know," she retorted with a saucy lift of her chin. "We're staying right here at Tassels, thank you. As for your cloak, it's in that cupboard over there. See?" She went and opened the door and removed his garment. "This backs up on the kitchen chimney, so we put anything wet or cold in it to dry out."

This time he openly hooted with laughter. "My girl, I just don't believe you're the same Nancy I married!" Then, seeing her expression, "Don't get angry. It's a compliment. I'm very proud of you."

"That's fine," she said, smiling. "Now, hurry off or Charles here is going to burst with impatience. Don't be too long; lunch is nearly ready."

He was almost out the door, his young nephew on his heels, before he turned back and said, "You know, Nance, I must get some proper country clothes to leave down here." It was her turn to grin. The suggestion was as good as a promise that he was beginning to feel as she did about Tassels. And if that was so, her dreams of their living here as a family might very well come true.

The air was crisp and surprisingly dry. Snow lay thick over the landscape, dressing the wide green leaves of laurel and privet, threaded in the needled branches of pine and fir, blurring the angular outlines of leafless oaks and elms. It crunched beneath their feet; intensified the weak winter sunlight until it was a thing of blazing glory. "This way," Charles said. "See, we've widened the path." The boy moved surefooted through territory with which he'd become completely familiar, and Roger followed with a deep sense of rightness of things that was inexplicable and unfamiliar.

Then, when they were on the way back after all the requisite, and deserved, praise had been heaped on the repaired river steps, Charles turned to his uncle and said, "It's really nice here, isn't it? I don't mind so much about leaving Yorkshire now that we've come down here."

Roger could find no words to reply. At that moment he could have murdered Mark with his bare hands. What diabolical madness had made his brother deprive this child of his birthright? The boy was his son, Roger's nephew, the next generation of Griffins, and he belonged in Harwood Hall. A sense of impotent fury rose in Roger's throat. Silently he wrapped an arm around the lad's small shoulders and walked beside him toward the house.

They were almost to the gate when he saw the stranger, a tall reed of a man wearing a fur-lined cloak that flared out over the flanks of his pure-white mount. Horse and rider had planted themselves squarely across the path to Tassels' front door. He seemed to spot Roger and Charles a split second before they saw him. "Good day to you," he called out. "Happy Christmas."

"Happy Christmas to you, sir," Roger said quietly. "I don't believe we've met."

The man jumped nimbly from his horse and extended his hand. "We have not. Antony Sheldon, good sir, your humble servant."

"Ah, of course." Roger shook the outstretched hand. "Lord Sheldon, I believe. I knew we were neighbors, but I'm not here often." Then he turned to his nephew. "Where are your manners, Charles? Can't you bid his lordship good day?"

"Good Christmas to you, milord," the boy managed. Memories of their last meeting, when this same nobleman had threatened to flay the skin from his back, were too fresh in the child's mind to allow for more. He darted off toward the house and ignored the greeting Sheldon called after him.

"You seem to have startled all courteousness out of him, milord. Sorry. Now, will you come inside for a sip of Christmas cheer? I'm sure my wife would be delighted to meet you. Or has she had that pleasure already?"

"Thank you, I'd be mightily pleased to take a drink with you. I've yet to meet your good wife. I'm sure the pleasure will be mine. Jamie!" he called over his shoulder. "Where are you?"

Roger was startled to see an enormous fellow shuffle out of the bushes. He'd thought their visitor quite alone.

"Here, now, see to my horse. That's a good boy." Sheldon dismounted and handed the reins to the servant he'd called Jamie. "Don't be alarmed by this giant, Captain Griffin. He's been with me for years. I know his appearance is unnerving. He's simple, poor chap. Mind of a ten-year-old child, but superb with horses."

The women had warning of his lordship's arrival. Charles had seen to that. Nancy was in the front room pouring claret, and the rest had chosen to make themselves scarce. Like Charles, they found their previous meeting with Antony Sheldon unforgettable. "Good Christmas to you, Mistress Griffin," the visitor said heartily. And then, over Nancy's shoulder, "and to you, Miss Laura. I rather hoped I'd see you again today."

Surprised, Nancy turned and saw the girl come forward into the room. Laura had managed to change into her best frock in the five minutes since Charles had announced Lord Sheldon's presence. "Good day, your lordship," she dropped a deep and graceful curtsy. "How very nice of you to call."

Roger found himself watching the man with a combination of amusement and annoyance. Sheldon's garb was flamboyant and not a little ridiculous, doublet and hose like some Elizabethan cavalier, and his mannerisms equally overdone. Nonetheless he carried off the masquerade with rare style. He was a true eccentric who seemed to thoroughly enjoy his self-appointed role—one couldn't help but admire the chap. And how he charmed the ladies! After five minutes' ordinary conversation he suddenly stood up and hurled himself across the room to bow deeply before Nancy. "My very dear madam," he said with feeling. "I have just realized in whose presence I am. You are Nancy Wilmott, aren't you? I only just recognized you. Perhaps because in this part of the world I simply never expected to meet in the flesh an artist I've so long admired across the footlights."

She laughed and made light of it, but there was no denying Nancy was delighted with the recognition. Roger knew her well enough to see that. He didn't know his seventeen-year-old niece half so thoroughly, but nonetheless he could recognize the symptoms of adoration she too was displaying. Laura was enchanted with this comic nobleman.

Needless to say, his lordship was invited to lunch. Happily, he refused. Happily at least for Roger, who'd had quite enough of the fellow's posturing after a quarter of an hour. Nancy and Laura didn't seem as glad to see him leave. They escorted Lord Sheldon to the door, one at each side like a particularly fetching guard of honor, and pressed on him invitations to come again.

"But why don't you like him, Roger?" Nancy asked. "He seemed quite charming to me. And amusing into the bargain."

"I don't dislike him. I never said I did. I just find that sort tolerable only in limited doses. Sitting down here in Surrey on his elegant backside and riding about the country in fancy dress...it's rather stupid behavior for a grown man, don't you think? I heard his estates are in a shocking condition. Fellow takes everything out and puts nothing in. You can't manage lands that way. Not and hang onto them."

"Oh? Where did you hear that?" They were alone in the big kitchen. The others were all off somewhere on pursuits of their own, and the warmth of the kitchen fire made a cozy background for the talk Roger wanted to have with his wife.

"Just here and there in the city," he answered, poking a log deeper into the flames. "I made inquiries after that first time I was down here. Remember, the Wadden couple told me Tassels was just next to Lord Sheldon's property. Naturally I wanted to know what sort of neighbor you had."

"Well, it doesn't matter. I've not seen hide nor hair of him before today, and doubtless won't until he pays another courtesy call next Christmas. Now, enough of that. I've been waiting and waiting to hear what's happening with you in the city. Begin at the beginning and tell me everything. Was there anything more heard of the *Queen Catherine?*"

"Nothing. But I shan't begin at the beginning, Nancy. That's not the important part of the story. I think I'd best begin somewhere around the middle." He rose and stood facing her. "I've taken a partner into Griffin's Importations. Someone you know—Benjamin Ahmet."

6.

At Roger's suggestion Nancy went to spend a few days in London soon after Christmas. "You can do some shopping," he said. "Get some things for the house, and for yourself and the baby if you like. You won't believe what you can buy ready-made in town these days. Come see, Nancy, it will do you good." She didn't bother to tell him that what did her most good was the realization that he wanted her in the city because he craved her company.

Nancy was astounded when she called at the George Alley premises. They had become a rabbit warren filled with hurrying figures busy moving sheafs of paper from one place to another, runners arriving every other minute from the docks and, never far from sight, one or another of the liveried watermen or handsome company representatives waiting for an assignment. It took her five minutes to work her way into the inner office where Roger sat issuing directives and making decisions like a general on a battlefield.

"Not I, pet," he amended when she said as much. "You shan't make me soldier, even in jest."

"Very well, an admiral then. But it comes to the same thing. You're too busy to take me to lunch, I suppose."

"At the moment I am, rather. Can you manage on your own? I'll be finished here about six this evening."

"That's fine. I'll shop, and call on Nell, I think. Or visit the theater if she's not available."

"Fine," he said heartily, turning back to his papers with what looked like relief. "Enjoy yourself."

She smiled and dropped a quick kiss to the top of his head. When she was almost out the door she turned back to him in sudden confusion. "Roger, I haven't any money! What do I shop with?"

"Good God! What an ass I am." He fished an elegant wallet

from the drawer of his desk. "Here, love, this will do for your expenses. Anything you buy just have sent around here. Tell them you're Mrs. Griffin and that I'll settle all the bills."

She raised her eyebrows at this evidence of his stature in the city, and a teasing remark was almost spoken before she thought better of it. Roger was taking himself very seriously these days. She only smiled and left.

But once she was strolling along Cheapside, accosted on every side by cries of costermongers hawking their wares and enticing shop windows, she decided on a different order of the day than she had indicated to Roger. London was seducing her, wooing her as one of its own. In the months she'd lived in Surrey she had forgotten how much this bustling busy city was part of her. Now she had an overwhelming urge to find herself once more among these Londoners "in the know." What she wanted, she realized, was gossip. News. Information about who, where, and what. "You there!" she called out, hurrying toward a hackney coachman. "Are you free? Good. Take me to Pall Mall. Mistress Gwyn's house. I presume you know where it is." The cries of the street peddlers followed her through the city.

"So I just have to be philosophical about the French bitch." Nell sighed and poured another cup of tea for both of them. "What do you think of this stuff? I think it's bitter and horrid myself, but everybody's drinking it." She didn't wait for an answer but went on chattering as she had for the last half hour. "Mind you, I don't let her get the best of me. Not in or out of court. Or in or out of bed, for that matter. But Charles won't send Mademoiselle de Kéroualle back to France, because he won't offend Louis. That's what he says, at any rate. But"—she sat back and patted her tummy—"I've another 'proof of affection' coming, so I can't complain."

"Oh Nell, how lovely! No wonder you're looking so radiant. In the light of that I'll have to forgive you for not coming to Tassels in all this time. You did promise, you know."

"I know I did, darling. And I meant to, but I just can't leave Charles while this Louise is around. She's perfectly awful, Nancy, really she is. No chin. And she hangs on him like a leech. Always wanting to stick her nose in his court business and trying to gain favors for Catholics."

"She's a Catholic, then?"

"What else? I told you she was a bitch."

"You're being very hard, Nell. All Catholics aren't awful, you know." Nancy couldn't help laughing. Nell's venom was so much a personal thing, with nothing of theology involved.

"I suppose not. You said you liked Roger's family that one time you met them, and they became Catholics. Still..."

Nancy dropped her eyes and busied herself stirring the tea. Had Nell called at Tassels, Nancy wouldn't have attempted to hide the presence of Clare and the children. She would trust Nell with anything. But since the other girl didn't know, there was no point in burdening her with the secret. To change the subject she said, "You haven't asked me about Tassels or my life there. Are you interested?"

"Oh, Nance, of course I am! I'm interested in anything to do with you. It's just that I have no one else I really trust. All this stuff about the French bitch has been brewing inside me with no one to talk to. Now tell me everything. How did you find the house?"

"A shambles. But it's lovely now. That's what I'm in London for. To buy furniture and such. But you must come to see us, Nell. You've not even met your little namesake."

"I know. And I feel quite awful about it. But you got the silver mug and porringer I sent for her?"

"Yes, I did. They're lovely. And save up your pennies for another. You see, darling," Nancy said and leaned forward conspiratorially, "I'm pregnant again too. And you're the first to know. I haven't even told Roger."

Nell threw her arms around Nancy with bruising enthusiasm. "Marvelous! But when are you going to tell him?"

"Tonight. If I can get him to pay attention to me rather than business."

"Oh, I daresay you'll manage that, my girl! But it is the only place to talk to a man, isn't it? In bed, I mean. You have to get them paying attention to the parts below their waist before you can make them open their ears. Now we simply must celebrate. Come along, Nancy. I shall take you to all the fashionable shops and we'll spend a pile of money. I know a little woman on Watling Street makes the most exquisite silk night dresses you've ever seen. Positively sinful...."

She kept gossiping while they got ready to leave and didn't stop even when they were in her coach riding toward town, until she was startled in midsentence by a vicious lurch that nearly threw both her and Nancy from their seats. "Where are we?" Nell demanded of the driver. "What's the trouble, Higgins?"

The coachman pushed open the flap separating him from his passengers. "It's the mob, Miss Nell. They're shoutin' and throwin' things again. Do ye want me to go on and run 'em down?"

"No, Higgins, that won't be necessary. What are they shouting? The usual things about damn the pope and his French lackey king?"

"Aye, that's it, Miss Nell."

By this time Nancy and Nell could hear the ruckus themselves. Not content with hurling insults, the crowd was making threatening motions. One small boy hurled a rotten orange. It splattered against the window and hung there for a moment before rolling away, leaving a trail of mud and juice. "See, it's as I told you," Nell said quietly to Nancy. "They know what this papist Kéroualle woman is really about. Don't worry, I'll soon put an end to this problem."

"Nell, don't!" Nancy shouted as the younger girl hastily rolled down the glass and leaned out the window. "You'll be killed!"

Nell ignored her. Her famous stage-trained voice rang out over the shouting and screeching of the angry throng clustered around the coach. "Be quiet, good people! Don't you see? It's me, Nell Gwyn. I'm the Protestant whore!"

Roger was laughing until the tears rolled down his cheeks. "She really said that? Really?"

"So help me God. And they went away quiet as lambs. After giving her a rousing three cheers, that is."

He rolled over and slung an arm across her breasts. They were in that same room at the Golden Bull they had occupied so often before. His quarters at George Alley were all right when he was on his own, but he wanted something a little more luxurious for this night that Nancy was spending in town. "It's the best story I've heard in years. I only wish I could tell it as you do."

"Well, all that stage training has to count for something. But I wonder if you should tell it. Is there really something evil brewing, Roger? Something to do with this de Kéroualle woman?"

"You mean, I take it, something to bode ill for Clare and the children. No, I don't think so. The Duchess of York is very ill. They say she's dying. Too bad for her, of course, but the best thing for James. He can wait a bit, then get himself a good Protestant wife and go on as before."

"Roger Griffin, you're a bastard! Would you bury me so easily and go looking for someone else to warm your bed?"

"Mmm, can't say. I think not, unless she was as talented in it as you are." She flung a pillow at him, and he feinted it aside. "Want a fight, do you? Well, then..."

Only later, after all the tumbling and laughing and love-making were at an end, did she tell him her news. And it was later still, while he slept with his hand clasped over her belly as if to protect both her and the baby, before she let herself truly relax. In the silent dark she savored the sensation of happiness that was growing inside her alongside the child. Mrs. Roger Griffin, beloved wife and mother, mistress of Tassels...not bad for an urchin from the Moorgate slums.

The winter wasn't a hard one. At Tassels they were warm and snug, and Nancy knew that Roger was grateful for the kind weather that made it easy for ship traffic in the port of London. She understood how critical this first year of his alliance with Benjamin Ahmet was, and knew they were being exceptionally lucky. "Sometimes," she confided to Clare one mild afternoon in late February, "I have to hug myself to prove it's all real."

"You're happy, then?" Clare didn't look up from the mortar and pestle she held in her lap.

"Unbelievably happy. What are you making?"

"A tonic for you. Sarah found the first green tops of some spring nettles showing down by the river. They're very healthful for expectant mothers."

"Nettles! Ugh...how do they taste?"

"Not at all bad. I shall brew them in a tisane for you to drink this evening. You'll see. And we must write the recipe in your stillroom book. That way you'll know how to do it when I'm gone."

"Don't talk about that. I can't bear to think of you going. Why can't you stay here?"

"Because Mark's sent for us. He's been given a small house on the Spanish legation's property. I have to be with him, Nancy. You understand that."

"Yes, of course. But it's so dangerous, Clare. I told you what happened when I was with Nell in London. The people

210

are so narrow-minded. They're looking for papists under their beds. Though what harm they can fear from you I can't imagine."

"It's politics, Nancy, all of it. I can't be worried about that. I just have to be with my husband." Clare stopped grinding her potion and tipped it into a basin. "Besides, when we're living on the property of the legation we're safe. And we can hear holy Mass."

"That's important then? This Mass of yours?"

"It's everything," she said simply. "But there is something else. I don't like leaving you alone here just now. Laura's offered to stay with you, if you'll have her. At least until the baby is born."

"Of course I'll have her. She's a dear girl, Clare, and I love her. But you must realize the real reason she wants to stay behind."

"Lord Sheldon. Yes, I know."

"And you approve? They ride together three or four times a week, don't they?"

"At least that. As for my approving, I can't see any reason not to. He's odd, I know, but..."

"Yes, odd." Nancy pursed her lips and said no more. Close as she was to Clare, the differences in their backgrounds made it impossible for her to admit what she suspected about Antony Sheldon. She resolved to try to talk to Laura sometime in the not too distant future.

The conversation Roger had with the Duke of York a few weeks later was far more frank and, in its way, more important to the future of Laura and all the family. Griffin was in James's private apartment above the navy office in Seething Lane. "I asked you here, Roger," the duke explained, "because it attracts less attention than the palace. You're not offended, I hope."

"Hardly, your highness. Any summons from you is an honor."

James smiled wryly. "No court manners, Roger. God knows I get enough of those. All fawning and bowing to my face...behind my back it's another matter."

"Not with me, sir," Roger said quietly.

"No, I know that. That's why I wanted to see you." Instead of explaining further he said, "You're looking very well. The life of a city merchant with a country estate agrees with you."

"I rather think it does," Roger admitted. "I'd never have expected it to, but then..."

"Yes, needs must where fate dictates. It's the way of the world. God's way, I think."

"God's, sir?" Roger found the comment surprising. James had never been given to piety.

"Yes. He does have some influence on our affairs, you know. I come to see that more and more."

This was a new York. Introspective and melancholy. Living up to the sobriquet "Dismal Jimmy" with which Nell Gwyn had christened him years before. It wasn't a side of his nature Roger had ever seen; he found it a bit unnerving. "You're looking tired, your highness, if I may be so bold. Perhaps a holiday..."

"Tired? Yes, I expect I am. But no holidays, Roger. Not now. The duchess is very ill. I suppose you've heard."

"Yes sir. I have. I needn't tell you of my sympathy."

"Save it for her, lad. You can't imagine, I couldn't tell you, what it's like. What she's going through." His eyes had a haunted look, like those of a man who had witnessed unspeakable things. And that from a battle-hardened military man.

"Is it . . . will it be long, sir? I mean no disrespect, but . . ."

"Yes, of course. We both know what dying is about. Better to have it over with. But Ann's not of that mind. She keeps saying she wants to suffer. To hang on the cross with Jesus for the salvation of souls. I know, it sounds like mawkish woman's talk. But if you could see her, hear her..." He stood up and pounded his fist hard on the table. "Enough of that. I didn't call you here to talk of this. Though the matter's related, I think. Poor Ann. The last thing she would have wanted was to set the dogs on Catholics. But that's just what her conversion did, isn't it? And it's going to get worse, Roger. That's what I wanted to tell you."

"I'm listening, sir."

"Parliament's going after blood again. God knows they do it often enough. Damned upstarts think they can tell the king how to rule the country. Anyway, that's an old story. The thing is they're petitioning his majesty for a new law. Bemoaning the growth of popery and demanding stricter enforcement of the recusancy laws. Charles will probably have to agree. These wars with the Dutch cost money, and the

Westminster jackasses have the power there. You understand?"

"Not really, sir. Not what it has to do with me, I mean. If you're thinking of my brother..."

"No, no, not that." James waved his hand in a gesture of impatience. "Your family's your own affair, no business of mine. It's trade, lad. Your trade. It may be that I'll have to fade from the public eye a bit, live more privately. You see how it is. My cousin Prince Rupert may be made lord high admiral. I just wanted you to know that he understands about our arrangement. He'll keep to it. No watermen in Griffin livery to be bothered by the press, and all that. Didn't want you to worry."

"Thank you, sir, I'm very grateful." He stared at James, but nothing in the man's face shed any further light on this extraordinary conversation. Why tightening the laws against recusancy should cause the king's brother to retreat from public office was as much a mystery when Roger left as it had been undreamed of when he entered. He walked to his luncheon meeting with Benjamin deep in thought.

7.

"He's quite marvelous, isn't he?" Laura threw off her shawl and flung herself down at Nancy's feet. "Did you see us this morning? He brought new horses. We rode for hours... like the wind... and spring flowers are coming up everywhere." She leaned back on her elbows, her young breasts thrusting against the lacings of her demure blue frock. "Johnny jump-ups and violets near the river, and some darling pink things I've never seen before. Antony says they grow only here in this part of Surrey."

"Antony, is it?" Nancy asked softly. "Not Lord Sheldon any longer?"

"Oh, not for ages. He insisted I call him by his Christian name when we first started riding together."

"And what does he call you?"

"Why, Miss Laura, of course! You mustn't think he's not been a perfect gentleman, Aunt Nancy. He has, really. But he's not a stuffy formal sort." She rolled over onto her stomach and cupped her chin in her hands. "He's so witty and charming and...well, I guess 'sweet' is the word. You do know what I mean, don't you? You know quite a lot about men." Then she flushed and stammered in confusion. "I mean..."

"I know what you mean. It's all right, Laura. I'm not offended. And frankly, you're right. I fancy I do know rather a lot about men. Which is why..."

"Yes?"

"Tell me something. Don't think I'm doubting you, I'm not. But has Lord Sheldon ever kissed you, or said anything of his future intentions?"

"No, he hasn't. And it's my turn to say I'm not offended. I'm glad you brought the matter up, Aunt Nance. I wanted to ask you about it anyway. I've had no experience with men at all. Not ever. Shouldn't he have tried to kiss me by now?"

Nancy countered with a question of her own. "Do you want to?"

"Yes I do. Very much. Does that make me a shameless tart?" The girl looked both defiant and terribly vulnerable. "Aren't I pretty enough, Aunt Nancy? Is that it?"

"You're quite lovely, my dear." She touched the girl's blond curls. "Your hair is like spun gold. I love to see it loose like that. No, you mustn't think it's got anything to do with your looks. As for being a tart, that's nonsense. Laura, since we're speaking so truthfully, do you want to wed Lord Sheldon?"

"More than anything in the world." The girl grasped both Nancy's hands in her own. "Tell me how to win him. Please. I'll do anything."

Here it was, the moment she had been dreading and expecting for weeks now. Laura deserved an answer, and the best one she knew would be the hardest for the girl to accept and understand. "I think," she began hesitantly, "that is, I suspect, that Lord Sheldon is different from most men."

"I know that! Of course he's different. That's why I care so for him."

It was no use. She couldn't begin to explain the truth to this innocent child. Particularly since she wasn't completely sure she was right. There would have to be some other way to deal with the situation. "Don't fret about it, Laura. Just go on being your beautiful, charming self. I'll think more about it and we can talk further some other time. Besides, I've news for you today. Your sister Sarah's coming to spend some time at Tassels. I had word from your mother this morning."

"That's lovely! But why? How come Sarah's coming here now? I should think mother would need her. There must be such a lot to do in the new house."

"Be that as it may, Sarah will be here day after tomorrow. I think now that spring is here she wants to set about remaking this garden just as she kept saying she would. Besides, it's difficult in London right now for those of your faith. You knew about the king's proclamation last week?"

"Yes, Antony told me. All Romish priests, particularly Jesuits, to leave England by the first of May. Everyone but Father Huddleston, that is. I've been wondering about the Cuttlebones."

"Who are they? And who's Father Huddleston?"

"The Cuttlebones are the family we stayed with when we first went to London. They're darlings, but quite... well, fanatical. And thick as thieves with the Jesuits. I hope they come through all this. Father Huddleston's a priest but not a Jesuit. He's a special favorite of the king's. He helped his majesty escape from Cromwell years ago. And you're right about this being a reason to ship Sarah down here. With that big mouth of hers, Lord knows what trouble she may cause."

The younger girl's arrival gave Nancy just the opportunity she needed. Sarah's visit was ostensibly to oversee the making of a proper garden at Tassels—a task she set about with enthusiasm, even though it seemed a strange job for a woman. "There's a proper orchard back behind that well, Aunt Nancy. You can hardly see the trees for the weeds and such, but they're there. I've told Mr. Wadden we must start clearing that part tomorrow. And I want to remake all the beds in the front of the house this week too."

"Sarah! That's impossible. It's far too much work for a young girl and an old man."

"Two young girls. I told Laura she must help. She'll just have to let that Lord Sheldon ride without her for a few days."

"Even so. It's too much work."

Sarah shrugged. "Still, we may as well make a start. Maybe you can get a garden boy to help soon."

Nancy looked at her quickly. That was the perfect opening. "Yes," she said firmly. "Maybe I can. And the sooner the better."

Less than three quarters of a mile separated Sheldon Park from Tassels, but still Nancy had never seen it. Now she urged the horse forward and gingerly adjusted her position in the old cart. Michael Wadden had brought the simple rig to Tassels some weeks previously. "Be good thing t'ave, ma'am," he'd insisted. "Ye kin get about by yerself if'n ye want to."

"Like this!" Nancy demanded, laughing and patting her swollen belly. "Maybe you haven't noticed, Michael. I'm going to have a baby in September."

"I knows that, ma'am. Just why I wanted ye t'ave this 'ere cart. Easier fer ye than a saddle it is."

She'd merely shaken her head and thanked him. It was no good trying to tell the old man she had no need to travel. He'd meant kindly. And in the end she had let him give her some lessons in driving the thing. So today, when she had decided to pay a call on her neighbor, she had been able to set off without saying a word to anyone.

"Whoa," she called out as they neared the front gate. "Just hold up a bit, boy." Carefully she climbed down and tied the horse to a nearby tree. She had no intention of bringing this inelegant equipage all the way to Lord Sheldon's door. Far more dignified to walk the rest of the way and arrive on her own two feet. Besides, it gave her an opportunity to assess the house in a more leisurely manner.

The drive leading from the gate to the door was a broad avenue lined with sycamore trees. It was quite wide enough to take two carriages full abreast, but there was no indication that any such fashionable vehicles had ever been along this path. The ground beneath Nancy's feet was stony and uneven. Clumps of nettles grew everywhere, and she had to walk a jagged course to avoid their stinging touch. In one place a rotten tree blocked her way and she had to venture into the high grass at the side to avoid climbing over it. Blown down in a winter gale, no doubt, and left to lie where it fell. The trees that yet stood were huge monsters, untamed by human hand. In places they met overhead and created a dense canopy of foliage and damp shade. Nancy drew her shawl closer about her shoulders. The air seemed somehow colder than outside the gates. Less like spring. There was no sign of the house until the path took a sharp turn. Then Sheldon Park lay ahead of her like a fortress guarding some unknown treasure.

It wasn't built of the soft rosy brick that marked so much of the local architecture, but of flinty gray stone rather like the kind she had seen in Yorkshire. It was a low square building with two crenellated towers interrupting the symmetrical facade. There were slits for bowmen in the towers, and involuntarily she drew back. It wouldn't surprise her in the least to see an arrow aimed through one of those openings. Don't be silly, she told herself, and raised her chin defiantly. There was no turning back now. The front door loomed before her, a huge thing of black oak with studs as big as her fist and a knocker almost hidden by a mass of the vining ivy that grew everywhere.

"You'll not gain access through that door, madam," Antony Sheldon's voice said from somewhere behind her. "It hasn't been opened for at least fifty years. Come around to the side with me. It's far more hospitable."

She had thought of the place as a fortress, but once inside she changed that opinion. It was a crumbling ruin, a shell that would disappear at the first push. Everywhere the decay was obvious and ugly. Holes in the floors, patches of moss growing on walls that dripped with moisture, threadbare furniture twice as old and decrepit as that Clare had pitched out of Tassels. Only in the small study Lord Sheldon led her to did some sign of human habitation remain.

"Shocking old pile, isn't it?" he commented cheerfully. "This is my sanctuary. Please sit down, Mrs. Griffin. I can assure you that sofa is very comfortable. Now what can I get you? A glass of sack, perhaps? It's a fine light sort from Portugal. I recommend it."

"Thank you, that would be most welcome." She seated herself as gracefully as her condition permitted and tried to look around without being obvious. In this room the walls were paneled in elaborately carved oak. There were two glass-paned doors leading to a small terrace, allowing sunlight to enter. The satin curtains and upholstery thus illuminated were faded, but to Nancy they looked still beautiful.

Perhaps they were made so by contrast with the rest of the house. She reached gratefully for the etched goblet filled with wine. "What a beautiful glass!" she exclaimed as the light caught the beaker's pale-rose glow. "I've never seen anything like it before."

"Nor anything like Sheldon Park, I'd venture," he replied, smiling wryly. "The glass is Venetian and quite rare. The rest"—he made a broad gesture that took in all their surroundings—"is the product of Sheldon madness of one sort and another."

"Madness? I'm afraid I don't understand."

"Oh, not the usual sort. Not the kind that makes them cart you off and lock you away. At least not if you're a nobleman. But madness nonetheless. My great-great-grandfather built this place. In 1590, if you can credit it. He tore down a perfectly serviceable Tudor home and erected this stone folly in its place. He fancied himself one of the knights of the round table. We're a Cornish family originally, you see. Styled himself John Pendragon, the old man did. Do you know the reference?"

"Yes." Nancy nodded. "I've played Guinevere once or twice. Pendragon was meant to be Arthur's title, wasn't it?"

"Exactly. The title of any ancient Briton chieftain or king, if it comes to that. Anyway, John Pendragon's son, my great-grandfather, didn't enjoy the role bequeathed him. He went off to live in Italy and only returned a few years before he died. Brought a few treasures back, however. That glass among them. To continue the saga...am I boring you, Mrs. Griffin?"

"Not at all. Please continue."

He refilled her glass while he spoke. "Well, the next chapter's rather dull until the end. Great-grandfather's son, Grandfather Sheldon, also an Antony by the way, lived here as quite an ordinary lord-of-the-manor type. Even took his seat in the Lords on occasion. But he had little head for business or management. There was a terrible drought in 1637. It wiped him out, and he promptly did the honorable thing and hung himself. From that rafter over there, I'm told." Nancy couldn't avoid looking and shuddering. "Oh, don't worry, I've never seen or heard of his ghost anywhere near the place," his lordship said lightly. "That brings us to my father. He was the second son and would never have inherited the place except that like his ancestors the elder son did rather fancy himself a knight in shining armor. Rode

218

off to do battle in the Stuart cause and was promptly slain at Worcester in 1651. We came to live here then. My mother and father and myself. I'm an only child, you see. My parents both died some years before the restoration. So now you are brought to the present, when I am lord of Sheldon Park and live here in solitary splendor. Bit of an anticlimax, I'm afraid. But then, life isn't much like the theater, is it?"

"I'd hardly call you an anticlimax, milord." Nancy was glad of his long tale. It had given her time to collect her wits and get over the shock of her first impressions. "It is, how shall I put it, rather surprising to find you living amid all this ruined glory."

"And not giving two hoots about it, you mean?" Sheldon laughed. "No, don't apologize. You're quite right. I don't. I have my little retreat in here and my horses. I'm quite content to let Sheldon Park fall down around my ears. Besides, I have very little choice."

"Why do you say that?"

"Why indeed? A woman's question, my dear lady. A man, particularly a man of affairs like your husband, would know instantly. Because I haven't a farthing with which to do anything about it. The Sheldon estates are bankrupt, Mrs. Griffin. Impoverished. I inherited a huge mass of debt, nothing more. Does that answer your question? More important, is it the answer you came here to seek?"

"No." She ran a finger along the rim of the glass. It was incredibly delicate, yet gave an impression of strength. "Not exactly. But you're quite right in assuming I did come here seeking information."

"Not a difficult deduction. Considering you've never called before, and it can't be easy for a woman in your condition to walk even the short distance from Tassels."

"I didn't walk. I've a horse and cart tied up down below near the front gate. I left them there because they seemed so inelegant."

"Then you arrived and discovered that nothing could be poorer than this." He laughed loudly again. "I like you, Mrs. Griffin. I really do. You've a refreshing frankness that quite charms me. Will you have some more wine?"

"No, thank you. And do call me Nancy. I'm glad you approve my frankness, milord. It makes the next question easier."

"Wait." He held up a cautionary hand. "You may ask

219

whatever you wish. But only on the condition you call me Antony."

"Very well, Antony then. Now tell me, Antony, why are you leading my niece on in this fashion? It's quite callous of you. And I rather think you're not normally a cruel or callous man."

"Leading her on, Miss Laura? Is that what you think?"

"What else is there to think? You realize, I'm sure, that she fancies herself in love with you, wants to marry you."

"And you think that impossible in the light of all this"—once more the broad gesture that indicated all around him—"this not so genteel poverty."

"Not because of that. That would be a surmountable obstacle if you chose to put your mind to it, I'm sure. No, we both know that's not why you will never marry Laura."

For the first time he treated her to that dark look Clare had described after her first meeting with Antony Sheldon in the deserted cabin. Sinister she'd called it, frightening. Now Nancy knew what she meant. Sheldon's whole character underwent some instantaneous transformation. "What are you implying, madam?" he asked. The words were simple, but the tone carried more than a little threat.

"I'm not implying anything." She was trembling inside, shocked by her own boldness. Years of theatrical experience came to her aid; there wasn't a hint of fear in her voice or manner. "I'm simply telling you that I recognize your personal preferences. In view of them I find your pursuit of my niece quite surprising and unacceptable."

"My personal preferences.... You have a nice turn of phrase, my dear. But I'll not be fenced with. What do you mean?"

"Stop it!" She rose and mustered as much dignity as her pregnancy allowed. "I've known many men of your type. A number of them are my friends. Like you they prefer to love other men rather than women. It's your own affair as long as you leave Laura out of it."

There was a long silence. Sheldon poured himself another drink and drained it dry before he spoke. When he finally did, it wasn't to her, but to some vague point above her head. "Yes, I guessed you knew. I guessed it the first time I met you. I don't know why I put you to the discomfort of saying it outright. I fancy I just wanted to see if you'd courage enough to do it. My apologies."

"I don't want your apologies. Nor do I condemn you for

your peculiarities. They don't matter in the least to me. Laura does."

"Oh yes, Laura." He sank down in his chair and leaned his head back against its faded brocade. "How can I explain to you about Laura?"

"I wish you'd try. If you don't I'll have no choice but to inform her father of what's going on. He will doubtless take her away from here immediately."

"Why haven't you done that before?"

"Because it would break her heart, and leave a scar she would carry for a lifetime. I'd far rather see the business die a natural death. As I think it would if you simply tapered off your attentions to her. What can you possibly want from her, anyway?"

"How I wish I could make you understand. Laura is like a breath of fresh air. She's so totally innocent. So good. Being with her is like being born again. I can't see that I'm hurting her in any way."

"Not hurting her! By using her as a balm to ease your sordid conscience. You astound me, milord."

"Antony. And why should I astound you? Don't you think even reprobate old sinners like me require absolution?"

"That's your problem. I'll not allow you to use Laura in some weird rite of your own devising. She is innocent, just as you say. I plan to see she remains so."

"Very well. What are you going to do? Tell her everything so she'll shrink from me in horror?"

"Not unless you force me to it. I have no desire to do that either to her or to you."

"Then what do you suggest?"

"Only that you stop seeing her. At least seeing her so often."

"I don't think she would take that very calmly. She is fond of me, just as you say."

"She's besotted with you," Nancy amended frankly. "Very well, I admit if you just stopped taking her about it would be particularly hard on her. Say you continue to call, but don't take Laura riding around the countryside, just the two of you alone like lovers. Come to Tassels, but make some excuse. Say you can't ride for a bit. See her in my company. Her sister Sarah is there, too. That should help to temper things a bit."

"Yes," he said after a pause of some length. "Yes, I guess

it should. I will do just as you say, Nancy. I promise. I never intended Laura to be hurt, believe me."

"I do believe you. I knew that all along or I should never have come here." Then, just as she prepared to leave, Nancy remembered the excuse she planned to give at home for making this call. "There's one other thing. We're starting to work on the gardens at Tassels. They're in a terrible state, as you know. My younger niece, Sarah, is a passionate gardener, and she's overseeing the work, but she needs help. I wondered if you could recommend a lad I might hire as a gardener's boy."

"Yes, I'm sure if I think about it I'll come up with someone. Young boys are my specialty, as you've guessed." She was shocked, and it showed on her face. "There," he said, rising, "that was a stupid and insulting thing for me to say to you. You didn't deserve it, and I'm apologizing yet again. I don't pervert children, Nancy. It's not my style. I only said that in ... I don't know ... anger, I guess. Stop worrying. Everything will be arranged just as you wish."

She let herself out the same way he'd brought her in. The house was deserted, eerie. God, how could anyone live in such a place? And were there no servants? Did he stay here quite alone? Then, just as she started down the path, she saw the big groom, the simpleton called Jamie. He was sitting motionless on the grass beneath the window of Sheldon's private study.

8.

The next morning was marked by a horrific thunderstorm. A great crashing, shuddering gale caused the trees to sway in threatening arcs and rain to beat in sheets against the windows. By ten the Waddens still hadn't arrived, and Nancy suspected the road between their cottage and Tassels to be washed out. It occurred to her that she and the girls might be isolated for some days, a miserable prospect. Both her nieces were already impatient for the weather to clear and allow them their planned pursuits.

"You'll not go riding in this, surely," Sarah said to her sister.

"I don't know. It will depend on what Antony says. Anyway, I wish it would stop. Storms like this frighten me."

"They don't do the garden any good either. After all our work in the orchard, this is going to take down branches and what-all. It'll be an awful mess to clean." Sarah scowled at the elements as if she could frighten the sun into appearing.

Nancy smiled in spite of her concerns. This younger Griffin girl was a force to be reckoned with at the best of times. Imagine God's having the audacity to send weather that didn't please her. Immediately she was distracted from her private joke by a loud rapping at the front door. "Is that someone come to call?" she said in astonishment. "On a morning like this?"

"I didn't hear anything." Laura tried to peer out the window, but it was impossible to see through the rain. "Shall I open the door?"

"Yes, but be careful. It's blowing straight in that direction." Nancy moved little Nell's crib closer to the fire. "Still, I'm sure I heard someone..."

The last of her words couldn't be heard above the noise of the storm. The moment Laura released the bolt the huge door flung itself back against the wall as if it were a wisp of straw, and the wind screamed into the room, alive and terrifying.

A man stood on the threshold, bracing himself against the force of the gale, waiting to be invited inside. "It's Jamie, Aunt Nancy," Laura shouted over her shoulder as she pulled the caller out of the rain. "Antony's Jamie."

The big man allowed himself to be dragged just inside the entrance and no further. There he stood, dripping rivers of water onto the floor and grinning his sweet but vacant grin. "His lordship sent me, ma'am." He clutched an old cloth cap in one massive hand and bowed in Nancy's direction. "Him said you be needin' a garden boy."

"Yes, but..." Then, noting Sarah and Laura struggling to close the door against the wind, "There, Jamie, help them!" He moved slowly in the girls' direction, took the massive door in one hand, and shut it easily. By the time that was done Nancy had recovered from her surprise. She led him into the

223

kitchen, and gave him a hot drink and instructions to dry himself by the fire.

In the front room Sarah was hugging herself with glee. "He'll do just splendidly! We'll get an enormous amount of things done with that mighty Jamie to help."

"But what a strange choice," Nancy murmured. "I expected him to send some lad from the village, not his own groom."

"Well..." Laura still wasn't over her pique at the fact that yesterday her aunt had gone alone to call at Sheldon Park. "What did you expect? I've told you how very generous Antony is."

"So you have. According to Jamie, however, we won't have the opportunity to thank him today. He's difficult to understand, but I think he was trying to tell me Lord Sheldon has hurt his foot and will be laid up for a bit."

"Oh dear!" Laura reached for her shawl even as she spoke. "I must go and see if he needs anything."

"You'll do no such thing, young lady!" Nancy's manner left no room for argument. "I wouldn't dream of letting you call on a man by yourself. What would your mother and father say?"

The arrival of Jamie as resident garden boy was but the first of many surprises. Years later Nancy was to look back on that summer of '72 as a time of contrasts. Still, neither then nor in retrospect could she see any way they could be interpreted as a warning.

After that single terrible storm, the weather turned glorious and stayed so for weeks on end. It was a golden, halcyon time of gentle night rains and mellow sunny days. Sarah was in her element. With Jamie and Michael Wadden to help, she hacked at the wilderness surrounding Tassels, and gradually even city-bred Nancy could recognize the outlines of the charming country garden Sarah was creating. The girl grew nut-brown, positively oozing health and contentment.

Laura, on the other hand, was soon a wraith, pale and wan and given to unprovoked fits of weeping or temper. All due, of course to the sudden change in her relationship with Lord Sheldon. The week after the storm he arrived at Tassels with his foot bandaged and using a cane. "No riding for me for some months, I'm afraid," he announced ruefully. What was yet worse for Laura was that he made an obvious and

224

successful effort to avoid being alone with her from that day forward.

Nancy grieved for the child. She knew how painful the whole experience must be. But she knew too that it was better than the terrible disillusionment of the truth. Nancy disciplined herself to wait out the time that must pass before her niece would recover from her melancholy. One always adjusted to such things. Perhaps she might not have so deluded herself were it not for her own very expectant motherhood.

For Nancy, carrying this second child was a totally different experience from the first pregnancy. Then she'd been introspective and afraid; this time was remarkable for the ease and self-assurance she felt throughout. Having produced a Griffin as perfect and adorable as little Nell, she wasn't in the least nervous about a repeat performance. "You're still applauding the last act," she told Roger one June afternoon while he sat under an ancient apple tree and dandled his baby daughter on his knee. "You're bound to like the encore."

"I'm sure I will," he agreed, laughing at the child's efforts to clasp his waistcoat buttons. "After all, I'm the author of the play, aren't I?"

"Well, the co-author at least. I had a hand in it too."

"That wasn't your hand, if memory serves me."

"Rude man!" she exclaimed with mock fury. "Wait till I've a big handsome son to defend me, you won't be so cheeky then."

He grew serious, "It doesn't matter, you know. Whether or not it's a son, I mean. Another daughter like this one will do fine."

"Mmm... I can't say for sure this time. I knew Nell was a girl from the first. This baby's less, how shall I put it, communicative."

"Good God! Do you mean to say you have some kind of conversation with the thing before it's born?"

His awestruck tone amused her. "It's just not something any man can understand, darling," she said sweetly. She secretly hugged herself when he looked properly respectful of the mystery she and her sex shared.

Roger's participation in this pregnancy was wholly different from the last time. Her husband was attentive and excited, not secretly resentful and worried as he had been with Nell. He adored his daughter. Nancy doubted that he had ever anticipated taking such enormous pleasure from fatherhood. And they were closer now than they had been before. Some new element had entered their love, a kind of shared partnership. That mutual respect was the most exciting experience she'd ever had.

So Nancy blossomed with rosy good health throughout her pregnancy, while Laura wasted away to a shadow of her former self. It got so obvious that eventually Roger questioned his wife about it. "She's suffering from unrequited love," Nancy explained. "It's horrid for her, of course, but it will pass."

"Unrequited love?" He thought for a moment. "Do you mean that Sheldon chap? You must. There's no one else but Jamie and old Wadden around here, and I don't see either of them firing a young girl's heart."

"Yes, it is Lord Sheldon."

"I thought he was Antony to you."

"He is most of the time. What difference does it make?"

"None. Christ! What can she see in that fop? But if she does care for him, how come it's unrequited? Laura's a little beauty. At least she is when she's not mooning around here like a sick puppy dog. Why in hell shouldn't Sheldon respond to her? There's damned little else in these parts. Nothing in Laura's class, certainly."

Nancy shrugged and averted her eyes. She had no intention of telling Roger what she knew to be true. He was wildly intolerant of men like Antony Sheldon. It was a blessing he was too stupid about such things to recognize the man for what he was. "I can't say, really. Maybe he's just biding his time. Or thinks himself too old for her, or something like that."

To Laura she said nothing. In fact, she avoided giving the girl any opportunity to confide her feelings. Much better, she had decided weeks ago, to allow Laura to suffer her private misery until it burned itself out. Then it would be over and she'd be content to marry whomever her father selected. No point in indulging in endless heart-to-heart talks that would only serve to fan the flames of her passion. Yes, it wanted only time to put matters finally to rights.

And there were still other things to claim her attention, things that happened in the larger world outside Tassels. Most made their effects felt even in remote Surrey sooner or later. For one thing, after issuing that bitter condemnation and banishment of all "Romish priests and Jesuits" in early spring, King Charles proceeded during the summer to turn about and disband Parliament and promulgate a sweeping declaration of indulgence. "Freedom of conscience," he declared firmly, "is to flourish in this realm." So the pressure was off Clare and Mark, along with so many others, and Sarah could safely have been returned to London at any time. It was she who elected to remain at Tassels and get on with the gardens.

At the same time that he declared his subjects free to follow their own lights so far as God was concerned, the king chose to remind them of their express duty to him. Against all advice and disregarding the state of his finances, Charles declared yet another war against the Dutch. It proved an expensive and unpopular business. How much so Nancy, like the rest of England, wasn't to know for some months. What she did know as soon as Antony brought the broadside announcing the war into the house was that it was much better for Sarah to be here in the country than in a London that would soon feel the pinch of siege economics. "I've been through this kind of thing before," she reminded her nieces. "In no time you can't get this or that in the shops and all you hear is how many dead and wounded there are on our side or theirs. It's quite horrid."

"Will that affect Uncle Roger's business?" Sarah asked. "The part about not being able to get this or that in the shops, I mean?"

"Good Lord, Sarah, I don't know! I just never thought of it."

As it happened, two things had saved Griffin's Importations from disaster when this third war with the Dutch began. The one was the warehouse space in Wapping, the other the extraordinary fit of melancholy that overtook the Duke of York shortly after his wife died.

The first time Griffin took his newly acquired partner to see the firm's storage facilities, Ahmet had stood in openmouthed astonishment. "Good God, man! You could house all of Whitehall in here."

"You could indeed. That's what sold me on the place."

"But it's madness. We'll never fill it. Why pay for so much unused space?"

"You're being short-sighted. My dear Benjamin, it simply never works that way. I've been involved in operations like this time and again. The recurrent problem is never too much space but too little. You'll see I'm right, mark my words.

Anyway, it's a moot point. I already have a signed lease, as I've told you."

So no more was said about Wapping, though Roger knew full well it remained a nagging worry for Ahmet. That is, until after one of Roger's long visits with James.

These sessions had become frequent and demanding. York had lately taken to using his former aide as a kind of father confessor, much as the queen had been accustomed to do. What quality in himself made others trust him thus Roger couldn't say. But he did know that it could prove a bloody nuisance as well as embarrassing. James had developed an introspective and slightly mawkish streak. He would send word for Roger to meet him at some obscure tavern where he was drinking incognito, then proceed to keep him prisoner for hours while he rambled on about his dead wife, his motherless daughters Mary and Ann, and his general unhappiness. Only once did Roger dare to mention that York had a string of mistresses to solace him. It was a mistake. The duke had instantly grown angry and sullen. "I never expected that from you, Roger," he said bitterly. "I thought you understood that none of that casual fucking has any effect on how a man really feels. Feels in here, I mean!" He thumped his breast with vigor, and the subject wasn't raised again. But neither did that one fall from grace cause James to stop sending for Roger.

"I can't very well say no," he told Benjamin. "He's the king's brother, after all. Besides, I have a real fondness for James, though he can be an old woman sometimes."

"I should think," Benjamin replied in that slow careful way he adopted when discussing anything he considered serious, "the wisest course would be to cultivate the man. As you point out, he's the second-highest-placed fellow in the country. It may mean something, Roger. Wait and see."

When, two months before the official declaration of war, James told Roger what was to happen, Ahmet's advice proved its worth. "It's part of the treaty, you see," the duke explained in ale-thickened speech. "That treaty of Dover has many parts none but the king and I know about. Now this isn't for anyone else to hear, you understand, but you're a good lad, Roger. Charles and I owe you something. Mustn't let all your loyalty go unrewarded. Shabby thing, chasing you out of court. I'd never have done it. But I'm not the king. Won't matter if you get some special advance warning.... Going to be war, lad. Louis XIV and Charles against the Dutch. Sometime in summer. All arranged in the treaty. Be forearmed, my friend, now you're forewarned."

They bought every scrap of cargo they could lay their hands on. Coffee and spices from Arabia, dried fruits from Turkey, even a first-time venture into chocolate purchased from the Dutch through the good offices of some of Ahmet's relatives. A veritable flotilla of vessels of every nationality pulled into the Wapping docks and emptied their holds into Griffin's cavernous warehouse. Few besides Benjamin and Roger knew of that mounting treasure. The company representatives were told nothing; none of the precious goods were yet offered for sale. "Wait till there's little else," the partners told each other. "Only stave off the creditors and wait."

They'd gone into fearsome debt to finance the operation. Just about every goldsmith in London had their signatures on a due bill of one size or another. Then, just when there might have been embarrassing demands for payment, the war turned in favor of the Dutch.

York often told Roger that on the battlefield his French allies were his worst enemies. "Can't follow the simplest bloody order. Stupid bastards just don't know right from left. You'd have to see it to credit it, boy, take my word on it."

He'd not believed it at first. It sounded like more of James's perennial complaining. Events proved it the truth. Things went from bad to worse, and by the end of July merchantmen flying the English flag sailed in constant peril. Roger and Benjamin paid a visit to the floor of the Exchange and left wearing broad grins of overwhelming self-confidence. Trade goods were so scarce as to be almost nonexistent, fancy foodstuffs were conspicuous by their absence. "Send Kendal and his hounds out on the streets, my friend," Benjamin said softly. "I think the fox is ready for the kill."

By September they were practically the only traders in London with goods to sell. And the Wapping warehouse wasn't empty yet. To crown it all, they had managed to bring in two new shipments from Turkey via Lisbon. Ahmet's relatives and Roger's old Portuguese ally, Alphonso da Gama, were pressed into service for that arrangement. It cost dearly, of course, but it was worth it. The night that cargo finally arrived the partners went themselves to supervise the unloading. Once it was safely stowed away, Roger felt like a man riding the tail of a whirlwind. Nothing could stop them now. He was almost ready to make a move on Harwood. He'd even made a mental selection of the solicitor he would use to initiate the anonymous contact with John Lane.

They hired a boat to ferry them back as far as London Bridge, then walked some of the way together. "A good night's work, Roger," Benjamin said by way of leavetaking when they parted at the corner of Fenchurch Street.

"Yes, and more than that. We're a fine team, Benjamin— we pull well in the same harness."

The other man chuckled softly. "Oxen, are we? Well, I'd rather be hitched to you than any man in England. Goodnight, Roger."

"Goodnight, Benjamin." He watched the slight figure move into the shadowy street and wondered for a moment about Ahmet's home. In all the months of their partnership he'd never been invited there, never met the sister of whom Ahmet had spoken that first day. He shrugged and moved on. Jews were known to be an odd lot. For some reason best known to himself Ahmet chose to keep his business and personal lives wholly separate. So be it.

In the distance he saw a watchman's swaying lantern and heard him call out, "Midnight and all's well on a chilly evening!" Midnight was it? Later than he'd thought. And it was chilly. He'd be glad to get home to a hot drink and a night's rest.

But he wasn't to get to bed so quickly as that. Young Sam Ludlow had apparently returned from his weekly trip to Tassels. The lad was curled up on the floor in a corner of Roger's office when he let himself into the George Alley premises. The boy heard him and jumped up, rubbing sleep from his eyes, as he spoke. "I been waitin' for ye, cap'n. Thought ye'd want the news straight away. Mistress Griffin's had her baby, sir. Another girl it is. Born yesterday afternoon. Mistress said to tell ye babe's name is Jennifer and she's waitin' to introduce ye soon as ye can come."

He planned to leave for Surrey the following day, just as soon as he made sure everyone would be able to manage without him. "Have some wine, Benjamin," he insisted when his partner called in midmorning. "Help me celebrate. I'm a father again."

"Congratulations," Ahmet said warmly, accepting the drink and downing it in one gulp. "Boy or girl?"

"A girl. Nancy's named her Jennifer, I hear. She never waits to consult me about these children's names, you know. Cheeky little baggage, my wife. But in the circumstances I can hardly complain."

"Not when she's just presented you with a second 'proof of affection,' certainly. Your good health, my friend." Ahmet raised his refilled glass. "And that of your wife and child."

He hadn't emptied his tumbler before the door burst open. "I gotta see Cap'n Griffin!" a voice shouted. "Lemme through or I'll smash yer silly face in!"

"What the hell's this all about?" Roger raced to the outer room just in time to see a disheveled and agitated Michael Wadden pull back his ancient fist and threaten a clerk at least twice his size. "Here, hold on, Michael! What are you doing here? Are you drunk, you old villain? You'd better come in and explain yourself if you can."

He got Wadden into his private office, and sent Ahmet to restore order outside. Roger could make no sense of the drama. The man didn't seem drunk. He sank into a chair, and his energy and belligerence drained away. While Roger watched, the old man crumpled like a haystack in a stiff breeze. "I never seen the like," he muttered through a sudden gush of tears. "Never in all me born days. There he was hangin' there. Wot was left of him, that is....There was pieces of him spread round the floor. Just like a side o' beef, cap'n. Blood everywhere. Never thought a man could have so much blood in him. And the little gel just standin' with a scythe in her hands. And her all covered in blood too...."

The only indication of the sick terror churning inside Roger was his white-knuckled grip on the old man's shoulders. His words were calm and deliberate. "Wadden, listen to me, one thing first. Mistress Nancy and the babies—where are they?"

"At Tassels, cap'n. Ye don't unnerstan'. 'Tain't Mistress or babies wot's dead. 'Tis his lordship. Butchered like a cow he is. Miss Laura took a scythe to 'im."

PART FOUR

A Nest of Gold

The builders did not know the uses to which
their work would descend; they made a new
house with the stones of the old.... year by
year, generation after generation, they enriched
and extended it; year by year the great
harvest...grew to ripeness....

—Evelyn Waugh,
Brideshead Revisited

1.

"It's a lunatic idea." Nancy looked very pale and tired. She lay in bed among a great clutter of pillows, the newborn Jennifer clasped to her breast and young Nell's crib close beside. "It makes no sense. Laura couldn't have killed him."

"Hush, darling." He stroked the auburn hair back from her forehead and allowed one finger to trail along the infant's velvet cheek. "Don't think about it now. Just rest. I'll take care of everything."

"But you have to understand, to believe me. Laura couldn't do a thing like that. There are things you don't know about, things I haven't told you...."

"Please, love, you mustn't, not now. Won't you trust me? I promise you I'll put all this to rights."

"You won't let the sheriff take Laura?"

"Of course not. Now, here's Sarah with a drink for you." He turned gratefully to his young niece, accepted the tumbler she offered, and held it to Nancy's lips. "Take the baby, Sarah," he murmured softly. "Put her in the cradle there." Jennifer didn't seem to mind this. She murmured once, then settled into sleep. They waited until Nancy's eyes closed too, then tiptoed from the bedroom. "Where's Ellen Wadden?" Roger asked, his sense of urgency showing for the first time.

"Gone to the village to fetch a wet nurse. She tried to find one yesterday, but no one was available. They told her the Jenks girl was nursing a babe in the next valley, and she's supposed to be back today." Sarah's eyes were red-rimmed, but her voice was calm, her manner collected.

"Fine," he said firmly. "That's just what Nancy needs. Now you go sit with her until Ellen returns."

"Yes, I will, but she'll nap for some time now. That was a sleeping draft I just gave her. I found the recipe in the book Mama left in the stillroom."

"Good girl. And Sarah...you mustn't worry. It's going to be all right. I'll see to that."

"Please, Uncle Roger." Her eyes were full of tears now; the surface calm was crumbling. "You must find Laura. Please."

"When did you see her last?"

"Not since..." She struggled with the words. "Since Michael ran into the house shouting about what was in the barn. I didn't understand what he was talking about, so I went out to see. Laura was standing there. I didn't say anything, I couldn't. She just looked at me, then ran. I...oh God! It was so horrible."

He hugged the girl for one fierce, protective moment. "All right, Sarah, don't give way now. Go sit with your aunt. I'll take care of everything."

It was easier said than done. The one thing Wadden had done before riding to London to fetch him had been to swing shut the big doors of the barn and draw the heavy bolt. When they arrived together back at Tassels the old man had looked at the place and said, shuddering, "I ain't goin' in there agin, cap'n. Ain't nothin' could make me."

"No need. Go into the house and get something to drink. Then make sure all the fires are tended. After that you can get some rest. But don't leave, Michael. I may want you. There's a cot in the dairy, isn't there? You can get a couple of hours' sleep." Then he'd gone to see his wife and his new daughter.

Now the moment could be put off no longer. He'd have to see for himself what had happened in the barn. Next he'd have to find his niece. After that he would decide what to do.

God knows he'd seen gore in plenty before this, on battlefields in France and Spain, on the deck of a fighting ship under fire. Many a time he'd stood his ground while men were writhing in death agony at his feet. When the Great Fire swept the city there were miraculously few people killed, but he had never forgotten one man he'd seen run from a burning house with his clothes in flames and his mouth open in an endless, tortured scream. None of that prepared him for the scene inside the barn.

What was left of Antony Sheldon hung on a great hook stuck into a rafter far overhead. His feet were just at Roger's eye level. At least they would have been if he'd still had

235

them. They'd been cut from the ankles and left sprawled at grotesque angles beneath the body. One severed arm lay nearby, next to a hunk of unidentifiable flesh that was covered with flies. It was less than twenty-four hours since Wadden had discovered the murder, but the blood was dried now, rust-colored and flaking from the floor beneath Roger's feet.

He'd expected a stench, but there was none. The cool weather, no doubt. Somehow the absence of any smell made the scene more horrible, more unreal. It was as if he were looking at some mad artist's conception of hell. Only the open staring eyes convinced him this was really a man who'd once lived and breathed, a man he'd known. "Sweet Christ," he murmured at last and turned to go. He didn't know if he was cursing or praying, only that he couldn't remain in this place a moment more.

Then, just before he reached the door, he stumbled over something lying in his path. Part of him didn't want to know what it was; another part, more compelling, insisted that he look closer and see. It was one more lump of dismembered flesh. Unbelieving, he prodded the thing with his toe. Sheldon's genitals, penis and testes still intact, almost free of blood. They'd been cut from him with what appeared one clean blow of that scythe now standing neatly propped against the wall. Roger stumbled into the open air and vomited his guts into a clump of gilly flowers.

"I put the scythe back in its place," she said softly. "Mama always says it's important to return things to their proper place."

He wanted to say something, but no words came. Laura sat before him on the floor of the cabin. Her dress was covered with ugly dark blotches. Blood, he realized, and caught himself idly wondering if the stains had seeped through to her petticoat. With an involuntary shudder he forced himself back to reality and reached out a hand to his niece. "Come, Laura," he said quietly. "We must go home now. Everyone's worried about you."

"Are they? Yes, of course. I'm sorry, I didn't mean to be any trouble." Her voice was that of a very young child. "Is Papa there?"

"Your father's in London, Laura. You know that."

"Oh yes. I remember now. We're not at the Hall any longer, are we?" She rose and reached out to take his hand. Hers was caked in dried blood. Roger fought against a return of that terrible wrenching nausea. Whatever Laura had done, she was his niece, his responsibility. He made himself avert his eyes and take her hand. Then he led her from the cabin.

Earlier, when he remembered this place young Charles had shown him some months before, it had been still afternoon. Now it was dusk, a peculiar purple twilight that he'd noticed before in these woods. Somewhere an owl called mournfully. That and the noise of dried leaves crunching beneath their feet were the only sounds. Laura stopped in the middle of the path and said without expression, "Have you seen them, Uncle Roger?"

"Seen who?" he asked gently. He expected her to refer to some persons out of the past. People from Harwood, probably. Just as she'd inquired about her father a few minutes ago. Laura seemed completely removed from the present horror.

Instead she said, "Why, Antony and Jamie, of course. They're both dead, you know. I tried and tried to make them alive again, but it wasn't any use."

"Jamie…" Careful, he told himself. She doesn't know what she's saying, what she's done. God knows how she'll react if she really remembers. "Jamie's all right, Laura. I'm sure he is." It occurred to him even while he spoke that he hadn't seen the big man since arriving at Tassels. No one mentioned him either.

"Is he? That's marvelous! But how can he be? The knife was in so deep. I tried to pull it out, but it wouldn't come."

He felt faint again. He was acting like an old woman, dammit! Must pull himself together. Must find out what she was talking about."Where was he, Laura, when you saw the knife?"

"In the barn, of course. Way in the back. He'd been spying on us. That's why…oh my God!" In the half-light he could see the change come over her face, as the memory revived in her mind. "Blessed Mother of God," she whispered. "Help me." Then, with her head thrown back and her mouth open in a scream that seemed to come from somewhere deep in her bowels, "Help me…"

2.

She was unconscious when he carried her back to the house. He kicked the front door open and shouted for Sarah. Then, noting her face when she came in and saw Laura in his arms, he feared he might have a second hysterical female to deal with. "Don't panic, for God's sake. She's just fainted."

He deposited the girl on a sofa. "Now listen to me, Sarah. There are a great many things to be done. Important things, if we're all going to survive this situation. With Nancy as she is you're the only one I can rely on. Will you help? And keep your wits about you no matter what?"

The girl took a deep breath. She was only fifteen, after all. Nothing, not even two years of living as a fugitive, had prepared her for this. Finally she said quietly, "Tell me what I'm to do, Uncle Roger."

"Good girl." He tilted her chin with his hand and managed a smile. "When all this is over I'll take you off somewhere, just the two of us, and you can have your own private rip-roaring session of hysterics." He saw her attempt at a grin and felt a real pride in the child's determination to soldier on.

Then they both heard Laura groan. Roger looked anxiously toward her. It didn't suit his plans to have Laura conscious now. "First thing," he told Sarah, "go to the stillroom. Make up that same sleeping potion you made Aunt Nancy earlier. But do it double-strength. Now hurry!"

He waited until she was gone to step to Laura's side. Obviously she'd soon be awake. He looked ruefully at the girl, such a delicate creature. He must be very careful not to do permanent damage. Slowly he drew back his fist and landed a delicate blow square on her chin. Laura didn't make a sound.

"Here it is." Sarah returned, carrying a tankard. "I made it as strong as I dared."

"And you were quick, too. You're doing fine, Sarah." He took the drink from her and forced it slowly down Laura's throat. "Have to be careful not to choke her," he explained. "She's still unconscious. Now, I forgot to ask you before. Is Ellen back?"

"Yes. And Maude Jenks too. They're with Aunt Nancy now. Maude's got plenty of milk, so that's all right, but they have to be sure baby Jennifer will nurse from her."

He hardly listened. Women's business. His concerns were of a different nature. "There, she's drunk the lot. Now, Sarah, I'm going to carry her to your room. Then I'm going to bring up a big kettle of water and you're to bathe her from head to toe. Thoroughly, you understand. There must be no . . ." He hesitated.

"I know," the girl said. "No traces of blood left. I'll do it."

He looked at the child with new respect. When all this was over he'd find some way to tell her how proud he was of her behavior. "Right. After you've done that I want you to take every scrap she has on and burn it. In the kitchen fire or in here. Wherever you can manage to do it without being seen. That's important, Sarah. No one must see you."

"I understand everything, Uncle Roger. Let's just stop talking and get on with it."

It took him half an hour to get things ready so Sarah could carry out his instructions. After that he was quite sure he could safely leave Laura to her younger sister. Ellen and the wet nurse were still in the bedroom with Nancy. Michael Wadden was asleep on the cot in the dairy, an empty tankard by his side.

Roger decided that was a very good idea indeed. But he wanted something stronger than ale. A few weeks ago he'd brought down a bottle of that French brandy he'd been introduced to by Ahmet. He was acquiring a real taste for the stuff. Yes, it was still in the larder where he'd left it. He poured himself a generous portion and stood for some moments before mustering the courage to do what he must. Then he turned on his heel and made for the barn. Much as he hated to do it, he had to check on Laura's claim that the charnel house outside concealed not one but two bodies.

Ten minutes later he was back in the kitchen downing

another very stiff brandy. This time he'd retched until he thought he'd strangle, but he hadn't actually vomited. More important, he'd discovered what he went to look for, Jamie's body. Just where Laura had said it was. For almost an hour he remained staring into the fire in deep thought.

He led the man to the very back of the barn and pointed to the big figure crumpled behind a half-rotted timber partition that had once marked a horse stall. In death Jamie looked no less vacant than he had in life, but, compared to the carnage all around him, his was a clean and simple dying. He lay curled up like an infant in a cradle. One hand still clutched the handle of the pruning knife that was buried up to the hilt in his chest.

"Killed himself, captain, that's what you think?"

"I do, sheriff. Moreover, my niece confirms the story. She ran in here when she heard the screams and tried to stop this butchery. Naturally she could do nothing."

"Naturally. Terrible experience for a young girl, I imagine."

"Indeed. She's been put to bed. You do understand that I'm reluctant to have her questioned about the matter again."

"Of course, Captain Griffin. Besides, all this is quite self-explanatory. Shall we, er...go outside?"

They hurried into the garden. There was a stench in the barn now, fetid and overpowering. Two days had made rot inevitable. Roger wiped his face with a silk handkerchief and noticed that the sheriff was trying hard not to retch. "Jamie wasn't to blame for his actions, you understand," Griffin said. "He was a mindless chap. Lord Sheldon kept him on as a kindness. A few months back his lordship sent Jamie here as a favor to my wife. She needed someone to help with the garden work."

"Lord Sheldon was a friend, then?"

"Indeed. As well as a neighbor. Apparently he came to call on the day of the tragedy and somehow Jamie lured him into the barn. As to what came over the poor imbecile to make him do that"—he gestured in the direction of the bodies—"I really can't say."

"Doubtless we'll never know. Thank you for your time, captain. I'm most sincerely sorry you've had all this unpleasantness. Please convey my regrets to your goodwife. I'll have the bodies removed today."

240

"He believed the story, then?" Nancy pulled herself up in the bed and looked intently at Roger. He'd thought to keep all this from her, but she insisted on knowing.

"Yes. I'm sure he did. Sent you his compliments and apologized for the 'unpleasantness.' He's an ambitious chap, wants to rise in the world. Before sending for him I made sure of that. And that he knew something of my affairs in town."

"Tell me something else, Roger. Do you believe it?"

He sat back in his chair and thought for a few moments before answering. When he spoke his voice was low and controlled. "Perhaps the truest answer is that I more or less believe it. I'm convinced that Laura didn't kill him. Once the shock passed and I thought about it, it didn't make sense. First of all, she'd never have had the strength to..." he stopped speaking. He'd avoided discussing the details with Nancy, and he didn't want to do so now.

"You needn't be so reticent, darling," she said softly. "I know the story. How they found him, I mean. Ellen Wadden told me. Michael told her."

"Damn the old hag! Doesn't she know better than to upset you at this time?"

"Shh, it's all right. I wanted to know. Weren't you going to say that Laura wouldn't have had the strength to wield that heavy scythe?"

"That, yes. More important, she'd not have been able to get him up on that high hook. Sheldon must have weighed close to one hundred and eighty pounds. But since we're talking about it, I'd best be frank. I said 'more or less true.' Not the whole truth. Oh, I think Jamie did the actual murder. He had the necessary strength. Moreover, I don't doubt he killed himself in a fit of terror and remorse afterward. But Laura's role in the affair is less clear. I don't for a moment believe that she merely happened on the scene. What provoked Jamie, Nancy? What part did Laura have in that?"

Two days later he still hadn't answered the question to his own satisfaction. What's more, Nancy had grown suddenly reluctant to discuss the matter. On his instructions Sarah was yet keeping Laura asleep most of the time. It seemed to him necessary to get the entire business expunged from Tassels, at least in a physical sense, before letting the girl regain consciousness and do battle with her demons. He'd never forget what he'd seen on her face that one moment in the woods when she'd suddenly recalled the whole horrifying scene.

The sheriff had been as good as his word. Both bodies were gone. Jamie had been carted away to a common gravesite outside the village. Antony Sheldon, albeit in pieces, was removed to his appointed place in the family vault at Sheldon Park.

Now Roger wanted to go up to London, even if it was only for a day. There were things that needed his attention. He couldn't expect Benjamin to carry the whole load indefinitely. The only thing stopping him was Nancy. He didn't know how she'd react to his leaving just yet. But she didn't seem to mind when he mentioned it. "Don't worry about us," she said firmly. "Now that I'm up and about we can manage very well."

"I don't want you doing too much. But it will only be for a day or so. Just to check on things. I'll return as quickly as I can. I think I'd best be here when Laura finally wakes up."

His wife looked at him pensively. "You needn't worry about that either," she said. "I've done a lot of thinking. I'm fairly sure I have the whole thing puzzled out. I can deal with Laura."

He was incredulous. "Have you? Then you're a damn sight smarter than I. I can't make any explanation fit all the facts. Of course I know she was infatuated with him, felt rejected. You told me all that months ago. But how does Jamie fit in? And that horror out there...something more than a young girl's fancy had to be involved in that." He saw her shudder. "Sorry, I shouldn't have mentioned it."

"No, it's all right. And it does fit. When you know all the facts, as I do."

"Then tell me, for God's sake!"

"Not now, Roger. Not until I've spoken to Laura. I owe her that. In a way I'm partly responsible. Roger, I can't say any more just now. Please be patient with me, trust me just a little bit."

He sighed. "As you wish. At least until I get back. One other thing—I've been wondering, should I send word to Clare when I'm in London?"

Nancy shook her head. "Not yet. Just a few more days, Roger, please."

"Yes, very well. But there's one matter I won't wait on. I've given Michael instructions to burn the barn. Down to the ground. I don't want any of us to see that place again. I certainly don't want Nell or Jennifer ever to hear about it."

Nancy looked over at the sleeping babies and had to smile. "Don't worry, darling. They are the two people in this house least likely to be affected by any of this."

3.

"We have to talk about it, Laura."

The girl shook her head and turned to stare out the window. Then, sensing Nancy's determination, she said, "I don't want to talk about it ever."

"But that's the very worst thing you can do, my dear. How can I make you understand..." She smoothed the hair back from the girl's brow. The fever was gone, but Laura still looked terribly ill; ashen skin and eyes burning with some strange and terrible light. "Laura, at least listen to me. There are things you don't understand, don't even know about. I kept them from you because I wanted to spare you heartbreak. In a way much of this is my fault."

"That's ridiculous. You don't know what happened. You weren't there. It's my fault, all of it. I shall burn in hell as a murderess." There was little expression in her voice, only a terrible certitude.

"Now you're being ridiculous. You didn't kill Antony. You couldn't have."

"I didn't..." She shuddered but went on speaking. "I didn't actually wield the weapon, if that's what you mean. But I killed him. Jamie too. It doesn't matter now. It's done, and talking won't undo it. Where's Sarah? She promised not to leave me."

"I sent her away. What I have to say is for your ears only. It isn't Sarah's business. Look at me, Laura." Nancy left her chair to sit on the bed and put both her hands on the girl's shoulders. "There's one thing you don't know, unless Antony told you before he died. Do you understand about the kind of man he was? Do you?" She was almost shaking those frail shoulders in her desperation to break through the barriers Laura had erected.

"He was a good and kind man. What else is there to know?"

"One other very important thing. Antony Sheldon was in one way a deviate. Different from most men. He could love only other men. Don't look at me like that, Laura. It's the truth. Surely you must heard of such things before."

"I don't...yes, I think so. I heard Papa talking once. But that's absurd. Antony wasn't mad. You know he wasn't."

"I never said he was. Such things aren't madness. It's only the stupid and naive who think they are. I've known many men like that over the years, Laura. Some of the players in the King's Company are like that. They aren't mad either."

"But how can you know if that was true of Antony?"

Nancy took a deep breath. This was the part she most dreaded explaining. How would Laura react to having been manipulated? Would she see it as a betrayal by someone she had trusted? There was no pulling back now no matter what the outcome might be. "I recognized this taste in Antony almost from the first moment I met him. As I told you, I've known many men of that stripe. When you told me he never kissed you or made any mention of the future in spite of all the time you spent together I knew I was right. The day I went to Sheldon Park alone I told him my suspicions to his face."

"And...?" She was staring intently at Nancy now, obviously wanting to know in spite of herself.

"And he admitted I was right. Flat out. There could be no mistake, Laura."

"Then why was he so attentive to me? If he didn't like women, why did he court me?"

"It was just that I wanted to know. That's why I went and confronted him as I did. I told him he was being grossly unfair to lead you on as he had." She took both Laura's hands in her own, hung on tight all the while she spoke. "He admitted his behavior had been quite reprehensible, but he also told me how deeply he cared for you. That's the part I so want you to understand, Laura. Antony wasn't capable of loving you as a normal man loves a woman, but he did love you in his own fashion. That's why he sought out your company."

"He did until after your visit to Sheldon Park. I never connected his later coolness to me with that until now. There was a connection, wasn't there, Aunt Nancy?"

"Yes. It's very hard for me to tell you this now, Laura. After what's happened I think I did a terribly wrong thing. It might have been better just to let matters come to a head on their own. As it was I wanted to protect you. I didn't want that experience to sour you on life. So I insisted that Antony stop seeing you alone. I made him promise me he would."

"And poor daft Jamie? What had he to do with it all?"

"From my point of view, nothing. At least so I thought. Now I see it was something different...." Her voice trailed off. She hadn't enough courage to say more just yet. "I asked for a garden boy. I'd no idea he would send Jamie. When he did I'd no idea what it meant."

"But now you do?" Laura had settled back against the pillows. Her attention seemed to be wandering again. "It doesn't matter. Nothing will bring them back."

"But it does matter! It matters because you are blaming yourself for something that was set in motion long before you ever knew Antony Sheldon. Listen to me, Laura! I'm convinced that Jamie was Antony's lover. He must have felt terribly rejected when Antony sent him to work here. But that's got nothing to do with you. I don't know why Antony did it either."

"His lover?" Laura was staring at her, understanding slowly dawning in her eyes. "You mean they did things together? Things a man and woman normally do?"

"Yes. I suspect it had gone on for years. Certainly since long before any of us came to Tassels."

Suddenly Laura was giggling. Harsh, humorless sounds spilled from her lips until she shoved her fist in her mouth to stop them. "And you think..." She was breathless, struggling to speak between unbidden hysterical gulps of laughter. "You think that absolves me of blame for what happened?"

"Of course it does. You must see that."

"Oh no, Aunt Nancy. No. I told you before, you don't know what happened. You see..." She was crying now, great tears rolling down her cheeks. "I lured Antony to the barn on the pretext of needing help with a garden tool. I told him I couldn't lift the scythe, asked him to get it for me. I didn't even know Jamie was in there." She raised herself to her elbows, staring at Nancy, unable to stop the flow of words. "Then I threw myself at him. Literally. I flung my arms

245

around his neck and kissed him, told him I loved him and asked why he'd been ignoring me. I didn't care how shameless it was. I just wanted to make him notice me again. And he kissed me back. Not just once but three times. He kept saying he loved me. That's when Jamie ran out from the back of the barn. That's when it happened."

She lay back exhausted. "I didn't know why the poor daft thing reacted so. It never dawned on me he was jealous. I only knew that something I'd done had caused him to go totally mad. Now I understand it all. Thank you, Aunt Nancy."

"But..." She had wanted to convince the girl she was blameless. Instead she had given her proof of her own suspicions. "But it wasn't just that. It couldn't have been."

Laura held up a small, thin hand to silence her. No matter what she did, Nancy couldn't make her discuss it further.

"How are things at home, Roger?"

"A bit calmer. It's been pretty horrible, however. Our neighbor, one Antony Sheldon, got himself hacked to pieces by one of his lunatic servants. Chose our barn to do it in, unfortunately."

"Not very neighborly," Ahmet said wryly. "And not very English. Doesn't sound a bit like your usual reticent and so polite manner."

"The fires burn below the surface, Benjamin, but they're there. Never doubt it."

"I begin to see how right you are. I've news for you too. Have you heard yet about James?"

"The Duke of York? No, nothing. What's he done?"

"Well, if the rumors are to be believed, gone over to Rome."

"What? Do you mean he's become a papist? Who says so?"

"Just about everyone. Apparently it happened some time past and he's managed to keep it a secret until now. The influence of the dying duchess, they claim. He's not taken Anglican communion for months. Seems last Sunday in the Royal Chapel the vicar made a great point of the fact. Preached on how the taking of the sacrament was a necessary thing for all good Protestants. James got up and walked out."

Roger sat down heavily and ran his fingers through his hair. "We must look quite mad to you," he said finally. "We so-called Christians. What a fine thing we make of the message of love and salvation we claim to have from God."

"In my experience," Ahmet said and shrugged, "it doesn't do to hold God responsible for the actions of his so-called followers. It can easily make one a devil worshiper. Have a brandy."

"Have you any idea what this will mean if it's true?"

"I can guess. James is heir to the throne, since Charles has no legitimate son. I wonder what the good English public will make of the possibility of another Catholic sovereign. How long has it been?"

Roger did some hasty calculations. "If I remember my lessons, Mary Tudor died in 1558. That makes it a hundred and what...fourteen years? They called her Bloody Mary, and with good cause. There's few will welcome the idea of a repeat performance."

"We can but hope that good King Charles has a long and healthy life. Shall we drink to that?"

Roger rose and smiled only a little cynically. "The king," he said, lifting his glass.

"The king." Benjamin took a long deep swallow, then raised his glass again. "And to Griffin's Importations. May its fortunes be as felicitous as those of his majesty."

"But they can't really be certain about James." Nancy took his hand and led him farther along the path between the apple trees. "Besides, what difference does it make, really? Why must it be such an issue?"

"They're certain enough. And James looks to be the next king unless Charles outlives him. No one any longer hopes that poor Catherine will produce a legitimate heir. Speaking of which, I've another tidbit will interest you. Louise de Kéroualle presented Charles with a son a while back. The king has owned the child as his."

"Oh dear...poor Nell. Have you any word of her?"

"Nothing specific. I only know she's still in her Pall Mall house and they say Charles yet calls there regularly."

"Still, she'll be hurt. She really cares so much for him. I wish I could go and see her."

"Why can't you? Jennifer's getting on all right with the wet nurse, isn't she? And I've been thinking. You should hire someone to take charge of the babies. A proper children's nurse. We can afford that these days."

"That's a good idea, but even so, I wouldn't leave Tassels now. There's Laura and Sarah to consider."

247

"Send them back to their mother in London. It's where they belong, after all."

"No, Roger, it isn't that simple." She drew him to a sawn-off tree trunk that acted as a bench in this still-wild section of the garden. "You see, I must tell you the whole story now. Much as I hate to talk about it."

He stared at the ground in silence for some moments when she finished speaking. "What I can't understand," he said finally, "is how you allowed the situation to progress to that state."

"But I didn't. Once I realized how serious Laura was becoming I put a stop to it, just as I told you."

A chance breeze blew a clutter of dead leaves over his boots. They made a soft rasping sound. Roger stared at them, a thin white line etching his set mouth. He seemed to be considering his words, controlling them perhaps. "Your way of stopping the situation was to allow Sheldon to visit here whenever he wished? To take his servant into the house as garden boy?"

She wanted to reply, but he gave her no opportunity. "Nancy, this story you've told me is so incredible I can't find words to tell you everything I'm thinking. Perhaps it's better if I don't. You are mistress here. When I'm in London the full responsibility for our children and this household is yours. On top of that you've made yourself guardian to my nieces, despite my early objections to that situation. Now you tell me you gave hospitality to a man you knew to be capable of the most base perversions. And that bad judgment ended in a gruesome murder. It's mind-boggling!"

His voice had been low and controlled throughout the speech. Nancy stared at the ground, not daring to look at him, choked with the words of her own defense and too furious to utter them. Then, before she could say anything, Roger rose and started to walk away.

Suddenly he turned back to her. "If you've made such a botch of running this simple little place, how are you to manage when we're back at Harwood Hall? That's the question I'm asking myself now. It's not a pleasant query for a man to have about his own wife."

4.

October. The charred remains of the old barn lay like a black
scar on the earth. Some days, if the wind and the sun were
right, they still smelled of burning. Laura hadn't seen the
actual blaze, but often she would go and stand beside the
ruins for hours at a time. Silent, introspective, she seemed
bent by the weight of her burden of sadness and guilt. A few
times Nancy tried to talk to her, but she gave it up. It was
impossible to break through the girl's shell.

Besides, the whole terrible business had left Nancy with
a deep unhappiness of her own to bear. To be sure she felt
some guilt for the deaths of the two men, but that she could
have accepted more readily than the acrid disappointment
engendered by Roger's reaction, just when she'd thought
things were going so well between them. Still, they had
achieved a truce of sorts within days of that bitter scene in
the orchard; the matter simply wasn't mentioned again. But
she knew Roger's feelings, and that knowledge was like a
suppurating wound.

Perhaps it was unhappiness which caused her to throw
herself into the day-to-day management of Tassels with a
fervor and zeal even greater than she'd displayed before. First
she followed Roger's advice and engaged Maude Jenks as
full-time nurse for the two babies. The children knew and
liked her, and she was an easygoing, loving sort. Nancy's
next move was to find a lad in the village, Thomas Harvey,
and hire him as garden boy and general dogsbody.

There was a second barn near the house, one that hadn't
been involved in the tragedy and had thus been allowed to
remain standing. Once when Roger returned for his now customary weekend visit he was astounded to find installed in
that rickety structure a gentle old milch cow, a nameless

local breed of soft golden hide and brown eyes. "Have you taken up farming?" he asked her incredulously.

"Not really. She's a good milker. Her name's Sally, and she supplies us with milk, cream, butter, and cheese. Young Tom tends to her."

"I see. And does this paragon of a lad do the churning and cheese making too?"

"Of course not. The girls and Ellen and I do that. We take turns. It works quite well."

"Ah yes, the girls. I've been thinking of that, Nancy. In spite of what I've said in the past I don't mind their being here with you now. That little Sarah is as tough and brave as more than half the men I've known. But it is a funny kind of arrangement. Don't their parents expect them to return home?"

"Yes, they do. I had word from Clare just this week. Laura and Sarah will be leaving the end of the month. They're just staying until then to help with the pickling and preserving. Sarah's vegetable gardens yielded very well indeed. We've a lot to put by for the winter."

"I see." He noted her preoccupied look and watched while she wandered off, ruffling through the big stack of household linen in her arms. Strange things were happening to Nancy. It was as if she was using this little country house and its mundane demands as setting for a new role she'd decided to play. In some ways he didn't like the new role as well as he had the old.

That night, upstairs in the big bed that dominated the now fully furnished master bedroom, he was reminded of that thought again. She yielded to his embraces willingly, but he couldn't rid himself of the idea that somehow Nancy was removed from him, holding back some part of herself he'd once possessed but did no longer. At the same time he found her yet more physically attractive. Motherhood had rounded some of the angular, boyish quality of her figure. The breasts were as high and firm as before, but her hips had widened, softened. To Roger the change was remarkably appealing— especially since it had been brought about, in a sense, by him. It was a bit as if he were some kind of god, fashioning a woman in his own image.

He nuzzled her neck and ran his finger lightly over the ivory skin of her midriff. "You smell delicious," he murmured. She smiled but didn't answer. "Let me throw back these coverings. I want to look at you."

"In the dark?"

"It's not dark. I can see you in the firelight. I know when you're smiling." Impulsively he sprang from the bed and padded naked across the carpet to the hearth. "Here, this'll make it even better." He tipped a full bucket of coal on the small blaze and waited until it flared up with a satisfying roar. "Now you can't be too cold," he said as he flung the blankets back from the bed and stood surveying her.

It was a moment when he would have expected her to stretch out her arms, make some show of desiring him as much as he obviously desired her. Instead she merely lay waiting, a languorous smile still on her lips. Suddenly, irrationally, he was angry. Without another word he covered her body with his and forced himself deep inside her without preamble of endearments or caresses. He heard her one sharp intake of breath and knew he'd hurt her. That didn't prevent him from raising and lowering his body over hers with greater and greater ferocity until, with a deep groan of satisfaction, he emptied himself into her belly.

He was thoroughly ashamed of himself then, and searched for some way to apologize. Nancy never gave him the opportunity. "Roger," she said matter-of-factly moments after he'd rolled off her to lie panting on his own side of the bed, "do you think you could bring me a few things from London when you come next week? I'd really like to have some of those nice bits you and Benjamin supply to all the households in town. Some figs and dates, perhaps. And maybe a hundred-weight of sugar. You could carry it all if you came by boat."

He brought the things she had requested the following Saturday, but by then she'd lost interest. A new and startling piece of information had reached Tassels in his absence, and Nancy was waiting for him in the big front room when he arrived. "Leave all that," she said quickly. "Just here in the hall. Ellen will see to it. Come, I've a hot drink waiting for you. The fire's lovely and warm, too. You must be cold."

She let him get his cloak off and down a tankard of mulled wine before she continued, but he could see impatience and excitement written all over her. "What is it?" he asked at last. "You've obviously got something you're dying to tell me. Not expecting again, are you?"

"No." She shook her head. "At least I don't think so. Anyway, it's nothing ordinary like that. It's much more serious.

Here, read this." She handed over a sheet of thick vellum paper, and the first thing he noted about it was the elaborate engraved heading. "Messrs. Timothy, Timothy, White, and Parsons," he read. "Solicitors and Representers of All Matters Legal to Lords, Ladies, and Gentlemen of Property. 27 Lincoln's Inn." He glanced over at his wife. She stood before the fire, tall and quite composed. Her long auburn hair was twisted into a bun atop her head, and her hands were folded primly at her waist. "Very impressive heading," he commented.

"Read it," she said quietly.

"Dear Madam," the letter began. "We have pleasure to inform you that we are attorneys to the late lamented Antony Blair Sheldon, Lord Sheldon, and as such are charged with executing all the instructions of his lordship's will after his lordship's untimely demise. You will doubtless be interested to learn that the last codicil to that will, created just a month before his lordship passed on, concerns yourself. In it you are made heir to that portion of the estate consisting of the house known as Sheldon Park and the land which runs between said house and that property known as Tassels, currently belonging to you by quitclaim deed tendered by his most gracious majesty Charles II.

"Be informed, most honored lady, that we await instructions from you as to the proper and convenient time of conveyancing the said house and lands to your ownership. If you would favor us by having your own solicitors call at our chambers, the matter can be expeditiously arranged.

"We remain, madam, your most humble servants,

"Timothy, Timothy, White, and Parsons."

"Bloody hell..." Roger said, sitting down hard in the nearest chair.

"Quite," Nancy agreed. She poured another glass of wine.

"But it's absurd! You must see that."

"No, I don't. Why is it absurd?"

"Because..." Roger ran his fingers through his hair and made a determined effort to control his temper. There was little to be gained from simply insisting she forget the whole thing. There'd be no peace in their lives if he did that. He had to make her understand the full problem. "Look, love, you can't just say, 'Thanks very much, that'll do nicely,' and go on as before. Accepting something like this is very complicated. First of all, there are inheritance taxes to pay. Huge ones that have to be tendered in hard currency. I simply can't afford that right now. Then there's the house and the land themselves. I've never seen Sheldon Park, but it must be rather a grand structure. It'll want care. Someone must live in it, staff it with servants."

"The house is a fallen-down old ruin. Any day now some good gale is going to come and blow it over. Antony told me himself that he inherited a monstrous debt and little more. That's why it's in such terrible condition. The only thing to do would be to tear it down."

"But good God, Nance! If that's true and you know it, why are we having this argument? What do you want with the place anyway? And where would we find the money to pay off all the creditors who doubtless have liens on the property, even supposing we managed to scrape together enough to pay the inheritance tax?"

"I don't care a fig for Sheldon Park itself. Maybe it could be sold to help raise some of this cash you're talking about. What I want is the land."

"Yes, the land. Let's see, it's something less than a mile from here to Sheldon Park, isn't it? Say he owned as much on either side...that'd be, what...nearly five hundred acres?"

"Seven hundred acres. That's how much property is between here and Sheldon Park. Michael told me. He once did some work with a surveyor that Antony employed. The land is roughly a rectangle, and the distance between here and Sheldon Park is less than the distance the other way."

"I see. You've discussed this with the servants, then?"

"No, of course not. I just asked about the land. Michael hadn't a clue why."

"Very well, forget that for the moment. What do you want those seven hundred acres for? That's what I don't understand."

"For Tassels. Don't you see? It would make the place a proper little estate. We could have a real farm and raise all our own foodstuffs right here on our own land. Besides, the land involved includes five tenant farmers, and their rents would help pay to run the place. You should know about all that better than I."

"I do. That's precisely the point. Nancy, this place, this Tassels, it's just a stopgap. Just a temporary home until I manage to buy back Harwood. What's the sense in saddling ourselves with a project like this?"

"I'm the one who'd be saddled with it. You could just go on as you are. You worry about Griffin's Importations and I'll look after Tassels. I can do it. Whatever you think." Her chin came up defiantly.

"And when the time came to move? To go home to Yorkshire?"

"Yorkshire was home to you, Roger, I understand that. But never to me."

He looked at her closely now. The full import of this conversation was reaching him at last. "Are you saying you want me to forget about Harwood?" he asked in a low voice. "To accept this worker's cottage in its stead?"

"Yes, Roger," she said firmly. "That's exactly what I'm saying."

"A most generous gift, sir, most generous indeed."

The solicitor, one Algernon Hume, was a dark oily-looking man. Something not quite English betrayed itself in his coloring and skin texture. At that moment Roger would have described him as lizardlike.

"Yes, I guess it was," he agreed. He'd be damned if he'd explain himself to this old bastard. Or defend his wife from the man's ill-hidden suspicions. He was an employee, someone whom Roger had hired. Nothing more. "Now, would you mind telling me the results of your visit to Messrs. Timothy, Timothy, White, and Parsons? I'm a busy man, Mr. Hume."

"Of course, Captain Griffin. Do forgive me. Well, it's quite a straightforward matter when all is said and done. The bequest is uncontested. Lord Sheldon had no family or heirs. The property in question is but a small part of the total estate—the house and those lands, seven hundred acres, that run between it and the property you presently own. Er..." He ruffled through some papers on his desk. "Tassels, I believe it's called. Another gift to Mistress Griffin, I see. A royal bequest at that. If I may say so, captain, you seem to have been most fortunate in your choice of a wife." He managed a slippery smile that looked decidedly obscene.

"You may not say, sir. Just content yourself with telling me the amount of cash necessary to realize this inheritance."

"Er...yes, of course.... Well, the inheritance taxes will amount to two hundred pounds. Give or take a few shillings, that is. I can't be entirely exact without checking a few more things, you understand. But a larger sum is involved, I'm afraid. Some fourteen hundred pounds owed to creditors would have to be paid before the title could be cleared and handed over to your good self. Timothy, Timothy, White, and Parsons tell me the entire estate is thus encumbered. Sadly the late lamented Lord Sheldon wasn't much of a business-man. To be fair, many of the debts go back to his father and grandfather. An ill-fated lot, the Sheldons, it seems." He sat back and smiled with satisfaction. Hume was the sort who always took enormous pleasure from discussing the misfor-tunes of others.

It was Benjamin who put it all into perspective for him later that evening. "It's not such a huge sum, Roger. We could certainly find the sixteen hundred pounds, if that's what's troubling you." He handed the other man a glass of brandy and returned to his seat. "But let me speak frankly, then you can get angry with me if you wish. It's not the money that's worrying you, is it? I rather suspect it's the whole idea of Lord Sheldon's leaving the house and land to Nancy in the first place that rankles. Am I right?"

"Partly. It does seem damned odd. He'd known her for less than a year. On the other hand, he was a great admirer of hers, seen her on stage, that sort of thing. It's the kind of whimsical gesture that was quite in character for him. Shel-don wasn't Nancy's lover or anything of the sort, if that's what you're thinking. He was a boy-lover, a pervert. That's how he met his gruesome end in the first place. Fell afoul of his male paramour. Christ, it disgusts me just to talk about it!"

Ahmet shrugged. "Each to his own poison, Roger. It's a good rule of life. Even if it weren't so, the idea wouldn't occur to me. I don't see Nancy making you cuckold. She's the most honest, straightforward woman I've ever met."

"You don't have to tell me that, I know it. Deceit's just not her style. Besides, these days she's positively besotted with that Tassels of hers. I find it hard enough to compete. I'd challenge any other man to do so."

"But is that a bad thing? With you so tied up here in the city much of the time, surely she needs something to occupy her."

"I know that too. But Tassels is just a little cottage, Benjamin. Oh, she's done a lot with it. I don't deny that. But still..."

"Still, it's not a patch on Harwood Hall. Is that it?"

"Yes, I suppose that's the final word."

"And she doesn't share your passion to return to the old family seat? No, you don't need to answer. I know Nancy well enough to guess that she'd start choking for air with every mile you took her north of London."

"She'd get over it."

"No doubt. But look, Roger, you're making a stick for your own back. Surely some kind of domestic peace is worth paying a price for?"

"Of course it is. That's why I consented to send Hume to talk with Sheldon's solicitors in the first place. But I didn't commit myself to more than that then, and I'm not prepared to do so now."

"Look at it this way." Ahmet leaned forward and punctuated his words by waving the glass he held. "You're not quite ready to make a move on Harwood yet, are you?"

"Not quite. I thought I might be, but a session with the account books convinced me otherwise. It'll take another year or more to put that kind of capital together."

"Right. But sixteen hundred to ransom Nancy's legacy and make her happy isn't anything like so difficult. And if you agree, give her her head, as it were, she may well present you with a Surrey property worth a handsome sum on the open market. Then, when you're ready for Yorkshire, it could be sold. Make a tidy profit, I shouldn't wonder."

"Perhaps. If she could do it. But I don't think either you or she is reckoning with what's really involved in estate management. It's no job for an amateur, believe me."

"No, you're probably right. But still, you have that expertise right in your own family. Hire your brother, Roger. Get him out of that Spanish embassy and put him on as manager of Tassels. Forgive me for sounding so much a Jew, but blood ties can't be ignored so lightly as you seem to think. He's your father's son, Roger. Just as you are. Whatever you think of his beliefs and behavior, he's your brother and Nancy's your wife."

5.

Nancy was half afraid of her own boldness. The terms under which Roger had agreed to allow her to accept the Sheldon bequest were that she recognize it meant no permanent commitment to Tassels as the family home. She had been willing enough to back down on that aspect of their argument. He who fights and runs away, she told herself placidly, lives to fight another day. The devil take Roger and his male ideas of "honor." If he chose to believe she'd eventually consent to selling the place and moving to that Yorkshire wilderness, then let him. One of these days he'd find out differently, but nothing would be served by having the final showdown now.

But she wasn't anything like so sure of her latest idea. It had come to her late one night; since then it would leave her no peace. It was such a sound idea, so right for everyone concerned, so wise a solution to the new problems she faced. The morning after her brainchild was born Nancy rode out to do her first thorough survey of the land she'd soon be officially acquiring.

The northern boundary of Tassels was a stand of beech and other hardwood trees running at a right angle to the river that formed the westernmost edge of the property. Through that copse of trees there was a path leading to the adjacent woods, those that had belonged to the Sheldon estate but would soon belong to the Griffins. She was thinking of that path while she made her way to the barn.

Nancy had taken to riding horseback a short time earlier. She still wasn't very sure of herself, but she was determined. The horse Michael Wadden had bought for her was a gentle old mare, in no way anxious for excitement. As long as Nancy made no demands for speed or jumps or anything foolish like that, the mare was content to do her part to see her mistress didn't land in a ditch. With this truce between them, Nancy and the horse got on quite well. On the morning of her tour of inspection she urged the old beast down the familiar path into the woods.

Autumn gales had whipped most of the trees bare, and today sunlight found its way through the interwoven branches and dappled the ground. Idly she noted the heavy crop of berries many of the low shrubs carried, and she remembered Ellen's comment that it meant a hard winter. The old woman was probably right. She knew things like that, had the inborn knowledge of the country-bred. Well, what of it? Tassels was well prepared for the winter. All kinds of root vegetables were buried in a deep pit near the house; the larder was stocked with other vegetables preserved in salt or vinegar. There were six huge cheeses ripening on the dairy shelves, two kegs full of cloth-wrapped wheels of butter laid down in brine, two more kegs filled with ground flour she'd purchased from the village mill. To add to her sense of satisfaction and security, just yesterday she'd seen the small room they called the meat safe hung with salted beef, pork, and bacon. Let winter do its worst; they were ready.

Lost in her thoughts, staring at the ground, she didn't realize the horse was taking a new path of its own choosing, through the woods to a high ridge of pine. Nancy only became aware of the unfamiliar surroundings when the light dimmed and the dense green of the trees replaced the scattered sunlight of the earlier part of the journey.

She looked up and pulled in the reins with a sharp exclamation. "Whoa, girl, whoa! Where the devil have you brought us? And why?" Carefully she edged farther along the narrow path. The horse seemed anxious to proceed in a particular direction. "Very well, old lady," she said softly. "Let's see what you have in mind. But be gentle. Remember who's up on your back, won't you?"

In minutes they had cleared the pine grove and were standing atop a hill overlooking a small valley of cultivated fields and farmhouses. Nancy counted six dwellings, each with its own bit of surrounding property. She looked around her and tried to fathom the location of this valley. She'd given up in despair—her sense of direction only worked in London, unfortunately—when she heard a deep voice from over to her left.

"Hallo there! It's old Tilly, then. Come for a look at yer old home, girl, haven't ye? Mornin', ma'am." The speaker was a boy of sixteen or seventeen. In dress and speech he was obviously local.

"Good morning," Nancy replied, smiling. "Do I take it you know my horse?"

"Tilly? Sure do, ma'am. Knowed her since I was a baby. Me father sold her just two months past. And if she's yer horse now, then ye must be Mistress Griffin of Tassels."

"I am. I didn't know about the horse. My man just arrived with her one day, said she was a good one for us to buy."

"Michael Wadden, ye means? Right. 'Twas him who bought Tilly from us. You've come to look us over, then? Now that yer to be new squire's lady, that is."

"Well, as a matter of fact I didn't. Not exactly. It was this horse that brought me. I wasn't paying much attention, and she just came along this way. I was just wondering whose land this was."

The boy grinned. "Yers, ma'am. If ye be mistress of Tassels, that is."

"I am. Well, well...." She looked with new appreciation at the pastoral scene in front of her. "It's quite a splendid patch at that. What's your name by the way?"

"Harry, ma'am. Harry Sparks. That's our place down there on the left. The cottage with all the chickens outside. 'Tis a good little place, ma'am. And me father pays rent regular, too. Ye ain't gonna put us off, are ye?"

"Of course not, Harry. None of you. Please see that all the tenants in the valley know that. But tell me something. I was told there were five tenants, so why do I see six houses? Does one of them not belong to Lord Sheldon—to us, that is?"

"Oh no, ma'am. They's all his. Rather, they's all yers now. But that one over at far end of the valley, that's Tupenny Cottage. Ain't nobody lives there now. Used to belong to Mr. White what was his lordship's estate manager. Then, when Mr. White left, place just sat empty. His lordship never seemed interested."

Nancy's eyes lit up. She put her hand up to shade the sun and peered at the place the boy indicated. "Tupenny Cottage... what a funny name! Why is it called that?"

"'Cause of the flowers, ma'am. The ones they call tupenny flowers. Grow right up to the front door, they do. Been Tupenny Cottage long as I knowed it."

"Harry, you are a veritable fount of information. Tell me, what are you doing right now?"

"Now, ma'am?" He held out the basket he carried. "Just

259

gatherin' blackberries, ma'am. Fer Ma to bake in a pie. We's allus gathered 'em in these woods. His lordship never said we couldn'."

"Fine. As far as I'm concerned you can continue to gather as many as you wish. But right now I've another job for you. Take me around, Harry. I want to see all the houses in the valley. Most particularly Tupenny Cottage. I'm very interested in that indeed."

"Sarah...where are you?" The kitchen door banged shut behind Nancy as if to punctuate her words. She was flushed and breathless after a ride home in which for the first time she'd urged the old horse to go at something approximating a gallop. "Sarah, listen, what are tupenny flowers?"

"I'm not sure, Aunt Nancy, wait a minute." The girl flew away to her bedroom and returned carrying a handsome leather-bound volume. "*Gerard's Herbal*—do you know it?"

"No. I'm afraid I don't."

"Well, it's perfectly marvelous. Everything that grows is listed. What it's good for, everything. Papa gave it me on my tenth birthday. I've Culpeper too, but Gerard is better, I think." She was ruffling the pages hastily while she spoke. "Yes, here it is! Shall I read it to you?" And when Nancy nodded her head, "The Latin name is *Lysimachia nummularia*. Gerard says, 'Boiled with wine and honey it cureth the wounds of the inward parts and ulcers of the lungs and in a word there is not a better wound herb.' Are we to grow some, Aunt Nancy? Here at Tassels?"

"No, pet, not exactly." Nancy paced the kitchen floor, her expressive hands fluttering with excitement. "But I'm going to cure a wound with these tupenny flowers. At least I'm going to try."

It was a blessing that Roger was due at Tassels the next day. Nancy could hardly have borne waiting longer for him. Yesterday she had been frightened by her own bold idea. Then, after she found Tupenny Cottage standing empty on their new land, the rightness of the scheme became so obvious she was sure Roger must see it. Still, she planned her campaign carefully. She knew she would have only one opportunity to state her case. A subject so explosive would not bear continuous persuasion.

He arrived just before noon, on horseback as he much preferred, and she immediately installed him in the comfortable front room with two-month-old Jennifer in a cradle by his feet and Nell in her favorite spot on his lap. At two, Roger's elder daughter adored her father quite as much as he did her. "Lunch will be ready soon," Nancy said, planting a kiss atop his head. "Hashed pullet in cream, your favorite. Will you have a glass of wine in the meantime?"

"Brandy, I think, if there's some about."

"Of course." She poured the French essence into a small glass and handed it to him sweetened by her brightest smile. "I'll just leave you with the babies then...."

Later, when the children had been carried to the nursery and Sarah and Laura were off on their own pursuits, she gave him another, yet more generous, portion of brandy and took a small one for herself. Outside the November sky was gray and threatening, but here by the fire it was as cozy as anyone could wish.

"Lunch was delicious, Nance," he said with a sigh of satisfaction as he stretched his legs before the blazing logs. "I still can't get over what a fine cook you've come to be."

"All thanks to Clare. But I must admit, Ellen still does most of the cooking."

"As well she should. You're to be mistress of this place, not maid of all work."

"Funny," she said softly. "Clare told me that very same thing a year ago. It's a harder lesson to learn than the actual doing of things. Managing the household servants takes skill. All management does, I expect." She watched him carefully over the rim of her glass.

"Yes." He seemed to be watching her just as intently. Suddenly it occurred to Nancy that he was somehow playing at the same game as she, setting her up for some kind of pronouncement, as it were. His next words intensified that impression. "Speaking of Clare, how is she? And how's Mark, for that matter? Still a porter at the Spanish legation?"

"Mmm...they're fine. I had a letter last week. But Clare says Mark hates the confinement of the job. In the heart of the city like that...when he's used to country life...."

"So I'd imagine. He's quite remarkably good at the job he was trained for, you know. Country squire, managing lands and tenants..."

Her gasp of astonishment caused the brandy to choke in her throat. It was as if Roger were reading her mind! She coughed until tears ran down her cheeks while her husband solicitously thumped her shoulders. "That's enough brandy for you," he said, removing the glass to a nearby table. "Too strong for ladies, I'm afraid. Shall I get you some sack?"

"No, nothing, thank you. I'm quite all right. But..."

"Yes? Something you wanted to say?"

There was no hiding it now. A smile most assuredly lurked around Roger's mouth. A teasing, self-satisfied smile. It was quite a different reaction from anything she'd anticipated. And she hadn't even sprung the trap yet! "Well," she began slowly, "there is something I wanted to discuss. Something important."

"Indeed. Go on, then, I'm listening. And here we are alone, well fed, cozy. Everyone far away as if they'd been given instructions before I came." He tapped his fingers on the arm of the chair and watched her with amusement no longer disguised. "It's most apparent you've something to discuss, my love, so out with it."

"I want..." She began boldly, but the words froze in her throat. Determined, she took a deep breath and started again. "I want to ask Mark..."

"To become manager of Tassels in its new dress as a country estate," he said, finishing her sentence before she could herself. "I know."

Nancy stared at him in astonishment. He really was smiling! "But how did you know?" she stuttered at last.

"Because," he said and reached out and pulled her on to his lap, "I had the very same idea myself. Last week. I've been rehearsing the plan in my mind for days. It makes good sense on every count."

"But I still don't see how you knew that was my idea." She pulled back slightly so she could watch his face while he answered.

He didn't reply at once, however. He was too busy laughing. When he finally spoke, the words came slowly, punctuated by his gestures as he unlaced her bodice and let his fingers caress her pink-tipped breasts. "My sweet, any man set up for the kill as artfully as you set me up today would know something was afoot. I merely put two and two together. Your hints at lunch were too broad to be mistaken, and as for your performance in here just now...I'd have been a fool to miss the point."

She ignored his questing hands a moment longer. "And you agree? I can make the proposition to Mark and Clare?"

"I agree. But I'd much prefer they not be in this house. I still don't feel I want such proximity to Mark. Not after everything that's happened."

"But that's no problem at all," she said happily. "I still have a surprise for you after all." She didn't tell him about Tupenny Cottage just then, however. First there were other matters to claim her attention. Her nipples were swollen beneath his touch, and she bent her head to kiss him with more ardor than she'd felt for many months.

By Christmas all the Yorkshire Griffins were ensconced in the small house in the valley. Andrew and Charles were quite delighted at being back in Surrey. They rediscovered old haunts, made friends with the children of the local farmers, and even managed to spend sufficient hours at their books each morning to please their father. Clare began in her customary fashion to turn the long-deserted cottage into a proper home, and she never once complained at the frequency with which she'd faced this same task in recent years. Nor did she make odious comparisons between the humble dwelling and the great manor house she had left behind.

For Sarah, Tupenny Cottage was yet another garden challenge, and she patiently explained to her aunt that many of the plants she'd carefully nursed back to health at Tassels would now provide seeds and cuttings to stock the beds surrounding the cottage. "And there are one or two really good things at Tupenny, too, Aunt Nance. A quite unusual little shrub with evergreen foliage I'm hoping to divide so you can have a bit here as well...." She was capable of spending hours with sheets of paper on which she drew endless plans for her horticultural endeavors. But they were nowhere near as precise or detailed as the drawings her father made and spread before Nancy on his frequent visits to Tassels.

"The land's good, Nance. No denying it." He moved an urgent finger across his homemade maps. "There's a stand of pine that wants thinning just here. We'll take out all but the young saplings and keep half for firewood. The rest will fetch upwards of twenty pounds at auction. I recommend we sell at Guildford market. Cheaper and easier transportation than going to London. That'll quite overshadow any slightly lower price we might get by selling in the country. And the profit can be used to start draining this fen here. See, just next to Sheldon Park itself. It's a bog, but it could be made into perfectly good growing land with only a little work."

"Mark..." Nancy put her hand over his and turned away from the map. "It all sounds marvelous, but let me change the subject just for a moment. How's Laura?"

He removed his hand from hers and rolled the long sheet into a neat cylinder before he spoke. "There's little point in lying to you," he said sadly. "She's not good, Nancy. I'm very worried, and so is Clare. I just don't understand why a girl as sane and sound as Laura can't get that gruesome business out of her mind. Put it behind her, forget about it."

"She was in love with him, you know. I'm afraid I mismanaged things very badly. I can't stop blaming myself for how Laura is now."

"That's ridiculous, Nancy. Neither Clare nor I think that. You must believe me. Whatever Laura felt for Lord Sheldon, he's dead and that's that. She's got to get over it and pick up her life. She will, you know, eventually. Everyone does."

His words were accurate, but not in any way that either he or Nancy would have imagined.

6.

The winter of 1673 slipped into spring. The countryside around Tassels erupted into new life, and as if to keep pace, Nancy told Roger she was pregnant again. "A son this time, I'm sure of it," she announced with that certitude he found so maddening.

"How the hell can you know that?" he demanded, though he knew her answer would be the usual enigmatic woman's nonsense.

"I know," she said, smiling.

He turned away in frustration. Nonetheless, he did rather think it would be marvelous to have a son. These days he had hopes of having something truly worthwhile to pass on to a male heir. "We're planning to enlarge the George Alley premises," he said, though her news had rather dwarfed his own small surprise. "The building next door went up for sale, and we grabbed it."

"That's splendid, Roger! You must be very proud of all you've accomplished."

"It's too soon for that. Griffin's Importations has been doing well, but so far we put more back in than we take out. It'll be like that for a while longer, I think. So does Ahmet."

"I'm so pleased about that." She turned and ran her fingers over the matted hair of his chest.

"What? That we're plowing the profits back into expansion? Any business worth its salt does as much."

"No, silly. I mean that you and Benjamin have gotten on so well together. I'm really very proud of that."

"I hate to tell you, madam, but you had nothing to do with it. It was merely a coincidence that Ahmet approached me shortly after you mentioned his name." He propped himself on his elbow and stared out the window at the path leading toward their door. It was a proper path now, wide and paved with local stone. On this May morning it was bordered with a profusion of tulips in riotous colors. "I can't deny that you were right, however. We make an excellent team. I don't remember any man I've ever thought more of than Benjamin. He's . . . Nancy! What in hell is that?" Coming slowly into view beneath their bedroom window was a horse-drawn cart piled perilously high with massive stones and what looked like wooden stage scenery.

Nancy bounded from the bed and stood by the window in nothing but her skin. "It's the bits of Sheldon Park!" she exclaimed happily. "All the good ones that were worth saving. I'd no idea they would be here today. Quick, Roger! Where's my frock? I've got to get downstairs and see they unload in the right place. . . . You see," she deigned to explain while she pulled on her clothes with more haste than usual, "I didn't tell you before, but we're expanding too. We've razed Sheldon Park to the ground. There's to be a sheepfold there. And everything decent from the old mausoleum is coming here to build a new wing." She was almost out the door before she turned back to him and said saucily, "I intend that your son will be born into a house suitable for a gentleman of property."

* * *

265

It was this new wing that induced her to pay a visit to London in June. "I can't find any upholstery fabrics suitable down here in the country," she explained. "I simply have to go to a proper London draper."

"Very well," Roger agreed with that air of amused tolerance he adopted whenever she spoke of Tassels. "But you might as well make it into a bit of a holiday and spend a few days in town with me. I'll book rooms at some inn and we can do a little celebrating. Go to the theater, for one thing. You'd like that, wouldn't you?"

"I should adore it," she agreed with enthusiasm. "And I can visit Nell too."

So it was arranged. Nancy left Maude Jenks in charge of the children, with instructions to call on Clare in the event of any emergency, and set out for London. She wore her best frock, grateful that her figure wasn't yet swollen with her third child. She knew Roger would be tied up with business until the evening, so she wasted no time going to George Alley after her arrival. "Let me off at Hungerford Stairs," she told the boatman. "And there's a penny extra if you'll carry my bag to Mistress Gwyn's house on Pall Mall."

"You see, Nance," Nell was explaining half an hour later when the two women sat together in the elegant drawing room, "Charles and I have an understanding now."

"I'm so glad. I really mean it, love. I was worried when I heard how much time he spent with...I mean..."

"You mean when you heard he was sleeping with Louise de Kéroualle. It's all right. I don't mind about it any more." Something wistful and sad in her tone belied the statement. "I...he really loves me, Nance. No one would believe that, but it's true. It's just that it isn't in Charles's nature to be faithful to any one woman. Besides..." She rose and walked to the carved marble mantelpiece, her back to Nancy. "With his own brother doing such terrible things to him, Charles needs all the understanding and loyalty I can give."

"His brother? What do you mean?"

"Don't tell me you haven't heard!" Nell whirled around, her pink satin frock making a flash of color in the afternoon sun. "Even down there in the country you must know what Dismal Jimmy's done now."

"Oh, that religion business? Is that what you mean?"

"Of course! And not just becoming a papist—there's more. Things you can't know, but I do. I'd like to flog the man, I

266

really would. How can he be such an imbecile? And so ungrateful...."

"Nell..." It was Nancy's turn to stand now. She walked toward her friend and took her beringed hand in her own. "Listen, darling, I think we'd best end this conversation just now. Before we quarrel. I appreciate your position and admire your loyalty to Charles, you know that. But York has been a most extraordinary friend to Roger, and thus to me. I feel...well, dishonest, to listen to criticism about him."

Nell pulled her hand away. Her expression was something between a grimace and a pout. That exquisitely mobile face that had captivated audiences had lost none of its ability to convey a whole range of emotions. "I guess I understand. But I can't say I approve, Nancy. Not after Charles has been so good to you...given you your home and everything..."

"But Nell!" This was a low blow, one she wouldn't have expected from Nell in any circumstances. "I'm the king's loyal subject! You know that better than anyone. How can you imply otherwise?"

"Oh, I don't mean to say you're not his 'loyal subject,' as you put it. Of course I don't. It's just that many who claim to be don't recognize the full implications of the statement. Mark my words, Nance, the time is coming when people are going to have to choose. Charles or James. The Church of England or popery. You'll see."

"Interesting," was Roger's first comment when she related the story later that evening. "I wonder how typical her reaction is."

Benjamin, who was dining with them in the Swan, a new eatery at Charing Cross, reached across the table to help himself to more pigeon pie. "I suspect," he said in his half-amused fashion, "Mistress Gwyn is more than usually typical."

"That's not proper English, Benjamin. If a thing is typical it can't be more typical." Nancy waved her fork to punctuate her statement. By this time she had consumed rather more wine than customary. Her cheeks were flushed, her eyes sparkled, and her speech was slightly slurred.

"Look who's telling me about proper English, will you, Roger? Don't forget, madam, I knew you when you still dropped your aitches and said 'ooh cor' at every opportunity!"

"You're wicked to remind me," Nancy said with a sigh. "These days I happily forget what it was like to live on the streets and never be sure where the next meal was coming from." She reached for Roger's hand and pressed it to her lips. "But all that's behind me now, thanks to you."

The gesture immediately quelled the slight irritation he had felt when Benjamin had referred to his early friendship with Nancy. Actually Roger had developed so much genuine affection for his partner that the thought seldom crossed his mind. Now he forgot his moment of jealousy and asked, "Seriously, Benjamin, what do you think of Nell's reaction? Do you think the furor over James's conversion will die down?"

Ahmet shrugged and sat back in his chair. "I don't know if my observations are worth much. I'm still a foreigner after all. But I rather suspect that things won't die down, because the Duke of York himself will not allow them to do so." Seeing his companions' puzzled expressions, the Turk warmed to his subject. "Look, no one knows better than the two of you that the whole Catholic thing is like a volcano below the surface, just waiting to erupt. As long as no one stirs the flames, people are content to forget about it. But let someone pour fuel on the embers, so to speak, and poof!" He threw up both his hands in an exaggerated gesture. "Fire everywhere. And the devil take the hindmost. Particularly if the poor wretch happens to be a papist."

"And that's what you think James will do?" Roger asked softly. "Pour fuel on the embers?"

"What else can I think? Haven't you heard he's sent to Italy for his second bride? Word has it he's proposed to Duke Francis II of Modena that a marriage be arranged with Francis's sister, Mary."

Roger looked stunned, Nancy puzzled. It was she who spoke first. "But I don't understand. What has that to do with anything? Surely no one can object to his marrying again."

"My dear girl, you've been in the country too long. All the juiciest bits of gossip pass you by. Mary of Modena is not only a Catholic, she's reputed to be the eldest bastard daughter of some former pope. I forget which one . . . not Clement . . ."

"No," Roger interrupted very softly. "Not Clement. Alexander VII. Died in 1667."

"How do you know that?" Nancy turned to her husband in astonishment. "Since when do you follow foreign whores and bastards so carefully?"

"I know," he said with no humor in his face or voice, "because James himself told me the story. About six weeks ago when he was assuring me he'd never make such a politically suicidal marriage. Benjamin, are you sure?"

Ahmet shrugged once more. "You know my sources, Roger. They're not infallible, but usually accurate."

"Yes, damn it. They usually are. Pray that this time you're wrong, my friend. If you care at all for this England you've adopted, pray you're wrong."

He tried for an audience with James on the following day, but to no avail. His highness the Duke of York was not receiving visitors at the moment. Frustrated at Whitehall, Roger went to the naval offices in Seething Lane. They were bolted and barred, and a funereal air hung about the empty halls. He was almost out of the narrow street when he had another idea and doubled back to knock firmly on the door of the house across from the office. "Good morning," he said to the young woman who opened the door. "My name is Captain Roger Griffin. I'm an old friend of Mr. Pepys. Is he in?"

There followed half an hour's conversation with Samuel in the man's comfortable study. Pepys was circumspect and cautious, as was always his style, but Roger was convinced that the man shared Ahmet's opinion of the truth of the rumor. "Good luck, Samuel," he said warmly when he left. "I wish you much fortune in the days ahead."

"And I you, Roger. I rather think we're both in need of some just now. It may not be the best of times to be friend to the Duke of York."

On June 15 the announcement was made that, for personal reasons, the Duke of York was withdrawing from all public office. His cousin, Prince Rupert, was made lord high admiral of the Royal Navy. It was exactly the scenario James had suggested to Roger two years earlier; it had merely taken a little longer for his enemies and York's own monumental bad judgment to bring it all about.

Naturally it was Ahmet who first brought him the news. He found Roger sitting in his sumptuous new office in the enlarged George Alley premises and told him the whole story in quick economic statements that instantly conveyed the facts. It was a verbal code at which the two men had become adept in recent years. It allowed them to transmit thoughts and feelings, as well as information, in a minimum of time—a talent as good for friendship as for business.

"I take it you're worried about this, then," Roger asked when Benjamin finished speaking.

"Yes. Aren't you?"

Griffin stretched and walked to the window that overlooked the busy thoroughfare of Cornhill just a few steps away. "I guess 'disappointed' is a better word. It bodes no good for James. Why the man must be such a self-destructive fool I'll never understand."

"Nor I. But let me ask you something more selfish. Do you think it bodes ill for Griffin's Importations?"

"Not if the old rules still apply. York told me long ago that this might happen. If it did I wasn't to worry. Rupert was party to our arrangement and would honor it."

"Good. But that's not all, is it?"

"No. There's much more. All England, in fact."

"Good Lord, Roger! Isn't that a bit dramatic?"

"Perhaps. I certainly hope so. I've lived through one civil war, and I don't fancy another."

7.

Mark Griffin mounted the little sorrel pony, adjusted his weight in the saddle, and, clucking softly to the beast, urged her forward. "It's not such a long journey to London, Robin," he told the pony gently. "You won't find it a hard trip." For him, however, the journey seemed very hard indeed.

Once, when they had climbed to the top of the pine ridge overlooking the valley, he reined in and turned to look at the somnolent landscape below. Tupenny Cottage had recently been given a fresh coat of white paint, and the nodding daisylike flowers which gave the house its name created a billowing yellow quilt at its feet. The scene sparkled high-summer-bright in the sun. Mark sighed. Somehow this leavetaking seemed more threatening than had that of the spring morning three years before when they'd quit Harwood Hall. This small cottage in the quiet Surrey valley spoke to him of peace and hard-won security. How precious those things were he'd learned well, but none of these misgivings stopped him from turning back to the path and continuing toward London.

He reached the Rose Inn in Covent Garden by early evening, and in this fashionable but relatively quiet part of town secured a room and the promise of a meal without any difficulty. The Rose had been chosen by Huddleston many months earlier as the best possible rendezvous. "If you need to meet with me, Mark, for any reason after you're down there at your brother's place, just send me a note saying, 'Sir, your rose plants are ready to be moved.' Sign it 'Smith.' I'll be at the Rose in Covent Garden every morning thereafter until I see you. It seems perhaps a bit theatrical, but prudence is a virtue."

A virtue indeed. Considering how reluctant he was to ask the priest what he must ask, Mark almost wished they hadn't been so thorough in their plans for any eventuality. He pushed the thought away when the old man slid into the seat next to him as he was breakfasting the next day. Huddleston wore ordinary clothes—the mood in London made his religious robes a liability right now—but other than that he seemed unchanged. The two men talked for over an hour. Then Mark paid his bill and left. The priest followed a few minutes later.

Laura was waiting for him near the bend in the river, almost a mile from the cottage and her mother's watchful eye. "Did you see him, Papa?" Mark nodded. "And will he do it?" Her father nodded again. "Thanks be to God!" the girl exclaimed with feeling.

"Laura..." He slid down from the saddle and gripped her shoulders. "You're sure? Absolutely sure? This isn't just some kind of wish to escape reality?"

"We've been over all this before, Papa," she said quietly.

271

"You know I'm sure. You promised you'd not stand in my way. You said if Father Huddleston agreed, you'd take it as a sign...."

"Yes, and I'll keep my word. But God help me, I don't know what I'm to say to your mother."

"A nun? Laura?" Nancy sat down heavily in the nearest chair. Her body, swollen with pregnancy, seemed to be playing tricks on her these warm August days. That was why she'd come to consult Clare this morning. She'd hoped her sister-in-law would be able to suggest some herbal tonic to perk her up. Then, the moment she walked through the door, she realized that she had interrupted a tense family scene.

Only Clare and Mark were at home; the children had apparently been banished some time earlier. Between the husband and wife distress crackled in the air like the early warnings of a thunderstorm. Clare's eyes were red with weeping, and Mark was drawn and very pale. Nancy tried to excuse herself and leave, but both insisted she remain. "You're indirectly involved," Mark explained. "You'll have to know sooner or later. It might as well be now." Then his startling pronouncement had sent the breath from her body as effectively as if he'd struck her.

"Tell him, Nancy," Clare begged. "Tell him it's madness and he mustn't let her do it!"

"I...Mark, are you going to allow this?"

"Allow it!" Clare didn't give him a chance to reply. "Not just that! He's encouraged her."

"That's not true, Clare. I've told you so repeatedly." He turned to Nancy, as if prepared to try another jury. "Laura spoke to me about this as long ago as Christmas. Surely you know what the girl's been like ever since last summer."

"That's exactly the point," Clare said, obviously taking up an oft-repeated chorus. "That's why she mustn't be allowed to make such a decision now. She's upset, distraught..."

"That's simply not an adequate explanation, Clare. I've told you that over and over. If she had given up the notion after some weeks it would be different." He turned back to Nancy. "Laura believes that God is calling her to join her aunt at that convent in France. She thinks He used the shocking experience with Lord Sheldon to show her the need for prayer and penance on behalf of suffering humanity.

It sounds very grandiose, I know." He shrugged helplessly.

"And very like an idealistic and impressionable young girl," Nancy said firmly. "I'm afraid I agree with Clare, Mark. It's none of my affair, but since you've spoken to me about it I can't hide my opinion. I think it very foolish of you to allow her to take such a step in her present state of mind."

Clare uttered a deep sigh of satisfaction and sat down hard, as if to say the matter was settled. "There, Mark, you see? I'm not such a fool after all."

"I never said you were a fool, my dear." He didn't feel impatient with his wife. He understood too well what the loss of Laura meant to her and knew too well how little sympathy she had for the whole idea of monastic life. "Believe me, I share your grief. I did everything I could to dissuade Laura. But finally we both agreed we'd leave it to Father Huddleston. If he said there was a way to get her to France and a likelihood that the St. Savior's nuns would accept her, then we would take that as a sign from heaven."

"A sign?" Clare was crying again. "A sign from the devil, more likely! He must like the idea of locking up young girls away from their homes and families. Away from any chance of their ever being wives and mothers..."

Nancy ignored this outburst and addressed herself to Mark. "I take it this Huddleston has promised to help?"

"Yes. He's to meet a French packet in Dover sometime soon. Some bit of royal business about which I know nothing. But it gives him an opportunity to get Laura out of England with no one the wiser. She's to travel to Kent on her own, then meet Father Huddleston. The French boat will take her over the Channel."

"I see. Mark, bear with me one more moment." Nancy's voice was very low, her sincerity apparent. "Just tell me how you can be sure it isn't merely that Laura is still upset by what happened."

"I can't. Not really. Maybe she is still suffering from shock. But maybe it is the voice of God she hears. How can I stand in the way of that? Try to understand, Nancy. Because of what Clare and I came to believe some four years ago, Laura lost everything—her home, all the wealth and position to which she'd been born, the prospects of the kind of marriage she could have expected before that. And not only did she raise no objection, she chose of her own free will, as did her

273

sister and brothers, to join us in our new faith. I see that as the hand of God, Nancy. I can't see it otherwise. Now I can't tell Laura that it's all right to follow the Lord part of the way, but not all the way. Not even if one believes, as she does, that He's asking. Don't you understand? It would make a mockery of everything that's gone before. Everything she's suffered because of her faith. And there's another thing. Since Huddleston's agreed to help her get to this nunnery, Laura's a changed girl. Even Clare commented on it a few days ago before she knew the cause. Laura's as happy as her old self. She's like a bride."

They were concerned about how Roger would take the news. Nancy saw no way to keep it from him, but she feared, as did Mark and Clare, that it would make him yet more bitter about his brother. It would tear irreparably the thin tissue of reconciliation that was slowly building between them. She worried for days about how best to tell him the story, created and rejected a dozen different plans.

Then the matter was taken out of her hands. Sarah arrived at Tassels on Sunday morning, a week after the revelations at Tupenny Cottage. Nancy had no idea what she intended. "Is Uncle Roger awake?" the girl asked. "I'd like to speak with him."

"Yes, of course, Sarah, he's in the study. You know where it is."

The girl nodded and hurried off to the new wing of the house. The expansion of Tassels was fast showing itself as a minor architectural triumph. One went down an old corridor past the stillroom and the dairy and stepped into a new world that somehow seemed to flow with effortless grace from the old. Here the walls were paneled with carved oak and the rooms larger and more spacious than in the original house, but their elegance and charm seemed to spring from the old root as naturally as a flower from a bud. The study in which Sarah found Roger was part of the new master suite, and it was light and airy with glass doors leading out to a small terraced garden which she herself had planned and executed.

"Oh," she said enthusiastically when her knock was answered by an invitation to enter. "The china roses are in bloom! I didn't really think they'd flower this first season!"

"So they are, my girl. A tribute to your horticultural skill. Is that what you've come about?"

"No, not at all. I want to talk to you, Uncle Roger. Is this a good time?"

"As good as any. Sit down." He smiled fondly at the niece he liked so well, waited until she'd settled herself in a chair before offering her a bit of refreshment. "Since you're here, have a drop of sack," he said, smiling. "I presume at sixteen you're considered old enough for that. We can toast your roses."

"Mmm, lovely stuff." She sipped the wine gratefully, then set the glass down and turned a serious face to her uncle. "I've come about Laura," she said firmly. "Everyone is pussyfooting about afraid to mention her to you, but I say that's nonsense. I think you should be told straight out, and I'm sure you'll understand."

"I see." He tried to keep the amusement from his voice. The child was so very serious; he didn't want to offend her. "What about her, then? It sounds very grave. Is your sister threatening the good name of Griffin with some mad indiscretion? Come, Sarah, out with it."

"Laura wants to become a nun. She's leaving for France next month."

The words hung in the air between them. Sarah didn't move an eyelash, only fixed him with her direct and challenging gaze. Roger watched her for some seconds, then asked, "Does anyone besides you know of these plans?"

"Everyone. That is, my mother and father and Aunt Nancy and Charles and Andrew. I don't think any of the servants or tenants know."

"I see." This information was more startling than her earlier pronouncement. Obviously the whole thing wasn't some girl's prank cooked up between Laura and Sarah, but a true decision to which the whole family was privy. "Why wasn't I told before now?" he asked.

"Because of just what I said. They all thought you'd make a fuss. Throw us out of the cottage. Tell the authorities and stop Laura from going. That sort of thing."

He rose and walked woodenly to the glass doors. The morning light had that limpid, innocent quality that promised a day when all things were possible. "And you?" he asked softly. "What do you think, Sarah?"

"That they're being ridiculous. Even Aunt Nancy, and she should know better. That's why I came."

"My dear child," he said finally. "That tongue of yours is going to get you into serious trouble someday. The time must come, little Sarah, when you learn that courage alone isn't enough with which to face the world. There is a need for prudence too."

Sarah shook her head with impatience. "Bother prudence!" she said firmly. "At least for now. You're not going to make a fuss, are you, Uncle Roger?"

He was silent for some seconds, and when he turned back to her there was a sadness in his voice. "No, Sarah, I'm not going to make a fuss. Frankly, I'm rather hurt to have been cast in the role of villain by everyone, including your Aunt Nancy. Did she know you were going to tell me all this?"

"Of course not. It would have been stupid of me to let her know."

"Mmm. Sarah, answer me something else. What do you think of Laura's plans?"

"Well..." The girl seemed suddenly less sure of herself. "I don't know, really. It's not anything I'd ever want to do. Lock myself up with a bunch of women and pray day and night..." She shuddered expressively. "But it's her life, after all. Why shouldn't she do what she likes with it? Better than marrying some man and letting him...I mean..." Sarah reddened with embarrassment.

Roger couldn't help but grin now. "So you don't fancy marriage, Sarah. What do you want, then?"

"Just to stay here and be with the family and work in the gardens," she answered quickly. "It's all I ever want." Typically, however, Sarah refused to be distracted from the reason for her visit. "Then it's all right about Laura, Uncle Roger? Will you tell everyone it's all right?"

"Yes, Sarah, yes I shall." He thought she must be going to kiss him, but that wasn't the girl's style. She merely smiled and left the room. Roger remained alone for some time, then he went to find his wife.

8.

The resourceful Huddleston had proposed that Laura travel to France on a ship which he knew full well would be sailing under the protection of King Louis XIV. He did not feel it necessary to inform Laura or her family what errand brought the ship to the English coast. His cryptic note bearing final instructions arrived at Tupenny Cottage on September 10. It said only, "October 3, midnight." There was no signature; none was required. Mark read the message and proceeded to consign the slip of paper to the fire.

The last time the brothers Griffin had spoken face to face was four years earlier in Harwood Hall, when Mark told Roger he and his family were to become Catholics. Since then it was through the agency of their wives or Mark's children that they made their way through the tangled skein of their parallel lives. Neither of them seemed to confront the fact with anything like directness until one morning in mid-September when Roger sat at his desk in George Alley and thought about the news his niece Sarah had imparted a few days earlier. "Laura's leaving on October third," she had said with a hint of wistfulness. "She's all excited and happy, but Mama is terribly upset."

He'd made some banal remark at the time and gone on playing with baby Jennifer. Today, in a moment of uncustomary quiet at the office, the words came back and prodded at his consciousness. What was it Sarah had told him originally, that first time in August when she explained about Laura's plans? Oh yes, that the girl was to make her way to Kent on her own and meet that fellow Huddleston there. The more he thought about it the more disturbed he became.

How was she getting to Kent? And how sure was she or

anyone else that this Huddleston was reliable? What if something went wrong? What if Laura was discovered in her flight by some zealous sheriff or justice of the peace? It was illegal for recusants to leave the country, particularly if they were planning to enroll in foreign religious schools or institutions. Surely this nunnery of Laura's came under that heading. And if the worst happened, what then? What of all the rest of them? "Damned likely all our heads will be in the noose!" he said aloud.

Roger marched into the outer chamber, slamming the door behind him. "Kendal!" he shouted loudly. "Come here, I want you."

The older man appeared at once. He was officially the leader of all the company representatives, but often he functioned as Roger's personal assistant as well. The two men worked well together despite dramatically different temperaments and styles of operation. "Some problem, captain?" he asked cheerfully. Monty rather liked problems.

"Yes, but not here. Tell me what's on in the next few days. Any reason I can't get away to Surrey for a bit?"

"You mean before the weekend?"

"Dammit, man! Of course that's what I mean. I shouldn't be asking these questions if it was just a regular trip down there."

"Well . . ." Kendal stroked his elegant white wig with equally elegant white hands. "Let's see. There's that shipment of oranges due in from Spain."

"Yes, but not till day after tomorrow. Anyway, Ahmet can meet that."

"Begging your pardon, captain, Mr. Ahmet's away, if you recall."

"Yes, of course. And not due back from where is it?—Bristol—until the beginning of the week. Well, as I said, the oranges aren't expected until Thursday. I could be back by then."

"In that case, sir, there seems nothing that will absolutely require your personal attention."

"Good. Send Ludlow over to the stables right away. Tell him I want a strong mount ready and saddled in half an hour."

He had the several hours of the journey in which to worry his problem. By the time he rounded the bend of the river he'd decided on a course of action. He paused for a moment to look at the path which would lead him to Tassels, the children, and Nancy's warm bed, then turned the horse's head in the direction of the tenants' valley and Tupenny Cottage.

They had finished supper and were sitting quietly by the fire when he arrived. Andrew and Charles were engrossed in the maneuvers of some wooden soldiers spread out before them. Sarah's nose was buried in a book of herbal lore. Laura sat with a pile of sewing in her lap, and it was obvious that his knock interrupted the game of backgammon that occupied Clare and Mark. "Roger!" his sister-in-law exclaimed in astonishment. "We certainly didn't expect you. Is something wrong?"

"No, nothing like that. Sorry to barge in, but don't worry, nothing's wrong." His brother was looking at him quizzically. This was the first time Roger had set foot in Tupenny Cottage. "Mark, I'd like to speak to you. Now, if it's convenient."

"Of course." The elder Griffin rose in his usual unhurried manner. "Excuse me, my dear. Will you come into the kitchen, Roger? The cottage doesn't have anything as grand as a gentleman's study." He led the way while he spoke.

Then, when they were in the small room at the rear and he'd lit a candle and poked at the fire, "Can I get you something to drink? I've a bit of fairly decent sack, if you've a mind for it. Or a glass of ale. That's the limit of our cellar, so make a choice." He was smiling as he spoke. The words seemed to Roger a catalogue of lessons on how the mighty had fallen, but it was apparent that Mark meant them not at all like that.

"Ale's fine," he said rather more gruffly than he'd intended. "It's been a long, thirsty ride."

"You've come from London, then?" Mark didn't pause for a reply. "And"—he gestured at Roger's heavy riding boots—"arrived straight here without a stop at Tassels, judging from the look of you. What's wrong, Roger?"

"It's this business with Laura."

"I see." He poured mugs of ale for both of them and joined Roger by the fire. "I was given to understand you have no objection to her plans. At least that's what Sarah told me."

"Sarah! Christ almighty, Mark, don't you see? That's what's wrong. There's been only women deciding this, telling you and me that. If it isn't Nancy or Clare it's one of your girls. My own would doubtless be in the act if they were old enough to speak!"

"Doubtless," Mark agreed, then grinned, which just en-

279

couraged Roger's pique. "But you and I haven't been speaking much to each other for some time now. We can hardly blame the ladies for seeking to fill the void."

"That's another matter. This is different. Look, Mark, Laura's your daughter, not mine. If you have no objection to her tossing her life down a cesspool it's no business of mine. A nunnery, for God's sake. . . . But that's not what's brought me hell-bent for leather all the way from London. I don't know why I didn't see it before, but I see it now. This scheme of hers is bloody dangerous. For all of us. May I ask if you've thought of that?"

Mark suddenly felt a deep sense of shame. "I can't blame you for the question. I know it seems to you that everything I've done for the past four years has been without any thought for the effect on you and your family."

"Forget all that! I told you I didn't come here to argue about your decisions or beliefs. I only want some assurance that this latest plan is being enacted with caution."

"Of course you do. I'm sorry . . . no, don't interrupt me. It needs to be said. I'm genuinely sorry I didn't come to you about all this myself weeks ago. You had a right to know the arrangements and approve them. I guess I've just grown so accustomed to our nonspeaking relationship it never occurred to me."

"Be that as it may, what are the plans? How trustworthy is this fellow Huddleston? Sarah tells me he's had a hand in the matter."

"Yes, that's correct. Do you know who he is?"

Roger shrugged. "Vaguely. Fellow who helped the king back in '51, isn't he? Got a life pension and a grace-and-favor posting as a result, didn't he?"

"That's the short of it. He's a Catholic priest, the only one who's cited as a specific exception in every law against them made by Parliament. At the moment he's chaplain to the queen at Somerset House. None of that is important except to explain that he's privileged to come and go as he pleases in and out of court."

"I thought that was every Englishman's birthright," Roger said. His words dripped cynicism. "At any rate, I'm prepared to accept that it's Huddleston's. How does that make him reliable in this matter?"

"He's a friend," Mark said simply. "If he says it's safe for Laura to leave on this French ship, then I'm convinced it is."

"Very well, I see that. The bit that worries me is how she gets to wherever she's to meet Huddleston."

"I'm taking her myself."

"Bloody marvelous. That way you can both be arrested."

"I've no reason to think we'll be arrested, Roger. Why should anyone bother about us? A man and a young girl traveling to Kent...who's to question us?"

"I don't know. But surely I don't need to tell you that there are those in England who look for papists under their beds at night. After this latest business with the Duke of York..." He rose and paced the room. "I don't know, it just worries me."

Mark refilled both their mugs. "Any suggestions?" he asked quietly after some minutes.

Roger slammed the mug down on Clare's well-scrubbed kitchen table. "Yes, dammit! I have a suggestion. Might as well be hung for a sheep as a lamb. If this crazy scheme's to come off without getting us all permanent lodgings in some dungeon, then we'd best give it a sporting chance."

The brothers talked for another thirty minutes. At the end of that time they were agreed on all the details. "That's settled, then," Roger said as he rose to go.

"Settled," Mark said as he walked with his visitor to the door. "And Roger...thank you. It seems the only thing to say."

Roger grinned impulsively, then thrust out his hand. "It'll take more than an army of witch hunters to catch a Griffin," he said, chuckling.

Mark gripped his brother's hand warmly, then opened the door on an evening that had developed the first hint of winter chill.

From Hampton Court Palace the River Thames flowed eastward to the open water along a course of some fifty miles. It cut between the flat banks of Middlesex on one side and Surrey on the other, then through the heart of London and out to Wapping and Deptford. After that the legendary royal river made her way between Essex and Kent, past the Isle of Sheppey and around that bulge of Kentish coast speckled with small seaside villages like Whitstable and Herne Bay, until, at Margate, one could smell the salt of the North Sea and the English Channel was but a stone's throw to the right.

"How much longer do you make it, Hart?" Roger asked.

His shoulders ached with rowing, and the poor fit of the borrowed clothes didn't help.

"'Bout another half hour, cap'n. See, ye kin spy the Dover lights down there on the horizon."

Like Roger, Mark squinted off in the direction the old sailor indicated, but he could see nothing, only the still form of his eldest daughter where she sat in her disguise of men's clothing. Laura hadn't spoken a word since the journey started. "Are you all right?" he asked her now.

"Fine, Papa."

"Not too cold?"

"No, Papa, I'm fine."

Listening to this interchange, Roger marveled. Mark certainly seemed to love this child of his. How could he permit her to take this step? How indeed could he have taken that irrevocable step that had, however indirectly, made them all actors in this bizarre farce? Roger turned his mind from the enigma he'd long since decided was insoluble and paid attention to the rowing.

Their craft was a small wherry, just big enough for the four of them and the one crate of Turkish figs Roger had loaded aboard to reinforce their subterfuge. He'd considered using one of the big Griffin barges and a legitimate crew of his own watermen—such a choice would have cut the time of the journey in half—but had opted for the greater secrecy of the small boat with only himself, Mark, and the faithful Hart to row. It had been easy enough to arrange for the wherry to be brought to Tassels's river landing. Household business he'd simply said.

The four conspirators wore Griffin livery, highly identifiable purple breeches and jerkin trimmed with gold braid, which had been easy to get once Roger determined to involve Hart in the venture. These days the old seaman was not just night watchman of the George Alley premises, but unofficial quartermaster as well. On hearing his employer's request he promptly told four of the regular watermen that their uniforms were a disgrace to the firm and were to be brought to him for cleaning. In truth the livery he'd acquired badly needed such attention. When they had donned the outfits prior to starting this trip, Mark and Roger had both commented on the smell. Laura struggled into the strange man's suit, held her nose, and said nothing.

They set out at dawn on the morning of October 3. Roger knew the trip would be slow and arduous for three rowers unused to the task. He'd considered leaving a day before the Dover rendezvous to give them opportunity for frequent stops and the inevitable mistakes. But that would have meant spending a long time waiting at the Dover end, possibly as much as a day if they made better time than expected, and that seemed to him the most dangerous part of the venture. So they gave themselves eighteen hours to complete the journey a proper crew could have done in seven. Thank God it had proved enough. They were in sight of Dover, and when last he'd checked the time it had been not quite ten.

In the main it had proved an uneventful progress along a river that chose to be kind as regards squalls and currents. There had been only one bad moment. Just outside of Deptford a frigate of the Royal Navy edged near and ran beside them for almost ten minutes. The one time he permitted himself to look up to her high deck, Roger saw a young lieutenant with a spyglass keeping them under surveillance. Finally, the frigate took a northerly tack and left the little wherry to herself, and the four breathed a collective sigh of relief.

It wasn't till then that Roger realized his mouth had gone powder-dry and his palms sweaty with fear. The others seemed to feel something the same, except for Hart, who said in a voice heavy with feeling, "That be Gingerman. Worst bastard for the press wot ever walked. He knew from first minute we wuz Griffin men, not to be took. Just hung by like that to fright us. Enjoys that sort o' thing, does Gingerman." He spat over the side.

Now it was almost over. Whatever fate awaited Laura would be her own choice. No repercussions could touch the rest of the family. The thought gave Roger renewed strength. Ignoring the burning ache in his shoulders, he pulled harder. The two other men responded to his stepped-up pace and the little wherry sped toward Dover.

9.

The tavern where he and Hart waited was called the Crow's Nest. It was a dingy waterfront place where the ale tasted poisonous and the other drinkers looked to be yet more lethal. One scarred oak counter was the only amenity; across its filthy expanse tankards of brew were slopped to customers required to stand while they tippled. Roger found a bit of vacant wall and leaned against it gratefully.

"How long ye think they'll be, cap'n?" Hart asked.

"Can't say. And no titles, Hart, it's not wise." Like the old man, Griffin had changed into buff breeches and jerkin and had hidden his livery and other baggage just outside the town. At least, he thought gratefully, the pair of them still looked enough like the seamen they'd once been to attract no attention in this hellhole of a public house.

They'd been waiting for over an hour. At first Roger was glad of the warmth and even the terrible ale; now he was as anxious as Hart for Mark to rejoin them and the party to be on its way. His brother had taken Laura to that rendezvous which was the object of this entire mad exercise, but all had agreed it was best if only Mark knew where that meeting was to be. Roger wanted as little complicity as possible in this tryst with a papist priest.

Another hour passed. They drank two more tankards of ale. Griffin became increasingly aware of Hart's anxious glances and the impatient scuffling of his feet. Where the hell was Mark, anyway? It was near to one in the morning. He'd been supposed to deliver Laura at midnight. Roger drained his glass dry and started toward the bar to order another. Suddenly he changed his mind and turned back to his companion. "C'mon, old friend," he said softly. "Better the devil you know than the one you don't. Let's go see what we can find out."

The street was thick with fog, cold and salt-laden, with the ability to make one breathless as well as blind. "Where to, cap'n?" Hart asked.

"The docks, if we can find them."

"This way. I been in this town plenty o' times. You just take hold o' me shoulder, cap'n, and I'll lead the way."

Soon they came to a bit of high ground where the mists cleared, and below them Griffin saw Dover harbor. They had landed the wherry at a cove Hart knew about a mile upwater and made the rest of the journey on foot. This was Roger's closest look at the busy port since they'd arrived. He scanned the scene for any evidence of trouble, but nothing out of the ordinary was apparent. Then, while he watched, a brigantine of unmistakable French lines moved ghostlike over the moon-lit horizon. Was his niece on that ship? Christ, he'd give a lot to know. And a lot more to learn his brother's whereabouts.

"Cap'n!" Hart's voice had taken on a sudden urgency. "Someone's comin'!"

They stepped off the path and waited. Soon Roger heard the thud of hooves, muffled by the mists below their piece of high ground. "Sounds like a carriage," he whispered.

"Aye, a big one. Least six horses."

In fact only four mighty chestnuts pulled the splendid coach, which rose out of the fog to pass them close enough for Roger to reach out and touch the side if he wished. The vehicle was only a few feet beyond them when the driver suddenly reined in the horses and leaned behind to speak to his passengers. "Fog's right thick, milord," the man whined. "Cain't say I kin make much headway this night."

"I'd suggest, my good fellow, you'd do well to try. That is, if you value your head. His highness won't take lightly any inconvenience to this lady."

With a start Roger recognized the speaker. It was the Earl of Peterborough, long an intimate of the Duke of York's. Seated next to him was the tiny figure of a young girl huddled into the protection of a sable cloak and hood. Griffin looked more closely at the equipage. Emblazoned on its side were the Stuart arms. No doubt about it, this was James's carriage. Moreover he'd be willing to wager his next year's profits that the girl inside was the infamous Mary of Modena, who was rumored to be James's next wife. In less time than it took him to reach these conclusions the carriage moved on. Griffin and Hart resumed their clumsy progress toward the harbor.

Within five minutes a wind came up and blew away the fog. It was easier walking now, but Roger was immensely relieved when he saw Mark coming toward them. "All's well?" he asked by way of greeting.

"Yes, thank God. Sorry for the delay. It seems we were but an insignificant part of some larger drama which was running into snags of its own. My friend"—Hart was out of earshot, but still Mark avoided mentioning Huddleston by name—"was come on some errand for the Duke of York, and Laura couldn't be boarded until another girl disembarked. Apparently she was reluctant to do so and took some persuading."

"Ha," Roger said bitterly. "I'd like to ring the necks of the persuaders. I just saw the passenger in question. Her carriage passed us on the road. It seems, brother mine, that our James has got himself his papist wife, whatever the rest of England thinks about it."

It was some weeks later that the nation learned of the arrival of the reluctant fifteen-year-old bride. Parliament raved, and chose to retaliate by denying Charles the money he needed to continue the war against the Dutch. They also passed a law forbidding the marriage. The London crowds, meanwhile, expressed their opinion by rioting in the streets and burning an effigy of the pope. None of it mattered. James contemptuously announced that he had already married Mary of Modena. The wedding had taken place in Italy on September 30. Admittedly the Earl of Peterborough had stood proxy for York, but the ceremony was legal and binding nonetheless.

Far from all this furor, Laura Griffin had her own concerns. Like her aunt before her, she went to the Abbey of St. Savior alone and unattended, preceded only by a note from the same Bishop Fermeau who had once sponsored Sophia. But unlike her aunt, Laura had absolutely no preconceptions about what she was to find inside the abbey walls.

"We've a special treat for you, *ma petite*," Sister Imelda, still the keeper of the gate to the outside world, announced when Laura arrived. "You're to have a visit with Sister Benedict before the actual entrance ceremony."

"Sister Benedict?" The girl had no idea who that might be, or why a visit with her was deemed a special privilege.

"Your aunt, my dear! Don't you know her name in religion?" Then, remembering the particular circumstances these English women had to deal with, she clapped her hand to her forehead in dismay. *"Mais certainement,* you know nothing! How could you? Dear Sister Benedict says she daren't write home for fear the wicked English king will slap you all in a dungeon."

"He's not wicked," Laura interrupted stiffly. "It's others who are at fault. You don't understand."

Imelda bit her lip. "No, *ma petite,* you are quite right. I understand nothing of this business. Forgive me if I've offended you, but permit me to explain what I do know. Your aunt was professed of her final vows last year. She is Sister Benedict of the Cross now. A holy nun and an example to us all.

"I cannot tell you what joy she had when she learned that God had called you to this place. Never mind, she will tell you herself."

She led the girl to a small room with one stiff wooden chair facing a heavy iron grille. Sister Imelda motioned Laura to sit down, then rang a small bell. "I will leave you now," she said finally. "Sister Benedict will be here straightaway. When you have finished your visit I will be waiting for you in the next room."

At first Laura didn't even recognize Sophia in the strange convent garb. But that lasted only a few seconds. Soon they were clasping hands through the iron bars and both talking at once in their anxiety to exchange as much news as possible in the brief time allotted. Sophia seemed most surprised to learn of the whereabouts of the various members of the family and how they now lived more or less together in Surrey. "Has Roger come into the faith, then?" she asked in wonder.

"No, nothing like that. It's just that his wife is a very good and understanding person and they've two little girls and Papa was needed once Antony left all that land to Aunt Nancy..."

Sophia shook her head in confusion. "It's too much," she said quickly. "I can't try to understand it all in this little time. I will ask mother if you may write me a long letter once you're inside. A long letter with all the news. Will you do that, Laura?"

"Of course. But a letter, when we're both in the same place...it seems so silly!"

Sophia laughed. "That's not the only thing that will seem silly to you, darling, until you're used to us and our ways. Just be patient. It will get easier as time goes by, I promise you."

Laura couldn't help but notice how completely her aunt identified with the nunnery. These strange French women were "us" while she was apparently "they." "Aunt Sophia," she asked shyly, aware that she should say "Sister Benedict" but somehow reluctant to give up the old ways just yet, "were you surprised? When they told you I was coming, I mean?"

The other woman cocked her head in a manner Laura found comfortingly familiar. "Not exactly. You see, I knew one of you was coming, but I rather suspected it was Sarah."

"Sarah! She thinks the whole idea of being a nun is positively daft! What do you mean you knew one of us was coming? Didn't that bishop say it was me?"

"Oh, certainly! By the time the letter from his lordship came it was clear it was you. I mean before that." She stumbled, sorry she'd started down this path. "When I...when the nun told me..." Laura continued to gaze at her inquisitively. "Oh, never mind! It doesn't matter. What matters is you're here and great days are coming! Great days for us and for England, Laura. Just wait and see!"

10.

It had always seemed odd to Roger that close as he and Ahmet were, he'd never met Benjamin's sister, Rachel. For the first two years of their relationship Benjamin never mentioned her. Then a chance encounter precipitated Roger's first sight of Rachel Ahmet, and he finally found himself invited to the Ahmet home in Ingram's Court just behind the herb market.

It happened because Griffin went to St. Paul's churchyard to buy a book on household management which his wife had requested. It was still a marvel to him that Nancy of all people should ask for such a book. When Roger found the stall selling the work there was a long queue in which he duly took his place, and for a moment he half regretted Nancy's new domesticity. Then he noticed an extremely beautiful young woman standing just in front of him. That helped to make the wait more tolerable.

She was tiny and appealingly curvaceous, but that wasn't what first attracted his eye. It was instead the woman's rather exotic, foreign look. Very dark, with a quality of something Roger could only identify as mystery. When her turn came, he heard her intriguingly accented English. It was amusing to pass the time by guessing where she might be from.

"Will these be all, ma'am?" the clerk inquired, surveying the stack of volumes the woman had chosen.

"Yes. For today, at least." She favored the bookseller with a smile that displayed two fetching dimples and said, "Please deliver them to the home of Mr. Benjamin Ahmet at 6 Ingram's Court."

"Here!" Roger couldn't restrain his surprise. "I beg your pardon—you aren't Mr. Ahmet's sister, by any chance?"

The woman turned to look at her questioner and said with that inflection he found quite devastating, "But of course I am. Should I know you, sir?"

Roger grinned. "You should, but sadly you don't. I'm Roger Griffin, Miss Ahmet."

By this time they had stepped out of the line to continue their conversation, and Rachel extended one tiny gloved hand. "I should indeed. Benjamin has spoken of you so often, Captain Griffin. What a pleasure to meet you at last."

They chatted a moment longer, and she left. It wasn't till then that Roger found to his annoyance he'd lost his place in the queue. He had to start at the rear all over again, but he didn't really mind. The thought of the woman's beauty stayed with him like a warm fire on a winter afternoon.

Later, when he mentioned the incident to Benjamin, he discovered the other man already knew about it. "Rachel told me the story," Ahmet explained. "And asked that you join us for dinner some night soon. You will come, I hope."

"Delighted," Roger said at once. He was rather surprised to find how genuinely delighted he really was.

Griffin's first visit to Ingram's Court took place early in December. It was a surprisingly mild Tuesday evening when he approached the little covey of half-timbered houses set around a cobbled square. Had Ahmet not given him precise directions he'd never have found the place. It seemed isolated, foreign, somehow removed from the bustling city roundabout.

Roger glanced at the slip of paper he held. Yes, number 6. It was just over there. He made his way to a doorway half hidden by some bare-stemmed vine that would, in summer, create a leafy framework for the entrance. While he waited for a reply to his knock, he glanced at the other houses in the court. On the neighboring property he noted a small placard inscribed with the name Levi, but before he could look at any others the door to number 6 opened and Rachel Ahmet stood before him framed in soft yellow candlelight.

She was more beautiful than he remembered, and more exotic. Her black hair was pulled straight back from her high forehead to hang down her back in a mass of ringlets. Her eyes were as black as her hair, her cheekbones high and elegant. Rachel had lips of dark red that reminded him of ripe plums in summer. "Do come in, Captain Griffin," she said in the accent he found so appealing. "We are both very pleased you could come."

She led him to a small room just off the entrance hall where Benjamin was waiting with the inevitable glass of brandy. It was, Roger noted, a room that suited them both. Books everywhere, not just on shelves that seemed specially built for the purpose, but scattered over tables and lying open on the arms of chairs. The curtains and upholstery were not the most expensive or the grandest in London, but certainly he'd never seen color used to such advantage. Everything was in soft shades of mauve or pink or blue; subdued, but warm and totally inviting. "What a beautiful room," he exclaimed.

"I'm glad you like it, Roger," Ahmet replied. "Like everything in the house it's Rachel's doing. Rather un-English-looking, I suspect—but for us a touch of home."

"You've been away from Turkey for a long time, haven't

290

you, Miss Ahmet?" Roger said to his hostess. "Do you find yourself homesick?"

"Please, you must call me Rachel. And to answer your question ... no, not really. It's just as true to say I've been in England a long time. In some ways we do try to keep the old ways alive, the Turkish customs I mean, but in most others both Benjamin and I have become thoroughly English."

It was true—and a fair analysis of the very blending he found so charming. Rachel was not locked away in some purdah exclusively for women as she would have been in the East, but neither was she wholly an English girl. She retained the kind of feminine shyness and reticence common to her sex in the culture from which she sprang, coupled with an alert and obviously intelligent mind. Her manner of deferring to her brother and even to him made Roger feel astonishingly protective toward her. He found the feeling pleasurable in the extreme. Rachel Ahmet's elegance and breeding showed in every word and gesture, but didn't conflict with the merriment and good fun that marked the dinner party.

"You must try some of this," she said, laughing as she passed him a dish of some vegetable concoction he'd never before seen. "It's very popular all over the East. It's called *imam bayildi.*"

"Careful, Roger," Benjamin warned. "The name means 'the holy man fainted.' Both the Ahmets laughed at Roger's reaction to this announcement.

"The question long debated by wise men of Turkey is simply this," Benjamin continued. "Did the holy man faint because of his pleasure at the taste of the dish, or anger with his wife for feeding him something so likely to divert his mind from higher things? Taste it and give us your verdict."

"But it's delicious!" Roger said in surprise after his first mouthful. "It looks so odd I'd never ... I mean ..." He blushed, and the Ahmets laughed some more.

Later they took him back to the small study and served him an assortment of meltingly sweet jams in tiny crystal goblets to be eaten with yet tinier silver spoons. The whole evening went thus; exotic, different, and a challenge to senses he hadn't known he'd possessed.

It was still later, after Rachel had left the two men alone with their final tiny bowls of thick sweet Turkish coffee, that Ahmet said, "I rather think you find us less English than you expected, Roger. Here at home we don't try to fit in, only to be ourselves. Perhaps that's why we seldom invite strangers to join us."

"Frankly, I had wondered about that."

"Yes, I'm sure you had. It's odd, you know—we Jews are traditionally hospitable. We even have a feast day in the year when we are supposed to open the door and shout as loud as we can, 'Let all who are hungry come and eat!'"

"And do you do that still? Here in London?"

"Would you believe it, yes. But perhaps not as loud as scripture commands. Just loud enough to be heard here in Ingram's Court. That's our protection, you see."

"I'm afraid I don't see."

"Roger, you surprise me. I thought you'd guessed. We own every house in the court. We being a group called B'nai Shalom, the Brotherhood of Peace. Admittedly that's not the name you'd find on the deeds. We had to use a proper English solicitor to act as what you'd call a 'front man,' but we own it nonetheless. Only Jews live here, Roger. We look out for each other, and that makes our position in your country tolerable. Do I shock you?"

"No," he answered slowly. "Not really. Now that you tell me the story it explains a lot of things. Makes sense, too."

"Yes, I expected you to see that. But never mind, I now declare you an honorary member of B'nai Shalom despite the fact that you're a *goy*, an outsider. You may come here whenever you wish, and know that the door is always open to you and yours."

Roger was genuinely touched. Somehow the evening had given him an insight into the full extent of the generosity behind Benjamin's words.

A week before Christmas the weather turned bitterly cold. The Thames froze from well below Whitehall as far as Wapping. Londoners, who had found little to celebrate in the past few months, proceeded to erect an ice fair on the frozen river and besport themselves on skates and sledges with rare enthusiasm. It was a nuisance for business, of course. No deliveries were possible as long as the river remained an icy wasteland. "To hell with it," Roger announced when Christmas was still five days off. "I'm closing the office until the New Year."

Getting to Tassels in those circumstances was rather difficult, but his horse was game despite the extra weight of the presents Roger carried in his saddlebags. It was nearly midnight when he arrived home, frozen and hungry and much in need of some wifely ministrations. There were none forthcoming, however; he rode up to the front door to find the house ablaze with lights and an air of desperation apparent as soon as he crossed the threshold.

"Here, Ellen..." He stopped the old servant as she was proceeding to ignore his unexpected arrival and hurry past him with the kettle of steaming water she carried. "What's going on? How come you're not all sleeping? Where's your mistress?"

"Mistress be in her bed, poor thing," the woman answered, looking at him as if he were a particularly objectionable bit of dirt that had managed to invade the house. "Ye should know...."

"I don't know a damn thing. I've just come from London. Now stop talking riddles and tell me what's the matter with my wife."

"Hmphh... only said ye should know, not that ye did.... Miss Nancy's abed with birthin' pains. Real bad they are. Been like this since yesterday. Not that I'd expect you or any man to care what ye causes with yer bit o' sport."

Roger ignored the rest of the tirade and took the stairs two at a time. Since they had moved their bedroom to the new wing it wasn't usually possible to hear a sound from the master suite until one had actually passed through the corridor of the old house and entered the new. But this night he got only as far as the landing before he heard Nancy's cries.

For an instant Roger felt himself back in the filthy little room in the Cock and Pie four years earlier. She sounded now just as she had then, as if she would gladly welcome death in place of the wracking agony of the moment. Instinct told him that this was no normal occurrence. He'd not been present at the birth of either of his daughters, but he was sure neither of them had been anything like this. If that opinion required confirmation, he found it in Clare's face when she met him at the door to his wife's bedchamber.

"Roger! I didn't expect you, but it's a blessing you've come.... I'm very worried."

"What is it, Clare? What's the matter? Surely it isn't like this every time?"

"No." His sister-in-law shook her head. "Nancy usually

has an easy labor. This time the baby's turned the wrong way around. Poor Nancy, she's been like this for hours. I'm not sure if she can go on much longer." As if to verify the words there was another heart-wrenching scream from the bed.

"Sweet Christ, Clare! Isn't there something you can do?"

"I've given her all the herbal drafts I know to help such things." Clare wrung her hands in a wholly uncharacteristic gesture of despair. "I just don't have any idea what else to do."

He was peeling off his cloak and gloves even while he spoke. "Who's with her now?"

"Sarah and Maude Jenks. Ellen should be coming back soon. She just went to get some more hot water. They say sometimes the steam helps."

"Get rid of them all," he said brusquely. "Send Sarah and Ellen downstairs, tell the Jenks girl to stay in the nursery with the babies. There's to be just you and me."

"What are you going to do?"

"Dammit, Clare, just do what I say. I don't know exactly what I'm going to do, but I'm not going to let her go on like that, and have a gaggle of cackling Cassandras acting like some kind of Greek chorus in the background. Now let's stop talking and get on with it."

At first he didn't think she recognized him. Then, in a moment of all too brief respite between the punishing waves of pain, she opened her eyes, saw him, and stretched out her hand. "Easy, love," he whispered. "Try to be easy. And hang on a bit longer, can't you? I'm going to try to help."

It seemed to him necessary to explain to her what he was going to do; to have, as it were, her approval for what might be a disastrous interference in a process he knew so little about. "Clare tells me," he said quietly, "the baby's turned the wrong way around. That's why you're having such a hard time. Once, years ago on the Continent, I was with some troops and we came across a local woman having a baby in the fields. We had a doctor with us, and he helped her. I think it was a similar situation, and I remember what he did. I'm going to try the same thing, if you'll let me, darling."

"Anything..." she managed to whisper before the pain returned and she could only scream in agony.

Later Clare told him it had only taken about five minutes.

While he lived through the nightmare it seemed to Roger to last for endless hours.

At the head of the bed was Clare, sitting behind Nancy, gripping her arms and shoulders as if she could tear the pain out of the girl and take it on herself. At the foot he stared in terror at his wife's straining, contorted body. It was as if the Nancy he knew, the Nancy of slim thighs and delicately curved hips, had been overlaid with some swollen, misshapen creature that wasn't quite human. He was engaged in a duel with that creature, that entity which was trying to steal from Nancy her very life.

There wasn't time to marvel at the extraordinary fact that this slim girl could so open her body that another human life could come forth. There was time only to take one deep breath and, as carefully as he could, repeat the procedure he'd seen another man perform years before.

Whether it was instinct or luck or the grace of God he couldn't say. He only knew that at that first tentative moment of probing he caught hold of something firm and definite. Later he would realize it had been the child's foot. Suddenly Nancy screamed again and strained with all her might to expel the creature that was causing her such agony. Without thought or calculation he pulled. For long seconds the struggle continued. Roger tugged as though not a tiny baby resisted him, but some huge line connected to a sail or an anchor. Through it all Nancy's single one-note scream went on and on. He thought that if it stopped, if she was silent, her life would stop too. Then it was over.

The baby lay on the sheets between its mother's legs, no longer resisting him, but lying motionless and inert beneath his hand. Slowly Roger let go the small foot and stared at the creature. It was is if he were looking at everything through the wrong end of a spyglass. The child seemed miniaturized, unreal and far away. He looked up and noted how silent the room had become. He could hear his own breathing, but no one else's. Nancy lay back against the battered pillows, her eyes closed, as motionless as the child.

Clare was the first to break the tableau. "It's all right, Roger. She's only fainted. Here, give me that place...." She had to physically shove him away from the bottom of the bed while her hands flew into the familiar routine. "Get that cloth over here. Bathe her face; I'll take care of the baby."

295

"Is it..." He couldn't formulate the words. His tongue wouldn't function.

"Not it, he. You've a son. And yes, he's alive." Even while she spoke Clare was cutting the cord that tied the infant to his mother, then wiping him down with motions that looked to Roger all too rough.

"He's getting around to introducing himself now, I think," she said softly. Then, so suddenly it made Roger jump, she delivered a swift slap to the tiny buttocks. For a second or two nothing happened, until at last the tiny mouth opened and let forth an ear-piercing shriek.

"Shall we call him Roger?"

It seemed to him quite incredible that this morning, just six hours after she'd struggled for life itself, Nancy was sitting up in bed nursing her baby boy and chatting with her husband as if the whole occurrence were quite the sort of thing she did every day.

"No," he managed to reply, despite the fact that he was still awestruck by the whole sequence of events. "This time, if you don't mind, I'd like to choose the name."

"Well, you've earned the right," Nancy answered, smiling. "I doubt that either young Master Griffin or I would be here now if it weren't for you."

"Thank God I was able to help," Roger said quietly. He'd not yet told Nancy that the occasion he had witnessed so long ago, the one that had provided him with the model for his own intervention in the birth, had resulted in an infant strangled by the cord wrapped around its tiny neck.

"Anyway, I've thought a bit about this one's name since you told me it was to be a boy. As the young man has chosen to prove his mother's a seer, I'd like him to have the name I've had in mind all along."

"Fine," Nancy agreed. "But I'm dying of suspense. What's it to be?"

"James."

"James? For the Duke of York, you mean?"

"Exactly."

"But... Dismal Jimmy, that's what Nell calls him. Do you fancy our son a Dismal Jimmy?"

"Not a bit of it. Nell's not the final authority, you know. I think James a fine, strong name. Don't you?"

Nancy made a small face. "I guess it's all right. But do

you think this a good time to be naming a poor little innocent after James? I rather hope our son will be more favored by providence."

"James it is," Roger pronounced firmly. "Never mind the braying of the London wolf pack. I only pray this young man turns out to be as loyal to his friends, and to York, as his namesake's been to us."

He never bothered to tell Nancy that had the baby been a girl he'd made up his mind to call her Rachel.

BOOK II

1678–1685

PART FIVE

The Lion's Roar

Here's pennyroyal and marigolds,
Come buy my nettle-tops.
Here's watercresses and scurvy grass,
Come buy my sage of virtue, ho!
Come, buy my wormwood and mugwort,
Here's all fine herbs of every sort,
And southernwood that's very good,
Dandelion and horseleek.
Here's dragon's tongue and horehound.
Let none despise the merry, merry wives
Of famous London Town.

—Old herb seller's ballad

1.

They'd been, on balance, good years, Roger Griffin decided. He couldn't say why, on this spring afternoon, he'd suddenly left the office and come here by the river to muse about the past. A sudden touch of melancholy perhaps, a sense of time passing, a need to assess his life?

Griffin leaned back against the grass and watched the busy traffic on the Thames. Without effort he could see four, no five, barges flying the purple-and-gold flag of Griffin's Importations. Surely that said something? He didn't need to meditate on the business to know it was a success. He needed only to check his account books or tally up the coins in money chests lodged at half a dozen different goldsmiths. If cash was the criterion the last four years had been remarkably productive.

But surely pounds, shillings, and pence weren't the only measure of a man. What then? Children? At seven Nell was a headstrong beauty so much like her mother that seeing her was seeing a sort of miniaturized Nancy. Jennifer, a year younger, was a different breed, soft-spoken, chubby, a little bit of fluff. James was only four; too soon to judge what sort of man he'd grow to be. Too soon too for Roger to take pride in the development of any of the three. Admittedly, he adored them. Nothing gave him more pleasure than an afternoon spent in their company; but they were no yardstick against which to test the limit of his present melancholy.

"Forget it!" he said aloud. Only a solitary chaffinch paid him any attention. "What I've got is spring fever. I need one of Clare's herbal tonics to put me right." He rose, dusted off his breeches, and started back toward George Alley. Nancy was meeting him in town this evening. There would be time for some work at his desk in what was left of the afternoon.

As he walked toward his office, his mood didn't lighten.

There were two other possible causes, both so obvious he chose to ignore them. There was the ongoing battle over Harwood Hall, fought on two separate fronts. Thus far no amount of money had succeeded in shifting John Lane from the place he'd usurped. And Nancy still insisted that if he did manage to buy back the place she wouldn't live in it. So Roger had contented himself with acquiring land that abutted Harwood—that piece just south of the Hall which Mark had intended to buy before all the trouble began. By itself the acreage wasn't worth much—it was only bare hills on which the old Kirkslee Priory had once stood—but when he regained the Hall it would be a handsome addition.

None of this was new. A problem of long standing could hardly explain his present mood. That left only the strange conversation he'd had with Benjamin yesterday. God knew Ahmet was no prophet of doom...it wasn't like the man to become so morose on the strength of vague premonitions, or, as he styled them, hunches.

"You can call me mad if you like, Roger, but I can feel it in my bones."

"Feel what, for God's sake? I just don't see what you're talking about."

The Jew slammed his fist against the arm of his chair in a rare gesture of frustration. "I keep telling you. Bigotry, persecution, Jew-baiting. The same old catalogue of sins that's been repeating itself for hundreds of years."

"Look," Roger said with as much patience as he could muster. "I know the history is all too plain. You've precedents enough on which to hang your argument, God knows. But what I don't see, Benjamin, is what makes you feel that such persecutions are nearer or more dangerous now than they were, say, last month or last year. What's happened? That's what I don't understand."

"Nothing's happened, I tell you. It's just a feeling I have...a 'sense,' for want of a better term."

"And what does this 'sense' tell you to do?"

"I'm not sure, except for one thing—I've got to get Rachel away from here."

"Rachel? But where would you send her? Where could she go?"

"I don't know exactly. I've thought of Amsterdam—we have relatives there. Maybe even the colonies in America."

"But surely it would grieve Rachel to go to any of those places, to leave you, England..."

"Yes, I know all that. Still, if I'm right the choice is clear. Leaving England is better than dying."

If Roger was honest, he could indeed pinpoint the reason for his mood. If Benjamin sent Rachel away, if he couldn't look forward to the two or three times a month when he was invited to Ingram's Court, it would leave a void in his life that nothing else could fill. That was the long and short of it. It didn't matter how much money he earned, how delightful were his children, how successful Nancy had been in turning Tassels into a showplace known throughout Surrey. What really mattered was Rachel Ahmet of the sparkling black eyes and the tinkling laugh. She it was who gave spice and pleasure to his days. The thought of losing even that innocent friendship was the black cloud that suddenly blotted out the April sun.

These days Nancy never went up to London by water. During the numerous changes and additions to Tassels which had occupied her since they had acquired the Sheldon land, a proper mews had evolved in the meadow behind the sycamores. Her original plan had been to use the facility much as it had been used at Harwood Hall, as a place to house the hawks and falcons and hounds which would someday provide young James with the sport that had fascinated his father and grandfather before him. Roger had derided the idea at first, then become fascinated with it and himself purchased the first birds and beasts to be installed in the mews. At four, however, Jamie was still too young to be introduced to the pleasure of the hunt, and Roger simply hadn't the time to take up his old games. The mews had become instead a stable. True, two of the horses were bought because they showed great promise as hunters, but the rest were work animals used mainly to pull the elegant carriage that was Nancy's proudest possession.

She had ordered the coach on her own, without consulting either Roger or Mark. The day she conceived the idea Nancy had been walking by the premises of a dealer in such wares and was forced to stop her progress while a graceful vehicle rolled out of the alley into the street. It was obviously a new carriage on the road for the first time. The single passenger was a lady whose dress and bearing marked her as nobility, and seeing the expression on the woman's face made Nancy quiver with longing. She marched inside and concluded the deal in twenty minutes.

The coach she chose was essentially a simple light equipage that could carry up to six persons. What made it special, at least from Nancy's point of view, was the decoration she commissioned. The moldings and footboards were to be colored in red and olive oils, the body japanned with silver flowers, and on each side the doors emblazoned with the Griffin coat of arms. No one was more astonished than she when she heard herself tell the painter, "Azure, a bend or. With two griffins rampant...."

Nancy hadn't seen that ancient symbol since her long-ago visit to Harwood Hall. Roger had chosen quite a different design to identify Griffin's Importations. When Nancy instructed the workman she simply dredged out of her memory the description Clare had recited eight years before. But the memory was absolutely clear, explicit in every detail. "There's a motto too," she said. "I want it worked into the design. *Regum in Via Recta Dirige*. You can do all that?"

"Certainly, ma'am. But you're sure those are your arms, your motto? Meaning no offense, ma'am, but there's penalties for usin' 'em if ye ain't entitled."

"No fear," she said, smiling. "I'm Mrs. Roger Griffin, and those are my husband's arms."

The carriage cost forty-three pounds and three shillings, and the decorating brought the total account to fifty-six pounds. The bill for the four coach horses was closer to a hundred. She bought those at Guildford market, again without consulting either Roger or Mark. Finally, she hired a young coachman, one Rudolph Duggins, late of Bolton in Yorkshire and come south to seek his fortune, who agreed to do double duty as stablemaster. Only when all that was accomplished and coach, horses, and driver were installed in the mews did she invite Roger to come and inspect her new acquisition.

He merely stared, circled the vision a time or two, then walked silently out to the orchard. She had to follow him down there before she could elicit any comment on her efforts.

"That boy has a Yorkshire accent," Roger said. "Where did you find him?"

"In London. Hanging around Nell's looking for work. Don't you think him suitable?"

"Suitable! The whole thing's like a bloody mirage. The coach looks quite grand enough to drive out of Whitehall.

How did you know about the coat of arms? Mark must have helped you with that."

"Mark didn't know a thing about it. He still doesn't, for that matter. I wanted you to see it first. I saw the arms that time we went to Harwood Hall. I just remembered them."

"I see."

She was disappointed, and it showed. "You don't like it, do you, any of it? They were wise purchases, Roger. I can show you what I spent, and I've worked it all out. The rig will pay for itself in eighteen months."

"It's not that. There's no reason you shouldn't have a carriage. We can afford it."

"Well, then?"

"I don't know exactly. It just startled me. I guess in my own mind I simply put all that aside until we're back at Harwood. It seems somehow out of place here."

"Rubbish!" Nancy's chin came up in customary defiance. "This is my home and that's my carriage. Every penny to pay for it was earned right here at Tassels. I used the profits from the spring sheep shearing."

They never discussed it again. Neither did Nancy ever again hire a boat to bring her to town. She rode to London behind Rudy Duggins, her plumed hat swaying in the gentle motion of the elegant coach that bore on its sides the proud blazon of two griffins rampant.

This afternoon the coach was filthy by the time it turned into Cheapside and headed for George Alley. The spring had been unusually warm and dry, making the road from Surrey a track of dust beneath the horses' hooves. "If ye won't be needin' me for a bit, ma'am, I kin get 'er washed down same place I water the horses."

"Yes, Rudy, that'll be fine. I shan't need you until morning. Captain Griffin and I will spend the night in town."

She was excited by the prospect. It had been months since she'd had such an outing. For one thing, she was very busy at Tassels; for another, Roger hadn't suggested it. He was busy too, she knew that. Still, her voice had been a bit wistful when she mentioned to him that Nell was to play Lady Squeamish in a new play by Otway, *Friendship in Fashion*.

"Come up for it by all means," Roger had said at once.

"We'll have a night out and you can stay over until morning."

Despite being a little hurt that the impetus had to come from her, Nancy jumped at the invitation. Nell had returned to the stage a year before, and everyone had greeted the event with cheers. "Pretty, witty Nell," the crowds and critics roared alike. Nancy was mad to see her act again.

George Alley was battened down for the night by the time she arrived, and Roger was waiting for her in the deserted office. "I've booked two theater seats for us," he said by way of greeting. "And supper and a room later on at the Golden Bull."

"Just the two of us?"

"Yes." He smiled more warmly than she was accustomed to of late. "Just the two of us."

A huge crowd was milling around the theater by the time they arrived. Nancy ran a practiced eye over the other women and decided she was satisfied. At thirty-four she knew herself to be at the zenith of her good looks. The auburn hair was as glorious as ever, though these days she wore it piled on top of her head, not loose down her back as she used to do. Life in the country had put permanent color in her cheeks, and her figure was improved by the few pounds she'd added since the birth of her children. Her frock of blue-and-white-striped silk had a lace ruffle edging the hem and short train as well as more ruffles to finish the elbow-length sleeves, and she'd exchanged her daytime hat for a cornet of matching lace that framed her face and fluttered gently over her bare shoulders. Yes, she thought as she flicked open her elegant fan and nodded to a lady she didn't really think she knew, I'll do.

Roger, however, was oblivious to his wife's appearance. He'd tried to shake his depressed mood before she arrived— he owed her that much on this rare evening in town—but wasn't entirely successful. It might have been better once they arrived at the theater except for one thing. Standing a few feet away, as yet unaware of the Griffins' presence, were Benjamin Ahmet and his sister. Rachel wore plum-colored brocade devoid of any ornament. Her head was bare, and when she turned, spotted Roger, and smiled, her expression seemed to him more dazzling than the accumulated sparkle of all the jewels on all the women present.

"Look, Roger!" Nancy whispered excitedly in his ear.

"There's Benjamin. I wonder who the woman with him is. She's a gorgeous creature. So exotic and foreign-looking."

"That's Rachel Ahmet, his sister. Come along, I'll introduce you."

2.

Nell was marvelous. It didn't require friendship to see that. She had the audience in the hollow of her hand from her first line to her last. They gave her a standing ovation at her entrance, and another, longer version when she took her final bow. "Roger tells me you know Miss Gwyn well," Rachel said shyly to Nancy as they rose to go. The four had managed to sit together, but the play had provided no opportunity for chatting. These were Rachel's first words since they were introduced two hours ago.

"Yes." Nancy found the younger girl's ingenuousness appealing. "We grew up together and acted together on this very stage."

"Oh, I wish I could have seen you. Benjamin's told me you were wonderful. But back then he always said I was too young to visit the theater."

Nancy laughed. It was easy for her to understand why Benjamin didn't want his little sister tailing along when he came to see Nancy in the old days. "Well, you're not too young now, but I'm too old. No more acting for me—Roger's seen to that!"

Rachel smiled. "I'm told your children are angels. You must be quite content to give up all this for them." She made a broad gesture encompassing the smoky theater and its tinseled glamour.

"Angels! Well, maybe he thinks that because he's not with them day and night. But come, Miss Ahmet, enough of this domestic chatter. Wouldn't you like to meet Nell and the rest of the cast?"

Rachel's black eyes widened in wonder. "Could I really?"

"Of course you can. Roger, Benjamin, let's go backstage. Miss Ahmet wants to meet everybody."

"Do you think that wise, Rachel?" Benjamin asked softly.

"Oh, why not?" his sister pleaded. "You're always whisking me away home just when things get exciting. Please, Benjamin...just for a minute."

There was no resisting her appeal. Roger looked less anxious than his partner to prolong this part of the evening, but he dutifully followed his wife, who was leading them all to the Green Room.

"Nancy!" a voice shouted as soon as she entered the door. "Did anyone know you were coming? Look, Nell, it's Nancy!" She was enveloped in familiar hugs and greetings, and for long minutes the other three could only stand awkwardly at the side. Then Nancy dragged them to the center of the throng.

"Nell, this is Rachel Ahmet. You remember Benjamin, don't you? She wanted to meet you." More greetings, more laughter. The players were in high spirits following the success of the evening. They swept the Griffins and Ahmets into their revels without hesitation.

Soon the entire party were in the Lion's Rest drinking each other's health and indulging in that kind of bonhomie which is peculiar to theater folk. "Give us a song, Nance," someone shouted from the rear. "C'mon! For old times' sake. Nell's made her comeback. Now it's your turn!"

"No comebacks for me," Nancy said in reply. "I'm a proper lady now." But even as she spoke she was being propelled to the front of the small room. "I haven't sung for years...nothing but lullabies."

"C'mon, Nance, pull the other leg! We know you can still sing."

"Very well," she answered finally. "But you remember you asked for it. Here, Jack, help me up on this thing." Nancy swung her skirts high above her knees, and a burly stagehand hoisted her atop a convenient keg of ale. "What will it be?" she asked.

"Anything as long as it's bold as brass and in the old Nancy Wilmott style," came the reply.

"That's right," someone else urged. "What about 'The Miller's Daughter'?" A dozen voices joined in that request, and finally someone managed to find a place for Nancy's old accompanist, Kevin Mitchell, and his lute. Kevin didn't wait for her to agree to sing "The Miller's Daughter." He merely grinned up at Nancy and plucked the opening chords.

> *"The miller's daughter riding to the fair*
> *Without a saddle upon a scurvy mare..."*

Her voice was a bit hesitant at first, but by the third line she'd found both her key and her old gusto.

> *"Cried, 'O Mother I'm quite undone,*
> *I'm all o'ergrown with hair.'"*

There was no stopping her now. Even if she had seen the expression in Roger's eyes she'd not have regretted giving in to the crowd's demands. It was marvelously exciting to be the center of attention again.

> *"Away you silly daughter*
> *'Tis ev'ry she's concern.*
> *And if you don't believe me*
> *Look here and you may learn."*

With a flourish Nancy swung her skirts over her head, then dropped them demurely. The crowd was loving it, clapping her rhythm with raucous enthusiasm.

> *"Then taking her aside*
> *She made the matter plain:*
> *'O Mother you're ten times worse,*
> *You ride upon the mane.'"*

The impromptu show went on for almost an hour. Two more songs by Nancy alone, then a duet with Nell, and finally the whole company singing, "I gave her cakes and I gave her ale and we were wondrous merry..."

Halfway through the performance Rachel Ahmet turned to Roger and whispered, "You must be very proud to have such a talented wife."

He knew her too well to imagine there was any sarcasm in the remark. He was surprised, however, that she didn't know him well enough to guess at the fury that was assailing him now. Nancy flaunting herself like any common whore,

310

singing bawdy songs with as much relish as a sailor. Roger turned to look at Rachel. The contrast between the two women was painful. With a guilty start he pulled his gaze away from Rachel and looked over to her brother. Benjamin paid them no attention. He was completely wrapped up in Nancy. At this moment she was leaning forward to kiss Sir Will D'Avenant, and the entire assembly got a good look at her breasts as she did so.

Hours later they said goodnight to the theater company and the Ahmets and made their way to the Golden Bull. Nancy had drunk quite a bit by then. She wasn't drunk, however, just pleasantly tipsy, as exhilarated by the events of the evening as by the wine. Roger had downed twice as much as she, but he wasn't drunk either. He felt instead that some great knot of controlled feeling was coming undone in his belly. The sensation alarmed him. Careful, one part of his mind kept saying, careful...she's your wife, the mother of your children....

"Oh, my!" Nancy flung herself across the bed. "That was fun. I haven't had such an evening in so long I'd quite forgotten what it feels like."

"You remembered very quickly," Roger answered quietly.

"Yes, I did." Nancy seemed totally unaware of his mood. "I haven't sung those songs in years, but once I started every word came back."

"Once a slut, always a slut," he said softly.

Nancy stared at him in silence. He was standing above her now, staring down at where she lay on the bed, menace in every line of his body. She didn't move, only kept staring at him while his vicious words hung in the air between them.

It was Roger who broke the tableau after some seconds. "Nancy, I'm sorry. Forgive me, please. I've had too much to drink."

"In vino veritas," she quoted. "Is that what you think, Roger? What you really think?"

"No, of course not. I told you, I've had too much to drink."

"Too much? No, I think not. Not enough, I'd say. Otherwise you'd not be backing off. You'd tell me the rest of what is on your mind. What you tell yourself in your heart of hearts."

She stood up while she spoke and began to undress. "Well, Roger, don't say I didn't warn you. Gentry marry gentry; when they don't there's trouble. You should have listened to me. Then you wouldn't be so miserable now. You should have arranged some sweet, docile highborn lady for a wife. That way you could have had me on the side for the one thing I'm good for." She stood naked before him with her firm breasts just inches from his chest. "Take your breeches off, Roger. Since you can't make your heart happy with your choice of a wife, you might as well let your cock enjoy its folly."

He wanted to shout at her, slap her if necessary. Anything to make her stop speaking. But no words came. His reaction was totally involuntary; his loins had a life of their own. One hand reached out to fondle her breasts even while the other was busy undoing his clothes. Within seconds they were writhing on the bed, locked together in that same passion that had first marked their union, but with none of the tenderness that had once tempered it. "I hate you, Roger Griffin," she whispered in his ear even as he drove himself into her. "I hate you for what you can't forgive in me...."

They didn't speak again. Roger left the room at dawn, and soon afterward Nancy had breakfast and sent a messenger to the stable where Rudy was waiting with the coach. "Straight home," she told him as soon as he arrived. "Straight back to Tassels."

3.

For Roger the morning brought the first summons from the Duke of York in almost eighteen months. James couldn't have chosen a worse moment. Roger was not only emotionally drained by the terrible scene with Nancy, he was in the throes of a ghastly hangover. To make matters worse, there were at least four letters in the file which Monty had marked urgent. They were staring up at him now as he gazed bemusedly from his desk to the pageboy waiting for a reply. "Yes, yes, of course," he said finally. "Tell his highness I shall be at the palace at three just as he requests."

The urgent letters proved to be less so than Monty's sense of the dramatic had indicated. A request for new instructions from an orange grower in Seville, two letters from Wapping accusing the night watchman at Griffin's warehouse of pilfering goods—both in the same hand and both unsigned—and an offer from a Turkish sea captain to sell them a cargo of cocoa beans at twice the going rate. He wrote to the man with the oranges that Griffin's would purchase the entire crop if he'd take three percent less than he was asking, tore up the anonymous tattlings but made a mental note to check the warehouse accounts, and dispatched the letter from the Turk to Benjamin, who could tell the man to go to hell in his own language.

By lunchtime nothing pressing remained. Roger left George Alley and proceeded along Fleet Street to a tavern with the unlikely name of the Devil and St. Dunstan. The place was noted for its fine food and distinguished clientele, but neither attraction was on Roger's mind at the moment. He hoped to find Pepys there. The fellow often lunched at the Devil, since he quite enjoyed rubbing elbows with the high born. Maybe Pepys could tell him what was in the wind. It wouldn't hurt to be somewhat prepared for the meeting with

York. No joy, Samuel was nowhere in evidence. Roger ordered a dish of oysters—someone had once told him they were good for a hangover—but left them untouched. Two glasses of the landlord's best ale did help, however. He felt somewhat revived by the time he started toward St. James's Palace.

Back in '73, when all the ruckus over James's marriage to Mary of Modena took place, both his enemies and his friends advised the duke to live quietly in the country with his new bride. James had effectively thumbed his nose at the lot of them. He moved Mary into St. James's Palace with much pomp and show. The couple were there yet, although of late the gossip around them seemed to be assuming rather more menace. In his customary fashion Roger eschewed the whole mess. He much preferred to keep a comfortable distance between himself and the intrigues at court. Today, apparently, he was not to be allowed to do so.

"It's good to see you, Roger. It's been some time."

"Yes, sir, since the wedding, in fact."

James made a face. "That damned wedding. I thought the girl would never stop crying."

It was no secret that when Mary, his eldest daughter by his first wife, was handed over to William, Prince of Orange, the impetus was politics rather than romance. It had been not James's choice, but Charles's. The king needed to placate his Dutch enemies, who were besting him in battle, and prod his French allies, who were inclined to take him too much for granted. Thus a marriage between a Stuart princess and the most powerful ruler among the Dutch. "You've a couple of daughters of your own, haven't you, Roger?" York asked.

"Yes, sir, two. Nell's seven and Jennifer's six. A son too, as you may recall."

"Ah, of course! My young namesake. How is he?"

"Fine, your highness. Growing a foot a week, it seems."

The idle chatter went on for some minutes. James inquired after Nancy, after Tassels, and finally after the progress of Griffin's Importations.

"I can't complain, sir. We've been fortunate."

"You're satisfied with that partner of yours, then...the Jew...what's his name?"

"Ahmet, sir, Benjamin Ahmet. More than satisfied. It was a lucky day for me when I tied up with Benjamin."

The duke tapped his chin with one ringed finger. "I see. Surprises me a bit, that. I rather thought Jews couldn't be trusted."

Roger tried to suppress the uncomfortable feeling developing in the pit of his stomach. "In my experience, sir, one does best to base trust on the man, not his race or religion."

"*Touché*, Roger," York said, smiling. "As always, the *mot juste*." Then suddenly, "What do you think will happen to Shaftesbury?"

Roger was thrown completely off guard. "Shaftesbury, sir? But he's in the tower. I mean, isn't he?"

"Oh yes! Both he and Buckingham. With, I might add, their cooks, valets, and other sundry servants as well as all the books they require and fresh linen every week. And thus does my brother think to cut the legs from this upstart Country Party that Shaftesbury leads in opposition to him. Damned Whigs! Do you see them rolling over and playing dead so easily, Roger? Well, do you?"

"I can't say, sir. You know I take little notice of such matters."

"That's a damned lie, Roger Griffin, and you should know better than to try it on me." York's words were harsh, but the expression in his eyes as well as his tone of voice tempered them. "Look, I know what you're trying to do. I've always known. Stay above it all and live your own life. Can't blame you, can't blame any man. A pox on both your houses...that sort of thing. But there comes a time, Roger, when it just won't do. Do you follow me?"

Roger sat back and tried to take a measure of the situation. After some seconds he spoke with slow deliberation. "Your highness, I'm not a political animal. You may recall I learned that years ago, to my distress. Frankly there doesn't seem to me much to choose between Shaftesbury and his Whig rabble and Danby and his Tories. Oh, the latter claim to support the king, I'll grant you that, but what are they? Nothing but a bunch of squabbling old women whose main concern is to be allowed to preserve the privileges their inherited wealth has secured for them." He rose and paced toward the window. This little speech was more frank than he'd intended, but he couldn't avoid warming to his subject. "A pox on both their houses, just as you said. As for me, sir, I'll stand on my loyalty to the king and the House of Stuart, but that doesn't mean I have to crawl into bed with the likes of Danby."

There was a long silence. Roger stood staring at the carpet; James remained seated with his elegantly booted feet stretched out before him and his face expressionless. Then he slowly raised his hands and began a measured spate of applause. "Well said, Roger," he commented finally. "Well said. Are you then ready to match the actions to the words?"

Here it was. James was calling in the many favors Roger owed him. It had to come sooner or later; he shouldn't be surprised. Only one answer was possible. "At any time, your highness. You know that."

"Yes." James stood up and joined him by the window. His voice was lowered to a whisper when he said, "I need you to go to France."

"To France, sir?"

"Shh...it's a matter of some secrecy. That's why you're the perfect choice. You must have some business there, some excuse for going."

"Well, yes, I suppose so. We import a few special sweet-meats from Paris once in a while. But it's usually all done by correspondence."

"Not this time." York punctuated his words by making stabbing motions with one long finger in the direction of Roger's chest. "This time you're going yourself. Say you're combining business with pleasure if you must. Take your wife, perhaps. Anyway, I want you to leave for Paris by the end of the week."

"What is it I'm to do there?"

"First, whatever it is that gives you the excuse for going. Don't forget that, Roger. Give no one on either side of the Channel reason to be suspicious of your actions. Secondly, you're to find an old woman whose name I'll give you. She lives just a few miles outside the city in the district known as the Île de France. I want you to interrogate her."

"But why? What old woman, sir? Interrogate her about what?"

"Her name's Marie Lavoie, and she was maid to that Welsh lass, Lucy Walter, who was Charles's mistress back in '48 when we were yet in exile."

Roger stared at York. Could it be the man was losing his wits? There seemed no sense whatever in this conversation. "I'm sorry, I just don't understand. What am I to ask this Lavoie woman, and why?"

York chuckled. "You think I've gone quite mad, don't you, Roger? Never fear, I'm as sane as you are. Think, man! Think! Lucy Walters died in '57, so no one can question her about anything. But in '48 she bore a son. Now Roger, pray tell me that young man's name."

316

"James, Duke of Monmouth," Roger answered quietly. The matter was becoming very clear.

"Exactly!" York actually whirled around the room in his excitement. Nothing of Dismal Jimmy about him at this moment. "The very same bastard whom my brother acknowledged as his son and whom Shaftesbury insists must be legitimated and made heir to the throne. Thus, says he, after Charles there'll be a Protestant king. But—and here's the rub of it, Roger—I have it on good authority that young Lucy spread her legs for any number of others while Charles was sniffing at her heels. Don't you see? If that's so, then there's doubt that Monmouth is the king's son after all. No Monmouth, no convenient alternate to me for Shaftesbury to hang his arguments on."

His excitement seemed to have exhausted him. James fell back in his seat and gestured vaguely to a decanter on a nearby table. "Pour us a dram o' that brandy there . . . that's a good lad. Now, Roger, what do you think?"

It was the most difficult question York had posed in this whole difficult meeting. To tell the duke the truth now would have taken a man more anxious for trouble than Roger Griffin. "I think it's brilliant, sir. I'll arrange to sail for France by Saturday."

There was no question of taking Nancy, not the way things were between them now. Anyway, the entire escapade was the most incredible nonsense. The Duke of Monmouth was a handsome and talented young ne'er-do-well with a huge fund of popular support to draw upon in any emergency. Once, years before, he and two others had murdered a London night watchman who took exception to their riotous merrymaking. Charles had been obliged to grant "a gracious pardon to our dear son James, Duke of Monmouth." If the great English public had swallowed that, they weren't likely to rise up and reject Monmouth on the strength of some old woman's tattle. Still, York wanted him to go to Paris, so go he must. He'd find this Lavoie person and talk to her. For the rest he could make no promises.

It was Thursday afternoon, two days before his planned departure, when he suddenly looked up from his desk to see Sam Ludlow sitting with his head bent over a book of figures. Sam was nineteen now. Three years previous he had come to Roger and announced that he'd taught himself to read and write. Ludlow wanted a better job with the firm than that of errand boy, and in the face of such prodigious application Roger had been delighted to grant the request. He'd promptly made Sam a clerk and gradually given him more and more responsibility. Now the young man, who'd shown an aptitude for figures, was his personal accountancy assistant. "Sam," Roger said, interrupting the boy's careful calculations, "how would you like to see Paris?"

The idea was as much of a shock to Ludlow as it had been an impulse for Roger, but both adjusted quickly enough. Naturally Sam was delighted with the scheme, and Roger was pleased with himself for thinking of it. They left for Dover at dawn on Saturday and took passage on the five-o'clock packet bound for Calais.

4.

It was their custom to take turns providing a venue for the meetings. This night the men of B'nai Shalom were gathered at 6 Ingram's Court. Women had no part in their business, but Rachel had prepared a table of refreshments before retiring. Spread out before the assembly were plates of tiny cakes stuffed with dates and walnuts, pastries made of ground almonds and dredged in honey, little bowls of hot sweet coffee, and platters of fruits and sweetmeats. Benjamin viewed the refreshments with satisfaction and added two decanters of French brandy. The traditionalists of the brotherhood wouldn't approve, but that wasn't the only element of his hospitality they would find to criticize. Damn the old reactionaries, he told himself. The devil take them.

Levi was holding forth in one corner of the room. Eleven of the sixteen members present were paying him rapt attention. The other four were arguing some obscure point of talmudic law, a dispute that had been going on since before

Benjamin was born; none of them noticed when he slipped out of the drawing room.

Swiftly Ahmet went toward his private study at the rear of the house. "I trust you're completely comfortable, sir," he inquired of his seventeenth guest—the one none of the others knew about.

"Quite comfortable, Mr. Ahmet. Your charming sister provided me with everything a man could desire."

"Fine. You'll not mind being patient, then. Just until I prepare the ground. It may take close to an hour."

"Not in the least. But tell me, you really think they'll consent to hear me?"

Ahmet shrugged. "I can't guarantee it, of course. I told you that from the first. But I think they will. It's certainly worth a try."

"I agree. Thank you, Mr. Ahmet. I shall await your summons."

In the drawing room the discussion had turned to Shaftesbury and his party of Whigs. Old Menachim Cohan had interests in many coffee houses in the city; since these were Whig strongholds and meeting places he considered himself an expert on the matter. "I tell you," he was declaiming in his heavily accented English, "imprisoning Shaftesbury will in the end do no more than that nonsense of trying to close the coffee houses. Englishmen are sick of this king and the papists around him. It's going to be '49 all over again, mark my words."

"We shall, Menachim," Benjamin said drily. "I hope few others have marked them. It wouldn't be healthy for you if Charles heard that you've predicted he'll lose his head. Now, gentlemen, if I may suggest that we begin..."

Most of the men already wore hats; they still followed the old custom of never removing them. A few, like Ahmet himself, had adopted the Western etiquette, which demanded a gentleman be bareheaded indoors. Those few now fumbled small skullcaps out of their pockets. Hiram de Jonghe, a young man from The Hague, looked ridiculously funny in his, since he also affected an elaborate shoulder-length wig. There was more shuffling about while the men withdrew their fringed prayer shawls, kissed the ends devoutly, and wrapped themselves in the traditional symbols of devotion. Not until they were all ready did Solomon Levi rise and take the place due him as the eldest present. Standing before the assembly, he looked from one to another, then—when he was quite sure all were ready—intoned the words of the ancient Hebrew prayer. "*Sh'ma Yisroel*... Hear O Israel the Lord our God, the Lord is one..."

The regular business was routine. The brotherhood's investments were discussed and pronounced sound, provision was made for a monthly stipend to be paid to the widow of one deceased member, a special long-term loan was granted to another who had fallen on hard times. Less than half an hour had passed when Menachim Cohan rose to introduce a matter of new business. "Gentlemen," he said, surveying the assembly with eyes half hidden behind thick spectacles, "it is my belief that we must set aside a special emergency fund."

"What kind of emergency, Menachim?" It was the first time the young de Jonghe had opened his mouth. He had been a member of the brotherhood for less than a year.

"Hah! For Jews, my young friend, there is only one kind of emergency. Escape."

"What are you rambling on about, you old fool?"

"Living in the past, that's what you're doing, Menachim. This is England, not Spain and not Portugal."

"Wait. Menachim may be right. Remember York? That was only a few hundred years ago, and they massacred every Jew in the place. Don't be too quick to dismiss the possibility."

"Gentlemen!" Ahmet's voice carried over their chattering. "Please, may I have your attention. First, Menachim, may I thank you for raising the subject that's on my own mind. Secondly, I'd like to tell all of you that I agree with our esteemed brother Cohan. I do not like to say it, my friends, but for Jews an escape route is always a necessity. In this time and place I believe it's vital."

"But why, Benjamin?" Solomon Levi's voice was thin with age, but it still carried the ring of authority. "Do you know something the rest of us don't? Does Menachim? If so, why have you waited so long to tell the brotherhood?"

The implied criticism wasn't a new element, it merely hadn't surfaced until now. Most of the others liked and respected Benjamin Ahmet. But to a man they were distrustful of his single break with their traditions. Ahmet had taken a non-Jew as a partner. That same non-Jew was a frequent visitor to his home. Such a thing was without precedent, and it made the rest nervous. One did business with *goyim*, outsiders, naturally; but one didn't take them into one's bosom.

Ahmet knew all this. He knew too that when he'd finished this night's work some of those present would curse his name for a lifetime. It didn't matter; he'd decided to act and the decision couldn't be reversed. "Listen to me, all of you." he said quietly. "There is going to be terrible trouble in England. You were talking about the Whigs and the Tories just a while ago. You all know that the king and Parliament are at sword's point over the matter of the succession and a possible Catholic monarch ruling this country. Don't you see that for them the easiest way out is to find a common enemy? Don't you know that choosing a scapegoat is older than history? Who do you think they are likely to pick when the need arises?" His voice was louder now, and his fist slammed the table in anger. "Who but us?"

"But why? We've done nothing. None of us take sides in the struggle between Danby and Shaftesbury." De Jonghe's voice was a whine.

"Don't be a fool, Hiram!" Ahmet told the young man in scorn. "We are enormously convenient for them. We're a small, identifiable group of foreigners. What's more, we have wealth and connections spread throughout Europe. Nothing can be easier than accusing us of a conspiracy. But it's not to say all this I've raised the issue—most of you know these things better than I. What I want to tell you is that I suggest a totally new kind of escape route. Gentlemen..." Ahmet paused, sure he had the attention of every man present. "I propose that now, before the trouble actually starts, we buy into a plantation in the New World."

"The New World?" Menachim said. "Do you mean America? Are you suggesting we go all the way to America if we must leave England?"

"Why not?" Benjamin asked.

"Because," old Levi said, thrusting a bony finger at Ahmet, "there is no reason to think we'll be better off there than we are here. America! It's crazy. A half-wild place full of savages. I once talked to a man who'd been there. He said in the winter the snow is over your head, and in the summer a man can die from the heat. You're talking rubbish, Benjamin. There's no future in America."

"I think there is, Solomon. I've invited someone who knows the place to speak to us about it."

"Invited..."

"Here, at this meeting?"

"You invited a stranger here? Told him about the brotherhood?"

The men were all talking at once, looking around the room as if they feared the interloper were hiding behind the curtains.

"Yes," Ahmet said loudly, and succeeded in regaining their attention. "I've done just that. Now hold on a minute before you start cursing me. Do any of you imagine that I'd do such a thing without careful thought?"

"You fool!" The usually silent Itzik Gomez rose to his feet in white-faced fury. "You yourself say we can be accused of conspiracy. Now you've given some stranger the very fuel needed to fire such a story. If this were the old days, Ahmet, I'd be prepared to stone you!"

"Be that as it may, Itzik," his host said calmly, "I've done it. Now, since this outsider already knows of our existence, since he's already in the house and presumably knows the presence and identity of each of you, what more is there to lose? Mightn't you just as well hear what he has to say?"

They mumbled and moaned for another five minutes until finally Levi spoke for the whole company. "Very well, Benjamin. You've maneuvered us into a situation where we have little choice. Bring on this man. We'll listen to him. One thing though—am I correct in assuming he's a *goy?*"

"He is." Benjamin nodded. "But not the sort of Christian you're accustomed to meeting. This is a man of enormous vision, my friends. I beg you, give him a fair hearing." He left then, and returned seconds later with the stranger who'd been the cause of so much controversy.

Ahmet's guest was a man of rather unprepossessing appearance, until one looked into his eyes. They burned with a zeal which had been consuming him since the age of twelve. Hardship, persecution in the service of his beliefs, he had withstood all of that; the experience was written on his face.

Ahmet stopped just before the door of the drawing room. "I should warn you, they're all dressed like this." He indicated his skullcap and prayer shawl. "It may sound strange, but for Jews to discuss and plan is, in a way, to pray. We wear the same garb in both cases."

The other man laughed softly. "My dear Ahmet, did you think that in *The Great Case of Liberty of Conscience* I meant anything other than what I said? It is totally your own affair how you dress or how you pray. That's why my new colony in America is being formed."

"Yes, of course." He leaned forward and pushed open the door. "Come in, sir. Gentlemen, I have the honor to present to you Mr. William Penn."

Roger hadn't been in France in almost twenty years, nor had he spoken the language in all that time, but after a day or two in Paris he felt quite at home once more. "Mind you," he told Sam Ludlow the second day, "I'm not saying I like the place. I don't. The French are too stuck on themselves and too polite by half. Still, the food and wine's quite good, and we're here, so we may as well make the best of it."

The best of it had proved better than anything young Sam had ever expected to experience. They called on two businessmen who had relations with the firm and in each case were treated like visiting royalty. The women in their powdered wigs and low-cut gowns were a feast for Sam's eyes as much as the victuals a feast for his stomach. "How long are we going to be here, cap'n?" the lad asked enthusiastically on the third day.

"Depends," Roger said. "I've another bit of business to take care of, and I can't say how long that'll take."

He was of two minds about bringing Ludlow with him to see the Lavoie woman, assuming he found her where York said she'd be. If the woman had anything worthwhile to report, then a second witness could certainly prove useful, but if this business backfired, as he feared it might, then the fewer who knew of the matter the better. In the end he determined on a compromise.

"I've a trip to the country to take, Sam," he told the boy. "Private business to do with the family. You come along for the ride and wait for me nearby." It was the best solution he could think of. If it turned out the woman had information worth reporting, he'd simply collect Sam from wherever he'd left him and make sure he heard it. If she didn't, Ludlow need never know exactly where he'd gone or why.

He could have saved himself all the bother. He found Marie Lavoie just where James told him she'd be, at an old farm near Chantilly where she lived with her grandson and his wife. At first they didn't want to let him in. After that obstacle was overcome by the simple expedient of money, Marie pretended to neither hear nor understand him.

"Come, you old witch," Roger finally said in exasperation. "I can tell you hear every word. You know just what I'm saying, too. Look." He extracted another bag of coins and dangled it before her rheumy old eyes. "What have you to lose by talking to me? Lucy Walters is dead. Nothing you say can hurt her. We just want to know about her son. Can you swear that King Charles was the boy's father?"

She seemed determined to go on ignoring him until suddenly, in a gesture impossibly quick for such aged hands, she snatched the bag of coins from him and flung it down the front of her dress. "Heh, heh . . ." Her chuckle was malevolent. "Young fool you are . . . just like he was then. . . ."

"The king, you mean? Was the king a fool? Was Lucy making him cuckold?"

"Not that." She shook her head. "He was like you . . . thought it all so important. Don't matter, none of it. Ye gets old and tired and it don't matter. . . ."

Roger sighed. "Yes, yes, I'm sure you're right. But just tell me this one thing. Did Lucy have other lovers?"

"Course I'm right. Ain't I old enough to be right? Very well, stop pesterin' me. I'll answer ye. Why shouldn't I? Mind you, the money's mine now. Ye ain't gettin' it back."

"I don't want it back. Just an answer."

She shrugged as if to say her amusement was over for the evening. She'd obviously taken a good deal of pleasure in stringing along this insistent Englishman. "Lucy never lay with nobody but the king," she said at last. "Loved him, she did. Never let another man near her. I'd swear that on the Holy Bible."

"What place is that over there?" Sam asked, pointing to a spire lit by moonlight about half a mile away.

"I don't know," Roger said impatiently. "Just drink your wine and let me think."

After his thoroughly unsatisfactory interview with Marie Lavoie, he'd rejoined the boy at the little *auberge* where he'd left him. Now Roger couldn't decide whether to spend the night in this place or ride back to Paris immediately. It mattered little. Neither option would save him having to return to London at the first opportunity and tell James his hopes were futile.

Sam knew Griffin well enough to be resigned to his moods. He merely shrugged and ignored his employer's rebuke. His curiosity about the ghostly-looking steeple persisted. When the innkeeper returned with more wine, Sam tried the few words of French he'd learned in the last few days. "What place is that?" he demanded.

"That, m'sieu...that's the Abbey of St. Savior." The man crossed himself piously. "Holy nuns live there. They sleep in their coffins and live on bread and water."

Roger looked up at him, startled. The words "Abbey of St. Savior" had penetrated his self-absorption. "How far away is it?" he asked.

"As the crow flies, m'sieu, perhaps a quarter of a mile. By road, about twice as long."

"I see. Landlord, this lad and I wish to spend the night. Have you a bed for us?"

5.

"There's an Englishman at the door, mother." Sister Imelda's agitation was apparent in her tone and manner. "He's asking to see Sophia and Laura Griffin!"

"An Englishman asking for Sister Benedict and Sister Damian," the abbess said calmly, "must be a relative. Tell them he's here."

"Oh no, mother! We mustn't!"

Mother Germaine's eyebrows rose dramatically. "Why ever not, Imelda? What's the matter with you?"

The nun sank to her knees beside the abbess's chair. "I'm so frightened for them, mother. I fear he's some official from their country, come to throw them in that Tower of theirs, the one where they make all the martyrs..."

"Imelda! You have far too much imagination for a nun. Now go see if you can find Benedict. Damian's sure to be in the kitchen."

"Yes, mother." Imelda walked dutifully to the door. "Oh,

I forgot one thing. He's not alone. The Englishman, I mean. There's another man with him, just a boy really."

Germaine was losing patience. "It makes no difference, sister. It must be two relatives. Please, just do as I say."

The doorkeeper hurried through the corridors to the kitchen. Sister Damian was indeed there, sorting through a mountain of early spring greens and singing softly to herself in the process. She heard the news with mounting excitement. "But didn't he give a name?" she asked while unpinning her apron and shaking loose the long skirt of her habit. "Didn't he say who he was?"

"I didn't ask." Imelda stared at the floor in shame. "Forgive me, sister, I was just so taken aback..."

The younger girl impulsively hugged her companion. "Never mind, darling. Whoever it is I shall be thrilled. It might be Papa. And the younger one could be Charles or Andrew. Oh, hurry, Imelda, do see if you can find Benedict. Maybe they can't stay long."

The girl was racing down the corridor by the time she spoke the last words, and this gave Imelda courage. Surely if Sister Damian was so anxious to meet her callers there was nothing to fear. Feeling much better, she turned to the task of finding Sister Benedict. This was never easy. The older of the two English nuns spent hours in prayer, sometimes even forgot to come for meals, though this was much against the rule. Still, Benedict was loved by the community. There was a transparent holiness about the woman. Imelda resolved to look in the garden first. There was a grape arbor some distance from the house that afforded solitude and privacy. She'd seen Benedict there once or twice. Wrapping a shawl around her shoulders against the morning chill, the old nun toddled off.

"But surely you can stay for lunch, Uncle Roger?"

"Well, Laura, I don't really know. It seems an imposition." He couldn't rid himself of a feeling of discomfort even after he became used to talking to his niece through the imposing iron grille and seeing her in the ridiculous outfit. "I should like to see Sophia before I leave, however."

"Oh, it's no imposition, I promise you! We can't eat with you, that's forbidden. But there's a dining room just for guests, and I'll come back and visit a bit longer after you've eaten. I think we'll have found Sister Benedict—I mean Aunt Sophia—by then too."

"Found her? I don't understand, Laura, how can she be lost? Don't you all live inside this place?"

Laura laughed gaily. "This place, as you call it, is an abbey. Yes, of course we all live inside. It's just that Aunt Sophia is given to going off by herself, and then she's hard to locate."

"Hmph," Roger snorted. "Nothing much changed with her, I see. She's been doing that sort of thing since she was a child."

"No, Uncle Roger." Laura looked grave. "It's not that at all. I should prepare you, I suppose. She's different. Different from what she was and from all of us. I don't know if you'll understand this, but Aunt Sophia's very holy. Very close to God. She sees things, knows things...it's terribly hard to explain," the girl ended, sighing.

"Yes, I expect it is." Roger hoped his disbelief didn't show in his voice. He didn't know quite what had brought him to this place to see his sister and niece. Maybe just the magnetism of finding himself so close. In any event, everything he'd seen and heard since his arrival in this so-called abbey confirmed his opinion. It was lunacy, all of it. A waste of time, and worse, a waste of life. Well, so be it. The choice hadn't been his. In any event he could see that Laura was well, and happy with her self-delusions. That news would please Clare enormously, and more than anything that was his motive for the visit. It had seemed unduly cruel to be so close to Sophia and Laura and not bring news of them back to the family.

"Very well, my dear," he said, smiling. "We'll accept your invitation to lunch. Meanwhile you see if you can't persuade my sister to put aside her trances for the moment and come to see me."

Laura grinned and pushed her face close to the wide-spaced bars of the grille for a quick kiss. "*Bon appetit*, Uncle Roger. I'll see you soon again."

Sam Ludlow viewed all that had happened this morning with a strong sense of disapproval. It seemed to him not at all a good idea to come visit this papist stronghold. Not the sort of thing any truly self-respecting Englishman should do. Not even in France. Oh, he knew the captain had some papist relatives. Everyone knew that. But to actually come and see them in this place was something else again.

While his employer went into the private parlor where he

327

met with his womenfolk, Sam was made to wait in an outer room that struck him as uncomfortably prisonlike. There were bars on the windows, and the furniture was of spartan simplicity, except for a huge cross with a particularly lifelike figure of the Lord pinned upon it. Idolaters, that's what all these papists were. And witches too, he shouldn't wonder. Certainly the ones in this place. Holy nuns...rubbish! Witches, more likely. Just look at the way they dressed.

"Come, Sam. We're to dine in that room over there. I trust you've brought your appetite with you."

The captain's sudden arrival startled him. No less the extraordinary announcement that they were actually going to take a meal in this spooky place. "Eat here, cap'n? But that innkeeper said they lived on bread and water."

"Yes, and slept in their coffins. Nonsense, all of it. Don't believe every bit of gossip you hear. You should have learned that by now. I've just seen my niece, and believe me she's quite healthy and fit. Doesn't look to me as if she's been fed a diet of bread and water. And I wager they'll manage something more substantial for us too."

They ate well, but Sam couldn't identify the bits of meat in savory sauce, nor was he familiar with the assortment of vegetables that accompanied it. "What you think this stuff is, cap'n? I heard these French folks eat all manner of strange things, snails even, and frogs' legs."

"Neither of those, I think," Roger said, smiling at the lad's obvious discomfort in these unfamiliar surroundings. "Rats, maybe. Never can tell about papists, you know." He nearly choked with laughter when he saw the boy's expression after that. "Oh, be sensible, Sam. Don't make me sorry I've brought you all this way," he said, laughing. "It's some perfectly ordinary meat in a rather good gravy. Now eat up and be done with it."

They were just finishing the excellent cheese with which the meal ended when the old nun who'd first admitted them came to the door of their dining room. "Please, m'sieu, if you are ready, Sister Benedict is waiting for you in the parlor now."

"Right." Roger rose and downed the last of his wine. "Wait here, Sam. I'm just going to have a visit with my sister and then we'll be off."

Sophia's appearance brought him up short the moment he entered the parlor. Even seen behind the partial concealment of the grille and swathed in the voluminous black robes of the nunnery she seemed to him to dominate everything around her. Roger had last seen Sophia when she stood before the front door of Harwood bidding him and Nancy goodbye during their visit to Yorkshire. He remembered very clearly how she had looked then—hysterical and self-absorbed, a spoiled child who wanted nothing so much as a good whipping to put her straight. Subconsciously he'd expected to see the same thing now, willful, headstrong Sophia intent on playing her self-appointed role as prophetess. It was nothing remotely like that.

Later, when he would try to explain it to the others, he could only say, "It was as though she'd somehow gone away...become transparent." Sophia didn't seem to him to be wholly present. It was as if she were instead replaced by something else, something that used her to shine through.

"Hello, Roger. It's marvelous to see you." Her voice was quite ordinary. Nothing like her appearance.

"I suppose Laura told you that I just happened to be in the neighborhood, Sophia. It seemed a fine opportunity to visit the pair of you and take news back to the family. You're well, I hope."

Sophia smiled. "Very well, thank you. And Sister Damian—Laura—too, as doubtless you saw." Her smile broadened. "Did you not know your errand would bring you near St. Savior's?"

"No." He looked at her quizzically. "What do you mean, my errand?"

Her laughter tinkled across the barrier separating them. "It doesn't matter. His highness need not worry about that. Anyway, I'm glad of the opportunity to tell you how grateful I am that you bought the land."

Roger stared at her. He knew he'd gone very pale. Sophia, on the other hand, didn't seem to think anything in this conversation remarkable. "What do you know of his highness's affairs? And what land? What are you talking about?"

She ignored the question about James. For the rest she simply said, "The land that abuts Harwood. The place where Kirkslee Priory stood. You've bought it, haven't you?"

"Yes, as a matter of fact I have. But how did you know? I'd quite forgotten the connection between that place and this. That old priory, Kirkslee, was the same order as this one, wasn't it?"

Sophia nodded. "That's why I'm so pleased and grateful."

"But how did you know?" he repeated.

"Oh, it doesn't matter. Look, here's Sister Damian." Laura entered just then, and Sophia obviously welcomed the diversion.

"I hoped I'd catch you before you left, Uncle Roger. I did want to give you this letter to bring back to Mama and Papa. You can do that, can't you?"

"Gladly." Roger took the envelope she poked through the bars.

Suddenly the three were enveloped in an awkward silence. Sophia stared at the letter in Roger's hand, and he could see her eyes fill with tears. "What is it, Sophia? What's wrong?"

"Nothing." She shook her head sadly. "Nothing is wrong. All is as God ordains. Goodbye, Roger." She started for the door.

It seemed to him a sudden and unceremonious leavetaking. "Sophia, I...it's good to have seen you. I may get to France again on business...."

She only smiled and left.

They were preparing to leave when a nun of regal bearing suddenly appeared with a small round monk in tow. "Captain Griffin, I am Mother Germaine, abbess of St. Savior's. I trust you found your sister and your niece in good health and spirits?"

"Very much so, milady. Thank you." Roger bowed and waited for the abbess to make the next move. He had no knowledge of the protocol of such situations.

"There is something, captain...I don't mean to delay you, but if you could just spare a moment more."

"Your humble servant, milady." He couldn't help but notice that the woman must have been a great beauty in her day. Even the weird outfit didn't hide that. And that voice...

"I should like to present Dom Pérignon," she said, smiling and drawing the monk forward. "You must forgive my meddling, captain, but you see, here in the convent we are like a family. We know everything about each other's relatives. For instance, I know, because Sister Damian has told us, that you are head of a company that imports foodstuffs to England. Is that not so?"

Her attempt to charm him wasn't subtle, but neither was it ineffective. Roger smiled. "That's so."

"Yes. That's why I wanted you to meet Dom Pérignon. He happened to have come to see us today on business. And you happened to arrive. Divine Providence, I say. Now, I shall leave you two."

The abbess slipped away quickly and Roger found himself left alone with the silent monk. The man had a cherubic look enhanced by the circle of shaven scalp that topped his chubby face. Outside Roger could hear Sam talking to the horses he'd gone to saddle. He hoped his impatience didn't show in his voice when he asked, "Is there something I can do for you, sir?"

The monk smiled. "No, *mon capitaine,* there is something I can do for you. I am cellarer at the Benedictine abbey of Hautvillers not far from here. If you will do me the honor of accompanying me there I can promise you a most extraordinary reward."

"I see." Roger looked closely at the man. "May I ask what that is?"

"A new wine, monsieur. A most remarkable new wine that is, I assure you, fit for angels. And"—his eyes twinkled—"no less for Englishmen."

6.

Nancy sent Rudy to Tupenny Cottage with the message, because he was the fastest horseman on the place.

"Mistress needs ye, ma'am," Rudy told Clare quickly. "She asks ye come straightaway."

"Of course." Clare put down the bunch of narcissi she'd been gathering and wiped her hands on her apron. "What's the trouble, Rudy? What should I bring?"

"Cain't say, ma'am. Leastwise not for sure. Young Master James, I think it be."

"An accident?"

"Don't think so, ma'am. Think the young master's been taken with some kind of fever."

Clare caught her breath. "Wait here, I won't be a moment."

She hurried off to find Mark, who was washing by the pump in the back garden after a tour of the estate. "There's trouble at Tassels," she said as soon as he was in earshot. "I'm going up there right now with Rudy."

"Of course." Mark straightened up and shook the droplets of water from his head and shoulders. At forty-eight he was still a man of muscle and toughness. "Shall I come with you?"

His wife shook her head. "No, I don't think that's wise. Rudy doesn't know exactly what's wrong, but he thinks little James has some kind of fever. If that's so we may have to isolate everybody at Tassels and you'll be needed here."

Mark nodded. "Yes, I see. Go ahead then, love. Send word as soon as you're able."

Twenty minutes later she was standing by the child's bedside with a sinking feeling in her stomach. "How long has he been like this?"

Nancy touched the boy's forehead. The baby-soft skin was burning with fever. "Just since breakfast. He complained of being sick at his stomach, and we gave him a purge and put him to bed. Then an hour or two ago this fever came on. What do you think, Clare?"

The older woman looked carefully at the child's reddened skin and the discoloration around his eyes. "I'm very much afraid it's smallpox, Nancy. I hate to tell you this, but you'll have to know."

Nancy sank to her knees beside the bed. "I feared that from the first." She swallowed hard and was silent for some moments, then she rose and said with all the calmness she could muster, "What do we do, Clare?"

"First get me something to write with. We'll need a great variety of herbs. I must get a message to Sarah." Then, while she was scratching her urgent requests, "Have you had the illness?"

"I'm not sure, really. I think I did once as a tiny child, it's a vague memory. But I was in London in '59 when it was very bad. I never got it then."

"Then we can hope you've had it and become immune." Clare looked up while folding her note. "You do understand that's how it happens? Once one has had the infection and bested it, it never returns. So we will get young Jamie through this attack and then we'll know he's safe for a lifetime." She smiled brightly. "Now, send someone to Sarah with this note. Then we'll move our little patient to your bedroom. We must isolate him completely, Nancy. From everyone else in the house and outside. That's the only way to prevent the spread of the disease. I've told Sarah to see that Mark knows what's happening. He'll make certain no one comes to Tassels or leaves it until this is over." She was working even while she spoke, and Nancy fell in beside her, grateful yet one more time for the strength and goodness of this remarkable woman.

The message was waiting for Griffin when he returned from Paris. Five cases of smallpox had surfaced at Tassels by then. All three children, their nursemaid, Maude Jenks, and a young stableboy. "How are they managing?" Benjamin asked when a white-faced Roger shared the terrible news.

"This note's from my brother. He says Clare and Nancy are doing all the nursing. They both seem immune....I...oh God, Benjamin..." He crumpled the letter and flung it against the wall. "Tell Ludlow I'll need a horse!"

"Roger, wait!" Ahmet strode to the door of the office to block Griffin's exit. "Have you had the disease?"

Roger shook his head. "No. Look, I know what you're thinking. But I can't just let them stay down there and me here. They're my children, Ahmet. For the love of God, man, don't you understand?"

"Of course I do. In your place I'd be tearing off for Surrey too. But it's madness, Roger. And it will likely do much more harm than good. How will it help your children or your wife if you're ill too? Where will they be without a husband and father as breadwinner? Have you thought of that?"

Griffin ran his fingers through his hair. There was no denying the weight of the argument. "But there must be something I can do," he said at last.

"Has a doctor been sent for?"

"I don't know, Mark doesn't say. He just says Nancy and Clare are doing everything that can be done."

"Look, I know a man, a doctor. He's a brilliant chap, I give you my word. We could go and see him. Maybe he'll ride down there and help."

"Thank you." Roger took a moment to press Benjamin's hand in gratitude, then the two men left George Alley together.

They located the doctor in a fetid alley near Moorgate. The man's house was as much a hovel as those of his neighbors, but once one was inside the difference was obvious. The place was scrubbed from top to bottom, aromatic rushes lay on the floor, and the faint scent of curative herbs was everywhere. The man himself was robust and cheerful, and he greeted Ahmet as an old friend. "Roger, this is Dr. Steven Winters. My friend and business partner, Roger Griffin."

"Welcome, gentlemen, please come in." He led them into a small parlor, then asked, "How can I help you?"

"It's I who need help, sir." Roger explained. "My family lives on a small estate in Surrey, Tassels by name, just a mile downstream from Hampton Court Palace. I returned from the Continent this morning and learned that smallpox had surfaced there."

"How many cases?" Winters asked.

"Five, according to the information I have. Among them a nursemaid, a stableboy, and all three of my children."

Winters nodded with more sympathy in his face than words could have conveyed. "I'll go today. My work here won't allow me to be gone for long, but at least I'll see what can be done. And you, sir, have you had the disease?"

Roger shook his head. "No."

"When were you last in contact with any of the sufferers?"

"Almost a month ago. I did see my wife a fortnight past, but she herself isn't ill."

"Good. One thing is clear. You must avoid your home at all costs till this thing is finished. Now, sir, if you'll be kind enough to tell me how I can find Tassels, I'll leave at once."

"We'll do better than that, Steven." It was the first time Ahmet had spoken. "One of our boats will await you at Trigg Stairs. The crew knows the way."

"Fine. Explain to them they'll be asked to come no farther than the riverbank once we arrive. They'll be safe there."

"He's a remarkable man, Roger. If anyone can help, I'm sure Winters can." They were sitting in Benjamin's study. He had insisted that Griffin accompany him there for something to eat and some rest.

"Who is he? How did you meet him?"

Roger wasn't really interested in anything but news from Tassels, but he seemed to need to keep talking. It was some kind of emotional purgative, Ahmet realized. "That's all part of a longer story I've been waiting to tell you," he said as he refilled their glasses. "Winters is a member of a sect called the Quakers. Ever heard of them?"

"Once or twice. Silence and brotherly love and no sermons or sacraments. Isn't that their practice?"

"I suppose it's something like that. More interesting to me is the tenet of complete freedom of conscience expounded by their leader, William Penn."

"Yes. I've heard of him too. Does most of his preaching from jail, doesn't he?"

Ahmet shrugged. "Sometimes. Don't dismiss him so easily, Roger. Or his coreligionists. You saw Winters's place. He lives in those awful slums so he can give free medical care to the poor."

Roger downed his brandy. "I didn't mean to sound scornful. God knows I'm grateful to him and to you for any help in this situation."

"I understand. Anyway, about this Penn...did you know he's founded a colony in America? Mostly others of his belief from Germany at the moment, but they're looking for more settlers from England. And Penn's likely to acquire yet more land in America. The king owes him sixteen thousand pounds. Charles borrowed that much from Penn's father, and the debt's not yet been repaid."

"You seem to know rather a lot about this Quaker," Roger said, smiling. "Are you thinking of joining his sect?"

"His sect, no. I shall die the Jew I was born, my friend, you know that. His settlements in the New World are of interest to me, however."

Roger had no time to reply to this remarkable statement. Rachel chose that moment to join them, and Ahmet touched his lips in a gesture that made it plain he didn't wish to discuss the subject in his sister's presence. "Come sit with us, my dear," he said instead. "We can use a bit of cheering at this moment."

The Ahmets insisted Roger move in with them until the emergency at Tassels passed. "It's no good for you to be alone in that room at George Alley," Rachel insisted. "You'll simply brood."

Griffin was too numb with worry to argue. He did as he was bidden but insisted on going into the office the following morning. It wasn't until he'd been there an hour that he realized he'd not yet reported to the Duke of York the results of his errand.

"Damn!" he cursed aloud when the idea forced its way into

his consciousness. The last thing Roger wanted to do was deal with a disappointed and angry James, but there was no help for it. Delaying things would only make the matter worse. He sent Ludlow to St. James's Palace with a note requesting an interview. He was enormously relieved when the boy came back and announced that his highness the Duke of York was with the king at Windsor Castle and not expected back until the end of the week.

This reprieve somewhat eased Roger's mind. He sat in thought for a moment or two, then went to the trunk he'd brought back from France but not yet unpacked. On the top were the presents he'd carried home for the children. He carefully avoided looking at those. Beneath them lay the two bottles of wine Dom Pérignon had given him. Roger extracted them from the trunk and placed one in the drawer of his desk. The other he tucked under his arm as he left the office.

Only Rachel was at Ingram's Court to greet him. Benjamin, she explained, had been called to Bristol on business relating to a big shipment of spices they were expecting. "He'll not be home until tomorrow," she said in that accented English he never tired of hearing. "But he left strict instructions you were to remain here. You will stay, won't you, Roger?"

"If you don't object."

"Of course I don't. Oh, I nearly forgot the most important thing! Dr. Winters called a little while ago. He couldn't wait, but he left you this note."

His fingers were trembling while he opened it:

Sir,
I have pleasure to inform you that things at Tassels are better than either of us hoped. Your son and your daughter Nell have passed the crisis and are well on the way to recovery. The little girl, Miss Jennifer, and her nursemaid are still very ill, but they exhibited symptoms of the disease much after the others. I have bled them both and there is reason to hope that they too will soon be broken of fever. Your wife and the lady called Mistress Clare are both well, albeit much exhausted by their nursing duties. I assure you, sir, that everything that can be done is being done. The ladies have shown much wisdom in their choice of herbal sim-

ples to treat the fever. I promised to return in three days' time and I shall then give you further news.

I remain, sir, your humble servant,

Steven Winters

Under Almighty God,

Doctor of Medicine and Physician of Healing.

"Good news?" Rachel asked, watching his face as he read the letter.

"Better than I hoped," Roger said with a grateful sigh. He handed her the missive to read for herself.

"But this is wonderful!" she exclaimed when she'd finished. "God be praised!"

"Indeed. You know, it's funny," he said with a hint of wistfulness in his voice. "You sound as if you know them, yet you've never met my children."

"I do feel as if I know them. You've spoken of them so often."

"I wish you'd come down to Surrey sometime."

Rachel shrugged. "It's not our custom for women to travel about thus."

"Particularly to the home of *goyim*," Roger added softly. "I know. I've come to understand all that since I've known you and Benjamin. But it's not contrary to your customs to have a drink with me in thanksgiving for this news, is it?" She shook her head and smiled so the two dimples in her cheeks were appealingly evident. "Watch this, Rachel—it's something special."

Roger withdrew Dom Pérignon's wine from his pocket and, using the tool the monk had given him for the purpose, began carefully extracting the bit of cork that sealed the bottle. "This was given me by a French monk I met while abroad. It's a remarkable new wine he's developed, and he thinks, as I do, that it may prove a profitable import for us. I want your opinion. Stand back now, here it goes!" The cork suddenly jumped from the bottle and landed halfway across the room. The wine started to foam out over Roger's hand, but he was quick to tip it into a glass as the Benedictine had shown him. "Here, now." He handed the goblet to Rachel. "He calls the stuff Champagne. See what you think of it."

7.

Despite the exceedingly large profits which the importation of Champagne eventually brought to Griffin's, Roger was never again able to drink the wine. So much flowed from that May night in Ingram's Court, so much that was at best painful, at worst unendurable.

Until that evening he'd never seen Rachel take more than a sip of claret, but Champagne she found much to her taste. After the third glass she was delightfully flushed and sparkling, her customary reserve evaporating in direct proportion to the lowered level of the bottle. "Do give me just a bit more," she said, holding out her glass. "It's the most delicious wine I've ever tasted."

"I really shouldn't be encouraging you," Roger said and laughed. He was pouring even as he spoke. Outside he heard the watchman call, "Midnight and all's well on a fine spring evening." It didn't seem that late. This Champagne had a heady quality; it was even affecting him. He downed another swallow and moved closer to Rachel.

The combination of drink, the intimate setting, and the tension of the past days provoked a question he'd often thought of but never voiced. "Tell me something...it's none of my business I know...but why have you never married? A woman like you, it's quite extraordinary."

She looked particularly thoughtful when she replied, "At first there was no one suitable in our community here. No one of the right age who was not already wed."

"In all England?" he asked in astonishment.

"I didn't say that. I said in our community."

"Oh, I see. He'd have to be a Jew, is that it?"

"Of course. I'm sorry if you find that odd, it's just the way it is. At least, most of the time."

Roger pressed the point. "All right, I accept that. But you

said, 'at first.' Was there another reason later? Did some male who might have been 'suitable,' as you put it, appear?"

"There's de Jonghe. He came last year, and my brother thought a match might be made. But..." She broke off and shrugged.

"But what? Has this de Jonghe prospects? Is he a decent sort?"

"I suppose Hiram is decent enough. I don't know him well. Certainly he has prospects. Still, I had to tell Benjamin it was impossible."

"How old are you?" Roger demanded suddenly.

"Twenty-one," she answered. "What has that to do with it?"

Twenty-one, the same age as his niece Sarah. He didn't say that. Only, "You're old enough to know that you must let your brother make such decisions. Surely he has your best interests at heart."

"Yes, he has," Rachel said softly. "That's why he understands, and wouldn't insist."

"I don't understand."

"Do you want me to marry, Roger?"

He found the question oddly disturbing. "I don't know. You should marry. You should have someone to look after you."

"Benjamin looks after me."

"That's different. I suppose he's never married because there aren't any Jewesses of the right sort available either?"

"It is a very strong rule among our people, Roger. In most instances it causes no hardship. Jews seldom mix with gentiles anyway."

"But sometimes? Sometimes it causes hardship?"

"Things are different in England. At least for Benjamin and me. There's you, for instance." Her voice was barely audible.

"Me?" He knew even as he spoke how dangerous the conversation was becoming. He couldn't restrain himself. "What have I to do with it?"

"We have such fondness for you, Benjamin and I. It's changed many of our ideas."

"Such as?"

Rachel lifted her glass and drained the wine. "It's made me realize that the idea of loving a gentile isn't as far-fetched as I once thought." Her words had a defiant ring, as if she'd responded to some self-imposed dare.

Roger stared at her. This had been the notion in the back of his mind when he began this conversation, some perverse need to probe the festering wound that was his feeling for Rachel Ahmet. Like biting hard on a sore tooth. Now the discussion was racing beyond those limits. Still he couldn't stop. "Do you care for me, Rachel?" he asked quietly. "Not as a friend, I know the answer to that. As a man."

"You're married," was her only response.

"Yes. But that's not an answer to my question."

"I love you, Roger," she said simply. "I have loved you since the first moment I saw you."

Three of the four candles that lit the room had gone out some time earlier. The fourth was sputtering its last, but they weren't in darkness. A full moon shone through the window. It limned Rachel's black hair and caused the string of pearls around her neck to shimmer with strange colors. By its light he could see that her eyes were wide open when he moved closer and took her in his arms.

They never moved from the study to one of the bedrooms upstairs. Had they done so the interruption might have returned them to their senses. Instead they simply slithered from the sofa to the hearth rug spread before the dying fire.

There was nothing hurried or frantic about the encounter. Roger pressed his mouth to hers with the deep satisfaction of tasting at last that for which he'd so long yearned. She didn't really know how to kiss a man, but the warmth of her response was unmistakable. Gently he opened her lips with his tongue. He felt the tremor that passed over her body and the way she pressed yet closer to him. A long time passed just so—kissing and touching and saying nothing aloud, but everything nonetheless.

It was she who finally loosed her bodice and exposed herself to him. The way she did so made the act almost holy. It was a gesture of giving unlike anything in his experience.

Her breasts were full, the nipples dark and pronounced. He stroked them lightly. The silky bronze-gold of her skin accented for him the truth that this was a woman wholly apart from any he had known. There was a moment then, fleeting but real, when he seemed to stand outside himself and see the whole scene. For the duration of perhaps one breath it occurred to him that he could yet stop this thing from happening, that he owed it to Rachel and everyone else to do so. Then he bent his head and kissed her dusky breast. Her flesh smelled of sandalwood and jasmine, and beneath his cheek he could feel her heart racing. There was no stopping after that.

He knew without asking that she was a virgin. He lifted her legs and wordlessly showed her how to clasp them around his hips. His first thrust was careful and very slow, the second more determined. Then he heard her gasp and felt himself penetrate that place where none had been before.

And later, much later, he said, "I'm sorry. Can you ever forgive me?"

"Don't say that ever. Do not imagine for one moment, my dearest, that any of this would have taken place if I didn't wish it." She smiled at him then, a smile he wasn't likely to forget. "I chose to have one night's happiness because it was the only thing available. I shall never regret that, and neither must you."

They both knew without discussion that this had been a unique experience, never to be repeated. He wasn't the sort of man to take a mistress; Rachel wasn't the sort of woman to become one. She rose and left the room, and Roger watched her go with a pain of loss he knew was never to heal.

By the end of the week, Dr. Winters told him he could go to Tassels.

Nancy looked paler and more worn than he'd ever seen her. "Maude Jenks died a few hours ago," were the first words she said to him. "We did everything we could, but we lost her."

"The children?"

"All on the road to full recovery," she replied with a tremor of wonder in her voice. "The stableboy too. I can hardly believe it."

"Thank God for you and Clare. Winters told me it was the pair of you that saved them."

"I only did what Clare told me to do. And thanked heaven every moment for her presence. I kept thinking...what if she wasn't here? What if they'd never come to Tassels, moved to Tupenny Cottage?"

"Yes." Roger's voice shook with relief. "I know what you mean. And that's all your doing. If you hadn't been so insistent years ago it might all have been different."

"That doesn't matter now." Nancy waved aside those comments impatiently. "But it's taught me so much, Roger. That last night in London, all the terrible quarrels we've had over the years. It's so stupid. When there's real trouble, then you come to see it. Now the children are given back to us, I think it's a miracle. We mustn't be such fools ever again. To destroy our own lives when there's so much evil outside ourselves waiting to do it for us..."

She sounded almost hysterical—a reaction to everything she'd been through, no doubt. Roger stepped forward and put his hands on her shoulders. "It's all right, Nance. Everything's going to be fine now. Stop worrying. Can I see the children?"

"Yes, of course. I didn't mean to confront you with all this the minute you arrived. It's just been on my mind. Come." She stretched out her hand and led him to the stairs. "They're waiting for you."

Jennifer was still very sickly and quiet, but she had no fever and even managed to smile at him when he entered the nursery. Jamie was sitting up in bed with a host of wooden soldiers spread over the coverlet. He was obviously enjoying his privileged invalid state. "I had smallpox, Papa," he announced with solemnity. "I was the very first to get it."

"So I heard." Roger hugged the boy fiercely, torn between amusement at Jamie's claim to distinction and an urge to cry from gratitude and relief. Jamie was bright-eyed and even had a bit of color in his cheeks. Best of all, his face seemed unmarked by the ravages of the usually disfiguring disease. "How..." Roger ran his hand over the child's clear skin.

"Clare guarded against that from the first moment," Nancy explained. "She tied their hands up in little muslin mitts and controlled the itching with salves."

"I scratched a tiny bit, Papa," Nell admitted as he moved to hug her in turn. "Just at first, before I understood." She sounded properly chagrined but determined to make her confession prior to any questions or accusations. "See?" Nell pushed her auburn hair back from her temple with a hand that looked to him painfully thin and wasted. Sure enough, about an inch of skin was marred by pocks.

"Never mind, darling." Nancy stepped forward and took the child's hand in hers. "Your curls will cover that." Later she explained to Roger that all three children had some pocking on their bodies where the bedclothes had rubbed against the sores. "We couldn't help that, but at least none of them is scarred where it shows."

"Just one of the many miracles we have to be grateful for," he said. "And now you must have some rest. I'm packing the lot of you off to Bath to take the waters and recuperate just as soon as Winters agrees the children can travel. Will you like that?"

"Yes," Nancy answered solemnly. "I will indeed. Will you join us?"

"At least part of the time. Now I'll just nip down to Tupenny and tell Mark my plans and make sure he can manage here on his own. No problem there, I expect, but anyway it will give me a chance to thank Clare and give her some news." Nancy looked interested. "I saw Laura and Sophia in France," Roger explained. "It was all rather accidental and rushed, but at least I can report to Clare and Mark that both are doing fine. It's a mighty queer life they've chosen, near as I can make out. But they seem happy in it, so that's that." He withdrew a slightly crumpled envelope from his jacket. "Laura even wrote them a letter."

"Oh, that's wonderful!" Nancy said enthusiastically. "It will please them all so much. Hurry down there, darling. I can't wait for them to have the news. As a matter of fact," she added and grabbed a shawl from a peg on the wall, "I'll come with you. Ellen can manage here for a bit."

They walked together the half mile that separated Tupenny Cottage from Tassels. The afternoon sun was warm; wild violets and bluebells dappled the grass of the woodland, and Roger Griffin told himself he was a fortunate man. There was little point in moaning over what might have been, longing for a woman he loved in a quite different way from his wife. It was time to start being grateful for what one had and to hell with the rest.

8.

It was a mark of Ahmet's preoccupation with the current political unrest and the Quakers' plans that he never noticed the change which came over his sister.

Spring passed to summer, and London was subjected to temperatures far above normal and a drought besides. Shaftesbury was released from the Tower, and he and Danby fought what amounted to pitched battles in the House of Lords. The Commons urged Charles to make war on France, anything to break down papist alliances and strength, and to legitimate Monmouth and ensure that the Catholic James would never be king. Charles went himself to address the Parliament. "On this subject, gentlemen," he said quietly, "I shall not yield."

"But why?" Rachel asked her brother when he reported the extraordinary statement. "Why won't he yield? Charles isn't a Catholic too, is he?"

Benjamin shrugged. "Some say secretly that's where his sympathies lie. No one really knows for sure. That's not the point. What the king sees himself defending, I think, is the whole question of the right of succession and the true Stuart line."

"But if Monmouth's the king's son, then he's a Stuart too."

"No, not with the right to succeed. Not a bastard. I must say, I can see Charles's point. If he declares Monmouth legitimate when he knows he isn't, merely to rearrange the future and make people happy, then the whole principle of true succession is undermined. A bastard's a bastard, after all."

Rachel dropped her eyes and left the room. Benjamin returned to the papers on his desk. Penn had sent him a report on the latest doings in America. There was a tract of land that seemed particularly interesting. It lay just south of the present Quaker colony and looked like particularly good farm country. "...If we can convince the king to deed it to us then I propose to call the place Sylvania, for the woods thereabouts are indeed marvelous...."

For a moment Ahmet looked up and stared at the door through which his sister had just left. Rachel had seemed quiet of late, melancholy even. What she needed, he told himself for the hundredth time, was a husband, children.... He must try once more to persuade her to allow him to open negotiations with de Jonghe. Surely there could be no question of transporting her to the wilds of America in her present unmarried state.

Rachel had been three years old when her parents died and she was sent to her brother in England. Despite having been raised without a mother, she was not ignorant of feminine things. In a community as closely knit as that of the Jews resident in England there were plenty of women to guide her education in such matters. She had learned to embroider, to play the harp, to sing, to oversee the kitchen and make sure that the strict laws of *kashruth* were obeyed. Separate utensils and crockery for flesh meats, no fish that lacked fins and scales...all as the Book of Leviticus commanded; as was written in the sacred Torah.

Other things too she learned from the ladies of Ingram's Court. They had the attitudes toward raising young girls that were common in the lands from which they came. Rachel knew how babies were made and born by the time she was seven. She had, therefore, no doubts in her mind now. She was pregnant with Roger's child, and that child would make its presence apparent within the next month or two.

For herself she considered this no shame. She was proud to bear Roger's child. For Benjamin, however, it would be an impossible situation that could destroy him personally and professionally. He would feel horribly betrayed by the two people closest to him. As for Roger, if he knew the truth it would cause him enormous pain and guilt. She knew him well enough to be sure of that. So only one solution was possible. Neither Roger nor Benjamin must ever know the truth.

For a while, in the very beginning, she had considered a hasty marriage to de Jonghe. No doubt Benjamin could arrange it; and if she gave birth after six or seven months of marriage who would know for certain that it wasn't de Jonghe's child, born before its time? The plan, though, was too risky to hold her attention for long. Roger might guess the truth when the baby was born. She didn't know de Jonghe particularly well, but it didn't seem fair to use him thus. Moreover, he might not prove a father worthy of Roger's child. No, the Dutchman was out. That decision gave rise to another scheme, one she much preferred.

Three days after Benjamin received the letter from Penn, Rachel again joined him in his study. "I have a proposal to make," she said seriously. "Can you discuss it with me now?"

"Of course, my dear." He put aside the book he'd been reading and waited.

"I know you are much taken with the idea of going to the colonies in America. Has it occurred to you that for me to undertake such a move unmarried might be very difficult?"

"But Rachel, of course it's occurred to me! Don't you know I'm always concerned about what's best for you?" He was genuinely hurt.

"Naturally I know that. Please, Benjamin, don't get excited. Just listen to me. I want to go to Amsterdam. To our relatives there. Right away."

He looked perplexed. "I don't understand."

"Don't you see? There are many more Jews there than here. I could find a husband. Then later we could perhaps join you in America."

Ahmet stared at her. "But why? I can arrange a marriage with de Jonghe whenever you wish. I'm sure he'd be amenable to the idea. And I know a bit about him. I know nothing of some stranger you might find in Amsterdam."

"But I don't wish to marry Hiram de Jonghe. I told you that ages ago. He doesn't suit me." Her usually gentle manner became more forceful. "Times are changing, Benjamin. It's a new age. I won't be sold off like a sheep or an ox."

"No one is suggesting that you're a sheep or an ox. What you're saying is ridiculous. Who will speak for you in Amsterdam?"

"Tante Miriam," she answered, referring to a very old aunt whom neither of them had met. "Or her husband, Avrum. Surely you'd trust them?"

"Well, yes, I suppose I would. But you're my responsibility, Rachel. Not theirs. I can't just wish you on them like some orphan with no one and nothing of her own."

"You needn't worry about that," she said calmly. "I've

346

already arranged it. I wrote to Tante Miriam last month and got a reply today. She's expecting me as soon as I can book passage."

When Roger heard that Rachel had left England, his first reaction was a dismaying sense of loss. He did his best to conceal it from Benjamin, who was telling him the story. His second reaction was indignation that she'd not even seen him to say goodbye. "But why didn't she tell me? I'd certainly have liked to say farewell, wish her Godspeed..."

"Yes, I know. I told her that very thing. But there wasn't any reasoning with my sister this past week. I'm sorry, Roger. I do know she's very fond of you. You mustn't think otherwise."

The innocence of that remark made Griffin wince. At first, weeks ago, he'd wondered if somehow Ahmet knew what had happened on that night he'd gone to Bristol. Soon he realized that his partner knew nothing, that Rachel wanted it that way. She was right, of course, but the deception sickened him. Now he simply said, "Yes, I know she is fond of me. And I return her feelings. Do you know what precipitated this trip to Amsterdam? It's just a holiday, I hope."

Ahmet shrugged. "I really can't answer either question. She simply insisted that she wanted to go. She said something about asking our aunt and uncle to find her a husband there, but frankly I don't believe it. My sister, I fear, isn't keen on marrying anyone. As to how long she'll stay, I don't know." Morosely he made a gesture of resignation that signaled the subject closed. Their talk turned to business.

Later, when he had time to think about it, Roger understood, or thought he understood, the wisdom of Rachel's move. Far better if the two of them were apart and thus beyond temptation. Better too, though the idea pained him, if she found a good husband and married. The thing's over and done with, he told himself firmly. It was one night's madness, that's all. He and Rachel belonged to different worlds, and it was best they both got on with their lives.

Toward the end of the month James summoned him once more. Roger hadn't seen the Duke of York since he'd given him the ill-received report that Marie Lavoie insisted Lucy Walters had been utterly faithful to the king. "Not your fault,

I suppose," James had said grudgingly, "but you're sure you did everything? Everything there was to do? You're sure, Roger?"

"I'm sorry, sir, if I could tell you differently I'd do so. But the truth is, the old woman's adamant and nothing will make her say otherwise."

James eyed him speculatively. "Nor you, I suppose. No, forget I said that. You'd not do it, and it would be madness anyway...."

Despite that instantaneous reversal, Roger was left with an uncomfortable feeling after the interview. However briefly, York had suggested he perjure himself. That he'd not jumped to the bait was, Roger thought, likely to tell against him in the future.

The notion lingered, and the summons to St. James's Palace on this Thursday in July wasn't welcome. It had to be obeyed, nonetheless.

"Tell me," the duke asked after the usual pleasantries, which, it seemed to Roger, had been just a bit cooler than usual. "What are your relatives doing these days? The ones who became Catholics...your brother and his wife, wasn't it?"

Roger stared at him. James knew damn well it was his brother. And all of the circumstances surrounding the affair. No one in London could forget an issue as notorious as that, least of all a man who'd been so close to the whole thing. "Yes," he answered after some seconds. "My brother and his wife. They're well, thank you. Living quietly and causing no further trouble."

His reluctance to speak of their actual whereabouts was probably obvious to York, he realized. Many people knew where Mark and Clare were, James probably among them. What all this was in aid of he couldn't fathom. Still, he would take what precautions were available to him. James smiled rather as if he could read all these thoughts in Griffin's face.

"Sometimes I don't think you're quite as nonpolitical an animal as you seem to be," he said. "Have you heard of Shaftesbury's latest ploy?"

"One hears every day of Shaftesbury's latest ploy," Roger answered wearily. "Then there's a new one the following day."

"Quite." The duke rose and offered his guest a tankard of ale. "Of course the Monmouth business looks dead now, since the king's been so adamant. 'I shall not yield,' he told them."

Roger accepted the drink and nodded. James went on speaking without any encouragement.

"Shaftesbury's best line of attack is through the queen. I've been saying that for months, and now the old blackguard seems to have thought of it for himself."

"My understanding was that Queen Catherine was living in seclusion at Somerset House. How can Shaftesbury make capital of that?"

"Oh, she is. Has been for some years, as you well know. His majesty's string of bedmates finally wore her down. Can't say I blame the poor woman." Roger refrained from commenting on York's own string of bedmates, or the fact that they seemed to have little effect on his wife, Mary of Modena.

"You see," James went on. "What Shaftesbury wants now is for Charles to divorce Catherine, marry a Protestant, and produce a Protestant heir. Very simple, isn't it?"

Roger shrugged. "That's hardly a new idea, sir. The queen's enemies have been suggesting it for years."

"Yes," James agreed. "But this time it's different. This time I think her majesty's enemies are prepared to press their case with vigor. I know you've always been loyal to Catherine. I feel obliged to tell you that things are in the wind. Catherine will need all the friends she can muster. Most particularly Protestant friends like yourself. Untainted by papist leanings. I trust you take my meaning."

Late summer, August 13, 1678. Masses of roses bloomed in the gardens of Whitehall. Honeysuckle scented the still, hot afternoon air. Charles, King of England, walked alone, his hands behind his back, his head bowed. The "merry monarch" wasn't particularly high-spirited this day. The intrigues and conspiracies that had plagued his reign seemed finally to be weighing him down. The exchequer was near bankruptcy, as usual, and the Parliament disinclined to fund it, also as usual. In this single year there had been three eclipses of the sun and two of the moon. Bad portents. Now it was so damnably hot. Not like England at all....

"Your majesty!" A slight, familiar figure darted forward from behind a tree. "I beg you, your majesty, a word if I may. Just one word..."

Behind the king a bevy of guards and footmen started forward. Charles held up his hand, and they halted. "Very well, what is it?" It had always been his style to deal thus with his subjects. This particular man was known to him, an assistant in the Royal Laboratory. No harm could come from a minute's conversation with the lad. Charles inclined his head and listened.

"I bring you grave news, sire." The voice shook with agitation. "Quite by chance I've learned of something ... terrible evil, sire. Terrible!"

"I see. Well, my young friend, what is it? I can hardly be expected to deal with the matter unless you acquaint me with the facts." Boring, all of it. But even fools must be dealt with when you're king.

"A plot, your majesty. A wicked plot to murder your gracious self."

"I see. No new idea, that. I've heard of many plots to murder me before now. As you can see, none of them has yet succeeded."

"I pray you, sire. Don't take my words lightly. 'Tis a real threat. It's only by the grace of almighty God that I've discovered the villains and can tell all."

"Very well." His impatience, he feared, was showing. "Who is it this time?"

"Papists, your majesty. 'Tis a popish plot intending to shoot you down. This very day, maybe. It's all led by Jesuits, but there's many involved, sire. Highborn and low. I can tell you any number of names."

PART SIX

The Eagle's Flight

They are here...that despicable corps of Angels
who were neither for God nor Satan; But only
for themselves....

—Dante Alighieri,
The Inferno

1.

"You've seen this thing?" Benjamin pushed the newsletter across the table toward Roger. Like the broadsheets that had carried information to Englishmen for decades, it was a large sheet of paper closely printed on both sides and containing whatever its enterprising author had determined would best titillate the masses. This one was perhaps more inflammatory than most.

"I've seen it." Roger eyed the thing with distaste. It purported to tell of a Jesuit plot to murder the king. All discovered by a fellow no one had ever heard of, name of Titus Oates. Roger dismissed the broadsheet with a wave of his hand and glanced around the familiar drawing room of the Ingram's Court house. Maybe he was simply imagining it, but it seemed to him the place had lost much of its warmth and charm now that Rachel was gone. "I can't say the doings of the papists particularly fascinate me. Any news of your sister?" He tried to make his voice ordinary.

"A letter a few days back. She's well, it's been a mild autumn in Amsterdam, and she's enjoying herself. No word of any future husband, I regret to say." Benjamin sighed and crossed to the window. A great elm stood in the center of the little courtyard. More than anything else this dignified and shapely tree created the impression that Ingram's Court was a place apart from the rest of the city. Today its leaves shone dull gold in the early October sun.

Ahmet knew that Roger could be terribly pigheaded sometimes. Nonetheless he was determined to try to interest his friend in the project which of late occupied all his thoughts. "I've invited someone else here this afternoon," he said. "Someone I want you to meet."

"Oh? Sounds interesting—who is he?"

"I've mentioned the chap to you before. That Quaker friend

of mine, the one with the land in America." He had no time to say more, for at that instant the maid announced Mr. William Penn. He was a gentleman, no doubt, but dressed very simply in the buff britches and jerkin of the working class.

Roger shook the man's hand with warmth. "I'm delighted to meet you, sir," he said, smiling. "Ahmet here has told me much about your plans. What's more, I owe a great debt to one of your coreligionists."

"The pleasure is mine, Captain Griffin. And I'm only too glad that Dr. Winters was able to help in the illness of your children. The happy outcome was most gratifying." His glance fell on the newsletter still lying on the table. "There'll be no happy outcome there, I fear." His manner changed entirely. "Black days are ahead for England."

"Black days," Roger repeated with a hint of scorn. "Over the doings of some lunatic Jesuits? I think not, Mr. Penn. We've been through this sort of thing too many times before."

"Indeed?" Penn sat down, and one stubby finger tapped an impatient rhythm on his leather-clad thigh. "You're wrong, captain. Forgive my blunt speech, but you're very wrong. You ignore these portents at your peril."

The corners of Roger's mouth turned up in a slight smile. "Eclipses of the sun and rumblings of thunder? We've been hearing about those all summer long."

Benjamin spoke for the first time. "Don't be so quick to dismiss them, Roger. Oh, I knew that'd be your attitude, that's why I asked William to join us here. I hoped he might help to convince you."

"I assure you, sir," Roger said, turning to look at Penn, "I mean you no insult merely because I disagree. Neither can I see anything to be gained by joining my voice to the chorus of idiocy reported in this rag." He pushed the newsletter away.

"I take no offense, captain, I assure you. Only hear me out." Roger nodded, and Penn rose to continue speaking with his back to the fireplace and looking for all the world like a minister preaching a sermon.

"This man, this Titus Oates, have you seen him? No? Then let me assure you, when you do—and I don't doubt that opportunity will come—you'll be more than ever convinced the whole 'plot' he claims to have uncovered is but a fiction born in his fevered brain. Ugly little dwarf of a man, looks quite like an evil wizard. How, you will say to yourself, can such a man have the ear of the king, the privy council, and the Parliament? I have no doubt, Captain Griffin, that such will be your reaction."

"Well, then?" Roger sat back and waited. Penn was an absorbing speaker whatever one thought of his subject.

"What matters is that you not let your natural incredulity prejudice your perception of the facts."

"What facts?" Griffin exploded. "Do you see what he says here? 'I saw'...'I carried a letter'...'I overheard'...on and on like that. Not a scrap of corroborating evidence anywhere. It's patent rubbish. Mind you, I don't doubt the Jesuit plots. I can believe anything of Jesuits. But I very much doubt that our Mr. Oates knows any more about them than I do."

"For God's sake, man!" Ahmet pounded on the table. "What does it take to convince you? Of course Oates's 'plot' is a fiction. Any thinking man knows it. But at this very moment London is sinking into hysteria. The town's about to burn to the ground, and you want to sit and fiddle!"

"I can't fiddle, Benjamin," Roger answered, chuckling. "It's a talent I never acquired. Now, now...don't get so angry with me. All right, tell me what you think we—or I—should do."

"We must get out of here. All of us," Ahmet said grimly. "Why do you think I agreed so readily to Rachel's going to Amsterdam? There are going to be terrible persecutions, Roger. Penn and I, we both belong to religions all too familiar with persecution. It's a lesson I hope you never learn. I want you to take your family and come with me to America."

It was almost a week later, walking along Pudding Lane, that Roger saw chains stretched across the road for the first time. The watch was no longer one old man with a lantern. Suddenly that ancient London institution had become a band of armed militia who stopped passersby at every corner and demanded to see proof of identity.

Two days ago a young man named Coleman, once York's private secretary and a known Catholic, had been sent to Newgate prison on the strength of letters he'd written to France some years before. Titus Oates had accused Coleman of being in a plot to murder the king; a search of his room had uncovered these old letters. There was nothing in them about any plot, but they did speak in glowing terms of the glorious time to come when James would sit on the English throne and the country would return to the old faith. "Treason!" bayed the hounds. Now Coleman was in irons.

Yesterday the body of Sir Edmund Berry Godfrey had been discovered at the foot of Primrose Hill. Nothing particularly unusual in that. Murders were committed in London with some frequency. But Godfrey was the same justice of the peace who had first taken Oates's sworn testimony, the now infamous eighty-three articles in which he "exposed" the scurrilous Popish Plot. And Godfrey had disappeared soon afterward. Now it was known that he'd been murdered, though not how or by whom, and everywhere it was being said that this proved the truth of Oates's accusations. Roger couldn't see how the one fact followed from the other; but he could see plain enough the effect the whole thing was having on the city.

"Armed men everywhere," he said grimly to Benjamin, who was waiting for him in George Alley. "And chains across the streets. The town's under siege."

Ahmet nodded and said nothing. He'd warned Roger. He knew only too well what was to follow. "God help the poor Catholics," he said quietly.

"Poor Catholics!" Griffin slammed his gloves down on the desk. "Poor Catholics indeed. They've brought this on themselves. You can't imagine the scheming and intriguing they've indulged in all these years. Now it's all come home to roost."

"You fool," Ahmet said softly. "You bloody fool. Don't you understand what this kind of thing is all about? Even now? It doesn't matter what group you care to name. Papists, Jews, Moors...Englishmen, for that matter. All you have to do is locate an identifiable bunch of people someplace where they're a minority and the game's off and running. Look." He rose and pointed out the window. His hand trembled with emotion. "They've just made it lawful for the home of anyone known to be a papist to be searched daily. And the mania's spreading. There must be a dozen men in Newgate already. It won't end there, Roger, mark my words."

"I don't know, Benjamin." Griffin ran his fingers through his hair. "I just can't believe it'll be as bad as you say. Good God, man, this is England! Not Spain or Portugal or some place like that. England! Besides," he added as he stood up and poured them both a drink, "it may well be a case of where there's smoke there's fire. Maybe there is a grain of truth in Oates's accusations."

The word of the so-called popish army came some days later. Oates told the House of Commons a new tale, one he'd not mentioned before. Once the Jesuits had assassinated his majesty there were hundreds of Catholic laymen waiting to rise up in arms. They'd already been appointed to cabinet posts and military ranks in a new government and army meant to take control of the realm.

Why hadn't he mentioned this before? He'd been tired, confused, distraught....Who were these Catholic laymen? Obligingly Titus named names—at least half a dozen peers of the realm and numerous others from a well-known actor to a barman at the Pheasant Tavern. No, he continued to insist, the Duke of York knew nothing of any of it. He wasn't involved. There was even a plan to replace him with some other Catholic king if he balked at gaining the throne in such a manner.

Parliament was in a frenzy. The lord chief justice was summoned, and all the doors and windows were barred by the sergeant-at-arms. No one was allowed to leave until the chief justice, Sir William Scroggs, had arrived and issued warrants for the arrest of those whom Oates had named. But that didn't stop the news from seeping into the streets.

Nothing seemed able to stem the tide of hysteria. By early December, York's secretary, the unfortunate Coleman of the indiscreet letters, had swung at Tyburn. So had another young Catholic, William Staley, scion of a wealthy family known to Roger as well as most other London businessmen. One afternoon, while very drunk in the Black Lion alehouse, he was overheard to say, "The king is a great heretic. I would kill him myself." A fortnight later he was hung, drawn, and quartered, his head impaled on London Bridge and his quarters on the four gates of the city. Nor was the mania confined to London. In Yorkshire an eighty-two-year-old priest was accused of baptizing a Catholic child. For this heinous crime he too was hung, drawn, and quartered.

By this time Griffin and Ahmet had ceased to argue the question or the advisability of emigrating to America, a suggestion Roger said was daft. Benjamin merely kept silent and watched, while Roger tried to fight off the sense of revulsion and shame that was swiftly overpowering him. Why, he asked himself repeatedly, did he always have this insane desire to pick at any wound? So the country was in the grip of some madness; why must he become involved? Ignore it, he told himself over and over. It will pass, such things always do. But he couldn't ignore it.

On the afternoon of December 17, Griffin found himself drawn to the Old Bailey, where four Jesuits and one layman were on trial. It was his first sight of Oates. The man was squat, bowlegged and bull-necked, with a jaw so enormous his mouth seemed to be hideously in the middle of his face. The voice that was sending so many to the gallows was a whine. Ahmet insisted that Oates was an active homosexual and, moreover, stark mad. At one time or another the man had been three or four different kinds of Protestant as well as a Catholic, and even, for a brief while, a seminarian with the Jesuits. They'd decided he was unsuitable and sent him away. Now they were reaping their reward.

At this trial, the most notorious to date, the lord chief justice himself was presiding. The accused were permitted no defense counsel. There was the usual jury of twelve, but were they peers of the men on trial? Certainly no Catholics sat on the jury, let alone any priests.

Roger stared at Scroggs and tried to fathom the judge's mentality. His full, sensual mouth seemed to relish the taste of his words, his corpulent frame to swell with self-importance when he made his summing-up speech to the jury. "What shall I say of these villains?" he roared. "They eat their God, they kill their king and saint the murderer!"

The verdict was guilty. What else would have been expected? The sentence, death. "You have done, gentlemen," Scroggs told the jurors, "like very good Christians; that is to say, very good Protestants. . . ." Roger left the Old Bailey soon afterward.

"Did ye hear, guvnor?" A man accosted him in the street anxious to tell someone, anyone, his news. "Did ye hear? Oates says the queen's really the one behind the plot. Queen Catherine herself it is wot's plottin' his majesty's murder!"

2.

"Where's the mistress?" Rudy didn't wait for the door of the kitchen to close before accosting Ellen at her place by the stove.

"Upstairs, in her room. What ails ye, lad? Mistress ain't to be disturbed now. She be doin' her accounts."

"There's somethin' funny happenin' down in the valley. I just seen a troop o' men ridin' down there. All armed."

Ellen's usually placid face hardened. "Quick!" She grabbed young Tom Harvey by his shirt collar. "Go get mistress. Don't waste no time or I'll have yer hide!"

Nancy returned with Tom to find a kitchen silent, in the grip of tension. "What is it, what's wrong?"

Rudy stepped forward. "Sorry to trouble ye, ma'am, but I was ridin' the new hunter, that chestnut we bought t'other day. Takin' her out for a bit o'exercise. Saw a parcel o' men ridin' into the valley. Armed, they were."

Nancy didn't waste time on further questions. "Saddle my horse," she said quickly.

"Beggin' yer pardon, ma'am . . . 'twould be better if ye rode up behind me. Faster."

"Very well," she agreed without argument. "You're right. Hurry, Rudy, let's go . . ."

The chestnut was a strong animal; they'd paid a substantial amount of money for her. This day Nancy realized she'd been worth it. Even with two riders on her back the horse flew like the wind over the rough terrain. Halfway to their destination Rudy turned the animal from the path onto a short cut across a field. Nancy gripped the coachman's waist. The mare responded to the challenge by taking three successive fences without putting a foot wrong. They were charging down the slope to the valley in less than ten minutes.

The men whom Rudy had seen were standing at the door

of Tupenny Cottage. They looked every bit as menacing as the young man's tone had indicated; tough, surly characters with swords and pistols at the ready. In their midst stood Mark Griffin, his arm around his wife and his expression as cool and collected as always.

"What is it, Mark?" Nancy slid down without waiting for any assistance. "Who are these people? What's going on?"

"This fellow here claims to be the sheriff, that one his sergeant-at-arms. For the rest, I can't say."

"My men, ma'am." The one whom Mark had identified as the sheriff bowed in Nancy's direction. "And you, I trust, are Mistress Griffin, Captain Roger Griffin's wife?"

"I am," She tried to make her voice and manner as calm as Mark's, as imperious as if she were onstage playing some ancient queen. Face and boldness were the only weapons at her command. She knew how inadequate they were. Cold terror was churning in her stomach, for she could guess the errand that brought these men here. She'd known it from the first words Rudy spoke. "What right have you to come here armed?" she demanded. "This is Griffin land. This gentleman is our estate manager."

"Yes, ma'am, I know that." The man's voice was unctuously polite. "But I'm afraid too that he's known to me and others as Mark Griffin, formerly squire of Harwood Hall, a known papist." He turned to Mark. "Do you deny that, sir?"

"No, I've never denied it."

"But we've been through all that," Nancy interjected in a frantic attempt to seize the initiative. "He's been adjudicated a recusant and fined for it. We were promised that was the end of the matter."

"It might have been." The sheriff was less polite now. His words had acquired a hint of menace, and two of his party had their pistols in hand. "If the squire had been content to leave it thus, it might have been the end of the matter. But..." He withdrew a scroll of paper from his jerkin and read from it. "You are known, sir, to have accepted a commission in an army of papists whose intention is first to murder his most gracious majesty Charles II and then to rise in rebellion against the lawful government and church of this realm. You are to be a captain in that army. You are a traitor." He spat out the words. "Seize him!" The sheriff gestured with one arm, and two burly men moved forward. "The woman too."

"Wait!" Nancy thrust herself in front of the man. "What proof have you of these accusations? It's lunacy."

"Be quiet, Nancy!" Mark's voice rang out over the confusion. He knew well that in times like these any defense of any victim could be disastrous for the defender. "There'll be time for such questions later....I trust, sir,"—his calm had returned, and he addressed himself once more to the sheriff— "that at some point I'll be allowed to face my accusers? Hear the evidence they claim to have against me?"

"That's not difficult." The man shrugged. With two fellows holding Griffin and his wife in firm armlocks, the sheriff could be magnanimous. "Your accuser is right here." He gestured. "A young man stepped out of a copse of trees and moved toward them.

"Sam Ludlow!" Nancy exclaimed. "What are you doing here?"

"I know what happened, that's what," the boy said with sullen defiance. "I knowed it all and I told."

Nancy stared at the youth, scorn and disdain in her eyes. "Just what nonsense are you talking, you evil little villain? When Captain Griffin hears about this he'll flog the skin off your back."

"No he won't," Ludlow said. "I know everything about the way these folks have conspired against the king and how Cap'n Griffin hisself helped. I wuz there when he took that letter from the French nun and agreed to bring it here."

Nancy's eyes widened in disbelief. Suddenly it was all too clear. The horror was far worse than she'd imagined. It wasn't merely a tissue of lies, but a distortion of facts. They would be twisted beyond recognition. She heard the sheriff give orders to search Tupenny Cottage, and his voice seemed to come from some far-distant place where truth had little meaning.

"It is totally beyond me how these things can be believed."

Nancy paced the floor in front of Roger's desk. With her in the George Alley office were her husband and Benjamin Ahmet. It was very late, nearly midnight. She'd arrived in town with the news only a few hours before. Then, after a hurried consultation with Roger, she had gone to Nell's. Now the three were gathered here to talk. At least discussion helped to ease their anxiety.

"You can see what's going on out there." Roger gestured to the street.

Nancy nodded her head. It had taken her almost an hour to make her way back from Pall Mall. Chains across the road, armed watchmen who stopped her at every corner. Only the pass she carried, given her earlier by Roger and signed by Prince Rupert in his capacity as lord high admiral, enabled her to get through the citadel of panic which London had become.

"I guess in some perverse kind of way it's logical." Benjamin sighed. "Doubtless Oates decided that it would look a bit odd if the Jesuits had no plan to subdue the country once the king was assassinated. So we get this ghost army...." He slapped a much-circulated newsletter on the table. "Here's the story Parliament heard some days ago. Printed for all to see, and to use in settlement of any private grudges they happen to have at hand."

"But that's another thing I don't understand," Nancy said. "What possible grudge can Sam Ludlow have against Mark and Clare? Against any of us, for that matter? My God! He's been with Griffin's since he was ten years old. It doesn't make any sense."

"Oh yes it does," Roger said. "In the present atmosphere it's happening every day. Bricklayers are suddenly remembering priest-holes they found years ago, a joiner claims he once found popish beads in a man's house...'The noble Brutus hath told you Caesar was ambitious,'" he quoted softly.

Nancy sank into a nearby chair. "Sam Ludlow? Ambitious for what?"

Roger shrugged. "Who knows? Esteem, notoriety, money...any or all of them. But of Master Ludlow's ambitious nature I have no doubt. With all this buzzing in the air he suddenly remembered our trip to France last spring. It must have seemed too good an opportunity to miss."

"How did he know about the letter?" Benjamin asked.

"I told him. Why the hell shouldn't I have done so? It's never been any secret that my brother and his family are papists. Ludlow was grumbling about our side trip to the abbey, and I simply mentioned to him, by way of explanation, that my niece gave me a letter to bring home to her mother and father. I thought no more about it from that day to this. It seemed such a trifling thing. Even now I can't feel guilty about it. Dammit! It *was* a trifling thing!"

"Of course it was," Nancy interjected. "Let's not make a

361

bad situation worse by blaming ourselves where no blame lies."

"Good advice, my dear," Benjamin said. "What did Nell have to say? Any joy there?"

"Yes, I guess so. At least as far as we're directly concerned. She's sure she can talk to Charles and that no one will bring any action against Roger as bearer of the wretched letter. As always," she added bitterly, "whom you know matters more than anything else. Nell and I go back too far to be made enemies over this lunacy, whatever her anti-papist feelings."

"Thank God for small favors," Roger said with feeling.

"Maybe large ones," Benjamin added, searching for a ray of hope. "If Nancy's right, perhaps your brother and his wife are fortunate too. They know someone who knows someone who's in the king's confidence."

It was a weak attempt at humor, but both Roger and Nancy smiled.

Roger stood up. "Nancy, what about Sarah and the boys? I've been so damned upset I never thought to ask."

"It's all right," she said quickly. "I should have told you as soon as I came. They're fine. Fortunately they weren't home when that beastly sheriff and his hoodlums appeared. I found them as soon as I could and explained what had happened. Naturally they're terribly upset and worried, but they're safe. I sent them to stay in the cabin. You remember, darling, the one we used to call Whitehall." Roger nodded. "They're there, and Rudy will act as messenger for them, bring them whatever they need. It won't do for more than a day or two, but meanwhile they're safe until we can find out if there are any threats to them."

"It's insane," Roger said glumly. "All of it."

"So," Benjamin sat down with an air of sadness. "You're finally convinced of that. I'd not have thought it would take so long."

Griffin leaned back in his chair and closed his eyes. Weariness of spirit matched that of body. "When it comes to the point where people are seriously accusing my brother of being involved in a plot to overthrow the rightful King of England, even I'm convinced, Benjamin. They might as well accuse him of jumping over the moon or swimming to China. Either would make as much sense."

"But they'll say it was Jesuit influence," Nancy whispered. "They'll drag up all that business in Yorkshire eight years ago and say that explains it. It won't matter how crazy the whole thing is. It won't matter a bit."

3.

They spent the night at George Alley. Benjamin stayed with them. He wouldn't go to Ingram's Court after Roger and Nancy refused his offer of hospitality. There was a terrible sense of waiting, though none of them could have said for what. Finally, much later in the day, a messenger arrived from Nell.

"Thank God," Nancy breathed as she read the note. "She's arranged for them to be transferred from Guildford prison to Newgate. It's much easier for Charles to intervene if they're right here in London."

"I guess it's something to be thankful for," Roger said quietly. "We've got to get word to Tassels. Sarah and the boys must be frantic."

"Shall I go?" Nancy asked at once.

"No, you stay here. If Nell needs to contact us it'll be you she wants. I'll go." He gave word for a horse to be made ready, then looked a question at Benjamin.

"No fear, Roger," the other man said quickly. "I shall be by Nancy's side every minute until you return. Either here or at Ingram's Court. Whatever seems best."

"Thank you. That eases my mind." He drew on his cloak and gave his wife one swift kiss before leaving.

It took a long time to get through London. The watch stopped him half a dozen times, but in each instance they were persuaded by the pass he carried to let him through. That pass had been given him by Rupert some weeks earlier. The hysteria had seemed bad enough then, but it was worse now. Roger blessed his luck in having the document and continued on his slow but steady way.

Once he was beyond Tuthill Fields and had left the city behind, the going was easier. Still it was near two in the morning when he rode onto his own land and started for the cabin in the woods.

"Stop right there," a voice said with cool menace. "If you come any farther I'll blow your head off."

Roger pulled up his horse in a sudden motion, making the animal rear back with a loud neigh of displeasure. "Who's there?" he demanded. "Who dares to threaten me on my own land?"

"Uncle Roger? Is that you?" Young Andrew stepped out of the shadows, his pistol still held at the ready.

"Of course it's me. Where the hell did you get that?" Roger dismounted as he spoke.

"It came from your study," the lad admitted. "I made Rudy bring it to me."

"I see. Have you shot anybody yet?" Roger asked drily.

"No. You're the first person I've had to challenge."

"That, at least, is good news." Roger slung an arm around Andrew's shoulders. "Where are the others?"

"In there." He motioned toward the cabin. "We've kept an armed watch since yesterday, but no one's come except Rudy."

They were walking toward the house when Andrew paused. "I'm sorry about taking your gun without permission, Uncle Roger. But it seemed the only thing to do, once we'd made up our minds."

"Made up your minds to what?" Roger asked.

The boy took a deep breath. "Not to be led like lambs to the slaughter the way everyone else is doing. We decided we'd rather fight and die."

"I see. I understand that, of course. But who are you fighting, Andrew? That's the point."

"The mob. All those lunatics out there who want our blood for no reason except our religion. We're not traitors, you know that. We've no part in any plot to overthrow the king or anyone else." His voice choked for the first time. "Neither have Mama or Papa, but they wouldn't believe them."

By this time they'd reached the door of the cabin. Charles and Sarah were huddled by the fire, wrapped in the blankets that had been left here six years before, when they used this place to hide from Roger. The thought made him shudder; he pushed it aside. "I've got some news," he said. "It offers a little hope."

For the first time the others looked animated. None had dared to ask him for news, because they were convinced that he must be bringing them word of something horrible. With this statement they stood and moved about and clamored for information.

"Look, they're not free yet, so don't get your hopes up. Aunt Nancy went to her friend Nell Gwyn. Miss Gwyn thinks it may be possible to get the king to intervene. She's arranged for your parents to be moved from Guildford to London where his majesty will have more control."

"Where in London?" Sarah asked without any expression in her voice.

Roger swallowed hard. "Newgate prison," he answered. "It was the best we could do."

His niece nodded. "You wouldn't believe what they did to the cottage."

"What who did to the cottage?"

"The sheriff and his men," Charles answered. "The bloody whoremasters! I hope they all burn in hell! They tore the place apart. Even ripped out some of the walls. Supposedly they were looking for some kind of 'evidence.'"

Roger gripped the boy's shoulders. "Listen to me, Charles, it may be important. What did they actually take? You must try to remember and tell me."

Andrew said, "The only things we know for sure that they took are a prayer book, a string of rosary beads, and Laura's letter. At least we presume they took the letter. Mama always kept it in her prayer book, and, as I've told you, they took that."

"It was all lying in plain sight on the table in Mama and Papa's room," Sarah added. "They'd no need to do what they did."

He persuaded them to return with him to Tassels itself. "No need for you to be miserable up here," he insisted. "We've no reason to suppose anyone's looking for you. If they were they'd have searched for you that same day. Besides, I'll feel better knowing the lot of you are in the house. Nancy's going to be needed in London until this thing is solved, and I don't like leaving the children with just the servants to look after them."

It was an appeal they understood, as he knew they would. Griffin loyalty was bred into these three as it was into their ancestors. By the time he'd had some sleep and prepared to ride back to London, Sarah had taken over as mistress of the manor and the boys were busy overseeing the business of the estate. "That's the best thing," Roger told Andrew in his last conference with his nephew. "Just try to act normally and keep everyone calm."

Andrew nodded. "Right, Uncle Roger. But there's something you'd better understand. What I said last night about not going like a lamb to the slaughter, I meant it. We all mean it."

"Very well, I understand that, and you're old enough to make the choice for yourself. Only one thing, Andrew. My three children are in the house with you. They're far too young to comprehend any of this. They can only rely on you, Charles, and Sarah for protection."

The lad nodded. "You don't need to tell me that," he said. "They'll come first, no matter what."

"Thank you. As for the servants, I think they can all be trusted. At least I hope so."

"Yes, I think so. The tenants too. They all loved Mama and Papa."

Roger felt a lump rise in his throat when the boy referred to Mark and Clare thus in the past tense. Doubtless he didn't even realize he'd done it. He'd turned away to mount when Andrew posed one last question. "Is Aunt Nancy all right?"

"Yes. She's fine. I left her in the care of my best friend. He'll look after her."

While he was riding down the path toward the London road the irony of those words struck him. That's just the sort of thing Benjamin might have said the night he went to Bristol and left his sister at Ingram's Court with a trusted house guest.

"How's Miss Rachel, sir?" someone might have asked in passing.

"Fine, she's with my best friend...."

Guilt rose in his gorge like vomit. He swallowed hard and rode on. It was too late to remedy any of that. He could only do what he could to prevent new outrages.

Despite Benjamin's promise to remain by Nancy's side, she was alone at George Alley when he returned. Roger still kept a bedchamber above his office and spent his nights there during the week when he was in London. It was in that room he found his wife, lying across the bed and staring at the ceiling. "Where's Ahmet?" he asked at once. Fear and foreboding were in the very air they breathed now. It made anything at all capable of invoking terror.

"He's gone to meet someone who claims to know something. He didn't want to go, but I insisted. An old man came looking for him here. I don't know who he was." She sat up and shook her auburn hair back from her forehead. "I tried to sleep, but I couldn't."

"Yes, I know." Roger sat beside her and took her hand. For some reason he couldn't name it occurred to him that he'd never loved her more than he did at this moment. "Was the fellow looking for Ahmet a cripple? With a black eyepatch?"

"Yes. He looked like an actor, too bizarre to be real."

Roger shrugged. "He's real enough. One of Ahmet's regular network of informers. He's been useful to us many times in the past. That makes me feel better. I'd be worried if it was someone I didn't know."

"What did you find at Tassels?"

He told her everything. She looked grave when he was finished, but somewhat less worried than before. "I'm glad they're at the house," she said firmly. "You did the right thing to move them there. It was silly of me to hide them in the cabin."

"You didn't have time to think it through, just to act. I'd probably have done the same."

She shook her head. "Still, this is better. Left to themselves they'd just get more and more depressed. God knows what they'd decide. This way they'll keep busy, and more important, they won't do anything that would endanger the children. That will act as a check on things."

"Yes, I thought so too." It didn't seem to him wise to say any more. The thing he really feared, and that he didn't want to discuss with Nancy, was Andrew and his white-knight personality. It would be just like the older boy to try to stage some dramatic rescue of his parents from prison. There seemed less danger of that now. Both the transfer to Newgate and the responsibility for Nell, Jennifer, and James militated against it. He said nothing of this. Only, "Have you eaten? I can send out for something."

Just then, however, Hart knocked on the door and announced that Ahmet was waiting for them downstairs. He looked terrible, glummer than Roger had ever seen him.

"Brace yourselves," Benjamin said, coming straight to the point. "It's bad. I found out what was in that damned letter. At least what they claim is in it." He fished a piece of scrap paper from his pocket. "Fellow I know is a friend of a friend of a clerk in Justice Scroggs's chambers. The letter's been turned over to him. Seems that somewhere it says..." He narrowed his eyes and read from the little paper, "'Aunt Sophia keeps saying wonderful things are going to happen in England. She knows things like that. Gets messages, if you understand what I mean. She says that in our lifetimes a Catholic king will be returned to the English throne. Wouldn't that be wonderful?'" He stopped reading and looked at them. "Is it likely to be a true quote?" he asked finally.

"Oh yes." Roger sank into a chair and his voice was barely audible. "An exact quote, I daresay. My sister, Sophia, thinks she hears voices, sees visions. She's no part of any plot, but God help us trying to prove that."

Nancy rushed into the silence that followed Roger's remarks. "But that letter was written five months ago! How can it relate to some plot supposed to exist now?"

Neither Benjamin nor Roger answered her. Each was busy with his own thoughts. Roger's were all of Chief Justice Scroggs and the impression he'd formed of him last week at the Old Bailey. Benjamin thought of young Coleman's letters. None were any worse than this one, and Coleman was already dead.

4.

Christmas came and went. Nancy paid a one-day visit to Tassels to bring presents for the children; Roger remained in London but sent Hart to accompany her through the hazards traveling now entailed. She found the household subdued but normal. Sarah had seen to it that the front room was decked with greens and a proper Christmas dinner prepared.

"She said she didn't want the little ones disappointed," Nancy told Roger when she returned to the city. "I couldn't find words to tell her how grateful I was."

"There's no one like Sarah in a crisis," he agreed. "I learned that years ago."

"She comes by that honestly," Nancy replied. "There's a lot of Clare in Sarah." Then for the first time she suddenly dissolved in tears. The mention of her sister-in-law's name snapped the tight web of control she'd exercised until now.

"Don't love, don't...it won't solve anything. You'll just make yourself sick." He rocked her in his arms and tried to find words of comfort. There were none for either of them. Finally, as much to distract her as anything, he asked, "What about the children? You haven't told me anything."

"They're fine. Missing us, of course, but fine. Nell sent a big kiss, and Jennifer said to tell you hers was even bigger. Your daughters think themselves rivals for your affection, I fear." She managed to laugh a little through her tears.

"And what of Jamie? No kisses from him, I'll warrant." Roger knew his son considered himself a man at the age of barely five.

"Not a chance. But..." Nancy hesitated and bit her lip. "That's the one thing that worried me. Jamie said something peculiar. Something about having kept the watch with Andrew the night before." She stared at Roger in perplexity. "He even mentioned a pistol. Do you think he's imagining things?"

"No, I don't." Roger sighed. "I told you what Andrew said. Doubtless he's mounted a watch every night at Tassels. He and Charles take turns, I expect. They may even have pressed Rudy and Tom Harvey into service. Jamie's bound to get involved in that. Any little boy would."

"Oh, Lord....Should we do something, Roger? I didn't think to say anything while I was there. Question Andrew or such?"

"Leave it alone." His voice was grim. "Maybe it's just as well they keep watch. This whole country's going stark mad. Andrew's instincts are sound. Protect your own and the devil take the hindmost."

"My God, Roger!" He heard her echoing the very words he'd spoken to Benjamin weeks before. "This is England, not some foreign country. I thought we were supposed to have laws here. Laws to protect the innocent."

On the first day of January 1679 there was yet one more of those natural accidents that had done so much to inflame tempers throughout the year. A freak series of storms raged over London, and suddenly, at eleven in the morning, the city was plunged into darkness. Crowds of people rushed through the streets shouting about the end of the world. Still other's bellowed, "It's the papists, they're attacking!"

"So now they credit the papists with controlling the weather." Nancy turned from the window in disgust. "The lot of them ought to be locked away. Lunatics, that's what they are, lunatics!"

"Careful, Nancy." Benjamin was at George Alley today, as he had been every day since the ordeal began. "If you're willing to lock them up because you think they're mad, what can you charge against their behavior?"

"Damn you, Benjamin. Don't be so logical. I can't tolerate it right now." She stamped her foot for emphasis, and the whole silly interchange nearly degenerated into a quarrel. Then Nancy bit her lip and pulled herself back from the brink of anger. Tensions running so high always forced arguments, she knew that. Moreover, both she and Benjamin were particularly on edge today. Roger had gone once more to try to see the Duke of York. They pinned such hopes on York's intervention; if only he could be reached. Since all this had begun the usually accessible James had shut himself away in his palace and refused to give any audiences.

When Hart opened the door they turned to him with heightened expectation. Any news would be welcome if it meant an end to this waiting. "It's Miss Nell, ma'am. Lookin' for ye."

Nell entered right behind him. Nancy saw at once the state she was in. "What is it? What's happened?"

"Quick, come with me! Right now. The trial's going on this very minute."

The three hurried into the street, Benjamin and Nancy pulling on their cloaks even as they ran. "We'll take my carriage," Nell said breathlessly. "The watchmen all recognize it and we'll make better time."

Still they lurched through the city streets at what seemed a snail's pace. No one challeneged them, but they had to wait time and again for the watch to take down the chains that barred the way. "The thing that most worried me," Nell took the opportunity to explain, "was what that young villain Ludlow would say about Roger. He carried the damned letter. It may have been possible to implicate him too."

"No..." Nancy went yet a further shade of pale, and Benjamin reached for her hand.

"Don't worry." There was grim satisfaction in Nell's voice. "His name won't be mentioned. I conveyed certain warnings to young Mr. Ludlow. But these things are so damned complicated. The very people who cooperated in persuading the little wretch to shut up insisted the trial must be speedy and unannounced. It's all so complicated," she repeated passing her hand over her brow. Nancy could see that the hand trembled.

Nell had never met Clare or Mark Griffin. She didn't even particularly like Roger. But her love for Nancy was unchanged, and Nell Gwyn's kind of loyalty made her suffer along with her friend. Nancy reached out and patted the girl's knee. "It's all right, darling. I know you did everything you could."

"Well, I'm not through yet," came the spirited reply. "A few heads will roll over this one. I was supposed to receive twenty-four hours' notice of the trial. Instead I just heard now..."

Her words were interrupted by the coachman. "We're here, ma'am. This entrance is best, I think."

Nancy had never before been inside the Old Bailey. It was a remarkable building, but she barely saw it. She saw only Mark and Clare, standing in the dock as calmly as they might have stood in the front garden of Tupenny Cottage.

Her eyes raked over them for any indication of the torture she'd so much feared. No, it didn't look as if they'd been tortured. Mark had a bruise over one eye, and the bodice of Clare's dress was torn, nothing more. Thankfully she breathed a sigh and looked around the room. There were few people, none of the crowds that usually came to these things. The men present, and she and Nell were the only women other than Clare, all looked official types, men who had reason to be here. "What's happening?" she whispered urgently to Benjamin. "It all seems so quiet."

"Look over there." He pointed to the seats reserved for the jury. They were empty. "They've gone out to deliberate the verdict, I'll warrant. Apparently all the evidence has been heard."

At that moment someone spied Nell Gwyn and turned to stare. Few faces were better known in London; she attracted this kind of attention wherever she went. One or two people smiled and nodded, as if they'd met her strolling in Pall Mall of a Sunday afternoon. Nancy turned her attention back to the dock. She wanted to catch Clare's eye, let her know that they were here. It might be some small comfort. Neither Clare nor Mark looked in her direction, however. Only at each other and at some distant point in space.

Suddenly there was a flurry of activity at the front of the courtroom. The low chatter stopped, and everyone was silent while the jury of twelve filed back to their seats. Then they all had to rise while the judge returned to his bench. "It's Scroggs," Benjamin whispered in her ear. "I'd hoped perhaps someone else..."

"Gentlemen of the jury, have you reached a verdict?"

"We have, milord."

Nancy held her breath and clenched her fists. Calm and strong, she must be calm and strong, just like Mark and Clare themselves. She wanted to look at them, but she couldn't. Nothing could give her enough courage for that. Instead she stared at the tips of her satin slippers. They were stained with mud. With utmost concentration she examined the exact shape and color of the stain. She felt Benjamin's arm circle her waist, and then she heard the words as if from very far away. "Guilty as charged," a voice intoned. A ripple of satisfaction passed over the court.

Scroggs leaned forward and addressed the prisoners in the ancient tradition, "Is there any reason why I should not pass sentence of death?"

"None!" a voice shouted from somewhere. "Hang 'em," another demanded. "Hang all these plotters!"

"Milord!" Nancy knew that voice. She looked up. Mark had leaned forward and was speaking to the chief justice. "Milord, may I speak?" Scroggs nodded and banged his gavel for silence.

"As to the verdict of this court," Mark said, "I cannot quarrel. We were charged with receiving a letter from our daughter. We did indeed receive such a letter, and cherished it, as any parent would cherish a message from a child forced into exile for no reason except the desire to follow her conscience in the worship of her God. And that, gentlemen, is the real crime of which we are accused and found guilty. Our faith. We are no plotters. You all know that." A chorus of derision interrupted him, but Scroggs gaveled again for silence.

"It is the prisoner's right to be heard," the chief justice said loudly. "In my court there'll be no perversion of justice."

"You all know we're no plotters," Mark repeated. "We are his majesty's loyal subjects and always have been. But for eight years we have been hounded and persecuted and made to suffer every kind of loss and deprivation, for one reason only—that we have returned to the faith of our forefathers. All our forefathers, yours as well as ours. For over a hundred years a virulent pox has infected this England we all profess to love. Hundreds of good men and true have been murdered..."

Another interruption by the listeners, and this time Mark himself shouted them to silence. "Yes, murdered! And for no crime other than their adherence to the faith that once was professed by every Christian in the realm. But you cannot snuff out that faith, gentlemen." His voice had lowered, but every word was heard by the suddenly hushed crowd. "Nothing you do can snuff it out. I say what has been said before, 'come rack, come rope, we will not yield!'"

Scroggs was leaning back, one finger tapping his cheek and the other hand resting on his gavel. He waited a moment or two to be sure that the prisoner's speech was ended. Then he ran his eye over the crowd and moved ponderously in his chair.

Finally, when he had the total attention of everyone present, he delivered the sentence he'd passed so often these past weeks. "You must go to the place from whence you came, there to remain until ye shall be drawn through the open city of London upon hurdles to the place of execution, and there be hanged and let down whilst still alive, and your entrails taken out and burnt in your sight; then your heads to be cut off and your bodies divided into four parts, to be disposed of at his majesty's pleasure. May God have mercy on your souls."

Roger was waiting for them when they returned. He knew where they'd been; Hart had told him. When Benjamin and Nancy entered the room he had only to look at them to know everything else. It was as bad as he'd expected. The trial he'd attended previously had prepared him.

Silently he crossed to Nancy and took both her hands in his. They felt damp, and when he looked down he could see that her palms were bleeding. She'd dug her nails into them. "Come," he said quietly, "sit down." He wiped her hands with his handkerchief and insisted she drink the brandy Benjamin poured. Then he sat beside her, and the three of them remained in silence for a long time.

"James promised he'd try," Roger said finally. His tone was so flat he might have been discussing the weather. "There's reason to hope the king might commute the sentence. Charles knows now the whole thing's a farce."

"Does he?" Benjamin asked. "How can you be sure?" He didn't look at Roger while he spoke, only at Nancy staring silently into space.

"York told me. He says the whole thing's being fanned by Shaftesbury, whose main targets are James and the queen. A while ago Oates suddenly claimed Catherine was implicated in the plot. Funny, I heard the same story myself on the street some days ago. Seems the king was furious. Oates claimed to have been in Somerset House and overheard the queen plotting with some Jesuits. Charles had him taken there and the little bastard couldn't identify one room in the palace. He was supposed to bring them to the spot where he'd overheard this conversation, but he couldn't find his way past the gatehouse."

"But things go on?" Benjamin asked incredulously.

Roger shrugged. "They've their own games to play. The stakes are more complicated than that lunatic Oates even imagines. In the end he's a pawn like so many others."

"When will James let you know?" They were Nancy's first words.

"Soon, darling," he said gently. "As soon as he can. He hopes to see the king today or tomorrow."

In faraway Amsterdam, Rachel Ahmet knew little of the drama that was unfolding in England. News was slow to travel across the water, and she had pressing concerns of her own.

It had been necessary, of course, to take the old aunt into her confidence almost immediately. "I'm pregnant, Tante Miriam," she announced frankly. "There's no point in my trying to hide it from you."

"And where is the baby's father?" the woman demanded.

Rachel shook her head. "That's not important. He's a married man; there's his wife and his other children to consider. I won't be responsible for shattering so many lives."

"Hmph," the old woman snorted with derision. "You young people of today! You're all crazy. No respect left. Nothing. No brains either. Didn't you think about this wife and these other children before you let this devil make you pregnant? What good is it worrying about that now?"

"He's not a devil, Tante Miriam. It's as much my fault as his."

"Ach, I suppose it's to be expected. You with no mother since a baby almost. And that fool of a brother of yours letting you go so long without a husband. What does he think now of his modern notions? Tell me that, will you?"

"He doesn't know, Tante. That's why I came to you. Please, please promise you'll help me to keep him from knowing. That's the only good thing that can come out of this. Please..."

The old woman was barely four feet tall and almost as wide. She had acquired a mustache in her late years, even the traces of a beard. It made her look like some caricature of one of the ancient patriarchs in the Bible. Now she was being asked to pronounce judgment, also like an ancient patriarch. "This man," she asked solemnly, "the baby's father. He's a Jew?"

Rachel had expected this. Understanding all the complexities behind the question, she had determined her answer long before now. "Of course," she replied without even a blush. "Of course he's a Jew."

"Yes, I thought he must be. Where would you even meet a *goy* to get involved with? Very well, child, you may stay with me and no one will know anything. Not Benjamin nor anyone else. We'll say you're married and here on a visit. Mind you," she added at the last, "if the father were a *goy* I'd not do this. But since it's one of our own there must be no scandal. Let the *goyim* make scandals, not us."

Now, six months after that conversation had taken place, Rachel lay in the deep feather bed in Amsterdam and waited for the birth of her child. She'd started into labor the night before. The pains were coming close together this morning. The midwife assured her this was a good sign.

"Soon, *mevrouw*," she kept repeating. "Very soon. You're doing fine. A strong and healthy girl you are. You'll have no trouble."

Rachel had learned only a minimum of Dutch since coming here. She couldn't have carried on a conversation with the midwife if she'd wanted to. In her aunt's house the family spoke the old Turkish dialect of her youth; she needed Dutch only on her rare sorties into town. But she had little need of words in this situation. She understood instinctively what the midwife wanted her to do. Dutifully she devoted all her attention to deep breaths and concentrated pushing. An hour later her son was born.

"It's a boy, Rachel," Tante Miriam was smiling despite her disapproval of the whole situation. "A beautiful boy. Congratulations."

Rachel smiled sweetly. Then she fell asleep.

"Neither my brother nor his wife is a traitor, sire. The suggestion is ludicrous." Roger had been totally astounded by this summons to Charles's presence, but now that he was here he had no intention of tempering his words.

"But a jury of their peers says they are traitors, Captain Griffin."

"Then the jury is mistaken."

"I see." The king ran one finger over his mustache. It was

376

a habit Roger remembered well. Charles had changed little in the eight years since Roger had last seen him. A bit looser in the jowl perhaps, slightly more careworn; that was all. "What is it you wish me to do?" the king asked in that direct manner that had always been his way.

"To grant them a royal pardon, sire." Roger remained where he was, standing and looking his sovereign straight in the eye.

"Yes, so my brother said. I didn't realize you and he continued to see so much of each other."

"His highness has been a most gracious friend to me, sire. I count myself very fortunate that such has been the case."

"Quite." Charles stopped toying with his mustache and began toying with a jeweled paperweight instead. It was an exquisite lapis lazuli bauble, and Roger found himself staring at the thing as if mesmerized.

"Can you give me any explanation for this letter they had in their possession?" the king demanded.

"The only explanation is the true one, sire. Their daughter, my niece, wrote the letter to them. It was a perfectly innocent thing."

"Innocent? I doubt that.... I've heard what it contains. Messages concerning my death, as I understand it."

"No, sire. Not as you mean. My niece was reporting what she'd heard from another member of the religious community with which she lives. This other woman fancies herself some kind of seer or prophetess. It's woman's nonsense, sire, nothing more. There were no messages from any other human beings and no plots involving my brother or his wife."

Charles was silent for some moments after this. Suddenly his manner changed. It was as if he'd taken off a garment he wore only as some kind of disguise. "Many things have happened since you left the court, Griffin," he said quietly. "Times are difficult, and even a king must sometimes be led where he would not go."

"Yes, sire, I understand that."

"There is a great deal at stake here. A great deal that I could not explain to you."

Roger recognized his own words to Ahmet. These days it seemed that someone was always reciting his own words back to him. Maybe Sophia wasn't the only prophet in the family.

"I have no wish to shed innocent blood," the king continued. "Still, there are those who must be appeased, controlled.

Tell me, the squire and his wife, they still proclaim themselves papists?"

"Yes, your majesty. I'm afraid they do." There was little point in denying it.

"Perhaps that's the escape route, then. Very well, captain." He rose, and Roger knew the interview was coming to an end. "We will see what can be done. You may leave it in our hands."

There followed long weeks of waiting when nothing, and everything, seemed to happen. In the matter of Mark and Clare Griffin, no action was taken. Nancy and Roger tried everything they could think of to obtain permission to visit them in Newgate, but without success.

If Nell had been in London it might have been different, but she wasn't. Suddenly she'd gone off to Paris with her youngest son in tow. Her hurried message to Nancy simply said that the child had a complaint of the leg that had thus far resisted all treatment and she was taking him to consult a French physician reputed to be expert in such matters. Without her good offices they were helpless. The Duke of York was unreachable. Rumors surrounded him, and James was virtually in hiding. None of Ahmet's contacts proved able to get them entry into the prison. They could only wait.

Roger and Nancy lived in a vague limbo in which their only consolation was the old truism about no news being good news. "I suppose I should go home," Nancy said after ten days of this. "Maybe I can be useful there."

"For a while, perhaps," Roger agreed. He understood her desire to be immediately available if anything happened, but he was anxious to get her away from the turmoil that beset London. "Go back for a few days and send me word when you're ready to return. I'll come to fetch you or send Hart. I don't want you traveling alone just now." It was agreed, and she departed for Tassels. He sent her home in a Griffin wherry, manned by his most trusted watermen, and, unbeknownst to Nancy, he armed them all.

In the larger drama of which their agony was but a small part a great deal was happening. Not only were the prisons across England filling up with dizzying speed, there were a dozen or more noblemen in the Tower. Naturally all were Catholics, but until now they had avoided being penalized for their faith. Adept politicians, they had managed to combine conscience and expediency until the comet named Titus Oates rose in their sky. To the crowds who roamed the streets crying out in fear and blood-hunger, the issue was clear. The papists were going to take over and all good Protestants would burn at Smithfield. To the more enlightened, the macabre death dance was being piped by an altogether different set of musicians.

"Politics!" Roger slammed the latest newsletter onto the table near Benjamin. "Stinking, rotten politics. Nothing more."

"When is it ever anything else?" Benjamin inquired calmly. "Power. How to get it if you haven't got it, how to hang onto what you've got. Read the Bible. I suggest the Book of Kings for starters. Nothing ever changes."

"You're still thinking it will be different in America?"

Ahmet shrugged. "Who knows? I just think it's worth a try. You're still certain you don't want to come? Even after this?"

"I don't know...I've thought of it some. But no, I don't think so. I'm an Englishman, and I can't imagine living anywhere else. Besides, look at everything we've built here. How can you want to walk out on all this?" He waved his arm around the comfortable office. Griffin's Importations was continuing to do very well, even during the current chaos. So well oiled was the machine they'd built that it continued to function efficiently even while its two top men virtually ignored it for other concerns.

"That," Ahmet said with feeling, "is a classic excuse to do nothing. If we managed to create this success here, why do you doubt we can repeat the exercise? It's us, Roger, you and me. We're the secret. Think of it! A virgin country where trade is barely getting started. Good God, man! We'll make a dozen fortunes in as many weeks."

Roger shook his head. "Not good enough. I don't doubt there's money to be made in the colonies. But I can't see myself or my family living in a log cabin with red Indians running wild everywhere. No, Benjamin, it's not for me. I require civilization to sweeten my porridge."

"What about freedom?"

"Why, Mr. Ahmet," Roger's words dripped sarcasm. "Haven't you heard? This is England. Gentlemen are free here. You forget, sir, that document called Magna Carta. Sadly," he sighed, "everyone else seems to have forgotten it as well."

*   *   *

His hopes for a return to that sense of balance and freedom
that he believed endemic to England rose on the twenty-
fourth of the month. Charles suddenly dissolved the Parliament that had sat for the past eighteen years and decreed
there should be elections for a new Parliament to convene on
March 6.

"Maybe some new blood will bring this nation to reason
again," Griffin told Ahmet.

Then, on that same afternoon, he saw the Jesuit William
Ireland and his assistant, a layman named John Grove, going
to their deaths at Tyburn. The pair were dragged through
the streets on contraptions like sledges, called hurdles, while
a raving mob engulfed them, spitting and cursing and hurling
refuse at the condemned.

It was a sight he was never to forget. Doubtless its poi-
gnancy was intensified because he could so easily imagine
Mark and Clare in the same position. Griffin watched the
procession as long as he could stand it. After some minutes
he stumbled away into an alley and retched.

6.

The election divided the realm on clear lines. One was either
for Shaftesbury and his Whigs, which was to say against any
notion of the Duke of York as the next king, or for Danby
and his Tories, and thus for Charles and the court. But one
was never, ever for popery and its plots.

Notwithstanding the fact that Charles had been furious
over the attempt to implicate Queen Catherine, it suited his
majesty's needs to be seen as opposing popery with as much
fervor as his subjects. Oates found himself possessed of a
grace-and-favor apartment at Whitehall and a life pension
of twelve hundred a year. Of course, Titus was no longer

alone. Dozens of other witnesses to the evildoings of the plotters had now come forward to be heard and believed and fawned over by the public. Bedloe and Prance were two more names spoken in tones of hushed awe. Any of these men could destroy a fellow human being merely by pointing an accusatory finger.

Most of the executions followed swiftly after the grim sentence was pronounced. Only Mark and Clare Griffin, it seemed to Roger, were denied this small mercy. He was beginning to wonder if his intervention on their behalf had been the greatest cruelty of all.

"Why doesn't the king act?" he demanded of Benjamin one day in February. "For God's sake, can't he do something to end this intolerable waiting?"

Ahmet pointed out the obvious. "At least there's still hope. That must be some consolation, though I don't doubt the waiting is far worse for them than for you."

"What galls me is that I don't know if they understand anything about it. I've never been able to find out if they even know the king's taken their case under advisement."

"They must, Roger. No place is more rife with rumors than a prison. Surely they must know."

"Sweet Christ, if only something would happen...."

Two days later something did.

"Have you heard?" Griffin found Benjamin at breakfast in Ingram's Court. "This just hit the streets."

"This" was the published text of a letter Charles had written to James. "It seems best to us for you to go abroad before the new Parliament convenes...."

"What do you think?" Roger demanded anxiously. "Is Charles capitulating completely?"

"Expediency, dear chap. Expediency," Ahmet said. "May I make a suggestion?" Griffin nodded. "I think you'd better send for Nancy. It seems to me that things are liable to break very soon." He tapped the broadsheet with a thoughtful finger. "The king seems to me ready to, how do you English put it, to 'seize the initiative.'"

Word that James and his duchess were being required to leave all their children behind, even the youngest, three-year-old Princess Isabella, was being vaunted in the streets two days after the publication of the letter. Nancy was expected in town in the afternoon—he'd sent Hart to fetch her the previous day—but Roger thought he could go to St. James's Palace and be back before she arrived.

"What can you hope to accomplish?" Ahmet asked.

"I don't know." Griffin ran his fingers through his hair. "It's all so miserable and petty. I want to offer York any help I can. And frankly, I want to remind him about Mark and Clare. God knows he's got trouble enough of his own right now, but surely it can't hurt to ask him to put in a final word."

During the past months it had become extremely difficult to secure an interview with York. He'd concluded his only defense was seclusion. Now that the game was effectively lost and exile pronounced, things had returned to their former status. Roger presented himself to the gatekeeper and was ushered into James's study fifteen minutes later.

"I'm glad you came." Dismal Jimmy he certainly looked today, drawn and pale, with great circles beneath his eyes as if he hadn't slept in weeks. "I hoped I'd have an opportunity to say goodbye."

"Surely not goodbye, your highness. Only farewell till next we meet." The words sounded hollow in his ears, but he didn't know what else to say.

"Perhaps." James managed a smile. "Meanwhile, sit down. You'll have some wine? Now tell me, what news of your family?"

Roger found the attempt at normalcy more daunting than pathos. He was tongue-tied and stumbling in his reply. "All's well, that is with my wife and children.... We're very disturbed, however. At the way things...I mean..."

"I know what you mean. It's all right, Roger. I'm resigned. The duchess too. If only we were allowed to take the baby...."

"Sir, listen...I've been thinking about that. It sounds mad, I know, but perhaps there's a way around it. I was thinking that it might be possible to...well, to smuggle the Princess Isabella out on a Griffin barge."

York held up his hand. "More plots, Roger? Now? No, thank you but I think not. You see, this isn't the end of the war, merely a battle lost. If I did what you're suggesting it would prejudice the future in a very dangerous way. You're a good enough tactician to see that."

"I suppose I do. It just seems such a spiteful and petty thing. Why should they do it? Why should the king do it?"

York shrugged. "It's all petty and spiteful. God knows we're not the only victims."

"No." This was his opening. Either he must speak now or maintain silence. "Sir, forgive me if the moment seems inopportune, but it may be the only chance I have.... My brother and his wife are yet in Newgate prison under sentence of death."

"Yes." James nodded. "I know. It is some small comfort that the sentence is not yet carried out."

"Frankly, I wonder. This waiting must be horrible. I haven't been able to get permission to visit them in prison, and for all I know they understand nothing of what's happening."

"That I can yet remedy." The duke took a slip of paper from his desk and wrote some hurried words. He signed the sheet with a flourish, affixed his seal, then handed it to Roger. "This will gain you access to Newgate. It's the only thing in my power now, lad. For the rest you, like all the rest of us, must wait on the king's pleasure."

The stairs were so narrow and winding she feared she'd lose her footing. Only Roger's firm grip on her elbow kept Nancy steady. He walked in front of her—there was no room to go two abreast—and behind the silent jailer.

If I were costuming a jail guard, Nancy thought, I'd make him look just like this one—filthy, unwashed, and dressed in rags. Did theater imitate life, she wondered, or the other way around? Newgate prison looked like a stage set too. It was hard to imagine that anything like this could really exist.

The stones ran with moisture. The only illumination came from high narrow slits placed at intervals along the hallways; there was no light at all on these stairs, only the jailer's lantern. The sounds of scurrying rats mingled with human moans heard from behind bolted doors, and above everything the all-pervasive, overpowering stench of death. No, she mustn't think of that, not that word. She had promised herself not to lose control for even an instant. Certainly Mark and Clare deserved that much.

They walked on in silence through a labyrinth of passages and locked doors which the jailer patiently opened with the series of keys that hung from his waist. "Here ye be." He unbolted one final door. "They's both in there waitin' for ye.

Twenty minutes. No more." He pocketed the generous tip Roger gave him without a word of thanks, waited until they were inside, then locked the door behind them.

The first few moments were confused and emotional. They hugged, kissed, cried...it was as if no quarrel had ever separated the two brothers, as if bonds stronger than mere in-law status united Nancy to the others.

It was Mark who turned the conversation toward practical things. "Do you bring any news?" he asked.

"Nothing really new," Roger said. "I don't know how much you already know."

"Little enough. When we were first brought here one of the guards that accompanied us from Surrey made a comment on our transfer's being a direct order from the king. I knew then you must be involved."

"It was Nancy," Roger hastened to explain. "She saw Nell Gwyn, and that's how it came about. Since then the king's promised to look into the matter. There's some hope for a royal pardon, Mark. Not a lot, I won't lie to you, but some hope."

There was too little time to waste any on spoken gratitude. Roger and Mark continued to talk legalities and tactics in hushed tones. Nancy tried to determine how the pair really were, but the dim light made it impossible to tell. "Are you well?" she asked Clare.

"Well enough. The only really bad thing is the dirt and the rats." She gave an involuntary shudder but suppressed it quickly. "That and not being together. We're kept in separate cells. But God knows, there are plenty worse off than we." Then she repeated the first question she'd asked. "You're sure the children are all right? You'd tell me the truth, wouldn't you, Nancy, if they've been arrested or anything? I want to know."

"They're fine. I give you my solemn oath on it, darling. They're staying at Tassels, and I don't know what I'd have done without them. I've been spending a lot of time in London, and your three have been virtually running everything. House, land, everything."

"Thank God. Nancy, one thing, one promise...whatever happens, promise me you'll look after them. Oh, I know they're grown up now, but still, they'll need someone. They mustn't be alone in the world."

"Nothing's going to happen," Nancy insisted firmly. "The

king knows you're innocent of any plot against him. He's going to issue a royal pardon. You'll see."

Clare smiled. "Be that as it may, and I certainly hope you're right, you do promise me...."

Roger had been speaking to Mark but he overheard Clare's request. "Listen," he said to both of them. "That's one worry you mustn't have. I give you my word nothing we can do for your children will ever be lacking." Mark gripped his hand, and Roger saw on his brother's wrist the terrible wounds left by the irons with which he was usually bound.

"We wanted to bring Sarah and the boys with us today," Nancy explained, "but it didn't seem wise."

"No," Mark agreed with her. "I'm sure it's best if they're kept wholly removed from this matter."

How matter-of-fact he sounded, Nancy thought. How sane and cool. The simple courage evident in their calm seemed to her worse than weeping and wailing would have been. She felt that lump of tears always so close to the surface these days rise in her throat once more. To combat it she said quickly, "Look, I've brought you some things. I didn't know if they'd let me give you anything, so..." She lifted the full skirt of her frock and displayed a silk bag suspended from her waist. "It's as much food as I could carry, and these things." She withdrew a handful of tiny packets. "Sarah put these together. She said you'd be able to use them."

"Oh yes!" Clare pressed the small parcel to her nose. "Healing herbs. Oh, bless Sarah! Trust her to think of it. There's any number of prisoners in here I'll be able to help with these...."

The words were a brief insight into the way Clare spent her days in this dreadful place. Before Nancy could comment they heard the tread of the guard's boots. "Oh no! Is it twenty minutes already?"

"Quick, Mark!" Clare moved to embrace her husband and stuff a portion of the foods and herbs down his shirtfront. They barely had time to kiss before the door was opened.

"Time's up." The jailor raised his lantern, and in its glow Nancy and Roger had a first really good look at the ravaged, prison-pale faces of their kin.

"For God's sake, man!" Roger approached the guard with a handful of coins. "Let us stay a little longer. What harm can it do?"

"Plenty. To me. I got me orders." The guard ignored the bribe and spat on the floor in contempt. "You highborn folks, yer all alike. Think ye can buy everything. Get a move on you two!" He became yet more hostile and prodded Mark with a vicious kick. "Miserable papists! Hangin's too good for ye!"

Roger clenched his fists and moved forward. Only Mark's words stopped him. "Don't, Roger, don't. It'll just make things worse. Go now, both of you. Go quickly and Godspeed."

7.

She'd named the boy Antony for no particular reason other than that it sounded to her very English. Roger's son should have a proper English name.

"Antony!" Tante Miriam exclaimed in disgust. "What kind of name is Antony for a Jewish boy?"

Rachel merely shrugged. "Times are changing, Tante Miriam. I want him to have a name like other people's."

But it was her own idea, not her indomitable aunt's, to make the child's second name Jacob. Both heritages are his, she told herself. I want him to love both. On the ninth day following his birth the *moyel* had come and performed the ritual circumcision that marked Antony Jacob as descendent from the patriarchs of old. And Uncle Avrum had his name read into the register at the synagogue. Antony Jacob had taken his place among the sons of Israel.

This latter rite had posed some problems for the old man. First, an illegitimate child had no claim to the ancient ceremony. Second, he must be cited as Antony Jacob *ben* somebody. "Son" of somebody. It was the law. A boy must be placed on the rolls of the children of the chosen people with his antecedents clearly stated. But this little Antony Jacob was *ben* who? Avrum didn't know, and his wife's stubborn niece refused to say. Very well, he told himself at first, it won't be done. If his own mother doesn't care, should I?

For a day or two he thought no more about it, but the idea continued to rankle. Such a sweet child, so innocent...and

Rachel's child. Descended of the proud house of Ahmet. Probably an equally proud heritage on his father's side if the truth were ever to be known. Was it the baby's fault if his parents were idiots overcome by a moment's lust? If they'd done this thing, was it for the child to suffer? You're an old fool, he told himself repeatedly. Does God need Avrum to tell Him of the child's birth? Does the maker of heaven and earth require a name to be read aloud in a synagogue before entering that name in the book of life?

Still, he continued his mental exercise in talmudic argument, if the ceremony was not important, would God have ordained it? Did not the tradition of fifteen hundred years deserve to be obeyed? But it was the tradition itself which denied Antony Jacob's right to have his name called out by the rabbi. What was one to do about that?

On the Saturday following the boy's circumcision, Avrum donned his skullcap and prayer shawl and went to pray. Some time later he heard with satisfaction the name of his grandnephew chanted from the altar. Antony Jacob *ben* Moses.

That had been, Avrum told himself modestly, a stroke of small genius. Wasn't the boy a son of Moses? Weren't all Jews sons of Moses? So what if there were a few names of more recent ancestors missing? What if the rabbi and all the congregation believed the Moses named to be the child's actual father? He'd never said that, had he? He merely told the rabbi, Antony Jacob *ben* Moses. Feeling enormously relieved, Avrum left the services amid the congratulations and well-wishes of his friends.

He told Rachel about it a few days later, and he could see she was pleased.

Weeks later, as news of the crisis in England became better known in Amsterdam, Rachel became more concerned about the demands of the present than the claims of the past. She craved news from her brother, but none came. "Don't worry," Tante Miriam said placidly. "This time it's Catholics they're after. For the moment Jews are safe. Let the *goyim* murder each other. What's that to us?"

"That's wicked!" Rachel said with feeling. "Don't you think God cares about people suffering if they're not Jews?"

The old woman chose to ignore the question. She said instead, "You know some Catholics perhaps? That's what's worrying you?"

"No, not exactly. It's just that a friend of ours, of Benjamin's and mine, has some people close to him that are Catholics...." Her voice trailed off, and she left the room. A plan had been formulating in the back of her mind, a scheme she knew was wild and almost surely doomed to failure. Still, it was the only thing she could think of.

Everyone knew that the Duke of York and his duchess were due to arrive in The Hague in a few days. King Charles had sent his brother into exile, and he was coming here. Not surprising; York's daughter Mary was married to William, Prince of Orange. The English refugees were going to receive a royal welcome.

Rachel made up her mind and went to the small desk in her room. It took her just ten minutes to compose the note. Then she folded it into the bosom of her gown and drew on her shawl. "I'm going out for a little walk," she told her aunt. "I won't be long."

She hurried along the canals to the heart of town. The building she sought was located in a superior position on the main shopping street. There was no sign outside; none was needed. This was the shop of the most famous diamond merchant in Europe. The rich, the royal, and the mighty knew how to find it without any sign. "Is Missen Rose in?" Rachel asked the man behind the counter.

"I believe so, *mevrouw*. You there!" He clapped his hands and a small boy came running. "Go upstairs and tell Missen Rose her cousin Mevrouw Rachel is asking for her."

A few minutes later Rachel was in the sitting room with the Dutch girl. Rose was the daughter of a distant cousin of Rachel's father. Their kinship wasn't close, but they had been introduced when Rachel arrived in Amsterdam. Had circumstances been different they might have become great friends. As it was, Rachel's pregnancy kept her secluded and the acquaintance had never ripened.

Rose was obviously surprised at this unexpected call. "I never thought to see you today, cousin Rachel," she said, smiling. "Are you well, and your child?"

"We're fine, thank you. I hope I haven't inconvenienced you by coming unannounced..." She broke off. These formal sparrings just wasted precious time. Tante Miriam would expect her home very soon. "Rose, listen to me...I need your help. But first you must promise to keep all this secret."

The other girl's eyes widened. Her life was ordinarily very placid. Settled and secure, of course, but dull. Now this beautiful relative whom she'd so recently met was offering to bring some small excitement into Rose's day. "Of course, cousin. Only tell me what I can do," was her breathless reply.

"This letter"—Rachel withdrew the note and laid it on the table between them—"must be delivered into the hands of the Duke of York when he arrives at The Hague."

"But why?" Rose stared at the innocent-looking envelope. "Why do you want to write to the Duke of York? And how could I manage such a thing?"

"Listen, terrible things are happening in England. Haven't you heard?" Rose nodded solemnly. "My brother is there, all our friends. . . . Oh, never mind all that, there isn't time now. What matters is that the Duke of York is a friend of a friend of mine. I know he'll tell me some news if I can only reach him."

"But I still don't see . . ." Rose made a perplexed face. "How could I get this to his highness? Why should you think I could?"

"Because messengers from this shop can go anywhere and be received," Rachel said insistently. "If someone brought the duke a parcel that looked to come from here, everyone would think it was diamonds. He'd be sure to accept and open it."

"You mean you want me to . . . ?"

"Exactly. Now listen, Rose, there must be someone among the staff you can trust. Someone who's particularly fond of you, perhaps. An admirer."

"Well, there's Piet, the errand boy. He's always mooning after me."

"Excellent. Now, I'll tell you what we'll do. . . ."

Nell returned to London from Paris on March 3. The next day she sent word for Nancy to come to the house in Pall Mall.

"I didn't forget about you, darling. I hope you didn't think so. It's just that little James's leg kept getting worse and worse. I had to do something."

"How is he?" Nancy asked, impatient to discuss her own concerns but aware of Nell's.

"A little better, I think. The doctors insisted he must remain in France for a long course of treatment, so I decided to come home. I saw Charles last night."

Nancy waited expectantly for the next words. Nell seemed a bit reluctant to go on. She fussed over pouring them some wine, rang a bell to demand a different bottle, and didn't settle back to conversation for some minutes. She was stalling. Nancy knew her too well not to recognize the fact. "Is it bad news?" she demanded finally. "You'd better tell me the worst. Has the king refused a pardon?"

"Oh no! Nothing like that." Nell turned back to her with what seemed to Nancy forced brightness. She was tugging at one curl when she said, "It can be settled very simply. Of course, Charles must have some sop to give the Parliament. You understand that. So he's going to offer Mark and Clare a royal pardon, with just one condition."

"What condition?" Nancy asked quietly.

"The only thing they have to do is renounce their Catholic faith. There, I told you it was simple."

"Are you sleeping?" By now she'd spent so many nights with Roger in the George Alley premises that they'd become as familiar as her bedroom at home in Tassels. By the light of the moon Nancy could make out the faint water stain on the wall, caused by a rainstorm when Roger had forgotten to close the window. Just like a man. So was his feigned slumber. She knew he wasn't really asleep.

"No. I thought you were."

"No." Then, after some seconds, "You still think there's no chance they'll take the pardon?"

She had wept so bitterly when he'd first stated that opinion he was reluctant to stick by it now. But there was little to be gained by lying. Nancy would know the truth soon enough. It was better if she had some time to adjust to the idea. "I know they won't."

"But how can you know? How can you be so sure? After all, they've been weeks in the hell of Newgate. Mightn't that have decided them to take any chance that's offered? For God's sake, Roger!" She rose on her elbow and stared at him as if willing him to agree with her. "It's not as if they'd have to mean it. They could say whatever they have to say. That wouldn't change what they believe."

"Don't you understand, Nancy? It's an oath. A solemn oath, and they must swear it. After that they have to attend Anglican services and take Anglican communion regularly."

"So what? We do that. I don't think we're damned to hell, and I'm quite sure Mark and Clare don't think we are either."

"That's different. We're not Catholics and never have been."

"I still don't think you're right. They may do it." Her stubbornness was born of her own need to hope.

"Darling, you have to face reality. It's only going to be harder if you don't. If my brother wouldn't swear an oath in which he didn't believe in order to save Harwood Hall for his children and all of us, you can be quite certain he won't do it just to save his own life or Clare's."

8.

There was yet no hint of spring in the air. The night chill pierced Ahmet's bones; he drew his cloak closer and quickened his pace. It seemed to him that here in the rabbit warren of slums surrounding Moor Fields the cold bit harder than elsewhere in London.

His thoughts were interrupted when a man fell into step beside him. "Ye be the feller wot's looking' fer Jack?"

"I am."

"Follow me."

He was led through a maze of alleys and paths—a route, he realized, deliberately made more confusing than it needed to be. No chances were being taken that he could afterward point to the exact spot where the deal had been made. The man he was on his way to meet intended to protect himself from the possibility that Ahmet was an informer. Subverting his majesty's justice was a treasonable offense.

"This be the place," his companion said at last. He pushed open a low wooden door. "Go in there and wait. Jack'll be along soon."

The place seemed to be a storeroom, for an alehouse or a tavern most likely. There were kegs everywhere; the air reeked of beer. It occurred to Benjamin that this experience might put him off the brew for the rest of his life. After this it would always be associated in his mind with death. Violent, ugly, and painful death.

"All right, guv'nor," a soft voice said close behind him. "Let's see the color of yer money. No, don't turn around! 'Tain't necessary fer ye to see my face."

"I don't give a damn for the look of your face," Ahmet replied without rancor. "It's how well you do your job and keep your word that matters to me."

"Better'n most, guv, better'n most. On both counts."

It was the only assurance he was going to get. There was no way to make certain this villain would keep his bargain. All he could do was gamble and hope for the best. It was better than doing nothing. "Here's your money." He passed a sack of coins back over his shoulder and heard them jingle when the other man tested the heft. "It's all there. One hundred pounds."

There was no reply for some minutes. He could tell from the sounds that the money was being counted. "Aye," the faceless voice said at last. "'Tis all here. Thanks, guv'nor."

"If you do as you've promised, you're welcome to it."

"I'll do it," the voice replied carelessly. "Why shouldn't I? What's it to me how long a couple o' papists take to die? Mind you," he went on, "it wouldn't do to have it happen too often. They'd be sayin' ole Jack didn' know his job....But once is all right. No one'll make too much fuss o'er once. Besides, ain't fer the money I'm doin' it. Not really. That Quaker feller, Dr. Winters, he saved me little girl a while back. I'm grateful fer that. Since he's the one asked me to help ye, I'm glad enough to do it. Pays him back, like."

There was silence again. Ahmet realized he was once more alone, waited for a while, rose and went outside. "All right, me bucko." The voice was that of the first man, the one who'd brought him here. "Just follow me and I'll get ye back to yer own part o' town. Wouldn' do to have ye end up a corpse on Moor Fields after ye come as our guest, so to speak." He chuckled malevolently and began walking. Ahmet followed in silence.

Roger wanted to forbid them all to go, Nancy as well as Sarah, Charles, and Andrew. He started on that line only to be met by a wall of defiance. In the end it was Benjamin who convinced him to recant. "You want to protect them, I know that. Spare them the horror. But it will only make it worse,

392

Roger. You're denying them the only consolation they can have now, that of standing firm in the face of the enemy the way your brother and his wife have. If they aren't there they'll always think they were cowards who ran away and hid. You must see it."

He did. When he admitted as much to Ahmet the other man clapped him on the shoulder and said, "Good. It's best that way. And Roger, for what it's worth, it may not be quite as bad as you think. Not as bad as it could be..." He broke off, unable to continue. He wanted to tell Griffin what he'd arranged, but he couldn't. Talking about it in detail seemed impossible. Ahmet turned away and left his friend to his private grief.

The morning of March 10 dawned bright and clear. Nancy thought it should be storming, not sunny with birds chirping as if nothing unusual were happening. But then nothing was. Just two more papists going to their death on Tyburn Hill.

The crowd had been treated to the scene frequently of late, but still it hadn't grown tired of blood. An execution was a holiday, an excuse to get out and see the sights. When the Griffins followed the hurdle from Newgate along High Holborn and out to the Oxford road at the edge of the city, they were lost in a jeering, shouting mass that was thoroughly enjoying itself.

A few times they almost lost each other. Roger kept as tight a grip on Nancy's arm as he dared, and he tried to keep Andrew's back always in sight. The boy was walking just ahead of them, hand in hand with his brother and sister, the three clinging together despite the surging throng that threatened to separate them. Once, when an egg thrown by some child hit Clare full in the face and splattered over her torn and filthy dress, he saw Sarah stagger as if she might faint. Andrew held her up, and they kept moving.

The distance was less than three miles, but the journey took as many hours. The crowd didn't want to lose one minute of the sport. They wanted everything done slowly so they could savor it. Finally the gallows were in view. Two nooses hung together over a raised platform, and a great brazier burned nearby. Those twin nooses were the one concession the king had granted after the Griffins refused to deny their popish beliefs. They would die together. It wouldn't be necessary for one to watch the other's sufferings.

Around the place of execution were hundreds of scaffolding seats. Now the masses of people rushed to secure places of comfort from which to watch the proceedings, and cursed those already there. Roger wrapped his arm tighter around his wife and let the hordes surge by them. In the end the family was left standing in a corner slightly off to one side, with only a few others nearby.

He never could remember exactly when the five of them had joined hands. Certainly no one had said anything to suggest it. It merely happened. They clasped each other not so much for mutual support as in silent defiance.

Is this really happening? Roger kept asking himself. Are we really here? Am I going to wake up soon and find it's all just a nightmare? It was Mark's familiar voice ringing out over the heads of the crowd that convinced him of the reality of it all. They'd told him how eloquent his brother had been the day of the trial. He'd not expected the same thing today, not after everything Mark had been through. But the condemned man's right to a final statement was a thing older even than Tyburn tree. The crowd expected it, looked forward to it. Squire Mark Griffin didn't disappoint them.

He was spattered with the mud, horse dung, and even human excrement that had been hurled at him during the long trek. Moreover, his imprisonment in Newgate had lasted almost ten weeks, a circumstance few were forced to endure. That ordeal had reduced him to a shadow of the man he'd been. Like his wife, Mark was so emaciated he seemed transparent. But the fires that burned in the man were apparent. He looked nothing short of radiant, and while Roger's mind rejected the notion as madness, his eyes persisted in seeing what was there to be seen. "Like Sophia," he whispered aloud, though not even Nancy heard him. "He looks like Sophia looked that day in France...."

"Good ladies and gentlemen," Mark repeated when the crowd had finally hushed to hear him. "I wish you God's blessing and pray you may all one day be good Catholics as your ancestors were before you. Neither I nor my wife hold any man blameworthy for our sufferings. We forgive you all and pray God to do the same. He who from the cross forgave His own tormentors will surely not neglect to forgive ours.

"If, however, it is possible that any words of mine might save others from such sufferings, then I feel I must speak them. If they impress even one among you as truth, then perhaps a change may come."

"Ah, get on wi' it!" A man shouted from the crowd. "Pray for the king and let's see how you die!"

A few voices took up the cry, but yet others silenced them. "Let him have his say. It's his right...."

"We are part of no plot." Mark's voice again rang over their heads. "There is no plot! Only those who wish to practice their religion, the true religion, in peace. It is for that we die here this day. That and nothing else."

A man cut across Roger's vision, old, gray-haired, with very blue eyes. He placed himself just next to them, though he in no way indicated that he knew who they were, and at that moment both Mark and Clare seemed momentarily to look in their direction. "Mama..." Roger heard Sarah whisper as if her mother could hear her last farewell. Then his attention was drawn back to his brother.

"We die as we have lived," Mark continued after a pause so short none seemed to have noticed it. "Loyal subjects of his most gracious majesty Charles II. But there is one king we recognize as higher even than he..."

"Yah!" A voice shouted. "That whore of Babylon, the pope!"

"Jesus Christ!" came Mark's reply. "Jesus Christ yesterday, today, and the same forever! God save the king!"

With those words he'd given the signal that his speech was at an end. Swiftly the hooded hangman stepped forward and knelt for the condemned to bless and forgive him. Seconds later he'd lowered the noose over both their heads.

Then Roger sensed movement from the old fellow nearby. He saw the man lean forward and, with his hand held waist high so only those next to him could notice, trace the sign of the cross in the air. *"Ego te absolvo,"* Roger heard him whisper.

The Catholic form of absolution. So one of their coreligionists had dared to come forward and give Mark and Clare the final rites of the religion they were about to witness with their blood. For the first time Roger felt tears coursing down his cheeks.

There was a sudden crack of sound, and the bodies of his brother and sister-in-law were dangling in the air. They twitched convulsively for a second or two and then were still.

"Cut 'em down!" Someone shouted. "Cut 'em down!"

The hangman was fumbling with his knife. More seconds ticked by. The inexplicable delay went on while an angry murmur rippled through the crowd. Finally the ropes were severed and the bodies dropped with a thud to the platform below.

"You stupid clod, Jack!" a man yelled in disgust. "It's too late! You got it wrong this time. They's already dead."

The rest of the grisly sentence was carried out as the law demanded, but it didn't matter. The anonymous voice had been speaking the truth. They were dead by the time they were cut down.

"Thank God," Nancy whispered. "Oh, thank God...."

Silently they turned away and started from the scene. Once Roger turned to look back and saw the old man, the one he now believed to be a priest, making his way toward the execution platform.

Many years later, after time had made it possible to talk about the thing, Sarah explained. "It was Father Huddleston," she told her uncle. "He came to give them absolution and the last rites of the Church. I've always thought they saw him and knew. Look." She showed Roger a scrap of cloth. "He gave me this later. It's his handkerchief. He dipped it in their blood."

PART SEVEN

Two Griffins Rampant

O never say that I was false of heart,
Though absence seemed my flame to qualify.
As easy might I from myself depart,
As from my soul which in thy breast doth lie....

—William Shakespeare,
Sonnet CIX

1.

For many weeks Roger's way of coping with the tragedy was to ignore it, push it from his mind. He insisted he no longer cared about the outrages being perpetrated in the name of justice. Mark and Clare were dead. Nothing could bring them back. Now, he told Benjamin, he didn't give much of a damn.

"Let them all hang," he said with more ice than bitterness in his words. "They've made their pact with Satan. The whole country can go to the devil and I'll not shed any tears."

Benjamin eyed him speculatively. "Do I take it, then, that you're considering coming to America after all?"

"No. I've told you my opinion of that scheme before."

"What, then? Since you're so disinterested in England's future, I mean."

"Nothing. I just want to be left alone to live my life and help my family live theirs." He slumped back in his seat and put his booted feet on the desk. "I'm tired, Benjamin. Sweet Christ, I'm tired."

To withdraw from the memory of those two twitching figures on the gallows was not Nancy's way. She threw herself into a whirlwind of activity both at Tassels and in London.

After all, she had to help Sarah, Andrew, and Charles bear their grief. Nancy knew there was very little she could really do. Time would be the only healer. That and the deep faith the three had that their parents were martyrs to their beliefs, not victims of a futile, senseless waste of life. But Nancy tried to keep the young people occupied and busy, deny them any time to brood.

Charles and Andrew she made joint estate managers in their father's place. "Just till we see what the future holds for you two," she said firmly. "I'll not have you spending your lives down here in this backwater. But it'll do for the time being...." Sarah became her right hand and surrogate mistress of the house, in addition to retaining all the horticultural responsibilities that had always been hers.

This was a good thing in itself, for Nancy was away from Tassels two or three times a week these days. She had begun seeing more of Nell than she had for a good many years.

"Why the sudden fascination with London society?" Roger asked her mildly.

"Because I want to know what's going on, that's why. I don't want to be caught out again by a storm we don't even anticipate."

"Suit yourself." Roger shrugged. "Anyway, it's nice to have you in town so often. Shall we take some little house here? Would you like that?"

"No." Nancy shook her head firmly. "I don't want any house but Tassels. George Alley suits me fine. Anyway, I don't know how long these frequent trips will last."

She looked so lost in her thoughts when she spoke that Roger couldn't help but suspect she was planning more than she was admitting. "What are you up to, Nance?" he asked. "You'd better tell me."

"Nothing, not really. It's just that I want to know things, as I told you. And there's Sarah to consider."

"Sarah? What's she to do with it?"

"Sarah will be twenty-two in a few months. Don't you realize we have to find her a husband? I can't very well do that down in Surrey."

"I see." He grinned ruefully. "May I ask if you've mentioned this to her? I remember her telling me a few years back that she detested the idea of marriage."

"I never heard such nonsense! Don't tell me you think she wants to be a nun, like Laura?"

"Not a bit of it. At least that's what she said. As far as I could gather, she only wanted to go on as she was, virginal and happy."

"Nonsense," Nancy repeated. "The two ideas are incompatible. One can't be a happy virgin. Anyway, that was long ago. She's older now."

"Not so long ago. Besides, I seem to recall that you weren't interested in having anybody arrange a marriage for you. You told me how independent you were often enough."

"That was different," Nancy said impatiently. "I was a woman of the world. Sarah's an innocent child. Someone has to take care of this for her."

He was going to make some teasing comment about her

not being very virginal either, but suddenly she changed the subject. "I saw Sam Ludlow today. Walking along Pall Mall not far from Nell's. He was all dressed up like a gentleman. Bucket boots, velvet coat, plumed hat, the lot. At first I wanted to run up and scratch his eyes out. But I couldn't. I kept thinking of what Mark said at the last. About holding no man blameworthy."

There was a thin white line around Roger's mouth when he said, "It's lucky for Ludlow it was you that saw him, not I. If I ever do, I'll kill him. I expect he knows that."

The Duke of York looked at the young Jewess and smiled. The sight of her always made him smile. "I haven't seen you for some time, Rachel," he said. "Have you been avoiding me? I thought we agreed you'd come sooner than this."

"It isn't easy for me to get to The Hague, your highness. Family responsibilities, as I've told you."

"Mmmm...and that's all you've told me. Never mind, I promised never to pry into your secrets, and I will keep my word. Now, walk with me and tell me amusing things. I've few enough amusements these days."

There had been at least half a dozen such meetings before this one. The young woman first made contact with him through a transparent little ruse involving a well-known Amsterdam diamond merchant, a letter smuggled in among some gems brought to him that he might "see the quality of the merchant's stock." Silly. Everyone knew the quality of the jewels sold by that particular Jew. Still, the whole business amused him. He sent for the writer of the letter and even bought one of the baubles.

The lady turned out to be the sister of Roger Griffin's business partner. She wanted only information. He was willing enough to accede to the request. Why not, when the inquirer was so beautiful and charming? The news he was able to give was all bad, however. Seeing Rachel's face when he told her of the fate of Griffin's brother and sister-in-law had given James much to think about. At the time, however, he merely called for brandy to revive her and then insisted she walk with him in the gardens until she recovered. York was never one to deny himself the company of a lovely and intelligent lady. He invited Rachel to visit him again, and he was delighted when she continued to do so.

Rachel found something likable in the duke's complex

character. Besides, the terrible conditions he described as existing in England made her terrified for the future of her brother and Roger and his family. It wouldn't hurt, she told herself, to cultivate this friendship. Admittedly James was in exile at the moment, but he remained the brother of the king and the heir apparent. Such an ally might prove invaluable at some time in the future. She visited him as frequently as she could, even played the coquette shamelessly. Rachel had no intention of giving in to James's less-than-subtle attempts to bed her, but neither did she intend to separate herself from this, her one real link with London.

"I wish I understood why you are so frightened, my dear," York said suddenly as they paused to admire a pair of swans gliding along the lake.

"Frightened? Why do you think that?"

"Come now, Rachel. I'm a man of wide experience. When a woman is so reluctant to tell anything of her life, I can only assume she has cause to fear. Tell me..." He turned and looked directly into her black eyes. "Are you married? Is the problem a jealous husband?"

She lowered her glance demurely. This could be tricky. She mustn't tell the duke a story that wouldn't jibe with that facade her aunt and uncle had created for her. Such a disparity in tales could cause real trouble later. "I..." She hesitated, then made up her mind. "I have no husband here, your highness."

York laughed softly. "An answer worthy of a barrister in court, my dear. No husband here indeed. And where is here? In this garden? In The Hague? In Amsterdam? You can't expect to fob me off with that bit of sophistry, Rachel."

But that was the only answer she would give him. No amount of pleading or probing could achieve more. Finally he could only laugh again and say, "Very well. You shall have your little intrigue, sweet Rachel. But I warn you, I'm an experienced player at this game. In the end I shall win and you will tell me all. I promise it."

For answer Rachel only curtsied and made her farewells. James watched her go with a pensive expression. He remained thus for some minutes, then turned and strode purposefully into the palace, where his daughter was queen and he was but an exiled foreigner. It was not the most comfortable of positions, but it wasn't without some limited authority. "You!" He summoned a page with a snap of his fingers. "Send my secretary to me at once."

The secretary was a young man who spoke both English and Dutch. Prince William had placed him in his father-in-law's service as soon as the Duke of York arrived in The Hague. James eyed him now with an air of careful appraisal. "Let's see how useful you can be, Hans," he said. "I have a job for you. A bit of investigating I wish done with every discretion. You can handle that?"

"I will do my best, your highness."

"Good. Now, I want you to go to Amsterdam. . . ."

Twenty minutes later the man had left on his errand. York smiled with satisfaction and poured himself a glass of excellent Dutch brandy. This whole business amused him. It took his mind from his own problems, and that was a most welcome diversion at present.

A week later he had the man's report. Rachel lived with an aunt and uncle in Amsterdam. She'd come there eighteen months before. No husband was ever seen, but the story was that she was married to someone in England. In any event, she had been pregnant at the time of her arrival and now she was the mother of a son born in January of '79. She lived quietly, the family were highly respected among their fellow Jews, and no breath of scandal was attached to the lady's name.

So. James fingered the single sheet of paper and pursed his lips. Perhaps his interest was piqued not only by the woman herself, but by the fact that her story had its roots in London. Like any exile, the Duke of York yearned for home. Whatever spoke to him of England commanded his attention.

2.

"No word, cap'n. Nothin' good, that is."

"Thank you, Hart. Keep your ear to the ground and let me know if anything changes." Roger watched the man leave. He was very old now, due a pension and a country cottage in return for his service. Griffin tapped the desk thoughtfully. The king had been ill for almost a week, at point of death some said. It gave the town something new to think about, at any rate.

Last month the high point in the macabre farce led by Titus Oates had occupied all their attention. Oates had accused the queen's physician, Sir George Wakeman, of conspiring with Catherine to poison Charles. But the trial had proved that the poison lay elsewhere. Even Scroggs seemed to recognize the absurdity of the charge. He cross-examined Oates with more than usual care, and the man was soon tripping himself up at every second sentence.

"Public discredit on the bastard at last!" Benjamin had said with satisfaction as he reported the street gossip to Roger. "Everyone that matters knows he's lying now."

"Everyone that mattered knew it before this," Roger said quietly.

"No, this is different. Oh, you're right, of course. They did know if they'd an ounce of brains. But this time the ordinary people seem to suspect they've been taken for fools. It's a good sign."

"If you say so."

On that day Roger had shrugged and changed the subject. Today, a month later, he wasn't so ready to play the disinterested observer. The old Griffin loyalty was in his blood, he couldn't change it. The king was dying, according to all reports, and meanwhile James was hundreds of miles away. Shaftesbury was unlikely to let the chance go by. He'd use every opportunity to snatch the crown from the true Stuart heir and bestow it where he chose. Roger thought a few minutes longer, then rose and walked out into the August sunshine.

"My very dear Roger." Catherine pressed her cheek to his. "It has been such a long time. And so much sadness in between."

"Yes, your majesty. For all of us. But you look well."

The queen smiled and indicated he should sit beside her. "I have learned patience and fortitude in my time here, Roger. Very English virtues, aren't they?"

He laughed. "So they say. We've been displaying few virtues of late, however."

"Madness," Catherine said, "isn't confined to any one race of people. Roger ... you know I did what I could. I'm only sorry it wasn't enough."

"I knew you would try, ma'am. It was some comfort."

"So much blood, so many martyrs." She rose and took his hand. "Come with me. I want to show you something."

Silently he followed her down a long corridor. He'd not been to see Catherine since she had returned to take up residence here in Whitehall, but he remembered this passage well enough. It led to her bedchamber. "Look," she said, throwing open the door and pointing to a group of paintings on the wall. "Do you recognize them?"

"The five Jesuits most recently executed at Tyburn," he replied quietly.

"Not executed, martyred. Martyred at Tyburn for no reason other than their Catholic faith.... Your brother and his wife could have their portraits there too," she added after some seconds. "They died in the same cause."

Griffin shrugged and turned aside. "I do not share your beliefs, ma'am, you know that. But I share your horror at all this senseless bloodshed. I'm grieved you see us English at such a sorry time in our history."

"That's not why I brought you here, Roger. I want to try to make you understand about my husband. He has almost no freedom of choice in this matter. You must believe that. I will tell you something no one else knows. Often, late at night, he comes here to this room and stands before those portraits. He weeps, Roger." Her voice trembled, and she was very pale. "The king weeps and begs forgiveness of those men."

"Please, milady, you must not upset yourself so." Roger feared she was going to faint. He took her hand and looked around for a chair.

"It's all right." She managed a smile. "I'm not going to have hysterics. Not now. Come, we will step out to the balcony for some air." Soon they stood leaning against the stone balustrade looking down at the river and the gardens below. "One final word in my husband's defense. . . . Do you realize that it is the crown itself that's at stake in this matter? It is the existence of the House of Stuart that Charles seeks to protect."

"I know that. That's why I've come."

"Yes. We must speak of that. When they told me you wanted an audience I could only think how glad I was that you'd come at last. Forgiven me, as it were, for the terrible ills done your family. But of course you have some other reason. Tell me, Roger."

"There is no question of forgiveness, your majesty. You must believe that. I've never blamed you or the king. It's all very much more complicated than that. But my errand is related nonetheless. I regret to cause you more pain, but I must ask outright. Will the king live? They say he's very ill."

"Very ill indeed." Her voice was calm. "I do not know if he will live. The doctors contradict each other every quarter of an hour."

"That's what I feared. What of the Duke of York, ma'am? Who is taking care that he knows of this and is ready to assume the crown?"

Catherine smiled. She was no longer a young woman, but age had been kinder to her than youth. Years before she'd had only an insipid prettiness that couldn't compete with the great beauties of the Stuart court. Today she had a grace and elegance few of them could match. "So, my gallant captain, loyal to York till the end? How like you."

"I am loyal to my country, ma'am. There's little extraordinary in that."

"After the way you've been used? I don't agree. It is virtue of an order seldom seen, dear Roger. But you didn't come here for flattery. To answer your question, it is rumored that Sunderland has sent word to James. Frankly, I'm not sure."

"No, neither am I. That's what worries me."

She turned to him then and took both his hands in hers. "Could you help, Roger? Is there something you could do? I've thought much about it, but every action of mine is watched. Besides, I'm of little use in these intrigues. I never have been."

"I can try, ma'am. I will try."

"God grant you success. Go now. Every moment is precious." Then, before he reached the door, "Roger, one more thing. They will know you've been to see me today. I told you, Shaftesbury's people watch me at every moment. He is determined that Monmouth shall succeed Charles, and he'll not hesitate to do anything necessary to ensure that. You must be careful."

"I intend to be, milady." He bowed low and left just as he'd entered, walking at an ordinary pace, head high and nodding to any face remotely familiar. Nothing furtive, nothing suspicious. He was an old friend of the queen's who'd come to offer his sympathy now her husband was so ill. Nothing more.

He left for Tassels immediately. Nancy was surprised to see him unexpectedly, but she was too busy to ask many questions. The month before she'd commissioned further additions to the house, and this evening she was consulting with the architect about a small snag in her plans. "He says the proper stone for the new facade must be brought from the north," she explained with an air of distraction. "Yorkshire stone's the only kind that's the right color for this." She thrust a sketch under Roger's nose, but he only glanced at it.

"Very well," he said quickly. "Do it if you think it's best. Tell them they can quarry on the land I bought there last year. You'll find the deeds in my study."

"Oh yes! I hadn't thought of that. It's a marvelous idea." Nancy hurried off to tell the architect she'd solved the problem, and Roger went on with the business that brought him here.

"You." He gestured to a youngster he'd not seen before. His wife had so enlarged the staff of this place that he often met servants whose names and faces were unknown to him. "You're a page, aren't you?"

"Yes sir, that I am. The mistress hired me two days past.

First page of the house." The boy drew himself up with self-importance.

"Very well, first page, go find Mr. Andrew. Tell him to come to me here straightaway."

"Yes sir," As he was leaving to execute the order, the boy turned back. "Begging your pardon, sir, who shall I say? I mean, I gotta tell Mr. Andrew who wants him, don't I?"

Roger chuckled. "You do indeed. And you don't know who I am, is that it? Tell him Captain Griffin wants him."

"Yes sir!" The lad's eyes widened at the thought of his terrible gaffe, but he said no more, merely hurried away.

Griffin spared no further thought for the page. He'd more important things on his mind. The critical point was whether or not Andrew was a wise choice. Well, only time would tell. Whatever happened, he'd made a decision; now he must back it. Griffin poured a brandy for himself and one for Andrew and waited.

His nephew arrived a few minutes later, letting himself into the front room—they called it the drawing room these days, and it was a far grander place than once it had been—and stretching out his hand in greeting with a kind of easy grace that Roger liked. "We didn't expect you, Uncle Roger," the lad said. "At least Aunt Nancy didn't mention your coming tonight."

"No, she didn't expect me. Here, I took the liberty of pouring you a brandy. Do you like the stuff?"

"Very much. Thank you." Andrew took the glass and waited.

In the months since his parents' deaths the boy—a young man really, twenty-one now—had developed a kind of reserve that overlay the hot-headed nature he'd always displayed. It was as if grief had banked the flames, taught him control. Roger looked at him carefully and liked what he saw. A Griffin to be reckoned with. Good, it's what was needed. "I want you to do something," he said finally. "It's dangerous but necessary. At least I think so. I will tell you the facts, and you must tell me if you think them worth risking your neck."

Nearly two hours and half a dozen brandies later the elder Griffin said, "That's settled then. You'll leave at dawn. I've arranged for one of our barges to pick you up at the landing stairs."

"And they take me straight through to Dover?" Andrew

407

asked. They'd been over the plan a number of times. He knew the answer; this was just a final check.

"Yes. And you get a packet from there. All quite straightforward and ordinary. Remember, Andrew, that's your best defense. No one has seen you. You've been down here in Surrey for years. Neither Shaftesbury's men nor Sunderland's will recognize you or have any reason to suspect you. These papers"—he tapped the envelope lying on the table between them—"prove you're on business for Griffin's Importations, but it's better if you don't even need to show them. Better to keep the Griffin name out of it entirely until you actually are face to face with York. Then tell him who you are. Until that time, travel as Andrew Dumont. Your mother's maiden name shouldn't be hard to remember."

"It won't be." He rose and started to leave. "I'd better get what sleep I can." Then, shyly, "Uncle Roger...thank you."

"For asking you to put your head on the block?" Roger smiled. "You're welcome, though I don't know what for."

"For trusting me."

Griffin sat alone for some time after his nephew left. His instincts, he decided, had been sound. It was a perfect choice. Mark's elder son was a blend of the best qualities the family ever produced. Daring and steadiness combined. And, more important in this instance, unswerving loyalty to the crown. For all Mark's peculiar religious ideas, he'd inculcated that into his boy.

Roger rose and started to snuff out the candles and bank the fire for the night. Then he had a thought and went to the door leading into the hall. Sure enough, the young page was waiting there. Waiting, Roger realized, to tidy the room after it was empty. He smiled. Nancy had finally made this house into an establishment run along the lines of the home of his youth. He'd have to get used to that all over again. Griffin nodded to the servant and started up the stairs.

3.

The Hague, Andrew decided, looked rather like thick cream fresh from the dairy. Pale ivory in color, flecked with yellow butterfat. The analogy made him laugh; he only wished he'd someone with whom to share the notion. In fact, everything about this adventure made him laugh—not least the purported danger he was in. That, he'd decided early on, was a joke. Oh, he'd seen a few Englishmen on the boat, and even here, who skulked around and managed to give the impression they were chaps to be reckoned with if one wanted trouble. But none of them paid him the least attention. They were all occupied with each other. He'd figured that out almost immediately.

So today he strode freely along the narrow little streets and admired the Dutch architecture. It appeared stolid and respectable and full of virtue—full of virtuous people, at any rate. Busy little round housewives and even busier little round men of affairs—both sorts were scurrying up and down the alleys of the town with self-satisfied expressions on their pudgy faces. Andrew laughed aloud again and continued his march toward the palace.

Three days earlier he'd gone to an inn near the royal residence and sat a long time over a glass of ale. Eventually he'd struck up a conversation with a fellow Englishman. The man wasn't one of the skulkers he'd noticed before, but a servant come here with the duke and duchess. After a few glasses of the potent local beer it had been easy to ascertain York's habits in this place of exile. "Spends a lot o' time just walkin' in the gardens, does his highness. Poor man, longin' for home just like all the rest o' us...."

Today Andrew planned to join James in one of those solitary strolls and offer him a way to assuage his homesickness. It was ridiculously easy to mingle with the crowds that went in and out the palace gates. Like Whitehall, this royal household was the center of a whirlpool of activity. Hundreds trafficked through the place on business ranging from affairs of state to deliveries to the palace kitchens. No one paid attention to a tall wiry young man who seemed to know exactly where he was going.

Of course the Prince and Princess of Orange were well guarded. They were the reigning monarchs; if he'd wanted to reach them unseen and unannounced Andrew would have had a much tougher task. But a foreign prince, sent from his own country in virtual disgrace, was a different matter. No one bothered about James. Andrew need only keep trotting about with the look of someone on a definite and unremarkable errand and eventually, he was convinced, he'd find the gardens where York walked.

His confidence wasn't misplaced. After about fifteen minutes he came on a pretty little lake bordered with willow trees and looking very much like the canal in St. James's Park back in London. He wasn't the least bit surprised to see a man pacing slowly along the embankment and to recognize that man as James, Duke of York.

"Your highness," he said quietly as he fell into step beside him. "It is important that I speak with you for a moment."

"Who the devil are you?" York asked with more curiosity than surprise in his voice.

"My name's Andrew Griffin, sir. Roger Griffin is my uncle."

"I see." York smiled. "You use a name I know well and one sure to gain my confidence. Can you prove your lineage?"

"My uncle expected you to ask that. He said to tell you that the name of the inn where you and he took shelter in '58, after the battle of Nieuport, was the Maiden's Tears. He said you both laughed much over the name and that you were sure to remember it."

"Yes. And no one else to know of the incident either. Besides, you've the look of a Griffin about you. Come, lad, we can sit over here and talk." He led the way to a bench beneath a sheltering elm tree. "What news do you bring?"

"Your brother the king, sir, he's very ill. Some fear he's dying."

"That much news even I have. The problem remains what to do about it."

"My uncle respectfully suggests, your highness, that it's imperative you return to England immediately. Unless you are actually present it will be impossible to stop Shaftesbury's forces from declaring Monmouth king. Once that transfer of power takes place your own claim to the crown will be most difficult to support."

"Yes, I know all that too. Sunderland sends me information here. But you must see that if I leave this place, if I try to return to England, Shaftesbury's men will attempt to assassinate me and thus solve their problem. I'm an exile. I haven't enough loyal men with me to guard against such a possibility. The Hague is crawling with English spies at this moment."

"True, sir. But I—that is, my uncle has a plan. No one knows or suspects me. Shaftesbury's men and Sunderland's are all busy watching each other. If you'll agree, sir, I think I can help you return to London without anyone's knowing about it."

It wasn't until later, leaning over the side of the small pinnace that was making her way across the North Sea carrying a cargo of spices bound for Griffin's Importations, that James was really struck by the physical resemblance. He looked at young Andrew's profile and realized that he was looking at the same thrusting jaw and square chin he'd first seen in France in '57. Twenty-two years had passed, and now here he was, in a battle of a different sort, with yet another Griffin at his side.

They were traveling as father and son, James and Andrew Dumont, employees of Griffin's Importations bound for home after a buying trip to the Indies. No one had questioned the story or looked at them twice. Of course the fact that they'd left behind a much-vaunted story that the Duke of York was ill and confined to his bed did help. James smiled when he thought about it. His wife could be counted on in such a situation. She had the true Italian love of drama and intrigue. Yes, his Mary was a reliable conspirator—she'd have them all believing the tale for as long as was necessary.

"The wind's sharp, sir." They were the first words Andrew had spoken in some time. "Shall I get you another cloak? Or would you prefer to go below?"

"Nothing, lad. I'm fine. Thank God for the sharp wind. It'll see us home quickly. That's all that matters." He kept his eyes glued to the young man while he spoke. Something was gnawing at the back of his mind, something he wanted to remember. Of course! Rachel's child....

A few weeks before, right after the secretary made his report, James had confronted the mysterious Rachel with the information he now had. She'd not been in the least nonplussed. She'd even brought the baby to see him one afternoon. He was a strapping little boy not quite a year old who possessed that same jaw and chin he was looking at now. He was sure of it. The baby, York realized with near conviction, must be Roger Griffin's bastard son. And he'd wager a year's income that Griffin knew nothing about it.

Dover by the gray light of early morning. Fog lay over the chalk cliffs, obscuring their whiteness, giving the whole scene a look of fantasy. Dream or nightmare? James wondered. Impossible to say, at least just yet. The slapping of waves against the side of their anchored ship seemed quiet and gentle, a lulling, comforting sound. They were waiting for the Griffin barge Andrew informed him was scheduled to meet them here. The captain of the pinnace was a docile enough fellow. He merely shrugged and dropped anchor when they told him to do so.

"They'll not be long, sir. I'm sure it's the fog that's held them up." Andrew looked anxiously at the duke as if afraid James would fear some kind of betrayal.

"Don't worry, lad," York said quietly. "I've waited this long. An hour or two more doesn't matter. Wait a minute...is that them now?" He pointed to a small rowboat just nosing out of the fog and heading toward the anchored merchant ship.

"I don't know. I don't think so. It doesn't look like a Griffin barge."

It wasn't, only a messenger craft from a larger vessel somewhere astern of theirs. "We've a letter for one Mr. James Dumont," a man called up as the rowboat pulled along side. "Is he aboard?"

Andrew felt a sick plunging sensation in the pit of his stomach. How could anyone know the name under which they were traveling?

"Right here," James shouted down while signaling his young companion to silence. "Send it up."

The man in the rowboat speared the envelope on a kind of halberd and thrust it up toward James, who leaned dangerously far over the side to retrieve the letter. "Thank you. There, got it! Hold on, my man. . . ." He reached into his purse and flicked a coin toward the crew of the tiny boat. "Where are you from?" he asked with easy good nature.

"That ship just over yonder." The same man did the speaking. "Cain't hardly see her for the fog. We'll be landing soon as it lifts."

Andrew peered at the speaker, trying to distinguish his features. Impossible in this murk. "Is it from my uncle, sir?" He turned anxiously to James, who was reading the letter.

"No, from my wife, the duchess." James read quickly, and by the time he reached the end of the message a broad grin had spread across his face. "By God! The girl's a prize if ever there was one. Guess who's on that ship, Andrew. The one that sent us this letter."

"I'm afraid I've no idea." The boy's bewilderment was obvious.

"The Duke of York, that's who. In disguise. A black wig, it says here, and accompanied by a mere handful of his most trusted associates."

"But I don't understand. . . ."

"A ruse, son! A ploy! A diversionary tactic! It's an elementary fact of war. And this child bride of mine—she's younger than you are my boy—this innocent babe thought of it all. And even arranged for us to have word." James walked away chuckling, and Andrew remained staring after him.

By midday the fog lifted and the Griffin barge pulled up beside them. The transfer was a bit tricky for Andrew, who'd never been at sea before this trip. James negotiated the rope ladder with ease. "Look," he said quietly to the boy when they were both aboard the barge. "Over there." The other vessel had docked, and they could make out a party of men going ashore with what seemed ostentatious secrecy.

Andrew only spent a moment watching the scene, then turned his attention back to their own concerns. "What news?" he asked the old man who stood beside them. Then, without waiting for a reply, "This is Hart, sir. My uncle's most trusted employee."

"Glad to find you here, Hart," James said amiably. His spirits had been outrageously high since he'd learned of Mary's trick. "I repeat young Andrew's question. What news? And where are we headed?"

"Not much news, yer highness." Hart ignored the man's

hurried indication that titles should be ignored. He knew how trustworthy the crew of the barge were, even if York didn't. "They say the king's neither better nor worse. He's at Windsor Castle now, and that's where we're takin ye. If'n that's all right, that is."

"Are those Captain Griffin's orders?"

"They are that, sir."

"Then carry on."

The news reached Roger the next morning. Word had been sent from Windsor, and now it was all over London. The king was up and about and very much alive and looking to stay that way. "Is it reliable, do you think?" he asked Monty, who had brought him the information.

"It seems so, captain."

"Thank God." He didn't add aloud his equally fervent prayer that James and Andrew were also safely delivered. He'd hoped for Hart's return before now, but so far there was no sight of the man, nor any of the crew of the barge sent to Dover. Well, it was too soon to worry. Griffin returned his attention to the papers on his desk.

Ten minutes later Hart was sitting with him. "All easy as you please, cap'n. And both parties we wuz sent to collect just fine. We dropped his highness at Windsor, then took Mr. Andrew back to Tassels. The mistress insisted we spend the night, and welcome it was, sir. The men was tired. Hope it was all right to stay."

"Of course." Roger wondered how much Nancy knew or guessed. He'd told her only that he was sending Andrew on company business.

"Just as well we was there anyway," Hart continued. "This message for ye came from Windsor this mornin'. Mistress said I was to put it straight in yer hands."

"Thank you." Roger reached for the envelope and recognized the handwriting, though there was neither royal seal nor other indication. "Meet me," he read, "at the heavenly place. Thursday, five o'clock."

There was no signature. He needed none. The venue and the code name James had given it were both familiar. The tavern to which he referred was the Angel on Tower Hill, a favorite of York's whenever he wished to drink or talk incognito. "Just like the old days," Roger muttered aloud with a slight smile on his face. Still, it was good news. If James was hanging about long enough to meet him at the Angel, then the king's reception of his banished brother couldn't have been too bad.

4.

"So I'm for Scotland." James smiled ruefully. "In the light of recent events, his majesty's decided I'll be better closer to home, but still out of sight, so to speak. Moreover, Monmouth is to be banished. My brother, you see, doesn't wish the plotters to have it so easy next time." He tugged the front of the ill-fitting leather jerkin that made up his disguise as a laborer and laughed lightly. "I'm grateful to you, Roger. Haven't had an opportunity to do this sort of thing in a long time. Drink up, man. The landlord's supply of ale can't be exhausted yet."

"I'm only glad it all worked out satisfactorily," Roger said. "There were moments when I wasn't sure the plan was wise. Particularly when I heard of the king's recovery. But all's well that ends well, as they say. And I'm delighted that Andrew had a chance to test his mettle. Your good report of him pleases me greatly. I'd always thought the lad was made of the right stuff."

"He is indeed. Tell me, what are your plans for his future?"

"Frankly, I don't know. His position is difficult."

James made a face of distaste. "To say the least. Branded a recusant at age twelve, son of convicted traitors..."

"That, sir, is an outrageous lie." Roger's anger was apparent.

"Hold your temper, my boy. No one knows that better than I. I speak only of the, how shall I put it, public situation. But I've been thinking, would you consider a court appointment for him? Say in the household of my brother-in-law the Duke of Modena?"

Roger toyed with his ale. "All the way to Italy. The family would miss him sorely. But his religion would be no detriment there, and God knows the lad deserves his chance at some kind of career. Yes sir, I guess the answer is I'd consider it gratefully."

"Good. Then it's done. I'll start the arrangements this week. Now, Roger, I think you'd best get us a couple of refills. I've other news for you, and I think you may need some fortification."

Griffin rose and took their empty tankards to the bar. Little point in speculating on what James planned to say; he'd find out soon enough. He noticed, however, the man's mood seem to become more guarded, more calculating.

The duke took a long pull of his ale, then said, "I met a few interesting people while in exile at my daughter's palace. Even some from London." His eyes narrowed, and he watched Griffin carefully. Roger was aware of the scrutiny but only sat and waited. He knew from experience there was no hurrying James in this sort of thing.

"That partner of yours, the Jew. Name's Ahmet, isn't it?"

"Yes." York knew Benjamin's name quite well. All this was merely the buildup. Roger braced himself.

"Has a sister, doesn't he?"

He felt the palms of his hands dampen with sweat. Rachel was in Amsterdam. Not far from The Hague. Whatever York was hinting at must have something to do with her. If he tried to make her one of his chain of mistresses...or worse, if he expected Roger to help him do so...None of these racing thoughts prepared him for York's next words.

"Never mind answering. I know he has a sister. I've met the lady a number of times. And her infant son."

Roger could only stare at him. The words didn't make any sense.

"Little boy just ten months old," James continued. "Born January last." He leaned forward and fixed his gaze on Roger's pale face. "Your son, I warrant. Though I should tell you the lady never even hinted that. I just guessed."

He spent the weekend in town, having sent word to Tassels that the press of business detained him. George Alley was manned by only a skeleton staff that recognized his all too obvious mood and left him strictly alone.

There were long hours spent lying on his bed staring at

the ceiling of the small room and looking for answers that didn't appear. Yet more hours walking beside the river, over on the quiet semideserted south bank. The turgid waters of the Thames offered no answers either. But if little in the way of definite plans for Rachel's future or that of their son presented themselves to him, one conviction did form. All the demands of honor and integrity compelled a single course of action. To do otherwise was to become someone very different from the man he believed himself to be, to violate irrevocably the essence of the values he claimed to profess. By Sunday evening he was walking slowly toward Ingram's Court.

"In some ways," he said quietly at last, "it seemed unnecessarily cruel to tell you I'd betrayed your trust. That's why I never said anything before this. But the boy's existence changes all that. I have no right to deny you knowledge of your nephew's birth. I don't ask you to forgive me, Benjamin. That would be too much. I do hope you can someday understand."

Ahmet had remained silent throughout the long and painful explanation. Only his face betrayed the changing emotions the story produced. Now he looked composed, if very pale. When Griffin rose to leave, Ahmet didn't stop him.

The week brought work. Roger did it automatically, through efficiency born of long habit rather than effort. Only pain convinced him he was still alive. The shock and numbness were gone now; in their place was a terrible aching, an almost overwhelming sense of loss.

Until all this he had not really realized what was meant by loyalty. Oh, he'd thought about it often enough, measured his own conduct on numerous occasions by the rigid Griffin legacy of fidelity to the crown and the family. What he'd missed, never understood, was the other side of that coin.

The most terrible thing about the news York had brought him was not his own failure; he'd had almost two years to accept the notion of his feet of clay. The thought that now pummeled his insides, made him want to scream aloud with anguish, was that he had forfeited the loyalty of the two people he'd most trusted in the world.

Ten years ago, when, as he saw it then, Mark had betrayed

him, he'd thought life was over. It was the first real breach in the seemingly impregnable sense of Griffin security. Then the king and the Duke of York had deserted him and he'd had a further taste of bitter injustice. Nancy had said something about it at the time—"You expect life to be fair and you're shocked when it isn't." He could hear her voice now as plainly as he had in that filthy little room in the Cock and Pie.

But she had helped him to trust again. From the time she had heard the news of the *Queen Catherine*'s sinking and left newborn Nell to join him in London to the moment she had stood steadfast by his side at Tyburn, Nancy had given him unswerving devotion. She'd taught him by her example to believe in people once more.

And so had Benjamin. A foreigner, a Jew, a man born to a different world, had become his best friend and most trusted ally. Now he had forfeited the love and respect of both of them. The sense of loss was unbearable.

Nearly a fortnight later, Ahmet still hadn't come near George Alley. Roger lived like a recluse, doing nothing because there seemed nothing to do. He couldn't bring himself to go home to Tassels.

Benjamin, he reasoned, had probably gone to Amsterdam. He'd want to see Rachel and the boy, make arrangements for their future. A future in which Roger would be allowed no part.

"So, Benjamin." The old man stroked his beard and leaned back in his chair. "What brings you here? I haven't seen you a guest in my house for a long time."

"I know, Menachim. I'm sorry. I've been so busy...." He shrugged and realized the apologies were hollow. He hadn't come before because the old man bored him, a reactionary fighting changing times. They both knew it. "I came tonight because I need to talk, Menachim," he finished simply.

"I see." Cohan poured a glass of wine for each of them and lifted his. "*L'chaim*," he said quietly.

"*L'chaim*," Benjamin echoed. It was a very ancient toast. It meant "To life." The thought made him wince.

"So?" The old man set his glass aside after the first careful sip. "You want to talk and you don't go to your new friends. To *goyim*. You come here to an old Jew who was your father's friend and your grandfather's. So talk, Benjamin. I'm listening."

"I want to ask you a question." He hesitated for only a moment. He'd been over this in his mind a dozen times. "What is betrayal, Menachim? What does the word really mean?"

Cohan pursed his lips and pressed his fingertips together in front of his dirty beard. If an artist wanted to portray Jews at their most Jewish he could have chosen nothing more fitting than this wizened elder with his skullcap slightly askew above watery eyes, half-rotten teeth, and a stained beard, his head full of biblical wisdom—and the dapper younger man, sophisticated, successful, yet waiting for the advice that was the legacy of thousands of years of adversity.

"Who," Cohan said at last, "who should know more about betrayal than a Jew?" He smiled and reached for a book. The answers to all questions could be found in a book.

"It's somewhere here...." He thumbed the pages hastily, the way someone does who knows the contents almost by heart. "Yes, here in the Book of Proverbs. Listen, Benjamin, the voice of Solomon himself....'The innocence of the upright guides them safely, the treacherous by their own plots are destroyed.'" He closed the book with an air of satisfaction. "What more can you ask? Betrayal only hurts the betrayer in the end."

Ahmet rose with a gesture of impatience. "That's not it at all. Treachery, plots...they're no part of this. Nothing was planned. It just happened."

"So? Sit down, Benjamin. You're making me nervous." Cohan refilled his guest's glass before saying more.

When he continued it was in a different tone. Something of amusement lurked behind his words. "You know," he said, almost laughing, "I just remembered something. When your father used to do that...that walking around the room as if he wanted to wear out the carpets...it always meant he knew he'd lost the argument." Cohan pressed one finger against his temple and cocked his head. He looked like a gnome, Ahmet thought. Or perhaps a cat about to pounce.

"I think," the old man continued, "you know you've lost the argument too. Not with me. With yourself. Tell me if you can, Benjamin, how can there be betrayal without forethought? Passion yes, error of course. Even serious error. But betrayal? No, that requires that a man plot and scheme. Just as it says in the holy book."

"It's that simple?" Ahmet asked scornfully.

Cohan nodded. "It's that simple. Only a fool makes bricks without straw, Benjamin. You are many things, but you are no fool."

He walked the few feet to his own door with those words ringing in his head. "Bricks without straw..." In his study, seated at his desk, master of all he surveyed, not a supplicant at the feet of an old sage, he repeated the words aloud. "Bricks without straw..." Indeed.

He sat silent for a long time, letting himself think rather than brood for the first time in days. Two problems needed sorting. Never mind his wounded feelings. Human nature was what it was. He knew that as well as anyone. As Menachim had said, he was no fool. The only things that mattered now were Rachel and the boy and his own relationship to Roger Griffin. The last was, perhaps, not as vital as the first two, but if he was honest he had to admit it weighed as heavily on his mind.

After some time he reached for writing materials and scrawled a brief message. Then he rang for a servant and dispatched the note to George Alley.

In the house on the other side of Ingram's Court, Menachim Cohan was writing too. His letter was addressed to a cousin in Amsterdam, a man somewhat younger than himself, but equally skilled in the art of discreet inquiry.

Was it not to Amsterdam that Ahmet's sister Rachel had gone so suddenly about two years ago? And almost no word about her since. Somehow Benjamin's anguish this night, the anguish that made him seek out an old man in his search for answers, was connected with that departure.

Menachim had learned from long experience to trust his hunches. He'd learned too to allow no opportunity to pass him by. The information might not matter now, might not matter ever. But one couldn't tell. He would find out what the mystery was if he could. Learn the impetus behind Benjamin's question. Then he would simply wait. Most likely he would never have occasion to use the knowledge once he had it. But just in case... Better to be prepared. Always better.

Roger Griffin, even if he had known of Cohan's inquiries, could not have imagined the extraordinary role they would give the old Jew in Griffin affairs.

* * *

Ahmet walked to the sideboard and poured two glasses of brandy, then turned back to his visitor. His first words were totally unexpected. "What did you say the child's name is?"

"According to James, Antony Jacob."

"Well then," he said and handed one of the glasses to Roger, "I propose we drink a toast to Antony Jacob."

More silence until finally Benjamin asked, "What do you propose to do?"

"I don't know." Roger could barely look at the man. "The only decision I seemed able to reach was to come here and tell you. Since that night I've done nothing. Nothing but wish I could turn the clock back, undo all the damage."

Benjamin nodded. "I know how you feel. That's what I've been thinking too. If only I'd never gone to Bristol that night. If only..." He shrugged. "What's the point? We both know life's full of 'if onlys.'"

Griffin buried his head in his hands. "Sweet Christ, Benjamin! Isn't there anything I can do?"

"Do? About what? Rachel, the baby, Nancy..."

"You've left out yourself." Griffin's words were barely audible. "I don't expect you to believe me, but I hate myself worst of all for betraying you."

"Betrayal." Ahmet leaned back in his chair, struggling with his own demons. "That's the word I used too. At first I did feel betrayed. My sister and my best friend bringing shame and disgrace on my name.... Wait." He held up his hand to forestall Roger's reply, ignored the other man's anguished groan. "I said, 'at first.' Then I talked to someone older and wiser than either of us. He pointed out a very simple truth. There can be real betrayal only when there's forethought. Without that it's error or rashness, maybe even tragedy. But not betrayal."

"You believe that?"

"Yes, Roger, I do. You see..." He rose and placed his hand on Griffin's shoulder. "If I don't believe it, what am I left with? Not you, not Rachel, not the boy.... I'm getting older, Roger. We're all getting older. I don't know about you, but for myself, there's no appeal in facing the rest of my life with that much aloneness, that much bitterness."

Griffin merely looked at him. There was nothing he could reply. After some seconds he clasped the other man's hand where it lay on his shoulder. They held the pose for some seconds, then Ahmet moved away and Griffin downed his untouched brandy.

"What do we do next?" he asked quietly. "I seem incapable of making any coherent plan."

"You know..." Benjamin ran one finger around the rim of his glass as if testing it for imperfections. "I think we are being rather short-sighted."

"I don't understand."

"We are speaking as if there are decisions remaining to us. The more I think about it the less I think that's true. It seems to me Rachel has made all the decisions."

"But that's mad! She ran because she wanted to spare either of us pain or shame. Now, knowing the truth, I can't let her just remain in hiding over there. Surely you must see that."

"Roger." Benjamin leaned back in his chair and looked at the other man intently. "One thing you haven't told me in all this. Do you love my sister?"

"Yes, in a kind of way I do."

"A kind of way?"

"A very important way, but different. I can't explain."

"Different from what you feel for Nancy. Is that what you're trying to say?"

"Yes." Griffin rubbed his forehead in a gesture of almost total weariness. "Yes, that's what I'm trying to say."

"Hmm...I understand that. It's what I expected." Ahmet rose and stood with his back to the fire. It was very late; the coals had burned into mere embers and the room was growing chilly though it was only the middle of September. "Listen to me, Roger. What I'm going to say now is something I prefer to discuss just this once. I propose that the subject never be mentioned between us again. I know my sister very well. I'm almost twenty-seven years older than she, you know. Rachel is the child of my father's second wife. They both died when she was barely three. We have had only each other for years. She's not an ordinary woman, Roger. If she gave herself to you she did so because she loved you. I don't for one moment doubt that bearing your son was a source of joy for her, regardless of the circumstances."

"But..."

"No. Let me finish. I know there is a common custom among you English of setting up a separate household for a mistress, acknowledging the children of the union...that sort of thing. Even the king does it."

422

"It never occurred to me to treat Rachel that way," Roger said stiffly. "I don't mistake her for some common mistress, I assure you."

"Yes. I believe that. If I didn't I'd have reacted very differently to this whole sorry tale. But I'm not the injured party, not really. It seems to me stupid to act as if I am."

"No, God help me, it's Rachel who's been injured. She who deserved it least of all."

"Perhaps. But I'm more concerned with the only really innocent victim in this entire affair. The child, my nephew, your son. He's the one that's totally blameless. It's his future that matters now."

"Yes, I see that."

"Then you must see too that in these first years of his life his mother is the best judge of what's good for him. She has elected to keep his existence secret from us, and to remain with him in Amsterdam. Have we any right to go blundering in and insist that be changed?"

"When you put it that way it's hard to disagree. But it seems so awful. She there and we here. Never knowing the boy, never being able to help her in his upbringing."

"Maybe"—Benjamin's voice was barely a whisper—"that's the penance you must do. And I'm not blameless in this, Roger. I should have seen what was coming. More important, I should have provided Rachel with a proper husband and father to her children years ago."

Roger wanted to say something, but nothing came.

"Look, here's what I propose," Ahmet continued. "Can James arrange to get money to Rachel? In such a way that she won't know from whom it really comes?"

"I don't know. I suppose so. I didn't think to ask him."

"Very well. Let's assume he can and will do that. I think it's a reasonable assumption. Further, let's assume that Rachel is content with the arrangements she's made for the present moment. For the rest I think it's best we do nothing."

"There's a soundness to your arguments. But for how long?"

"I can't really say. A year or two, certainly. By then…"

Roger looked at him quizzically. "By then what?"

"Perhaps the circumstances will be different. This plan of enn's for a settlement in America looks to be going ahead.

If it does, I'm going to join him. You'll hardly be surprised at that."

"No. Grieved, but not surprised."

"Well then, it seems to me the time may be right just about then for me to go see Rachel and tell her what we know. I would hope to persuade her to bring the child and join me in the New World. A new beginning for both of them doesn't seem a bad plan."

"No." Roger sighed and was silent for some seconds. Finally he said, "I suppose I must admit it's a good plan. But for me the hardest course of action is to do nothing."

"Yes, I realize that. If you did something, anything, it would make you feel better, convince you amends were being made. Money seems a small solace in place of action."

"It's so bloody easy!"

"Exactly. And that's the greatest sacrifice you can make. All your instincts are those of a fighter, my friend. I've always known that. Now you're being told to suppress them. As I said, it's a hard penance. But a necessary one."

"Very well. I agree to the plan. There seems little choice."

"No. There isn't much." Benjamin passed his hand over his eyes. "One further question, though it's none of my business. Are you going to tell Nancy?"

"Of course it's your business. The answer is, no, I'm not. Not unless you force me to it."

"I'd never do that."

"I hoped you wouldn't. What would be served by telling her? Just more pain for more innocent bystanders. I'd feel better and she'd feel worse."

"Good." Ahmet even managed a smile. "I'm glad you see that. Now, I think we both need some sleep. Don't bother to go back to George Alley, Roger. The guest room is at your disposal. As always. Nothing's really changed."

"It almost never does." Roger walked with his old friend toward the stairs.

October had spilled its golden glow over England before the Duke of York was actually ready to depart for Scotland and take up his post as royal commissioner. Before that he'd had a number of meetings with Griffin.

They discussed Andrew's future first. York had secured the boy a place as aide to one of the chief ministers of the Duke of Modena. "It'll be a good beginning for him," he told

Roger. "He'll learn about government and diplomacy. Then someday when I'm . . . well, let's just say in the future it will prove useful."

"As I've said before, your highness, I'm grateful. And Andrew's beside himself with pleasure and excitement. We're all grateful."

At later meetings, the question of Rachel Ahmet was raised. James was surprised that Griffin didn't intend to summon her back to London and publicly acknowledge the child as his.

It was a decision James did not approve, but he had concerns of his own and this business was, after all, not his affair. It seemed to him rather shabby treatment just to send the girl money. Still, he owed Griffin much, and he didn't refuse to make the arrangement. "I've one or two people I can trust in The Hague," he said. "I'll see they get the funds to her."

"Thank you, sir."

"Can't say I approve, Roger. You're not being as straightforward about this as I'd have expected."

"I'm sorry if I disappoint you. I can only repeat, it seems to me what the lady would prefer."

"Oh, very well. Give me the money, I'll get it to her. And not a word about where it comes from. She'll think it a gift from me."

5.

By Easter of 1680, Nancy's latest additions to Tassels were complete. No one who had seen the place when the Griffins first moved there would recognize it now. The recent work had changed the entire appearance of the onetime cottage. Over the jumble of wings and differing rooflines a symmetrical facade had been erected, pure classical simplicity with a column of Grecian pillars at ground level and one long sweeping gable. The whole was executed in the flinty gray York-shire granite they had quarried from Roger's hillside and carted here three hundred miles south.

"Moving the stone's costing a fortune," she had admitted to Roger while the work was in progress. "And it's so slow....But considering that we don't have to pay for the materials themselves, it's all coming out about the same."

"They found enough granite for their needs, then?" he'd asked somewhat absentmindedly. Work on the house always fascinated Nancy, but not him.

"Oh yes, plenty. Uncovered some old ruins, I believe."

Roger had looked up at her with startled recognition in his eyes. "Of course! Kirkslee Priory. I'd quite forgotten that was the site of the old nunnery."

"Oh dear." Nancy bit her lip in consternation. "I remember now too. Wasn't there a wing of Harwood built of that stone? And didn't Sophia say..."

"Yes," he interrupted her very firmly. "I know what Sophia said. But that's the end of that discussion. I don't want to hear any more about it now or ever. I'll have no talk of hauntings at Tassels."

"No, of course not. Besides, I don't want the children frightened."

They never mentioned the matter again.

"Isn't it lovely?" she asked Sarah, who stood beside her in the spring sunshine the first morning after the workmen had finally departed.

"Beautiful," the girl agreed. "You should be very proud of all you've done, Aunt Nancy. No one would think it possible from the little place you had to work with."

"I am proud of it. And I want to show it off. Sarah," she said, turning to the girl with a burst of enthusiasm, "I want to give a party. Would that offend you? Would you think it too soon after your parents' death?"

"Not a bit," the sensible Sarah replied quickly. "It's a year, after all. If Mama were here she'd say the same thing. I know Charles will agree too."

"And Andrew's too far away for us to consult him, so that's settled. Tell me, darling, do you remember parties when you were a child? At Harwood, I mean."

Sarah stooped to pluck a dead leaf from a shrub by the side of the front walk. "I can't say I really do. I was thirteen when we left, and the only thing I really remember is Christmas. There were always lots of guests at Christmas."

"Yes. Well, actually, for most of your growing-up years Cromwell and the Puritans were in power. They didn't hold much with parties. But I do." She hugged the girl impulsively. "And I've a wonderful plan for this one. It's going to be a masquerade ball. What do you think of that?"

"Sounds lovely," Sarah answered, smiling at the older woman's enthusiasm. "Will we all have to come in costume?"

"Of course. And I've just the right thing in mind for you, too. Come inside, love, we've simply piles of things to do!"

They scheduled the ball for May 10. Roger was consulted after a fashion, but this, like so many domestic arrangements, he considered Nancy's province. He merely nodded his head and took no part in the arrangements. Nancy noticed that he seemed preoccupied of late; for the past six months, in fact. She put it down to Benjamin's insistence that he was leaving England for America in the near future. Doubtless Roger was worried about how the business would do without Ahmet. Well, she wasn't worried. Roger would do fine on his own, and anyway, Tassels was financially independent these days. Now that the latest building work was completed and paid for, it might even start showing some profit. There was nothing to fuss about. Roger was just being moody. Nancy put the notion aside and went on with her plans.

There was more than just the desire for a good time behind her masquerade ball. Since she'd been spending so much time with Nell in London she'd met all sorts of young men who might be suitable husbands for Sarah. Nancy planned to invite them and see what she could promote. She never mentioned this to Sarah, however. The girl would just get nervous and hostile if faced with such a suggestion. Instead she kept her own counsel and involved Sarah in discussions of decorations and refreshments.

"What about our costumes?" the girl asked suddenly one day. "You've not said anything about what you plan to wear. Should I be thinking of something for myself?"

"Of course not, pet! I've arranged everything. I wanted it to be a surprise, but maybe I should have consulted with you. I've got a dressmaker in London doing a French milkmaid's

427

dress for you. Lovely and ruffly. You'll look charming. Is that all right?"

"It sounds fine." Sarah smiled when she asked, "I suppose you've got Uncle Roger and Charles all suited up too? And that you're going to keep your own costume a secret?"

"Yes to both queries," Nancy answered, laughing. "Now, what about flowers for the dining hall? What do you have in mind for that?"

"Well, it's a bit difficult at this time of year. May's too early for roses, though I'd have chosen them if I could. As it is, I think we should use the same theme throughout the house. Daffodils and laurel. There'll be plenty of both, and they can look quite charming."

"Perfect! And I like the theme idea. Better than having a bit of this and that. Masses of daffodils. In fact, let's call it the Daffodil Ball!"

It was May 2 when Roger mentioned casually to his wife, "I'll have to stay in town next weekend. A French chap's coming over to talk about selling us his wine. We've done so well with Champagne that we're thinking of adding a line of claret."

"Claret! Next weekend! Roger, how could you? Don't you realize that Saturday night is the ball?"

"Oh Lord! I'd quite forgotten. Sorry, darling, I just don't know what to do."

"Well, I do. Bring your Frenchman here. He can spend the weekend and you can talk business on Sunday."

"Fine. I'll do that. But wait a minute—he won't have a costume."

"Oh, never mind. Tell him he can come as a French wine merchant!"

Roger chuckled. "Good, that's just what I'll tell him. What am I to wear, by the way? You've never told me, but I presume you've everything arranged."

"Naturally. And don't you worry about it. Just get here on Saturday and it will all work out."

This conversation was taking place in Roger's study. It was still the same charming room that Nancy had built the year young James was born. And it was delightfully close to their bedroom. He looked at her now, flushed and happy with the plans for her great ball, and suddenly he realized how convenient that arrangement was. He'd like nothing better than to bed his wife this very instant. There'd been too little of that lately. He must put this business about Rachel and the little boy out of his mind, start paying more attention to Nancy.... He'd actually risen and gone to plant a tender kiss on her cheek when there was a knock on the door.

"Come in." Roger hoped his annoyance didn't show in his voice.

"It's me." Sarah stepped inside. There was an unwieldy paper-wrapped parcel under her arm. "I hope I'm not interrupting...I can come back later if it's more convenient."

"No, no, Sarah. It's fine. What is it?"

"Well..." the girl seemed stricken with a sudden bout of shyness. She who was always so forthright and direct. "I want to give you something. Both of you. Could you come downstairs?"

"Downstairs?" Nancy asked. "Couldn't you give it to us here?"

"I'd rather not. That is, if you don't mind. Downstairs in the new dining hall."

The trotted dutifully behind her. Obviously the package under her arm had something to do with this business, but Nancy couldn't guess what it might be.

When they were in the vast oak-lined room, Sarah stepped to the long table and looked around her for a moment before speaking. There was much to admire. The walls of the room were paneled in carved wood, and the ceiling was a masterpiece of the plasterer's art. The motif throughout was of fruit, swags of carved and molded grapes and pears and apples that looked lifelike enough to eat. "It's such a beautiful room," Sarah said softly. "That's why I thought of this."

"Thought of what, Sarah?" Roger asked with just a hint of impatience. He was still thinking of his wife and the seduction that had been interrupted.

Sarah ignored his question and went on speaking. "You see, when the sheriff's men ransacked Tupenny Cottage, this was almost ruined. Mama had it carefully stored, but they ripped it. Walked on it, even." While she spoke she was unwrapping the mysterious parcel. A folded swathe of brilliant blue was suddenly revealed in the afternoon sunlight.

"It's the coat of arms," Nancy exclaimed with a sudden gasp of recognition.

"Yes. This corner was badly torn, but I've been mending it all these months." Sarah spread the great cloth over the table. "I think it could hang here now."

"Sweet Christ," Roger whispered, stepping forward and touching the ancient banner with reverence. "I'd no idea the thing was still in the family."

"You didn't think Mama and Papa would leave it?" Sarah asked incredulously. "Not this. We took it with us when we left the Hall. We've had it ever since. I know Mama and Papa would want you to have it now."

"Azure a bend or. With two griffins rampant." Nancy repeated the old formula and stepped closer to admire the exquisite workmanship of the Griffin needlewomen. "Is this the bit you mended? I'd no idea you could sew so beautifully."

"Not as well as Mama or Laura, but well enough. At least it had to be well enough. I was the only one to do it." Sarah smiled. "See, it's this bit of the field and the motto I had to do. There was a big hole in the *Via* of *Regum in Via Recta Dirige* . . . 'Guide Straight the King' . . . I've always loved that part."

For some moments the three stood silently looking at the tapestry. Then Roger spoke. "I think it will look splendid hanging on that wall over there. Can you have that arranged, Nancy?"

"Of course. I'll get it done tomorrow."

"Good." He turned to Sarah with a smile. "My dear, I think you've put the final word on an argument your aunt and I have been having for ten years." Then he turned to his wife. "You win, darling. This is home. Hang up the arms and make it official." Quietly he turned and walked away.

Nancy watched him go. There was a sadness in his step, she couldn't help but see it, but there was hope too. "Thank you," she whispered, hugging Sarah tightly. "Thank you for more than you can ever know."

6.

He found the costume laid out in his dressing room when he went upstairs to change for the ball. It had probably been there earlier, but he'd been too occupied with his French guest to notice.

The fellow was a bit eccentric, full of strange-sounding theories about winemaking of which Roger understood very little. But Gaston DuMars seemed a decent enough sort, fairly plain-spoken for a Frenchman—not as devious as Roger usually thought that breed to be. "If he agrees to guarantee us his entire output, then I think we'll have a contract," he called over his shoulder to Nancy, who had accompanied him upstairs. "Bloody hell!" He lifted a great metal shield that lay across his path. "What the devil is this?"

"Your costume. At least, part of it. You're to be a Roman general. I couldn't arrange for an admiral. They didn't have admirals in ancient Rome."

"Thank God! This is bad enough. Do you really expect me to wear all this regalia?"

"I certainly do. You'll look splendid."

"But how does it all go? What are these?" He held up two long leather strands.

"The thongs for tying your sandals. See, here they are. Oh, never mind. You don't have to understand it all. I've explained everything to young Tom, and he's going to help you dress. Now, don't waste time, darling. I'm going to change. I'll meet you on the landing in forty-five minutes. We must be downstairs before any of the guests arrive."

"Very well," he said somewhat crossly. "It's my own fault for not making you tell me what you'd in mind earlier. I shall look bloody ridiculous, but I won't spoil your fun at this late date."

"You'll look marvelous," she insisted, kissing him lightly. "See you in forty-five minutes."

"Wait a minute. Nancy, what are you wearing?"

"You'll see." She was gone before he could ask any further questions.

When he met her in the hall he realized he should have guessed. She was dressed as Cleopatra, in the very same costume he'd first seen her wearing so many years before on the stage of the Drury Lane Theater. "You're even more beautiful now," he said, smiling at her with affection. "But I still like your own hair better than that black wig."

"Whoever heard of a redheaded Cleopatra?" she rejoined quickly. "Now, are you coming, Mark Antony?"

"Of course, your royal highness." He offered her his arm and they descended the stairs.

In the enormous ballroom that had been built to run the length of the east wing of the house there was a high balcony at one end. This was the musician's gallery, and Nancy had hired the instrumentalists of the King's Company of Players to provide the music for the evening. They were all in place now, tuning their strings and testing their cymbals in a weird cacophony of sound. Sarah was in the room too, putting the final touches to a last vase of the golden daffodils that were everywhere.

"Oh look, Roger! Doesn't she look charming?"

"She does indeed. You will turn the head of every young man in sight, my dear."

Sarah tugged inelegantly at the skirt of her blue frock, which was tucked up all around to display a lacy petticoat beneath. "I don't think this is a very practical dress for milking," she said with some pique. "Do they really wear such things? Long full sleeves, and the bodice has so many bones I can't breathe."

"Stop fussing, Sarah," Nancy said firmly. "You look adorable. The dressmaker copied the design from a French book, so it must be authentic. Where's Charles?"

"Checking to make sure the servants brought enough wine up from the cellar. He says you brought Champagne, Uncle Roger. Are we really to have it tonight?"

"We are indeed. And unless I'm very much mistaken, that wonderful-looking Elizabethan that's just come in is none other than your brother Charles."

"Sir Walter Raleigh at your service, my noble Roman."
Charles tried to bow, but the exercise was less graceful than
it might have been. "Oof... this doublet's so stiff and padded
I can't bend!"

"Well, go off somewhere and practice, love," Nancy said.
"You must be able to bow properly. Now, you three stay here
and wait for the first guests. I'm just going to have one last
peek into the nursery to make sure the children are all right."

"They're not to be allowed downstairs, then?" Roger asked
somewhat wistfully. He'd been having visions of his two
daughters in costume, being admired by all and sundry. "Not
even little Nell?"

"Certainly not!" Nancy exclaimed with feeling. "Balls are
not suitable for little girls of eight and nine." And with this
pronouncement she left the room.

"Don't worry, Uncle Roger," Charles stage-whispered after
his aunt was gone. "I have it on reliable authority that young
Jamie's got himself a page's outfit and plans to put in an
appearance despite his mother's rules."

"Good for him!" Roger laughed. "Did he think of that all
by himself? Not bad for six years old."

"Well, maybe not entirely by himself." Charles grinned
in conspiratorial fashion.

Roger slung an arm around the boy's shoulders. "Come
along, Sir Walter. Let's see about loosening you up a bit so
you can at least bow."

The array was stunning. Nell Gwyn as a Spanish princess
in a great wide skirt and masses of diamonds; any number
of ladies as queens of one sort or another—dazzling jewels
and well-exposed bosoms seemed to be the necessary elements of that costume. There were a few Arab sheikhs and
at least a dozen red-coated dragoons of different regiments.
Three different men had elected to wear the plaid—fortunately they'd all chosen different clans—and twice that number were dressed as Elizabethan courtiers. There were strolling minstrels, Eastern potentates, and one very amusing
mandarin with a long braid and even longer fingernails.

"How did he manage that?" Sarah asked with customary
practicality.

"I haven't a clue," Charles answered. "But better him than
me. It must be damned uncomfortable."

"Not as uncomfortable as those two." Sarah pointed to a

pair of men who had all but stolen the show. They were costumed as red Indians, complete with feathers and beads and warpaint and not much else. "They must be freezing."

In another corner of the room Roger and his guest, Gaston DuMars, were also discussing the Indians. "Must be bloody cold," Roger said, echoing his niece's sentiments and those of practically everyone at the ball.

"No doubt," the Frenchman agreed with a shrug. "But think of it, *mon capitaine,* to be young and so well muscled and to have an opportunity to display it thus. Ah, I think they consider any discomfort worthwhile."

"I suspect you're right. I say, will you excuse me, DuMars? That fellow there is my partner. The one done up like a Turkish sultan. I want to bring him over to meet you."

Roger started across the crowded room, and DuMars found himself alone in the midst of the gorgeous throng. He'd never expected such glamorous entertainment in England. And the musicians knew all the dances, too. Bransles and courantes with their formal measured paces, and a rousing athletic thing they called a jig. They were beginning a new one now. Suddenly a voice at his elbow said, "Are you enjoying yourself, Monsieur DuMars? Can I get you anything?"

It was the little niece of Captain Griffin. All afternoon she had been preoccupied with her flower arrangements, not a bit like the flirting, coquettish women he was accustomed to. "I'm enjoying myself very much indeed, Mademoiselle Sarah. But I have only one regret."

"Oh, what's that?"

She expected him to say something about not being in costume, but instead he said, "That you've not yet danced with me. Please..." He extended his arm.

"I'm sorry. I don't dance."

"But of course you dance. All lovely young ladies dance."

"This is French, isn't it? This new dance..." Her tone was just a bit wistful.

"Yes. And since you are dressed as a French milkmaid, I insist you must dance with me. Never mind if you've not done this one before. I shall show you."

The crowds jostled them; great clouds of feathers from one costume even blinded DuMars at one point in his attempt to lead Sarah to the dance floor. But eventually they made their way to the center of the ballroom and were hesitantly involved in the complex steps. "See?" he said as they linked arms for one of the movements. "You're doing very well indeed."

"Thank you. Tell me, what kind of soil do you grow your grapes in?"

He didn't know her well enough to realize this abrupt change of subject was quite normal for Sarah. "Kind of soil?"

The demands of the dance separated them for a moment, but when they came together again she took up the same theme. "Yes. I mean, is it light or heavy? Sweet or sour? I've read that grapevines do best in heavy soils, but frosts can then be a problem."

"You astound me, *chère mademoiselle!* Do such matters interest you?"

"They are the only things that interest me," Sarah said frankly. "I oversee all the gardens here at Tassels. Most of them I planted myself a few years back."

"Indeed... No, no, my dear, put out the left foot now..."

"Oh bother! I told you I don't dance."

"Yes, well, come, Mademoiselle Sarah. We will find a quiet corner, I will get you a glass of your uncle's excellent Champagne, and I will tell you about the problems of grapevines on heavy soil. That will please you?"

"Very much indeed." Sarah grinned at him and took his arm. She quite ignored her Aunt Nancy, making her way toward them with frantic gestures intended to attract Sarah's attention, towing with her one of the red Indians.

"You certainly make an authentic-looking Turkish sultan."

"Not very original of me, I suppose." Benjamin laughed. "But easy. And may I say you're an astoundingly convincing Roman. Something in the nose and jawline, I think."

"My dear Benjamin, you know enough history to realize that we all have something Roman in our jawlines! A leftover of the common foot soldier's notion of how to enforce the Pax Romana. Have you seen Nancy?"

"I'm not sure. In this disguised crush it's hard to tell. I did spot a fetching Cleopatra that reminded me of the lady. Ah, but of course! Antony and Cleopatra."

"How perceptive of you. Come, we'll get you some Champagne and a little relief from the mob. There's someone I want you to meet. The French chap I told you about, the one with the vineyards."

"Oh yes. Claret isn't it? You think it will do well for us?"

"I'm sure of it. More important, I think we can get a decent long-term contract from the fellow. Here." He stopped a passing footman, and handed Benjamin a glass of sparkling wine. "Supper's to be served at midnight, I think. There's just time to find DuMars and talk a bit before then."

Gaston, however, was nowhere to be seen. They didn't think to try the orchard, where, in fact, the Frenchman was walking with Sarah and discussing crop yields.

"Never mind," Roger said after a lot of futile pushing and shoving and searching. "You're staying the night, aren't you? Good, so is he. We can talk tomorrow." At that moment four of the musicians blew a trumpet fanfare and supper was announced. The partners had no further opportunity to talk, but once during the sumptuous meal Roger caught Benjamin's eye and nodded to where DuMars sat laughing and chatting with Sarah.

A dozen or so guests had been asked to spend the night, and a good number more were invited to be guests of Nell Gwyn at nearby Hampton Court Palace. There was much to-ing and fro-ing the following day, and business discussions received short shrift. Roger could find only fifteen minutes alone with DuMars before he left to return to London.

"I don't feel we've had as much time together as I would have wished, monsieur, but I hope you enjoyed yourself."

"Very much. I must thank you for a wonderful visit, Captain Griffin."

"Delighted. Now, can you see me at my office this week so we may complete our discussions?"

"Well . . ." The man hemmed and hawed a bit. "Truth is, I've many things to occupy my time in town this week. Other business. You understand. Is it possible you might be able to see me next weekend?"

"Next weekend? Well, certainly, if that's the soonest you can arrange."

"Good! Good! I hope your wife won't think I've abused her hospitality coming two weeks running. Thank you, sir. Until Saturday, then." DuMars bowed and left before Roger could speak another word.

Nancy found him staring open-mouthed after the departing Frenchman. "What's happened? You look as though you've been thoroughly outfoxed. Did that fellow get the best of you in a bargain?"

"Not exactly. We've not come to hard negotiations yet. But he just wangled an invitation down here for next Saturday in the most blatant way possible. I'm thoroughly astounded. He seemed gentleman enough until now."

"I see. . . ." Nancy looked reflective, then broke into a broad grin. "Well, why not! He's a little old for her, but why not?"

"Why not what? Too old for whom?"

"Oh, darling, you're so dense I sometimes wonder how you manage to survive." She sighed patiently. "Haven't you noticed that he's spent every moment possible with Sarah?"

"Sarah? You mean you think DuMars is interested in Sarah? That's why he wants to come back here?"

"Naturally. What's wrong with that?"

"Nothing, dammit! But sweet Christ, Nancy, I'm trying to do business with the man! This is no time for him to be paying attention to Sarah."

Nancy giggled. "In matters of this sort, darling, one can't choose one's time."

7.

Apparently the production of claret was the most complicated of arts, and to devise a contract to sell the wine equally complex. There were endless negotiations about whether the blending of one year's vintage with another was to be allowed, what additives were to be permitted. There was even a long series of talks about labeling the bottles. It all meant that Gaston DuMars was a regular visitor to Tassels. Seemingly his other English commitments allowed him only the weekends to deal with Griffin.

Roger, who by now recognized the truth of Nancy's earlier assessment, complied patiently with DuMars's tactics. "Still no firm contract for the claret," he reported repeatedly to Ahmet.

"Might I ask if you plan to negotiate with this chap forever?" Benjamin asked mildly one afternoon.

"If that's what I'm instructed to do," Roger answered. "You can think me spineless if you like, but you're not married to Nancy."

"No." Ahmet laughed heartily. "I'm not. I take it she's decided that Sarah is to marry the fellow."

"Definitely. However, I don't think she's told Sarah yet. That's the bit that really puzzles me. The girl acts oblivious to the whole scheme. Oh, she seems to like DuMars well enough, even spends quite a bit of time with him. But I'm convinced she hasn't a notion of what's really going on."

It was mid-June before Nancy saw fit to explain the realities to Sarah.

"Marry Gaston!" the girl repeated with shock. "I shall certainly not do any such thing! I don't intend to marry anyone."

"But you care for him, don't you?"

"I like him very much," Sarah said. "He's a fine gentleman, very kind and knowledgeable about gardening. But I'd never let him . . . well, you know what I mean. Now, don't argue with me, Aunt Nancy. I'm quite firm in what I say."

It was time to intervene. Nancy chose her moment carefully, and the following Saturday afternoon DuMars found himself alone with his hostess in her private sitting room. "This is a charming room, Madame Griffin," he said appreciatively. "In fact, your entire house is quite the most charming I've seen in England."

Nancy smiled. "I'm delighted you like it, Monsieur DuMars, but I do think it's not just Tassels that appeals to you here in Surrey."

"So," the Frenchman said and shook his head ruefully, "I'm that transparent, am I? Do you think me quite impertinent even to imagine that the young Mademoiselle Sarah might entertain my suit?"

"Not at all. In fact, monsieur, I shall be very frank and hope I do not shock you. Both my husband and I believe such a match to be an excellent idea. You know, of course, that we are Sarah's guardians. Both her mother and father are dead."

"I heard that story," he said quietly. "The kind Monsieur Ahmet thought it important that I know so that I would not unwittingly wound any of you, and he told me some time ago. It is a great tragedy, madame. I offer my sympathy, for what it's worth."

"Thank you. It was the greatest of tragedies for all of us, and while we've learned to live with it, none of us find it easy. Not even Sarah; despite the fact that she's a most sensible young lady. And she has the teachings of her religion to sustain her. You are of the same persuasion as she, are you not, monsieur?"

"I am French, madame. I am therefore a Catholic, though I can't claim to be a holy or devout man."

"That's your affair, sir. I only mention the matter because it is one more thing that you and my niece have in common. That and your love of plants and horticulture."

"Dare I think, Madame Griffin, that you are suggesting I should propose to mademoiselle? I've been on the edge of doing so any number of times. But frankly, the lady gives me little encouragement. At least not the type a gentleman expects in such an affair." For the first time he seemed embarrassed.

"I know exactly what you mean. You mustn't feel it's any lack of affection on Sarah's part. In fact, monsieur, she cares deeply for you. But..." Nancy rose and stood with her back to the room. "There are elements of marriage that she doesn't understand, even fears. I have tried to enlighten her, but she won't listen. And I should tell you that neither my husband nor I would force the girl to marry you or anyone." She turned now and faced the man directly. "It is up to the prospective husband to convince her that her terrors are groundless, monsieur. I trust you take my meaning."

DuMars rose and bowed. "I understand everything you have said, madame. And I am deeply grateful for your trust. Moreover, I promise you I shall not abuse it." He left the room with great dignity. Despite this, and the serious nature of his last words, the Frenchman was smiling broadly.

"Well, the fat's in the fire now," Nancy muttered aloud, sinking to the couch and kicking off her elegant satin slippers. "I only hope the old boy's got some of that famous French expertise one hears about."

"Often you have promised to show me the rest of the estate, Mademoiselle Sarah. It's such a beautiful afternoon, could we not take a little walk in the woods?"

"Oh, that sounds lovely," the girl agreed with enthusiasm. "There's a stand of wild violets up near a cabin we used to use as children. They should be in bloom now, and I could take you there. But won't you be wanting to see Uncle Roger this afternoon?"

"Ah, mademoiselle, I must confess to you that I'm a weak man. On such a day I simply refuse to put business before pleasure. Come, let us leave immediately before anyone even sees us go."

One of the nicest things about Gaston DuMars, Sarah had decided weeks ago, was that he didn't need to be chattering all the time. He was as content as she simply to walk and observe and listen. They made their way in leisurely, companionable silence along the deep carpet of pine needles that covered the woodland path. It was almost fifteen minutes later, after the pines had melted into the oaks and elms of this part of the forest, that she wordlessly parted a screen of leaves and pointed to the clusters of velvet purple flowers at their feet.

"Exquisite," DuMars said appreciatively. "And how wise of you to leave them here and not force them to live in your garden."

"I don't think one can force nature," Sarah replied. "It never works. See, here they live in glory and peace." She knelt to inhale the sweet aroma of the blossoms, and DuMars knelt beside her.

"Exquisite," he repeated. "May I gather just a few for you?" The girl nodded, and he carefully picked a handful of the violets, stood, and drew her up beside him. "Now, I think they will be happy to be just here." Before she knew what he intended he lodged the tiny nosegay in the bodice of her dress to nestle between her breasts.

It all happened so quickly and was so unexpected. Sarah turned away in confusion. She could feel her cheeks reddening, and that made her angry with him and with herself. "Would you like to see the cabin I told you about?" she asked quickly to cover her awkwardness.

"Very much."

They resumed their walk in silence, and a few moments later she was showing him into the primitive little structure she'd not visited since the night they had hidden here from the sheriff's men.

Sarah never expected the place to upset her, but suddenly she found herself trembling. It was almost as if she could see Antony Sheldon standing just over there as he had the very first day she saw him. And her mother, so calm and protective and unwilling to allow anything or anyone to threaten her children. Now, less than ten years later, they were both dead. And Papa too. Violent, wicked deaths....Laura had been there near the window that first time they had met Lord Sheldon. Now Laura was locked away doing penance for a crime she'd not committed. Andrew was gone too, driven from his native country by his beliefs....

"My dear Sarah..." DuMars put his arm around her quickly. "What is it? You're shaking. What's the matter?"

"I'm sorry. It's this place. I never thought it would affect me so. But Mama was here with us so often, and Lord Sheldon..."

"Come." He didn't wait for any further explanation but led her outside. "We will sit here in the fresh air and sunshine until you are feeling better." He spread his jacket and gently forced her to the ground. "Now, *chérie,* you do not have to say anything at all, but if you wish to speak, if it is some comfort for you, I will listen."

For a while she said nothing. Then, slowly at first but with increasing speed, as if a dam had been broken, she told him the whole story. Beginning not with the cabin but with that long-ago gray day in a Yorkshire November when the justice of the peace had demanded they swear an oath they could not swear. The years of running and hiding, the comparative peace of Tassels that was shattered first by the murder of Antony Sheldon and then by the terrible scene at Tyburn. A great, cathartic outpouring that left her weak and pale but enormously relieved.

Gaston was holding her hand, stroking the hair back from her forehead. "So, dear little Sarah," he said, "you have decided to trust no one, to love no one. Is that how you think to bear your pain?"

"No, that's not true. I love my family, my brothers, my sister, Aunt Nancy and Uncle Roger..."

"Shh." He pressed a finger over her lips. "You know that's not what I mean. You care for all of them with the affection of a child. But you will not allow yourself to care for a man with the affection of a woman."

"Why do you say that?"

"Because it's true. Do I not know how you rebuff me, do

not allow me to speak the things in my heart? My dear Sarah, you know I wish to marry you. You have known it for some time."

"You must not say such things! I won't have it! I don't intend to marry anyone, ever. If you'd asked, I'd have told you that long ago." She sat up abruptly and started to move away, but DuMars firmly pulled her back beside him.

"You are talking nonsense, *ma petite*. But it is enough. Enough fear and enough words." Swiftly he smothered her reply with a long deep kiss.

At first Sarah struggled. She was a lean, strong girl. Years of working out of doors had made her tanned and well muscled. This impertinent Frenchman would find she was no shrinking maiden who capitulated to him just because he wore breeches! Her nails clawed his face, and when that had no effect she pummeled his chest with her fists.

It was to remove that target from her reach that DuMars stretched himself full-length over her writhing form. He did not intend to rape the girl. He loved her; it was no part of his plan to do violence to either her body or her senses, only to break through the defenses she'd erected. If Sarah had struggled but a moment longer he'd have withdrawn and apologized. Instead she grew suddenly still beneath him. Then, as he kissed her a second time, he felt her arms steal around his neck and her lips part beneath his.

The warmth crept up from her toes to engulf her. Sarah had never experienced anything remotely like it. Without warning she found the sensation Gaston was producing in her body both overwhelming and totally delightful. Perhaps it was because the whole thing followed so closely on the terrible upset of the visit to the cabin and her outpouring of talk. Even later, when she looked back on the events of the afternoon from a calm distance, she could never be sure of that. At the time the thing was happening she didn't try to analyze it. It was as if her mind, her careful, controlled approach to life, had shut itself off and her physical being had taken over.

She heard a long sigh and realized it had come from her. The violets that Gaston had tucked in her bosom were being crushed beneath his weight, giving off a heady scent that seemed to envelop her. The pressure of his body against hers was wonderful. It was comforting in a way she'd not felt comfort since she was a small child. Sarah arched herself to drink yet more deeply of that wondrous solace of touch.

"Chérie..." she heard him whisper. Then he spoke her name, and she recognized the question in his low voice. For reply she pressed herself yet closer to him. What she wanted most of all, more than anything in the world, she realized with astonishment, was to be naked. To feel this marvelous, healing balm of touch on her bare flesh. When he started to loosen the ties of her bodice she offered no resistance.

By the time her nude body lay beneath his, she had ceased to think at all. There was only the feel of the soft velvet jacket beneath her back and buttocks, the tickling of some ferns where her bare legs extended beyond the fabric. A thrush trilled overhead, and the scents of the woodland mingled with that of the violets. Instinctively she spread her legs to welcome her lover, and the momentary pain when he plunged himself inside her was but an instant's counterpoint in the symphony of feeling. Close, so close. Touching her everywhere, warming her, covering her, possessing her. Sarah yielded the essence of herself with joy.

It was almost dusk, and the air had grown chill. Gaston placed his jacket over the thin fabric of her frock before they started back to the house. They had lain together in silence for a long time. Now everything was understood between them with no need for words. He said simply, "I shall ask your uncle's permission to marry you as soon as it can be arranged. Then we will go home to France together. I feel certain he will agree."

Sarah only nodded and placed her hand in his. Together they walked away from the cabin. Behind them the crushed and scattered violets lay forgotten on the ground.

8.

Nancy had her heart set on a lovely big wedding at Tassels, but it wasn't possible. Both Gaston and Sarah wanted a Catholic ceremony, and that was much easier to arrange in France than in England.

"Would you permit, *mon capitaine,* that Mademoiselle Sarah travel with me to France before we are wed?" Gaston asked with grave seriousness. "I assure you I shall guard the lady with my life, and marry her the moment we are on French soil."

"I see no reason why not," Roger said. The man's dignity and propriety rather amused him. "I'm sure Sarah's honor won't be irrevocably compromised by such a brief trip." And later, to Nancy, "I almost told him how I'd carted you the length of England before we were married, but somehow he doesn't seem the type to see the humor of it."

"Oh," she said absently, studying her face in the dressing-room mirror and trying her hair in a new fashion, "I don't think he's quite as priggish as you imagine. A different sort altogether in private, I suspect."

"Hmm...as usual you seem to know something I don't. Anyway, he and Sarah should be good for each other. She seems quite content with the arrangement. Frankly, I never thought she'd agree to marry him."

"Yes, well, that just shows how little you men know of women." She turned to him with a broad grin. "Anyway, it's all settled. No big celebrations here, though, more's the pity. I was quite looking forward to it."

Nancy was not to be denied all the fun of the wedding, however. At her suggestion the whole family accompanied the engaged couple as far as Dover when, at the end of June, Sarah and Gaston departed for France. At first Roger didn't think the trip wise. It was still technically illegal for a known recusant such as Sarah to leave the country. A large group would attract more attention than two people alone. But the hysteria that had gripped England for eighteen months was fast dying. Just this month a number of "plot" suspects had been quietly released from prison for lack of evidence. These days Oates was far enough discredited so that judges demanded more than just his word about someone's guilt. Parliament had even drastically reduced the fellow's life pension, though he still had his Whitehall apartment.

"Of course," Roger explained to Nancy, "it's the anti-James forces in court that keep the thing alive still. They're the real plotters."

She displayed the knowledge of politics she had acquired in London. "With Charles making that public declaration that he never married Monmouth's mother, a lot of wind's gone out of their sails. Without a legitimate Monmouth, who can they offer as heir in James's place?"

"I don't know. What does Nell say? She's always been a supporter of the bastard duke."

"Yes, she has. I don't think she's really such an anti-papist as she pretends. I think she just doesn't like James. It's a subject we agreed a long time ago not to talk about. We'd only quarrel. I suspect the hope is still for Charles to divorce Catherine, marry a Protestant, and produce an heir."

"That idea's been around for a long time. He'll never agree to it."

"No, you're right. Even Nell says so. She knows the king better than anyone, and she confided to me that she's convinced he'll never divorce Catherine."

"Stalemate," Roger said quietly. "For the moment, at least."

So the two factions seemed to have fought themselves to a draw, and tensions eased enough for Roger to agree to the celebration trek to Dover.

They set out in three coaches, each with a great pile of trunks and hampers strapped to its roof. "What the hell is all this stuff?" Griffin demanded on the morning of the departure. He'd arrived from town late the previous night, and this was the first he'd seen of preparations for the journey. "Are we all moving to France?"

"Don't be silly. It's Sarah's dowry. You didn't expect me to let her go to a foreign country empty-handed, did you? She'll need proper English linen and woolens and crockery and..."

"My dear girl, you can take my word for it, France is a civilized place, not a wilderness. You act as if she's headed for the American colonies!"

Nancy only snorted in derision at the notion that any place could rival England, and Roger chuckled. He'd never admit it, but secretly he was pleased and touched at the care Nancy took of his niece. It was a Griffinlike thing to do, this loyalty to the memory of Mark and Clare and willingness to be surrogate mother to their children. He was proud of his wife.

Sometimes, late at night, he thought about his own lapses in that old tradition. First there had been his early unwillingness to stand by his brother when the whole mess began. He'd become more and more ashamed of that as the years went by, particularly after he'd seen the awe-inspiring display of steadfast loyalty to belief Mark had displayed. But it was too late to change any of that. The other thing that tormented him in the dark hours was more immediate. Rachel and the child—his unacknowledged, unseen son. No matter how much he thought about that tortuous maze of conflicting obligations, no solution better than the one he'd adopted presented itself. Eventually, he could only roll over and try to sleep.

On the trip east to Dover he had no time for such musings. All three children were in the coach with him—Nancy rode with Sarah in the second and Charles and Gaston in the third—and they kept him fully occupied. The opportunity to spend so much time alone with Nell, Jennifer, and Jamie was a rare treat. By the time they reached Dover, however, the youngsters had begun squabbling among themselves and his patience was wearing thin. He was delighted to see the harbor spread out before them in the early-summer sun.

DuMars had booked places on a packet leaving the following day, so they took rooms at an inn near the quay. Roger immediately had a long consultation with the landlord to arrange a properly festive supper.

Nancy had brought a nursemaid from home, and she was instructed to take the children on a long walk, to let them rid themselves of some of the cooped-up energy. "See they have plenty of fresh air and exercise," she told the girl. "I want a peaceful evening."

"It will indeed be a peaceful evening," Roger said firmly. He'd played indulgent papa long enough; he intended to brook no further nonsense from the three. "Now, DuMars," he said, turning to the Frenchman, "if you can tear yourself away from your bride for an hour or two, I'd be glad of a private word with you." The two men retired to the taproom, and Nancy was left alone with Charles and Sarah.

"I wish Gaston had told us more of his home," she said wistfully. "I'd feel better if I knew you had everything you need with you."

"I'm sure it's fine," Sarah said; she was by far the calmest member of the party. "Mostly we've talked about the gardens. There are acres and acres of grapevines, of course, but a big park too. Gaston says they don't do as much with herbs and flowers as we do in England. That's why I've brought so much seed with me."

"What else?" Charles commented. "Trust you to think of that."

He seemed to Nancy a bit moody and depressed. Doubtless it was sad for Charles to be the last of the elder Griffin children left at home. No time to deal with that now. She returned to domestic discussion with Sarah. Just before they were due to join the two men downstairs, she said, "I guess you'll be able to visit Laura and Sophia, won't you? When you're living in France, I mean."

"Yes. Gaston's house is some hundred miles away from their abbey, but he has promised I may make the journey."

"You'll give them my love," Nancy said wistfully. "Especially Laura."

"Of course." Sarah's tone was emotionless, but Nancy knew she understood.

The three little ones returned from their excursion not much subdued, but a look from their father told them the time for cavorting was past. They behaved well for the rest of the evening. The meal proved every bit as gay as Nancy could have hoped.

By next morning, when they saw the couple board the small packet bound for Calais, the happy mood in which they'd set out returned. They waited until the ship had hoisted anchor and set sail before starting on the long trek back to Surrey. Nancy arranged things so that for the first part of the journey she was alone with Roger. "Did you have a good talk with Gaston?" she asked as soon as they were underway.

"Yes. Very good. The first shipment of claret will arrive this autumn."

"Claret!"

"Of course, claret. That's what I'm buying from the man, isn't it?"

"Buying...Roger Griffin, you're horrid! Here you are in a last conversation with the man who's marrying your niece and ward and you talk about business."

"What did you expect me to say? I don't think DuMars needs me to instruct him in his conjugal duties."

"Oh, I suppose not. Still..." She stared petulantly out the window and didn't speak again for almost an hour. Then, quite abruptly, "What are your plans for Charles?"

They'd been married for eleven years, and he was used to her mercurial changes of mood. "I've been thinking about it. It seems to me there's a place for him in the business. I think he's got a good steady head for that sort of thing."

"Yes, I've thought that too. And with Benjamin so determined to leave for the colonies, Charles will be a real asset to you. Are you going to talk to him about it soon? I think he's feeling a bit left out of things with the other birds flown the nest."

"Yes, soon." It was Roger's turn to retreat into morose silence. The mention of Ahmet stirred up all his other, secret, concerns.

"Penn thinks the king's getting ready to grant him the tract he wants," Benjamin said, watching Roger's reactions closely. "As I've told you, it's to be in repayment of a debt Charles owes the family. Penn wants to call the place Sylvania."

They were quenching a midsummer thirst in the Boar's Head tavern. Griffin looked around him at the comfortable old hostelry and said softly, "I'll never understand how you can leave all this for that wilderness."

Ahmet shrugged. "In my blood, perhaps. Leaving, wandering...the Jewish curse. I take it, then, you won't reconsider, come with me?"

"No."

"I thought not. Roger, it's time I speak to Rachel. I want to go to Amsterdam this week. I'll not do it without your agreement."

"I agreed to that a long time ago."

"Very well, then it's settled. You can manage without me for about a fortnight?"

"I'll soon have to manage without you permanently," Roger said sadly. "It'll be good practice."

"You'll do fine." Benjamin smiled. "I don't have any worries about Griffin's Importations. There is one thing, though...."

"What?"

"I'm sorry, I know this is painful. Look, I think it best if I don't tell Rachel that you know about the boy. I'll just tell her that I learned of his existence through my own sources. She won't question that."

"No." Roger's voice was barely audible. "I expect she won't. And will you tell her you know the identity of the child's father?"

"Not directly. She may guess, but I won't mention it. It'll only lead to discussions I think it best not to have."

"As you wish," Roger answered. "I seem to have forfeited any rights in this matter."

Unexpected business delayed Ahmet's departure for Amsterdam a few weeks. By the time he returned it was the end of August. He'd been gone a little longer than the fortnight he'd originally scheduled for the trip, and this made Roger anxious. He was so terribly hungry for news about Rachel and the child, so afraid that it wouldn't be good news. The morning that Benjamin finally returned and walked into George Alley, Roger only had to look at him to know there was trouble.

"Sit down," he said. He rose immediately, shut the door of his office, and poured a glass of brandy for his friend. "Here, drink this. You look awful."

"Had the bad luck of a very choppy crossing, and a ghastly trip from Dover." Ahmet motioned out to the street, where rain was sluicing down in a flood. "The road was nothing but mud."

"Not surprising; it's been going on like this for the past week. Was the weather in Amsterdam any better?"

"A bit. By comparison at least. Cool and gray, but dry."

Roger couldn't tolerate the small talk any longer. "Rachel..." he said with all his questions in the single word.

"She and the child are both well. He's a fine healthy lad, and Rachel seems to have made a tolerable life for both of hem. Naturally she was terribly shocked to see me at first.

449

Said she'd always considered the possibility but thought I'd write and give her some warning."

"You say 'at first.' How did she react after she'd had some time to adjust?"

Benjamin smiled for the first time. "Like herself. All sweet calm and reason."

"Then...I mean, why..."

"Why do I look like this?" Ahmet stretched and walked to the window. The glass ran with rain, nothing else could be seen. "We can't keep much from each other, can we, my friend?" he said softly. "You may as well know now as later. Rachel won't come with me to America."

"Won't...but that's insane! What does she want to do?" Even while he spoke the words a secret place in his heart was rejoicing. She'd not be going thousands of miles away from him after all.

"My aunt and uncle, the couple with whom she's living, are very old. She feels now that it's her duty to remain with them and 'comfort their old age,' as she put it."

"It's like her."

"Yes, it is. But for the life of me I can't fathom what kind of future she envisions for the boy."

"You didn't tell her..."

"Any of the things we agreed I shouldn't tell her? No, I didn't. Neither that I knew you to be the father of her son nor your own awareness of the situation. Nothing I'd have said could have changed her mind, so all the former arguments against telling seemed valid."

"Benjamin..." Roger hesitated, not wanting to sound as if he were pressuring the other man. "What about you? Are you still determined to go?"

"I've been thinking about that for a week. I just made up my mind this morning. Yes, I will go. As soon as Penn gives the word. You see..." He turned to face Roger. "It seems to me that with you here Rachel has a backup protection that's real even though she's unaware of it. I see nothing to be gained by staying in England."

The wholehearted friendship and trust in those words made Roger feel very humbled.

450

9.

Despite having learned to ride at rather a late date, Nancy had become a passable horsewoman. She was no longer afraid to mount even the frisky hunters stabled in the mews behind the sycamore trees. Early on the morning of June 20, 1681, she had Rudy saddle the big chestnut called Eleanor's Glory, a thoroughbred Arabian out of Dame Eleanor and Tom's Glory Boy, and set out to ride.

"Anyplace special ye be goin', ma'am?" Rudy asked with some concern in his voice. "Ellie's been mighty cantankerous of late."

"No, no place special. I just want to ride. Don't worry, Rudy." She looked fondly at the man. He was devoted to her, and she appreciated it. "We'll be fine. Won't we, girl?" she added, patting the creature's silky mane and accepting a leg-up into the saddle. "You know," she said and turned to the stable man with a smile, "Captain Griffin has a sister who used to ride all over Yorkshire full astride, like a man."

"No! You're not thinkin' of tryin' that, ma'am!"

"Of course not." She wasn't feeling particularly gay, but the incredulous horror in his face did make her laugh. "I'd look pretty silly doing that in this skirt, don't you think? She used to wear breeches." With this astounding statement she rode off, leaving a shocked Rudy staring after her.

The chuckle Nancy got out of that was the first one she'd enjoyed in many weeks. Lately she'd been blue and despondent without really knowing why. Today she at least had an identifiable reason for her sadness. It was just one year exactly since she'd bid goodbye to Sarah at the Dover harborside. She'd not have believed then how deeply she would miss the girl.

This year Charles had gone to live in London and work in Griffin's Importations. He had rooms in High Holborn Street and even a couple of servants of his own. At twenty-one Charles had become quite the young man about town. Roger said, however, that he never let pleasure interfere with business. The lad had become invaluable to him now that Ahmet was gone.

They'd had a letter from Benjamin just a fortnight past. He was very enthusiastic about the prospects in the new colony, and seemed to be thoroughly enjoying himself. Everyone seemed to be enjoying themselves but her, Nancy thought as she urged the horse down the wooded path leading to the tenants' valley. Andrew's letters from Italy were every bit as cheerful and hopeful as Benjamin's.

"Why is it, Ellie," she questioned the horse, "that I feel like an old has-been that's been put out to pasture?" The animal neighed a friendly response, but it wasn't much comfort.

"At least you're not a bit cantankerous, whatever Rudy said," she told Ellie softly. "You and I know our place, don't we, girl? Just get on about our business and do what we're told. Bloody boring, isn't it?" After that she didn't chatter to the horse, just rode on in silence. When they reached the pine ridge overlooking the valley, she reined in and looked down.

Once one was actually in the deep depression between the wooded hills, each of the cottages had a good deal of privacy from gardens and hedgerows; from this vantage point they could all be seen, like little pastel squares on a green patchwork quilt. The five families who lived in the tenant houses were unchanged from the day the Griffins had acquired the land. One or two old men had died and been replaced by their sons, that was all. At the far end of the valley, halfway up a gentle hill, there was a new house built just this past year. The estate manager they'd hired six months previously, a fellow called Matthew Chalmers, lived there with his wife and seven children.

Nancy had been reluctant to hire a new man. Irrational though she knew it to be, she couldn't help feeling it was a violation of Mark's memory. But with both the boys and Sarah gone she'd had to allow Roger to persuade her of the need. She'd come to like Chalmers well enough, and she found him competent, but she had nothing like the close involvement with him, and thus the estate, she'd had with Mark back in the days when they'd hewed a paying proposition from a derelict wilderness.

The one thing she'd refused to do, however, was install Chalmers and his family in Tupenny Cottage. Roger had agreed with her, and they'd built the man his own place at the other end of the valley. Today, in the pastoral scene below, Tupenny Cottage could barely be seen. "Gently, girl," Nancy said, starting the horse down the steep, rocky incline. "Let's go have a visit."

On that terrible day two years ago the sheriff and his men had done their job of destruction with evil thoroughness. It had been sheer malice, of course. There was no need for them to break the windows and hack down the walls of the cottage in their search for "evidence," but they'd done it nonetheless.

At first it hadn't occurred to Nancy to repair the damage. She'd had too many other things on her mind. Besides, with the children living at Tassels there'd been no need. When she finally thought about it, it had seemed superfluous. The ruins had become overgrown with ivy and ferns, and there were wild roses clambering over the rubble. Tupenny Cottage had become a verdant outcropping in its secluded corner of the landscape. It seemed to Nancy a fitting memorial for Mark and Clare, and she left it as it was.

"Whoa..." She reined in and dismounted. The scent of honeysuckle filled the air and bees flitted busily from one blossom to the next. A great fat toad, sunning himself on a rock, didn't even open an eye when Nancy walked by. An indignant blackbird scolded her. Who was she to intrude in this place? Nancy took a crust of bread from her pocket and dropped it on the grass as a peace offering. "Here, Mama Bird, take this home to your nestlings. Hurry, soon they'll fly away...."

And that was the thing hardest to bear about the passage of time. It seemed to her that for every day that went by, someone needed her less. Oh, Nell and Jennifer and Jamie still depended on her. They were only ten, nine, and eight, after all. But how quickly they'd be grown and gone! Just as Clare's children were.

She could remember them on the day they'd first come to Tassels. She'd been alone in the front room of the tumbledown old cottage the house had been, and the four of them had been but children.

They'd grown together in this place. She and they, each

developing into changed people. Now they were all gone and she was left. It wasn't hard to imagine the time when her own three would be gone too. Soon, sooner than she thought she could bear.

If only she'd had more children. Roger would have liked that too. But after the difficult time she'd had with Jamie she'd simply never conceived again. "I'd give anything," she whispered, "for at least one more." One more little face to look trustingly to her for all its wants. One more child to stave off the inevitable moment when she would be alone.

It was nearly noon when she started back to the house. Perhaps it was because she had stayed away longer than she intended, or maybe it was only her melancholy mood demanding something, anything, to dispel the gloom. Without really thinking about it, she let the horse break into first a brisk trot, and soon a gallop. Before many minutes had passed they were flying over the open field. Nancy knew the old stone fences were there. She'd been over this ground a hundred times. Always before she'd taken the jumps with care and caution. Today she didn't give them a thought.

Ellie knew they were there too. She dashed toward them with positive relish and took the first two without a moment's break in her stride. "C'mon, girl!" Nancy shouted into the wind of their swift progress. "C'mon. Show me what you can do!" The horse gathered all her strength for the final and highest hurdle. Nancy could feel the animal's muscles rippling with the effort. Suddenly a pheasant darted from cover and dashed directly across their path. Ellie neighed loudly in startled anger. All sixteen hands of her great height reared back on her hind legs. Nancy was thrown before she had a chance to know what had happened. She lay very still beneath the hot midday sun.

Noon in the Abbey of St. Savior. The tolling bell sent its message over the countryside; it was the time of the Angelus... "The angel of the Lord declared unto Mary...Behold the handmaid of the Lord, be it done unto me according to thy word..."

The summons to pause and remember rolled over the sunlit somnolent countryside. Not many heard, fewer responded. One farmer leaned a moment on his hoe and crossed himself piously, another snorted in derision. Somewhere a woman paused before putting her bread in the oven. She held the long wooden paddle with its burden of loaves in midair while she closed her eyes and soundlessly moved her lips.

In the silent abbey the nuns were scrubbing, washing, cooking, mending—doing the work of daily life. But they all heard, and each one paused and remembered that God became man that man might become more like God. Each whispered *Ave* was offered not for the speaker alone, but for the thousands upon thousands outside the walls who could not or would not pray.

One nun had finished her morning's chores. She knelt alone in the whitewashed chapel, the high wooden sides of her choir stall almost hiding her from view. Her Angelus mingled with the great stream of prayer in which she was immersed. The inexplicable sense of "presence" in which she found herself was beyond her ability to understand, but she had learned to yield to it, to mingle the essence of herself with the otherness of the One loved and loving.

"Sister Benedict." A voice intruded upon her contemplation, and the woman opened her eyes. "I have something to tell you."

"Yes?" Benedict of the Cross, once Sophia Griffin, looked at the other nun and waited. She had been visited thus in the chapel many times. It came as no surprise.

"You must get a message to your brother."

"My brother? Why? Is something wrong?"

"Not yet. Later, perhaps...never mind. Just do as I say. Tell him the boy mustn't be sent to America. At least not yet."

"What boy?"

"Your brother's son."

"Roger's son? James? He's only eight years old. Why should they send him to America? I don't understand."

"Not James. The other one."

Sophia stared. "But there isn't another one. There's only James. I don't understand," she repeated.

"Of course you don't, not now. But you will. All things are arranged, little sister. There are no accidents, no mistakes."

"America." Sophia repeated the word as if the idea had just penetrated her consciousness. "So far away, a heathen, alien land..."

455

The other nun, the one who had never changed since the first day Sophia saw her in the west wing of Harwood Hall, smiled. "It will not always be so. Particularly not for the Griffins. America promises much for your family. But not now, not for some years. You must see to it. The boy mustn't be sent to America."

"But how can you expect me to do anything about that? I don't even know what child you mean."

The old woman smiled. "You still ask so many questions? Even after all these years?"

"Well..." Sophia smiled too. "You are rather puzzling, you know. Like a conjurer's trick, now I see you, now I don't."

"But you see me now."

"Naturally. But no one else would. If any of my sisters came here now they'd say, 'Poor Benedict, her mind's going. Caught her talking to herself in the chapel.'"

The Kirkslee nun laughed. The tinkling sound, like herself, was unchanged by time. "It doesn't matter. They won't see you."

"No, I know that. Is that all you've come to tell me?"

"Yes, but it's very important. You will do as I say?"

"Of course. If I can find a way."

"You will."

The Kirkslee nun was gone. Sophia returned to her prayer, but the sense of presence was gone. All was dry and mechanical now. It didn't matter. "Behold the handmaid of the Lord; be it done unto me according to thy word..."

That same day Amsterdam whispered death. Oh, not all of it. Not the whole city. Just odd corners here or there, mostly in the oldest quarter of town, the center which had once been the heart of the medieval settlement. Here the canals were so narrow one could almost reach across and touch the opposite bank. The ancient houses overhung the waterways so that no sunlight ever reached them. It was from those fetid streams that the faint warning rose. Not a real clamor, at least not yet. But a portent of tragedy for anyone sensitive to such things.

It was along the embankment of just such a place that Rachel walked this dull-gray afternoon. She was headed for home, her arms laden with fresh vegetables and fruits purchased at the market nearby, and she smelled fear without immediately understanding its cause. In this innermost section of the city where her aunt and uncle had their small but comfortable house, the populace were almost all Jews. Few outsiders, *goyim,* came here. Suddenly Rachel saw a party of officials leave one house in obvious haste. Swiftly they slammed the door behind them, and all but one hurried away. The man they'd left behind spent a moment painting a black cross on the door before he ran after his companions.

Smallpox! Rachel stared at the dreaded warning on the door, then, drawing her skirts as close to her as she could, hastened on. Once home she said nothing; there was little point in alarming the old people. But right after lunch she sat down to compose a letter to her cousin Rose.

Antony Jacob was to be sent on the first leg of a long and difficult journey. His mother couldn't possibly know that it was to take him halfway around the world, involve him in events and decisions no one yet dreamed possible. The little child who giggled and played while his mother prepared to send him to her cousin Rose for a visit would have a role in shaping that new world so far away.

They never knew how long Nancy had lain there before Rudy finally discovered her. It had been one o'clock when he gave in to his feeling of nagging unease and set out to look for his mistress. He'd found her almost immediately after that. The great horse had been standing nearby, chewing an occasional mouthful of grass, waiting patiently for Nancy to get up and mount. "If only I'd stopped her takin' the bugger," Rudy exclaimed over and over. "I knowed Ellie was in a funny mood. I should've stopped her."

"Don't blame yourself," Roger insisted. "I'm sure there was little you could have done to change the mistress's mind."

He had plenty of guilts of his own to deal with in the weeks he kept vigil beside his wife's bed. She was delirious much of the time, moaning and whimpering, sometimes speaking whole sentences with seeming lucidity. All her fear and loneliness and worry poured out as it never would have were she conscious. Roger became painfully aware of how badly he'd failed her.

"If only I'd realized," he told himself repeatedly. "Involved her more in my own life and plans...." The only thing he could think of to do now was sit beside her. He left the office and all its concerns to young Charles and stayed at Tassels. They had nurses, of course, hired from the village and vetted by Ellen Wadden, who knew them all. Capable enough women, but none filled him with much confidence.

Roger had considered sending for Sarah, but she was expecting her first child any day now. It was unthinkable for her to undertake the journey from France in such a condition. So he contented himself with keeping an eagle eye on the ministrations of the hired nurses and doing as much as possible for Nancy with his own hands.

Dr. Winters he'd summoned the very first day. Mercifully the man hadn't gone to America with Penn. He came as frequently as he could, but he patiently explained that time was the only real healer in such cases. "We can only wait. When and if the fever breaks and Mistress Nancy comes to herself, we'll have cause to hope. She's still young and strong. The broken bones will knit if she can only be rid of the fever."

Then, one morning when Roger returned to the bedside after snatching a few hours sleep in his study, he looked into Nancy's face and saw that she recognized him. She was as pale as death. The once-glorious auburn hair hung in lank strands to her shoulders. But her brown eyes were clear for the first time in almost two months. As if to confirm his joy, she managed a weak smile and fluttered her hand, so thin it was almost transparent, where it lay on the coverlet.

"Darling..." He couldn't find anything else to say. The hand fluttered once more, and he reached for it gently. Yes, there was no mistake about it, she responded to his touch with an answering pressure. Barely perceptible, but real.

The letter from Benjamin arrived that same day.

10.

"It is with much grief," Ahmet wrote, "that I must tell you terrible news. Word reached me here just yesterday. My sister Rachel died a few weeks back. There was an outbreak of smallpox in my uncle's part of Amsterdam, and he and his wife both contracted the disease. Rachel sent her son to other cousins and remained to nurse the old people. They died a few days later and she a fortnight after them. The boy is safe with the relatives I mentioned. It is they who informed me of these sad events."

Rachel dead... he could hardly believe it. Shock came before grief. This on top of the long vigil he'd just kept beside Nancy. Roger walked slowly out to the garden carrying the letter he'd not yet finished reading. The sun was shining, flowers bloomed in all the well-tended gardens of Tassels. Behind him the elegant facade of the house conveyed a sense of permanence and position. Roger turned to look back at it, proud and beautiful and seeming set for all time to remain exactly as it was. The illusion of immortality. He walked slowly away from that promise he knew to be empty.

In the orchard, amid the gnarled old trees and the young saplings growing side by side, he sat for a long time trying to come to terms with the turmoil of emotions the news caused. Rachel was dead, and whatever debt he'd owed her was now canceled. He need never again worry about her, nor mourn for the havoc he'd wrought in her life. Neither would he ever again be tempted to compare the differing love he felt for her and for his wife. And this, he was honest enough to admit, was a profound relief.

But what of justice, virtue, honor? Was there no payment due Rachel? No amends yet to be made? Until today he'd always thought of the whole dilemma as one not solved, only held in abeyance for the moment of reckoning and retribution. And now this. The problem swept away, expunged from the slate, as if it had never happened. It seemed monstrous to be thus delivered from one's own destiny.

Sighing, he made himself read the rest of the letter. After a little more discussion of Rachel and the circumstances of her death, Ahmet went on to say, "There remains, of course, the question of young Antony. My cousins have offered to keep him and raise him themselves in Holland, or to arrange that the child be brought to me here in America. Of those two proposals I'd choose the latter, but I do not feel I can make such a choice without consulting you."

So there it was. The problem wasn't solved as he'd first thought. That short-sighted reaction had come about because whenever he thought about this whole business he thought of Rachel. It was she who was real to him; her situation that he'd most worried about. But that was stupid. As Ahmet had pointed out when Roger first told him of the situation, the child was the only innocent victim of circumstances in the entire affair.

Roger stared at the paper in his hand. Benjamin had spelled out only two alternative futures for the boy; he could be left in Amsterdam or sent to America. But there was a third possibility implicit in the letter. Roger could acknowledge the child as his, and bring him to England to be raised as his son.

He looked up toward the house. The top floor could be seen through the trees. In that room to the left, his wife lay, just barely pulled back from the precipice of death. He did not yet know if she would ever again be wholly well and herself. Now he was being asked to burden her with the secret he'd kept hidden all this time. How old was the boy now...just over two and a half years. Could Nancy be expected to accept such a child into her life? Had he any right even to pose the question?

Roger could not make up his mind what course to take, so he did nothing. About a week after the yet-unanswered letter had arrived he decided Nancy seemed well enough for him to leave her and pay a quick visit to town.

"I'll be away only a couple of days," he said anxiously. "You're sure you don't mind."

"Of course not. You've been wonderful, darling. I'm sorry to be such a burden."

"Shh...none of that. Just get well, that's all that matters. I'll leave tomorrow morning and be back before you've had a chance to miss me." He smiled at her and touched her cheek. "Shall I bring a surprise from London? What would you like?"

"You. That's all." Nancy could sit up now. One of her legs had been badly broken in the fall. It was yet splinted and immobile, but apart from that she was making a rapid recovery. She leaned her head back on the pillows and answered her husband's smile with her own. "I'm so grateful, Roger."

"Grateful? For what?"

"For you...even for this"—she gestured at her own bruised body—"strange as it sounds. It's taught me a lot."

"Me too. Look, love," he leaned forward and took her hand. "There are things we must talk about as soon as you're well enough. Things you said while you were ill and delirious...and other things."

"Tell me."

"No, not yet. When I return. When there's more time."

He found things at George Alley in better control than he'd expected. Charles had acquitted himself well. "Everything's shipshape, Uncle Roger," the boy said with justifiable pride. "I've left a full report on your desk, more of a diary actually. I've been keeping it daily."

"An excellent idea," Roger said with enthusiasm. "Tell you what, if you've nothing pressing for me at the moment, I'll spend a couple of hours with your diary, then we can have lunch together somewhere. It'll give me a chance to ask you questions."

The folio was on his desk, a leather-bound volume filled with Charles's sloppy script, but readable. It catalogued the daily business of Griffin's Importations with absolute fidelity. A shipment of figs delivered on a Tuesday, the same shipment mentioned again four days later when it was delivered about town by the watermen. Painstaking detail, absolute accounting of every ha'penny. The kind of work one could never expect from a hired hand. If he'd needed convincing of Charles's suitability for business, this would have done it. Moreover, it dramatized those flesh-and-blood-bred loyalties that no amount of money could buy. Roger resolved while reading it to offer the lad a partnership before the end of the year. He deserved no less.

The third-from-last entry had been made in the book the day before yesterday. It concerned a consignment of Champagne from France. Charles noted the exact number of bottles, even their precise place of storage in the Wapping warehouse. He'd added another bit of information as well.

"The Benedictine monk, Dom Pérignon, accompanied the wine here from France. He says he's on business for his order. England first, then Spain. Called at George Alley and asked to see Captain Griffin. Informed him R.G. at Tassels and suggested he visit there if convenient."

"Did he not come," Charles asked later over the huge steak-and-kidney pudding they were sharing at the Devil and St. Dunstan tavern. "I rather thought he would."

"Can't say," Roger explained between mouthfuls. "He may have arrived at Tassels after I'd left to come here. Sorry to toss the old boy about so. Did he say why he wanted to see me? Any problems about the Champagne? Damned profitable line. I'd not like the imports interrupted."

"No, nothing like that. He didn't actually say, but I got the feeling it was a personal matter. As for tossing him about, console yourself. I gave the good monk a most excellent lunch at the Cardinal's Hat."

"Did you! All the way up in Lombard Street? I hope the fellow wasn't wearing his monastic robes when you carted him on that journey."

"No chance." Charles refilled both their glasses from the bottle of claret on the table. "He knows more about England than that. Came all done up like any ordinary French *bourgeois* off to see the world. Speaking of which..." He gestured toward the bottle. "This stuff's not a patch on what Gaston produces. We ought to send some of DuMars's claret for the landlord to try. I'll wager we could get the contract."

"I'll wager the same," Roger said, grinning. "See that you do it, Charles. Soon."

Three nights later, he returned to Tassels. Nancy was asleep. She looked better than when he'd left her. There was a hint of color in the cheeks illumined by the moon that shone through the window. He stood watching her for some minutes, then silently undressed and lay beside her. He didn't

462

intend to stay the night. He'd soon go and sleep in his temporary bed in the study, just as he had all the months she'd been ill. He only wanted to remain with her for a little while, take comfort from her regular breathing and the faint smile on her lips.

"Roger, is that you, love?"

"Yes. Sorry, I didn't mean to wake you."

"It's all right, I'm glad you did."

He leaned over to kiss her. She smelled of lavender and other flowers. "You've fixed your hair." He ran his fingers through the auburn tresses. They were silky and shining again, as they had always been before the accident.

"Mmm...Ellen helped me. We did it right here in the bed. I was especially glad of it when that man came. I'd have hated to shame you by looking like a kitchen maid."

"What man?" He was tired from the long journey home. There was only idle curiosity in the question.

"Oh, I forgot you couldn't know. A Frenchman. Said his name was Dom Something-or-other. I can't recall exactly, but I've written it down somewhere."

"Dom Pérignon?"

"Yes, that was it! How did you know?"

He explained about Charles's diary.

"Well, he did come," she went on. "Arrived just a few hours after you'd left and was very sorry to have missed you. I told him you'd be returning shortly and asked him to stay, but he wouldn't. Said he had to get to Bristol and after that Spain. Business of his order. Is he really a monk? He didn't look it."

"Yes, really. I gather he thought it safer not to announce the fact in England."

"Can't say I blame him."

"Did he say what he wanted with me?" Roger asked. "It must have been important for him to make a detour all the way down here."

"Well, he did, but I warn you, it's very strange." She propped herself on one elbow and looked at her husband. "He said he was asked to give you an urgent message from Sophia. He said she wants you to know the boy mustn't be sent to America. What does that mean? Have you any idea?"

Roger was silent for many minutes. Finally he rose, lit a candle, and returned to sit beside his wife's bed. "I've never really believed in Sophia's visions before now," he said softly. "But this just can't be explained any other way. It's a long and difficult story, my dearest. You won't like it. Are you strong enough?"

Nancy nodded, and he began speaking.

She listened through a curtain of differing emotions. Shock first, then incredulity followed by sorrow. And finally anger. She stormed at him, belabored him with his infidelity...the whole catalogue of responses women have made to such revelations from time immemorial. He remained silent while she spoke. Nothing she said was any worse than what he'd told himself since that long-ago night in Ingram's Court. He had explained in some detail about those circumstances, an attempt to convey his vulnerability. It was perhaps the bitterest truth of all for Nancy.

"What I can't forgive," she said, "what I can never forgive, is the thought of you with that foreign woman while I was here alone fighting to save the lives of our children."

She struggled to a sitting position in the bed. Automatically Roger tried to help her. Angrily she pushed him away. "Don't you touch me, Roger Griffin! Don't you ever touch me again. I know what you are now. It's taken me almost twelve years to learn, but I know." Her voice carried the conviction behind her words, the years onstage bearing fruit even now when she was being as honest as ever in her life.

"The way you were when I dragged you out of that tavern after York slapped your hands. A sniveling, self-pitying coward, that's what! All your talk of Griffin honor! It's just a screen to hide behind..." She was gasping for breath, the strain of emotion added to illness, but the words would not be stopped. Anger was a flood tide that would not be dammed. "Your 'honor' is intact as long as you get your own way. A little adversity and you fall apart. Get out of here. Go back to London, or go to hell for all I care. I don't want to see you again ever."

Exhausted, she fell back on the bed. There was nothing for him to do but leave.

It was from George Alley that he wrote to Benjamin a few days later. "How I wish you were here, old friend—your counsel is badly needed. One thing only is certain. I will acknowledge the boy as mine, give him my name and a legal claim to the legacy he's due. As to his immediate future, I just don't know. When I tell you that my sister, Sophia, the one who's a nun in France, has had a vision and says the lad must not be sent to America, you'll no doubt think me mad. But it's true, and so help me, Benjamin, I'm chilled at the idea of ignoring that warning.

"I will travel to Amsterdam this week and make whatever arrangements seem practical. If your relations there are agreeable to keeping the child, at least temporarily, I'll naturally arrange payment for his board and expenses...."

PART EIGHT

Shared Triumph

The long imprisonment, the fetid dungeon, the weary suspense, the tyrannous trial, the barbarous sentence, the savage execution...O my God, are they to have no reward?

—John Henry Newman,
The Second Spring

1.

In the purple and gold of early-summer twilight the Yorkshire dales are a spectacle to ravish the heart. Surely paradise must look something like this; perhaps the same delicate grayed colors flowing one into the other with the exquisite shimmering quality of a rainbow. On this evening the warm, moist air was alive with the song of a hundred different birds.

A man stood on the peak of one hill and surveyed the countryside with bitterness. Failure was a sour taste in his mouth. Spread before him was not only the magnificent workmanship of nature, but also the art of man, in its way almost as beautiful. Harwood Hall—proud, defiant of change, mellowed by centuries but never conquered. The great house and its lands filled the man's eyes. Once they were symbol of his triumph, today they mirrored his defeat.

His enemies would level many charges against John Lane; being a fool had never been one of them. Throughout the fourteen years of his tenure as master of Harwood he had resisted every attempt to trick him out of the Hall either by money or threat. In each case, he had known who was behind the scheme. The mere thought of that now was enough to increase his anger and his despair. Lane spat on the ground, as if to wash the unspoken name of Griffin from his mouth, and turned away. In the end it was not the Griffins who had defeated him, but the king they championed. Him and his Tory lackies.

Long ago Lane had thrown in his lot with the Whigs. Some months back a number of Whigs had been discovered in a plot to murder both Charles and James and place James's daughter Anne on the throne. Suddenly the world turned upside down for Lane and his ilk. Charles could at last tak revenge on those who had so long opposed him. Most important, he could decimate opposition to the succession of James.

Every known Whig in the realm was swiftly stripped of office, great fortunes were tumbled with a stroke of the king's pen. Lane's was among them. Now he was virtually bankrupt, no longer justice of the peace and magistrate, deeply in debt—the very real threat of prison was a whisper away.

The only thing left was Harwood. For the past week he had attempted to raise cash by mortgaging the house, but the stink of failure hung about him like a shroud. No one would lend him a farthing, not even with the great manor as collateral. At least not in Yorkshire. Lane decided to make one last attempt.

Dark crept over the dales. He'd best get moving. He called to the horse waiting patiently a few yards away, mounted, and set off on the long ride to London.

At the same moment that Lane set out on his journey, young Charles Griffin was totally occupied with a pair of lips as red as ripe plums yielding beneath his own.

"Ooh! Are you always in such a hurry, sir," the girl demanded, pulling back. Her fashionable frock made a sensuous rustling sound against the satin covering of the sofa as she moved away and gracefully adjusted her skirts and bodice.

"But, Marissa, I'm mad for you! Truly I am."

"Nonsense! You never laid eyes on me until this very evening."

"What has that to do with it?" Charles leaned forward and reached for her once more. "What does time matter in affairs of love?"

The girl laughed and twirled out of his reach in a flurry of ruffles and petticoats. "You're quite mad, sir. But you amuse me. You shan't have your way tonight. But you may call on me Wednesday at five." She smiled coquettishly as she left the room without waiting for a reply.

Charles sat back and exhaled a disappointed sigh. Then he grinned. Ah well, one couldn't always win. Might as well go back to the party. He made his way from the deserted morning room to the front of the house, where half a hundred guests were merrily, and noisily, disporting themselves.

Lord Michael's gatherings were famous throughout the city. Here in his magnificent house on the Strand he entertained an assortment of Londoners invited for their ability to be either decorative or amusing. Their very divergence of backgrounds contributed to the spice of the evenings. Charles found himself rubbing shoulders with dukes and earls, a few actors and actresses, and at least half a dozen men of business like himself.

The women were less easy to classify. They were all beauties, some few even had wit, but suddenly they didn't interest him. His failure with the lovely Marissa had soured him on feminine wiles for this night. Besides, it was too late to begin again the tedious business of conquest.

He helped himself to a glass of Champagne—a Griffin import, he noted with some satisfaction. Only Dom Pérignon produced Champagne of this fine pale color and quality, and only Griffin's brought Dom Pérignon's Champagne to England. Charles sipped his drink. Surveying the throng, he noticed one man he'd not before seen. A newcomer to these parties; that might prove interesting. He sidled toward the stranger. Could even be a Jew from the look of him. A very affluent and elegantly turned-out Jew. Trust Lord Michael to find such a person. "How do you do, sir," he said when he finally reached the man's elbow. "I don't believe we've met. My name is Charles Griffin."

"Hiram de Jonghe," the man said, bowing gracefully. The two strolled off in casual chatter.

Despite a lifetime in Yorkshire, John Lane was not ignorant of London ways. True, while Sir John Dewinters had been alive he'd been the one to handle the complicated affairs of both of them in this part of the world. Theirs had been an alliance not of trust or friendship, but of mutual greed. Still, it had worked well enough to create a tangled but profitable net of intrigue and dealing from one end of England to the other. But Dewinters was dead these two years past. A hunting accident with a backfiring gun was the official verdict. Lane, and many others, suspected retribution on the part of some person or persons unknown. Men like Dewinters and himself couldn't avoid making enemies. So be it. This time he'd have to arrange things himself.

He took lodgings at a modest inn near Trigg Stairs and set about his quest. The coffee houses were the place to start. That's where one could find those possessed of cash and ready to lend it if the terms were right. For two days he drank endless pints of the thick dark brew, watched, and listened. Finally he determined to approach one bewigged gentleman he was convinced was dealing in just the sort of transaction he had in mind.

"Harwood Hall, you say?" the fellow inquired after listening to the Yorkshire man for some minutes. "And you want to raise capital on it?" Lane nodded. The other eyed him shrewdly. "I think, sir, if the place is all you claim it to be, it should be easy for you to find such sums as you require closer to home." Lane said nothing. The stranger continued, "I wonder why you've come so far? That is to say, I don't really wonder, I know. You're a Whig, aren't you?" The man took a bejeweled snuffbox from his waistcoat pocket and spent some seconds inhaling two carefully measured pinches. Then, after a mighty and apparently satisfying sneeze, he spoke again. "Permit me to offer some advice, sir. Free of charge. There's no money in London for Whigs. It isn't a prudent investment these days to count on a Whig's ability to repay. Good day to you, sir."

Lane watched the man's retreating back and gripped his bowl of coffee with trembling hands. It was just then that a very odd-looking chap seated himself in the chair the other Londoner had vacated. "Forgive the interruption, sir." The old man's clothes were of foreign cut, his English was faintly accented, and he had an extraordinary white beard covering the lower half of his face. "I couldn't help overhearing. Perhaps I could be of assistance. My name is Menachim Cohan. I can sometimes arrange matters such as I believe you are concerned with."

A Jew. He should have guessed. So it had come to this— dealing with Jews. No help for it. "Then you're just the man I'm looking for," Lane answered with no attempt at subtlety. 'I need ten thousand pounds. Just temporary-like. Me name's John Lane, and I've me house and lands to offer for collat-ral."

"Yes, so I heard." Menachim stroked his beard. He didn't ike the look of this *goy*. Still, business was business. But not ilways, not every single time. Something was nagging at the ￼ack of his mind. Something he should try to remember. A ragment of conversation that had taken place years before. What did you say was the name of this house of yours?" he sked.

"I didn't. Not to you. It's Harwood Hall. Finest manor in

all Yorkshire. Worth ten times what I want to borrow. More, maybe."

"Harwood Hall...." Cohan sipped his bowl of coffee and watched the stranger over the rim. There was definitely something he should remember. "I tell you what," he said quietly. "Let me think about it, make some inquiries. Ten thousand pounds is a lot of money."

"If ye ain't got the cash what are yer botherin' me for?" Lane demanded with ill grace.

"Did I say I didn't have the cash?" Lane shook his head. "Then I suggest you learn some manners and a little patience, my friend. I will meet you here at this same time the day after tomorrow." The Jew walked slowly to the door and left the Yorkshireman by himself.

It was less than twenty-four hours later that another Jew lifted the brass knocker of the door of 22 High Holborn Street. It fell with a resounding thud, and very quickly a liveried manservant appeared. "Yes, sir?"

"This is the residence of Mr. Charles Griffin, is it not?"

"It is, sir."

"I wish to see Mr. Griffin. I'm a friend, Hiram de Jonghe. Please tell him I'm here."

"Very well, sir. If you'll just step inside...."

De Jonghe took the opportunity to examine what he could see of the rooms Griffin occupied. Nice. Very nice. Tastefully and expensively decorated, but nothing ostentatious. That fitted in with everything he'd learned in the ten days since he'd first made the young man's acquaintance. Landed gentry. The genuine article, Norman stock. Fell on hard times when he was a lad and his whole family became recusants. Hadn't kept them down for long, though. One brother, this lad's uncle apparently, had become a wealthy businessman. Now young Charles was a full partner in the firm. And earned a handsome few shillings, from the look of this place. The servant returned and interrupted his musings.

"Mr. Griffin will see you in a few moments, sir. Kindly follow me and wait in here."

The drawing room was small but even more impressive than what he'd seen so far. Hiram had an eye for furniture. That was a magnificent writing table over there in the corner. Inlaid mahogany. French, he'd wager. And there were three or four other pieces equally as good. Yes, his instincts had been sound. Charles Griffin was the contact he'd been watching and waiting for, the one who could assist him out of the narrow world of the Jewish community of London into the wider mainstream, where there was yet more money to be made. The gods had smiled on Hiram. They'd put him in the way of doing the lad a good turn at no cost to himself.

Half an hour later Charles Griffin bid his caller farewell. He pressed the older man's hand in gratitude and watched him walk away. Then Charles hurried off in the direction of George Alley. By the time he'd gone a quarter of the distance he broke into a run. Damn the curious onlookers of the crowded streets. The devil take the lot of them—this was worth running after.

2.

"It's the Hall, sir." He gasped for breath but didn't pause. "John Lane's in town trying to raise money on it."

Roger stared hard at him. "Harwood? You're sure?"

"Yes, dead sure. Hiram de Jonghe just came and told me. I ran most of the way here."

Griffin had been working late at his desk when Charles arrived. Now he looked at his nephew—sweating, disheveled, and gasping for breath—rose, poured the boy a brandy, and made him sit down. "Drink this. Collect your wits and tell me again from the beginning. Who's de Jonghe?"

Charles gulped the brandy in one swallow, coughed, then began to speak with more deliberation. "About a week and a half ago I met him at one of Lord Michael's parties. He's a Jew from Amsterdam, nice enough sort far as I could tell. We chatted a bit. Then about an hour ago he appeared on my doorstep. I think we exchanged addresses the night of the party, I don't really remember. Anyway, tonight there he was. Said he knew my family had once owned Harwood Hall

473

in Yorkshire and thought I'd be interested to know that a man named John Lane was trying to borrow money using Harwood as collateral." The boy paused long enough to accept a second brandy and sip it gratefully.

"How did de Jonghe know about it? Did Lane try to borrow the money from him?" Roger was pacing the room as he spoke, his mind racing ahead of his words.

"I'm not sure—I don't think so." Charles fished into his waistcoat pocket. "He gave me a name. Yes, here it is. Menachim Cohan. De Jonghe implied this was the man who knew the details."

Roger reached for the slip of paper and studied it. "Yes, I know the name. I think I heard Benjamin mention the chap once or twice."

"Well, that'll help, won't it?"

"Maybe. It depends on who stands to gain what. Tell me one more thing. Have you any idea why de Jonghe came to you? Seems a lot of trouble for a casual acquaintance."

"I know, I've been puzzling about that too. Can't really come up with a definitive answer. I think he just wants to be in the way of any profit that's going. Exactly how isn't clear."

"No, but I suspect you're right." Roger grabbed his coat from a hook on the wall and started for the door. "In any case, the next step is obvious. I'm going to try to find Cohan. You go home and wait for me. I'll come by as soon as I've anything to tell."

"Can't I come with you?"

"No, I don't think that's wise. One man stands in a better bargaining position than two. But Charles..." He approached the lad and placed both hands on his shoulders. "Well done. Well done indeed."

These past months had made Griffin a frequent wanderer through the London night. Nancy refused to recant on her edict of banishment, and he could never bring himself to insist on his rights. He had visited Tassels once or twice to see the children, but he never stayed long. It was too painful, served to remind him of all the unsolved problems of their lives.

Now, without having to think about it, he made his way through the darkened streets toward Pope's Head Alley. The name Menachim Cohan didn't just ring a bell in connection with Benjamin. Griffin was sure he'd seen it written over a small goldsmith's shop.

But each of the premises in the tiny street was bolted. The names of the proprietors were obscured or entirely covered by the heavy shutters pulled down over the doors. It was not surprising, considering the nature of the trade carried on behind them. Neither was the fast-approaching figure of a heavily armed watchman.

"Sorry, guv'nor," the man said, eyeing Roger's rich clothes and deciding some tact was called for. "All locked up fer the night. You'll have t' come back in the mornin'."

"I'm looking for Menachim Cohan. It's an emergency. Can you tell me where to find him?"

The watchman shrugged. "Sorry, ain't never heard of him. Don't know most of these gents. Just the fellow what pays me wages."

He mentioned a name Roger didn't recognize. No joy there. The watchman continued to stare; Griffin turned away and walked slowly out of the alley. At this very moment Lane might be getting the money he needed and setting out for Yorkshire. The opportunity of a lifetime would be lost. If only Benjamin were here. But he wasn't. Griffin decided on the next best thing.

It took him ten minutes to walk to Ingram's Court. By the time he reached his destination the only illumination was another watchman's swinging lantern. "Eleven o'clock on a fine warm evening," he heard the man call. Hell of a time to appear at somebody's door, especially a near stranger's. Not that the lateness of the hour was going to stop him. He raised his hand and gave the brass knocker three firm strokes. Then he waited, studying the small plaque that said "Levi."

The young maidservant who answered his summons obviously thought him mad. She was in her nightclothes, tangled curls peeking out of an askew mobcap and a thin wrapper barely protecting her modesty. Pretty little thing—Levi did himself well. But she wasn't cooperative. No, she couldn't call her master at this hour. He could come back in the morning. What was he thinking of? Decent folk were all abed by now.

"I'm sorry, really I am. But I assure you, it is urgent." Roger stood his ground, his foot wedged firmly in the door so she couldn't close it in his face. Eventually she'd have to give in just to get rid of him.

There was no need. From the rear of the hall he heard a voice say quietly, "What is it, Jane? What's the matter?"

"Gentleman to see you, sir. I told him to go away and come back in the morning, but he won't."

"All right, Jane. Just go to bed. I'll see to this." Levi took the maid's place in the doorway and peered into the gloom. "Ah, Captain Griffin. I thought I recognized your voice. I never forget voices."

"Good evening Mr. Levi. I'm flattered that you remember me after all these years. Sorry to disturb you so late, but..."

"Yes, yes, I know. It's urgent. Come in, we can't talk on the doorstep."

He led the way to another door, candle held aloft creating a path of dim yellow light. Finally, when they were in a comfortable study, he lit a few more candles and brought a tray with a decanter and two glasses.

"Now, you'll have some wine. It's a very good claret. Produced by a fellow named DuMars in France." The old man's eyes twinkled as he let Roger know he was well informed.

Griffin didn't feel inclined to join in the repartee. Time was too short. "I won't keep you long, Mr. Levi. I'm looking for a compatriot of yours."

"Yes," Levi said. "Menachim Cohan."

"How do you know that?" Roger asked in astonishment.

"The same way I know of young Hiram's visit to your nephew earlier this evening. It's my business to know such things. And in this case it is also..." He stopped speaking while he poured the claret.

"Yes?" Roger leaned forward eagerly. "Also what?"

"Also..." Again Levi paused. He wouldn't continue until Griffin accepted a glass of the wine and took a sip. "Also part of the plan that we all should know."

Roger leaned back in his seat and told himself to relax. Something was afoot, more than he'd first realized. Nothing to do now but play along. But first he'd score a small point of his own, just to let Levi know he wasn't dealing with a naive amateur. "I don't know what plan you refer to, but I think I can guess who 'we' are. B'nai Shalom, the Brotherhood of Peace. Am I correct?"

Levi was unperturbed. "Quite correct, captain. Now make yourself comfortable and enjoy your wine. I'll send someone to tell Menachim you're here."

"One thing I don't understand." Roger looked from one old Jew to the other. "If you knew I was involved, why didn't you just come to me directly? Why all these elaborate charades?"

"But there have been no charades, captain," Cohan said easily. "As I told you, I talked with the man in a coffee house just yesterday. It would have been a straightforward enough arrangement—still could be—though for Whigs the interest must necessarily be quite high. But that aside, the name Harwood Hall stuck in my memory, though I couldn't say why. So I told the man, this John Lane, he'd have to wait, and I came to talk with my friend Solomon here." Cohan stopped speaking long enough to nod at Levi sitting silently beside him. "He remembered a little more than I did. One or two things we'd been told by Ahmet some years ago. But not all. We're getting old." He shrugged expressively. "It can't be helped. Our memories aren't what they once were.

"So," he went on even as he poured himself a second glass of claret, "we talked to one or two others. Solomon tells me you are familiar with our organization, captain. Is that correct?"

"Yes." Roger fought for the control he needed in this situation. Every instinct urged him to get over all this detail and get to the negotiations, but he knew he must play the game according to the older men's rules. They held most of the cards. "Yes, I know of B'nai Shalom. Benjamin Ahmet told me years ago. You must not see that as any kind of betrayal of trust. Benjamin wasn't just my partner. He was—is—my best friend."

"We know that." Cohan took up his narrative again. "A few other members remembered more than we did. Eventually the story was pieced together. The most interesting thing we learned was that another of our group had been asking similar questions recently. Hiram de Jonghe."

"That's the part I don't understand at all," Roger said. "What has de Jonghe to do with it? Did you send him to see my nephew?"

"No, nothing like that." Cohan chuckled softly. "We're much more subtle than that, captain. We've learned to be in order to survive. But Hiram is young. He's yet to learn some of the lessons about being a Jew and surviving. He's ambitious. He made your nephew's acquaintance quite by chance at some party or other." The old man's tone conveyed eloquently his opinion of a Jew who went to such parties with *goyim.*

"It was obvious to us," he continued, "that, in view of the questions he'd been asking, he planned to find some way to use that meeting to his advantage. Now, don't misunderstand me, Captain Griffin—de Jonghe's not a villain. There's nothing sinister in his plans. He's merely ambitious, as I said before. He yearns for wider pastures than those provided by the brotherhood. So be it. It's on his own head. We only used that desire to help him do what he wanted to do anyway. We saw to it that Hiram learned of my talk with John Lane, and we left him to do the rest. As we expected, he went to see young Mr. Charles. He wishes the young man to be indebted to him, to feel gratitude. As doubtless he does. So you see, everyone's ends have been served."

"No, I don't see. It just brings me back to my first question. Why didn't you come to me directly?"

Cohan leaned forward and fixed Griffin's eyes with his own watery brown ones. His beard was stained yellow around the mouth, and two front teeth were missing. Still the man had the dignity of an Old Testament patriarch. "Because we've learned better. For thousands of years we've been hounded and persecuted and destroyed like vermin in a hole. We don't walk into traps, Captain Griffin, no matter how cleverly they're baited. We wait for the hunters to come to us."

Roger was silent. On the mantel of the fireplace a clock with a heavy brass pendulum ticked away the seconds. It was the only sound in the room until Griffin said at last, "Gentlemen, I have no weapon but the truth. No oath to give you but my word as an Englishman. There is no trap. No plot. No scheme except the one Lane has proposed to you. My family and I are wholly the innocent victims in this matter. That we have learned this much is only thanks to you. Otherwise we'd have known nothing." Unable to sit still any longer, he rose and went to stand by the fireplace. "That is a crime I've vowed to avenge if it takes the rest of my life. Harwood Hall doesn't belong to John Lane. It isn't his to mortgage. Oh, he holds the deeds, all right, I don't deny that. But by trickery and subterfuge and malice.

"The Hall belongs to me and mine. It is ours by right of birth. My ancestor started building the place in 1077, over six hundred years ago. It has been the home of the Griffins ever since. My brother was forced to choose between protecting that legacy and following his conscience. He chose the latter, and because of that lost not only Harwood but his life. At the time I disagreed bitterly. For many years we didn't even speak. But that passed, thank God, some time before he died. Mark Griffin was willing to shed his blood to witness his beliefs. It is that right which John Lane and his ilk tried to deny him—the right to worship his God according to his own conscience. They didn't succeed in that, but they did manage to take from him, from all of us, the home of our forefathers. Now it is up to you whether they continue to succeed in that treachery."

Neither Cohan nor Levi looked at each other, only at Griffin. They seemed to communicate without saying a word. Could this man, this *goy*, be trusted? Completely, as they would trust one of their own? As Benjamin Ahmet had trusted him? Or would they find that Ahmet had been mistaken, that Griffin was a betrayer, a man who would use their actions against them at the first opportunity?

Levi spoke first. "If we don't lend him the money it is certain that Lane can get it nowhere else. Whigs can't raise a farthing these days, whatever their collateral. But it doesn't seem to me anything like so certain that if he loses this Harwood Hall you will get it back."

"It isn't," Roger agreed. "If Lane is thrown into debtor's prison the Hall will probably escheat to the crown."

"Escheat...?" Menachim spoke the word hesitantly. "I don't know this term. What is escheat?"

"A point of English law. If a man can't keep the title to property it reverts to the ownership of the sovereign or"—he paused for emphasis—"that of the rightful heirs."

"And you are the rightful heir?" Menachim asked.

"No, strictly speaking I'm not. My nephew is the rightful heir. Andrew is the eldest son of the eldest son. Harwood belongs to him."

"And that satisfies you?" Levi was peering at Roger over a pair of gold-framed pince-nez he'd donned in the last ten minutes, as if the glasses could help him see into the other man's soul. "You don't want the place for yourself? Only for this Andrew?"

Griffin chuckled for the first time in two hours. "Forgive me. It seems a funny way to put it. It isn't just for Andrew. It's for all of us. Harwood belongs to us. Andrew would be squire, but all of us share in the life of the Hall. Me, my wife, our children, theirs....It's hard to explain. It doesn't mean we'd live there. My wife and I have our own home in Surrey, for instance. It's only that Harwood would be in Griffin hands. That's what matters."

"Yes." Menachim nodded slowly. "I understand that. We Jews understand about family and blood ties. Your children, your sons, would benefit from the return of the place to your family. Is that what you're saying? Both your sons?" He spoke the words slowly and distinctly and stared at Griffin once more. "You have two sons, I believe?"

It was out. They knew about Antony Jacob. That's why they'd gone so far to help him. Loyalty to Benjamin and the house of Ahmet was behind it all. "Yes," Roger said solemnly. "It is my belief that both my sons would be immeasurably enriched if the Hall was returned to us."

"But my dear captain." Levi's voice was pitched low, every word distinct. "It is true, is it not, that your youngest son doesn't even live with you? He is, I believe, in Amsterdam with his mother's relations."

Roger nodded. Cohan took up the same theme. "Tell me, Captain Griffin, is this right, do you think? Is it what you English consider an equitable arrangement? A boy cheated out of his birthright that way...."

"Gentlemen, there's no question of cheating the child of what is his under law. If you know this much, surely you must know I've acknowledged the lad as mine. His name is Griffin. No court in the realm will deny him his share of inheritance."

Cohan spat noisily into a brass cuspidor before continuing. He showed anger for the first time, his face red, his breathing stertorous. "We are not speaking of courts, young man. If courts could be relied on for justice you could go to them to get your precious Harwood Hall returned, couldn't you?"

Griffin nodded. "I take your point."

"And my point about this boy too? Understand us, captain. We care not a farthing for your six hundred years of residence in this place in Yorkshire, this Harwood Hall. We can claim thousands of years of residence in the Holy Land, but that doesn't prevent us from being homeless, from wandering the face of the earth. The experience has taught us much, I assure you. We always take care of our own. Rachel Ahmet was one of us. My own family helped raise the girl. Her son will not stay an orphan refused the shelter of his father's roof. Not if you wish us to help you."

Roger ran his fingers through his hair and sank heavily into the nearest chair. "You don't know everything," he said after some seconds. "I've been to see the child a number of times. I feel about him as I do about my other three children. Whatever you think, in my own fashion I loved his mother. But she's dead and my wife is alive. How can I force her to accept another woman's child?"

Levi shrugged. "That's your affair. But if you want our cooperation we must have your word that the boy will be brought to England. That he'll be raised with the same advantages your other children enjoy."

For some minutes there was silence. Then Roger said, "You have my solemn oath it will be so."

3.

Never was Roger more grateful for having a course of action forced upon him. It wasn't just the Hall. That was important, of course. But it could not approach the significance of Antony Jacob.

The lad was almost four, a skinny stick of a toddler with nothing of baby pudginess about him. Already he displayed the Griffin ranginess. His eyes and his hair were Rachel's, great black eyes like two huge saucers, and lashes that curled up like the tips of a Turkish sultan's slippers. They made him look astonishingly exotic.

"I can't help it, captain... I so hate to see him go...." The young woman sniffled loudly and wiped her eyes with a sodden handkerchief.

"I understand, of course, Miss Rose. And I can never repay you for caring so well for him all this while. But it's time he came to England, met his brother and sisters...."

"Yes, I know." She started to hand the boy over to his father, then paused. "One more thing. I've been trying to teach him English, but he doesn't speak it well yet. You must be patient."

"I assure you, Miss Rose, we will be very patient." He smiled at the boy now gripped firmly in his arms. "You'll learn quickly once you're home, won't you, son?" Antony Jacob was too puzzled to do anything but nod.

"Captain's here, ma'am," Ellen Wadden told her mistress when she found her in the stillroom. "Just arrived and wants you to join him in his study."

"Well, I don't want to join him. Tell him I'm busy."

"Beggin' yer pardon, ma'am, I think you'd best go. Captain looks right determined. And he's brought..." The old servant hesitated. She had no desire to be the one to break such news to the mistress.

"Brought what?" When Ellen refused to answer, Nancy slammed down the basket of lavender blossoms she had been sorting and left. It was easier to see for herself what this was all about than to prise the information out of Ellen.

"You wanted me, Roger?" she asked coolly as she let herself into the study without knocking. "I hope this can be handled quickly."

"No, Nancy, I'm afraid it can't." He was calm but, as Ellen said, he looked very determined. "There's no easy way to tell you this, so I'll get straight to the point. I've brought Antony Jacob home from Amsterdam. He's in the nursery with the others right now."

She went white. For some seconds she was speechless. "You've brought... I don't believe it. I just don't believe you'd do this thing to me, to your children. Not even you..."

"Nancy, please! For God's sake, at least hear me out! And sit down. You look as though you're going to faint."

She let him help her into a chair because she had no choice. Since the accident she walked with a limp, and some measure of pain was a permanent companion. A shock like this quickly pushed her to the limits of her physical endurance.

"Why?" she asked while he stood over her, staring at her as if he hadn't seen her in years rather than months. "Why would you want to rub salt into my wounds? What have I done to deserve such treatment, Roger?"

He ignored her queries. Seeing her like this made him aware again of how desperately he'd missed her, how much a part of himself she was. Involuntarily he found his finger tracing the familiar line of her cheek. "I've missed you so, Nancy...."

She didn't push his hand away. Her eyes were locked with his. She wanted to move, to look elsewhere, but she couldn't. "Why?" she repeated after some seconds. It was a question about everything that had been, not just the day's events. They both knew it.

"I don't know. Not all of it...." He shook his head sadly. "We're so often at loggerheads, you and I, so often enemies."

"I've never been your enemy, Roger."

"I know that. When James told me about the boy that's what hurt most. Thinking that I'd betrayed you, lost your loyalty. I wish you could understand."

She dropped her eyes. "Why have you brought him here?" she asked again.

He told her the story about Lane and Harwood Hall and the old Jews who held the future in their hands. She listened in silence, never looking up, never meeting his gaze. Not until he said, "But that's not all of it. It provoked me into taking action, but sooner or later I'd have done so anyway. I couldn't help it. The boy's my son, Nancy. No amount of regret can change that. If I'm honest I have to say I wouldn't want it to. I love him. He's an adorable child. I'm proud of him. Just as I am of Nell and Jennifer and Jamie. Can't you understand?"

Nancy was staring at him now, seeing all kinds of truths written in his eyes. Still she was silent.

"Look," he pleaded, "if one of the other three had been fathered by someone else, born of some other woman, but given to you when still an infant, would you feel any differently about the child? Love him or her any less?" She shook her head. "It's rather like that. I don't know any other way to put it."

"He's not just some other woman's child," she whispered. "He's yours. Can't you see the difference? How can I look at him and forget that you preferred his mother to me?"

"But that's not true! It's never been true!" He dropped to his knees beside her chair, squeezing her hands as if he could transmit by touch things he couldn't say. "What I felt for Rachel never had anything to do with you. It was separate. Entirely another matter. I love you, Nance. I've loved you from the first moment I set eyes on you. That's part of me. The essential core. Everything else just flows over the top. Sweet Christ, I don't know how to put it in words."

"What did you tell the children?" she asked, ignoring his last speech but not removing her hands from his.

"The plain truth. Here's your baby brother come to live with us."

"We'd better go see how they're getting on," she said quietly. "With no warning or preparation I can't think how they'll react."

They were halfway down the corridor leading to the nursery when they heard the wails. It sounded as if all the children were yelling together. Despite her limp Nancy ran toward the door. Roger got there first. He entered the room to find a melee of tangled arms and legs and a harassed-looking nursemaid doing her ineffectual best to restore order.

"Quiet!" Roger roared above their cries. "Quiet at once! Now, what's going on in here?"

They obeyed his command for silence, but no one made any move to answer his question. His gaze traveled over each red-faced youngster in turn. Only the three eldest were to be seen. The newcomer was missing.

"Where's Antony Jacob?" Roger demanded. "What have you done to him?"

"He's under the bed," Jennifer volunteered. "He won't come out."

"Why not?" No reply. Roger fixed Jamie with his sternest look. "Jamie, you're the oldest boy. Now you tell me what's going on, young man, or I'll paddle your bottom until you can't sit down for a month!"

"I hit her, sir." Jamie turned on Nell with an accusatory finger. "I don't care if she is a girl. She was horrid. Kept pulling that boy's hair and telling him he was a bastard."

"I see." Roger turned to her. Nell stared at him defiantly, ignoring the sheltering arm the nursemaid held out and her mother's sympathetic expression.

"It's true, isn't it?" The girl hissed through clenched teeth. "You said he was our brother, so he must be a bastard." Nell's whole body shook with rage.

"He's a Griffin," her father answered in slow measured words. "A Griffin just as you are. I give you my word, Nell, if you ever again call him a bastard, I'll make you sorry you were born. Is that understood?"

She didn't answer him, just dropped her eyes to stare at the hem of her frock. Roger strode forward and took her by the shoulders. "I asked you a question, young lady. I'm waiting for an answer."

For some seconds more she continued to defy him. Then, just when Nancy feared Roger might actually strike the girl, she said, "Yes, Papa."

"Very well. And that goes for all of you." He might have said more, but Nancy interrupted. "For God's sake, Roger! Get that baby out from under the bed. He must be terrified."

Griffin had, of course, quite forgotten the little boy in his determination to make the older children understand the principle involved. Now it was Jamie who dived below the heavy mahogany bedstead and pulled the cowering Antony Jacob into their midst. "It's all right," he said matter-of-factly. "Mama and Papa are here now. Nell will leave you alone."

Nancy couldn't help but smile. Trust Jamie to do and say the simple, straightforward thing. At nine he displayed the same sympathy for the underdog that she always felt. Now this funny-looking child had fallen heir to Jamie's protection.

The stranger, however, didn't feel protected. He was trembling with fear. Being dragged into the center of all these people, seeing them all looking straight at him, only exaggerated it. "Where's Auntie Rose?" he suddenly wailed aloud. "I want Auntie Rose." But he said it in Dutch. None of them understood a word.

Nancy didn't need to understand him to know what was wrong. She only hesitated a few seconds, staring briefly at Roger, before her glance returned to the child wracked with heartbroken sobs.

"Oh, for God's sake! Give him to me, Jamie." She snatched the boy from his elder brother and cradled him in her arms. "He's frightened half out of his wits, and small wonder. You should be ashamed. All of you!" She included her husband in that condemnation and promptly marched out of the room. Roger heard her crooning soft comforting noises to the weeping child.

A few days later she went to the study. Roger hadn't yet returned to London—he felt he couldn't leave until he was sure of the household's peace—but he was sleeping in the same makeshift bed he'd used all during her illness.

Outside the glass doors a quarter moon shed an eerie half-ight over the China roses. Nancy walked to the window and surveyed the scene for some moments. "The stars look close enough to touch," she said at last.

"Yes. It's a beautiful night. You're beautiful too." He looked at her hungrily. Her auburn hair flowed freely down her back...the way she used to wear it years ago. Above the pale blue of her sleeping gown he could see her breasts, milk-white in the moonlight.

Wordlessly Nancy turned to him and opened her arms. He kissed her then. A long slow kiss intended to tell her the gratitude and love in his heart. It became something more. It seemed to Roger he could taste all the past on her lips. Bitter and sweet, but shared.

4.

It was a slow process. Roger had known it would be. He'd gone first to James.

"Remarkable turn of events, remarkable," the duke commented, rubbing his hands with satisfaction. "So here's another of the bloody bastards getting their comeuppance. Former magistrate, you say. The one who turned your brother and his family out of their home?"

"The very same. You remember Sir John Dewinters, the fellow who died in that hunting accident couple of years back? He and Lane were hand in glove. The pair of them staged the eviction of my brother and his family so that..." Roger broke off. Why remind York how easily the Stuarts had capitulated to Dewinters's blackmail?

James didn't need reminding. He looked at his visitor and nodded sadly. "Yes, I remember all that." His smile was only slightly forced. "It's all spilt milk nowadays, isn't it? A great deal has changed since '69."

"A great deal, sir, but not everything. Harwood Hall remains the Griffin legacy. With Lane bankrupt it will escheat to the crown..."

"Or the rightful heir," York finished for him. "Exactly who is the rightful heir? I can't keep all you Griffins straight."

"Andrew, sir. The lad you sent to Modena. He's my late brother's eldest son."

"Andrew!" James slapped his knee in loud good humor. "Andrew!" he bellowed a second time. "Well, I'll be damned. I like that, Roger. I really do. The boy deserves it. He'll make a fine squire."

"I agree. If he inherits."

"Yes, if indeed. It'll take a signed order from his majesty, you realize that?"

"I do."

"And our young Andrew is still a recusant, after all...." James looked thoughtful. "It's going to take time, Roger. You'll have to be patient."

Roger smiled. "We've waited fourteen years, sir. That should be some evidence of patience."

"Right!" York clapped him heartily on the shoulder. "Just leave it to me. One way or another we'll put matters right."

That conversation took place in July. Not till November did Roger finally learn that Lane had been taken to debtors' prison in York. Those few retainers he had maintained until the end had been sent away, the tenants who farmed various pieces of the estate allowed to remain. The property would thus be kept in good order. The Hall itself was empty; Roger thought of it as waiting for the return of its own.

"What are you going to do next?" Nancy inquired anxiously.

"Nothing. Wait on the king's good pleasure. What else is there to do?"

"I don't know," she said. "I find it hard to think of the whole thing as real."

Her own concerns were bound up with Tassels, her children, and the complex relationships between them and their new brother. Jamie and Jennifer accepted the little boy. Jamie had even given him that pet name which everyone now used, Tonyjay. It was much easier to say than Antony Jacob. Nell's hostility, however, was never far below the surface. Roger understood all Nancy's fears. He repeated now what he'd told her many times. "You know I won't go back on my word, whatever happens? You do believe that?"

Nancy nodded her head and smiled. From the first he'd

assured her that they would remain at Tassels. "I know," she whispered, taking the opportunity to kiss him softly and lean her head against his chest for a brief moment. No one would understand it, perhaps, but the coming of Tonyjay had set the final seal on their love and their marriage. The son Rachel Ahmet had borne was the instrument that brought Nancy and Roger to a fully ripe and mature union. Strange, but true.

He held her a bit away from him now. Her auburn hair was still beautiful, her eyes were lovely as ever, her delicate skin remarkably fresh. "Here you are," he said teasingly, "an old hag of thirty-eight and you're still as pretty as a lass. How do you do it, Mistress Griffin?"

"Ah, sir," she said with a broad imitation of his clipped Yorkshire accent. "I be like fine wine or cheese. Get better with age."

Time passed, nothing seemed to happen. Until finally the months brought them to June 18 in the year of grace 1684. Titus Oates stood in the dock at the Old Bailey. No one had yet bothered to tot up the numbers of men and women who, on his say-so alone, had stood there before him. In the rear of the crowded courtroom one man among many watched the accused, not so much with hatred as with incredulity.

Oates pawed the ground like a caged animal, his dwarfed body not still a moment, his bizarre long square jaw working continuously up and down. No words issued from that misplaced mouth. In contrast, Oates's accuser sat calmly in the front of the room, chatting amiably with his retinue of attendants. His royal highness James, Duke of York, seemed confident of the outcome of the trial.

The scene, Roger thought to himself with astonishment, was hardly to be believed. After the plots and counterplots, after miscarriages of justice, after the heir to the throne had to face banishment and exile... after all that, the man responsible stood in the dock accused of nothing more than *scandalum magnatum,* great scandal. The crime the jury had now retired to consider was that in April of 1680, at the Bishop of Ely's dinner table, Oates was heard to refer to James as "that traitor, the Duke of York."

Griffin closed his eyes and leaned his head back against the wall. What did it matter in the end? If they were trying him for a hanging offense, if Oates were made to follow his countless victims to Tyburn, would it change anything? Would it resurrect Mark and Clare, remove the stain on English justice, make Charles a nobler king, convince the realm they should be pleased with the notion of a Catholic as heir to the throne? No, none of it.

Just as they had from the beginning of the long nightmare, forces beyond Oates's control now ordered his destiny. Shaftesbury was dead, the Whigs totally discredited. Of late prisons and jails across the land had disgorged their cache of sufferers interned for no reason other than their popery. And James, returned to London and all his former offices and duties, was emboldened to bring suit against Oates for having once called him a traitor.

Around him Roger sensed a change in the buzz of voices. He opened his eyes to see the jury filing back to their places. With the rest, Griffin stood.

"Gentlemen, how say ye?"

"Guilty as charged."

A ripple of satisfaction among the onlookers, an audible sigh of pleasure from York, then silence. Everywhere, even in the dock. The prisoner seemed to will himself to stillness; yet his misshapen body twitched and shuddered. Justice Jeffries leaned forward and studied Oates through narrowed eyes.

The judge was not a prepossessing man. His wig was always slightly askew, and one corner of his mouth was afflicted with a noticeable tic. His robes were usually stained with remnants of his breakfast porridge. But when he tapped his gavel in the palm of one bony hand he overcame all that by the sheer force of his power and personality. Jeffries willed the court to silence; he had no need to command it. When the quiet was complete, when the only sound was that of breathing, he spoke.

"I remind ye, gentlemen," he told the jury, "of my earlier remarks concerning the need to make an example of this person." His eyes slid in Oates's direction, then returned to the jurors. "With that in mind I ask, have ye fixed the damages?"

"We have, milord." The foreman's tone carried an air of confidence; he seemed in no doubt that the information he conveyed would please the powerful justice. "We charge the felon to pay over to his royal highness James, Duke of York, the sum of one hundred thousand pounds in damages and twenty..." His voice was interrupted by a shout of jubilation from the gallery and a high-pitched whine of pain and terror from the dock. "Twenty shillings," the foreman shouted, "legal costs."

Jeffries leaned back in his high perch. No smile could be seen on his face, but there was a smile in his voice when he asked, "Mr. Oates, can ye pay?"

That tortured, whining voice, as shrill in defeat as it had been in triumph. "I cannot, milord. Not immediately, that is. If I had some time, perhaps..." The last was barely audible.

Jeffries tapped one finger rhythmically on the mellow oak of the bench. Finally he looked at James. "Your highness, you have heard the prisoner say he cannot pay the damages. Have you any instructions for the court?"

It was York's royal prerogative to be magnanimous if he chose. He could indicate that he was satisfied with the fact of the judgment, prepared to forgive the actual payment of the damages. The duke busied himself adjusting the elaborate lace cuffs that showed below the sleeves of his sumptuous velvet coat. His silence spoke loud enough for Jeffries.

"Very well." The justice turned back to the prisoner. "Since, sir, ye cannot pay, my duty is clear. I hereby order that ye be taken to debtors' prison. There to remain until the sum is paid." His gavel cracked one final time, and a squealing, whimpering Oates was led away. Jeffries rose and the assembly with him. Only when his black-robed figure was out of sight did the sound of a hundred people speaking at once break the silence.

Griffin remained in the rear, watching James. He didn't blame the man. He knew what Oates had inflicted on York. Still, Charles would have acted otherwise. Given the same circumstances, the elder Stuart would have waved a gracious hand and caused all England to love him better for it. That wasn't York's nature, never had been. Griffin regretted it. Particularly now when the man stood so firmly next to the throne.

The royal party was moving slowly toward the back of the chamber, James pausing to accept congratulations on all sides. They were still some distance from the door when his eyes met Roger's, and he smiled a greeting. A barely perceptible nod of the head indicated that he wished to meet him outside.

"So, Roger." York smiled broadly. "Are you pleased?"

Griffin shrugged. York knew him too well to expect pandering; he felt no need to disguise his opinion. "That your highness is vindicated, certainly. For the rest..."

"The rest? I see...you'd have advised me to forgive the debt."

"I suppose I would, sir. What difference does it make?"

York thumped his walking stick on the cobblestones. "I'll tell you what difference. I've the satisfaction of knowing that foul, black-hearted villain is languishing among the vermin in the Fleet. God knows he deserves no better and perhaps a good deal worse."

"Yes sir. I understand that."

"So you should, my friend, so you should." York slung a companionable arm over Griffin's shoulders to indicate his acceptance of their divergent opinions. One might often doubt James's wisdom or even his charity, but never his loyalty. "Now, enough of that. Come with me, lad. We'll lunch together. It's months since I've seen you. I've things to report. That Harwood business...I think things are moving ahead at last."

5.

He said nothing to anyone until the weekend. Then, pressed close to Nancy beneath the warmth of the feather quilt, he told her what James had said. She was silent. Roger stared out the window at the cold, starry November night.

"One thing I do want to do," he said softly, speaking more to himself than to her. "I'm going to see if I can bring Andrew home for a visit. I want to tell him what's happening. It just doesn't seem prudent to commit all this to writing. I've not told him a thing up to now."

"But won't it be dangerous for him? To travel back to

England, I mean. He's a known recusant, and he's been in the employ of a foreign power. It must be dangerous."

"I don't really think so. Not the way things are at the moment. I'll talk to James, ask if he can guarantee Andrew safe passage. Then we'll see."

Andrew arrived in Surrey a few days before Christmas. He brought with him the biggest surprise of the holiday—an exquisite little slip of a wife, Louisa Beatriz Maria Gabrelli by name, a name far too long for such a tiny girl. The family immediately adopted Andrew's pet name for her, Lulu. She was the daughter of a Venetian trader, he explained, and they had been married a month before.

Nancy cast a speculative eye over the girl. She didn't look pregnant; that wasn't likely to be the cause of the hasty wedding. Still, it had been so hurried Andrew had not even notified the family. And what a beauty she was. Masses of straight blue-black hair swept back from a high forehead to hang loose down her back. Spirited vitality was evident in every inch of her miniature but well-curved frame. Yet there was something odd about the girl, something not really Italian. She had almond eyes and fine high cheekbones.... Well, what difference did it make? Nancy hugged the new bride and welcomed her to Tassels.

Not until they'd rested from their journey and Andrew had shown his wife a bit of the place did Roger summon his nephew to the conference that had been the object of the trip. "You too, Charles," Griffin said. "We'd best tell Andrew all this together."

The three retired to the study, and Nancy was left alone with Lulu. Nell and Jen were in the kitchen helping with the preparations for the enormous Christmas feast, and Jamie was off somewhere with Tonyjay at his heels. The little sitting room was blissfully quiet. Nancy hunted about for something to say. "Do you like tea, Lulu?" she inquired finally. "I know in your country it's not very popular, but it's catching on fast here in England. I could brew some if you'd like to try it."

"I should very much enjoy some tea, Mistress Griffin," the girl said in her stiffly formal English. "I like it very much."

Nancy busied herself with the spirit lamp and kettle she had acquired for the preparation of this newly fashionable drink. "Oh no, please!" the girl exclaimed when her hostess lifted the pitcher of milk. "Nothing to dilute the tea!"

"Really?" Nancy was surprised. "You like it just plain? How extraordinary."

"Not really." Lulu's voice was barely audible. "It is the custom among my people." She sipped the tea with grace, and Nancy noted her hands for the first time. Cupped around the porcelain bowl they were even more delicate and finely made than the china. After some moments the almond eyes were raised and Lulu replaced the bowl on the table. "I think I should explain, Mistress Griffin. Andrew intended to do so, but he is very busy with his esteemed uncle..."

"Look," Nancy interrupted. "You can explain or not explain whatever you wish. That's entirely up to you. You're Andrew's wife, and that's enough for us. But there is one thing I would like you to do."

"Anything, esteemed Mistress..."

"That's just it. We're a plain-spoken family, my dear. Not given to titles. I'm Nancy and my husband is Roger. Aunt Nancy and Uncle Roger, if you prefer. But not esteemed anything." She grinned at the girl, and was enormously gratified to see her grin back.

"I would still like to explain..."

"Suit yourself, pet." Nancy curled her legs beneath her with fine disregard for propriety and listened.

Lulu's father was a Venetian. Her mother was a Chinese princess whom he'd met in Cathay. They'd fallen in love and run away together. For many years they had lived in peace in Venice. Last year, the man had died. Lulu, the only child of the union, had been just fifteen.

"But what a wonderfully romantic story!" Nancy exclaimed at the end. "What happened to your mother?"

"She returned to Cathay just a few weeks ago. It was her own choice, you see. With my father dead she really wanted to go back. She only protested at first because of me. Then"— the girl made an expressive gesture—"when Andrew took me as his wife everything was settled."

Nancy laughed with pleasure. "It's marvelous, Lulu! You're marvelous!" Secretly she was chuckling at the thought of this Chinese-Italian child as the squire's lady in staid settled Yorkshire, but she didn't feel up to explaining that.

* * *

The same subject occupied the three men in the study down the hall. "It's a lot to assimilate in one gulp," Andrew said. "Harwood, me as squire—I never expected it."

"No," Roger answered. "And you still shouldn't expect it. We don't know for sure it will come to pass. Everything depends on the king."

"But you must think there's a good chance," Andrew said. "Otherwise you'd not have sent for me."

"Yes, I think there's an excellent chance." He watched his eldest nephew carefully. Andrew was twenty-six; Charles, two years his junior, looked to be older and more settled of the two. Andrew the white knight, born a few centuries too late, Mark had often said.

"What's the matter, son?" Roger asked finally. "Doesn't the idea of being squire of Harwood please you?"

Andrew didn't answer right away. Knowing what the prospect of the Hall's return meant to his uncle, he chose his words carefully. "I think in all the world there can be no place more beautiful than Harwood Hall. I was twelve when we left. I've not seen the place in fourteen years, yet I dream about it at least once or twice a month. Always I see it as it looked in the evening, with the sun setting behind the west wing and the stones looking as if they were hewn from gold."

"The way it looks from the hill across the valley," Roger added. "Yes, I know just the view you mean."

Andrew sat up in his chair and looked his uncle straight in the eye. "But for the life of me I can't see myself going back there now. Not permanently. There's Lulu to consider. She's not cut out for such a life. Her story's very involved— I'll tell you all about it later, but for the moment just accept what I say. And there's my career. I've done well in Modena, Uncle Roger. I'm the duke's first aide. I believe I can look forward to being the Modena equivalent of lord chancellor someday. I'm good at it, and I thoroughly enjoy it. Meeting people, traveling, negotiating...affairs of state have turned out to be my métier. I hope that doesn't make you think me an ungrateful traitor."

"No," Roger said, "nothing like that. But you must admit it presents us with a problem."

Charles chuckled softly. It was a sound without mirth. "Rather an understatement. Tell me, Andrew, what do you suggest we tell his majesty? 'Sorry, sire, we've changed our minds, we don't want the Hall back after all. Never mind the fact that Griffins have lived there for six hundred years, the present heir doesn't fancy being squire.'"

"It's nothing like that!" Andrew's temper was rising. Anyone who knew him could recognize the signs.

"Then what is it?" the younger brother demanded. "You can put any face on the thing you care to, Andrew, it doesn't change the facts. You're asking us to kiss farewell to an income of thousands a year, a house and lands worth a hundred times as much on the open market. All because you want to remain lackey to some posturing Italian duke."

"So that's it." Andrew rose and stood staring at Charles. "It's not the family honor at stake, not for you. Just pounds, shillings, and pence. Wouldn't Papa be proud."

"Are you suggesting he'd prefer your attitude? Me for myself alone and the devil take the hindmost!"

"That's quite enough." Roger, still seated behind his desk, didn't even raise his voice, but both his nephews recognized the command in his words. They settled back in their seats and waited for him to continue.

"At this moment, gentlemen," Griffin said with controlled rage, "your father would be a great deal less than proud of both of you. You're throwing the words 'Griffin honor' around while behaving like fishwives in the Cornhill road. You disgust me!" He stood up and leaned forward, resting his tall frame on his clenched fists, looking a much bigger man than either of his nephews. "Let me tell you what Griffin honor really means. It's not pretending to be a saint. It's no guarantee against making errors of judgment. It is the willingness to do anything in your power to put those errors right. More than that, it means putting nothing"—he paused for a long moment—"do you hear me, absolutely nothing, ahead of the family and its concerns. Now, gentlemen, I bid you good evening. We'll talk again tomorrow. Perhaps you'll have reflected upon your positions more thoroughly by then."

Both boys rose to go. Roger stopped them before they reached the door. "One last thing. I think you should realize, Charles, that if Andrew will not step into the role for which he was born, then you are next in line."

"Very well." Andrew spoke quietly, bitterness apparent in his tone. "I'll do it."

Rain beat relentlessly against the windows, cold, icy December rain. Roger stared at the wind-whipped trees outside his study and didn't turn to face the boys when he asked, "Why, Andrew? What's changed your mind? Have the attractions of the Modena court paled during the night?"

"You've made it quite clear where you consider my duty to lie," Andrew answered. "What do you expect me to say?"

"Well..." He spun around and stared at the lad. "For a start I'd expect some joy, some pleasure in the prospect of taking back what your father always meant you to have and worked the better part of a lifetime to prepare for you."

"I said I'd do it, Uncle Roger. You can command me to a course of action. My feelings are no man's to dictate."

"Hang your bloody feelings!" Charles jumped to his feet, his anger not cooled since the evening before. "You're sitting there looking like a noble martyr and blaming Uncle Roger for insisting that an income of thousands can't be ignored as if it were the price of a pint of ale. What kind of world do you live in, Andrew? Do gold guineas grow on the trees in Modena?"

"Sit down, Charles," Roger said quietly. "Frankly I'm no more impressed with you in this instance than I am with your brother. I'm a little sick of hearing Harwood referred to as a money chest. It's a good deal more than that. You're a fool if you don't recognize it."

"Uncle Roger," Andrew broke in before Charles could reply, "permit me a further word. I've learned something in Modena despite my brother's opinion. In diplomacy one has always to look for the possible compromise. I wonder if that's the answer here." He turned and looked at the younger man. "Charles, Uncle Roger made a good point last night. You're next in line. What would you say to my resigning in your favor? Just think, you could control all that precious income yourself."

"Well, Charles?" Roger asked. "What about it? Supposing that's what was decided, would you accept?"

Charles stared at the floor, his face an expressionless mask. "I'll do whatever is necessary."

Roger tapped an idle finger on his desk. "I see. And will you hold to that promise when I tell you—tell you both, by the way—that it won't make a farthing's difference to the income of any of us whoever is squire at the Hall?"

His nephews stared at him astonished. Roger chose not to answer their questions until they were spoken aloud.

"How can that be?" Charles demanded. "Don't tell me that bastard Lane ran the place into the ground. Is there no income left?"

"You must realize, Uncle Roger," Andrew added, "that if Harwood produces no income I can't possibly take it on. I have a wife to support."

"Sit down, you two. Sit down and keep your mouths shut. It seems that you understood very little of what I told you last night. Permit me to spell it out, since you are apparently both doddering idiots.

"To take your point first, Charles, Lane did no financial damage to the Hall. The estate produces a fine income, just as you were at such pains to remind us."

"That's all right, then," Andrew said.

"No, Andrew. It's not all right because you both seem to be of the opinion that whoever takes over as squire will have that income to do with as he chooses. I daresay Charles here has even decided that such a bonanza is sufficient reason to give up his pleasant life in London. But he's wrong. You're both wrong.

"Neither of you will become squire without first signing an agreement that places the earnings from Harwood in a special fund administered by Griffin's Importations. In other words, by me."

"That's not fair!" they both spoke together.

"So, a veritable Greek chorus of dissent."

"Uncle Roger"—Charles again—"both Andrew and I are of legal age. You can't expect us to accept such an arrangement. We're not children to be put in the hands of some self-styled prince regent."

Roger took no offense at the remark. "Tell me something, Charles. You've been in the business with me for almost five years now. Have I ever attempted to control your income, examine your personal accounts?"

"No, never," the boy admitted. "You've always been fair, Uncle Roger. You can't accuse me of ever saying any different."

"No, I can't. That's why I find it so strange you should jump to the conclusions you've apparently reached. I want to show you something." He took a ledger from the drawer and pushed it across the desk.

The brothers examined the ledger. Andrew spoke first. "It's some kind of account book. With the names of each of us heading up a page."

"Exactly. Not just the two of you, but both your sisters, your Aunt Sophia, and my four children. I take it you've noted all that?" They nodded. "Don't you understand? Those are records of monies held by various goldsmiths in London.

497

They are your share of the profits of Griffin's Importations. You will note that you two are on exactly the same level as Jamie and Tonyjay."

Roger walked to the window and stared at the endless rain. His voice was choked, but his words were clear. "The last time I saw your father alive I promised him I would treat both of you exactly as if you were my own sons. I've tried to keep my word."

He sat down heavily before continuing. The memory of that terrible morning at Tyburn was in the room with them. It hovered in the air, stronger than blood.

"Please note too that Sophia and Laura show rather little in their accounts. The reason is that two years ago I paid over a large sum to their abbey on behalf of both of them. It's customary for women to bring a dowry to those places. At the time they went to France neither your father nor I had money to pay such a dowry. It was always his intention that it should be paid when possible. Admittedly I have little sympathy for the life they've chosen. But it wouldn't occur to me to ignore Mark's wishes for that reason. He considered it a debt. I've discharged it as soon as I could.

"You're all Griffins," Roger said softly. "It is just this I intend to see done with the income from Harwood, whoever is squire. Naturally the person in that role will have the largest share of the profits. That will be his right, just as it's mine, and to a lesser degree yours, Charles, to have a wage from the business. The balance will be divided among the rest of the family." Having said that, he dismissed them both with a wave of his hand.

6.

For some days Roger allowed them no opportunity to discus the matter. At least not with him. What Charles and Andre might be saying between themselves he couldn't guess. B he recognized the need for a cooling-off period before anything could be settled.

The morning of Christmas Eve dawned bright and sunny, the first such day in weeks. "Can you have both boys ready for an outing, Nance?" Roger asked as soon as he opened his eyes and saw sunlight pouring through the bedroom window. "Within the hour?"

"Yes, of course. What sort of outing?"

"To the woods, wife! Where else can we be expected to find a proper Yule log? And you'd best tell Rudy and young Tom I'll be needing them too. Can't expect much muscle power from Jamie and Tonyjay yet."

They returned by lunchtime dragging an enormous tree-trunk behind them on an improvised sledge. "Hmph," Ellen snorted when they approached the house. "What they need a sledge for? Ain't no snow hereabouts."

Roger seemed to have anticipated her question. He announced their arrival with a loud cry. "Come see, Nancy! We've a perfect beast of a Yule log. It'll burn for a week. And we've brought it home on a sledge just as we did in Yorkshire when I was a boy. Hang these snowless Surrey winters!"

"It snows here lots of times, Papa," Jamie insisted. "Just not this year."

"Well, that's not going to spoil our Christmas," Roger said. "Not on your life. Where are your mother and your sisters? I want them to see the thing before we put it in the house."

Ellen went after her mistress, who was supervising the making of mince tarts. "Best come, ma'am. Master's brung home half a tree and says it'll burn for a week. Smoke for a week, more likely. Maybe they's fool enough to burn green wood up there in Yorkshire. Down here we knows better."

Roger was wiser than the cantankerous old woman suspected. "It's perfect, Nance," he said with pride as she looked open-mouthed at the enormous elm trunk. "It must have come down in a storm some years past. We found it under a clump of bushes, and it's as dry and well seasoned as you could wish."

"And that's not all, Mama," Jamie added, fairly dancing with excitement. "Look at all the greens we found." He gathered up an armload of pine and cedar branches and started in the direction of the house.

"Put them in the front hall, Jamie," Nancy called after him. "We'll all help decorate after lunch." Laughing, she turned to the smaller boy. "Well, Tonyjay, did you have a good time?"

In the two years since he'd arrived at Tassels the child had learned to speak English with no trace of accent, a feat he'd never have accomplished if he'd started later in life. He'd be six the following month, and no one could have guessed that he had not been born in England. But his personality had changed little. He remained a gentle, soft-spoken little boy. Often Nancy suspected that great depth lurked behind that shy exterior. He was always doing things that surprised her. This day was no exception.

"I brought these for you," Tonyjay said, pulling a small bouquet of bright-red partridge berries and shining holly from beneath his coat. "They're just for you. Not to decorate the house."

She dropped to her knees and hugged the boy before accepting the offering. "Thank you, darling. I shall put them in my sitting room. They're beautiful. Now run along and help Jamie."

When she looked up, Roger was watching her. There was a suspicious glow in his eyes, almost the hint of tears. "Thank you," he said softly. "For everything."

Nancy smiled. "There's nothing to thank me for. He's impossible not to love."

"Does Nell share that opinion at last?" he asked in a more serious vein.

"Nell is what she is, there's not much point in expecting different. Headstrong and willful, I know, but I think she'll outgrow it."

"I guess we'll just have to muddle through till then." Roger laughed as he spoke. He had no intention of letting any serious conversation mar this day. No problems with his children or his nephews could prevent him from enjoying this Christmas.

Eventually they'd eaten the last of the succulent goose, devoured the final crumb of mince tart, quaffed the last of the wassail bowl with its delicious apples soaked in hot spiced ale. It was time to return to the unsolved problem of Harwood.

"Well," he asked Charles and Andrew a few days later, "any further thoughts?"

The older boy looked rather tired and pale. Had it not been for the matter of the Hall, Roger would have attributed it the appeal of his exquisite little wife and the lure of the marriage bed. As it was he suspected Andrew's drawn look to be the result of worry and a guilty conscience.

"I've thought of little else, Uncle Roger. I can't tell you I'm delighted with the prospect—that would be a lie, and you deserve better. But I'll take it on. And I'll do my damnedest to be as good a squire as my father was."

"Well done, lad. Spoken like a Griffin." He expected that to close the discussion, but Charles had other ideas.

"Wait a minute, please. Both of you. I've done plenty of thinking too. And I've something to say. May I speak freely, Uncle Roger?"

He nodded and waited for the boy to continue.

"It's a bad plan. Wait." He held up his hand as both his brother and his uncle began speaking at once. "Hear me out at least. Now look, if things had gone as everyone had a right to expect years ago, Andrew would have taken over as a matter of course. And if something had prevented that, I'd have stepped into his shoes. We both would have expected it, been trained for it. But God or fate or what you will took a hand, and everything changed. Andrew and I never had a chance to grow into that plan, that direction."

Charles paused for a moment to light the pipe he'd lately affected. Both his listeners waited silently for him to continue. "You've shown us how important it is that Harwood come back into Griffin hands, and we know it's a lot more than money. That doesn't alter the fact that Andrew sees himself as a statesman, not a gentleman farmer. And frankly, I'm a Londoner. I daresay you won't contradict me if I add that I'm good at business and that Griffin's Importations would be the poorer without me. Whatever you may think of some of the things I've said this past week."

Roger smiled faintly and nodded his head.

"So what's to be done?" Charles continued. "It seems to me we have to take a look at the next candidates in line for the role. Jamie's your man, Uncle Roger. He's the Griffin best cut out to be squire."

"Jamie," Roger said, "is eleven years old. I don't wish to belabor the obvious, but that's a bit young for what you're suggesting."

"All the better. Here he is being reared in the country on an estate that's rather like a Harwood in miniature. Don't forget, Uncle Roger. I've been beside the boy since he was born. I warrant I know him even better than you do. He loves the land, the countryside. He's a born genius with people and is growing into a passable horseman. Guide his education aright and Jamie's a natural. And if something happens, if he isn't able to take over, there's Tonyjay to rely on. They're both young enough to be groomed for the part."

There was a great deal of truth in everything Charles had said. But one major problem remained. "Even if we follow your plan," Roger said, "we've only devised a scheme for the future, not solved the present dilemma. You can't let a place like Harwood sit empty for eight or nine years. It's unthinkable."

"Of course it is." Charles leaned forward and waved his pipe for emphasis. "That brings me to the second part of my thesis. Now see what you think of this...."

It was nearly two hours more before the three of them shook hands and rose to leave the study. Each went to his bed thoroughly satisfied with the course of action they'd determined to follow. Each had a deeper understanding of the real meaning of the Griffin legacy.

7.

The scheme involved dealings in France; Andrew was the logical choice as emissary. He and Lulu could return to Modena via Paris. They carried travel documents bearing the seal of the Duke of Modena and a guarantee of safe passage within England bestowed by the Duke of York. Their path would be smooth and untroubled.

Soon after Christmas they went by coach to Dover and thence by packet to France. Nancy was sorry their visit had been so brief, but she was delighted with the story Roger had told her. If they could make it work it seemed a most satis factory solution to the problem. And a just one.

"Of course we must first have Harwood returned," Roge

commented in an introspective moment. "Otherwise it's all for naught."

"What do you really think about that part of it?" she asked. "Really, in your heart of hearts?"

Roger paused a moment before answering. "If it's up to James, it'll be done. First, he's a papist himself and doesn't hold with people's losing their property on the grounds of being Catholics. If James has his way, every papist in the realm can look for such restorations of former glory." He shook his head in amazement at another of life's ironies. "Strange that I of all people should benefit from an ascendancy of the papists. I've never been able to stomach them. That aside, James would do it for me regardless of the religious issue. I know his faults, but he's as loyal to his friends as he is bitter about his enemies."

"Then you think it's all but settled? The Griffins will return to Harwood?"

"Not exactly. Not all settled. I said *if* it depended on James. It's Charles who has the final word, and his majesty's nothing like so easy to predict."

"But you've always claimed Charles was a just king."

"True. According to his own lights and the way the political wind may be blowing. I simply don't know, Nancy. We'll have to wait and see."

They were nearly the same words Andrew used in speaking to the lady abbess of St. Savior's. "You understand, milady, nothing is yet settled. We must wait on the English king's good pleasure."

"I understand, Mr. Griffin. We will wait and pray with you. All will be as *le bon Dieu* ordains. What more can we ask?"

Andrew thought about that after she left him and while he waited for his sister and his aunt to come to the parlor. Laura and Aunt Sophia—no, he must remember, Sisters Damian and Benedict—would be as astonished at the news as he had been. And as joyful as the lady abbess at the proposition being made. Was all that the result of their prayers in the years they had been in this place? Ten for Laura, thirteen for Sophia...a lot of *Paters* and *Aves* must have been said in that time. Still, he thought the real power behind the sudden turn of events to be something else—the martyrdom of his parents at Tyburn and Uncle Roger's absolute refusal to let old crimes go unpunished, old debts unpaid.

The astonishment he had anticipated didn't quite materialize, however. Oh, there was joy enough, not only at the news but at the reunion. Andrew had seen neither Sophia nor Laura since they'd left England. But little in the way of astonishment was manifest. "Aren't you surprised?" he finally asked. "I was bowled over when Uncle Roger told me the story. I'd never imagined we'd be faced with such a possibility."

His sister chuckled. "Truth to tell, Andrew, we may be shut away in here, but we have our sources. At least Sister Benedict does...."

He looked inquiringly at his aunt, who only smiled and said nothing relating to the topic under discussion. Instead she leaned forward and said, "Tell me about Roger's youngest child."

"You mean Tonyjay?" Andrew asked. "I didn't know that you knew about him."

"Sarah comes to visit occasionally," Laura explained. "She had a letter from Aunt Nancy, and she told us."

"Yes." Sophia was glad of the explanation, which spared her any others. "How is he doing, Andrew? It's important. I can't say why, but I know it is."

"Well, you have to remember I saw him for the first time this visit. But near as I could tell, he seemed a pleasant child. He's a bit timid, but very bright and appealing."

"How does he get on with the others? Roger's other children?"

"They seem to like him well enough. Except Nell. She resents him. Jamie, on the other hand, is devoted to him. You mustn't worry about it, Aunt Sophia," he said finally. "I'm sure the family can cope. Now I've another bit of news for you. And if you tell me your mysterious 'sources' have revealed this too I shall give up and enter a monastery myself."

But they knew nothing of his marriage. They were surprised and enthusiastic when he brought Lulu in to meet them.

Only when they left did Lulu ask, "Where are we going now, husband?"

Andrew shook his head in annoyance. "You promised me you'd stop doing that."

"Doing what?" Lulu's black eyes opened wide in consternation. "How have I displeased you, husband?"

"There, you've done it again! Don't call me 'husband' like that. It's so formal and foreign-sounding. Call me 'Andrew' or 'darling' or what you wish, but not 'husband.' We're going to see my sister Sarah in Burgundy. And I promise if you go on with that 'husband' business you won't get on with Sarah at all. She's as no-nonsense and down-to-earth an Englishwoman as you'll ever meet."

Lulu smiled but said nothing. She was beginning to realize that the women of her husband's family were strong-willed, independent types. Doubtless that's why Andrew had fallen in love with her. The contrast must have appealed. She resolved to stop calling him "husband," since it annoyed him, but for the rest she didn't intend to change a bit. It was her mother's oriental legacy. She'd stay the way she was and ensure that her husband would always do just what she wanted!

It was January 15, 1685, when Roger received a message from Andrew. It was delivered to his George Alley office and said simply, "All is arranged. A." Roger sighed with satisfaction and immediately wrote a note asking for an interview with James. After some thinking and discussion with Charles it had been determined to tell the duke about the plans for Harwood should it be returned to them.

"Admittedly there's some risk," Charles summed up after their long talk on the subject. "James may not feel so dutybound to speak for us if he knows Andrew isn't immediately going to be installed as squire. But on balance I think it'll help. I rather think this idea will appeal to his highness."

Roger had agreed; now he was going to act. But before he'd had time to find someone to carry his request for a meeting to St. James's Palace, another note was placed on his desk.

"Come at once. Urgent. York." Griffin fingered the heavy wax seal and looked thoughtful. Then he rose and wrapped himself in a warm cloak against the frosty winter air. It was snowing by the time he reached London Bridge and engaged a waterman to carry him upriver.

"Here it is, lad, signed and sealed by his majesty this very morning. I can't tell you how sorry I am I couldn't do better...."

Roger took the folded document, and his hand trembled. The look on York's face was enough to tell him what the papers contained. An order claiming Harwood for the crown and disallowing for all time the rights to the property of the family Griffin. He stared at the heavy parchment through eyes blurred with unashamed tears. To have come so close, to have raised all their hopes—and now this.

"Well, aren't you going to read it?" James said quietly.

Griffin shook his head. "I can guess what it contains."

"But you must read it, lad. I insist. There are things you must understand, Roger. Go on, read it. It's all in there."

Slowly he unfolded the papers and spread them on a nearby table. There was the usual formal opening:

"I, Charles II, by the grace of God King of England, do hereby solemnly proclaim that in the matter of Squire Mark Griffin late of Harwood Hall, deceased with his wife in the year of our lord sixteen hundred and seventy nine..."

Roger looked up at James, who was watching him without expression. "I don't understand, sir. Why go into the business of Mark?"

"Read on," James replied.

Roger ran his eyes over the document as quickly as he could. The phrases began to jump out at him from the page.

"Said squire was unjustly accused and grievously executed by enemies of the crown.... We do hereby grant full pardon to him and to his wife...make it known before God and our subjects that said persons did no crime...harbored no ill will toward our sacred person...grant full and solemn pardon to them both...."

"I can't believe it...." He was crying openly now, and he didn't care what James thought of that.

"Go on, lad," the duke said, smiling at last. His little joke was over and apparently he was fully gratified with its effect. "There's more."

"...in reparation for grievous injustice it is our solemn decree that said Harwood Hall, all its demesne, lands, and chattel, be forthwith returned to the legal heir of said Squire Mark Griffin to be held by him and his progeny in perpetuity. Said heir to have full rights of ownership, tenancy, and all comforts guaranteed to him by the rightful laws of this our kingdom...."

"I don't know what to say, sir...." Roger didn't wait to be invited to sit. He couldn't, for his knees had turned to water. He sank into the nearest chair.

James poured them both a brandy. "Don't say anything, lad. It isn't necessary. You've got no more than you deserved. All things considered, perhaps less."

"I wish I knew some way to thank you." He downed the brandy in one fast swallow.

"No need. I'm glad to have been able to help. But in fairness you should know it didn't take much to persuade the king. Frankly, Roger, his majesty isn't well. I fear for him. And he seems anxious to do what he can to make amends for many things. As if..."

"As if what, sir?" Softly. Knowing what the answer would be.

"As if he wanted to put things right so he could meet his Maker in peace."

Roger didn't reply. He merely looked at the man who might soon be king and wondered what his reign held in store for both of them and for England.

8.

The afternoon of Thursday, February 5. Just three weeks since James had confided to Roger Griffin that he thought the king to be very ill. Since then Charles had confounded his doctors by improving sufficiently to walk in the gardens of Whitehall at least twice a day despite the wintry weather. Then, last Sunday evening, his majesty spent a restless night. The following morning he was stricken with a terrible fit of apoplexy and confined to his bed.

James was at his side now. Inexplicably, he and his brother were alone but for a few unobtrusive servants.

Charles's bastard sons, all but Monmouth, who remained banished, had come, bid their father farewell, and left. The two mistresses who had survived in his affections, Louise de Kéroualle and Nell Gwyn, had not been permitted access to the royal chamber. Some propriety had to be preserved, even for a monarch as openly merry as Charles. The queen was in her own apartment, prostrate with grief. The doctors, statesmen, and bishops had all disappeared.

James looked about the half-empty room and moved closer to the bedside. Charles seemed to be sleeping; perhaps he was unconscious. Throughout this illness he had had many lucid periods. Just this morning, when they were bleeding him yet again and applying red-hot blistering agents to all parts of his body, he'd found the wit to quip, "I'm sorry, gentlemen, that I take such an unconscionable long time dying...."

Now he was motionless and silent, and James alone kept vigil by his bed. The last to leave had been the bishops of the Church of England. Since the first of the week they'd been doing their best to give the dying man the solace of religion, urging him to take Anglican communion to no avail. "There's time enough for that," the king said repeatedly.

James moistened his lips and consulted his conscience for a final time. He knew what he must do. Louise de Kéroualle had reminded him of it just this morning. Louise, 'the papist whore', knew Charles's heart in religious matters better than anyone alive. "He is as much a believer in the Catholic religion as you or I," she told York. "I beg you to see that he dies in the faith."

James cared little for the woman. She was a scheming, lying bitch; he'd never thought otherwise. But in this instance he was convinced she spoke the truth. If he ignored that now, how could he face his own death? Still, in his position...a future king with more enemies than friends in court and throughout the realm...At this moment nearly every man, woman, and child in England was praying for a miraculous recovery for Charles. It wasn't just that they feared his successor; the people loved Charles. Whatever his faults he'd been able to inspire devotion and affection. They'd none for his brother.

To reconcile anyone to the Roman Church was a treasonable offense punishable by death. Could a man in James's position give such a weapon to his enemies? But had he any choice? For long minutes he agonized over the dilemma. He must act soon if at all. This brief time alone with the king was bound to end. Suddenly Charles stirred, moaned softly, and opened his eyes. James put his lips to the king's ear. "Do you want me to bring a Catholic priest?"

Charles's answer was a faint whisper. "For God's sake do...and please lose no time...."

James looked wildly around him for a moment, then saw the door just beside the bed. It led to the queen's chambers, a private passage seldom used.

Catherine was surrounded by attendants; at James's urgings she sent everyone away. When she heard his request she nodded, rang for a servant, then settled back on the pillows with a faint smile playing about her lips. It was for this she had prayed, endured her long martyrdom as barren Queen of England.

In minutes they were joined by Father Huddleston. In all the realm he was the one man whom they could wholly trust. So familiar was Huddleston in court that most had forgotten the fact that he was a Catholic priest. The old man's privileges had been in place so long, they had the disguise of familiarity. No one even questioned James when he ushered Huddleston into the king's bedchamber.

"Sire," the priest said in a voice only Charles could hear. "Years ago it was my great good fortune to help save your life. If you wish it I can now save your soul." The king nodded and raised his hand in assent. The hurried rites began.

One of the servants slipped unnoticed from the room and sped along the corridors to the chambers of the Earl of Chesterfield. Breathless and frightened, he burst into the room. "Sir! Come quickly, I beg you...they're making the king a Catholic! And him too ill and feeble to do a thing about it...."

"Calm yourself, good fellow. If they've brought him a priest they only confirm in word what has long been a fact in the spirit. The king has always been a Catholic. Let him die in peace...."

In the royal chamber, Huddleston had finished and gone. James remained by the bedside on his knees. Gradually the others returned. The room was soon full. Suddenly Charles exhibited another period of clearheadedness, seemed almost like his old self. One of the bishops came forward and offered him yet again the Anglican communion. "I hope, milord," was the answer, "I've already made my peace with God...."

After midnight Charles motioned once more for York. "Treat Catherine kindly, I beg you," he whispered. "England's never had a nobler queen. And my children, don't forget them when you're king...." Then the final words: "And Nell, James. See poor Nell doesn't starve."

His eyes closed. Two of the doctors bent over him for some moments, then the eldest of them raised his head and spoke. "His most gracious majesty Charles II is dead."

The bishops murmured pious words; James openly crossed himself in the Catholic manner. The Earl of Chesterfield stepped to the window to make the announcement to the masses of people crowded into the courtyard below. "The king is dead," he shouted into the February dawn. "Long live the king. God save James II of England, Scotland and Wales."

They buried him in quiet, with none of the pomp or panoply that had marked his restoration twenty-five years before. No lying in state, no elaborate funeral, not even a name on his tomb in Westminster Abbey.

"They knew," James told Roger Griffin late the next evening. "They knew he'd died a Catholic. It was the one thing they couldn't forgive him. That and leaving me as his heir."

The summons to James's side on this particular night hadn't surprised Roger—merely a renewal of his old role as father confessor—but the bitterness in the new king's voice did. "Does it matter now, sire? You're king. Surely the rest is unimportant."

"Not to me it isn't. I'll show them all, Roger. God's truth I will."

"That you'll be a great king, sire? I've no doubt of it."

James smiled. "Sometimes, lad, you've the makings of a diplomat about you after all. Could be it was a mistake ever to let you leave court. Well, too late for that now, I warrant. Tell me, how are things with Harwood Hall? The plan you told me about, is it working?"

"Rather soon to say, sire. But I had word from France today. My sister Sophia and my niece Laura have left for England with three other members of their community. They will go straight to Harwood and live there as private persons until the times are such that it is possible for us to rebuild their old priory on the adjacent land."

"And in the meantime you'll ready your son James to become squire when he's a bit older." The king smiled. "It's an excellent idea, Roger. I shall watch the progress with interest. I need not tell you that no Griffin will ever want for a friend in the king."

IT WAS A NEW COUNTRY,
A NEW WORLD TO CONQUER....

The Griffins, long the favorites of kings, now face ruinous scandal. Their only hope is the new family that Tonyjay has founded in the wilds of the Massachusetts colony.

With Lizzie, a woman as strong and untamed as the land she was born in, Tonyjay vows to protect the shipping empire and teach his children the Griffin lessons of loyalty and honor. Then the dark stirrings of his past lead him into the arms of a passionate aristocratic seductress. And Lizzie must win him back—to her and to his Griffin destiny....

The Adventurer

The next volume in the exciting Griffin Saga

by

Beverly Byrne

Soon to be a Fawcett Gold Medal original

GREAT ADVENTURES IN READING